THE

LANCASHIRE WITCHES

A ROMANCE OF PENDLE FOREST

By WILLIAM HARRISON AINSWORTH

WITH ILLUSTRATIONS BY

SIR JOHN GILBERT, R.A.

Northern Classic Reprints

Printwise Publications Ltd.
1992

This edition published 1992 by
PRINTWISE PUBLICATIONS LTD. and
PHOENIX BOOKS LIMITED
40-42 Willan Industrial Estate, Vere Street,
(off Eccles New Road), SALFORD, M5 2GR.
Tel: 061-745 9168 Fax: 061-737 1755

Originally published 1884
By George Routledge and Sons Limited

Reprint chosen and organised by

Cliff Hayes

Cover Illustration: The Incantation

ISBN No. 1 872226 55 8

Printed and bound by
The Guernsey Press Co. Ltd, Guernsey, Channel Islands

This book is reproduced from the 1882 edition of this much sought after book. I'm sure the enthralling and intriguing story far outweighs any slight blemishes on a few pages, which have been reproduced in the interests of authenticity.

INTRODUCTION

Out of all his novels Harrison Ainsworth is perhaps best known for The Lancashire Witches. It was at the recommendation of his friend James Crossley who suggested that he should use the account of the witches' trial at Lancaster in 1612, written by the Clerk of the Courts – Pott's Discoveries of Witches as the basis for a story. He spent two years collecting material and planning the book. With all this background preparation Ainsworth was able to create in this book perfect descriptions of the wild scenery of Pendle Forest, and a thrilling account of rites practised by the witches. The story is full of characters whose names we all seem familiar with, Mistress Nutter, Mother Chattox, Mother Demdick, The Abbot of Whalley, Alizon Devices and others. A romantic story so true to life that it seems that it really did happen. Maybe it did, William Harrison Ainsworth was a master of his craft.

When it was finished in 1841 the story was taken by The Sunday Times for serial publication, the price paid being one thousand pounds, a very large sum for that time. But it must have been worth it as thousands followed the story week by week. William Harrison Ainsworth wrote nearly 40 novels, each one a fascinating tale, each one with a flowing storyline, the same mix of fact and fiction, filled with characters real and not so real. Don't worry about the mixture, just enjoy the thrilling story and be transported back to Lancashire of the 1600's, when superstition, spells and fear ruled the lives of the ordinary people living around The Pendle Hill, back to that time now always referred to as the time of . . .

THE LANCASHIRE WITCHES

NAN REDFERNE AND MOTHER CHATTOX. P. 110

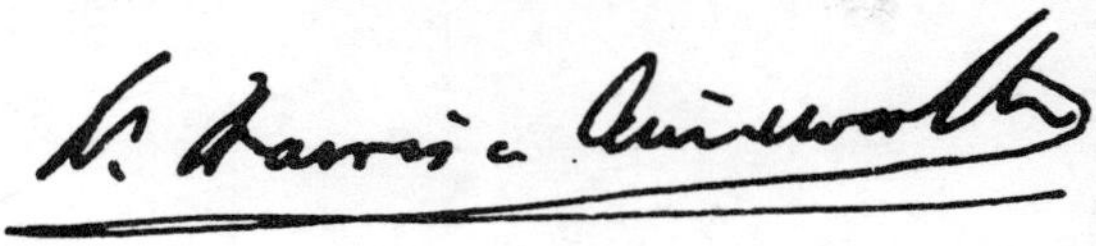

ABOUT THE THE AUTHOR

Born at 21 King Street, Manchester on the 4th February 1805 Harrison Ainsworth was the eldest son of an eminent lawyer. The house is long gone but the National Westminster Bank which stands on the spot carries a proud blue plaque on its wall to denote the event.

When two years old his family moved to Beech Hall in Cheetham because the family wanted more country air. It was this house Ainsworth re-purchases in later life. Ainsworth was a literary giant of the time and his popularity even outshone Charles Dickens (who Ainsworth met in 1834 and encouraged and helped to set his first book in print).

Although pushed by his father into the family firm of Solicitors, Messrs Ainsworth Crossley and Sudlow, his love of books and history was always a strong pull and many hours were spent at Chetham's Library, not only reading but absorbing the ideas and thoughts of the great men of the time.

Ainsworth wrote 39 novels though novel does not seem the right word as the leading ones had so much real facts and real people, all woven into great stories full of romance, drama and sadness that all good Victorian novels revelled in. His first book 'Rockwood' published in 1834 has an account of Dick Turpin riding from London to York on Black Bess. The story caught the imagination of the public and many will say to this day that it was true, although a thorough search reveals it never actually happened. Rockwood was well received and following its success he was the toast of London and was found in all the best society houses.

Married twice and both unhappy, Ainsworth was a 'dandy' and fashion leader. He moved to London in 1826 and it was there he finally gave up the legal profession and moved into publishing about 1830. Many quotes at the time refer to how good looking he was, and how fair and unmarked his skin was; "the Adonis of booksellers" said one. "As thorough a gentleman as his native city of Manchester ever sent forth" was another much quoted at the time.

Success followed success, but in 1853 he left London and spent life quietly researching and writing novel after novel. He spent two years preparing his most re-printed book "The Lancashire Witches" and indeed it was Ainsworth who brought Dickens to Manchester, and Lancashire, introducing him to William and Daniel Grant who were later to appear as the Cheeryble Brothers in Nicholas Nickleby.

One measure of his popularity was a public banquet given by the City of Manchester in 1881 to honour this famous Mancunian. The Mayor in his welcome informed the distinguished guests that "in our Manchester Public Free Libraries there are 250 volumes of Mr Ainsworths works. In the last year these have been read 7,660 times, mostly by the artisan class of readers. This means that 20 books are perused in Manchester by readers of the Free Libraries every day all year through". No Small Fete.

Harrison Ainsworth died in 1882 in Reigate after being almost a recluse for his last years, but left behind a marvellous collection of literature. His Lancashire books follow one another in gathering the History of the County from "The Lancashire Witches" (1600) through to "The Manchester Rebels" and "Mervyn Clitheroe" 1800.

P.S. More details about Harrison Ainsworth may be found in "Stories of Great Lancastrians".

Cliff Hayes

CONTENTS

INTRODUCTION: THE LAST ABBOT OF WHALLEY

BOOK I: ALIZON DEVICE

BOOK II: PENDLE FOREST

CONTENTS

THE LANCASHIRE WITCHES.

INTRODUCTION.

The Last Abbot of Whalley.

CHAPTER I.—THE BEACON ON PENDLE HILL.

THERE were eight watchers by the beacon on Pendle Hill in Lancashire. Two were stationed on either side of the north eastern extremity of the mountain. One looked over the castled heights of Clithero; the woody eminences of Bowland; the bleak ridges of Thornley; the broad moors of Bleasdale; the Trough of Bolland, and Wolf Crag; and even brought within his ken the black fells overhanging Lancaster. The other tracked the stream called Pendle Water, almost from its source amid the neighbouring hills, and followed its windings through the leafless forest, until it united its waters to those of the Calder, and swept on in swifter and clearer current, to wash the base of Whalley Abbey. But the watcher's survey did not stop here. Noting the sharp spire of Burnley Church, relieved against the rounded masses of timber constituting Townley Park; as well as the entrance of the gloomy mountain gorge, known as the Grange of Cliviger; his far-reaching gaze passed over Todmorden, and settled upon the distant summits of Blackstone Edge.

Dreary was the prospect on all sides. Black moor, bleak fell, straggling forest, intersected with sullen streams as black as ink, with here and there a small tarn, or moss-pool, with waters of the same hue—these constituted the chief features of the scene. The whole district was barren and thinly-populated. Of towns, only Clithero, Colne, and Burnley—the latter little more than a village—were in view. In the valleys there were a few hamlets and scattered cottages, and on the uplands an occasional "booth," as the hut of the herdsman was termed; but of more important mansions there were only six, as Merley, Twistleton, Alcancoats, Saxfeld, Ightenhill, and Gawthorpe. The "vaccaries" for the cattle, of which the herdsmen had the care, and the "lawnds," or parks within the forest, appertaining to some of the halls before mentioned, offered the only evidences of cultivation. All else was heathy waste, morass, and wood.

Still, in the eye of the sportsman—and the Lancashire gentlemen of the sixteenth century were keen lovers of sport—the country had a strong interest. Pendle forest abounded with game. Grouse, plover, and bittern were found upon its moors; woodcock and snipe on its marshes; mallard, teal, and widgeon upon its pools. In its chases ranged herds of deer, protected by the terrible forest-laws, then in full force: and the hardier huntsman might follow the wolf to his lair in the mountains; might spear the boar in the oaken glades, or the otter on the river's brink; might unearth the badger or the fox, or smite the fierce cat-a-mountain with a quarrel from his bow. A nobler victim sometimes, also, awaited him in the shape of a wild mountain bull, a denizen of the forest, and a remnant of the herds that had once browsed upon the hills, but which had almost all been captured, and removed to stock the park of the Abbot of Whalley. The streams and pools were full of fish: the stately heron frequented the meres; and on the craggy heights built the kite, the falcon, and the kingly eagle.

There were eight watchers by the beacon. Two stood apart from the others, looking to the right and the left of the hill. Both were armed with swords and arquebuses, and wore steel caps and coats of buff. Their sleeves were embroidered with the five wounds of Christ, encircling the name of Jesus—the badge of the Pilgrimage of Grace. Between them, on the verge of the mountain, was planted a great banner, displaying a silver cross, the chalice, and the Host, together with an ecclesiastical figure, but wearing a helmet instead of a mitre, and holding a sword in place of a crosier, with the unoccupied hand pointing to the two towers of a monastic structure, as if to intimate that he was armed for its defence. This figure, as the device beneath it showed, represented John Paslew, Abbot of Whalley, or, as he styled himself in his military capacity, Earl of Poverty.

There were eight watchers by the beacon. Two have been described. Of the other six, two were stout herdsmen carrying crooks, and holding a couple of mules, and a richly-caparisoned war-horse by the bridle. Near them stood a broad-shouldered, athletic young man, with the fresh complexion, curling brown hair, light eyes, and open Saxon countenance, best seen in his native county of Lancaster. He wore a Lincoln-green tunic, with a bugle suspended from the shoulder by a silken cord; and a silver plate engraved with the three luces, the ensign of the Abbot of Whalley, hung by a chain from his neck. A hunting knife was in his girdle, and an eagle's plume in his cap, and he leaned upon the but-end of a crossbow, regarding three persons who stood together by a peat fire, on the sheltered side of the beacon. Two of these were elderly men, in the white gowns and scapularies of Cistertian monks, doubtless from Whalley, as the abbey belonged to that order. The third and last, and evidently their superior, was a tall man in a riding dress, wrapped in a long mantle of black velvet, trimmed with minever, and displaying the same badges as those upon the sleeves of the sentinels, only wrought in richer material. His features were strongly marked and stern, and bore traces of age; but his eye was bright, and his carriage erect and dignified.

The beacon, near which the watchers stood, consisted of a vast pile of logs of timber, heaped upon a circular range of stones, with openings to admit air, and having the centre filled with fagots, and other quickly combustible materials. Torches were placed near at hand, so that the pile could be lighted on the instant.

The watch was held one afternoon at the latter end of November, 1536. In that year had arisen a formidable rebellion in the northern counties of England, the members of which, while engaging to respect the person of the king, Henry VIII., and his issue, bound themselves by solemn oath to accomplish the restoration of Papal supremacy throughout the realm, and the restitution of religious establishments and lands to their late ejected possessors. They bound themselves, also, to punish the enemies of the Romish church, and suppress heresy. From its religious character the insurrection assumed the name of the Pilgrimage of Grace, and numbered among its adherents all who had not embraced the new doctrines in Yorkshire and Lancashire. That such an outbreak should occur on the suppression of the monasteries, was not marvellous. The desecration and spoliation of so many sacred structures—the destruction of shrines and images long regarded with veneration—the ejection of so many ecclesiastics, renowned for hospitality and revered for piety and learning—the violence and rapacity of the commissioners appointed by the Vicar-General Cromwell to carry out these severe measures—all these outrages were regarded by the people with abhorrence, and disposed them to aid the sufferers in resistance. As yet the wealthier monasteries in the north had been spared, and it was to preserve them from the greedy hands of the visiters, Doctors Lee and Layton, that the insurrection had been undertaken. A simultaneous rising took place in Lincolnshire, headed by Makarel, Abbot of Barlings, but it was speedily quelled by the vigour and skill of the Duke of Suffolk, and its leader executed. But the northern outbreak was better organized, and of greater force, for it now numbered thirty thousand men, under the command of a skilful and resolute leader named Robert Aske.

As may be supposed, the priesthood were main movers in a revolt having their especial benefit for its aim; and many of them, following the example of the Abbot of Barlings, clothed themselves in steel instead of woollen garments, and girded on the sword and the breastplate for the redress of their grievances and the maintenance of their rights. Amongst these were the Abbots of Jervaux, Furness, Fountains, Rivaulx, and Salley, and, lastly, the Abbot of Whalley, before mentioned; a fiery and energetic prelate, who had ever been constant and determined in his opposition to the aggressive measures of the king. Such was the Pilgrimage of Grace, such its design, and such its supporters.

Several large towns had already fallen into the hands of the insurgents. York, Hull, and Pontefract had yielded; Skipton Castle was besieged, and defended by the Earl of Cumberland; and battle was offered to the Duke of Norfolk and the Earl of Shrewsbury, who headed the king's forces at Doncaster. But the object of the Royalist leaders was to temporise, and an armistice was offered to the rebels and accepted. Terms were next proposed and debated.

During the continuance of this armistice all hostilities ceased; but beacons were reared upon the mountains, and their fires were to be taken as a new summons to arms. This signal the eight watchers expected.

Though late in November, the day had been unusually fine, and, in consequence, the whole hilly ranges around were clearly discernible, but now the shades of evening were fast drawing on.

"Night is approaching," cried the tall man in the velvet mantle, impatiently; "and still the signal comes not. Wherefore this delay? Can Norfolk have accepted our conditions? Impossible. The last messenger from our camp at Scawsby Lees brought word that the duke's sole terms would be the king's pardon to the whole insurgent army, provided they at once dispersed—except ten persons, six named and four unnamed."

"And were you amongst those named, lord abbot?" demanded one of the monks.

"John Paslew, Abbot of Whalley, it was said, headed the list," replied the other, with a bitter smile. "Next came William Trafford, Abbot of Salley. Next Adam Sudbury, Abbot of Jervaux. Then our leader, Robert Aske. Then John Eastgate, Monk of Whalley—"

"How, lord abbot!" exclaimed the monk. "Was my name mentioned?"

"It was," rejoined the abbot. "And that of William Haydocke, also Monk of Whalley, closed the list."

"The unrelenting tyrant!" muttered the other monk. "But these terms could not be accepted?"

"Assuredly not," replied Paslew; "they were rejected with scorn. But the negotiations were continued by Sir Ralph Ellerker and Sir Robert Bowas, who were to claim on our part a free pardon for all; the establishment of a Parliament and courts of justice at York; the restoration of the Princess Mary to the succession; the Pope to his jurisdiction; and our brethren to their houses. But such conditions will never be granted. With my consent no armistice should have been agreed to. We are sure to lose by the delay. But I was overruled by the Archbishop of York and the Lord Darcy. Their voices prevailed against the Abbot of Whalley—or, if it please you, the Earl of Poverty."

"It is the assumption of that derisive title which has drawn upon you the full force of the king's resentment, lord abbot," observed Father Eastgate.

"It may be," replied the abbot. "I took it in mockery of Cromwell and the ecclesiastical commissioners, and I rejoice that they have felt the sting. The Abbot of Barlings called himself Captain Cobbler, because, as he affirmed, the state wanted mending like old shoon. And is not my title equally well chosen? Is not the Church smitten with poverty? Have not ten thousand of our brethren been driven from their homes to beg or to starve? Have not the houseless poor, whom we fed at our gates, and lodged within our wards, gone away hungry and without rest? Have not the sick, whom we would have relieved, died untended by the hedge-side? I am the head of the poor in Lancashire, the redresser of their grievances, and therefore I style myself Earl of Poverty. Have I not done well?"

"You have, lord abbot," replied Father Eastgate.

"Poverty will not alone be the fate of the Church, but of the whole realm, if the rapacious designs of the monarch and his heretical counsellors are carried forth," pursued the abbot. "Cromwell, Audeley, and Rich, have wisely ordained that no infant shall be baptised without tribute to the king; that no man who owns not above twenty pounds a year shall consume wheaten bread, or eat the flesh of fowl or swine without tribute; and that all ploughed land shall pay tribute likewise. Thus the Church is to be beggared, the poor plundered, and all men burthened, to fatten the king, and fill his exchequer."

"This must be a jest," observed Father Haydocke

"It is a jest no man laughs at," rejoined the abbot, sternly; "any more than the king's counsellors will laugh at the Earl of Poverty, whose title they themselves have created. But wherefore comes not the signal? Can aught have gone wrong? I will not think it. The whole country, from the Tweed to the Humber, and from the Lune to the Mersey, is ours; and, if we but hold together, our cause must prevail."

"Yet we have many and powerful enemies," observed Father Eastgate; "and the king, it is said, hath sworn never to make terms with us. Tidings were brought to the abbey this morning, that the Earl of Derby is assembling forces at Preston, to march upon us."

"We will give him a warm reception if he comes," replied Paslew, fiercely. "He will find that our walls have not been kernelled and embattled by licence of good King Edward the Third for nothing; and that our brethren can fight as well as their predecessors fought in the time of Abbot Holden, when they took tithe by force from Sir Christopher Parsons of Slaydburn. The abbey is strong, and right well defended, and we need not fear a surprise. But it grows dark fast, and yet no signal comes."

"Perchance the waters of the Don have again risen, so as to prevent the army from fording the stream," observed Father Haydocke; "or it may be that some disaster hath befallen our leader."

"Nay, I will not believe the latter," said the abbot; "Robert Aske is chosen by Heaven to be our deliverer. It has been prophesied that a 'worm with one eye' shall work the redemption of the fallen faith, and you know that Robert Aske hath been deprived of his left orb by an arrow."

"Therefore it is," observed Father Eastgate, "that the Pilgrims of Grace chant the following ditty:—

"'Forth shall come an Aske with one eye,
He shall be chief of the company—
Chief of the northern chivalry.'"

"What more?" demanded the abbot, seeing that the monk appeared to hesitate.

"Nay, I know not whether the rest of the rhymes may please you, lord abbot," replied Father Eastgate.

"Let me hear them, and I will judge," said Paslew. Thus urged, the monk went on:—

"'One shall sit at a solemn feast,
Half warrior, half priest,
The greatest there shall be the least.'"

"The last verse," observed the monk, "has been added to the ditty by Nicholas Demdike. I heard him sing it the other day at the abbey gate."

"What, Nicholas Demdike of Worston?" cried the abbot; "he whose wife is a witch?"

"The same," replied Eastgate.

"Hoo be so ceawnted, sure eno," remarked the forester, who had been listening attentively to their discourse, and who now stepped forward; "boh dunna yo think it. Beleemy, lort abbut, Bess Demdike's too yunk an too protty for a witch."

"Thou art bewitched by her thyself, Cuthbert," said the abbot, angrily. "I shall impose a penance upon thee, to free thee from the evil influence. Thou must recite twenty paternosters daily, fasting, for one month; and afterwards perform a pilgrimage to the shrine of our Lady of Gilsland. Bess Demdike is an approved and notorious witch, and hath been seen by credible witnesses attending a devil's sabbath on this very hill—Heaven shield us! It is therefore that I have placed her and her husband under the ban of the Church; pronounced sentence of excommunication against them; and commanded all my clergy to refuse baptism to their infant daughter, newly born."

"Wea's me! ey knoas 't reet weel, lort abbut," replied Ashbead, "and Bess taks t' sentence sore ta 'ert!"

"Then let her amend her ways, or heavier punishment will befall her," cried Paslew, severely. "'*Sortilegam non patieris vivere,*' saith the Levitical law. If she be convicted she shall die the death. That she is comely I admit; but it is the comeliness of a child of sin. Dost thou know the man with whom she is wedded—or supposed to be wedded—for I have seen no proof of the marriage? He is a stranger here."

"Ey knoas neawt abowt him, lort abbut, 'cept that he cum to Pendle a twalmont agoa," replied Ashbead; "boh ey knoas fu' weel that t'eawtcumbling felly robt me ot prottiest lass i' aw Lonkyshiar—aigh, or i' aw Englondshiar, fo' t' matter o' that."

"What manner of man is he?" inquired the abbot.

"Oh, he's a feaw teyke—a varra feaw teyke," replied Ashbead; "wi' a feace as black as a boggart, sooty shiny hewr loike a mowdywarp, an' een loike a stanniel. Boh for running, rostling, an' throwing t' stoan, he'n no match i' this keawntry. Ey'n triet him at aw three gams, so ey con speak. For't most part he'n a big, black bandyhewit wi' him, and, by th' Mess, ey canna help thinkin he meys free sumtoimes wi' yor lortship's bucks."

"Ha! this must be looked to," cried the abbot. "You say you know not whence he comes? 'Tis strange."

"T' missmannert carl 'll boide naw questionin', odd rottle him!" replied Ashbead. "He awnsurs wi' a gibe, or a thwack o' his staff. Whon ey last seet him, he threatened t' raddle me booans weel, boh ey sooan lowert him a peg."

"We will find a way of making him speak," said the abbot.

"He can speak, and right well if he pleases," remarked Father Eastgate; "for though ordinarily silent and sullen enough, yet when he doth talk it is not like one of the hinds with whom he consorts, but in good set phrase; and his bearing is as bold as that of one who hath seen service in the field."

"My curiosity is aroused," said the abbot. "I must see him."

"Noa sooner said than done," cried Ashbead, "for, be t' Lort Harry, ey see him stonding be yon moss poo' o' top t' hill, though how he'n getten theer t' Dule owny knoas."

And he pointed out a tall dark figure standing near a little pool on the summit of the mountain, about a hundred yards from them.

"Talk of ill, and ill cometh," observed Father Haydocke. "And see, the wizard hath a black hound with him! It may be his wife, in that likeness."

"Naw, ey knoas t' hount reet weel, Feyther Haydocke," replied the forester; "it's a Saint Hubert, an' a rareun fo' fox or badgert.

Odds loife, feyther, whoy that's t' black bandyhewit I war speaking on."

"I like not the appearance of the knave at this juncture," said the abbot; "yet I wish to confront him, and charge him with his midemeanours."

"Hark; he sings," cried Father Haydocke. And as he spoke a voice was heard chanting,—

> "One shall sit at a solemn feast,
> Half warrior, half priest,
> The greatest there shall be the least."

"The very ditty I heard," cried Father Eastgate; "but list, he has more of it." And the voice resumed,—

> "He shall be rich, yet poor as me,
> Abbot, and Earl of Poverty.
> Monk and soldier, rich and poor,
> He shall be hang'd at his own door."

Loud derisive laughter followed the song.

"By our Lady of Whalley, the knave is mocking us," cried the abbot; "send a bolt to silence him, Cuthbert."

The forester instantly bent his bow, and a quarrel whistled off in the direction of the singer; but whether his aim were not truly taken, or he meant not to hit the mark, it is certain that Demdike remained untouched. The reputed wizard laughed aloud, took off his felt cap in acknowledgment, and marched deliberately down the side of the hill.

"Thou art not wont to miss thy aim, Cuthbert," cried the abbot, with a look of displeasure. "Take good heed thou producest this scurril knave before me, when these troublous times are over. But what is this?—he stops—ha! he is practising his devilries on the mountain's side."

It would seem that the abbot had good warrant for what he said, as Demdike, having paused at a broad green patch on the hill-side, was now busied in tracing a circle round it with his staff. He then spoke aloud some words, which the superstitious beholders construed into an incantation, and after tracing the circle once again, and casting some tufts of dry heather, which he plucked from an adjoining hillock, on three particular spots, he ran quickly downwards, followed by his hound, and leaping a stone wall, surrounding a little orchard at the foot of the hill, disappeared from view.

"Go and see what he hath done," cried the abbot to the forester, "for I like it not."

Ashbead instantly obeyed, and on reaching the green spot in question, shouted out that he could discern nothing: but presently added, as he moved about, that the turf heaved like a sway-bed beneath his feet, and he thought—to use his own phraseology—

would "brast." The abbot then commanded him to go down to the orchard below, and if he could find Demdike to bring him to him instantly. The forester did as he was bidden, ran down the hill, and, leaping the orchard wall as the other had done, was lost to sight.

Ere long, it became quite dark, and as Ashbead did not re-appear, the abbot gave vent to his impatience and uneasiness, and was proposing to send one of the herdsmen in search of him, when his attention was suddenly diverted by a loud shout from one of the sentinels, and a fire was seen on a distant hill on the right.

"The signal! the signal!" cried Paslew, joyfully. "Kindle a torch!—quick, quick!"

And as he spoke, he seized a brand and plunged it into the peat fire, while his example was followed by the two monks.

"It is the beacon on Blackstone Edge," cried the abbot; "and look! a second blazes over the Grange of Cliviger—another on Ightenhill—another on Boulsworth Hill—and the last on the neighbouring heights of Padiham. Our own comes next. May it light the enemies of our holy Church to perdition!"

With this, he applied the burning brand to the combustible matter of the beacon. The monks did the same; and in an instant a tall, pointed flame, rose up from a thick cloud of smoke. Ere another minute had elapsed, similar fires shot up to the right and the left, on the high lands of Trawden Forest, on the jagged points of Foulridge, on the summit of Cowling Hill, and so on to Skipton. Other fires again blazed on the towers of Clithero, on Longridge and Ribchester, on the woody eminences of Bowland, on Wolf Crag, and on fell and scar all the way to Lancaster. It seemed the work of enchantment, so suddenly and so strangely did the fires shoot forth. As the beacon flame increased, it lighted up the whole of the extensive table-land on the summit of Pendle Hill; and a long lurid streak fell on the darkling moss-pool near which the wizard had stood. But when it attained its utmost height, it revealed the depths of the forest below, and a red reflection, here and there, marked the course of Pendle Water. The excitement of the abbot and his companions momently increased, and the sentinels shouted as each new beacon was lighted. At last, almost every hill had its watch-fire, and so extraordinary was the spectacle, that it seemed as if weird beings were abroad, and holding their revels on the heights.

Then it was that the abbot, mounting his steed, called out to the monks—"Holy fathers, you will follow to the abbey as you may. I shall ride fleetly on, and despatch two hundred archers to Huddersfield and Wakefield. The abbots of Salley and Jervaux, with the Prior of Burlington, will be with me at midnight, and at daybreak we shall march our forces to join the main army. Heaven be with you!"

"Stay!" cried a harsh, imperious voice. "Stay!"

And, to his surprise, the abbot beheld Nicholas Demdike standing before him. The aspect of the wizard was dark and forbidding, and, seen by the beacon light, his savage features, blazing eyes, tall gaunt frame, and fantastic garb, made him look like something unearthly. Flinging his staff over his shoulder, he slowly approached, with his black hound following close by at his heels.

"I have a caution to give you, lord abbot," he said; "hear me speak before you set out for the abbey, or ill will befall you."

"Ill *will* befall me if I listen to thee, thou wicked churl," cried the abbot. "What hast thou done with Cuthbert Ashbead?"

"I have seen nothing of him since he sent a bolt after me at your bidding, lord abbot," replied Demdike.

"Beware lest any harm come to him, or thou wilt rue it," cried Paslew. "But I have no time to waste on thee. Farewell, fathers. High mass will be said in the convent church before we set out on the expedition to-morrow morning. You will both attend it."

"You will never set out upon the expedition, lord abbot," cried Demdike, planting his staff so suddenly into the ground before the horse's head that the animal reared and nearly threw his rider.

"How now, fellow, what mean you?" cried the abbot, furiously.

"To warn you," replied Demdike.

"Stand aside," cried the abbot, spurring his steed, "or I will trample you beneath my horse's feet."

"I might let you ride to your own doom," rejoined Demdike, with a scornful laugh, as he seized the abbot's bridle. "But you shall hear me. I tell you, you will never go forth on this expedition. I tell you that, ere to-morrow, Whalley Abbey will have passed for ever from your possession; and that, if you go thither again, your life will be forfeited. Now will you listen to me?"

"I am wrong in doing so," cried the abbot, who could not, however, repress some feelings of misgiving at this alarming address. "Speak, what would you say?"

"Come out of earshot of the others, and I will tell you," replied Demdike. And he led the abbot's horse to some distance further on the hill.

"Your cause will fail, lord abbot," he then said. "Nay, it is lost already."

"Lost!" cried the abbot, out of all patience. "Lost! Look around. Twenty fires are in sight—ay, thirty, and every fire thou seest will summon a hundred men, at the least, to arms. Before an hour, five hundred men will be gathered before the gates of Whalley Abbey."

"True," replied Demdike; "but they will not own the Earl of Poverty for their leader."

"What leader will they own, then?" demanded the abbot, scornfully.

"The Earl of Derby," replied Demdike. "He is on his way thither with Lord Mounteagle from Preston."

"Ha!" exclaimed Paslew, "let me go meet them, then. But thou triflest with me, fellow. Thou canst know nothing of this. Whence gott'st thou thine information?"

"Heed it not," replied the other; "thou wilt find it correct. I tell thee, proud abbot, that this grand scheme of thine and of thy fellows, for the restitution of the Catholic Church, has failed—utterly failed."

"I tell thee thou liest, false knave!" cried the abbot, striking him on the hand with his scourge. "Quit thy hold, and let me go."

"Not till I have done," replied Demdike, maintaining his grasp. "Well hast thou styled thyself Earl of Poverty, for thou art poor and miserable enough. Abbot of Whalley thou art no longer. Thy possessions will be taken from thee, and if thou returnest thy life also will be taken. If thou fleest, a price will be set upon thy head. I alone can save thee, and I will do so on one condition."

"Condition! make conditions with thee, bond-slave of Satan!" cried the abbot, gnashing his teeth. "I reproach myself that I have listened to thee so long. Stand aside, or I will strike thee dead."

"You are wholly in my power," cried Demdike with a disdainful laugh. And as he spoke he pressed the large sharp bit against the charger's mouth, and backed him quickly to the very edge of the hill, the sides of which here sloped precipitously down. The abbot would have uttered a cry, but surprise and terror kept him silent.

"Were it my desire to injure you, I could cast you down the mountain-side to certain death," pursued Demdike. "But I have no such wish. On the contrary, I will serve you, as I have said, on one condition."

"Thy condition would imperil my soul," said the abbot, full of wrath and alarm. "Thou seekest in vain to terrify me into compliance. *Vade retro, Sathanas.* I defy thee and all thy works."

Demdike laughed scornfully.

"The thunders of the Church do not frighten me," he cried. "But, look," he added, "you doubted my word when I told you the rising was at an end. The beacon fires on Boulsworth Hill and on the Grange of Cliviger are extinguished; that on Padiham Heights is expiring—nay, it is out; and ere many minutes all these mountain watch-fires will have disappeared like lamps at the close of a feast."

"By our Lady, it is so," cried the abbot, in increasing terror. "What new jugglery is this?"

"It is no jugglery, I tell you," replied the other.

"The waters of the Don have again arisen; the insurgents have accepted the king's pardon, have deserted their leaders, and dispersed. There will be no rising to-night or on the morrow. The abbots of Jervaux and Salley will strive to capitulate, but in vain. The Pilgrimage of Grace is ended. The stake for which thou playedst is lost. Thirty years hast thou governed here, but thy rule is over. Seventeen abbots have there been of Whalley —the last thou!—but there shall be none more."

"It must be the Demon in person that speaks thus to me," cried the abbot, his hair bristling on his head, and a cold perspiration bursting from his pores.

"No matter who I am," replied the other; "I have said I will aid thee on one condition. It is not much. Remove thy ban from my wife, and baptise her infant daughter, and I am content. I would not ask thee for this service, slight though it be, but the poor soul hath set her mind upon it. Wilt thou do it?"

"No," replied the abbot, shuddering; "I will not baptise a daughter of Satan. I will not sell my soul to the powers of darkness. I adjure thee to depart from me, and tempt me no longer."

"Vainly thou seekest to cast me off," rejoined Demdike. "What if I deliver thine adversaries into thine hands, and revenge thee upon them? Even now there are a party of armed men waiting at the foot of the hill to seize thee and thy brethren. Shall I show thee how to destroy them?"

"Who are they?" demanded the abbot, surprised.

"Their leaders are John Braddyll and Richard Assheton, who shall divide Whalley Abbey between them, if thou stayest them not," replied Demdike.

"Hell consume them!" cried the abbot.

"Thy speech shows consent," rejoined Demdike. "Come this way."

And, without awaiting the abbot's reply, he dragged his horse towards the but-end of the mountain. As they went on, the two monks, who had been filled with surprise at the interview, though they did not dare to interrupt it, advanced towards their superior, and looked earnestly and inquiringly at him, but he remained silent; while to the men-at-arms and the herdsmen, who demanded whether their own beacon-fire should be extinguished as the others had been, he answered moodily in the negative.

"Where are the foes you spoke of?" he asked with some uneasiness, as Demdike led his horse slowly and carefully down the hill-side.

"You shall see anon," replied the other.

"You are taking me to the spot where you traced the magic circle," cried Paslew in alarm. "I know it from its unnaturally green hue. I will not go thither."

"I do not mean you should, lord abbot," replied Demdike, halting. "Remain on this firm ground. Nay, be not alarmed; you are in no danger. Now bid your men advance, and prepare their weapons."

The abbot would have demanded wherefore, but at a glance from Demdike he complied, and the two men-at-arms, and the herdsmen, arranged themselves beside him, while Fathers Eastgate and Haydocke, who had gotten upon their mules, took up a position behind.

Scarcely were they thus placed, when a loud shout was raised below, and a band of armed men, to the number of thirty or forty, leapt the stone wall, and began to scale the hill with great rapidity. They came up a deep dry channel, apparently worn in the hill-side by some former torrent, and which led directly to the spot where Demdike and the abbot stood. The beacon-fire still blazed brightly, and illuminated the whole proceeding, showing that these men, from their accoutrements, were royalist soldiers.

"Stir not, as you value your life," said the wizard to Paslew; "but observe what shall follow."

CHAPTER II.—THE ERUPTION.

DEMDIKE went a little further down the hill, stopping when he came to the green patch. He then plunged his staff into the sod at the first point where he had cast a tuft of heather, and with such force that it sank more than three feet. The next moment he plucked it forth, as if with a great effort, and a jet of black water spouted into the air; but, heedless of this, he went to the next marked spot, and again plunged the sharp point of the implement into the ground. Again it sank to the same depth, and, on being drawn out, a second black jet sprung forth.

Meanwhile the hostile party continued to advance up the dry channel before mentioned, and shouted on beholding these strange preparations, but they did not relax their speed. Once more the staff sank into the ground, and a third black fountain followed its extraction. By this time, the royalist soldiers were close at hand, and the features of their two leaders, John Braddyll and Richard Assheton, could be plainly distinguished, and their voices heard.

"'Tis he! 'tis the rebel abbot!" vociferated Braddyll, pressing forward. "We were not misinformed. He has been watching by the beacon. The devil has delivered him into our hands."

"Ho! ho!" laughed Demdike.

"Abbot no longer—'tis the Earl of Poverty you mean," responded Assheton. "The villain shall be gibbeted on the spot where he has fired the beacon, as a warning to all traitors."

"Ha, heretics!—ha, blasphemers!—I can at least avenge myself upon you," cried Paslew, striking spurs into his charger. But ere he could execute his purpose, Demdike had sprung backward, and, catching the bridle, restrained the animal by a powerful effort.

"Hold!" he cried, in a voice of thunder, "or you will share their fate."

As the words were uttered, a dull, booming, subterranean sound was heard, and instantly afterwards, with a crash like thunder, the whole of the green circle beneath slipped off, and from a yawning rent under it burst forth with irresistible fury, a thick inky-coloured torrent, which, rising almost breast high, fell upon the devoted royalist soldiers, who were advancing right in its course. Unable to avoid the watery eruption, or to resist its fury when it came upon them, they were instantly swept from their feet, and carried down the channel.

A sight of horror was it to behold the sudden rise of that swarthy stream, whose waters, tinged by the ruddy glare of the beacon-fire, looked like waves of blood. Nor less fearful was it to hear the first wild despairing cry raised by the victims, or the quickly stifled shrieks and groans that followed, mixed with the deafening roar of the stream, and the crashing fall of the stones, which accompanied its course. Down, down went the poor wretches, now utterly overwhelmed by the torrent, now regaining their feet only to utter a scream, and then be swept off. Here a miserable struggler, whirled onward, would clutch at the banks and try to scramble forth, but the soft turf giving way beneath him, he was hurried off to eternity.

At another point where the stream encountered some trifling opposition, some two or three managed to gain a footing, but they were unable to extricate themselves. The vast quantity of boggy soil brought down by the current, and which rapidly collected here, embedded them and held them fast, so that the momently deepening water, already up to their chins, threatened speedy immersion. Others were stricken down by great masses of turf, or huge rocky fragments, which, bounding from point to point with the torrent, bruised or crushed all they encountered, or, lodging in some difficult place, slightly diverted the course of the torrent, and rendered it yet more dangerous.

On one of these stones, larger than the rest, which had been stopped in its course, a man contrived to creep, and with difficulty kept his post amid the raging flood. Vainly did he extend his hand to such of his fellows as were swept shrieking past him. He could not lend them aid, while his own position was so desperately hazardous that he did not dare to quit it. To leap on either bank was impossible, and to breast the headlong stream certain death.

On goes the current, madly, furiously, as if rejoicing in the work of destruction, while the white foam of its eddies presents a fearful contrast to the prevailing blackness of the surface. Over the last declivity it leaps, hissing, foaming, crashing like an avalanche. The stone wall for a moment opposes its force, but falls the next, with a mighty splash, carrying the spray far and wide, while its own fragments roll onwards with the stream. The trees of the orchard are uprooted in an instant, and an old elm falls prostrate. The outbuildings of a cottage are invaded, and the porkers and cattle, divining their danger, squeal and bellow in affright. But they are quickly silenced. The resistless foe has broken down wall and door, and buried the poor creatures in mud and rubbish.

The stream next invades the cottage, breaks in through door and window, and filling all the lower part of the tenement, in a few minutes converts it into a heap of ruin. On goes the destroyer, tearing up more trees, levelling more houses, and filling up a small pool, till the latter bursts its banks, and, with an accession to its force, pours itself into a mill-dam. Here its waters are stayed until they find a vent underneath, and the action of the stream, as it rushes downwards through this exit, forms a great eddy above, in which swim some living things, cattle and sheep from the fold not yet drowned, mixed with furniture from the cottages, and amidst them the bodies of some of the unfortunate men-at-arms which have been washed hither.

But, ha! another thundering crash. The dam has burst. The torrent roars and rushes on furiously as before, joins its forces with Pendle Water, swells up the river, and devastates the country far and wide.*

The abbot and his companions beheld this work of destruction with amazement and dread. Blanched terror sat in their cheeks, and the blood was frozen in Paslew's veins; for he thought it the work of the powers of darkness, and that he was leagued with them. He tried to mutter a prayer, but his lips refused their office. He would have moved, but his limbs were stiffened and paralysed, and he could only gaze aghast at the terrible spectacle.

Amidst it all he heard a wild burst of unearthly laughter, proceeding, he thought, from Demdike, and it filled him with new dread. But he could not check the sound, neither could he stop his ears, though he would fain have done so. Like him, his companions were petrified and speechless with fear.

After this had endured for some time, though still the black torrent rushed on impetuously as ever, Demdike turned to the abbot and said,—

"Your vengeance has been fully gratified. You will now baptise my child?"

"Never, never, accursed being!" shrieked the abbot. "Thou mayst sacrifice her at thine own impious rites. But see, there is

* A similar eruption occurred at Pendle Hill in August, 1669, and has been described by Mr. Charles Townley, in a letter cited by Dr. Whitaker in his excellent "History of Whalley." Other and more formidable eruptions had taken place previously, occasioning much damage to the country. The cause of the phenomenon is thus explained by Mr. Townley: "The colour of the water, its coming down to the place where it breaks forth between the rock and the earth, with that other particular of its bringing nothing along but stones and earth, are evident signs that it hath not its origin from the very bowels of the mountain; but that it is only rain water coloured first in the moss-pits, of which the top of the hill, being a great and considerable plain, is full, shrunk down into some receptacle fit to contain it, until at last by its weight, or some other cause, it finds a passage to the sides of the hill, and then away between the rock and swarth, until it break the latter and violently rush out."

one poor wretch yet struggling with the foaming torrent. I may save him."

"That is John Braddyll, thy worst enemy," replied Demdike. "If he lives he shall possess half Whalley Abbey. Thou hadst best also save Richard Assheton, who yet clings to the great stone below, as if he escapes he shall have the other half. Mark him, and make haste, for in five minutes both shall be gone."

"I will save them if I can, be the consequence to myself what it may," replied the abbot.

And, regardless of the derisive laughter of the other, who yelled in his ears as he went, "Bess shall see thee hanged at thy own door!" he dashed down the hill to the spot where a small object, distinguishable above the stream, showed that some one still kept his head above water, his tall stature having preserved him.

"Is it you, John Braddyll?" cried the abbot, as he rode up.

"Ay," replied the head. "Forgive me for the wrong I intended you, and deliver me from this great peril."

"I am come for that purpose," replied the abbot, dismounting, and disencumbering himself of his heavy cloak.

By this time the two herdsmen had come up, and the abbot, taking a crook from one of them, clutched hold of the fellow, and, plunging fearlessly into the stream, extended it towards the drowning man, who instantly lifted up his hand to grasp it. In doing so Braddyll lost his balance, but, as he did not quit his hold, he was plucked forth from the tenacious mud by the combined efforts of the abbot and his assistant, and with some difficulty dragged ashore.

"Now for the other," cried Paslew, as he placed Braddyll in safety.

"One-half the abbey is gone from thee," shouted a voice in his ears as he rushed on.

Presently he reached the rocky fragment on which Ralph Assheton rested. The latter was in great danger from the surging torrent, and the stone on which he had taken refuge tottered at its base, and threatened to roll over.

"In Heaven's name, help me, lord abbot, as thou thyself shall be holpen at thy need!" shrieked Assheton.

"Be not afraid, Richard Assheton," replied Paslew. "I will deliver thee as I have delivered John Braddyll."

But the task was not of easy accomplishment. The abbot made his preparations as before; grasped the hand of the herdsman and held out the crook to Assheton; but when the latter caught it, the stream swung him round with such force that the abbot must either abandon him or advance further into the water. Bent on Assheton's preservation, he adopted the latter expedient, and instantly lost his feet; while the herdsman, unable longer to hold him, let go the crook, and the abbot and Assheton were swept down the stream together.

Down—down they went, destruction apparently awaiting them; but the abbot, though sometimes quite under the water, and bruised by the rough stones and gravel with which he came in contact, still retained his self-possession, and encouraged his companion to hope for succour. In this way they were borne down to the foot of the hill, the monks, the herdsmen, and the men-at-arms having given them up as lost. But they yet lived—yet floated—though greatly injured, and almost senseless, when they were cast into a pool formed by the eddying waters at the foot of the hill. Here, wholly unable to assist himself, Assheton was seized by a black hound belonging to a tall man who stood on the bank, and who shouted to Paslew, as he helped the animal to bring the drowning man ashore, "The other half of the abbey is gone from thee. Wilt thou baptise my child if I send my dog to save thee?"

"Never!" replied the other, sinking as he spoke.

Flashes of fire glanced in the abbot's eyes, and stunning sounds seemed to burst his ears. A few more struggles, and he became senseless.

But he was not destined to die thus. What happened afterwards he knew not; but when he recovered full consciousness, he found himself stretched, with aching limbs and throbbing head, upon a couch in a monastic room, with a richly-painted and gilded ceiling, with shields at the corners emblazoned with the three luces of Whalley, and with panels hung with tapestry from the looms of Flanders, representing divers Scriptural subjects.

"Have I been dreaming?" he murmured.

"No," replied a tall man standing by his bedside; "thou hast been saved from one death to suffer another more ignominious."

"Ha!" cried the abbot, starting up and pressing his hand to his temples; "thou here?"

"Ay, I am appointed to watch thee," replied Demdike. "Thou art a prisoner in thine own chamber at Whalley. All has befallen as I told thee. The Earl of Derby is master of the abbey; thy adherents are dispersed; and thy brethren are driven forth. Thy two partners in rebellion, the abbots of Jervaux and Salley, have been conveyed to Lancaster Castle, whither thou wilt go as soon as thou canst be moved."

"I will surrender all—silver and gold, land and possessions—to the king, if I may die in peace," groaned the abbot.

"It is not needed," rejoined the other. "Attainted of felony, thy lands and abbey will be forfeited to the crown, and they shall be sold, as I have told thee, to John Braddyll and Richard Assheton, who will be rulers here in thy stead."

"Would I had perished in the flood!" groaned the abbot.

"Well mayst thou wish so," returned his tormentor; "but thou wert not destined to die by water. As I have said, thou shalt be hanged at thy own door, and my wife shall witness thy end."

"Who art thou? I have heard thy voice before," cried the

abbot. "It is like the voice of one whom I knew years ago, and thy features are like his—though changed—greatly changed. Who art thou?"

"Thou shalt know before thou diest," replied the other, with a look of gratified vengeance. "Farewell, and reflect upon thy fate."

So saying, he strode towards the door, while the miserable abbot arose, and marching with uncertain steps to a little oratory adjoining, which he himself had built, knelt down before the altar, and strove to pray.

CHAPTER III.—WHALLEY ABBEY.

A SAD, sad change hath come over the fair Abbey of Whalley. It knoweth its old masters no longer. For upwards of two centuries and a half hath the "Blessed Place"* grown in beauty and riches. Seventeen abbots have exercised unbounded hospitality within it, but now they are all gone, save one!—and he is attainted of felony and treason. The grave monk walketh no more in the cloisters, nor seeketh his pallet in the dormitory. Vesper or matin-song resound not as of old within the fine conventual church. Stripped are the altars of their silver crosses, and the shrines of their votive offerings and saintly relics. Pyx and chalice, thuribule and vial, golden-headed pastoral staff, and mitre embossed with pearls, candlestick and Christmas ship of silver; salver, basin, and ewer—all are gone—the splendid sacristy hath been despoiled.

A sad, sad change hath come over Whalley Abbey. The libraries, well stored with reverend tomes, have been pillaged, and their contents cast to the flames; and thus long laboured manuscript, the fruit of years of patient industry, with gloriously illuminated missal, are irrecoverably lost. The large infirmary no longer receiveth the sick; in the locutory sitteth no more the guest. No longer in the mighty kitchens are prepared the prodigious supply of meats destined for the support of the poor or the entertainment of the traveller. No kindly porter stands at the gate, to bid the stranger enter and partake of the munificent abbot's hospitality, but a churlish guard bids him hie away, and menaces him if he tarries with his halbert. Closed are the buttery-hatches and the pantries; and the daily dole of bread hath ceased. Closed, also, to the brethren is the refectory. The cellarer's office is ended. The strong ale which he brewed in October, is tapped in March by roystering troopers. The rich muscadel and malmsey, and the wines of Gascoigne and the Rhine, are no longer quaffed by the abbot and his more honoured guests, but drunk to his destruction by his foes. The great gallery, a hundred and fifty feet in length, the pride of the abbot's lodging, and a model of architecture, is

* Locus Benedictus de Whalley.

filled, not with white-robed ecclesiastics, but with an armed earl and his retainers. Neglected is the little oratory dedicated to Our Lady of Whalley, where night and morn the abbot used to pray. All the old religious and hospitable uses of the abbey are foregone. The reverend stillness of the cloisters, scarce broken by the quiet tread of the monks, is now disturbed by armed heel and clank of sword; while in its saintly courts are heard the ribald song, the profane jest, and the angry brawl. Of the brethren, only those tenanting the cemetery are left. All else are gone, driven forth, as vagabonds, with stripes and curses, to seek refuge where they may.

A sad, sad change has come over Whalley Abbey. In the plenitude of its pride aud power has it been cast down, desecrated, despoiled. Its treasures are carried off, its ornaments sold, its granaries emptied, its possessions wasted, its storehouses sacked, its cattle slaughtered and sold. But, though stripped of its wealth and splendour; though deprived of all the religious graces that, like rich incense, lent an odour to the fane, its external beauty is yet unimpaired, and its vast proportions undiminished.

A stately pile was Whalley—one of the loveliest as well as the largest in the realm. Carefully had it been preserved by its reverend rulers, and where reparations or additions were needed they were judiciously made. Thus age had lent it beauty, by mellowing its freshness and toning its hues, while no decay was perceptible. Without a struggle had it yielded to the captor, so that no part of its wide belt of walls or towers, though so strongly constructed as to have offered effectual resistance, were injured.

Never had Whalley Abbey looked more beautiful than on a bright clear morning in March, when this sad change had been wrought, and when, from a peaceful monastic establishment, it had been converted into a menacing fortress. The sunlight sparkled upon its grey walls, and filled its three great quadrangular courts with light and life, piercing the exquisite carving of its cloisters, and revealing all the intricate beauty and combinations of the arches. Stains of painted glass fell upon the floor of the magnificent conventual church, and dyed with rainbow hues the marble tombs of the Lacies, the founders of the establishment, brought thither when the monastery was removed from Stanlaw in Cheshire, and upon the brass-covered gravestones of the abbots in the presbytery. There lay Gregory de Northbury, eighth abbot of Stanlaw and first of Whalley, and William Rede, the last abbot; but there was never to lie John Paslew. The slumber of the ancient prelates was soon to be disturbed, and the sacred structure within which they had so often worshipped up-reared by sacrilegious hands But all was bright and beauteous now, and if no solemn strains were heard in the holy pile, its stillness was scarcely less reverential and awe-inspiring. The old abbey wreathed itself in all its attractions, as if to welcome back its former ruler, whereas it was only to receive him as a captive doomed to a felon's death.

But this was outward show. Within all was terrible preparation. Such was the discontented state of the country, that fearing some new revolt, the Earl of Derby had taken measures for the defence of the abbey, and along the wide-circling walls of the close were placed ordnance and men, and within the grange stores of ammunition. A strong guard was set at each of the gates, and the courts were filled with troops. The bray of the trumpet echoed within the close, where rounds were set for the archers, and martial music resounded within the area of the cloisters. Over the great north-eastern gateway, which formed the chief entrance to the abbot's lodging, floated the royal banner. Despite these warlike proceedings the fair abbey smiled beneath the sun, in all, or more than all, its pristine beauty, its green hills sloping gently down towards it, and the clear and sparkling Calder dashing merrily over the stones at its base.

But upon the bridge, and by the river side, and within the little village, many persons were assembled, conversing gravely and anxiously together, and looking out towards the hills, where other groups were gathered, as if in expectation of some afflicting event. Most of these were herdsmen and farming men, but some among them were poor monks in the white habits of the Cistertian brotherhood, but which were now stained and threadbare, while their countenances bore traces of severest privation and suffering. All the herdsmen and farmers had been retainers of the abbot. The poor monks looked wistfully at their former habitation, but replied not except by a gentle bowing of the head to the cruel scoffs and taunts with which they were greeted by the passing soldiers; but the sturdy rustics did not bear these outrages so tamely, and more than one brawl ensued, in which blood flowed, while a ruffianly arquebussier would have been drowned in the Calder but for the exertions to save him of a monk whom he had attacked.

This took place on the eleventh of March, 1537—more than three months after the date of the watching by the beacon before recorded—and the event anticipated by the concourse without the abbey, as well as by those within its walls, was the arrival of Abbot Paslew and Fathers Eastgate and Haydocke, who were to be brought on that day from Lancaster, and executed on the following morning before the abbey, according to sentence passed upon them.

The gloomiest object in the picture remains to be described, but yet it is necessary to its completion. This was a gallows of unusual form and height, erected on the summit of a gentle hill, rising immediately in front of the abbot's lodgings, called the Holehouses, whose rounded, bosomy beauty it completely destroyed. This terrible apparatus of condign punishment was regarded with abhorrence by the rustics, and it required a strong guard to be kept constantly round it to preserve it from demolition.

Amongst a group of rustics collected on the road leading to the north-east gateway, was Cuthbert Ashbead, who, having been deprived of his forester's office, was now habited in a frieze doublet and hose, with a short camlet cloak on his shoulder, and a fox-skin cap, embellished with the grinning jaws of the beast on his head.

"Eigh, Ruchot o' Roaph's," he observed to a bystander, "that's a fearfo seet that gallas. Yoan been up to t' Holehouses to tey a look at it, beloike?"

"Naw, naw, ey dunna loike such seets," replied Ruchot o'Roaph's; "besoide there wor a great rabblement at t' geate, an one o' them lunjus archer chaps knockt meh o' t' nob wi' his poike, an towd me he'd hong me wi' t' abbut, if ey didna keep owt ot wey."

"An sarve te reet too, theaw craddinly carl!" cried Ashbead, doubling his horny fists. "Odds flesh! whey didna yo ha' a tussle wi' him? Mey honts are itchen for a bowt wi' t' heretic robbers. Walladey! walladey! that we should live to see t' oly feythers driven loike hummobees owt o' t' owd neest. Whey they sayn ot King Harry hon decreet ot we're to ha' naw more monks or friars i' aw Englondshiar. Ony think o' that. An dunna yo knoa that t' Abbuts o' Jervaux an Salley wor hongt o' Tizeday at Loncaster Castle?"

"Good lorjus bless us!" exclaimed a sturdy hind, "we'n a protty king. Furst he chops off his woife's heaod, an then hongs aw t' priests. Whot'll t' warlt cum to?

"Eigh by t' mess, whot *win* it cum to?" cried Ruchot o' Roaph's. "But we darrna oppen owr mows fo' fear o' a gog."

"Naw, beleady! boh eyst oppen moine woide enuff," cried Ashbead; "an' if a dozen o' yo chaps win join me, eyn try to set t' poor abbut free whon they brinks him here."

"Ey'd as leef boide till to-morrow," said Ruchot o'Roaph's, uneasily.

"Eigh, thou'rt a timmersome teyke, os ey towd te efore," replied Ashbead. "But whot dust theaw say, Hal o' Nabs?" he added, to the sturdy hind who had recently spoken.

"Ey'n spill t' last drop o' meh blood i' t' owd abbut's keawse," replied Hal o' Nabs. "We winna stond by, an see him hongt loike a dog. Abbut Paslew to t' reskew, lads!"

"Eigh, Abbut Paslew to t' reskew!" responded all the others, except Ruchot o' Roaph's.

"This must be prevented," muttered a voice near them. And immediately afterwards a tall man quitted the group.

"Whoa wor it spoake?" cried Hal o' Nabs. "Oh, ey seen, that he-witch, Nick Demdike."

"Nick Demdike here!" cried Ashbead, looking round in alarm. "Has he owerheert us?"

"Loike enow," replied Hal o' Nabs. "But ey didna moind him efore."

"Naw ey noather," cried Ruchot o' Roaph's, crossing himself, and spitting on the ground. "Owr Leady o' Whalley shielt us fro' t' warlock!"

"Tawkin o' Nick Demdike," cried Hal o' Nabs, "yo'd a strawnge odventer wi' him t' neet o' t' great brast o' Pendle Hill, hadna yo, Cuthbert?"

"Yeigh, t' firrups tak' him, ey hadn," replied Ashbead. "Theawst hear aw abowt it if t' will. Ey wur sent be t' abbut down t' hill to Owen o' Gab's, o' Perkin's, o' Dannel's, o' Noll's, o' Oamfrey's orchert i' Warston lone, to luk efter him. Weel, whon ey gets ower t' stoan wa', whot dun yo think ey sees! twanty or throtty poikemen stonding behint it, an they deshes at meh os thick os leet, an efore ey con roor oot, they blintfowlt meh, an clap an iron gog i' meh mouth. Weel, I con noather speak nor see, boh ey con use meh feet, soh ey punses at 'em reet an' laft; an be mah troath, lads, yood'n a leawght t' hear how they roart, an ey should a roart too, if I couldn, whon they began to thwack me wi' their raddling pows, and ding'd meh so abowt t' heoad, that ey fell i' a swownd. Whon ey cum to, ey wur loyin o' meh back i' Rimington Moor. Every booan i' meh hoide wratcht, an meh hewr war clottert wi' gore, boh t' eebond an t' gog wur gone, soh ey gets o' meh feet, and daddles along os weel os ey con, whon aw ot wunce ey spies a leet glenting efore meh, an dawncing abowt loike an awf or a wull-o'-whisp. Thinks ey, that's Friar Rush an' his lantern, an he'll lead me into a quagmire, soh ey stops a bit, to consider where ey'd getten, for ey didna knoa t' reet road exactly; boh whon ey stood still, t' leet stood still too, on then ey meyd owt that it cum fro an owd ruint tower, an whot ey'd fancied wur one lantern proved twanty, fo' whon ey reacht t' tower an peept in thro' a brok'n winda, ey beheld a seet ey'st neer forgit—apack o' witches—eigh, witches!—sittin' in a ring, wi' their broomsticks an lanterns abowt em!"

"Good lorjus deys!" cried Hal o' Nabs. "An whot else didsta see, mon?"

"Whoy," replied Ashbead, "t'owd hags had a little figure i' t' midst on 'em, mowded i' cley, representing t' abbut o' Whalley, —ey knoad it be't moitre and crosier,—an efter each o' t' varment had stickt a pin i' its 'eart, a tall black mon stepped for'ard, an teed a cord rownd its throttle, an hongt it up."

"An' t' black mon," cried Hal o' Nabs, breathlessly,—"t' black mon wur Nick Demdike?"

"Yoan guest it," replied Ashbead, "'t wur he! Ey wur so glopp'nt, ey couldna speak, an' meh blud fruz i' meh veins, when ey heerd a fearfo voice ask Nick wheere his woife an' chilt were. 'The infant is unbaptised,' roart t' voice, 'at the next meeting it must be sacrificed. See that thou bring it.' Demdike then bowed to Summat I couldna see, an axt when t' next meeting wur to be held. 'On the night of Abbot Paslew's execution,' awnsert t' voice. On hearing this, ey could bear nah lunger, boh shouted out, 'Witches! devils! Lort deliver us fro' ye!' An' os ey spoke, ey tried t' barst thro' t' winda. In a trice, aw t' leets went out; thar wur a great rash to t' dooer; a whirrin sound i' th' air loike a covey o' partriches fleeing off; and then ey heerd nowt more; for a great stoan fell o' meh scoance, an' knockt me down senseless. When I cum' to, I wur i' Nick Demdike's cottage, wi' his woife watching ower me, and th' unbapteesed chilt i' her arms."

All exclamations of wonder on the part of the rustics, and inquiries as to the issue of the adventure, were checked by the approach of a monk, who, joining the assemblage, called their attention to a priestly train slowly advancing along the road.

"It is headed," he said, "by Fathers Chatburne and Chester, late bursers of the abbey. Alack! alack! they now need the charity themselves which they once so lavishly bestowed on others."

"Waes me!" ejaculated Ashbead. "Monry a broad merk han ey getten fro 'em."

"They'n been koind to us aw," added the others.

"Next come Father Burnley, granger, and Father Haworth, cellarer," pursued the monk; "and after them Father Dinkley, sacristan, and Father Moore, porter."

"Yo remember Feyther Moore, lads," cried Ashbead.

"Yeigh, to be sure we done," replied the others; "a good mon, a reet good mon! He never sent away t' poor—naw he!"

"After Father Moore," said the monk, pleased with their warmth, "comes Father Forrest, the procurator, with Fathers Rede, Clough, and Bancroft, and the procession is closed by Father Smith, the late prior."

"Down o' yer whirlybooans, lads, as t' oly feythers pass," cried Ashbead, "and crave their blessing."

And as the priestly train slowly approached, with heads bowed down, and looks fixed sadly upon the ground, the rustic assemblage fell upon their knees, and implored their benediction. The foremost in the procession passed on in silence, but the prior stopped, and extending his hands over the kneeling group, cried in a solemn voice,

"Heaven bless ye, my children! Ye are about to witness a sad spectacle. You will see him who hath clothed you, fed you, and taught you the way to heaven, brought hither a prisoner, to suffer a shameful death."

"Boh we'st set him free, oly prior," cried Ashbead. "We'n meayed up our moinds to 't. Yo just wait till he cums."

"Nay, I command you to desist from the attempt, if any such you meditate," rejoined the prior; "it will avail nothing, and you will only sacrifice your own lives. Our enemies are too strong. The abbot himself would give you like counsel."

Scarcely were the words uttered than from the great gate of the abbey there issued a dozen arquebussiers with an officer at their head, who marched directly towards the kneeling hinds, evidently with the intention of dispersing them. Behind them strode Nicholas Demdike. In an instant the alarmed rustics were on their feet, and Ruchot o' Roaph's, and some few among them, took to their heels, but Ashbead, Hal o' Nabs, with half a dozen others, stood their ground manfully. The monks remained in the hope of preventing any violence. Presently the halberdiers came up.

"That is the ringleader," cried the officer, who proved to be Richard Assheton, pointing out Ashbead; "seize him!"

"Naw mon shall lay honts o' meh," cried Cuthbert.

And as the guard pushed past the monks to execute their leader's order, he sprang forward, and, wresting a halbert from the foremost of them, stood upon his defence.

"Seize him, I say!" shouted Assheton, irritated at the resistance offered.

"Keep off," cried Ashbead; "yo'd best. Loike a stag at bey ey'm dawngerous. Waar horns! waar horns! ey sey."

The arquebussiers looked irresolute. It was evident Ashbead would only be taken with life, and they were not sure that it was their leader's purpose to destroy him.

"Put down thy weapon, Cuthbert," interposed the prior; "it will avail thee nothing against odds like these."

"Mey be, 'oly prior," rejoined Ashbead, flourishing the pike: "boh ey'st ony yield wi' loife."

"I will disarm him," cried Demdike, stepping forward.

"Theaw!" retorted Ashbead, with a scornful laugh, "Cum on, then. Hadsta aw t' fiends i' hell at te back, ey shouldna fear thee."

"Yield!" cried Demdike in a voice of thunder, and fixing a terrible glance upon him.

"Cum on, wizard," rejoined Ashbead undauntedly. But, observing that his opponent was wholly unarmed, he gave the pike to Hal o' Nabs, who was close beside him, observing, "It shall never be said that Cuthbert Ashbead feawt t' dule himsel unfairly. Nah, touch me if theaw dar'st."

Demdike required no further provocation. With almost supernatural force and quickness he sprung upon the forester, and seized him by the throat. But the active young man freed himself from the gripe, and closed with his assailant. But though of Herculean build, it soon became evident that Ashbead would have the worst of it; when Hal o' Nabs, who had watched the struggle with intense interest, could not help coming to his friend's assistance, and made a push at Demdike with the halbert.

Could it be that the wrestlers shifted their position, or that the wizard was indeed aided by the powers of darkness? None could tell, but so it was that the pike pierced the side of Ashbead, who instantly fell to the ground, with his adversary upon him. The next instant his hold relaxed, and the wizard sprang to his feet unharmed, but deluged in blood. Hal o' Nabs uttered a cry of keenest anguish, and, flinging himself upon the body of the forester, tried to staunch the wound; but he was quickly seized by the arquebussiers, and his hands tied behind his back with a thong, while Ashbead was lifted up and borne towards the abbey, the monks and rustics following slowly after; but the latter were not permitted to enter the gate.

As the unfortunate keeper, who by this time had become insensible from loss of blood, was carried along the walled enclosure leading to the abbot's lodging, a female with a child in her arms was seen advancing from the opposite side. She was tall, finely formed, with features of remarkable beauty, though of a masculine and somewhat savage character, and with magnificent but fierce black eyes. Her skin was dark, and her hair raven black, contrasting strongly with the red band wound around it. Her kirtle was of murrey-coloured serge; simply, but becomingly fashioned. A glance sufficed to show her how matters stood with poor Ashbead, and, uttering a sharp angry cry, she rushed towards him.

"What have you done?" she cried, fixing a keen reproachful look on Demdike, who walked beside the wounded man.

"Nothing," replied Demdike with a bitter laugh; "the fool has been hurt with a pike. Stand out of the way, Bess, and let the men pass. They are about to carry him to the cell under the chapter-house."

"You shall not take him there," cried Bess Demdike, fiercely. "He may recover if his wound be dressed. Let him go to the infirmary—ha, I forgot—there is no one there now."

"Father Bancroft is at the gate," observed one of the arquebussiers; "he used to act as chirurgeon in the abbey."

"No monk must enter the gate except the prisoners when they arrive," observed Assheton; "such are the positive orders of the Earl of Derby."

"It is not needed," observed Demdike, "no human aid can save the man."

"But can other aid save him?" said Bess, breathing the words in her husband's ears.

"Go to!" cried Demdike, pushing her roughly aside; "wouldst have me save thy lover?"

"Take heed," said Bess, in a deep whisper; "if thou save him not, by the devil thou servest! thou shalt lose me and thy child."

Demdike did not think proper to contest the point, but, approaching Assheton, requested that the wounded man might be conveyed to an arched recess, which he pointed out. Assent being given, Ashbead was taken there, and placed upon the ground, after which the arquebussiers and their leader marched off; while Bess, kneeling down, supported the head of the wounded man upon her knee, and Demdike, taking a small phial from his doublet, poured some of its contents down his throat. The wizard then took a fold of linen, with which he was likewise provided, and, dipping it in the elixir, applied it to the wound.

In a few moments Ashbead opened his eyes, and looking round wildly, fixed his gaze upon Bess, who placed her finger upon her lips to enjoin silence, but he could not, or would not, understand the sign.

"Aw's o'er wi' meh, Bess," he groaned; "but ey'd reyther dee thus, wi' thee besoide meh, than i' ony other wey."

"Hush!" exclaimed Bess, "Nicholas is here."

"Oh! ey see," replied the wounded man, looking round; "boh whot matters it? Ey'st be gone soon. Ah, Bess, dear lass, if theawdst promise to break thy compact wi' Satan—to repent and save thy precious sowl—ey should dee content."

"Oh, do not talk thus!" cried Bess. "You will soon be well again.

"Listen to me," continued Ashbead, earnestly; "dust na knoa that if thy babe be na bapteesed efore to-morrow neet, it'll be sacrificed to t' Prince o' Darkness. Go to some o' t' oly feythers—confess thy sins an' implore heaven's forgiveness—an' mayhap they'll save thee an' thy infant."

"And be burned as a witch," rejoined Bess, fiercely. "It is useless, Cuthbert; I have tried them all. I have knelt to them, implored them, but their hearts are hard as flints. They will not heed me. They will not disobey the abbot's cruel injunctions, though he be their superior no longer. But I shall be avenged upon him—terribly avenged.

"Leave meh, theaw wicked woman," cried Ashbead; "ey dunna wish to ha' thee near meh. Let meh dee i' peace."

"Thou wilt not die, I tell thee, Cuthbert," cried Bess; "Nicholas hath staunched thy wound."

"He stawncht it, seyst to?" cried Ashbead, raising. "Ey'st never owe meh loife to him."

And before he could be prevented he tore off the bandage, and the blood burst forth anew.

"It is not my fault if he perishes now," observed Demdike, moodily.

"Help him—help him!" implored Bess.

"He shanna touch meh," cried Ashbead, struggling and increasing the effusion. "Keep him off, ey adjure thee. Farewell, Bess," he added, sinking back utterly exhausted by the effort.

"Cuthbert!" screamed Bess, terrified by his looks, "Cuthbert!

art thou really dying? Look at me, speak to me! Ha!" she cried, as if seized by a sudden idea, "they say the blessing of a dying man will avail. Bless my child, Cuthbert, bless it!"

"Give it me!" groaned the forester.

Bess held the infant towards him; but before he could place his hands upon it all power forsook him, and he fell back and expired.

"Lost! lost! for ever lost!" cried Bess, with a wild shriek.

At this moment a loud blast was blown from the gate-tower, and a trumpeter called out,

"The abbot and the two other prisoners are coming."

"To thy feet, wench!" cried Demdike, imperiously, and seizing the bewildered woman by the arm; "to thy feet, and come with me to meet him!"

CHAPTER IV.—THE MALEDICTION.

THE captive ecclesiastics, together with the strong escort by which they were attended, under the command of John Braddyll, the high sheriff of the county, had passed the previous night at Whitewell, in Bowland Forest; and the abbot, before setting out on his final journey, was permitted to spend an hour in prayer in a little chapel on an adjoining hill, overlooking a most picturesque portion of the forest, the beauties of which were enhanced by the windings of the Hodder, one of the loveliest streams in Lancashire. His devotions performed, Paslew, attended by a guard, slowly descended the hill, and gazed his last on scenes familiar to him almost from infancy. Noble trees, which now looked like old friends, to whom he was bidding an eternal adieu, stood around him. Beneath them, at the end of a glade, couched a herd of deer, which started off at sight of the intruders, and made him envy their freedom and fleetness as he followed them in thought to their solitudes. At the foot of a steep rock ran the Hodder, making the pleasant music of other days as it dashed over its pebbly bed, and recalling times, when, free from all care, he had strayed by its wood-fringed banks, to listen to the pleasant sound of running waters, and watch the shining pebbles beneath them, and the swift trout and dainty umber glancing past.

A bitter pang was it to part with scenes so fair, and the abbot spoke no word, nor even looked up, until, passing Little Mitton, he came in sight of Whalley Abbey. Then, collecting all his energies, he prepared for the shock he was about to endure. But nerved as he was, his firmness was sorely tried when he beheld the stately pile, once his own, now gone from him and his for ever. He gave one fond glance towards it, and then painfully averting his gaze, recited, in a low voice, this supplication:—

"*Miserere mei, Deus, secundum magnam misericordiam tuam. Et secundum multitudinem miserationum tuarum, dele iniquitatem meam. Amplius lava me ab iniquitate meâ, et à peccato meo munda me.*"

But other thoughts and other emotions crowded upon him, when he beheld the groups of his old retainers advancing to meet him: men, women, and children pouring forth loud lamentations, prostrating themselves at his feet, and deploring his doom. The abbot's fortitude had a severe trial here, and the tears sprung to his eyes. The devotion of these poor people touched him more sharply than the severity of his adversaries.

"Bless ye! bless ye! my children," he cried; "repine not for me, for I bear my cross with resignation. It is for me to bewail your lot, much fearing that the flock I have so long and so zealously tended will fall into the hands of other and less heedful pastors, or, still worse, of devouring wolves. Bless ye, my children, and be comforted. Think of the end of Abbot Paslew, and for what he suffered."

"Think that he was a traitor to the king, and took up arms in rebellion against him," cried the sheriff, riding up, and speaking in a loud voice; "and that for his heinous offences he was justly condemned to death."

Murmurs arose at this speech, but they were instantly checked by the escort.

"Think charitably of me, my children," said the abbot; "and the blessed Virgin keep you steadfast in your faith. Benedicite!"

"Be silent, traitor, I command thee," cried the sheriff, striking him with his gauntlet in the face.

The abbot's pale cheek burnt crimson, and his eye flashed fire, but he controlled himself, and answered meekly,—

"Thou didst not speak in such wise, John Braddyll, when I saved thee from the flood."

"Which flood thou thyself caused to burst forth by devilish arts," rejoined the sheriff. "I owe thee little for the service. If for naught else, thou deservest death for thy evil doings on that night."

The abbot made no reply, for Braddyll's allusion conjured up a sombre train of thought within his breast, awakening apprehensions which he could neither account for, nor shake off. Meanwhile, the cavalcade slowly approached the north-east gateway of the abbey—passing through crowds of kneeling and sorrowing bystanders;—but so deeply was the abbot engrossed by the one dread idea that possessed him, that he saw them not, and scarce heard their woful lamentations. All at once the cavalcade stopped, and the sheriff rode on to the gate, in the opening of which some ceremony was observed. Then it was that Paslew raised his eyes, and beheld standing before him a tall man, with a woman beside him bearing an infant in her arms. The eyes of the pair were fixed upon him with vindictive exultation.

He would have averted his gaze, but an irresistible fascination withheld him.

"Thou seest all is prepared," said Demdike, coming close up to the mule on which Paslew was mounted, and pointing to the gigantic gallows, looming above the abbey walls; "wilt thou now accede to my request?" And then he added, significantly—"on the same terms as before."

The abbot understood his meaning well. Life and freedom were offered him by a being, whose power to accomplish his promise he did not doubt. The struggle was hard; but he resisted the temptation, and answered firmly,—

"No."

"Then die the felon death thou meritest," cried Bess, fiercely; "and I will glut mine eyes with the spectacle."

Incensed beyond endurance, the abbot looked sternly at her, and raised his hand in denunciation. The action and the look were so appalling, that the affrighted woman would have fled if her husband had not restrained her.

"By the holy patriarchs and prophets; by the prelates and confessors; by the doctors of the church; by the holy abbots, monks, and eremites, who dwelt in solitudes, in mountains, and in caverns; by the holy saints and martyrs, who suffered torture and death for their faith, I curse thee, witch!" cried Paslew "May the malediction of Heaven and all its hosts alight on the head of thy infant—"

"Oh! holy abbot," shrieked Bess, breaking from her husband, and flinging herself at Paslew's feet, "curse me, if thou wilt, but spare my innocent child. Save it, and we will save thee."

"Avoid thee, wretched and impious woman," rejoined the abbot; "I have pronounced the dread anathema, and it cannot be recalled. Look at the dripping garments of thy child. In blood has it been baptised, and through blood-stained paths shall its course be taken."

"Ha!" shrieked Bess, noticing for the first time the ensanguined condition of the infant's attire. "Cuthbert's blood—oh!"

"Listen to me, wicked woman," pursued the abbot, as if filled with a prophetic spirit. "Thy child's life shall be long—beyond the ordinary term of woman—but it shall be a life of woe and ill."

"Oh! stay him—stay him; or I shall die!" cried Bess.

But the wizard could not speak. A greater power than his own apparently overmastered him.

"Children shall she have," continued the abbot, "and children s children, but they shall be a race doomed and accursed—a brood of adders, that the world shall flee from and crush. A thing accursed, and shunned by her fellows, shall thy daughter be—evil reputed and evil doing. No hand to help her—no lip to bless her—life a burden; and death—long, long in coming—finding her in a dismal dungeon. Now, depart from me, and trouble me no more."

Bess made a motion as if she would go, and then turning, partly round, dropped heavily on the ground. Demdike caught the child ere she fell.

"Thou hast killed her!" he cried to the abbot.

"A stronger voice than mine hath spoken, if it be so," rejoined Paslew. "*Fuge miserrime, fuge malefice, quia judex adest iratus.*"

At this moment the trumpet again sounded, and the cavalcade being put in motion, the abbot and his fellow-captives passed through the gate.

Dismounting from their mules within the court, before the chapter-house, the captive ecclesiastics, preceded by the sheriff, were led to the principal chamber of the structure, where the Earl of Derby awaited them, seated in the Gothic carved oak chair, formerly occupied by the Abbots of Whalley on the occasions of conferences or elections. The earl was surrounded by his officers, and the chamber was filled with armed men. The abbot slowly advanced towards the earl. His deportment was dignified and firm, even majestic. The exaltation of spirit, occasioned by the interview with Demdike and his wife, had passed away, and was succeeded by a profound calm. The hue of his cheek was livid, but otherwise he seemed wholly unmoved.

The ceremony of delivering up the bodies of the prisoners to the earl was gone through by the sheriff, and their sentences were then read aloud by a clerk. After this the earl, who had hitherto remained covered, took off his cap, and in a solemn voice spoke:—

"John Paslew, somewhile Abbot of Whalley, but now an attainted and condemned felon, and John Eastgate and William Haydocke, formerly brethren of the same monastery, and confederates with him in crime, ye have heard your doom. To-morrow you shall die the ignominious death of traitors; but the king in his mercy, having regard not so much to the heinous nature of your offences towards his sovereign majesty as to the sacred offices you once held, and of which you have been shamefully deprived, is graciously pleased to remit that part of your sentence, whereby ye are condemned to be quartered alive, willing that the hearts which conceived so much malice and violence against him should cease to beat within your own bosoms, and that the arms which were raised in rebellion against him should be interred in one common grave with the trunks to which they belong."

"God save the high and puissant king, Henry the Eighth, and free him from all traitors!" cried the clerk.

"We humbly thank his majesty for his clemency," said the abbot, amid the profound silence that ensued: "and I pray you, my good lord, when you shall write to the king concerning us, to say to his majesty that we died penitent of many and grave offences, amongst the which is chiefly that of having taken up arms unlawfully against him, but that we did so solely with the view of freeing his highness from evil counsellors, and of re-establishing our holy church, for the which we would willingly die, if our death might in anywise profit it."

"Amen!" exclaimed Father Eastgate, who stood with his hands crossed upon his breast, close behind Paslew. "The abbot hath uttered my sentiments."

"He hath not uttered mine," cried Father Haydocke. "I ask no grace from the bloody Herodias, and will accept none. What I have done I would do again, were the past to return—nay, I would do more—I would find a way to reach the tyrant's heart, and thus free our church from its worst enemy, and the land from a ruthless oppressor."

"Remove him," said the earl; "the vile traitor shall be dealt with as he merits. For you," he added, as the order was obeyed, and addressing the other prisoners, "and especially you, John Paslew, who have shown some compunction for your crimes, and to prove to you that the king is not the ruthless tyrant he hath been just represented, I hereby in his name promise you any boon, which you may ask consistently with your situation. What favour would you have shown you?"

The abbot reflected for a moment.

"Speak thou, John Eastgate," said the Earl of Derby, seeing that the abbot was occupied in thought.

"If I may proffer a request, my lord," replied the monk, "it is that our poor distraught brother, William Haydocke, be spared the quartering block. He meant not what he said."

"Well, be it as thou wilt," replied the earl, bending his brows, "though he ill deserves such grace. Now, John Paslew, what wouldst thou?"

Thus addressed, the abbot looked up.

"I would have made the same request as my brother, John Eastgate, if he had not anticipated me, my lord," said Paslew; but since his petition is granted, I would, on my own part, entreat that mass be said for us in the convent church. Many of the brethren are without the abbey, and, if permitted, will assist at its performance."

"I know not if I shall not incur the king's displeasure in assenting," replied the Earl of Derby, after a little reflection; "but I will hazard it. Mass for the dead shall be said in the church at midnight, and all the brethren who choose to come thither shall be permitted to assist at it. They will attend, I doubt not, for it will be the last time the rites of the Romish Church will be performed in those walls. They shall have all required for the ceremonial."

"Heaven's blessings on you, my lord," said the abbot.

"But first pledge me your sacred word," said the earl, "by the holy office you once held, and by the saints in whom you trust, that this concession shall not be made the means of any attempt at flight."

"I swear it," replied the abbot, earnestly.

"And I also swear it," added Father Eastgate.

"Enough," said the earl. "I will give the requisite orders. Notice of the celebration of mass at midnight shall be proclaimed without the abbey. Now remove the prisoners."

Upon this the captive ecclesiastics were led forth. Father Eastgate was taken to a strong room in the lower part of the chapter-house, where all acts of discipline had been performed by the monks, and where the knotted lash, the spiked girdle, and the hair shirt had once hung; while the abbot was conveyed to his old chamber, which had been prepared for his reception, and there left alone.

CHAPTER V.—THE MIDNIGHT MASS.

DOLEFULLY sounds the All Souls' bell from the tower of the convent church. The bell is one of five, and has obtained the name because it is tolled only for those about to pass away from life. Now it rings the knell of three souls to depart on the morrow. Brightly illumined is the fane, within which no taper hath gleamed since the old worship ceased, showing that preparations are made for the last service. The organ, dumb so long, breathes a low prelude. Sad is it to hear that knell—sad to view those gloriously-dyed panes—and to think why the one rings and the other is lighted up.

Word having gone forth of the midnight mass, all the ejected brethren flock to the abbey. Some have toiled through miry and scarce passable roads. Others have come down from the hills, and forded deep streams at the hazard of life, rather than go round by the far-off bridge, and arrive too late. Others, who conceive themselves in peril from the share they have taken in the late insurrection, quit their secure retreats, and expose themselves to capture. It may be a snare laid for them, but they run the risk. Others, coming from a yet greater distance, beholding the illuminated church from afar, and catching the sound of the bell tolling at intervals, hurry on, and reach the gate breathless and wellnigh exhausted. But no questions are asked. All who present themselves in ecclesiastical habits are permitted to enter, and take part in the procession forming in the cloister, or proceed at once to the church, if they prefer it.

Dolefully sounds the bell. Barefooted brethren meet together, sorrowfully salute each other, and form in a long line in the great area of the cloisters. At their head are six monks bearing tall lighted candles. After them come the quiristers, and then one carrying the Host, between the incense-bearers. Next comes a youth holding the bell. Next are placed the dignitaries of the church, the prior ranking first, and the others standing two and two, according to their degrees. Near the entrance of the refectory, which occupies the whole south side of the quadrangle, stand a band of halberdiers, whose torches cast a ruddy glare on the opposite tower and buttresses of the convent church, revealing the statues not yet plucked from their niches, the crosses on the pinnacles, and the gilt image of Saint Gregory de Northbury, still holding its place over the porch. Another band are stationed near the mouth of the vaulted passage, under the chapter-house and vestry, whose grey, irregular walls, pierced by numberless richly ornamented windows, and surmounted by small turrets, form a beautiful boundary on the right; while a third party are planted on the left, in the open space, beneath the dormitory, the torchlight flashing ruddily upon the hoary pillars and groined arches sustaining the vast structure above them.

Dolefully sounds the bell. And the ghostly procession thrice tracks the four ambulatories of the cloisters, solemnly chanting a requiem for the dead.

Dolefully sounds the bell. And at its summons all the old retainers of the abbot press to the gate, and sue for admittance, but in vain. They, therefore, mount the neighbouring hill commanding the abbey, and as the solemn sounds float faintly by, and glimpses are caught of the white-robed brethren gliding along the cloisters, and rendered phantom-like by the torchlight, the beholders half imagine it must be a company of sprites, and that the departed monks have been permitted for an hour to assume their old forms, and revisit their old haunts.

Dolefully sounds the bell. And two biers, covered with palls, are borne slowly towards the church, followed by a tall monk.

The clock was on the stroke of twelve. The procession having drawn up within the court in front of the abbot's lodging, the prisoners were brought forth, and at sight of the abbot the whole of the monks fell on their knees. A touching sight was it to see those reverend men prostrate before their ancient superior, —he condemned to die, and they deprived of their monastic home, —and the officer had not the heart to interfere. Deeply affected, Paslew advanced to the prior, and raising him, affectionately embraced him. After this, he addressed some words of comfort to the others, who arose as he enjoined them, and at a signal from the officer, the procession set out for the church, singing the "*Placebo.*" The abbot and his fellow captives brought up the rear, with a guard on either side of them. All Souls' bell tolled dolefully the while.

Meanwhile an officer entered the great hall, where the Earl of Derby was feasting with his retainers, and informed him that the hour appointed for the ceremonial was close at hand. The earl arose and went to the church attended by Braddyll and Assheton. He entered by the western porch, and, proceeding to the choir, seated himself in the magnificently-carved stall formerly used by Paslew, and placed where it stood, a hundred years before, by John Eccles, ninth abbot.

Midnight struck. The great door of the church swung open, and the organ pealed forth the "*De profundis*." The aisles were filled with armed men, but a clear space was left for the procession, which presently entered in the same order as before, and moved slowly along the transept. Those who came first thought it a dream, so strange was it to find themselves once again in the old accustomed church. The good prior melted into tears.

At length the abbot came. To him the whole scene appeared like a vision. The lights streaming from the altar—the incense loading the air—the deep diapasons rolling overhead—the well-known faces of the brethren—the familiar aspect of the sacred edifice—all these filled him with emotions too painful almost for endurance. It was the last time he should visit this holy place—the last time he should hear those solemn sounds—the last time he should behold those familiar objects—ay, the last! Death could have no pang like this! And with heart wellnigh bursting, and limbs scarcely serving their office, he tottered on.

Another trial awaited him, and one for which he was wholly unprepared. As he drew near the chancel, he looked down an opening on the right, which seemed purposely preserved by the guard. Why were those tapers burning in the side chapel? What was within it? He looked again, and beheld two uncovered biers. On one lay the body of a woman. He started. In the beautiful, but fierce features of the dead, he beheld the witch, Bess Demdike. She was gone to her account before him. The malediction he had pronounced upon her child had killed her.

Appalled, he turned to the other bier, and recognised Cuthbert Ashbead. He shuddered, but comforted himself that he was at least guiltless of his death; though he had a strange feeling that the poor forester had in some way perished for him.

But his attention was diverted towards a tall monk in the Cistertian habit, standing between the bodies, with the cowl drawn over his face. As Paslew gazed at him, the monk slowly raised his hood, and partially disclosed features that smote the abbot as if he had beheld a spectre. Could it be? Could fancy cheat him thus? He looked again. The monk was still standing there, but the cowl had dropped over his face. Striving to shake off the horror that possessed him, the abbot staggered forward, and reaching the presbytery, sank upon his knees.

The ceremonial then commenced. The solemn requiem was sung by the choir; and three yet living heard the hymn for the repose of their souls. Always deeply impressive, the service was unusually so on this sad occasion, and the melodious voices of the singers never sounded so mournfully sweet as then—the demeanour of the prior never seemed so dignified, nor his accents so touching and solemn. The sternest hearts were softened.

But the abbot found it impossible to fix his attention on the service. The lights at the altar burnt dimly in his eyes—the loud antiphon and the supplicatory prayer fell upon a listless ear. His whole life was passing in review before him. He saw himself as he was when he first professed his faith, and felt the zeal and holy aspirations that filled him then. Years flew by at a glance, and he found himself sub-deacon; the sub-deacon became deacon; and the deacon, sub-prior, and the end of his ambition seemed plain before him. But he had a rival; his fears told him a superior in zeal and learning: one who, though many years younger than he, had risen so rapidly in favour with the ecclesiastical authorities, that he threatened to outstrip him, even now, when the goal was full in view. The darkest passage of his life approached: a crime which should cast a deep shadow over the whole of his brilliant after-career. He would have shunned its contemplation, if he could. In vain. It stood out more palpably than all the rest. His rival was no longer in his path. How he was removed the abbot did not dare to think. But he was gone for ever, unless the tall monk were he!

Unable to endure this terrible retrospect, Paslew strove to bend his thoughts on other things. The choir was singing the "*Dies Iræ*," and their voices thundered forth:—

> Rex tremendæ majestatis,
> Qui salvandos salvas gratis,
> Salva me, fons pietatis!

Fain would the abbot have closed his ears, and, hoping to stifle the remorseful pangs that seized upon his very vitals with the sharpness of serpents' teeth, he strove to dwell upon the frequent and severe acts of penance he had performed. But he now found that his penitence had never been sincere and efficacious. This one damning sin obscured all his good actions; and he felt if he died unconfessed, and with the weight of guilt upon his soul, he should perish everlastingly. Again he fled from the torment of retrospection, and again heard the choir thundering forth—

> Lacrymosa dies illa,
> Quâ resurget ex favillâ
> Judicandus homo reus.
> Huic ergo parce, Deus!
> Pie Jesu Domine!
> Dona eis requiem.

"Amen!" exclaimed the abbot. And bowing his head to the ground, he earnestly repeated—

"Pie Jesu Domine!
Dona eis requiem."

Then he looked up, and resolved to ask for a confessor, and unburthen his soul without delay.

The offertory and post-communion were over; the "*requiescant in pace*"— awful words addressed to living ears—were pronounced; and the mass was ended.

All prepared to depart. The prior descended from the altar to embrace and take leave of the abbot; and at the same time the Earl of Derby came from the stall.

"Has all been done to your satisfaction, John Paslew?" demanded the earl, as he drew near.

"All, my good lord," replied the abbot, lowly inclining his head; "and I pray you think me not importunate, if I prefer one other request. I would fain have a confessor visit me, that I may lay bare my inmost heart to him, and receive absolution."

"I have already anticipated the request," replied the earl," "and have provided a priest for you. He shall attend you, within an hour, in your own chamber. You will have ample time between this and daybreak, to settle your accounts with Heaven, should they be ever so weighty."

"I trust so, my lord," replied Paslew; "but a whole life is scarcely long enough for repentance, much less a few short hours. But in regard to the confessor," he continued, filled with misgiving by the earl's manner, "I should be glad to be shriven by Father Christopher Smith, late prior of the abbey."

"It may not be," replied the earl, sternly and decidedly. "You will find all you can require in him I shall send."

The abbot sighed, seeing that remonstrance was useless.

"One further question I would address to you, my lord," he said, "and that refers to the place of my interment. Beneath our feet lie buried all my predecessors—Abbots of Whalley. Here lies John Eccles, for whom was carved the stall in which your lordship hath sat, and from which I have been dethroned. Here rests the learned John Lyndelay, fifth abbot; and beside him his immediate predecessor, Robert de Topcliffe, who, two hundred and thirty years ago, on the festival of Saint Gregory, our canonised abbot, commenced the erection of the sacred edifice above us. At that epoch were here enshrined the remains of the saintly Gregory, and here were also brought the bodies of Helias de Workesley and John de Belfield, both prelates of piety and wisdom. You may read the names where you stand, my lord. You may count the graves of all the abbots. They are sixteen in number. There is one grave yet unoccupied—one stone yet unfurnished with an effigy in brass."

"Well?" said the Earl of Derby.

"When I sat in that stall, my lord," pursued Paslew, pointing to the abbot's chair; "when I was head of this church, it was my thought to rest here among my brother abbots."

"You have forfeited the right," replied the earl, sternly. "All the abbots, whose dust is crumbling beneath us, died in the odour of sanctity; loyal to their sovereigns, and true to their country," whereas you will die an attainted felon and rebel. You can have no place amongst them. Concern not yourself further in the matter. I will find a fitting grave for you,—perchance at the foot of the gallows."

And, turning abruptly away, he gave the signal for general departure.

Ere the clock in the church tower had tolled one, the lights were extinguished, and of the priestly train who had recently thronged the fane, all were gone, like a troop of ghosts evoked at midnight by necromantic skill, and then suddenly dismissed. Deep silence again brooded in the aisles; hushed was the organ; mute the melodious choir. The only light penetrating the convent church proceeded from the moon, whose rays, shining through the painted windows, fell upon the graves of the old abbots in the presbytery, and on the two biers within the adjoining chapel, whose stark burthens they quickened into fearful semblance of life.

CHAPTER VI.—TETER ET FORTIS CARCER.

Left alone, and unable to pray, the abbot strove to dissipate his agitation of spirit by walking to and fro within his chamber; and while thus occupied, he was interrupted by a guard, who told him that the priest sent by the Earl of Derby was without, and immediately afterwards the confessor was ushered in. It was the tall monk, who had been standing between the biers, and his features were still shrouded by his cowl. At sight of him, Paslew sank upon a seat and buried his face in his hands. The monk offered him no consolation, but waited in silence till he should again look up. At last Paslew took courage and spoke.

"Who, and what are you?" he demanded.

"A brother of the same order as yourself," replied the monk, in deep and thrilling accents, but without raising his hood; "and I am come to hear your confession by command of the Earl of Derby."

"Are you of this abbey?" asked Paslew, tremblingly.

"I was," replied the monk, in a stern tone; "but the monastery is dissolved, and all the brethren ejected."

"Your name?" cried Paslew.

"I am not come here to answer questions, but to hear a confession," rejoined the monk. "Bethink you of the awful situation in which you are placed, and that before many hours you must answer for the sins you have committed. You have yet time for repentance, if you delay it not."

"You are right, father," replied the abbot. "Be seated, I pray you, and listen to me, for I have much to tell. Thirty and one years ago I was prior of this abbey. Up to that period my life had been blameless, or, if not wholly free from fault, I had little wherewith to reproach myself—little to fear from a merciful judge—unless it were that I indulged too strongly the desire of ruling absolutely in the house in which I was then only second. But Satan had laid a snare for me, into which I blindly fell. Among the brethren was one named Borlace Alvetham, a young man of rare attainment, and singular skill in the occult sciences. He had risen in favour, and at the time I speak of was elected sub-prior."

"Go on," said the monk.

"It began to be whispered about within the abbey," pursued Paslew, "that on the death of William Rede, then abbot, Borlace Alvetham would succeed him, and then it was that bitter feelings of animosity were awakened in my breast against the sub-prior, and, after many struggles, I resolved upon his destruction."

"A wicked resolution," cried the monk; "but proceed."

"I pondered over the means of accomplishing my purpose," resumed Paslew, "and at last decided upon accusing Alvetham of sorcery and magical practices. The accusation was easy, for the occult studies in which he indulged laid him open to the charge. He occupied a chamber overlooking the Calder, and used to break the monastic rules by wandering forth at night upon the hills. When he was absent thus one night, accompanied by others of the brethren, I visited his chamber, and examined his papers, some of which were covered with mystical figures and cabalistic characters. These papers I seized, and a watch was set to make prisoner of Alvetham on his return. Before dawn he appeared, and was instantly secured, and placed in close confinement. On the next day he was brought before the assembled conclave in the chapter-house, and examined. His defence was unavailing. I charged him with the terrible crime of witchcraft, and he was found guilty."

A hollow groan broke from the monk, but he offered no other interruption.

"He was condemned to die a fearful and lingering death," pursued the abbot; "and it devolved upon me to see the sentence carried out."

"And no pity for the innocent moved you?" cried the monk. "You had no compunction?"

"None," replied the abbot; "I rather rejoiced in the successful accomplishment of my scheme. The prey was fairly in my toils, and I would give him no chance of escape. Not to bring scandal upon the abbey, it was decided that Alvetham's punishment should be secret."

"A wise resolve," observed the monk.

"Within the thickness of the dormitory walls is contrived a small, singularly-formed dungeon," continued the abbot. "It consists of an arched cell, just large enough to hold the body of a captive, and permit him to stretch himself upon a straw pallet. A narrow staircase mounts upwards to a grated aperture in one of the buttresses to admit air and light. Other opening is there none. '*Teter et fortis carcer*' is this dungeon styled in our monastic rolls, and it is well described, for it is black and strong enough. Food is admitted to the miserable inmate of the cell by means of a revolving stone, but no interchange of speech can be held with those without. A large stone is removed from the wall to admit the prisoner, and once immured, the masonry is mortised, and made solid as before. The wretched captive does not long survive his doom, or it may be he lives too long, for death must be a release from such protracted misery. In this dark cell one of the evil-minded brethren, who essayed to stab the Abbot of Kirkstall in the chapter-house, was thrust, and ere a year was over, the provisions were untouched—and the man being known to be dead, they were stayed. His skeleton was found within the cell when it was opened to admit Borlace Alvetham."

"Poor captive!" groaned the monk.

"Ay, poor captive!" echoed Paslew. "Mine eyes have often striven to pierce those stone walls, and see him lying there in that narrow chamber, or forcing his way upwards, to catch a glimpse of the blue sky above him. When I have seen the swallows settle on the old buttress, or the thin grass growing between the stones waving there, I have thought of him."

"Go on," said the monk.

"I scarce can proceed," rejoined Paslew. "Little time was allowed Alvetham for preparation. That very night the fearful sentence was carried out. The stone was removed, and a new pallet placed in the cell. At midnight the prisoner was brought to the dormitory, the brethren chanting a doleful hymn. There he stood amidst them, his tall form towering above the rest, and his features pale as death. He protested his innocence, but he exhibited no fear, even when he saw the terrible preparations. When all was ready he was led to the breach. At that awful moment, his eye met mine, and I shall never forget the look. I might have saved him if I had spoken, but I would not speak. I turned away, and he was thrust into the breach. A fearful cry then rang in my ears, but it was instantly drowned by the mallets of the masons employed to fasten up the stone."

There was a pause for a few moments, broken only by the sobs of the abbot. At length, the monk spoke.

"And the prisoner perished in the cell?" he demanded in a hollow voice.

"I thought so till to-night," replied the abbot. "But if he escaped it, it must have been by miracle; or by aid of those powers with whom he was charged with holding commerce."

"He did escape!" thundered the monk, throwing back his hood. "Look up, John Paslew. Look up, false abbot, and recognise thy victim."

"Borlace Alvetham!" cried the abbot. "Is it, indeed, you?"

"You see, and can you doubt?" replied the other. "But you shall now hear how I avoided the terrible death to which you procured my condemnation. You shall now learn how I am here to repay the wrong you did me. We have changed places, John Paslew, since the night when I was thrust into the cell, never, as you hoped, to come forth. You are now the criminal, and I the witness of the punishment."

"Forgive me! oh, forgive me! Borlace Alvetham, since you are, indeed, he!" cried the abbot, falling on his knees.

"Arise, John Paslew!" cried the other, sternly. "Arise, and listen to me. For the damning offences into which I have been led, I hold you responsible. But for you I might have died free from sin. It is fit you should know the amount of my iniquity. Give ear to me, I say. When first shut within that dungeon, I yielded to the promptings of despair. Cursing you, I threw myself upon the pallet, resolved to taste no food, and hoping death would soon release me. But love of life prevailed. On the second day I took the bread and water allotted me, and ate and drank; after which I scaled the narrow staircase, and gazed through the thin barred loophole at the bright blue sky above, sometimes catching the shadow of a bird as it flew past. Oh, how I yearned for freedom then! Oh, how I wished to break through the stone walls that held me fast! Oh, what a weight of despair crushed my heart as I crept back to my narrow bed! The cell seemed like a grave, and indeed it was little better. Horrible thoughts possessed me. What if I should be wilfully forgotten? What if no food should be given me, and I should be left to perish by the slow pangs of hunger? At this idea I shrieked aloud, but the walls alone returned a dull echo to my cries. I beat my hands against the stones, till the blood flowed from them, but no answer was returned; and at last I desisted from sheer exhaustion. Day after day, and night after night, passed in this way. My food regularly came. But I became maddened by solitude; and with terrible imprecations invoked aid from the powers of darkness to set me free. One night, while thus employed, I was startled by a mocking voice which said,

"'All this fury is needless. Thou hast only to wish for me, and I come.'

ALVETHAM AND JOHN PASLEW.

P. 40

"It was profoundly dark. I could see nothing but a pair of red orbs, glowing like flaming carbuncles.

"'Thou wouldst be free,' continued the voice. 'Thou shalt be so. Arise, and follow me.'

"At this I felt myself grasped by an iron arm, against which all resistance would have been unavailing, even if I had dared to offer it, and in an instant I was dragged up the narrow steps. The stone wall opened before my unseen conductor, and in another moment we were upon the roof of the dormitory. By the bright starbeams shooting down from above, I discerned a tall shadowy figure standing by my side.

"'Thou art mine,' he cried, in accents graven for ever on my memory; 'but I am a generous master, and will give thee a long term of freedom. Thou shalt be avenged upon thine enemy—deeply avenged.'

"'Grant this, and I am thine,' I replied, a spirit of infernal vengeance possessing me. And I knelt before the fiend.

"'But thou must tarry for awhile,' he answered, 'for thine enemy's time will be long in coming; but it *will* come. I cannot work him immediate harm; but I will lead him to a height from which he will assuredly fall headlong. Thou must depart from this place; for it is perilous to thee, and if thou stayest here, ill will befall thee. I will send a rat to thy dungeon, which shall daily devour the provisions, so that the monks shall not know thou hast fled. In thirty and one years shall the abbot's doom be accomplished. Two years before that time thou mayst return. Then come alone to Pendle Hill on a Friday night, and beat the water of the moss pool on the summit, and I will appear to thee and tell thee more. Nine and twenty years, remember!'

"With these words the shadowy figure melted away, and I found myself standing alone on the mossy roof of the dormitory. The cold stars were shining down upon me, and I heard the howl of the watch-dogs near the gate. The fair abbey slept in beauty around me, and I gnashed my teeth with rage to think that you had made me an outcast from it, and robbed me of a dignity which might have been mine. I was wroth also that my vengeance should be so long delayed. But I could not remain where I was, so I clambered down the buttress, and fled away."

"Can this be?" cried the abbot, who had listened in rapt wonderment to the narration. "Two years after your immurement in the cell, the food having been for some time untouched, the wall was opened, and upon the pallet was found a decayed carcase in mouldering, monkish vestments."

"It was a body taken from the charnel, and placed there by the demon," replied the monk. "Of my long wanderings in other lands and beneath brighter skies I need not tell you; but neither absence nor lapse of years cooled my desire of vengeance, and when the appointed time drew nigh I returned to my own country, and came hither in a lowly garb, under the name of Nicholas Demdike."

"Ha!" exclaimed the abbot.

"I went to Pendle Hill, as directed," pursued the monk, "and saw the Dark Shape there as I beheld it on the dormitory roof. All things were then told me, and I learnt how the late rebellion should rise, and how it should be crushed. I learnt also how my vengeance should be satisfied."

Paslew groaned aloud. A brief pause ensued, and deep emotion marked the accents of the wizard as he proceeded.

"When I came back, all this part of Lancashire resounded with praises of the beauty of Bess Blackburn, a rustic lass who dwelt in Barrowford. She was called the Flower of Pendle, and inflamed all the youths with love, and all the maidens with jealousy. But she favoured none except Cuthbert Ashbead, forester to the Abbot of Whalley. Her mother would fain have given her to the forester in marriage, but Bess would not be disposed of so easily. I saw her, and became at once enamoured. I thought my heart was seared; but it was not so. The savage beauty of Bess pleased me more than the most refinéd charms could have done, and her fierce character harmonised with my own. How I won her matters not, but she cast off all thoughts of Ashbead, and clung to me. My wild life suited her; and she roamed the wastes with me, scaled the hills in my company, and shrank not from the weird meetings I attended. Ill repute quickly attended her, and she became branded as a witch. Her aged mother closed her doors upon her, and those who would have gone miles to meet her, now avoided her. Bess heeded this little. She was of a nature to repay the world's contumely with like scorn, but when her child was born the case became different. She wished to save it. Then it was," pursued Demdike, vehemently, and regarding the abbot with flashing eyes—"then it was that I was again mortally injured by you. Then your ruthless decree to the clergy went forth. My child was denied baptism, and became subject to the fiend."

"Alas! alas!" exclaimed Paslew.

"And as if this were not injury enough," thundered Demdike, "you have called down a withering and lasting curse upon its innocent head, and through it transfixed its mother's heart. If you had complied with that poor girl's request, I would have forgiven you your wrong to me, and have saved you."

There was a long, fearful silence. At last Demdike advanced to the abbot, and, seizing his arm, fixed his eyes upon him, as if to search into his soul.

"Answer me, John Paslew!" he cried; "answer me, as you shall speedily answer your Maker. Can that malediction be recalled? Dare not to trifle with me, or I will tear forth your black heart, and cast it in your face. Can that curse be recalled? Speak!"

"It cannot," replied the abbot, half dead with terror.

"Away, then!" thundered Demdike, casting him from him. "To the gallows!—to the gallows!" And he rushed out of the room.

CHAPTER VII.—THE ABBEY MILL.

FOR a while the abbot remained shattered and stupefied by this terrible interview. At length he arose, and made his way, he scarce knew how, to the oratory. But it was long before the tumult of his thoughts could be at all allayed, and he had only just regained something like composure when he was disturbed by hearing a slight sound in the adjoining chamber. A mortal chill came over him, for he thought it might be Demdike returned. Presently, he distinguished a footstep stealthily approaching him, and almost hoped that the wizard would consummate his vengeance by taking his life. But he was quickly undeceived, for a hand was placed on his shoulder, and a friendly voice whispered in his ears, "Cum along wi' meh, lort abbut. Get up, quick—quick!"

Thus addressed, the abbot raised his eyes, and beheld a rustic figure standing beside him, divested of his clouted shoes, and armed with a long bare wood-knife.

"Dunna yo knoa me, lort abbut?" cried the person. "Ey'm a freent—Hal o' Nabs, o' Wiswall. Yo'n moind Wiswall, yeawr own birthplace, abbut? Dunna be feert, ey sey. Ey'n getten a steigh clapt to yon windaw, an' you con be down it i' a trice—an' along t' covert way be t' river soide to t' mill."

But the abbot stirred not.

"Quick! quick!" implored Hal o' Nabs, venturing to pluck the abbot's sleeve. "Every minute's precious. Dunna be feert. Ebil Croft, t' miller, is below. Poor Cuthbert Ashbead would ha' been here i'stead o' meh if he couldn; boh that accursed wizard, Nick Demdike, turned my hont agen him, an' drove t' poike head intended for himself into poor Cuthbert's side. They clapt meh i' a dungeon, boh Ebil monaged to get me out, an' ey then swore to do whot poor Cuthbert would ha' done, if he'd been livin'—so here ey am, lort abbut, cum to set yo free. An' neaw yo knoan aw abowt it, yo con ha nah more hesitation. Cum, time presses, an ey'm feert o' t' guard owerhearing us."

"I thank you, my good friend, from the bottom of my heart," replied the abbot, rising; "but, however strong may be the temptation of life and liberty which you hold out to me, I cannot yield to it. I have pledged my word to the Earl of Derby to make no attempt to escape. Were the doors thrown open, and the guard removed, I should remain where I am."

"Whot!" exclaimed Hal o' Nabs, in a tone of bitter disappointment; "yo winnaw go, neaw aw's prepared. By th' Mess, boh yo shan. Ey'st nah go back to Ebil empty-handed. If yo'n sworn to stay here, ey'n sworn to set yo free, and ey'st keep meh oath. Willy nilly, yo shan go wi' meh, lort abbut!"

"Forbear to urge me further, my good Hal," rejoined Paslew. "I fully appreciate your devotion; and I only regret that you and Abel Croft have exposed yourselves to so much peril on my account. Poor Cuthbert Ashbead! when I beheld his body on the bier, I had a sad feeling that he had died in my behalf."

"Cuthbert meant to rescue yo, lort abbut," replied Hal, "and deed resisting Nick Demdike's attempt to arrest him. Boh, be aw t' devils!" he added, brandishing his knife fiercely, "t' warlock shall ha' three inches o' cowd steel betwixt his ribs, t' furst time ey cum across him."

"Peace, my son," rejoined the abbot, "and forego your bloody design. Leave the wretched man to the chastisement of Heaven. And now, farewell! All your kindly efforts to induce me to fly are vain."

"Yo winnaw go?" cried Hal o' Nabs, scratching his head.

"I cannot," replied the abbot.

"Cum wi' meh to t' windaw, then," pursued Hal, "and tell Ebil so. He'll think ey'n failed else."

"Willingly," replied the abbot.

And with noiseless footsteps he followed the other across the chamber. The window was open, and outside it was reared a ladder.

"Yo mun go down a few steps," said Hal o' Nabs, "or else he'll nah hear yo."

The abbot complied, and partly descended the ladder.

"I see no one," he said.

"T' neet's dark," replied Hal o' Nabs, who was close behind him. "Ebil canna be far off. Hist! ey hear him—go on."

The abbot was now obliged to comply, though he did so with reluctance. Presently he found himself upon the roof of a building, which he knew to be connected with the mill by a covered passage running along the south bank of the Calder. Scarcely had he set foot there, than Hal o' Nabs jumped after him, and, seizing the ladder, cast it into the stream, thus rendering Paslew's return impossible.

"Neaw, lort abbut," he cried, with a low, exulting laugh, "yo hanna brok'n yor word, an ey'n kept moine. Yo're free agen your will."

"You have destroyed me by your mistaken zeal," cried the abbot, reproachfully.

"Nowt o't sort," replied Hal; "ey'n saved yo' fro' destruction. This way, lort abbut—this way."

And taking Paslew's arm he led him to a low parapet, over

looking the covered passage before described. Half an hour before it had been bright moonlight, but, as if to favour the fugitive, the heavens had become overcast, and a thick mist had arisen from the river.

"Ebil! Ebil!" cried Hal o' Nabs, leaning over the parapet.

"Here," replied a voice below. "Is aw reet? Is he wi' yo?"

"Yeigh," replied Hal.

"Whot han yo dun wi' t' steigh?" cried Ebil.

"Never yo moind," returned Hal, "boh help t' abbut down."

Paslew thought it vain to resist further, and with the help of Hal o' Nabs and the miller, and further aided by some irregularities in the wall, he was soon safely landed near the entrance of the passage. Abel fell on his knees, and pressed the abbot's hand to his lips.

"Owr Blessed Leady be praised, yo are free," he cried.

"Dunna stond tawking here, Ebil," interposed Hal o' Nabs, who by this time had reached the ground, and who was fearful of some new remonstrance on the abbot's part. "Ey'm feerd o' pursuit."

"Yo' needna be afeerd o' that, Hal," replied the miller. "T' guard are safe enough. One o' owr chaps has just tuk em up a big black jack fu' o' stout ele; an ey warrant me they winnaw stir yet awhoile. Win it please yo to cum wi' me, lort abbut?"

With this, he marched along the passage, followed by the others, and presently arrived at a door, against which he tapped. A bolt being withdrawn, it was instantly opened to admit the party, after which it was as quickly shut, and secured. In answer to a call from the miller, a light appeared at the top of a steep, ladder-like flight of wooden steps, and up these Paslew, at the entreaty of Abel, mounted, and found himself in a large, low chamber, the roof of which was crossed by great beams, covered thickly with cobwebs, whitened by flour, while the floor was strewn with empty sacks and sieves.

The person who held the light proved to be the miller's daughter, Dorothy, a blooming lass of eighteen, and at the other end of the chamber, seated on a bench before a turf fire, with an infant on her knees, was the miller's wife. The latter instantly arose on beholding the abbot, and, placing the child on a corn bin, advanced towards him, and dropped on her knees, while her daughter imitated her example. The abbot extended his hands over them, and pronounced a solemn benediction.

"Bring your child also to me, that I may bless it," he said, when he concluded.

"It's nah my child, lort abbut," replied the miller's wife, taking up the infant and bringing it to him; "it wur brought to me this varry neet by Ebil. Ey wish it wur far enough, ey'm sure, for it's a deformed little urchon. One o' its een is lower set than t' other; an t' reet looks up, while t' laft looks down."

And as she spoke she pointed to the infant's face, which was disfigured as she had stated, by a strange and unnatural disposition of the eyes, one of which was set much lower in the head than the other. Awakened from sleep, the child uttered a feeble cry, and stretched out its tiny arms to Dorothy.

"You ought to pity it for its deformity, poor little creature, rather than reproach it, mother," observed the young damsel.

"Marry kem eawt!" cried her mother, sharply, "yo'n getten fine feelings wi' your larning fro t' good feythers, Dolly. Os ey said efore, ey wish t' brat wur far enough."

"You forget it has no mother," suggested Dorothy, kindly.

"An naw great matter, if it hasn't," returned the miller's wife, "Bess Demdike 's neaw great loss."

"Is this Bess Demdike's child?" cried Paslew, recoiling.

"Yeigh," exclaimed the miller's wife. And mistaking the cause of Paslew's emotion, she added, triumphantly, to her daughter, "Ey towd te, wench, ot t' lort abbut would be of my way o' thinking. T' chilt has got the witch's mark plain upon her. Look, lort abbut, look!"

But Paslew heeded her not, but murmured to himself:—

"Ever in my path, go where I will. It is vain to struggle with my fate. I will go back and surrender myself to the Earl of Derby."

"Nah,—nah!—yo shanna do that," replied Hal o' Nabs, who, with the miller, was close beside him. "Sit down o' that stoo' be t' fire, and take a cup o' wine t' cheer yo, and then we'n set out to Pendle Forest, where ey'st find yo a safe hiding-place. An t' ony reward ey'n ever ask for t' sarvice shan be, that yo'n perform a marriage sarvice fo' me and Dolly one of these days." And he nudged the damsel's elbow, who turned away, covered with blushes.

The abbot moved mechanically to the fire, and sat down, while the miller's wife, surrendering the child with a shrug of the shoulders and a grimace to her daughter, went in search of some viands and a flask of wine, which she set before Paslew. The miller then filled a drinking-horn, and presented it to his guest, who was about to raise it to his lips, when a loud knocking was heard at the door below.

The knocking continued with increased violence, and voices were heard calling upon the miller to open the door, or it would be broken down. On the first alarm Abel had flown to a small window whence he could reconnoitre those below, and he now returned with a face white with terror, to say that a party of arquebussiers, with the sheriff at their head, were without, and that some of the men were provided with torches.

"They have discovered my evasion, and are come in search of me," observed the abbot rising, but without betraying any anxiety. "Do not concern yourselves further for me, my good friends, but open the door, and deliver me to them."

"Nah, nah, that we winnaw," cried Hal o' Nabs, "yo're neaw taen yet, feyther abbut, an' ey knoa a way to baffle 'em. If y'on let him down into t' river, Ebil, ey'n manage to get him off."

"Weel thowt on, Nab," cried the miller, "theawst nah been mey mon seven year fo nowt. Theaw knoas t' ways o' t' pleck."

"Os weel os onny rotten abowt it," replied Hal o' Nabs. "Go down to t' grindin'-room, an ey'n follow i' a troice."

And as Abel snatched up the light, and hastily descended the steps with Paslew, Hal whispered in Dorothy's ears—

"Tak care neaw one fonds that chilt, Dolly, if they break in. Hide it safely; an whon they're gone, tak it to't church, and place it near t' altar, where no ill con cum to it or thee. Mey life may hong upon it."

And as the poor girl, who, as well as her mother, was almost frightened out of her wits, promised compliance, he hurried down the steps after the others, muttering, as the clamour without was redoubled—

"Eigh, roar on till yo're hoarse. Yo winnaw get in yet awhile, ey'n promise ye."

Meantime, the abbot had been led to the chief room of the mill, where all the corn formerly consumed within the monastery had been prepared, and which the size of the chamber itself, together with the vastness of the stones used in the operation of grinding, and connected with the huge water-wheel outside, proved to be by no means inconsiderable. Strong shafts of timber supported the flooring above, and were crossed by other boards placed horizontally, from which various implements in use at the mill depended, giving the chamber, imperfectly lighted as it now was by the lamp borne by Abel, a strange and almost mysterious appearance. Three or four of the miller's men, armed with pikes, had followed their master, and, though much alarmed, they vowed to die rather than give up the abbot.

By this time Hal o' Nabs had joined the group, and proceeding towards a raised part of the chamber where the grinding-stones were set, he knelt down, and laying hold of a small ring, raised up a trapdoor. The fresh air which blew up through the aperture, combined with the rushing sound of water, showed that the Calder flowed immediately beneath; and, having made some slight preparation, Hal let himself down into the stream.

At this moment a loud crash was heard, and one of the miller's men cried out that the arquebussiers had burst open the door.

"Be hondy, then, lads, and let him down!" cried Hal o' Nabs, who had some difficulty in maintaining his footing on the rough, stony bottom of the swift stream.

Passively yielding, the abbot suffered the miller and one of the stoutest of his men to assist him through the trapdoor, while a third held down the lamp, and showed Hal o' Nabs, up to his middle in the darkling current, and stretching out his arms to receive the burden. The light fell upon the huge black circle of the water-wheel now stopped, and upon the dripping arches supporting the mill. In another moment the abbot plunged into the water, the trapdoor was replaced, and bolted underneath by Hal, who, while guiding his companion along, and bidding him catch hold of the wood-work of the wheel, heard a heavy trampling of many feet on the boards above, showing that the pursuers had obtained admittance.

Encumbered by his heavy vestments, the abbot could with difficulty contend against the strong current, and he momently expected to be swept away; but he had a stout and active assistant by his side, who soon placed him under shelter of the wheel. The trampling overhead continued for a few minutes, after which all was quiet, and Hal judged that, finding their search within ineffectual, the enemy would speedily come forth. Nor was he deceived. Shouts were soon heard at the door of the mill, and the glare of torches was cast on the stream. Then it was that Hal dragged his companion into a deep hole, formed by some decay in the masonry, behind the wheel, where the water rose nearly to their chins, and where they were completely concealed. Scarcely were they thus ensconced, than two or three armed men, holding torches aloft, were seen wading under the archway; but after looking carefully around, and even approaching close to the water-wheel, these persons could detect nothing, and withdrew, muttering curses of rage and disappointment. By-and-by the lights almost wholly disappeared, and the shouts becoming fainter and more distant, it was evident that the men had gone lower down the river. Upon this, Hal thought they might venture to quit their retreat, and accordingly, grasping the abbot's arm, he proceeded to wade up the stream.

Benumbed with cold, and half dead with terror, Paslew needed all his companion's support, for he could do little to help himself, added to which, they occasionally encountered some large stone, or stepped into a deep hole, so that it required Hal's utmost exertion and strength to force a way on. At last they were out of the arch, and though both banks seemed unguarded, yet, for fear of surprise, Hal deemed it prudent still to keep to the river. Their course was completely sheltered from observation by the mist that enveloped them; and after proceeding in this way for some distance, Hal stopped to listen, and while debating with himself whether he should now quit the river, he fancied he beheld a black object swimming towards him. Taking it for an otter, with which voracious animal the Calder, a stream swarming with trout, abounded, and knowing the creature would not meddle with them unless first attacked, he paid little attention to it; but he was soon made sensible of his error. His arm was suddenly seized by a large black hound, whose sharp fangs met in his flesh. Unable to repress a cry of pain, Hal strove to disengage himself from his assailant, and, finding it impossible, flung himself into the water, in the hope of drowning him, but, as the hound still maintained his hold, he searched for his knife to slay him. But he could not find it, and in his distress applied to Paslew.

"Ha yo onny weepun abowt yo, lort abbut," he cried, "wi' which ey con free mysel fro' this accussed hound?"

"Alas! no, my son," replied Paslew, "and I fear no weapon will prevail against it, for I recognise in the animal the hound of the wizard, Demdike."

"Ey thowt t' dule wur in it," rejoined Hal; "boh leave me to fight it owt, an do you gain t' bonk, an mey t' best o' your way to t' Wiswall. Ey'n join ye os soon os ey con scrush this varment's heaod agen a stoan. Ha!" he added, joyfully, "Ey'n found t' thwittle. Go—go. Ey'n soon be efter ye."

Feeling he should sink if he remained where he was, and wholly unable to offer any effectual assistance to his companion, the abbot turned to the left, where a large oak overhung the stream, and he was climbing the bank, aided by the roots of the tree, when a man suddenly came from behind it, seized his hand, and dragged him up forcibly. At the same moment his captor placed a bugle to his lips, and winding a few notes, he was instantly answered by shouts, and soon afterwards half a dozen armed men ran up, bearing torches. Not a word passed between the fugitive and his captor; but when the men came up, and the torchlight fell upon the features of the latter, the abbot's worst fears were realised. It was Demdike.

"False to your king!—false to your oath!—false to all men!" cried the wizard. "You seek to escape in vain!"

"I merit all your reproaches," replied the abbot; "but it may be some satisfaction to you to learn, that I have endured far greater suffering than if I had patiently awaited my doom."

"I am glad of it," rejoined Demdike, with a savage laugh; "but you have destroyed others beside yourself. Where is the fellow in the water? What, ho, Uriel!"

But as no sound reached him, he snatched a torch from one of the arquebussiers and held it to the river's brink. But he could see neither hound nor man.

"Strange!" he cried. "He cannot have escaped. Uriel is more than a match for any man. Secure the prisoner while I examine the stream."

With this, he ran along the bank with great quickness, holding his torch far over the water, so as to reveal any thing floating within it, but nothing met his view until he came within a short distance of the mill, when he beheld a black object struggling in the current, and soon found that it was his dog making feeble efforts to gain the bank.

"Ah recreant! thou hast let him go," cried Demdike, furiously.

Seeing his master the animal redoubled its efforts, crept ashore, and fell at his feet, with a last effort to lick his hands.

Demdike held down the torch, and then perceived that the hound was quite dead. There was a deep gash in its side, and another in the throat, showing how it had perished.

"Poor Uriel!" he exclaimed; "the only true friend I had. And thou art gone! The villain has killed thee, but he shall pay for it with his life."

And hurrying back he dispatched four of the men in quest of the fugitive, while accompanied by the two others he conveyed Paslew back to the abbey, where he was placed in a strong cell, from which there was no possibility of escape, and a guard set over him.

Half an hour after this, two of the arquebussiers returned with Hal o' Nabs, whom they had succeeded in capturing after a desperate resistance, about a mile from the abbey, on the road to Wiswall. He was taken to the guard-room, which had been appointed in one of the lower chambers of the chapter-house, and Demdike was immediately apprised of his arrival. Satisfied by an inspection of the prisoner, whose demeanour was sullen and resolved, Demdike proceeded to the great hall, where the Earl of Derby, who had returned thither after the midnight mass, was still sitting with his retainers. An audience was readily obtained by the wizard, and, apparently well pleased with the result, he returned to the guard-room. The prisoner was seated by himself in one corner of the chamber, with his hands tied behind his back with a leathern thong, and Demdike approaching him, told him that, for having aided the escape of a condemned rebel and traitor, and violently assaulting the king's lieges in the execution of their duty, he would be hanged on the morrow, the Earl of Derby, who had power of life or death in such cases, having so decreed it. And he exhibited the warrant.

"Soh, yo mean to hong me, eh, wizard?" cried Hal o' Nabs, kicking his heels with great apparent indifference.

"I do," replied Demdike; "if for nothing else, for slaying my hound."

"Ey dunna think it," replied Hal. "Yo'n alter your moind. Do, mon. Ey'm nah prepared to dee just yet."

"Then perish in your sins," cried Demdike, "I will not give you an hour's respite."

"Yo'n be sorry when it's too late," said Hal.

"Tush!" cried Demdike, "my only regret will be that Uriel's slaughter is paid for by such a worthless life as thine."

"Then whoy tak it?" demanded Hal. "'Specially whon yo'n lose your chilt by doing so."

"My child!" exclaimed Demdike, surprised. "How mean you, sirrah?"

"Ey mean this," replied Hal, coolly; "that if ey dee to-morrow mornin' your chilt dees too. Whon ey ondertook this job ey calkilated mey chances, an' tuk precautions eforehond. Your chil't a hostage fo mey safety."

"Curses on thee and thy cunning," cried Demdike; "but I will not be outwitted by a hind like thee. I will have the child, and yet not be baulked of my revenge."

"Yo'n never ha' it, except os a breathless corpse, 'bowt mey consent," rejoined Hal.

"We shall see," cried Demdike, rushing forth, and bidding the guards look well to the prisoner.

But ere long he returned with a gloomy and disappointed expression of countenance, and again approaching the prisoner said, "Thou hast spoken the truth. The infant is in the hands of some innocent being over whom I have no power."

"Ey towdee so, wizard," replied Hal, laughing. "Hoind os ey be, ey'm a match fo' thee,—ha! ha! Neaw, mey life agen t' chilt's. Win yo set me free?"

Demdike deliberated.

"Harkee, wizard," cried Hal, "if yo're hatching treason ey'n dun. T' sartunty o' revenge win sweeten mey last moments."

"Will you swear to deliver the child to me unharmed, if I set you free?" asked Demdike.

"It's a bargain, wizard," rejoined Hal o' Nabs; "ey swear. Boh yo mun set me free furst, fo' ey winnaw tak your word."

Demdike turned away disdainfully, and addressing the arquebussiers, said, "You behold this warrant, guard. The prisoner is committed to my custody. I will produce him on the morrow, or account for his absence to the Earl of Derby."

One of the arquebussiers examined the order, and vouching for its correctness, the others signified their assent to the arrangement, upon which Demdike motioned the prisoner to follow him, and quitted the chamber. No interruption was offered to Hal's egress, but he stopped within the court-yard, where Demdike awaited him, and unfastened the leathern thong that bound together his hands.

"Now go and bring the child to me," said the wizard.

"Nah, ey'st neaw bring it ye myself," rejoined Hal. "Ey knoas better nor that. Be at t' church porch i' half an hour, an t' bantlin shan be delivered to ye safe an sound."

And without waiting for a reply, he ran off with great swiftness.

At the appointed time Demdike sought the church, and as he drew near it there issued from the porch a female, who hastily placing the child, wrapped in a mantle, in his arms, tarried for no speech from him, but instantly disappeared. Demdike, however, recognised in her the miller's daughter, Dorothy Croft.

CHAPTER VIII.—THE EXECUTIONER.

DAWN came at last, after a long and weary night to many within and without the abbey. Every thing betokened a dismal day. The atmosphere was damp, and oppressive to the spirits, while the raw cold sensibly affected the frame. All astir were filled with gloom and despondency, and secretly breathed a wish that the tragical business of the day were ended. The vast range of Pendle was obscured by clouds, and ere long the vapours descended into the valleys, and rain began to fall; at first slightly, but afterwards in heavy continuous showers. Melancholy was the aspect of the abbey, and it required no stretch of imagination to fancy that the old structure was deploring the fate of its former ruler. To those impressed with the idea—and many there were who were so—the very stones of the convent church seemed dissolving into tears. The statues of the saints appeared to weep, and the great statue of Saint Gregory de Northbury over the porch seemed bowed down with grief. The grotesquely carved heads on the spouts grinned horribly at the abbot's destroyers, and spouted forth cascades of water, as if with the intent of drowning them. So deluging and incessant were the showers, that it seemed, indeed, as if the abbey would be flooded. All the inequalities of ground within the great quadrangle of the cloisters looked like ponds, and the various water-spouts from the dormitory, the refectory, and the chapter-house, continuing to jet forth streams into the court below, the ambulatories were soon filled ankle-deep, and even the lower apartments, on which they opened, invaded.

Surcharged with moisture, the royal banner on the gate drooped and clung to the staff, as if it too shared in the general depression, or as if the sovereign authority it represented had given way. The countenances and deportment of the men harmonized with the weather; they moved about gloomily and despondently, their bright accoutrements sullied with the wet, and their buskins clogged with mire. A forlorn sight it was to watch the shivering sentinels on the walls; and yet more forlorn to see the groups of the abbot's old retainers gathering without, wrapped in their blue woollen cloaks, patiently enduring the drenching showers, and awaiting the last awful scene. But the saddest sight of all was on the hill, already described, called the Holehouses. Here two other lesser gibbets had been erected during the night, one on either hand of the loftier instrument of justice, and the carpenters were yet employed in finishing their work, having been delayed by the badness of the weather. Half drowned by the torrents that fell upon them, the poor fellows were protected from interference with their disagreeable occupation by half a dozen well-mounted and well-armed troopers, and by as many halberdiers; and this company, completely exposed to the weather, suffered severely from wet and cold. The rain beat against the gallows, ran down its tall naked posts, and collected in pools at its feet. Attracted by some strange instinct, which seemed to give them a knowledge of the object of these terrible preparations, two ravens wheeled screaming round the fatal tree, and at length one of them settled on the cross-beam, and could with difficulty be dislodged by the shouts of the men, when it flew away, croaking hoarsely. Up this gentle hill, ordinarily so soft and beautiful, but now abhorrent as a Golgotha, in the eyes of the beholders, groups of rustics and monks had climbed over ground rendered slippery with moisture, and had gathered round the paling encircling the terrible apparatus, looking the images of despair and woe.

Even those within the abbey, and sheltered from the storm, shared the all-pervading despondency. The refectory looked dull and comfortless, and the logs on the hearth hissed and sputtered, and would not burn. Green wood had been brought instead of dry fuel by the drowsy henchman. The viands on the board provoked not the appetite, and the men emptied their cups of ale, yawned and stretched their arms, as if they would fain sleep an hour or two longer. The sense of discomfort was heightened by the entrance of those whose term of watch had been relieved, and who cast their dripping cloaks on the floor, while two or three savage dogs, steaming with moisture, stretched their huge lengths before the sullen fire, and disputed all approach to it.

Within the great hall were already gathered the retainers of the Earl of Derby, but the nobleman himself had not appeared. Having passed the greater part of the night in conference with one person or another, and the abbot's flight having caused him much disquietude, though he did not hear of it till the fugitive was recovered; the earl would not seek his couch until within an hour of daybreak, and his attendants, considering the state of the weather, and that it yet wanted full two hours to the time appointed for the execution, did not think it needful to disturb him. Braddyll and Assheton, however, were up and ready; but, despite their firmness of nerve, they yielded like the rest to the depressing influence of the weather, and began to have some misgivings as to their own share in the tragedy about to be enacted. The various gentlemen in attendance paced to and fro within the hall, holding but slight converse together, anxiously counting the minutes, for the time appeared to pass on with unwonted slowness, and ever and anon glancing through the diamond panes of the window at the rain pouring down steadily without, and coming back again hopeless of amendment in the weather.

If such were the disheartening influence of the day on those who had nothing to apprehend, what must its effect have been on the poor captives! Woful indeed. The two monks suffered a complete prostration of spirit. All the resolution which Father Haydocke had displayed in his interview with the Earl of Derby, failed him now, and he yielded to the agonies of despair. Father Eastgate was in little better condition, and gave vent to unavailing lamentations, instead of paying heed to the consolatory discourse of the monk who had been permitted to visit him.

The abbot was better sustained. Though greatly enfeebled by the occurrences of the night, yet in proportion as his bodily strength decreased, his mental energies rallied. Since the confession of his secret offence, and the conviction he had obtained that his supposed victim still lived, a weight seemed taken from his breast, and he had no longer any dread of death. Rather he looked to the speedy termination of existence with hopeful pleasure. He prepared himself as decently as the means afforded him permitted for his last appearance before the world, but refused all refreshment except a cup of water, and being left to himself was praying fervently, when a man was admitted into his cell. Thinking it might be the executioner come to summon him, he arose, and to his surprise beheld Hal o' Nabs. The countenance of the rustic was pale, but his bearing was determined.

"You here, my son," cried Paslew. "I hoped you had escaped."

"Ey'm i' nah dawnger, feyther abbut," replied Hal. "Ey'n getten leef to visit ye fo a minute only, so ey mun be brief. Mey yourself easy, ye shanna dee be't hongmon's honds."

"How, my son!" cried Paslew. "I understand you not."

"Yo'n onderstond me weel enough by-and-by," replied Hal. "Dunnah be feart whon ye see me next; an comfort yoursel that whotever cums and goes, your death shall be avenged o' your warst foe."

Paslew would have sought some further explanation, but Hal stepped quickly backwards, and striking his foot against the door, it was instantly opened by the guard, and he went forth.

Not long after this, the Earl of Derby entered the great hall, and his first inquiry was as to the safety of the prisoners. When satisfied of this, he looked forth, and shuddered at the dismal state of the weather. While he was addressing some remarks on this subject, and on its interference with the tragical exhibition about to take place, an officer entered the hall, followed by several persons of inferior condition, amongst whom was Hal o' Nabs, and marched up to the earl, while the others remained standing at a respectful distance.

"What news do you bring me, sir?" cried the earl, noticing the officer's evident uneasiness of manner. "Nothing hath happened to the prisoners? God's death! if it hath, you shall all answer for it with your bodies."

"Nothing hath happened to them, my lord," said the officer, "but——"

"But what?" interrupted the earl. "Out with it quickly."

"The executioner from Lancaster and his two aids have fled," replied the officer.

"Fled!" exclaimed the earl, stamping his foot with rage; "now, as I live, this is a device to delay the execution till some new attempt at rescue can be made. But it shall fail, if I string up the abbot myself. Death! can no other hangmen be found? ha!"

"Of a surety, my lord; but all have an aversion to the office, and hold it opprobrious, especially to put churchmen to death," replied the officer.

"Opprobrious or not, it must be done," replied the earl. "See that fitting persons are provided."

At this moment Hal o' Nabs stepped forward.

"Ey'm willing t' ondertake t' job, my lord, an' t' hong t' abbut, without fee or rewort," he said.

"Thou bears't him a grudge, I suppose, good fellow," replied the earl, laughing at the rustic's uncouth appearance; "but thou seem'st a stout fellow, and one not likely to flinch, and may discharge the office as well as another. If no better man can be found, let him do it," he added to the officer.

"Ey humbly thonk your lortship," replied Hal, inwardly rejoicing at the success of his scheme. But his countenance fell when he perceived Demdike advance from behind the others.

"This man is not to be trusted, my lord," said Demdike, coming forward; "he has some mischievous design in making the request. So far from bearing enmity to the abbot, it was he who assisted him in his attempt to escape last night."

"What!" exclaimed the earl, "is this a new trick? Bring the fellow forward, that I may examine him."

But Hal was gone. Instantly divining Demdike's purpose, and seeing his chance lost, he mingled with the lookers-on, who covered his retreat. Nor could he be found when sought for by the guard.

"See you provide a substitute quickly, sir," cried the earl, angrily, to the officer.

"It is needless to take further trouble, my lord," replied Demdike; "I am come to offer myself as executioner."

"Thou!" exclaimed the earl.

"Ay," replied the other. "When I heard that the men from Lancaster were fled, I instantly knew that some scheme to frustrate the ends of justice was on foot, and I at once resolved to undertake the office myself rather than delay or risk should occur. What this man's aim was, who hath just offered himself, I partly guess, but it hath failed; and if your lordship will intrust the matter to me, I will answer that no further impediment shall arise, but that the sentence shall be fully carried out, and the law satisfied. Your lordship can trust me."

"I know it," replied the earl. "Be it as you will. It is now on the stroke of nine. At ten, let all be in readiness to set out for Wiswall Hall. The rain may have ceased by that time, but no weather must stay you. Go forth with the new executioner, sir," he added to the officer, "and see all necessary preparations made."

And as Demdike bowed, and departed with the officer, the earl sat down with his retainers to break his fast.

CHAPTER IX.—WISWALL HALL.

SHORTLY before ten o'clock a numerous cortège, consisting of a troop of horse in their full equipments, a band of archers with their bows over their shoulders, and a long train of barefoot monks, who had been permitted to attend, set out from the abbey. Behind them came a varlet with a paper mitre on his head, and a lathen crosier in his hand, covered with a surcoat, on which was emblazoned, but torn and reversed, the arms of Paslew; argent, a fess between three mullets, sable, pierced of the field, a crescent for difference. After him came another varlet bearing a banner, on which was painted a grotesque figure in a half-military, half-monastic garb, representing the "Earl of Poverty," with this distich beneath it:—

Priest and warrior—rich and poor,
He shall be hanged at his own door.

Next followed a tumbrel, drawn by two horses, in which sat the abbot alone, the two other prisoners being kept back for the present. Then came Demdike, in a leathern jerkin and blood-red hose, fitting closely to his sinewy limbs, and wrapped in a houppeland of the same colour as the hose, with a coil of rope round his neck. He walked between two ill-favoured personages habited in black, whom he had chosen as assistants. A band of halberdiers brought up the rear. The procession moved slowly along,—the passing-bell tolling each minute, and a muffled drum sounding hollowly at intervals.

Shortly before the procession started the rain ceased, but the air felt damp and chill, and the roads were inundated. Passing out at the north-eastern gateway, the gloomy train skirted the south side of the convent church, and went on in the direction of the village of Whalley. When near the east end of the holy edifice, the abbot beheld two coffins borne along, and, on inquiry, learnt that they contained the bodies of Bess Demdike and Cuthbert Ashbead, who were about to be interred in the cemetery. At this moment his eye for the first time encountered that of his implacable foe, and he then discovered that he was to serve as his executioner.

At first Paslew felt much trouble at this thought, but the feeling quickly passed away. On reaching Whalley, every door was found closed, and every window shut; so that the spectacle was lost upon the inhabitants; and after a brief halt, the cavalcade set out for Wiswall Hall.

Sprung from an ancient family residing in the neighbourhood of Whalley, Abbot Paslew was the second son of Francis Paslew of Wiswall Hall, a great gloomy stone mansion, situated at the foot of the south-western side of Pendle Hill, where his brother Francis still resided. Of a cold and cautious character, Francis Paslew, second of the name, held aloof from the insurrection, and when his brother was arrested he wholly abandoned him. Still the owner of Wiswall had not altogether escaped suspicion, and it was probably as much with the view of degrading him as of adding to the abbot's punishment, that the latter was taken to the hall on the morning of his execution. Be this as it may, the cortège toiled thither through roads bad in the best of seasons, but now, since the heavy rain, scarcely passable; and it arrived there in about half an hour, and drew up on the broad green lawn. Window and door of the hall were closed; no smoke issued from the heavy pile of chimneys; and to all outward seeming the place was utterly deserted. In answer to inquiries, it appeared that Francis Paslew had departed for Northumberland on the previous day, taking all his household with him.

In earlier years, a quarrel having occurred between the haughty abbot and the churlish Francis, the brothers rarely met, whence it chanced that John Paslew had seldom visited the place of his birth of late, though lying so near to the abbey, and, indeed, forming part of its ancient dependencies. It was sad to view it now; and yet the house, gloomy as it was, recalled seasons with which, though they might awaken regret, no guilty associations were connected. Dark was the hall, and desolate, but on the fine old trees around it the rooks were settling, and their loud cawings pleased him, and excited gentle emotions. For a few moments he grew young again, and forgot why he was there. Fondly surveying the house, the terraced garden, in which, as a boy, he had so often strayed, and the park beyond it, where he had chased the deer; his gaze rose to the cloudy heights of Pendle, springing immediately behind the mansion, and up which he had frequently climbed. The flood-gates of memory were opened at once, and a whole tide of long-buried feelings rushed upon his heart.

From this half-painful, half-pleasurable retrospect he was aroused by the loud blast of a trumpet, thrice blown. A recapitulation of his offences, together with his sentence, was read by a herald, after which the reversed blazonry was fastened upon the door of the hall, just below a stone escutcheon on which was carved the arms of the family; while the paper mitre was torn and trampled under foot, the lathen crosier broken in twain, and the scurril banner hacked in pieces.

While this degrading act was performed, a man in a miller's white garb, with the hood drawn over his face, forced his way towards the tumbrel, and while the attention of the guard was otherwise engaged, whispered in Paslew's ear,

"Ey han failed i' mey scheme, feyther abbut, boh rest assured ey'n avenge you. Demdike shan ha' mey Sheffield thwittle i' his heart 'efore he's a day older."

"The wizard has a charm against steel, my son, and indeed is proof against all weapons forged by men," replied Paslew, who recognised the voice of Hal o' Nabs, and hoped by this assertion to divert him from his purpose.

"Ha! say yo so, feythur abbut?" cried Hal. "Then ey'n reach him wi' summot sacred." And he disappeared.

At this moment, word was given to return, and in half an hour the cavalcade arrived at the abbey in the same order it had left it.

Though the rain had ceased, heavy clouds still hung overhead, threatening another deluge, and the aspect of the abbey remained gloomy as ever. The bell continued to toll; drums were beaten; and trumpets sounded from the outer and inner gateway, and from the three quadrangles. The cavalcade drew up in front of the great northern entrance; and its return being announced within, the two other captives were brought forth, each fastened upon a hurdle, harnessed to a stout horse. They looked dead already, so ghastly was the hue of their cheeks.

The abbot's turn came next. Another hurdle was brought forward, and Demdike advanced to the tumbrel. But Paslew recoiled from his touch, and sprang to the ground unaided. He was then laid on his back upon the hurdle, and his hands and feet were bound fast with ropes to the twisted timbers. While this painful task was roughly performed by the wizard's two ill-favoured assistants, the crowd of rustics who looked on, murmured and exhibited such strong tokens of displeasure, that the guard thought it prudent to keep them off with their halberts. But when all was done, Demdike motioned to a man standing behind him to advance, and the person who was wrapped in a russet cloak complied, drew forth an infant, and held it in such way that the abbot could see it. Paslew understood what was meant, but he uttered not a word. Demdike then knelt down beside him, as if ascertaining the security of the cords, and whispered in his ear:—

"Recall thy malediction, and my dagger shall save thee from the last indignity."

"Never," replied Paslew; "the curse is irrevocable. But I would not recall it if I could. As I have said, thy child shall be a witch, and the mother of witches—but all shall be swept off—all!"

"Hell's torments seize thee!" cried the wizard, furiously.

"Nay, thou hast done thy worst to me," rejoined Paslew, meekly, "thou canst not harm me beyond the grave. Look to thyself, for even as thou speakest, thy child is taken from thee."

And so it was. While Demdike knelt beside Paslew, a hand was put forth, and, before the man who had custody of the infant could prevent it, his little charge was snatched from him. This the abbot saw, though the wizard perceived it not. The latter instantly sprang to his feet.

"Where is the child?" he demanded of the fellow in the russet cloak.

"It was taken from me by yon tall man who is disappearing through the gateway," replied the other, in great trepidation.

"Ha! *he* here!" exclaimed Demdike, regarding the dark figure with a look of despair. "It is gone from me for ever!"

"Ay, for ever!" echoed the abbot, solemnly.

"But revenge is still left me—revenge!" cried Demdike, with an infuriated gesture.

"Then glut thyself with it speedily," replied the abbot; "for thy time here is short."

"I care not if it be," replied Demdike; "I shall live long enough if I survive thee."

CHAPTER X.—THE HOLEHOUSES.

At this moment the blast of a trumpet resounded from the gateway, and the Earl of Derby, with the sheriff on his right hand, and Assheton on the left, and mounted on a richly caparisoned charger, rode forth. He was preceded by four javelin-men, and followed by two heralds in their tabards.

To doleful tolling of bells—to solemn music—to plaintive hymn chanted by monks—to roll of muffled drum at intervals—the sad cortège set forth. Loud cries from the bystanders marked its departure, and some of them followed it, but many turned away, unable to endure the sight of horror about to ensue. Amongst those who went on was Hal o' Nabs, but he took care to keep out of the way of the guard, though he was little likely to be recognised, owing to his disguise.

Despite the miserable state of the weather, a great multitude was assembled at the place of execution, and they watched the approaching cavalcade with moody curiosity. To prevent disturbance, arquebussiers were stationed in parties here and there, and a clear course for the cortège was preserved by two lines of halberdiers with crossed pikes. But notwithstanding this, much difficulty was experienced in mounting the hill. Rendered slippery by the wet, and yet more so by the trampling of the crowd, the road was so bad in places that the horses could scarcely drag the hurdles up it, and more than one delay occurred. The stoppages were always denounced by groans, yells, and hootings from the mob, and these neither the menaces of the Earl of Derby, nor the active measures of the guard, could repress.

At length, however, the cavalcade reached its destination. Then the crowd struggled forward, and settled into a dense compact ring, round the circular railing enclosing the place of execution, within which were drawn up the Earl of Derby, the sheriff, Assheton, and the principal gentlemen, together with Demdike and his assistants; the guard forming a circle three deep round them.

Paslew was first unloosed, and when he stood up, he found Father Smith, the late prior, beside him, and tenderly embraced him.

"Be of good courage, Father Abbot," said the prior; "a few moments, and you will be numbered with the just."

"My hope is in the infinite mercy of Heaven, father," replied Paslew, sighing deeply. "Pray for me at the last."

"Doubt it not," returned the prior, fervently. "I will pray for you now and ever."

Meanwhile, the bonds of the two other captives were unfastened, but they were found wholly unable to stand without support. A lofty ladder had been placed against the central scaffold, and up this Demdike, having cast off his houppeland, mounted and adjusted the rope. His tall gaunt figure, fully displayed in his tight-fitting red garb, made him look like a hideous scarecrow. His appearance was greeted by the mob with a perfect hurricane of indignant outcries and yells. But he heeded them not, but calmly pursued his task. Above him wheeled the two ravens, who had never quitted the place since daybreak, uttering their discordant cries. When all was done, he descended a few steps, and, taking a black hood from his girdle to place over the head of his victim, called out in a voice which had little human in its tone, "I wait for you, John Paslew."

"Are you ready, Paslew?" demanded the Earl of Derby.

"I am, my lord," replied the abbot. And embracing the prior for the last time, he added, "*Vale, carissime frater, in æternum vale! et Dominus tecum sit in ultionem inimicorum nostrorum!*"

"It is the king's pleasure that you say not a word in your justification to the mob, Paslew," observed the earl.

"I had no such intention, my lord," replied the abbot.

"Then tarry no longer," said the earl; "if you need aid you shall have it."

"I require none," replied Paslew, resolutely.

With this he mounted the ladder, with as much firmness and dignity as if ascending the steps of a tribune.

Hitherto nothing but yells and angry outcries had stunned the ears of the lookers-on, and several missiles had been hurled at Demdike, some of which took effect, though without occasioning him discomfiture; but when the abbot appeared above the heads of the guard, the tumult instantly subsided, and profound silence ensued. Not a breath was drawn by the spectators. The ravens alone continued their ominous croaking.

Hal o' Nabs, who stood on the outskirts of the ring, saw thus far, but he could bear it no longer, and rushed down the hill. Just as he reached the level ground, a culverin was fired from the gateway, and the next moment a loud wailing cry bursting from the mob told that the abbot was launched into eternity.

Hal would not look back, but went slowly on, and presently afterwards other horrid sounds dinned in his ears, telling that all was over with the two other sufferers. Sickened and faint, he leaned against a wall for support. How long he continued thus, he knew not, but he heard the cavalcade coming down the hill, and saw the Earl of Derby and his attendants ride past. Glancing toward the place of execution, Hal then perceived that the abbot had been cut down, and, rousing himself, he joined the crowd now rushing towards the gate, and ascertained that the body of Paslew was to be taken to the convent church, and deposited there till orders were to be given respecting its interment. He learnt, also, that the removal of the corpse was intrusted to Demdike. Fired by this intelligence, and suddenly conceiving a wild project of vengeance, founded upon what he had heard from the abbot of the wizard being proof against weapons forged by men, he hurried to the church, entered it, the door being thrown open, and rushing up to the gallery, contrived to get out through a window upon the top of the porch, where he secreted himself behind the great stone statue of Saint Gregory.

The information he had obtained proved correct. Ere long a mournful train approached the church, and a bier was set down before the porch. A black hood covered the face of the dead, but the vestments showed that it was the body of Paslew.

At the head of the bearers was Demdike, and when the body was set down he advanced towards it, and, removing the hood, gazed at the livid and distorted features.

"At length I am fully avenged," he said.

"And Abbot Paslew, also," cried a voice above him.

Demdike looked up, but the look was his last, for the ponderous statue of Saint Gregory de Northbury, launched from its pedestal, fell upon his head, and crushed him to the ground. A mangled and breathless mass was taken from beneath the image, and the hands and visage of Paslew were found spotted with blood dashed from the gory carcass. The author of the wizard's destruction was suspected, but never found, nor was it positively known who had done the deed till years after, when Hal o' Nabs, who meanwhile had married pretty Dorothy Croft, and had been blessed by numerous offspring in the union, made his last confession, and then he exhibited no remarkable or becoming penitence for the act, neither was he refused absolution.

Thus it came to pass that the abbot and his enemy perished together. The mutilated remains of the wizard were placed in a shell, and huddled into the grave where his wife had that morning been laid. But no prayer was said over him. And the superstitious believed that the body was carried off that very night by the Fiend, and taken to a witch's sabbath in the ruined tower on Rimington Moor. Certain it was, that the unhallowed grave was disturbed. The body of Paslew was decently interred in the north aisle of the parish church of Whalley, beneath a stone with a Gothic cross sculptured upon it, and bearing the piteous inscription:—"**Miserere mei.**"

But in the belief of the vulgar the abbot did not rest tranquilly. For many years afterwards a white-robed monastic figure was seen to flit along the cloisters, pass out at the gate, and disappear with a wailing cry over the Holehouses. And the same ghostly figure was often seen to glide through the corridor in the abbot's lodging, and vanish at the door of the chamber leading to the little oratory. Thus Whalley Abbey was supposed to be haunted, and few liked to wander through its deserted cloisters, or ruined church, after dark. The abbot's tragical end was thus recorded:—

Johannes Paslew: Capitali Affectus Supplicio.

12o *Mensis Martii*, 1537.

As to the infant, upon whom the abbot's malediction fell, it was reserved for the dark destinies shadowed forth in the dread anathema he had uttered: to the development of which the tragic drama about to follow is devoted, and to which the fate of Abbot Paslew forms a necessary and fitting prologue. Thus far the veil of the Future may be drawn aside. That infant and her progeny became the LANCASHIRE WITCHES.

END OF THE INTRODUCTION.

THE LANCASHIRE WITCHES.

BOOK THE FIRST.

Alizon Device.

CHAPTER I.—THE MAY QUEEN.

ON a May-day in the early part of the seventeenth century, and a most lovely May-day. too, admirably adapted to usher in the merriest month of the year, and seemingly made expressly for the occasion, a wake was held at Whalley, to which all the neighbouring country folk resorted, and indeed many of the gentry as well, for in the good old times, when England was still merry England, a wake had attractions for all classes alike, and especially in Lancashire; for, with pride I speak it, there were no lads who, in running, vaulting, wrestling, dancing, or in any other manly exercise, could compare with the Lancashire lads. In archery, above all, none could match them; for were not their ancestors the stout bowmen and billmen whose cloth-yard shafts, and trenchant weapons, won the day at Flodden? And were they not true sons of their fathers? And then, I speak it with yet greater pride, there were few, if any, lasses who could compare in comeliness with the rosy-cheeked, dark-haired, bright-eyed lasses of Lancashire.

Assemblages of this kind, therefore, where the best specimens of either sex were to be met with, were sure to be well attended, and in spite of an enactment passed in the preceding reign of Elizabeth, prohibiting "piping, playing, bear-baiting, and bull-baiting on the Sabbath-days, or on any other days, and also superstitious ringing of bells, wakes, and common feasts," they were not only not interfered with, but rather encouraged by the higher orders. Indeed, it was well known that the reigning monarch, James the First, inclined the other way, and, desirous of checking the growing spirit of Puritanism throughout the kingdom, had openly expressed himself in favour of honest recreation after evening prayers and upon holidays; and, furthermore, had declared that he liked well the spirit of his good subjects in Lancashire, and would not see them punished for indulging in lawful exercises, but that ere long he would pay them a visit in one of his progresses, and judge for himself, and if he found all things as they had been represented to him, he would grant them still further licence. Meanwhile, this expression of the royal opinion removed every restriction, and old sports and pastimes, May-games, Whitsun-ales, and morris-dances, with rush-bearings, bell-ringings, wakes, and feasts, were as much practised as before the passing of the obnoxious enactment of Elizabeth. The Puritans and Precisians discountenanced them, it is true, as much as ever, and would have put them down if they could, as savouring of papistry and idolatry, and some rigid divines thundered against them from the pulpit; but with the king and the authorities in their favour, the people little heeded these denunciations against them, and abstained not from any "honest recreation" whenever a holiday occurred.

If Lancashire was famous for wakes, the wakes of Whalley were famous even in Lancashire. The men of the district were in general a hardy, handsome race, of the genuine Saxon breed, and passionately fond of all kinds of pastime, and the women had their full share of the beauty indigenous to the soil. Besides, it was a secluded spot, in the heart of a wild mountainous region, and though occasionally visited by travellers journeying northward, or by others coming from the opposite direction, retained a primitive simplicity of manners, and a great partiality for old customs and habits.

The natural beauties of the place, contrasted with the dreary region around it, and heightened by the picturesque ruins of the ancient abbey, part of which, namely, the old abbot's lodgings, had been converted into a residence by the Asshetons, and was now occupied by Sir Ralph Assheton, while the other was left to the ravages of time, made it always an object of attraction to those residing near it; but when on the May-day in question, there was not only to be a wake, but a May-pole set on the green, and a rush-bearing with morris-dancers besides, together with Whitsun-ale at the abbey, crowds flocked to Whalley from Wiswall, Cold Coates, and Clithero, from Ribchester and Blackburn, from Padiham and Pendle, and even from places more remote. Not only was John Lawe's of the Dragon full, but the Chequers, and the Swan also, and the roadside alehouse to boot. Sir Ralph Assheton had several guests at the abbey, and others were expected in the course of the day, while Doctor Ormerod had friends staying with him at the vicarage.

Soon after midnight, on the morning of the festival, many young persons of the village, of both sexes, had arisen, and, to the sound of horn, had repaired to the neighbouring woods, and there gathered a vast stock of green boughs and flowering branches of the sweetly-perfumed hawthorn, wild roses, and honeysuckle, with baskets of violets, cowslips, primroses, blue-bells, and other wild flowers, and returning in the same order they went forth, fashioned the branches into green bowers within the churchyard, or round about the May-pole set up on the green, and decorated them afterwards with garlands and crowns of flowers. This morning ceremonial ought to have been performed without wetting the feet: but though some pains were taken in the matter, few could achieve the difficult task, except those carried over the dewy grass by their lusty swains. On the day before the rushes had been gathered, and the rush cart piled, shaped, trimmed, and adorned by those experienced in the task, (and it was one requiring both taste and skill, as will be seen when the cart itself shall come forth,) while others had borrowed for its adornment, from the abbey and elsewhere, silver tankards, drinking-cups, spoons, ladles, brooches, watches, chains, and bracelets, so as to make an imposing show.

Day was ushered in by a merry peal of bells from the tower of the old parish church, and the ringers practised all kinds of joyous changes during the morning, and fired many a clanging volley. The whole village was early astir; and as these were times when good hours were kept; and as early rising is a famous sharpener of the appetite, especially when attended with exercise, so an hour before noon the rustics one and all sat down to dinner, the strangers being entertained by their friends, and if they had no friends, throwing themselves upon the general hospitality. The alehouses were reserved for tippling at a later hour, for it was then customary for both gentleman and commoner, male as well as female, as will be more fully shown hereafter, to take their meals at home, and repair afterwards to houses of public entertainment for wine or other liquors. Private chambers were, of course, reserved for the gentry; but not unfrequently the squire and his friends would take their bottle with the other guests. Such was the invariable practice in the northern counties in the reign of James the First.

Soon after mid-day, and when the bells began to peal merrily again (for even ringers must recruit themselves), at a small cottage in the outskirts of the village, and close to the Calder, whose waters swept past the trimly kept garden attached to it, two young girls were employed in attiring a third, who was to represent Maid Marian, or Queen of May, in the pageant then about to ensue. And, certainly, by sovereign and prescriptive right of beauty, no one better deserved the high title and distinction conferred upon her than this fair girl. Lovelier maiden in the whole county, and however high her degree, than this rustic damsel, it was impossible to find; and though the becoming and fanciful costume in which she was decked could not heighten her natural charms, it certainly displayed them to advantage. Upon her smooth and beautiful brow sat a gilt crown, while her dark and luxuriant hair, covered behind with a scarlet coif, embroidered with gold, and tied with yellow, white, and crimson ribands, but otherwise wholly unconfined, swept down almost to the ground. Slight and fragile, her figure was of such just proportion that every movement and gesture had an indescribable charm. The most courtly dame might have envied her fine and taper fingers, and fancied she could improve them by protecting them against the sun, or by rendering them snowy white with paste or cosmetic, but this was questionable; nothing certainly could improve the small foot and finely-turned ankle, so well displayed in the red hose and smart little yellow buskin, fringed with gold. A stomacher of scarlet cloth, braided with yellow lace in cross bars, confined her slender waist. Her robe was of carnation-coloured silk, with wide sleeves, and the gold-fringed skirt descended only a little below the knee, like the dress of a modern Swiss peasant, so as to reveal the exquisite symmetry of her limbs. Over all she wore a surcoat of azure silk, lined with white, and edged with gold. In her left hand she held a red pink as an emblem of the season. So enchanting was her appearance altogether, so fresh the character of her beauty, so bright the bloom that dyed her lovely cheeks, that she might have been taken for a personification of May herself. She was indeed in the very May of life—the mingling of spring and summer in womanhood; and the tender blue eyes, bright and clear as diamonds of purest water, the soft regular features, and the merry mouth, whose ruddy parted lips ever and anon displayed two rows of pearls, completed the similitude to the attributes of the jocund month.

Her handmaidens, both of whom were simple girls, and though not destitute of some pretensions to beauty themselves, in nowise to be compared with her, were at the moment employed in knotting the ribands in her hair, and adjusting the azure surcoat.

Attentively watching these proceedings sat on a stool, placed in a corner, a little girl, some nine or ten years old, with a basket of flowers on her knee. The child was very diminutive, even for her age, and her smallness was increased by personal deformity, occasioned by contraction of the chest, and spinal curvature, which raised her back above her shoulders; but her features were sharp and cunning, indeed almost malignant, and there was a singular and unpleasant look about the eyes, which were not placed evenly in the head. Altogether she had a strange old-fashioned look, and from her habitual bitterness of speech, as well as from her vindictive character, which, young as she was, had been displayed, with some effect, on more than one occasion, she was no great favourite with any one. It was curious now to watch the eager and envious interest she took in the progress of her sister's adornment—for such was the degree of relationship in which she stood to the May Queen—and when the surcoat was finally adjusted, and the last riband tied, she broke forth, having hitherto preserved a sullen silence.

THE MAY QUEEN.

P. 66

"Weel, sister Alizon, ye may a farrently May Queen, ey mun say," she observed, spitefully, "but to my mind other Suky Worseley, or Nancy Holt, here, would ha' looked prottier."

"Nah, nah, that we shouldna," rejoined one of the damsels referred to; "there is na a lass i' Lonkyshiar to hold a condle near Alizon Device."

"Fie upon ye, for an ill-favort minx, Jennet," cried Nancy Holt; "yo're jealous o' your protty sister."

"Ey jealous," cried Jennet, reddening, "an whoy the firrups should ey be jealous, ey, thou saucy jade! Whon ey grow older ey'st may a prottier May Queen than onny on you, an so the lads aw tell me."

"And so you will, Jennet," said Alizon Device, checking, by a gentle look, the jeering laugh in which Nancy seemed disposed to indulge—"so you will, my pretty little sister," she added, kissing her; "and I will 'tire you as well and as carefully as Susan and Nancy have just 'tired me."

"Mayhap ey shanna live till then," rejoined Jennet, peevishly, "and when ey'm dead an' gone, an' laid i' t' cowld churchyard, yo an they win be sorry fo having werreted me so."

"I have never intentionally vexed you, Jennet, love," said Alizon, "and I am sure these two girls love you dearly."

"Eigh, we may allowance fo her feaw tempers," observed Susan Worseley; fo we knoa that ailments an deformities are sure to may folk fretful."

"Eigh, there it is," cried Jennet, sharply. "My high shoulthers an sma size are always thrown i' my feace. Boh ey'st grow tall i' time, an get straight—eigh straighter than yo, Suky, wi' your broad back an short neck—boh if ey dunna, whot matters it? Ey shall be feared at onny rate—ay, feared, wenches, by ye both."

"Nah doubt on't, theaw little good-fo'-nothin piece o' mischief," muttered Susan.

"Whot's that yo sayn, Suky?" cried Jennet, whose quick ears had caught the words. "Tak care whot ye do to offend me, lass," she added, shaking her thin fingers, armed with talon-like claws, threateningly at her, "or ey'll ask my granddame, Mother Demdike, to quieten ye."

At the mention of this name a sudden shade came over Susan's countenance. Changing colour, and slightly trembling, she turned away from the child, who, noticing the effect of her threat, could not repress her triumph. But again Alizon interposed.

"Do not be alarmed, Susan," she said, "my grandmother will never harm you, I am sure; indeed, she will never harm any one; and do not heed what little Jennet says, for she is not aware of the effect of her own words, or of the injury they might do our grandmother, if repeated."

"Ey dunna wish to repeat them, or to think of em," sobbed Susan.

"That's good, that's kind of you, Susan," replied Alizon, taking her hand. "Do not be cross any more, Jennet. You see you have made her weep."

"Ey'm glad on it," rejoined the little girl, laughing; "let her cry on. It'll do her good, an teach her to mend her manners, and nah offend me again."

"Ey didna mean to offend ye, Jennet," sobbed Susan, "boh yo're so wrythen an marr'd, a body canna speak to please ye."

"Weel, if ye confess your fault, ey'm satisfied," replied the little girl; "boh let it be a lesson to ye, Suky, to keep guard o' your tongue i' future."

"It shall, ey promise ye," replied Susan, drying her eyes.

At this moment a door opened, and a woman entered from an inner room, having a high-crowned, conical-shaped hat on her head, and broad white pinners over her cheeks. Her dress was of dark red camlet, with high-heeled shoes. She stooped slightly, and being rather lame, supported herself on a crutch-handled stick. In age she might be between forty and fifty, but she looked much older, and her features were not at all prepossessing from a hooked nose and chin, while their sinister effect was increased by a formation of the eyes similar to that in Jennet, only more strongly noticeable in her case. This woman was Elizabeth Device, widow of John Device, about whose death there was a mystery to be inquired into hereafter, and mother of Alizon and Jennet, though how she came to have a daughter so unlike herself in all respects as the former, no one could conceive; but so it was.

"Soh, ye ha donned your finery at last, Alizon," said Elizabeth. "Your brother Jem has just run up to say that t' rush-cart has set out, and that Robin Hood and his merry men are comin' for their Queen."

"And their Queen is quite ready for them," replied Alizon, moving towards the door.

"Neigh, let's ha' a look at ye fust, wench," cried Elizabeth, staying her; "fine fitthers may fine brids—ey warrant me now yo'n getten these May gewgaws on, yo fancy yourself a queen in arnest."

"A queen of a day, mother; a queen of a little village festival; nothing more," replied Alizon. "Oh, if I were a queen in right earnest, or even a great lady—"

"Whot would yo do?" demanded Elizabeth Device, sourly.

"I'd make you rich, mother, and build you a grand house to live in," replied Alizon; "much grander than Browsholme, or Downham, or Middleton."

"Pity yo're nah a queen then, Alizon," replied Elizabeth, relaxing her harsh features into a wintry smile.

"Whot would ye do fo me, Alizon, if ye were a queen?" asked little Jennet, looking up at her.

"Why, let me see," was the reply; "I'd indulge every one of your whims and wishes. You should only need ask to have."

"Poh—poh—yo'd never content her," observed Elizabeth, testily.

"It's nah your way to try an content me, mother, even whon ye might," rejoined Jennet, who, if she loved few people, loved her mother least of all, and never lost an opportunity of testifying her dislike to her.

"Awt o'pontee, little wasp," cried her mother; "theaw desarves nowt boh whot theaw dustna get often enough—a good whipping."

"Yo hanna towd us whot yo'd do fo yurse'f if yo war a great lady, Alizon?" interposed Susan.

"Oh, I haven't thought about myself," replied the other, laughing.

"Ey con tell ye what she'd do, Suky," replied little Jennet, knowingly; "she'd marry Master Richard Assheton, o' Middleton."

"Jennet!" exclaimed Alizon, blushing crimson.

"It's true," replied the little girl; "ye knoa ye would, Alizon. Look at her feace," she added, with a screaming laugh.

"Howd te tongue, little plague," cried Elizabeth, rapping her knuckles with her stick, "and behave thyself, or theaw shanna go out to t' wake."

Jennet dealt her mother a bitterly vindictive look, but she neither uttered cry, nor made remark.

In the momentary silence that ensued the blithe jingling of bells was heard, accompanied by the merry sound of tabor and pipe.

"Ah! here come the rush-cart and the morris-dancers," cried Alizon, rushing joyously to the window, which, being left partly open, admitted the scent of the woodbine and eglantine by which it was overgrown, as well as the humming sound of the bees by which the flowers were invaded.

Almost immediately afterwards a frolic troop, like a band of masquers, approached the cottage, and drew up before it, while the jingling of bells ceasing at the same moment, told that the rush-cart had stopped likewise. Chief amongst the party was Robin Hood clad in a suit of Lincoln green, with a sheaf of arrows at his back, a bugle dangling from his baldric, a bow in his hand, and a broad-leaved green hat on his head, looped up on one side, and decorated with a heron's feather. The hero of Sherwood was personated by a tall, well-limbed fellow, to whom, being really a forester of Bowland, the character was natural. Beside him stood a very different figure, a jovial friar, with shaven crown, rubicund cheeks, bull throat, and mighty paunch, covered by a russet habit, and girded in by a red cord, decorated with golden twist and tassel. He wore red hose and sandal shoon, and carried in his girdle a wallet, to contain a roast capon, a neat's tongue, or any other dainty given him. Friar Tuck, for such he was, found his representative in Ned Huddlestone, porter at the abbey, who, as the largest and stoutest man in the village, was chosen on that account to the part. Next to him came a character of no little importance, and upon whom much of the mirth of the pageant depended, and this devolved upon the village cobbler, Jack Roby, a dapper little fellow, who fitted the part of the Fool to a nicety. With bauble in hand, and blue coxcomb hood adorned with long white asses' ears on head, with jerkin of green, striped with yellow; hose of different colours, the left leg being yellow, with a red pantoufle, and the right blue, terminated with a yellow shoe; with bells hung upon various parts of his motley attire, so that he could not move without producing a jingling sound, Jack Roby looked wonderful indeed; and was constantly dancing about, and dealing a blow with his bauble. Next came Will Scarlet, Stukely, and Little John, all proper men and tall, attired in Lincoln green, like Robin Hood, and similarly equipped. Like him, too, they were all foresters of Bowland, owning service to the bowbearer, Mr. Parker of Browsholme hall; and the representative of Little John, who was six feet and a half high, and stout in proportion, was Lawrence Blackrod, Mr. Parker's head keeper. After the foresters came Tom the Piper, a wandering minstrel, habited for the occasion in a blue doublet, with sleeves of the same colour, turned up with yellow, red hose, and brown buskins, red bonnet, and green surcoat lined with yellow. Beside the piper was another minstrel, similarly attired, and provided with a tabor. Lastly came one of the main features of the pageant, and which, together with the Fool, contributed most materially to the amusement of the spectators. This was the Hobby-horse. The hue of this spirited charger was a pinkish white, and his housings were of crimson cloth hanging to the ground, so as to conceal the rider's real legs, though a pair of sham ones dangled at the side. His bit was of gold, and his bridle red morocco leather, while his rider was very sumptuously arrayed in a purple mantle, bordered with gold, with a rich cap of the same regal hue on his head, encircled with gold, and having a red feather stuck in it. The hobby-horse had a plume of nodding feathers on his head, and careered from side to side, now rearing in front, now kicking behind, now prancing, now gently ambling, and in short indulging in playful fancies and vagaries, such as horse never indulged in before, to the imminent danger, it seemed, of his rider, and to the huge delight of the beholders. Nor must it be omitted, as it was matter of great wonderment to the lookers-on, that by some legerdemain contrivance the rider of the hobby-horse had a couple of daggers stuck in his cheeks, while from his steed's bridle hung a silver ladle, which he held now and then to the crowd, and in which, when he did so, a few coins were sure to rattle. After the hobby-horse came the May-pole, not the tall pole so called and which was already planted in the green, but a stout staff elevated some six feet above the head of the bearer, with a coronal of flowers atop, and four long garlands hanging down, each held by a morris-dancer. Then came the May Queen's gentleman usher, a fantastic personage in habiliments of blue guarded with white, and holding a long willow wand in his hand. After the usher came the main troop of morris-dancers—the men attired in a graceful costume, which set off their light active figures to advantage, consisting of a slashed jerkin of black and white velvet, with cut sleeves left open so as to reveal the snowy shirt beneath, white hose, and shoes of black Spanish leather with large roses. Ribands were every where in their dresses—ribands and tinsel adorned their caps, ribands crossed their hose, and ribands were tied round their arms. In either hand they held a long white handkerchief knotted with ribands. The female morris-dancers were habited in white, decorated like the dresses of the men; they had ribands and wreaths of flowers round their heads, bows in their hair, and in their hands long white knotted kerchiefs.

In the rear of the performers in the pageant came the rush-cart drawn by a team of eight stout horses, with their manes and tails tied with ribands, their collars fringed with red and yellow worsted, and hung with bells, which jingled blithely at every movement, and their heads decked with flowers. The cart itself consisted of an enormous pile of rushes, banded and twisted together, rising to a considerable height, and terminated in a sharp ridge, like the point of a Gothic window. The sides and top were decorated with flowers and ribands, and there were eaves in front and at the back, and on the space within them, which was covered with white paper, were strings of gaudy flowers, embedded in moss, amongst which were suspended all the ornaments and finery that could be collected for the occasion: to wit, flagons of silver, spoons, ladles, chains, watches, and bracelets, so as to make a brave and resplendent show. The wonder was how articles of so much value would be trusted forth on such an occasion; but nothing was ever lost. On the top of the rush-cart, and bestriding its sharp ridges, sat half a dozen men, habited somewhat like the morris-dancers, in garments bedecked with tinsel and ribands, holding garlands formed by hoops, decorated with flowers, and attached to poles ornamented with silver paper, cut into various figures and devices, and diminishing gradually in size as they rose to a point, where they were crowned with wreaths of daffodils.

A large crowd of rustics, of all ages, accompanied the morris-dancers and rush-cart.

This gay troop having come to a halt, as described, before the cottage, the gentleman-usher entered it, and, tapping against the inner door with his wand, took off his cap as soon as it was opened, and bowing deferentially to the ground, said he was come to invite the Queen of May to join the pageant, and that it only awaited her presence to proceed to the green. Having delivered this speech in as good set phrase as he could command, and being the parish clerk and schoolmaster to boot, Sampson Harrop by name, he was somewhat more polished than the rest of the hinds; and having, moreover, received a gracious response from the May Queen, who condescendingly replied that she was quite ready to accompany him, he took her hand, and led her ceremoniously to the door, whither they were followed by the others.

Loud was the shout that greeted Alizon's appearance, and tremendous was the pushing to obtain a sight of her; and so much was she abashed by the enthusiastic greeting, which was wholly unexpected on her part, that she would have drawn back again, if it had been possible; but the usher led her forward, and Robin Hood and the foresters having bent the knee before her, the hobby-horse began to curvet anew among the spectators, and tread on their toes, the fool to rap their knuckles with his bauble, the piper to play, the taborer to beat his tambourine, and the morris-dancers to toss their kerchiefs over their heads. Thus the pageant being put in motion, the rush-cart began to roll on, its horses' bells jingling merrily, and the spectators cheering lustily.

CHAPTER II.—THE BLACK CAT AND THE WHITE DOVE.

LITTLE Jennet watched her sister's triumphant departure with a look in which there was far more of envy than sympathy, and, when her mother took her hand to lead her forth, she would not go, but saying she did not care for any such idle sights, went back sullenly to the inner room. When there, however, she could not help peeping through the window, and saw Susan and Nancy join the revel rout. with feelings of increased bitterness.

"Ey wish it would rain an spile their finery," she said, sitting down on her stool, and plucking the flowers from her basket in pieces. "An yet, why canna ey enjoy such seets like other folk? Truth is, ey've nah heart for it."

"Folks say," she continued, after a pause, "that grandmother Demdike is a witch, an con do os she pleases. Ey wonder if she made Alizon so protty. Nah, that canna be, fo' Alizon's na favourite o' hern. If she loves onny one it's me. Why dunna she make me good-looking, then? They say it's sinfu' to be a witch—if so, how comes grandmother Demdike to be one? Boh ey'n observed that those folks os caws her witch are afeard on her, so it may be pure spite o' their pert."

As she thus mused, a great black cat belonging to her mother, which had followed her into the room, rubbed himself against her, putting up his back, and purring loudly.

"Ah, Tib," said the little girl, "how are ye, Tib? Ey didna knoa ye were here. Lemme ask ye some questions, Tib?"

The cat mewed, looked up, and fixed his great yellow eyes upon her.

"One 'ud think ye onderstud whot wos said to ye, Tib," pursued little Jennet. "We'n see whot ye say to this! Shan ey ever be Queen o' May, like sister Alizon?"

The cat mewed in a manner that the little girl found no difficulty in interpreting the reply into "No."

"How's that, Tib?" cried Jennet, sharply. "If ey thought ye meant it, ey'd beat ye, sirrah. Answer me another question, ye saucy knave. Who will be luckiest, Alizon or me?"

This time the cat darted away from her, and made two or three skirmishes round the room, as if gone suddenly mad.

"Ey con may nowt o' that," observed Jennet, laughing.

All at once the cat bounded upon the chimney board, over which was placed a sampler, worked with the name "ALIZON."

"Why Tib really seems to onderstond me, ey declare," observed Jennet, uneasily. "Ey should like to ask him a few more questions, if ey durst," she added, regarding with some distrust the animal, who now returned, and began rubbing against her as before. "Tib—Tib!"

The cat looked up, and mewed.

"Protty Tib—sweet Tib," continued the little girl, coaxingly. "Whot mun one do to be a witch like grandmother Demdike?"

The cat again dashed twice or thrice madly round the room, and then stopping suddenly at the hearth, sprang up the chimney.

"Ey'n frightened ye away ot onny rate," observed Jennet, laughing. "And yet it may mean summot," she added, reflecting a little, "fo ey'n heerd say os how witches fly up chimleys o' broomsticks to attend their sabbaths. Ey should like to fly i' that manner, an change myself into another shape—onny shape boh my own. Oh that ey could be os protty os Alizon! Ey dunna knoa whot ey'd nah do to be like her!"

Again the great black cat was beside her, rubbing against her, and purring. The child was a good deal startled, for she had not seen him return, and the door was shut, though he might have come in through the open window, only she had been looking that way all the time, and had never noticed him. Strange!

"Tib," said the child, patting him, "thou hasna answered my last question—how is one to become a witch?"

As she made this inquiry the cat suddenly scratched her in the arm, so that the blood came. The little girl was a good deal frightened, as well as hurt, and, withdrawing her arm quickly, made a motion of striking the animal. But starting backwards, erecting his tail, and spitting, the cat assumed such a formidable appearance, that she did not dare to touch him, and she then perceived that some drops of blood stained her white sleeve, giving the spots a certain resemblance to the letters J. and D., her own initials.

At this moment, when she was about to scream for help, though she knew no one was in the house, all having gone away with the May-day revellers, a small white dove flew in at the open window, and skimming round the room, alighted near her. No sooner had the cat caught sight of this beautiful bird, than instead of preparing to pounce upon it, as might have been expected, he instantly abandoned his fierce attitude, and, uttering a sort of howl, sprang up the chimney as before. But the child scarcely observed this, her attention being directed towards the bird, whose extreme beauty delighted her. It seemed quite tame too, and allowed itself to be touched, and even drawn towards her, without an effort to escape. Never, surely, was seen so beautiful a bird—with such milkwhite feathers, such red legs, and such pretty yellow eyes, with crimson circles round them! So thought the little girl, as she gazed at it, and pressed it to her bosom. In doing this, gentle and good thoughts came upon her, and she reflected what a nice present this pretty bird would make to her sister Alizon on her return from the merry-making, and how pleased she should feel to give it to her. And then she thought of Alizon's constant kindness to her, and half reproached herself with the poor return she made for it, wondering she could entertain any feelings of envy towards one so good and amiable. All this while the dove nestled in her bosom.

While thus pondering, the little girl felt an unaccountable drowsiness steal over her, and presently afterwards dropped asleep, when she had a very strange dream. It seemed to her that there was a contest going on between two spirits, a good one and a bad, —the bad one being represented by the great black cat, and the good spirit by the white dove. What they were striving about she could not exactly tell, but she felt that the conflict had some relation to herself. The dove at first appeared to have but a poor chance against the claws of its sable adversary, but the sharp talons of the latter made no impression upon the white plumage of the bird, which now shone like silver armour, and in the end the cat fled, yelling as it darted off—"Thou art victorious now, but her soul shall yet be mine."

Something awakened the little sleeper at the same moment, and she felt very much terrified at her dream, as she could not help thinking her own soul might be the one in jeopardy, and her first impulse was to see whether the white dove was safe. Yes, there it was still nestling in her bosom, with its head under its wing.

Just then she was startled at hearing her own name pronounced by a hoarse voice, and, looking up, she beheld a tall young man standing at the window. He had a somewhat gipsy look, having a dark olive complexion, and fine black eyes, though set strangely in his head, like those of Jennet and her mother, coal black hair, and very prominent features, of a sullen and almost savage cast. His figure was gaunt but very muscular, his arms being extremely long, and his hands unusually large and bony—personal advantages, which made him a formidable antagonist in any rustic encounter, and in such he was frequently engaged, being of a very irascible temper, and turbulent disposition. He was clad in a holiday suit of dark-green serge, which fitted him well, and carried a nosegay in one hand, and a stout blackthorn cudgel in the other. This young man was James Device, son of Elizabeth, and some four or five years older than Alizon. He did not live with his mother in Whalley, but in Pendle Forest, near his old relative, Mother Demdike, and had come over that morning to attend the wake.

"Whot are ye abowt, Jennet?" inquired James Device, in tones naturally hoarse and deep, and which he took as little pains to soften, as he did to polish his manners, which were more than ordinarily rude and churlish.

"Whot are ye abowt, ey sey, wench?" he repeated, "Why dunna ye go to t' green to see the morris-dancers foot it round t' May-pow? Cum along wi' me."

"Ey dunna want to go, Jem," replied the little girl.

"Boh yo shan go, ey tell ey," rejoined her brother; "ye shan see your sister dawnce. Ye con sit a whoam onny day; boh May-day cums ony wonst a year, an Alizon winna be Queen twice i' her life. Soh cum along wi' me, dereckly, or ey'n may ye."

"Ey should like to see Alizon dance, an so ey win go wi' ye, Jem," replied Jennet, getting up, "otherwise your orders shouldna may me stir, ey con tell ye."

As she came out, she found her brother whistling the blithe air of "Green Sleeves," cutting strange capers, in imitation of the morris-dancers, and whirling his cudgel over his head instead of a kerchief. The gaiety of the day seemed infectious, and to have seized even him. People stared to see Black Jem, or Surly Jem, as he was indifferently called, so joyous, and wondered what it could mean. He then fell to singing a snatch of a local ballad at that time in vogue in the neighbourhood:—

"If thou wi' nah my secret tell,
  Ne bruit abroad i' Whalley parish,
And swear to keep my counsel well,
  Ey win declare my day of marriage."

"Cum along, lass," he cried stopping suddenly in his song, and snatching his sister's hand. "What han ye getten there, lapped up i' your kirtle, eh?"

"A white dove," replied Jennet, determined not to tell him any thing about her strange dream.

"A white dove!" echoed Jem. "Gi' it me, an ey'n wring its neck, an get it roasted for supper."

"Ye shan do nah such thing, Jem," replied Jennet. "Ey mean to gi' it to Alizon."

"Weel, weel, that's reet," rejoined Jem, blandly, "it'll may a protty offering. Let's look at it."

"Nah, nah," said Jennet, pressing the bird gently to her bosom, "neaw one shan see it efore Alizon."

"Cum along then," cried Jem, rather testily, and mending his pace, "or we'st be too late fo' t' round. Whoy yo'n scratted yourself," he added, noticing the red spots on her sleeve

"Han ey?" she rejoined, evasively. "Oh now ey rekilect, it wos Tib did it."

"Tib!" echoed Jem, gravely, and glancing uneasily at the marks.

Meanwhile, on quitting the cottage, the May-day revellers had proceeded slowly towards the green, increasing the number of their followers at each little tenement they passed, and being welcomed every where with shouts and cheers. The hobby-horse curveted and capered; the Fool fleered at the girls, and flouted the men, jesting with every one, and when failing in a point rapping the knuckles of his auditors; Friar Tuck chucked the pretty girls under the chin, in defiance of their sweethearts, and stole a kiss from every buxom dame that stood in his way, and then snapped his fingers, or made a broad grimace at the husband; the piper played, and the taborer rattled his tambourine; the morris-dancers tossed their kerchiefs aloft; and the bells of the rush-cart jingled merrily; the men on the top being on a level with the roofs of the cottages, and the summits of the haystacks they passed, but in spite of their exalted position jesting with the crowd below. But in spite of these multiplied attractions, and in spite of the gambols of Fool and Horse, though the latter elicited prodigious laughter, the main attention was fixed on the May Queen, who tripped lightly along by the side of her faithful squire, Robin Hood, followed by the three bold foresters of Sherwood, and her usher.

In this way they reached the green, where already a large crowd was collected to see them, and where in the midst of it, and above the heads of the assemblage, rose the lofty May-pole, with all its flowery garlands glittering in the sunshine, and its ribands fluttering in the breeze. Pleasant was it to see those cheerful groups, composed of happy rustics, youths in their holiday attire, and maidens neatly habited too, and fresh and bright as the day itself. Summer sunshine sparkled in their eyes, and weather and circumstance as well as genial natures disposed them to enjoyment. Every lass above eighteen had her sweetheart, and old couples nodded and smiled at each other when any tender speech, broadly conveyed but tenderly conceived, reached their ears, and said it recalled the days of their youth. Pleasant was it to hear such honest laughter, and such good homely jests.

Laugh on, my merry lads, you are made of good old English stuff, loyal to church and king, and while you, and such as you, last, our land will be in no danger from foreign foe! Laugh on, and praise your sweethearts how you will. Laugh on, and blessings on your honest hearts!

The frolic train had just reached the precincts of the green, when the usher waving his wand aloft, called a momentary halt, announcing that Sir Ralph Assheton and the gentry were coming forth from the Abbey gate to meet them.

CHAPTER III.—THE ASSHETONS.

BETWEEN Sir Ralph Assheton of the Abbey and the inhabitants of Whalley, many of whom were his tenants, he being joint lord of the manor with John Braddyll of Portfield, the best possible feeling subsisted; for though somewhat austere in manner, and tinctured with Puritanism, the worthy knight was sufficiently shrewd, or, more correctly speaking, sufficiently liberal-minded, to be tolerant of the opinions of others, and being moreover sincere in his own religious views, no man could call him in question for them; besides which, he was very hospitable to his friends, very bountiful to the poor, a good landlord, and a humane man. His very austerity of manner, tempered by stately courtesy, added to the respect he inspired, especially as he could now and then relax into gaiety, and, when he did so, his smile was accounted singularly sweet. But in general he was grave and formal; stiff in attire, and stiff in gait; cold and punctilious in manner, precise in speech, and exacting in due respect from both high and low, which was seldom if ever, refused him. Amongst Sir Ralph's other good qualities, for such it was esteemed by his friends and retainers, and they were, of course, the best judges, was a strong love of the chase, and perhaps he indulged a little too freely in the sports of the field, for a gentleman of a character so staid and decorous; but his popularity was far from being diminished by the circumstance; neither did he suffer the rude and boisterous companionship into which he was brought by indulgence in this his favourite pursuit in any way to affect him. Though still young, Sir Ralph was prematurely grey, and this, combined with the sad severity of his aspect, gave him the air of one considerably past the middle term of life, though this appearance was contradicted again by the youthful fire of his eagle eye. His features were handsome and strongly marked, and he wore a pointed beard and mustaches, with a shaved cheek. Sir Ralph Assheton had married twice, his first wife being a daughter of Sir James Bellingham of Levens, in Northumberland, by whom he had two children; while his second choice fell upon Eleanor Shuttleworth, the lovely and well-endowed heiress of Gawthorpe, to whom he had been recently united. In his attire, even when habited for the chase or a merry-making, like the present, the Knight of Whalley affected a sombre colour, and ordinarily wore a quilted doublet of black silk, immense trunk hose of the same material, stiffened with whalebone, puffed out well-wadded sleeves, falling bands, for he eschewed the ruff as savouring of vanity, boots of black flexible leather, ascending to the hose, and armed with spurs with gigantic rowels, a round-crowned small-brimmed black hat, with an ostrich feather placed in the side and hanging over the top, a long rapier on his hip, and a dagger in his girdle. This buckram attire, it will be easily conceived, contributed no little to the natural stiffness of his thin tall figure.

Sir Ralph Assheton was great grandson of Richard Assheton, who flourished in the time of Abbot Paslew, and who, in conjunction with John Braddyll, fourteen years after the unfortunate prelate's attainder and the dissolution of the monastery, had purchased the abbey and domains of Whalley from the Crown, subsequently to which, a division of the property so granted took place between them, the abbey and part of the manor falling to the share of Richard Assheton, whose descendants had now for three generations made it their residence. Thus the whole of Whalley belonged to the families of Assheton and Braddyll, which had intermarried; the latter, as has been stated, dwelling at Portfield, a fine old seat in the neighbourhood.

A very different person from Sir Ralph was his cousin, Nicholas Assheton of Downham, who, except as regards his Puritanism, might be considered a type of the Lancashire squire of the day. A precisian in religious notions, and constant in attendance at church and lecture, he put no sort of restraint upon himself, but mixed up fox-hunting, otter-hunting, shooting at the mark, and perhaps shooting with the long-bow, foot-racing, horse-racing, and, in fact, every other kind of country diversion, not forgetting tippling, cards, and dicing, with daily devotion, discourses, and psalm-singing in the oddest way imaginable. A thorough sportsman was Squire Nicholas Assheton, well versed in all the arts and mysteries of hawking and hunting. Not a man in the county could ride harder, hunt deer, unkennel fox, unearth badger, or spear otter, better than he. And then, as to tippling, he would sit you a whole afternoon at the alehouse, and be the merriest man there, and drink a bout with every farmer present. And if the parson chanced to be out of hearing, he would never make a mouth at a round oath, nor choose a second expression when the first would serve his turn. Then, who so constant at church or lecture as Squire Nicholas—though he did snore sometimes during the long sermons of his cousin, the Rector of Middleton? A great man was he at all weddings, christenings, churchings, and funerals, and never neglected his bottle at these ceremonies, nor any sport in doors or out of doors, meanwhile. In short, such a roystering Puritan was never known. A good-looking young man was the Squire of Downham, possessed of a very athletic frame, and a most vigorous constitution, which helped him, together with the prodigious exercise he took, through any excess. He had a sanguine complexion, with a broad, good-natured visage, which he could lengthen at will in a surprising manner. His hair was cropped close to his head, and the razor did daily duty over his cheek and chin, giving him the roundhead look, some years later, characteristic of the Puritanical party. Nicholas had taken to wife Dorothy, daughter of Richard Greenacres of Worston, and was most fortunate in his choice, which is more than can be said for his lady, for I cannot uphold the squire as a model of conjugal fidelity. Report affirmed that he loved more than one pretty girl under the rose. Squire Nicholas was not particular as to the quality or make of his clothes, provided they wore well and protected him against the weather, and was generally to be seen in doublet and hose of stout fustian, which had seen some service, with a broad-leaved hat, originally green, but of late bleached to a much lighter colour; but he was clad on this particular occasion in ash-coloured habiliments fresh from the tailor's hands, with buff boots drawn up to the knee, and a new round hat from York with a green feather in it. His legs were slightly embowed, and he bore himself like a man rarely out of the saddle.

Downham, the residence of the squire, was a fine old house, very charmingly situated to the north of Pendle Hill, of which it commanded a magnificent view, and a few miles from Clithero. The grounds about it were well-wooded and beautifully broken and diversified, watered by the Ribble, and opening upon the lovely and extensive valley deriving its name from that stream. The house was in good order and well maintained, and the stables plentifully furnished with horses, while the hall was adorned with various trophies and implements of the chase; but as I propose paying its owner a visit, I shall defer any further description of the place till an opportunity arrives for examining it in detail.

A third cousin of Sir Ralph's, though in the second degree, likewise present on the May-day in question, was the Reverend Abdias Assheton, Rector of Middleton, a very worthy man, who, though differing from his kinsmen upon some religious points, and not altogether approving of the conduct of one of them, was on good terms with both. The Rector of Middleton was portly and middle-aged, fond of ease and reading, and by no means indifferent to the good things of life. He was unmarried, and passed much of his time at Middleton Hall, the seat of his near relative Sir Richard Assheton, to whose family he was greatly attached, and whose residence closely adjoined the rectory.

A fourth cousin, also present, was young Richard Assheton of Middleton, eldest son and heir of the owner of that estate. Possessed of all the good qualities largely distributed among his kinsmen, with none of their drawbacks, this young man was as tolerant and bountiful as Sir Ralph, without his austerity and sectarianism; as keen a sportsman and as bold a rider as Nicholas, without his propensities to excess; as studious, at times, and as well read as Abdias, without his laziness and self-indulgence; and as courtly and well-bred as his father, Sir Richard, who was esteemed one of the most perfect gentlemen in the county, without his haughtiness. Then he was the handsomest of his race, though the Asshetons were accounted the handsomest family in Lancashire, and no one minded yielding the palm to young Richard, even if it could be contested, he was so modest and unassuming. At this time, Richard Assheton was about two-and-twenty, tall, gracefully and slightly formed, but possessed of such remarkable vigour, that even his cousin Nicholas could scarcely compete with him in athletic exercises. His features were fine and regular, with an almost Phrygian precision of outline; his hair was of a dark brown, and fell in clustering curls over his brow and neck; and his complexion was fresh and blooming, and set off by a slight beard and mustache, carefully trimmed and pointed. His dress consisted of a dark-green doublet, with wide velvet hose, embroidered and fringed, descending nearly to the knee, where they were tied with points and ribands, met by dark stockings, and terminated by red velvet shoes with roses in them. A white feather adorned his black broad-leaved hat, and he had a rapier by his side.

Amongst Sir Ralph Assheton's guests were Richard Greenacres, of Worston, Nicholas Assheton's father-in-law; Richard Sherborne of Dunnow, near Sladeburne, who had married Dorothy, Nicholas's sister; Mistress Robinson of Raydale House, aunt to the knight and the squire, and two of her sons, both stout youths, with John Braddyll and his wife, of Portfield. Besides these there was Master Roger Nowell, a justice of the peace in the county, and a very active and busy one too, who had been invited for an especial purpose, to be explained hereafter. Head of an ancient Lancashire family, residing at Read, a fine old hall, some little distance from Whalley, Roger Nowell, though a worthy, well-meaning man, dealt hard measure from the bench, and seldom tempered justice with mercy. He was sharp-featured, dry, and sarcastic, and being adverse to country sports, his presence on the occasion was the only thing likely to impose restraint on the revellers. Other guests there were, but none of particular note.

The ladies of the party consisted of Lady Assheton, Mistress Nicholas Assheton of Downham, Dorothy Assheton of Middleton, sister to Richard, a lovely girl of eighteen, with light fleecy hair, summer blue eyes, and a complexion of exquisite purity, Mistress Sherborne of Dunnow, Mistress Robinson of Raydale, and Mistress Braddyll of Portfield, before mentioned, together with the wives and daughters of some others of the neighbouring gentry; most noticeable amongst whom was Mistress Alice Nutter of Rough Lee, in Pendle Forest, a widow lady and a relative of the Assheton family.

Mistress Nutter might be a year or two turned of forty, but she still retained a very fine figure, and much beauty of feature, though of a cold and disagreeable cast. She was dressed in mourning, though her husband had been dead several years, and her rich dark habiliments well became her pale complexion and raven hair. A proud poor gentleman was Richard Nutter, her late husband, and his scanty means not enabling him to keep up as large an establishment as he desired, or to be as hospitable as his nature prompted, his temper became soured, and he visited his ill humours upon his wife, who, devotedly attached to him, to all outward appearance at least, never resented his ill treatment. All at once, and without any previous symptoms of ailment, or apparent cause, unless it might be over-fatigue in hunting the day before, Richard Nutter was seized with a strange and violent illness, which, after three or four days of acute suffering, brought him to the grave. During his illness he was constantly and zealously tended by his wife, but he displayed great aversion to her, declaring himself bewitched, and that an old woman was ever in the corner of his room mumbling wicked enchantments against him. But as no such old woman could be seen, these assertions were treated as delirious ravings. They were not, however, forgotten after his death, and some people said that he had certainly been bewitched, and that a waxen image made in his likeness, and stuck full of pins, had been picked up in his chamber by Mistress Alice and cast into the fire, and as soon as it melted he had expired. Such tales only obtained credence with the common folk; but as Pendle Forest was a sort of weird region, many reputed witches dwelling in it, they were the more readily believed, even by those who acquitted Mistress Nutter of all share in the dark transaction.

Mistress Nutter gave the best proof that she respected her husband's memory by not marrying again, and she continued to lead a very secluded life at Rough Lee, a lonesome house in the heart of the forest. She lived quite by herself, for she had no children, her only daughter having perished somewhat strangely when quite an infant. Though a relative of the Asshetons, she kept up little intimacy with them, and it was a matter of surprise to all that she had been drawn from her seclusion to attend the present revel. Her motive, however, in visiting the Abbey, was to obtain the assistance of Sir Ralph Assheton, in settling a dispute between her and Roger Nowell, relative to the boundary line of part of their properties which came together; and this was the reason why the magistrate had been invited to Whalley. After hearing both sides of the question, and examining plans of the estates, which he knew to be accurate, Sir Ralph, who had been appointed umpire, pronounced a decision in favour of Roger Nowell, but Mistress Nutter refusing to abide by it, the settlement of the matter was postponed till the day but one following, between which time the landmarks were to be investigated by a certain little lawyer named Potts, who attended on behalf of Roger Nowell; together with Nicholas and Richard Assheton, on behalf of Mistress Nutter. Upon their evidence it was agreed by both parties that Sir Ralph should pronounce a final decision, to be accepted by them, and to that effect they signed an agreement. The three persons appointed to the investigation settled to start for Rough Lee early on the following morning.

A word as to Master Thomas Potts. This worthy was an attorney from London, who had officiated as clerk of the court at the assizes at Lancaster, where his quickness had so much pleased Roger Nowell, that he sent for him to Read to manage this particular business A sharp-witted fellow was Potts, and versed in all the quirks and tricks of a very subtle profession—not over-scrupulous, provided a client would pay well; prepared to resort to any expedient to gain his object, and quite conversant enough with both practice and precedent to keep himself straight. A bustling, consequential little personage was he, moreover; very fond of delivering an opinion, even when unasked, and of a meddling, make-mischief turn, constantly setting men by the ears. A suit of rusty black, a parchment-coloured skin, small wizen features, a turn-up nose, scant eyebrows, and a great yellow forehead, constituted his external man. He partook of the hospitality at the Abbey, but had his quarters at the Dragon. He it was who counselled Roger Nowell to abide by the decision of Sir Ralph, confidently assuring him that he must carry his point.

This dispute was not, however, the only one the knight had to adjust, or in which Master Potts was concerned. A claim had recently been made by a certain Sir Thomas Metcalfe of Nappay, in Wensleydale, near Bainbridge, to the house and manor of Raydale, belonging to his neighbour, John Robinson, whose lady, as has been shown, was a relative of the Asshetons. Robinson himself had gone to London to obtain advice on the subject, while Sir Thomas Metcalfe, who was a man of violent disposition, had threatened to take forcible possession of Raydale, if it were not delivered to him without delay, and to eject the Robinson family. Having consulted Potts, however, on the subject, whom he had met at Read, the latter strongly dissuaded him from the course, and recommended him to call to his aid the strong arm of the law; but this he rejected, though he ultimately agreed to refer the matter to Sir Ralph Assheton, and for this purpose he had come over to Whalley, and was at present a guest at the vicarage. Thus it will be seen that Sir Ralph Assheton had his hands full, while the little London lawyer, Master Potts, was tolerably well occupied. Besides Sir Thomas Metcalfe, Sir Richard Molyneux, and Mr. Parker of Browsholme, were guests of Dr. Ormerod at the vicarage.

Such was the large company assembled to witness the May-day revels at Whalley, and if harmonious feelings did not exist amongst all of them, little outward manifestation was made of enmity. The dresses and appointments of the pageant having been provided by Sir Ralph Assheton, who, Puritan as he was, encouraged all harmless country pastimes, it was deemed necessary to pay him every respect, even if no other feeling would have prompted the attention, and therefore the troop had stopped on seeing him and his guests issue from the Abbey gate. At pretty nearly the same time Doctor Ormerod and his party came from the vicarage towards the green.

No order of march was observed, but Sir Ralph and his lady, with two of his children by the former marriage, walked first. Then came some of the other ladies, with the Rector of Middleton, John Braddyll, and the two sons of Mistress Robinson. Next came Mistress Nutter, Roger Nowell and Potts walking after her, eyeing her maliciously, as her proud figure swept on before them. Even if she saw their looks or overheard their jeers, she did not deign to notice them. Lastly came young Richard Assheton, of Middleton, and Squire Nicholas, both in high spirits, and laughing and chatting together.

"A brave day for the morris-dancers, cousin Dick," observed Nicholas Assheton, as they approached the green, "and plenty of folk to witness the sport. Half my lads from Downham are here, and I see a good many of your Middleton chaps among them. How are you, Farmer Tetlow?" he added to a stout, hale-looking man, with a blooming country woman by his side—"brought your pretty young wife to the rush-bearing, I see."

"Yeigh, squoire," rejoined the farmer, "an mightily pleased hoo be wi' it, too."

"Happy to hear it, Master Tetlow," replied Nicholas, "she'll be better pleased before the day's over, I'll warrant her. I'll dance a round with her myself in the hall at night."

"Theere now, Meg, whoy dunna ye may t' squoire a curtsy, wench, an thonk him," said Tetlow, nudging his pretty wife, who had turned away, rather embarrassed by the free gaze of the squire. Nicholas, however, did not wait for the curtsy, but went away, laughing, to overtake Richard Assheton, who had walked on.

"Ah, here's Frank Garside," he continued, espying another rustic acquaintance. "Halloa, Frank, I'll come over one day next week, and try for a fox in Easington Woods. We missed the last, you know. Tom Brockholes, are you here? Just ridden over from Sladeburne, eh? When is that shooting match at the bodkin to come off, eh? Mind, it is to be at twenty-two roods' distance. Ride over to Downham on Thursday next, Tom. We're to have a foot-race, and I'll show you good sport, and at night we'll have a lusty drinking bout at the alehouse. On

Friday, we'll take out the great nets, and try for salmon in the Ribble. I took some fine fish on Monday—one salmon of ten pounds' weight, the largest I've got the whole season.—I brought it with me to-day to the Abbey. There's an otter in the river, and I won't hunt him till you come, Tom. I shall see you on Thursday, eh?"

Receiving an answer in the affirmative, squire Nicholas walked on, nodding right and left, jesting with the farmers, and ogling their pretty wives and daughters.

"I tell you what, cousin Dick," he said, calling after Richard Assheton, who had got in advance of him, "I'll match my dun nag against your grey gelding for twenty pieces, that I reach the boundary line of the Rough Lee lands before you to-morrow. What, you won't have it? You know I shall beat you—ha! ha! Well, we'll try the speed of the two tits the first day we hunt the stag in Bowland Forest. Odds my life!" he cried, suddenly altering his deportment and lengthening his visage, "if there isn't our parson here. Stay with me, cousin Dick, stay with me. Give you good-day, worthy Mr. Dewhurst," he added, taking off his hat to the divine, who respectfully returned his salutation, "I did not look to see your reverence here, taking part in these vanities and idle sports. I propose to call on you on Saturday, and pass an hour in serious discourse. I would call to-morrow, but I have to ride over to Pendle on business. Tarry a moment for me, I pray you, good cousin Richard. I fear, reverend sir, that you will see much here that will scandalise you; much lightness and indecorum. Pleasanter far would it be to me to see a large congregation of the elders flocking together to a godly meeting, than crowds assembled for such a profane purpose. Another moment, Richard. My cousin is a young man, Mr. Dewhurst, and wishes to join the revel. But we must make allowances, worthy and reverend sir, until the world shall improve. An excellent discourse you gave us, good sir, on Sunday: viii. Rom. 12 and 13 verses: it is graven upon my memory, but I have made a note of it in my diary. I come to you, cousin, I come. I pray you walk on to the Abbey, good Mr. Dewhurst, where you will be right welcome, and call for any refreshment you may desire—a glass of good sack, and a slice of venison pasty, on which we have just dined—and there is some famous old ale, which I would commend to you, but that I know you care not, any more than myself, for creature comforts. Farewell, reverend sir. I will join you ere long, for these scenes have little attraction for me. But I must take care that my young cousin falleth not into harm."

And as the divine took his way to the Abbey, he added, laughingly, to Richard,—"A good riddance, Dick. I would not have the old fellow play the spy upon us.—Ah, Giles Mercer," he added, stopping again,—"and Jeff Rushton—well met, lads! what, are you come to the wake? I shall be at John Lawe's in the evening, and we'll have a glass together—John brews sack rarely, and spareth not the eggs."

"Boh yo'n be at th' dawncing at th' Abbey, squoire," said one of the farmers.

"Curse the dancing!" cried Nicholas—"I hope the parson didn't hear me," he added, turning round quickly. "Well, well, I'll come down when the dancing's over, and we'll make a night of it." And he ran on to overtake Richard Assheton.

By this time the respective parties from the Abbey and the Vicarage having united, they walked on together, Sir Ralph Assheton, after courteously exchanging salutations with Dr. Ormerod's guests, still keeping a little in advance of the company. Sir Thomas Metcalfe comported himself with more than his wonted haughtiness, and bowed so superciliously to Mistress Robinson, that her two sons glanced angrily at each other, as if in doubt whether they should not instantly resent the affront. Observing this, as well as what had previously taken place, Nicholas Assheton stepped quickly up to them, and said—

"Keep quiet, lads. Leave this dunghill cock to me, and I'll lower his crest."

With this he pushed forward, and elbowing Sir Thomas rudely out of the way, turned round, and, instead of apologising, eyed him coolly and contemptuously from head to foot.

"Are you drunk, sir, that you forget your manners?" asked Sir Thomas, laying his hand upon his sword.

"Not so drunk but that I know how to conduct myself like a gentleman, Sir Thomas," rejoined Nicholas, "which is more than can be said for a certain person of my acquaintance, who, for aught I know, has only taken his morning pint."

"You wish to pick a quarrel with me, Master Nicholas Assheton, I perceive," said Sir Thomas, stepping close up to him, "and I will not disappoint you. You shall render me good reason for this affront before I leave Whalley."

"When and where you please, Sir Thomas," rejoined Nicholas, laughing. "At any hour, and at any weapon, I am your man."

"At this moment, Master Potts, who had scented a quarrel afar, and who would have liked it well enough if its prosecution had not run counter to his own interests, quitted Roger Nowell, and ran back to Metcalfe, and plucking him by the sleeve, said, in a low voice—

"This is not the way to obtain quiet possession of Raydale House, Sir Thomas. Master Nicholas Assheton," he added, turning to him, "I must entreat you, my good sir, to be moderate. Gentlemen, both, I caution you that I have my eye upon you. You well know there is a magistrate here, my singular good friend and honoured client, Master Roger Nowell, and if you pursue this quarrel further, I shall hold it my duty to have you bound over by that worthy gentleman in sufficient securities to keep the peace towards our sovereign lord the king and all his lieges, and particularly towards each other. You understand me, gentlemen?"

"Perfectly," replied Nicholas. "I drink at John Lawe's to-night, Sir Thomas."

So saying, he walked away. Metcalfe would have followed him, but was withheld by Potts.

"Let him go, Sir Thomas," said the little man of law; "let him go. Once master of Raydale, you can do as you please. Leave the settlement of the matter to me. I'll just whisper a word in Sir Ralph Assheton's ear, and you'll hear no more of it."

"Fire and fury!" growled Sir Thomas. "I like not this mode of settling a quarrel; and unless this hot-headed psalm-singing puritan apologises, I shall assuredly cut his throat."

"Or he yours, good Sir Thomas," rejoined Potts. "Better sit in Raydale Hall, than lie in the Abbey vaults."

"Well, we'll talk over the matter, Master Potts," replied the knight.

"A nice morning's work I've made of it," mused Nicholas, as he walked along; "here I have a dance with a farmer's pretty wife, a discourse with a parson, a drinking-bout with a couple of clowns, and a duello with a blustering knight on my hands. Quite enough, o' my conscience! but I must get through it the best way I can. And now, hey for the May-pole and the morris-dancers!"

Nicholas just got up in time to witness the presentation of the May Queen to Sir Ralph Assheton and his lady, and like every one else he was greatly struck by her extreme beauty and natural grace.

The little ceremony was thus conducted. When the company from the Abbey drew near the troop of revellers, the usher taking Alizon's hand in the tips of his fingers as before, strutted forward with her to Sir Ralph and his lady, and falling upon one knee before them, said,—"Most worshipful and honoured knight, and you his lovely dame, and you the tender and cherished olive branches growing round about their tables, I hereby crave your gracious permission to present unto your honours our chosen Queen of May."

Somewhat fluttered by the presentation, Alizon yet maintained sufficient composure to bend gracefully before Lady Assheton, and say in a very sweet voice, "I fear your ladyship will think the choice of the village hath fallen ill in alighting upon me; and, indeed, I feel myself altogether unworthy the distinction; nevertheless I will endeavour to discharge my office fittingly, and therefore pray you, fair lady, and the worshipful knight, your husband, together with your beauteous children, and the gentles all by whom you are surrounded, to grace our little festival with your presence, hoping you may find as much pleasure in the sight as we shall do in offering it to you."

"A fair maid, and modest as she is fair," observed Sir Ralph, with a condescending smile.

"In sooth is she," replied Lady Assheton, raising her kindly, and saying, as she did so—

"Nay, you must not kneel to us, sweet maid. You are queen of May, and it is for us to show respect to you during your day of sovereignty. Your wishes are commands; and, in behalf of my husband, my children, and our guests, I answer, that we will gladly attend your revels on the green."

"Well said, dear Nell," observed Sir Ralph. "We should be churlish, indeed, were we to refuse the bidding of so lovely a queen."

"Nay, you have called the roses in earnest to her cheek, now, Sir Ralph," observed Lady Assheton, smiling. "Lead on, fair queen," she continued, "and tell your companions to begin their sports when they please.—Only remember this, that we shall hope to see all your gay troop this evening at the Abbey, to a merry dance."

"Where I will strive to find her majesty a suitable partner," added Sir Ralph. "Stay, she shall make her choice now, as a royal personage should; for you know, Nell, a queen ever chooseth her partner, whether it be for the throne or for the brawl. How say you, fair one? Shall it be either of our young cousins, Joe or Will Robinson of Raydale; or our cousin who still thinketh himself young, Squire Nicholas of Downham."

"Ay, let it be me, I implore of you, fair queen," interposed Nicholas.

"He is engaged already," observed Richard Assheton, coming forward. "I heard him ask pretty Mistress Tetlow, the farmer's wife, to dance with him this evening at the Abbey."

A loud laugh from those around followed this piece of information, but Nicholas was in no wise disconcerted.

"Dick would have her choose him, and that is why he interferes with me," he observed. "How say you, fair queen! Shall it be our hopeful cousin? I will answer for him that he danceth the coranto and lavolta indifferently well."

On hearing Richard Assheton's voice, all the colour had forsaken Alizon's cheeks; but at this direct appeal to her by Nicholas, it returned with additional force, and the change did not escape the quick eye of Lady Assheton.

"You perplex her, cousin Nicholas," she said.

"Not a whit, Eleanor," answered the squire; "but if she like not Dick Assheton, there is another Dick, Dick Sherburne of Sladeburn; or our cousin, Jack Braddyll; or, if she prefer an older and discreeter man, there is Father Greenacres of Worsten, or Master Roger Nowell of Read—plenty of choice."

"Nay, if I must choose a partner, it shall be a young one," said Alizon.

"Right, fair queen, right," cried Nicholas, laughing. "Ever choose a young man if you can. Who shall it be?"

"You have named him yourself, sir," replied Alizon, in a voice which she endeavoured to keep firm, but which, in spite of all her efforts, sounded tremulously—"Master Richard Assheton."

"Next to choosing me, you could not have chosen better," observed Nicholas, approvingly. "Dick, lad, I congratulate thee."

"I congratulate myself," replied the young man. "Fair queen," he added, advancing, "highly flattered am I by your choice, and shall so demean myself, I trust, as to prove myself worthy of it. Before I go, I would beg a boon from you—that flower."

"This pink," cried Alizon. "It is yours, fair sir."

Young Assheton took the flower and took the hand that offered it at the same time, and pressed the latter to his lips; while Lady Assheton, who had been made a little uneasy by Alizon's apparent emotion, and who with true feminine tact immediately detected its cause, called out: "Now, forward—forward to the May-pole! We have interrupted the revel too long."

Upon this the May Queen stepped blushingly back with the usher, who, with his white wand in hand, had stood bolt upright behind her, immensely delighted with the scene in which his pupil—for Alizon had been tutored by him for the occasion—had taken part. Sir Ralph then clapped his hands loudly, and at this signal the tabor and pipe struck up; the Fool and the Hobby-horse, who, though idle all the time, had indulged in a little quiet fun with the rustics, recommenced their gambols; the Morris-dancers their lively dance; and the whole train moved towards the May-pole, followed by the rush-cart, with all its bells jingling, and all its garlands waving.

As to Alizon, her brain was in a whirl, and her bosom heaved so quickly, that she thought she should faint. To think that the choice of a partner in the dance at the Abbey had been offered her, and that she should venture to choose Master Richard Assheton! She could scarcely credit her own temerity. And then to think that she should give him a flower, and, more than all, that he should kiss her hand in return for it! She felt the tingling pressure of his lips upon her finger still, and her little heart palpitated strangely.

As she approached the May-pole, and the troop again halted for a few minutes, she saw her brother James holding little Jennet by the hand, standing in the front line to look at her.

"Oh, how I'm glad to see you here, Jennet!" she cried.

"An ey'm glad to see yo, Alizon," replied the little girl. "Jem has towd me whot a grand partner you're to ha' this e'en." And, she added, with playful malice, "Who was wrong whon she said the queen could choose Master Richard——"

"Hush, Jennet, not a word more," interrupted Alizon, blushing.

"Oh! ey dunna mean to vex ye, ey'm sure," replied Jennet. "Ey've got a present for ye."

"A present for me, Jennet," cried Alizon; "what is it?"

"A beautiful white dove," replied the little girl.

"A white dove! Where did you get it? Let me see it," cried Alizon, in a breath.

"Here it is," replied Jennet, opening her kirtle.

"A beautiful bird, indeed," cried Alizon. "Take care of it for me till I come home."

"Which winna be till late, ey fancy," rejoined Jennet, roguishly. "Ah!" she added, uttering a cry.

The latter exclamation was occasioned by the sudden flight of the dove, which, escaping from her hold, soared aloft. Jennet followed the course of its silver wings, as they cleaved the blue sky, and then all at once saw a large hawk, which apparently had been hovering about, swoop down upon it, and bear it off. Some white feathers fell down near the little girl, and she picked up one of them and put it in her breast.

"Poor bird!" exclaimed the May Queen.

"Eigh, poor bird!" echoed Jennet, tearfully. "Ah, ye dunna knoa aw, Alizon."

"Weel, there's neaw use whimpering abowt a duv," observed Jem, gruffly. "Ey'n bring ye another t' furst time ey go to Cown."

"There's nah another bird like that," sobbed the little girl. "Shoot that cruel hawk fo' me, Jem, win ye."

"How conney wench, whon its flown away?" he replied. "Boh ey'n rob a hawk's neest fo ye, if that'll do os weel."

"Yo dunna understand me, Jem," replied the child, sadly.

At this moment, the music, which had ceased while some arrangements were made, commenced a very lively tune, known as "Round about the May-pole," and Robin Hood, taking the May Queen's hand, led her towards the pole, and placing her near it, the whole of her attendants took hands, while a second circle was formed by the morris-dancers, and both began to wheel rapidly round her, the music momently increasing in spirit and quickness. An irresistible desire to join in the measure seized some of the lads and lasses around, and they likewise took hands, and presently a third and still wider circle was formed, wheeling gaily round the other two. Other dances were formed here and there, and presently the whole green was in movement.

"If you come off heart-whole to-night, Dick, I shall be surprised," observed Nicholas, who with his young relative had approached as near the May-pole as the three rounds of dancers would allow them.

Richard Assheton made no reply, but glanced at the pink which he had placed in his doublet.

"Who is the May Queen?" inquired Sir Thomas Metcalfe, who had likewise drawn near, of a tall man holding a little girl by the hand.

"Alizon, dowter of Elizabeth Device, an mey sister," replied James Device, gruffly.

"Humph!" muttered Sir Thomas, "she is a well-looking lass. And she dwells here—in Whalley, fellow?" he added.

"Hoo dwells i' Whalley," responded Jem, sullenly.

"I can easily find her abode," muttered the knight, walking away.

"What was it Sir Thomas said to you, Jem?" inquired Nicholas, who had watched the knight's gestures, coming up.

Jem related what had passed between them.

"What the devil does he want with her?" cried Nicholas. "No good, I'm sure. But I'll spoil his sport."

"Say boh t' word, squoire, an ey'n break every boan i' his body," remarked Jem.

"No, no, Jem," replied Nicholas. "Take care of your pretty sister, and I'll take care of him."

At this juncture, Sir Thomas, who, in spite of the efforts of the pacific Master Potts to tranquillise him, had been burning with wrath at the affront he had received from Nicholas, came up to Richard Assheton, and, noticing the pink in his bosom, snatched it away suddenly.

"I want a flower," he said, smelling at it.

"Instantly restore it, Sir Thomas!" cried Richard Assheton, pale with rage, "or——"

"What will you do, young sir?" rejoined the knight tauntingly, and plucking the flower in pieces. "You can get another from the fair nymph who gave you this."

Further speech was not allowed the knight, for he received a violent blow on the chest from the hand of Richard Assheton, which sent him reeling backwards, and would have felled him to the ground if he had not been caught by some of the bystanders. The moment he recovered, Sir Thomas drew his sword, and furiously assaulted young Assheton, who stood ready for him, and after the exchange of a few passes, for none of the bystanders dared to interfere, sent his sword whirling over their heads through the air.

"Bravo, Dick," cried Nicholas, stepping up, and clapping his cousin on the back, "you have read him a good lesson, and taught him that he cannot always insult folks with impunity, ha! ha!" And he laughed loudly at the discomfited knight.

"He is an insolent coward," said Richard Assheton. "Give him his sword and let him come on again."

"No, no," said Nicholas, "he has had enough this time. And if he has not, he must settle an account with me. Put up your blade, lad."

"I'll be revenged upon you both," said Sir Thomas, taking his sword, which had been brought him by a bystander, and stalking away.

"You leave us in mortal dread, doughty knight," cried Nicholas, shouting after him, derisively—"ha! ha! ha!"

Richard Assheton's attention was, however, turned in a different direction, for the music suddenly ceasing, and the dancers stopping, he learnt that the May Queen had fainted, and presently afterwards the crowd opened to give passage to Robin Hood, who bore her inanimate form in his arms.

CHAPTER IV.—ALICE NUTTER.

THE quarrel between Nicholas Assheton and Sir Thomas Metcalfe had already been made known to Sir Ralph by the officious Master Potts, and though it occasioned the knight much displeasure, as interfering with the amicable arrangement he hoped to effect with Sir Thomas for his relatives the Robinsons, still he felt sure that he had sufficient influence with his hot-headed cousin, the squire, to prevent the dispute from being carried further, and he only waited the conclusion of the sports on the green, to take him to task. What was the knight's surprise and annoyance, therefore, to find that a new brawl had sprung up, and, ignorant of its precise cause, he laid it entirely at the door of the turbulent Nicholas. Indeed, on the commencement of the fray he imagined that the squire was personally concerned in it, and full of wroth, flew to the scene of action; but before he got there, the affair, which, as has been seen, was of short duration, was fully settled, and he only heard the jeers addressed to the retreating combatant by Nicholas. It was not Sir Ralph's way to vent his choler in words, but the squire knew in an instant, from the expression of his countenance, that he was greatly incensed, and therefore hastened to explain.

"What means this unseemly disturbance, Nicholas?" cried Sir Ralph, not allowing the other to speak. "You are ever brawling like an Alsatian squire. Independently of the ill example set to these good folk, who have met here for tranquil amusement, you have counteracted all my plans for the adjustment of the differences between Sir Thomas Metcalfe and our aunt of Raydale. If you forget what is due to yourself, sir, do not forget what is due to me, and to the name you bear."

"No one but yourself should say as much to me, Sir Ralph," rejoined Nicholas somewhat haughtily; "but you are under a misapprehension. It is not I who have been fighting, though I should have acted in precisely the same manner as our cousin Dick, if I had received the same affront, and so I make bold to say would you. Our name shall suffer no discredit from me; and as a gentleman,

I assert, that Sir Thomas Metcalfe has only received due chastisement, as you yourself will admit, cousin, when you know all."

"I know him to be overbearing," observed Sir Ralph.

"Overbearing is not the word, cousin," interrupted Nicholas, "he is as proud as a peacock, and would trample upon us all, and gore us too, like one of the wild bulls of Bowland, if we would let him have his way. But I would treat him as I would the bull aforesaid, a wild boar, or any other savage and intractable beast, hunt him down, and poll his horns, or pluck out his tusks."

"Come, come, Nicholas, this is no very gentle language," remarked Sir Ralph.

"Why, to speak truth, cousin, I do not feel in any very gentle frame of mind," rejoined the squire; my ire has been roused by this insolent braggart, my blood is up, and I long to be doing."

"Unchristian feelings, Nicholas," said Sir Ralph, severely, "and should be overcome. Turn the other cheek to the smiter. I trust you bear no malice to Sir Thomas."

"I bear him no malice, for I hope malice is not in my nature, cousin," replied Nicholas, "but I owe him a grudge, and when a fitting opportunity occurs—"

"No more of this, unless you would really incur my displeasure," rejoined Sir Ralph; "the matter has gone far enough, too far, perhaps for amendment, and if you know it not, I can tell you that Sir Thomas's claims to Raydale will be difficult to dispute, and so our uncle Robinson has found since he hath taken counsel on the case."

"Have a care, Sir Ralph," said Nicholas, noticing that Master Potts was approaching them, with his ears evidently wide open, "there is that little London lawyer hovering about. But I'll give the cunning fox a double. I'm glad to hear you say so, Sir Ralph," he added, in a tone calculated to reach Potts, "and since our uncle Robinson is so sure of his cause, it may be better to let this blustering knight be. Perchance, it is the certainty of failure that makes him so insensate.

"This is meant to blind me, but it shall not serve your turn, cautelous squire," muttered Potts; "I caught enough of what fell just now from Sir Ralph to satisfy me that he hath strong misgivings. But it is best not to appear too secure.—Ah, Sir Ralph," he added, coming forward, "I was right, you see, in my caution. I am a man of peace, and strive to prevent quarrels and bloodshed. Quarrel if you please—and unfortunately men are prone to anger—but always settle your disputes in a court of law; always in a court of law, Sir Ralph. That is the only arena where a sensible man should ever fight. Take good advice, fee your counsel well, and the chances are ten to one in your favour. That is what I say to my worthy and singular good client, Sir Thomas; but he is somewhat headstrong and vehement, and will not listen to me. He is for settling matters by the sword, for making forcible entries and detainers, and ousting the tenants in possession, whereby he would render himself liable to arrest, fine, ransom, and forfeiture; instead of proceeding cautiously and decorously as the law directs, and as I advise, Sir Ralph, by writ of *ejectione firmæ* or action of trespass, the which would assuredly establish his title, and restore him the house and lands. Or he may proceed by writ of right, which perhaps, in his case, considering the long absence of possession, and the doubts supposed to perplex the title—though I myself have no doubts about it—would be the most efficacious. These are your only true weapons, Sir Ralph—your writs of entry, assise, and right—your pleas of novel disseisin, post-disseisin, and re-disseisin—your remitters, your præcipes, your pones, and your recordari faciases. These are the sword, shield, and armour of proof of a wise man."

"Zounds! you take away one's breath with this hail-storm of writs and pleas, master lawyer!" cried Nicholas. "But in one respect I am of your 'worthy and singular good' client's, opinion, and would rather trust to my own hand for the defence of my property than to the law to keep it for me."

"Then you would do wrong, good Master Nicholas," rejoined Potts, with a smile of supreme contempt; "for the law is the better guardian and the stronger adversary of the two, and so Sir Thomas will find if he takes my advice, and obtains, as he can and will do, a perfect title *juris et seisinæ conjunctionem*."

"Sir Thomas is still willing to refer the case to my arbitrement, I believe, sir?" demanded Sir Ralph, uneasily.

"He was so, Sir Ralph," rejoined Potts, "unless the assaults and batteries, with intent to do him grievous corporeal hurt, which he hath sustained from your relatives, have induced a change of mind in him. But as I premised, Sir Ralph, I am a man of peace, and willing to intermediate."

"Provided you get your fee, master lawyer," observed Nicholas, sarcastically.

"Certainly, I object not to the *quiddam honorarium*, Master Nicholas," rejoined Potts; "and if my client hath the *quid pro quo*, and gaineth his point, he cannot complain.—But what is this? Some fresh disturbance!"

"Something hath happened to the May Queen," cried Nicholas.

"I trust not," said Sir Ralph, with real concern. "Ha! she has fainted. They are bringing her this way. Poor maid! what can have occasioned this sudden seizure?"

"I think I could give a guess," muttered Nicholas. "Better remove her to the Abbey," he added aloud to the knight.

"You are right," said Sir Ralph. "Our cousin Dick is near her, I observe. He shall see her conveyed there at once."

At this moment Lady Assheton and Mrs. Nutter, with some of the other ladies, came up.

"Just in time, Nell," cried the knight. "Have you your smelling-bottle about you? The May Queen has fainted."

"Indeed!" exclaimed Lady Assheton, springing towards Alizon, who was now sustained by young Richard Assheton; the forester having surrendered her to him. "How has this happened?" she inquired, giving her to breathe at a small phial.

"That I cannot tell you, cousin," replied Richard Assheton, "unless from some sudden fright."

"That was it, Master Richard," cried Robin Hood; "she cried out on hearing the clashing of swords just now, and, I think, pronounced your name, on finding you engaged with Sir Thomas, and immediately after turned pale, and would have fallen if I had not caught her."

"Ah, indeed!" exclaimed Lady Assheton, glancing at Richard, whose eyes fell before her inquiring gaze. "But see, she revives," pursued the lady. "Let me support her head."

As she spoke Alizon opened her eyes, and perceiving Richard Assheton, who had relinquished her to his relative, standing beside her, she exclaimed, "Oh! you are safe! I feared"—And then she stopped, greatly embarrassed.

"You feared he might be in danger from his fierce adversary," supplied Lady Assheton; "but no. The conflict is happily over, and he is unhurt."

"I am glad of it," said Alizon, earnestly.

"She had better be taken to the Abbey," remarked Sir Ralph, coming up.

"Nay, she will be more at ease at home," observed Lady Assheton with a significant look, which, however, failed in reaching her husband.

"Yes, truly shall I, gracious lady," replied Alizon, "far more so. I have given you trouble enough already."

"No trouble at all," said Sir Ralph, kindly; "her ladyship is too happy to be of service in a case like this. Are you not, Nell? The faintness will pass off presently. But let her go to the Abbey at once, and remain there till the evening's festivities, in which she takes part, commence. Give her your arm, Dick."

Sir Ralph's word was law, and therefore Lady Assheton made no remonstrance. But she said quickly, "I will take care of her myself."

"I require no assistance, madam," replied Alizon, "since Sir Ralph will have me go. Nay, you are too kind, too condescending," she added, reluctantly taking Lady Assheton's proffered arm.

And in this way they proceeded slowly towards the Abbey, escorted by Richard Assheton, and attended by Mistress Braddyll and some others of the ladies.

Amongst those who had watched the progress of the May Queen's restoration with most interest was Mistress Nutter, though she had not interfered; and as Alizon departed with

Lady Assheton, she observed to Nicholas, who was standing near,

"Can this be the daughter of Elizabeth Device, and grand-daughter of—"

"Your old Pendle witch, Mother Demdike," supplied Nicholas; "the very same, I assure you, Mistress Nutter."

"She is wholly unlike the family," observed the lady, "and her features resemble some I have seen before."

"She does not resemble her mother, undoubtedly," replied Nicholas, "though what her grand-dame may have been some sixty years ago, when she was Alizon's age, it would be difficult to say.—She is no beauty now."

"Those finely modelled features, that graceful figure, and those delicate hands, cannot surely belong to one lowly born and bred?" said Mistress Nutter.

"They differ from the ordinary peasant mould, truly, replied Nicholas. "If you ask me for the lineage of a steed, I can give a guess at it on sight of the animal, but as regards our own race I'm at fault, Mistress Nutter."

"I must question Elizabeth Device about her," observed Alice. "Strange, I should never have seen her before, though I know the family so well."

"I wish you did not know Mother Demdike quite so well, Mistress Nutter," remarked Nicholas—"a mischievous and malignant old witch, who deserves the tar barrel. The only marvel is, that she has not been burned long ago. I am of opinion, with many others, that it was she who bewitched your poor husband, Richard Nutter."

"I do not think it," replied Mistress Nutter, with a mournful shake of the head. "Alas, poor man! he died from hard riding, after hard drinking. That was the only witchcraft in his case. Be warned by his fate yourself, Nicholas."

"Hard riding after drinking was more likely to sober him than to kill him," rejoined the squire. "But, as I said just now, I like not this Mother Demdike, nor her rival in iniquity, old Mother Chattox. The devil only knows which of the two is worst. But if the former hag did not bewitch your husband to death, as I shrewdly suspect, it is certain that the latter mumbling old miscreant killed my elder brother, Richard, by her sorceries."

"Mother Chattox did you a good turn then, Nicholas," observed Mistress Nutter, "in making you master of the fair estates of Downham."

"So far, perhaps, she might," rejoined Nicholas, "but I do not like the manner of it, and would gladly see her burned; nay, I would fire the fagots myself."

"You are superstitious as the rest, Nicholas," said Mistress Nutter. "For my part I do not believe in the existence of witches."

"Not believe in witches, with these two living proofs to the contrary!" cried Nicholas, in amazement. "Why, Pendle Forest swarms with witches. They burrow in the hill-side like rabbits in a warren. They are the terror of the whole country. No man's cattle, goods, nor even life, are safe from them; and the only reason why these two old hags, who hold sovereign sway over the others, have 'scaped justice so long, is because every one is afraid to go near them. Their solitary habitations are more strongly guarded than fortresses. Not believe in witches! Why I should as soon misdoubt the Holy Scriptures."

"It may be because I reside near them that I have so little apprehension, or rather no apprehension at all," replied Mistress Nutter; "but to me Mother Demdike and Mother Chattox appear two harmless old women."

"They're a couple of dangerous and damnable old hags, and deserve the stake," cried Nicholas, emphatically.

All this discourse had been swallowed with greedy ears by the ever-vigilant Master Potts, who had approached the speakers unperceived; and he now threw in a word.

"So there are suspected witches in Pendle Forest, I find," he said. "I shall make it my business to institute inquiries concerning them, when I visit the place to-morrow. Even if merely ill-reputed, they must be examined, and if found innocent cleared; if not, punished according to the statute. Our sovereign lord the king holdeth witches in especial abhorrence, and would gladly see all such noxious vermin extirpated from the land, and it will rejoice me to promote his laudable designs. I must pray you to afford me all the assistance you can in the discovery of these dreadful delinquents, good Master Nicholas, and I will care that your services are duly represented in the proper quarter. As I have just said, the king taketh singular interest in witchcraft, as you may judge if the learned tractate he hath put forth, in form of a dialogue, intituled "*Dæmonologie*," hath ever met your eye; and he is never so well pleased as when the truth of his tenets are proved by such secret offenders being brought to light, and duly punished."

"The king's known superstitious dread of witches makes men seek them out to win his favour," observed Mistress Nutter. "They have wonderfully increased since the publication of that baneful book!"

"Not so, madam," replied Potts. "Our sovereign lord the king hath a wholesome and just hatred of such evil-doers and traitors to himself and heaven, and it may be dread of them, as indeed all good men must have; but he would protect his subjects from them, and therefore, in the first year of his reign, which I trust will be long and prosperous, he hath passed a statute, whereby it is enacted 'that all persons invoking any evil spirit, or consulting, covenanting with, entertaining, employing, feeding, or rewarding any evil spirit; or taking up dead bodies from their graves to be used in any witchcraft, sorcery, charm, or enchantment; or killing or otherwise hurting any person by such infernal arts, shall be guilty of felony without benefit of clergy, and suffer death.' This statute, madam, was intended to check the crimes of necromancy, sorcery, and witchcraft, and not to increase them. And I maintain that it has checked them, and will continue to check them."

"It is a wicked and bloody statute," observed Mrs. Nutter, in a deep tone, "and many an innocent life will be sacrificed thereby."

"How, madam!" cried Master Potts, staring aghast. "Do you mean to impugn the sagacity and justice of our high and mighty king, the head of the law, and defender of the faith?"

"I affirm that this is a sanguinary enactment," replied Mistress Nutter, "and will put power into hands that will abuse it, and destroy many guiltless persons. It will make more witches than it will find."

"Some are ready made, methinks," muttered Potts, "and we need not go far to find them. You are a zealous advocate for witches, I must say, madam," he added aloud, "and I shall not forget your arguments in their favour."

"To my prejudice, I doubt not," she rejoined, bitterly.

"No, to the credit of your humanity," he answered, bowing, with pretended conviction.

"Well, I will aid you in your search for witches, Master Potts," observed Nicholas; "for I would gladly see the country rid of these pests. But I warn you the quest will be attended with risk, and you will get few to accompany you, for all the folk hereabouts are mortally afraid of these terrible old hags."

"I fear nothing in the discharge of my duty," replied Master Potts, courageously, "for as our high and mighty sovereign hath well and learnedly observed—'if witches be but apprehended and detained by any private person, upon other private respects, their power, no doubt, either in escaping, or in doing hurt, is no less than ever it was before. But if, on the other part, their apprehending and detention be by the lawful magistrate upon the just respect of their guiltiness in that craft, their power is then no greater than before that ever they meddled with their master. For where God begins justly to strike by his lawful lieutenants it is not in the devil's power to defraud or bereave him of the office or effect of his powerful and revenging sceptre.' Thus I am safe; and I shall take care to go armed with a proper warrant, which I shall obtain from a magistrate, my honoured friend and singular good client, Master Roger Nowell. This will obtain me such assistance as I may require, and for due observance of my authority, I shall likewise take with me a peace-officer, or constable."

"You will do well, Master Potts," said Nicholas; "still you must not put faith in all the idle tales told you, for the common folk hereabouts are blindly and foolishly superstitious, and fancy they discern witchcraft in every mischance, however slight, that befalls them. If ale turn sour after a thunder-storm, the witch hath done it; and if the butter cometh not quickly, she hindereth it. If the meat roast ill the witch hath turned the spit; and if the lumber pie taste ill she hath had a finger in it. If your sheep have the foot-rot—your horses the staggers or string-halt—your swine the measles—your hounds a surfeit—or your cow slippeth her calf—the witch is at the bottom of it all. If your maid hath a fit of the sullens, or doeth her work amiss, or your man breaketh a dish, the witch is in fault, and her shoulders can bear the blame. On this very day of the year—namely, May Day,—the foolish folk hold any aged crone who fetcheth fire to be a witch, and if they catch a hedge-hog among their cattle, they will instantly beat it to death with sticks, concluding it to be an old hag in that form come to dry up the milk of their kine."

"These are what Master Potts's royal authority would style mere old wives' trattles about the fire,'" observed Mistress Nutter, scornfully.

"Better be over-credulous than over-sceptical," replied Potts. "Even at my lodging in Chancery Lane I have a horseshoe nailed against the door. One cannot be too cautious when one has to fight against the devil, or those in league with him. Your witch should be put to every ordeal. She should be scratched with pins to draw blood from her; weighed against the church bible, though this is not always proof; forced to weep, for a witch can only shed three tears, and those only from the left eye; or, as our sovereign lord the king truly observeth—no offence to you, Mistress Nutter—'Not so much as their eyes are able to shed tears, albeit the womenkind especially be able otherwise to shed tears at every light occasion when they will, yea, although it were dissemblingly like the crocodile;' and set on a stool for twenty-four hours, with her legs tied across, and suffered neither to eat, drink, nor sleep during the time. This is the surest way to make her confess her guilt next to swimming. If it fails, then cast her with her thumbs and toes tied across into a pond, and if she sink not then is she certainly a witch. Other trials there are, as that by scalding water—sticking knives across—heating of the horseshoe—tying of knots—the sieve and the shears; but the only ordeals safely to be relied on, are the swimming and the stool before mentioned, and from these your witch shall rarely escape. Above all, be sure and search carefully for the witch-mark. I doubt not we shall find it fairly and legibly writ in the devil's characters on Mother Demdike and Mother Chattox. They shall undergo the stool and the pool, and other trials, if required. These old hags shall no longer vex you, good Master

Nicholas. Leave them to me, and doubt not I will bring them to condign punishment."

"You will do us good service then, Master Potts," replied Nicholas. "But since you are so learned in the matter of witchcraft, resolve me, I pray you, how it is, that women are so much more addicted to the practice of the black art than our own sex."

"The answer to the inquiry hath been given by our British Solomon," replied Potts, "and I will deliver it to you in his own words. 'The reason is easy,' he saith; 'for as that sex is frailer than man is, so it is easier to be entrapped in those gross snares of the devil, as was overwell proved to be true, by the serpent's deceiving of Eva at the beginning, which makes him the homelier with that sex sensine.'"

"A good and sufficient reason, Master Potts," said Nicholas, laughing; "is it not so, Mistress Nutter?"

"Ay, marry, if it satisfies you," she answered, drily. "It is of a piece with the rest of the reasoning of the royal pedant, whom Master Potts styles the British Solomon."

"I only give the learned monarch the title by which he is recognised throughout Christendom," rejoined Potts, sharply.

"Well, there is comfort in the thought, that I shall never be taken for a wizard," said the squire.

"Be not too sure of that, good Master Nicholas," returned Potts. "Our present prince seems to have had you in his eye when he penned his description of a wizard, for, he saith, 'A great number of them that ever have been convict or confessors of witchcraft, as may be presently seen by many that have at this time confessed, are some of them rich and worldly-wise; some of them fat or corpulent in their bodies; and most part of them altogether given over to the pleasures of the flesh, continual haunting of company, and all kinds of merriness, lawful and unlawful.' This hitteth you exactly, Master Nicholas."

"Zounds!" exclaimed the squire, "if this be exact, it toucheth me too nearly to be altogether agreeable."

"The passage is truly quoted, Nicholas," observed Mistress Nutter, with a cold smile. "I perfectly remember it. Master Potts seems to have the 'Dæmonologie' at his fingers' ends."

"I have made it my study, madam," replied the lawyer, somewhat mollified by the remark, "as I have the statute on witchcraft and indeed most other statutes."

"We have wasted time enough in this unprofitable talk," said Mistress Nutter, abruptly quitting them without bestowing the slightest salutation on Potts.

"I was but jesting in what I said just now, good Master Nicholas," observed the little lawyer, nowise disconcerted at the slight; "though they were the king's exact words I quoted. No one would suspect you of being a wizard—ha!—ha! But I am resolved to prosecute the search, and I calculate upon your aid, and that of Master Richard Assheton, who goes with us."

"You shall have mine, at all events, Master Potts," replied Nicholas; "and I doubt not, my cousin Dick's, too."

"Our May Queen, Alizon Device, is Mother Demdike's granddaughter, is she not?" asked Potts, after a moment's reflection.

"Ay, why do you ask?" demanded Nicholas.

"For a good and sufficing reason," replied Potts. "She might be an important witness; for, as King James saith, 'bairns or wives may, of our law, serve for sufficient witnesses and proofs.' And he goeth on to say, 'For who but witches can be proofs, and so witnesses of the doings of witches?'"

"You do not mean to aver that Alizon Device is a witch, sir?" cried Nicholas, sharply.

"I aver nothing," replied Potts; "but, as a relative of a suspected witch, she will be the best witness against her."

"If you design to meddle with Alizon Device, expect no assistance from me, Master Potts," said Nicholas, sternly, "but rather the contrary."

"Nay, I but threw out the hint, good Master Nicholas," replied Potts. "Another witness will do equally well. There are other children, no doubt. I rely on you, sir—I rely on you. I shall now go in search of Master Nowell, and obtain the warrant and the constable."

"And I shall go keep my appointment with Parson Dewhurst, at the Abbey," said Nicholas, bowing slightly to the attorney, and taking his departure.

"It will not do to alarm him at present," said Potts, looking after him, "but I'll have that girl as a witness, and I know how to terrify her into compliance. A singular woman, that Mistress Alice Nutter. I must inquire into her history. Odd, how obstinately she set her face against witchcraft. And yet she lives at Rough Lee, in the very heart of a witch district, for such Master Nicholas Assheton calls this Pendle Forest. I shouldn't wonder if she has dealings with the old hags she defends—Mother Demdike and Mother Chattox. Chattox! Lord bless us, what a name! —There's caldron and broomstick in the very sound! And Demdike is little better. Both seem of diabolical invention. If I can unearth a pack of witches, I shall gain much credit from my honourable good lords the judges of assize in these northern parts, besides pleasing the King himself, who is sure to hear of it, and reward my praiseworthy zeal. Look to yourself, Mistress Nutter, and take care you are not caught tripping. And now, for Master Roger Nowell.

With this, he peered about among the crowd in search of the magistrate, but though he thrust his little turned-up nose in every direction, he could not find him, and therefore set out for the Abbey, concluding he had gone thither.

As Mistress Nutter walked along, she perceived James Device among the crowd, holding Jennet by the hand, and motioned him to come to her. Jem instantly understood the sign, and quitting his little sister, drew near.

"Tell thy mother," said Mistress Nutter, in a tone calculated only for his hearing, "to come to me, at the Abbey, quickly and secretly. I shall be in the ruins of the old convent church. I have somewhat to say to her, that concerns herself as well as me. Thou wilt have to go to Rough Lee and Malkin Tower to-night."

Jem nodded, to show his perfect apprehension of what was said and his assent to it, and while Mistress Nutter moved on with a slow and dignified step, he returned to Jennet, and told her she must go home directly, a piece of intelligence which was not received very graciously by the little maiden; but nothing heeding her unwillingness, Jem walked her off quickly in the direction of the cottage; but while on the way to it, they accidentally encountered their mother, Elizabeth Device, and therefore stopped.

"Yo mun go up to th' Abbey directly, mother," said Jem, with a wink, "Mistress Nutter wishes to see ye. Yo'n find her i' t' ruins o' t' owd convent church. Tak kere yo're neaw seen. Yo onderstond."

"Yeigh," replied Elizabeth, nodding her head significantly, "ey'n go at wonst, an see efter Alizon ot t' same time. Fo ey'm towd hoo has fainted, an been ta'en to th' Abbey by Lady Assheton."

"Never heed Alizon," replied Jem, gruffly. Hoo's i' good hands. Ye munna be seen, ey tell ye. Ey'm going to Malkin Tower to-neet, if yo'n owt to send."

"To-neet, Jem," echoed little Jennet.

"Eigh," rejoined Jem, sharply. "Howd te tongue, wench. Dunna lose time, mother."

And as he and his little sister pursued their way to the cottage, Elizabeth hobbled off towards the Abbey, muttering, as she went, "I hope Alizon an Mistress Nutter winna meet. Nah that it matters, boh still it's better not. Strange, the wench should ha' fainted. Boh she's always foolish an timmersome, an ey half fear has lost her heart to young Richard Assheton. Ey'n watch her narrowly, an if it turn out to be so, she mun be cured, or he secured—ha! ha!"

And muttering in this way, she passed through the Abbey gateway, the wicket being left open, and proceeded towards the ruinous convent church, taking care as much as possible to avoid observation.

CHAPTER V.—MOTHER CHATTOX.

NOT far from the green where the May-day revels were held, stood the ancient parish church of Whalley, its square tower surmounted with a flag-staff and banner, and shaking with the joyous peals of the ringers. A picturesque and beautiful structure it was, though full of architectural incongruities; and its grey walls and hoary buttresses, with the lancet-shaped windows of the choir, and the ramified tracery of the fine eastern window, could not fail to please any taste not quite so critical as to require absolute harmony and perfection in a building. Parts of the venerable fabric were older than the Abbey itself, dating back as far as the eleventh century, when a chapel occupied the site; and though many alterations had been made in the subsequent structure at various times, and many beauties destroyed, especially during the period of the Reformation, enough of its pristine character remained to render it a very good specimen of an old country church. Internally, the cylindrical columns of the north aisle, the construction of the choir, and the three stone seats supported on rounded columns near the altar, proclaimed its high antiquity. Within the choir were preserved the eighteen richly-carved stalls once occupying a similar position in the desecrated conventual church; and though exquisite in themselves, they seemed here sadly out of place, not being proportionate to the structure. Their elaborately-carved seats projected far into the body of the church, and their crocketed pinnacles shot up almost to the ceiling. But it was well they had not shared the destruction in which almost all the other ornaments of the magnificent fane they once decorated were involved. Carefully preserved, the black varnished oak well displayed the quaint and grotesque designs with which many of them—the Prior's stall in especial—were embellished. Chief among them was the abbot's stall, festooned with sculptured vine wreaths and clustering grapes, and bearing the auspicious inscription:

Semper gaudentes sint ista sede sedentes:

singularly inapplicable, however, to the last prelate who filled it. Some fine old monuments, and warlike trophies of neighbouring wealthy families, adorned the walls, and within the nave was a magnificent pew, with a canopy and pillars of elaborately-carved oak, and lattice-work at the sides, allotted to the manor of Read, and recently erected by Roger Nowell; while in the north and south aisles were two small chapels, converted since the reformed faith had obtained, into pews—the one called Saint Mary's Cage, belonging to the Assheton family; and the other appertaining to the Catterals of Little Mitton, and designated Saint Nicholas's

Cage. Under the last-named chapel were interred some of the Paslews of Wiswall, and here lay the last unfortunate Abbot of Whalley, between whose grave, and the Assheton and Braddyll families, a fatal relation was supposed to subsist. Another large pew, allotted to the Towneleys, and designated Saint Anthony's Cage, was rendered remarkable, by a characteristic speech of Sir John Towneley, which gave much offence to the neighbouring dames. Called upon to decide as to the position of the sittings in the church, the discourteous knight made choice of Saint Anthony's Cage, already mentioned, declaring, "My man, Shuttleworth of Hacking, made this form, and here will I sit when I come; and my cousin Nowell may make a seat behind me if he please, and my son Sherburne shall make one on the other side, and Master Catteral another behind him, and for the residue the use shall be, first come first speed, and that will make the proud wives of Whalley rise betimes to come to church." One can fancy the rough knight's chuckle, as he addressed these words to the old clerk, certain of their being quickly repeated to the "proud wives" in question.

Within the churchyard grew two fine old yew-trees, now long since decayed and gone, but then spreading their dark-green arms over the little turf-covered graves. Reared against the buttresses of the church was an old stone coffin, together with a fragment of a curious monumental effigy, likewise of stone; but the most striking objects in the place, and deservedly ranked amongst the wonders of Whalley, were three remarkable obelisk-shaped crosses, set in a line upon pedestals, covered with singular devices in fretwork, and all three differing in size and design. Evidently of remotest antiquity, these crosses were traditionally assigned to Paullinus, who, according to the Venerable Bede, first preached the Gospel in these parts, in the early part of the seventh century; but other legends were attached to them by the vulgar, and dim mystery brooded over them.

Vestiges of another people and another faith were likewise here discernible, for where the Saxon forefathers of the village prayed and slumbered in death, the Roman invaders of the isle had trodden, and perchance performed their religious rites; some traces of an encampment being found in the churchyard by the historian of the spot, while the north boundary of the hallowed precincts was formed by a deep foss, once encompassing the nigh-obliterated fortification. Besides these records of an elder people, there was another memento of bygone days and creeds, in a little hermitage and chapel adjoining it, founded in the reign of Edward III., by Henry, Duke of Lancaster, for the support of two recluses and a priest to say masses daily for him and his descendants; but this pious bequest being grievously abused in the subsequent reign of Henry VI., by Isole de Heton, a fair widow, who in the first transports of grief, vowing herself to heaven, took up her abode in the hermitage, and led a very disorderly life therein, to the great scandal of the Abbey, and the great prejudice of the morals of its brethren, and at last, tired even of the slight restraint imposed upon her, fled away "contrary to her oath and profession, not willing, nor intending to be restored again;" the hermitage was dissolved by the pious monarch, and masses ordered to be said daily in the parish church for the repose of the soul of the founder. Such was the legend attached to the little cell, and tradition went on to say that the anchoress broke her leg in crossing Whalley Nab, and limped ever afterwards; a just judgment on such a heinous offender. Both these little structures were picturesque objects, being overgrown with ivy and woodbine. The chapel was completely in ruins, while the cell, profaned by the misdoings of the dissolute votaress Isole, had been converted into a cage for vagrants and offenders, and made secure by a grated window, and a strong door studded with broad-headed nails.

The view from the churchyard, embracing the vicarage-house, a comfortable residence, surrounded by a large walled-in garden, well stocked with fruit-trees, and sheltered by a fine grove of rook-haunted timber, extended on the one hand over the village, and on the other over the Abbey, and was bounded by the towering and well-wooded heights of Whalley Nab. On the side of the Abbey, the most conspicuous objects were the great north-eastern gateway, with the ruined conventual church. Ever beautiful, the view was especially so on the present occasion, from the animated scene combined with it; and the pleasant prospect was enjoyed by a large assemblage, who had adjourned thither to witness the concluding part of the festival.

Within the green and flower-decked bowers which, as has before been mentioned, were erected in the churchyard, were seated Doctor Ormerod and Sir Ralph Assheton, with such of their respective guests as had not already retired, including Richard and Nicholas Assheton, both of whom had returned from the abbey; the former having been dismissed by Lady Assheton from further attendance upon Alizon, and the latter having concluded his discourse with Parson Dewhurst, who, indeed, accompanied him to the church, and was now placed between the Vicar and the Rector of Middleton. From this gentle elevation the gay company on the green could be fully discerned, the tall May-pole, with its garlands and ribands, forming a pivot, about which the throng ever revolved, while stationary amidst the moving masses, the rush-cart reared on high its broad green back, as if to resist the living waves constantly dashed against it. By-and-by a new kind of movement was perceptible, and it soon became evident that a procession was being formed. Immediately afterwards, the rush-cart was put in motion, and winded slowly along the narrow street leading to the church, preceded by the morris-dancers and the other May-day revellers, and followed by a great concourse of people, shouting, dancing, and singing.

On came the crowd. The jingling of bells, and the sound of music grew louder and louder, and the procession, lost for awhile behind some intervening habitations, though the men bestriding the rush-cart could be discerned over their summits, burst suddenly into view; and the revellers entering the churchyard, drew up on either side of the little path leading to the porch, while the rush-cart coming up the next moment, stopped at the gate. Then four young maidens dressed in white, and having baskets in their hands, advanced and scattered flowers along the path; after which ladders were reared against the sides of the rush-cart, and the men, descending from their exalted position, bore the garlands to the church, preceded by the vicar and the two other divines, and followed by Robin Hood and his band, the morris-dancers, and a troop of little children singing a hymn. The next step was to unfasten the bundles of rushes, of which the cart was composed, and this was very quickly and skilfully performed, the utmost care being taken of the trinkets and valuables with which it was ornamented. These were gathered together in baskets and conveyed to the vestry, and there locked up. This done, the bundles of rushes were taken up by several old women, who strewed the aisles with them, and placed such as had been tied up as mats in the pews. At the same time, two casks of ale set near the gate, and given for the occasion by the vicar, were broached, and their foaming contents freely distributed among the dancers and the thirsty crowd. Very merry were they, as may be supposed, in consequence, but their mirth was happily kept within due limits of decorum.

When the rush-cart was wellnigh unladen Richard Assheton entered the church, and greatly pleased with the effect of the flowery garlands with which the various pews were decorated, said as much to the vicar, who smilingly replied, that he was glad to find he approved of the practice, "even though it might savour of superstition;" and as the good doctor walked away, being called forth, the young man almost unconsciously turned into the chapel on the north aisle. Here he stood for a few moments gazing round the church, wrapt in pleasing meditation, in which many objects, somewhat foreign to the place and time, passed through his mind, when, chancing to look down, he saw a small funeral wreath, of mingled yew and cypress, lying at his feet, and a slight tremor passed over his frame, as he found he was standing on the ill-omened grave of Abbot Paslew. Before he could ask himself by whom this sad garland had been so deposited, Nicholas Assheton came up to him, and with a look of great uneasiness cried, "Come away instantly, Dick. Do you know where you are standing?"

"On the grave of the last Abbot of Whalley," replied Richard, smiling.

"Have you forgotten the common saying," cried Nicholas—"that the Assheton who stands on that unlucky grave shall die within the year? Come away at once."

"It is too late," replied Richard, "I have incurred the fate, if such a fate be attached to the tomb; and as my moving away will not preserve me, so my tarrying here cannot injure me further. But I have no fear."

"You have more courage than I possess," rejoined Nicholas. "I would not set foot on that accursed stone for half the county. Its malign influence on our house has been approved too often. The first to experience the fatal destiny were Richard Assheton and John Braddyll, the purchasers of the Abbey. Both met here together on the anniversary of the abbot's execution—some forty years after its occurrence, it is true, and when they were both pretty well stricken in years—and within that year, namely 1578, both died, and were buried in the vault on the opposite side of the church, not many paces from their old enemy. The last instance was my poor brother Richard, who, being incredulous as you are, was resolved to brave the destiny, and stationed himself upon the tomb during divine service, but he too died within the appointed time."

"He was bewitched to death—so, at least, it is affirmed," said Richard Assheton, with a smile. "But I believe in one evil influence just as much as in the other."

"It matters not how the destiny be accomplished, so it come to pass," rejoined the squire, turning away. "Heaven shield you from it!"

"Stay!" said Richard, picking up the wreath. "Who, think you, can have placed this funeral garland on the abbot's grave?"

"I cannot guess!" cried Nicholas, staring at it in amazement—"an enemy of ours, most likely. It is neither customary nor lawful in our Protestant country so to ornament graves. Put it down, Dick."

"I shall not displace it, certainly," replied Richard, laying it down again; "but I as little think it has been placed here by a hostile hand, as I do that harm will ensue to me from standing here. To relieve your anxiety, however, I will come forth," he added, stepping into the aisle. "Why should an enemy deposit a garland on the abbot's tomb, since it was by mere chance that it hath met my eyes?"

"Mere chance!" cried Nicholas; "every thing is mere chance with you philosophers. There is more than chance in it. My mind misgives me strangely. That terrible old Abbot Paslew is as troublesome to us in death, as he was during life to our predecessor. Richard Assheton. Not content with making his tombstone a weapon of destruction to us, he pays the Abbey itself an occasional visit, and his appearance always betides some disaster to the family. I have never seen him myself, and trust I never shall; but other people have, and have been nigh scared out of their senses by the apparition."

"Idle tales, the invention of overheated brains," rejoined Richard. "Trust me, the abbot's rest will not be broken till the day when all shall rise from their tombs; though if ever the dead (supposing such a thing possible) could be justified in injuring and affrighting the living, it might be in his case, since he mainly owed his destruction to our ancestor. On the same principle it has been held that church-lands are unlucky to their lay possessors; but see how this superstitious notion has been disproved in our own family, to whom Whalley Abbey and its domains have brought wealth, power, and worldly happiness."

"There is something in the notion, nevertheless," replied Nicholas; "and though our case may, I hope, continue an exception to the rule, most grantees of ecclesiastical houses have found them a curse, and the time may come when the Abbey may prove so to our descendants. But, without discussing the point, there is one instance in which the malignant influence of the vindictive abbot has undoubtedly extended long after his death. You have heard, I suppose, that he pronounced a dreadful anathema upon the child of a man who had the reputation of being a wizard, and who afterwards acted as his executioner. I know not the whole particulars of the dark story, but I know that Paslew fixed a curse upon the child, declaring it should become a witch, and the mother of witches. And the prediction has been verified. Nigh eighty years have flown by since then, and the infant still lives—a fearful and mischievous witch—and all her family are similarly fated—all are witches."

"I never heard the story before," said Richard, somewhat thoughtfully; "but I guess to whom you allude—Mother Demdike of Pendle Forest, and her family."

"Precisely," rejoined Nicholas; "they are a brood of witches."

"In that case Alizon Device must be a witch," cried Richard; "and I think you will hardly venture upon such an assertion after what you have seen of her to-day. If she be a witch, I would there were many such—as fair and gentle. And see you not how easily the matter is explained? 'Give a dog an ill name and hang him'—a proverb with which you are familiar enough. So with Mother Demdike. Whether really uttered or not, the abbot's curse upon her and her issue has been bruited abroad, and hence she is made a witch, and her children are supposed to inherit the infamous taint. So it is with yon tomb. It is said to be dangerous to our family, and dangerous no doubt it is to those who believe in the saying, which, luckily, I do not. The prophecy works its own fulfilment. The absurdity and injustice of yielding to the opinion are manifest. No wrong can have been done the abbot by Mother Demdike, any more than by her children, and yet they are to be punished for the misdeeds of their predecessor."

"Ay, just as you and I, who are of the third and fourth generation, may be punished for the sins of our fathers," rejoined Nicholas. "You have Scripture against you, Dick. The only thing I see in favour of your argument is, the instance you allege of Alizon. She does not look like a witch, certainly; but there is no saying. She may be only the more dangerous for her rare beauty, and apparent innocence!"

"I would answer for her truth with my life," cried Richard, quickly. "It is impossible to look at her countenance, in which candour and purity shine forth, and doubt her goodness."

"She hath cast her spells over you, Dick, that is certain," rejoined Nicholas, laughing; but to be serious. Alizon, I admit, is an exception to the rest of the family, but that only strengthens the general rule. Did you ever remark the strange look they all —save the fair maid in question—have about the eyes?"

Richard answered in the negative.

"It is very singular, and I wonder you have not noticed it," pursued Nicholas; "but the question of reputed witchcraft in Mother Demdike has some chance of being speedily settled; for Master Potts, the little London lawyer, who goes with us to Pendle Forest to-morrow, is about to have her arrested and examined before a magistrate."

"Indeed!" exclaimed Richard, "this must be prevented."

"Why so?" exclaimed Nicholas, in surprise.

"Because the prejudice existing against her is sure to convict and destroy her," replied Richard. "Her great age, infirmities, and poverty, will be proofs against her. How can she, or any old enfeebled creature like her, whose decrepitude and misery should move compassion rather than excite fear—how can such a person defend herself against charges easily made, and impossible to refute? I do not deny the possibility of witchcraft, even in our own days, though I think it of very unlikely occurrence; but I would determinately resist giving credit to any tales told by the superstitious vulgar, who, naturally prone to cruelty, have so many motives for revenging imaginary wrongs. It is placing a dreadful weapon in their hands, of which they have cunning enough to know the use, but neither mercy nor justice enough to restrain them from using it. Better let one guilty person escape, than many innocent perish. So many undefined charges have been brought against Mother Demdike, that at last they have fixed a stigma on her name, and made her an object of dread and suspicion. She is endowed with mysterious power, which would have no effect if not believed in; and now must be burned because she is called a witch, and is doting and vain enough to accept the title."

"There is something in a witch difficult, nay, almost impossible to describe," said Nicholas, "but you cannot be mistaken about her. By her general ill course of life, by repeated acts of mischief, and by threats, followed by the consequences menaced, she becomes known. There is much mystery in the matter, not permitted human knowledge entirely to penetrate; but, as we know from the Scriptures that the sin of witchcraft did exist, and as we have no evidence that it has ceased, so it is fair to conclude, that there may be practisers of the dark offence in our own days, and such I hold to be Mother Demdike and Mother Chattox. Rival potentates in evil, they contend which shall do most mischief, but it must be admitted the former bears away the bell."

"If all the ill attributed to her were really caused by her machinations, this might be correct," replied Richard, "but it only shows her to be more calumniated than the other. In a word, cousin Nicholas, I look upon them as two poor old creatures, who, persuaded they really possess the supernatural power accorded to them by the vulgar, strive to act up to their parts, and are mainly assisted in doing so by the credulity and fears of their audience."

"Admitting the blind credulity of the multitude," said Nicholas, "and their proneness to discern the hand of the witch in the most trifling accidents; admitting also, their readiness to accuse any old crone unlucky enough to offend them of sorcery; I still believe that there are actual practisers of the black art, who, for a brief term of power, have entered into a league with Satan, worship him and attend his sabbaths, and have a familiar, in the shape of a cat, dog, toad, or mole, to obey their behests, transform themselves into various shapes—as a hound, horse, or hare,—raise storms of wind or hail, maim cattle, bewitch and slay human beings, and ride whither they will on broomsticks. But, holding the contrary opinion, you will not, I apprehend, aid Master Potts in his quest of witches."

"I will not," rejoined Richard. "On the contrary, I will oppose him. But enough of this. Let us go forth."

And they quitted the church together.

As they issued into the churchyard, they found the principal arbours occupied by the morris-dancers, Robin Hood and his troop, Doctor Ormerod and Sir Ralph having retired to the vicarage-house.

Many merry groups were scattered about, talking, laughing, and singing; but two persons, seemingly objects of suspicion and alarm, and shunned by every one who crossed their path, were advancing slowly towards the three crosses of Paullinus, which stood in a line, not far from the church-porch. They were females, one about five-and-twenty, very comely, and habited in smart holiday attire, put on with considerable rustic coquetry, so as to display a very neat foot and ankle, and with plenty of ribands in her fine chestnut hair. The other was a very different person, far advanced in years, bent almost double, palsy-stricken, her arms and limbs shaking, her head nodding, her chin wagging, her snowy locks hanging about her wrinkled visage, her brows and upper lip frore, and her eyes almost sightless, the pupils being cased with a thin white film. Her dress, of antiquated make and faded stuff, had been once deep red in colour, and her old black hat was high-crowned and broad-brimmed. She partly aided herself in walking with a crutch-handled stick, and partly leaned upon her younger companion for support.

"Why, there is one of the old women we have just been speaking of—Mother Chattox," said Richard, pointing them out, "and with her, her grand-daughter, pretty Nan Redferne."

"So it is," cried Nicholas, "what makes the old hag here, I marvel! I will go question her."

So saying, he strode quickly towards her.

"How now, Mother Chattox!" he cried. "What mischief is afoot? What makes the darkness-loving owl abroad in the glare of day? What brings the grisly she-wolf from her forest lair? Back to thy den, old witch! Ar't crazed, as well as blind and palsied, that thou knowest not that this is a merry-making, and not a devil's sabbath? Back to thy hut, I say! These sacred precincts are no place for thee."

"Who is it speaks to me?" demanded the old hag, halting, and fixing her glazed eyes upon him.

"One thou hast much injured," replied Nicholas. "One into whose house thou hast brought quick-wasting sickness and death by thy infernal arts. One thou hast good reason to fear; for learn, to thy confusion, thou damned and murtherous witch, it is Nicholas, brother to thy victim, Richard Assheton of Downham, who speaks to thee."

"I know none I have reason to fear," replied Mother Chattox; "especially thee, Nicholas Assheton. Thy brother was no victim of mine. Thou wert the gainer by his death, not I. Why should I slay him?"

"I will tell thee why, old hag," cried Nicholas; "he was inflamed by the beauty of thy grand-daughter Nancy here, and it was to please Tom Redferne, her sweetheart then, but her spouse since, that thou bewitchedst him to death."

"That reason will not avail thee, Nicholas," rejoined Mother Chattox, with a derisive laugh. "If I had any hand in his death, it was to serve and pleasure thee, and that all men shall know, if I am questioned on the subject—ha! ha! Take me to the crosses, Nance."

"Thou shalt not 'scape thus, thou murtherous hag," cried Nicholas, furiously.

"Nay, let her go her way," said Richard, who had drawn near during the colloquy. "No good will come of meddling with her."

"Who's that?" asked Mother Chattox, quickly.

"Master Richard Assheton, o' Middleton," whispered Nan Redferne.

"Another of these accursed Asshetons," cried Mother Chattox. "A plague seize them!"

"Boh he's weel-favourt an kindly," remarked her granddaughter.

"Well-favoured or not, kindly or cruel, I hate them all," cried Mother Chattox. "To the crosses, I say!"

But Nicholas placed himself in their path.

"Is it to pray to Beelzebub, thy master, that thou wouldst go to the crosses?" he asked.

"Out of my way, pestilent fool!" cried the hag.

"Thou shalt not stir till I have had an answer," rejoined Nicholas. "They say those are Runic obelisks, and not Christian crosses, and that the carvings upon them have a magical signification. The first, it is averred, is written o'er with deadly curses, and the forms in which they are traced, as serpentine, triangular, or round, indicate and rule their swift or slow effect. The second bears charms against diseases, storms, and lightning. And on the third is inscribed a verse which will render him who can read it rightly, invisible to mortal view. Thou shouldst be learned in such lore, old Pythoness. Is it so?"

The hag's chin wagged fearfully, and her frame trembled with passion, but she spoke not.

"Have you been in the church, old woman?" interposed Richard.

"Ay, wherefore?" she rejoined.

"Some one has placed a cypress wreath on Abbot Paslew's grave. Was it you?" he asked.

"What! hast thou found it?" cried the hag. "It shall bring thee rare luck, lad—rare luck. Now let me pass."

"Not yet," cried Nicholas, forcibly grasping her withered arm.

The hag uttered a scream of rage.

"Let me go, Nicholas Assheton," she shrieked, "or thou shalt rue it. Cramps and aches shall wring and rack thy flesh and bones; fever shall consume thee; ague shake thee—shake thee—ha!"

And Nicholas recoiled, appalled by her fearful gestures.

"You carry your malignity too far, old woman," said Richard severely.

"And thou darest tell me so," cried the hag. "Set me before him, Nance, that I may curse him," she added, raising her palsied arm.

"Nah, nah—yo'n cursed ower much already, grandmother," cried Nan Redferne, endeavouring to drag her away. But the old woman resisted.

"I will teach him to cross my path," she vociferated, in accents shrill and jarring as the cry of the goat-sucker.

"Handsome he is, it may be, now, but he shall not be so long. The bloom shall fade from his cheek, the fire be extinguished in his eyes, the strength depart from his limbs. Sorrow shall be her portion who loves him—sorrow and shame!"

"Horrible!" exclaimed Richard, endeavouring to exclude the voice of the crone, which pierced his ears like some sharp instrument.

"Ha! ha! you fear me now," she cried. "By this, and this, the spell shall work," she added, describing a circle in the air with her stick, then crossing it twice, and finally scattering over him a handful of grave dust, snatched from an adjoining hillock. "Now lead me quickly to the smaller cross, Nance," she added, in a low tone.

Her grand-daughter complied, with a glance of deep commiseration at Richard, who remained stupefied at the ominous proceeding.

"Ah! this must indeed be a witch!" he cried, recovering from the momentary shock.

"So you are convinced at last," rejoined Nicholas. "I can take breath now the old hell-cat is gone. But she shall not escape us. Keep an eye upon her, while I see if Simon Sparshot, the beadle, be within the churchyard, and if so he shall take her into custody, and lock her in the cage."

With this, he ran towards the throng, shouting lustily for the beadle. Presently a big, burly fellow, in a scarlet doublet, laced with gold, a black velvet cap trimmed with red ribands, yellow hose, and shoes with great roses in them, and bearing a long silver-headed staff, answered the summons, and upon being told why his services were required, immediately roared out at the top of a stentorian voice, "A witch, lads!—a witch!"

All was astir in an instant. Robin Hood and his merry men, with the morris-dancers, rushed out of their bowers, and the whole churchyard was in agitation. Above the din was heard the loud voice of Simon Sparshot, still shouting, "A witch!—a witch!—Mother Chattox!"

"Where—where?" demanded several voices.

"Yonder," replied Nicholas, pointing to the further cross.

A general movement took place in that direction, the crowd being headed by the squire and the beadle, but when they came up, they found only Nan Redferne standing behind the obelisk.

"Where the devil is the old witch gone, Dick?" cried Nicholas, in dismay.

"I thought I saw her standing there with her grand-daughter," replied Richard, "but in truth I did not watch very closely."

"Search for her—search for her," cried Nicholas.

But neither behind the crosses, nor behind any monument, nor in any hole or corner, nor on the other side of the churchyard wall, nor at the back of the little hermitage or chapel, though all were quickly examined, could the old hag be found.

On being questioned, Nan Redferne refused to say aught concerning her grandmother's flight or place of concealment.

"I begin to think there is some truth in that strange legend of the cross," said Nicholas. "Notwithstanding her blindness, the old hag must have managed to read the magic verse upon it, and so have rendered herself invisible. But we have got the young witch safe."

"Yeigh, squoire!" responded Sparshot, who had seized hold of Nance—"hoo be safe enough."

"Nan Redferne is no witch," said Richard Assheton, authoritatively.

"Neaw witch, Mester Ruchot!" cried the beadle in amazement.

"No more than any of these lasses around us," said Richard. "Release her, Sparshot."

"I forbid him to do so, till she has been examined," cried a sharp voice. And the next moment Master Potts was seen pushing his way through the crowd. "So you have found a witch, my masters. I heard your shouts, and hurried on as fast as I could. Just in time, Master Nicholas—just in time," he added, rubbing his hands gleefully.

"Lemme go, Simon," besought Nance.

"Neaw, neaw, lass, that munnot be," rejoined Sparshot.

"Help—save me, Master Richard!" cried the young woman.

By this time the crowd had gathered round her, yelling, hooting, and shaking their hands at her, as if about to tear her in pieces; but Richard Assheton planted himself resolutely before her, and pushed back the foremost of them.

"Remove her instantly to the Abbey, Sparshot," he cried, and let her be kept in safe custody till Sir Ralph has time to examine her. Will that content you, masters?"

"Neaw—neaw," responded several rough voices; "swim her! —swim her!"

"Quite right, my worthy friends, quite right," said Potts. "*Primo*, let us make sure she is a witch—*secundo*, let us take her to the Abbey."

"There can be no doubt as to her being a witch, Master Potts," rejoined Nicholas; "her old grand-dame, Mother Chattox, has just vanished from our sight."

"Has Mother Chattox been here?" cried Potts, opening his round eyes to their widest extent.

"Not many minutes since," replied Nicholas. "In fact, she may be here still for aught I know."

"Here!—where?" cried Potts, looking round.

"You wont discover her for all your quickness," replied Nicholas. "She has rendered herself invisible, by reciting the magical verses inscribed on that cross."

"Indeed!" exclaimed the attorney, closely examining the mysterious inscriptions. "What strange, uncouth characters! I can make neither head nor tail, unless it be the devil's tail, of them."

At this moment a whoop was raised by Jem Device, who, having taken his little sister home, had returned to the sports on the green, and now formed part of the assemblage in the churchyard. Between the rival witch potentates, Mothers Demdike and Chattox, it has already been said a deadly enmity existed, and the feud was carried on with equal animosity by their descendants; and though Jem himself came under the same suspicion as Nan Redferne, that circumstance created no tie of interest between them, but the contrary, and he was the most active of her assailants. He had set up the above-mentioned cry from observing a large rat running along the side of the wall.

"Theere hoo goes," whooped Jem, "t' owd witch, i' th' shape ov a rotten!—loo-loo-loo!"

Half the crowd started in pursuit of the animal, and twenty sticks were thrown at it, but a stone cast by Jem stayed its progress, and it was instantly despatched. It did not change, however, as was expected by the credulous hinds, into an old woman, and they gave vent to their disappointment and rage in renewed threats against Nan Redferne. The dead rat was hurled at her by Jem, but missing its mark, it hit Master Potts on the head, and nearly knocked him off the cross, upon which he had mounted to obtain a better view of the proceedings. Irritated by this circumstance, as well as by the failure of the experiment, the little attorney jumped down, and fell to kicking the unfortunate rat, after which, his fury being somewhat appeased, he turned to Nance, who had sunk for support against the pedestal, and said to her—"If you will tell us what has become of the old witch your grandmother, and undertake to bear witness against her, you shall be set free."

"Ey'n tell ye nowt, mon," replied Nance, doggedly. "Put me to onny trial ye like, ye shanna get a word fro me."

"That remains to be seen," retorted Potts, "but I apprehend we shall make you speak, and pretty plainly too, before we've done with you.—You hear what this perverse and wrong-headed young witch declares, masters," he shouted, again clambering upon the cross. "I have offered her liberty, on condition of disclosing to us the manner of her diabolical old relative's evasion, and she rejects it."

An angry roar followed, mixed with cries from Jem Device, of "swim her!—swim her!"

"You had better tell them what you know, Nance," said Richard, in a low tone, "or I shall have difficulty in preserving you from their fury."

"Ey darena, Master Richard," she replied, shaking her head; and then she added firmly, "Ey winna."

Finding it useless to reason with her, and fearing also that the infuriated crowd might attempt to put their threats into execution, Richard turned to his cousin Nicholas, and said: "We must get her away, or violence will be done."

"She does not deserve your compassion, Dick," replied Nicholas; "she is only a few degrees better than the old hag who has escaped. Sparshot here tells me she is noted for her skill in modelling clay figures."

"Yeigh, that hoo be," replied the broad-faced beadle; "hoo's unaccountable cliver ot that sort o' wark. A clay figger os big os a six months' barn, fashiont i' th' likeness o' Farmer Grimble o' Briercliffe lawnd, os died last month, war seen i' her cottage, an monny others besoide. Amongst 'em a moddle o' your lamented brother, Squoire Ruchot Assheton o' Downham, wi' t' yeod pood off, and th' 'eart pierct thro' an' thro' wi' pins and needles."

"Ye lien i' your teeth, Simon Sparshot!" cried Nance, regarding him furiously.

"If the head were off, Simon, I don't see how the likeness to my poor brother could well be recognised," said Nicholas, with a half smile. "But let her be put to some mild trial—weighed against the church Bible."

"Be it so," replied Potts, jumping down; "but if that fail, we must have recourse to stronger measures. Take notice that, with all her fright, she has not been able to shed a tear, not a single tear—a clear witch—a clear witch!"

"Ey'd scorn to weep fo t' like o' yo!" cried Nance, disdainfully, having now completely recovered her natural audacity.

"We'll soon break your spirit, young woman, I can promise you," rejoined Potts.

As soon as it was known what was about to occur, the whole crowd moved towards the church porch, Nan Redferne walking between Richard Assheton and the beadle, who kept hold of her arm to prevent any attempt at escape; and by the time they reached the appointed place, Ben Baggiley, the baker, who had been despatched for the purpose, appeared with an enormous pair of wooden scales, while Sampson Harrop, the clerk, having visited the pulpit, came forth with the church Bible, an immense volume, bound in black, with great silver clasps.

"Come, that's a good big Bible at all events," cried Potts, eyeing it with satisfaction. "It looks like my honourable and singular good Lord Chief-Justice Sir Edward Coke's learned 'Institutes of the Laws of England,' only that that great legal tome is generally bound in calf—law calf, as we say."

"Large as the book is, it will scarce prove heavy enough to weigh down the witch, I opine," observed Nicholas, with a smile.

"We shall see, sir," replied Potts. "We shall see."

By this time, the scales having been affixed to a hook in the porch by Baggiley, the sacred volume was placed on one side, and Nance set down by the beadle on the other. The result of the experiment was precisely what might have been anticipated—the moment the young woman took her place in the balance, it sank down to the ground, while the other kicked the beam.

"I hope you are satisfied now, Master Potts," cried Richard Assheton. "By your own trial her innocence is approved."

"Your pardon, Master Richard, this is Squire Nicholas's trial, not mine," replied Potts. "I am for the ordeal of swimming. How say you, masters! Shall we be content with this doubtful experiment?"

"Neaw—neaw," responded Jem Device, who acted as spokesman to the crowd, "swim her—swim her!"

"I knew you would have it so," said Potts, approvingly. "Where is a fitting place for the trial?"

"Th' Abbey pool is nah fur off," replied Jem, "or ye con tay her to th' Calder."

"The river, by all means—nothing like a running stream," said Potts. "Let cords be procured to bind her."

"Run fo 'em quickly, Ben," said Jem to Baggiley, who was very zealous in the cause.

"Oh!" groaned Nance, again losing courage, and glancing piteously at Richard.

"No outrage like this shall be perpetrated," cried the young man, firmly; "I call upon you, cousin Nicholas, to help me. Go into the church," he added, thrusting Nance backward, and presenting his sword at the breast of Jem Device, who attempted to follow her, and who retired muttering threats and curses; "I will run the first man through the body who attempts to pass."

As Nan Redferne made good her retreat, and shut the church-door after her, Master Potts, pale with rage, cried out to Richard, "You have aided the escape of a desperate and notorious offender—actually in custody, sir, and have rendered yourself liable to indictment for it, sir, with consequences of fine and imprisonment, sir—heavy fine and long imprisonment, sir. Do you mark me, Master Richard?"

"I will answer the consequences of my act to those empowered to question it, sir," replied Richard, sternly.

"Well, sir, I have given you notice," rejoined Potts, "due notice. We shall hear what Sir Ralph will say to the matter, and Master Roger Nowell, and—"

"You forget me, good Master Potts," interrupted Nicholas, laughingly; "I entirely disapprove of it. It is a most flagrant breach of duty. Nevertheless, I am glad the poor wench has got off."

"She is safe within the church," said Potts, "and I command Master Richard, in the king's name, to let us pass. Beadle!

Sharpshot, Sparshot, or whatever be your confounded name do your duty, sirrah. Enter the church, and bring forth the witch."

"Ey darna, mester," replied Simon; "young mester Ruchot ud slit mey weasand os soon os look ot meh."

Richard put an end to further altercation, by stepping back quickly, locking the door, and then taking out the key, and putting it into his pocket.

"She is quite safe now," he cried, with a smile at the discomfited lawyer.

"Is there no other door?" inquired Potts of the beadle, in a low tone.

"Yeigh, theere be one ot t'other soide," replied Sparshot, "boh it be locked, ey reckon, an maybe hoo'n getten out that way."

"Quick, quick, and let's see," cried Potts; "justice must not be thwarted in this shameful manner."

While the greater part of the crowd set off after Potts and the beadle, Richard Assheton, anxious to know what had become of the fugitive, and determined not to abandon her while any danger existed, unlocked the church-door, and entered the holy structure, followed by Nicholas. On looking around, Nance was nowhere to be seen, neither did she answer to his repeated calls, and Richard concluded she must have escaped, when all at once a loud exulting shout was heard without, leaving no doubt that the poor young woman had again fallen into the hands of her captors. The next moment a sharp, piercing scream in a female key confirmed the supposition. On hearing this cry, Richard instantly flew to the opposite door, through which Nance must have passed, but on trying it he found it fastened outside; and filled with sudden misgiving, for he now recollected leaving the key in the other door, he called to Nicholas to come with him, and hurried back to it. His apprehensions were verified; the door was locked. At first Nicholas was inclined to laugh at the trick played them; but a single look from Richard checked his tendency to merriment, and he followed his young relative, who had sprung to a window looking upon that part of the churchyard whence the shouts came, and flung it open. Richard's egress, however, was prevented by an iron bar, and he called out loudly and fiercely to the beadle, whom he saw standing in the midst of the crowd, to unlock the door.

"Have a little patience, good Master Richard," replied Potts, turning up his provoking little visage, now charged with triumphant malice. "You shall come out presently. We are busy just now—engaged in binding the witch, as you see. Both keys are safely in my pocket, and I will send you one of them when we start for the river, good Master Richard. We lawyers are not to be overreached you see—ha! ha!"

"You shall repent this conduct when I do get out," cried

Richard, furiously. "Sparshot, I command you to bring the key instantly."

But, encouraged by the attorney, the beadle affected not to hear Richard's angry vociferations, and the others were unable to aid the young man, if they had been so disposed, and all were too much interested in what was going forward to run off to the vicarage, and acquaint Sir Ralph with the circumstances in which his relatives were placed, even though enjoined to do so.

On being set free by Richard, Nance had flown quickly through the church, and passed out at the side door, and was making good her retreat at the back of the edifice, when her flying figure was descried by Jem Device, who, failing in his first attempt, had run round that way, fancying he should catch her.

He instantly dashed after her with all the fury of a bloodhound, and, being possessed of remarkable activity, speedily overtook her, and, heedless of her threats and entreaties, secured her.

"Lemme go, Jem," she cried, "an ey win do thee a good turn one o' these days, when theaw may chonce to be i' th' same strait os me." But seeing him inexorable, she added, "My grand-dame shan rack thy boans sorely, lad, for this."

Jem replied by a coarse laugh of defiance, and, dragging her along, delivered her to Master Potts and the beadle, who were then hurrying to the other door of the church. To prevent interruption, the cunning attorney, having ascertained that the two Asshetons were inside, instantly gave orders to have both doors locked, and the injunctions being promptly obeyed, he took possession of the keys himself, chuckling at the success of the stratagem. "A fair reprisal," he muttered; "this young milksop shall find he is no match for a skilful lawyer like me. Now, the cords—the cords!"

It was at the sight of the bonds, which were quickly brought by Baggiley, that Nance uttered the piercing cry that had roused Richard's indignation. Feeling secure of his prisoner, and now no longer apprehensive of interruption, Master Potts was in no hurry to conclude the arrangements, but rather prolonged them to exasperate Richard. Little consideration was shown the unfortunate captive. The new shoes and stockings of which she had been so vain a short time before, were torn from her feet and limbs by the rude hands of the remorseless Jem and the beadle, and bent down by the main force of these two strong men, her thumbs and great toes were tightly bound together, crosswise, by the cords. The churchyard rang with her shrieks, and, with his blood boiling with indignation at the sight, Richard redoubled his exertions to burst through the window and fly to her assistance. But though Nicholas now lent his powerful aid to the task, their combined efforts to obtain liberation were unavailing; and with rage almost amounting to frenzy, Richard beheld the poor young woman borne shrieking away by her captors. Nor was Nicholas much less incensed, and he swore a deep oath when he did get at liberty that Master Potts should pay dearly for his rascally conduct.

CHAPTER VI.—THE ORDEAL BY SWIMMING.

Bound hand and foot in the painful posture before described, roughly and insolently handled on all sides, in peril of her life from the frightful ordeal to which she was about to be subjected, the miserable captive was borne along on the shoulders of Jem Device and Sparshot, her long, fine chestnut hair trailing upon the ground, her white shoulders exposed to the insolent gaze of the crowd, and her trim holiday attire torn to rags by the rough treatment she had experienced. Nance Redferne, it has been said, was a very comely young woman; but neither her beauty, her youth, nor her sex, had any effect upon the ferocious crowd, who were too much accustomed to such brutal and debasing exhibitions, to feel any thing but savage delight in the spectacle of a fellow-creature so scandalously treated and tormented, and the only excuse to be offered for their barbarity, is the firm belief they entertained that they were dealing with a witch. And when even in our own day so many revolting scenes are enacted to gratify the brutal passions of the mob, while prize-fights are tolerated, and wretched animals goaded on to tear each other in pieces, it is not to be wondered at that, in times of less enlightenment and refinement, greater cruelties should be practised. Indeed, it may be well to consider how far we have really advanced in civilisation since then; for until cruelty, whether to man or beast, be wholly banished from our sports, we cannot justly reproach our ancestors, or congratulate ourselves on our improvement.

Nance's cries of distress were only answered by jeers, and renewed insults, and wearied out at length, the poor creature ceased struggling and shrieking, the dogged resolution she had before exhibited again coming to her aid.

But her fortitude was to be yet more severely tested. Revealed by the disorder of her habiliments, and contrasting strongly with the extreme whiteness of her skin, a dun-coloured mole was discovered upon her breast. It was pointed out to Potts by Jem Device, who declared it to be a witch-mark, and the spot where her familiar drained her blood.

"This is one of the 'good helps' to the discovery of a witch, pointed out by our sovereign lord the king," said the attorney, narrowly examining the spot. "'The one,' saith our wise prince, 'is the finding of their mark, and the trying the insensibleness thereof. The other is their fleeting on the water.' The water-ordeal will come presently, but the insensibility of the mark might be at once attested."

"Yeigh, that con soon be tried," cried Jem, with a savage laugh.

And taking a pin from his sleeve, the ruffian plunged it deeply into the poor creature's flesh. Nance winced, but she set her teeth hardly, and repressed the cry that must otherwise have been wrung from her.

"A clear witch!" cried Jem, drawing forth the pin; "not a drop o' blood flows, an hoo feels nowt!"

"Feel nowt?" rejoined Nance, between her ground teeth. "May ye ha a pang os sharp i' your cancart eart, ye villain."

After this barbarous test, the crowd, confirmed by it in their notions of Nan's guiltiness, hurried on, their numbers increasing as they proceeded along the main street of the village leading towards the river; all the villagers left at home rushing forth on hearing a witch was about to be swum, and when they came within a bow-shot of the stream, Sparshot called to Baggiley to lay hold of Nance, while he himself, accompanied by several of the crowd, ran over the bridge, the part he had to enact requiring him to be on the other side of the water.

Meantime, the main party turned down a little footpath protected by a gate on the left, which led between garden hedges to the grassy banks of the Calder, and in taking this course they passed by the cottage of Elizabeth Device. Hearing the shouts of the rabble, little Jennet, who had been in no very happy frame of mind since she had been brought home, came forth, and seeing her brother, called out to him, in her usual sharp tones, "What's the matter, Jem? Who han ye getten there?"

"A witch," replied Jem, gruffly. "Nance Redferne, Mother Chattox's grand-daughter. Come an see her swum i' th' Calder."

Jennet readily complied, for her curiosity was aroused, and she shared in the family feelings of dislike to Mother Chattox and her descendants.

"Is this Nance Redferne?" she cried, keeping close to her brother, "Ey'm glad yo'n caught her at last. How dun ye find yersel, Nance?"

"Ill at ease, Jennet," replied Nance, with a bitter look; "boh it ill becomes ye to jeer me, lass, seein' yo're a born witch yoursel."

"Aha!" cried Potts, looking at the little girl, "So this is a born witch—eh, Nance?"

"A born an' bred witch," rejoined Nance; "jist as her brother Jem here is a wizard. They're the gran-childer o' Mother Demdike o' Pendle, the greatest witch i' these parts, an childer o' Bess Device, who's nah much better. Ask me to witness agen 'em, that's aw."

"Howd thy tongue, woman, or ey'n drown thee," muttered Jem, in a tone of deep menace.

"Ye canna, mon, if ey'm the witch ye ca' me," rejoined Nance. "Jennet's turn'll come os weel os mine, one o' these days. Mark my words."

"Efore that ey shan see ye burned, ye faggot," cried Jennet, almost fiercely.

"Ye'n getten the fiend's mark o' your sleeve," cried Nance "Ey see it written i' letters ov blood."

"That's where our cat scratted me," replied Jennet, hiding her arm quickly.

"Good!—very good!" observed Potts, rubbing his hands. "'Who but witches can be proof against witches?' saith our sagacious sovereign. I shall make something of this girl. She seems a remarkably quick child—remarkably quick—ha, ha!"

By this time, the party having gained the broad flat mead through which the Calder flowed, took their way quickly towards its banks, the spot selected for the ordeal lying about fifty yards above the weir, where the current, ordinarily rapid, was checked by the dam, offering a smooth surface, with considerable depth of water. If soft natural beauties could have subdued the hearts of those engaged in this cruel and wicked experiment, never was scene better calculated for the purpose than that under contemplation. Through a lovely green valley meandered the Calder, now winding round some verdant knoll, now washing the base of lofty heights feathered with timber to their very summits, now lost amid thick woods, and only discernible at intervals by a glimmer amongst the trees. Immediately in front of the assemblage rose Whalley Nab, its steep sides and brow partially covered with timber, with green patches in the uplands where sheep and cattle fed. Just below the spot where the crowd were collected, the stream, here of some width, passed over the weir, and swept in a foaming cascade over the huge stones supporting the dam, giving the rushing current the semblance and almost the beauty of a natural waterfall. Below this the stream ran brawling on in a wider, but shallower channel, making pleasant music as it went, and leaving many dry beds of sand and gravel in the midst; while a hundred yards lower down, it was crossed by the arches of the bridge. Further still, a row of tall cypresses lined the bank of the river, and screened that part of the Abbey, converted into a residence by the Asshetons; and after this came the ruins of the refectory, the cloisters, the dormitory, the conventual church, and other parts of the venerable structure, overshadowed by noble lime-trees and elms. Lovelier or more peaceful scene could not be imagined. The green meads, the bright clear stream, with its white foaming weir, the woody heights reflected in the glassy waters, the picturesque old bridge, and the dark grey ruins beyond it, all might have engaged the attention and melted the heart. Then the hour, when evening was coming on, and when each beautiful object, deriving new beauty from the medium through which it was viewed, exercised a softening influence, and awakened kindly emotions. To most the scene was familiar, and therefore could have no charm of novelty. To Potts, however, it was altogether new; but he was susceptible of few gentle impressions, and neither the tender beauty of the evening, nor the wooing loveliness of the spot, awakened any responsive emotion in his breast. He was dead to every thing except the ruthless experiment about to be made.

Almost at the same time that Jem Device and his party reached the near bank of the stream, the beadle and the others appeared on the opposite side. Little was said, but instant preparations were made for the ordeal. Two long coils of rope having been brought by Baggiley, one of them was made fast to the right arm of the victim, and the other to the left; and this done, Jem Device, shouting to Sparshot to look out, flung one coil of rope across the river, where it was caught with much dexterity by the beadle. The assemblage then spread out on the bank, while Jem, taking the poor young woman in his arms, who neither spoke nor struggled, but held her breath tightly, approached the river.

"Dunna drown her, Jem," said Jennet, who had turned very pale.

"Be quiet, wench," rejoined Jem, gruffly.

And without bestowing further attention upon her, he let down his burden carefully into the water; and this achieved, he called out to the beadle, who drew her slowly towards him, while Jem guided her with the other rope.

The crowd watched the experiment for a few moments in profound silence, but as the poor young woman, who had now reached the centre of the stream, still floated, being supported either by the tension of the cords, or by her woollen apparel, a loud shout was raised that she could not sink, and was, therefore, an undeniable witch.

"Steady, lads—steady a moment," cried Potts, enchanted with the success of the experiment; "leave her where she is, that her buoyancy may be fully attested. You know, masters," he cried, with a loud voice, "the meaning of this water ordeal. Our sovereign lord and master the king, in his wisdom, hath graciously vouchsafed to explain the matter thus: 'Water,' he saith, 'shall refuse to receive them (meaning witches, of course) in her bosom, that have shaken off their sacred water of baptism, and wilfully refused the benefit thereof.' It is manifest, you see, that this diabolical young woman hath renounced her baptism, for the water rejecteth her. *Non potest mergi*, as Pliny saith. She floats like a cork, or as if the clear water of the Calder had suddenly become like the slab, salt waves of the Dead Sea, in which nothing can sink. You behold the marvel with your own eyes, my masters."

"Ay, ay!" rejoined Baggiley and several others.

"Hoo be a witch fo sartin," cried Jem Device. But as he spoke, chancing slightly to slacken the rope, the tension of which maintained the equilibrium of the body, the poor woman instantly sank.

A groan, as much of disappointment as sympathy, broke from the spectators, but none attempted to aid her; and on seeing her sink, Jem abandoned the rope altogether.

But assistance was at hand. Two persons rushed quickly and furiously to the spot. They were Richard and Nicholas Assheton. The iron bar had at length yielded to their efforts, and the first use they made of their freedom was to hurry to the river. A glance showed them what had occurred, and the younger Assheton, unhesitatingly plunging into the water, seized the rope dropped by Jem, and calling to the beadle to let go his hold, dragged forth the poor half-drowned young woman, and placed her on the bank, hewing asunder the cords that bound her hands and feet with his sword. But though still sensible, Nance was so much exhausted by the shock she had undergone, and her muscles were so severely strained by the painful and unnatural posture to which she had been compelled, that she was wholly unable to move. Her thumbs were blackened and swollen, and the cords had cut into the flesh, while blood trickled down from the puncture in her breast. Fixing a look of inexpressible gratitude upon her preserver, she made an effort to speak, but the exertion was too great; violent hysterical sobbing came on, and her senses soon after forsook her Richard called loudly for assistance, and the sentiments of the most humane part of the crowd having undergone a change since the failure of the ordeal, some females came forward, and took steps for her restoration. Sensibility having returned, a cloak was wrapped around her, and she was conveyed to a neighbouring cottage and put to bed, where her stiffened limbs were chafed and warm drinks administered, and it began to be hoped that no serious consequences would ensue.

Meanwhile, a catastrophe had wellnigh occurred in another quarter. With eyes flashing with fury, Nicholas Assheton pushed aside the crowd, and made his way to the bank whereon Master Potts stood. Not liking his looks, the little attorney would have taken to his heels, but finding escape impossible, he called upon Baggiley to protect him. But he was instantly in the forcible gripe of the squire, who shouted, "I'll teach you, mongrel hound, to play tricks with gentlemen."

"Master Nicholas," cried the terrified and half-strangled attorney, "my very good sir, I entreat you to let me alone. This is a breach of the king's peace, sir. Assault and battery, under aggravated circumstances, and punishable with ignominious corporal penalties, besides fine and imprisonment, sir. I take you to witness the assault, Master Baggiley. I shall bring my ac—ac—ah—o—o—oh!"

"Then you shall have something to bring your ac—ac—action for, rascal," cried Nicholas. And, seizing the attorney by the nape of the neck with one hand, and the hind wings of his doublet with the other, he cast him to a considerable distance into the river, where he fell with a tremendous splash.

"He is no wizard, at all events," laughed Nicholas, as Potts went down like a lump of lead.

But the attorney was not born to be drowned; at least, at this period of his career. On rising to the surface, a few seconds after his immersion, he roared lustily for help, but would infallibly have been carried over the weir, if Jem Device had not flung him the rope now disengaged from Nance Redferne, and which he succeeded in catching. In this way he was dragged out; and as he crept up the bank, with the wet pouring from his apparel, which now clung tightly to his lathy limbs, he was greeted by the jeers of Nicholas.

"How like you the water-ordeal—eh, Master Attorney? No occasion for a second trial, I think. If Jem Device had known his own interest, he would have left you to fatten the Calder eels; but he will find it out in time."

"You will find it out too, Master Nicholas," rejoined Potts, clapping on his wet cap. "Take me to the Dragon quickly, good fellow," he added, to Jem Device, "and I will recompense thee for thy pains, as well as for the service thou hast just rendered me. I shall have rheumatism in my joints, pains in my loins, and rheum in my head, oh dear—oh dear!"

"In which case you will not be able to pay Mother Demdike your purposed visit to-morrow," jeered Nicholas. "You forgot you were to arrest her, and bring her before a magistrate."

"Thy arm, good fellow, thy arm!" said Potts, to Jem Device.

"To the fiend wi' thee," cried Jem, shaking him off roughly. "The squoire is reet. Wouldee had let thee drown."

"What, have you changed your mind already, Jem?" cried Nicholas, in a taunting tone. "You'll have your grandmother's thanks for the service you've rendered her, lad—ha! ha!"

"Fo' t' matter o' two pins ey'd pitch him again," growled Jem, eyeing the attorney askance.

"No, no, Jem," observed Nicholas, "things must take their course. What's done is done. But if Master Potts be wise, he'll take himself out of court without delay."

"You'll be glad to get me out of court one of these days, squire," muttered Potts, "and so will you too, Master James Device.—A day of reckoning will come for both—heavy reckoning. Ugh! ugh!" he added, shivering, "how my teeth chatter!"

"Make what haste you can to the Dragon," cried the good-natured squire; "get your clothes dried, and bid John Lawe brew you a pottle of strong sack, swallow it scalding hot, and you'll never look behind you."

"Nor before me either," retorted Potts, "Scalding sack! This bloodthirsty squire has a new design upon my life!"

"Ey'n go wi' ye to th' Dragon, mester," said Baggiley; "lean o' me."

"Thanke'e friend," replied Potts, taking his arm. "A word at parting, Master Nicholas. This is not the only discovery of witchcraft I've made. I've another case, somewhat nearer home. Ha! ha!"

With this, he hobbled off in the direction of the alehouse, his steps being traceable along the dusty road like the course of a watering-cart.

"Ey'n go efter him," growled Jem.

"No you won't, lad," rejoined Nicholas, "and if you'll take my advice, you'll get out of Whalley as fast as you can. You will be safer on the heath of Pendle than here, when Sir Ralph and Master Roger Nowell come to know what has taken place. And mind this, sirrah—the hounds will be out in the forest to-morrow. D'ye heed?"

Jem growled something in reply, and, seizing his little sister's hand, strode off with her towards his mother's dwelling, uttering not a word by the way.

Having seen Nance Redferne conveyed to the cottage, as before mentioned, Richard Assheton, regardless of the wet state of his own apparel, now joined his cousin, the squire, and they walked to the Abbey together, conversing on what had taken place, while the crowd dispersed, some returning to the bowers in the churchyard, and others to the green, their merriment in nowise damped by the recent occurrences, which they looked upon as part of the day's sport. As some of them passed by, laughing, singing, and dancing, Richard Assheton remarked, "I can scarcely believe these to be the same people I so lately saw in the churchyard. They then seemed totally devoid of humanity."

"Pshaw! they are humane enough," rejoined Nicholas; "but you cannot expect them to show mercy to a witch, any more than to a wolf, or other savage and devouring beast."

"But the means taken to prove her guilt were as absurd as iniquitous," said Richard, "and savour of the barbarous ages. If she had perished, all concerned in the trial would have been guilty of murder."

"But no judge would condemn them," returned Nicholas; "and they have the highest authority in the realm to uphold them. As to leniency to witches, in a general way, I would show none. Traitors alike to God and man, and bond slaves of Satan, they are out of the pale of Christian charity."

"No criminal, however great, is out of the pale of Christian charity," replied Richard; but such scenes as we have just witnessed are a disgrace to humanity, and a mockery of justice. In seeking to discover and punish one offence, a greater is committed. Suppose this poor young woman really guilty—what then? Our laws are made for protection, as well as punishment of wrong. She should be arraigned, convicted, and condemned before punishment."

"Our laws admit of torture, Richard," observed Nicholas.

"True," said the young man, with a shudder, "and it is another relic of a ruthless age. But torture is only allowed under the eye of the law, and can be inflicted by none but its sworn servants. But, supposing this poor young woman innocent of the crime imputed to her, which I really believe her to be, how, then, will you excuse the atrocities to which she has been subjected?"

"I do not believe her innocent," rejoined Nicholas; "her relationship to a notorious witch, and her fabrication of clay images, make her justly suspected."

"Then let her be examined by a magistrate," said Richard; "but, even then, woe betide her! When I think that Alizon Device is liable to the same atrocious treatment, in consequence of her relationship to Mother Demdike, I can scarce contain my indignation."

"It is unlucky for her, indeed," rejoined Nicholas; "but of all Nance's assailants the most infuriated was Alizon's brother, Jem Device."

"I saw it," cried Richard—an uneasy expression passing over his countenance. "Would she could be removed from that family!"

"To what purpose?" demanded Nicholas, quickly. "Her family are more likely to be removed from her if Master Potts stay in the neighbourhood."

"Poor girl!" exclaimed Richard.

And he fell into a reverie which was not broken till they reached the Abbey.

To return to Jem Device. On reaching the cottage, the ruffian flung himself into a chair, and for a time seemed lost in reflection. At last he looked up, and said gruffly to Jennet, who stood watching him, "See if mother be come whoam?"

"Eigh, eigh, ey'm here, Jem," said Elizabeth Device, opening the inner door and coming forth. "So, ye ha been swimmin' Nance Redferne, lad, eh! Ey'm glad on it—ha! ha!"

Jem gave her a significant look, upon which she motioned Jennet to withdraw, and the injunction being complied with, though with evident reluctance, by the little girl, she closed the door upon her.

"Now, Jem, what hast got to say to me, lad, eh?" demanded Elizabeth, stepping up to him.

"Neaw great deal, mother," he replied; "boh ey keawnsel ye to look weel efter yersel. We're aw i' dawnger."

"Ey knoas it, lad, ey knoas it," replied Elizabeth; "boh fo my own pert ey'm nah afeerd. They darna touch me; an' if they dun, ey con defend mysel reet weel. Here's a letter to thy gran-mother," she added, giving him a sealed packet. "Take care on it."

"Fro Mistress Nutter, ey suppose?" asked Jem.

"Eigh, who else should it be from? rejoined Elizabeth. "Your gran-mother win' ha' enough to do to neet, an so win yo, too, Jem, lettin alone the walk fro here to Malkin Tower."

"Weel, gi' me mey supper, an ey'n set out," rejoined Jem. "So ye ha' seen Mistress Nutter?"

"Ey found her i' th' Abbey garden," replied Elizabeth, "an we had some tawk together, abowt th' boundary line o' th' Rough Lee estates, and other matters."

And, as she spoke, she set a cold pasty, with oat cakes, cheese, and butter, before her son, and next proceeded to draw him a jug of ale.

"What other matters dun you mean, mother?" inquired Jem, attacking the pasty. "War it owt relatin' to that little Lunnon lawyer, Mester Potts?"

"Theawst hit it, Jem," replied Elizabeth, seating herself near him. "That Potts means to visit thy gran-mother to morrow."

"Weel!" said Jem, grimly.

"An arrest her," pursued Elizabeth.

"Easily said," laughed Jem, scornfully, "boh neaw quite so easily done."

"Nah quite, Jem," responded Elizabeth, joining in the laugh. "'Specially when th' owd dame's prepared, as she win be now."

"Potts may set out 'o that journey, boh he winna come back again," remarked Jem, in a sombre tone.

"Wait till yo'n seen your gran-mother efore ye do owt, lad," said Elizabeth.

"Ay, wait," added a voice.

"What's that?" demanded Jem, laying down his knife and fork.

Elizabeth did not answer in words, but her significant looks were quite response enough for her son.

"Os ye win, mother," he said in an altered tone. After a pause, employed in eating, he added, "Did Mistress Nutter put onny questions to ye about Alizon?"

"More nor enough, lad," replied Elizabeth; "fo what had ey to tell her? She praised her beauty, an said how unlike she wur to Jennet an thee, lad—ha! ha!—An wondert how ey cum to ha such a dowter, an monny other things besoide. An what could ey say to it aw, except—"

"Except what, mother?" interrupted Jem.

"Except that she wur my child just os much os Jennet an thee!"

"Humph!" exclaimed Jem.

"Humph!" echoed the voice that had previously spoken.

Jem looked at his mother, and took a long pull at the ale-jug.

"Any more messages to Malkin Tower?" he asked, getting up.

"Neaw—mother will onderstond," replied Elizabeth. "Bid her be on her guard, fo' the enemy is abroad."

"Meanin' Potts?" said Jem.

"Meaning Potts," answered the voice.

"There are strange echoes here," said Jem, looking round suspiciously.

At this moment, Tib came from under a piece of furniture, where he had apparently been lying, and rubbed himself familiarly against his legs.

"Ey needna be afeerd o' owt happenin to ye, mother," said Jem, patting the cat's back. "Tib win tay care on yo."

"Eigh, eigh," replied Elizabeth, bending down to pat him, "he's a trusty cat." But the ill-tempered animal would not be propitiated, but erected his back, and menaced her with his claws.

"Yo han offended him, mother," said Jem. "One word efore ey start. Are ye quite sure Potts didna owerhear your conversation wi' Mistress Nutter?"

"Why d'ye ask, Jem?" she replied.

"Fro' summat the knave threw out to Squoire Nicholas just now," rejoined Jem. "He said he'd another case o' witchcraft nearer whoam. Whot could he mean?"

"Whot, indeed?" cried Elizabeth, quickly.

"Look at Tib," exclaimed her son.

As he spoke, the cat sprang towards the inner door, and scratched violently against it.

Elizabeth immediately raised the latch, and found Jennet behind it, with a face like scarlet.

"Yo'n been listenin, ye young eavesdropper," cried Elizabeth, boxing her ears soundly; "take that fo' your pains—an that."

"Touch me again, an Mester Potts shan knoa aw ey'n heer'd," said the little girl, repressing her tears.

Elizabeth regarded her angrily; but the looks of the child were so spiteful, that she did not dare to strike her. She glanced too at Tib; but the uncertain cat was now rubbing himself in the most friendly manner against Jennet.

"Yo shan pay for this, lass, presently," said Elizabeth.

"Best nah provoke me, mother," rejoined Jennet in a determined tone; "if ye dun, aw secrets shan out. Ey knoa why Jem's goin' to Malkin-Tower to-neet—an why yo're afeerd o' Mester Potts."

"Howd thy tongue or ey'n choke thee, little pest," cried her mother, fiercely.

Jennet replied with a mocking laugh, while Tib rubbed against her more fondly than ever.

"Let her alone," interposed Jem. "An now ey mun be off. So, fare ye weel, mother,—an yo, too, Jennet." And with this, he put on his cap, seized his cudgel, and quitted the cottage.

CHAPTER VII.—THE RUINED CONVENTUAL CHURCH.

BENEATH a wild cherry-tree, planted by chance in the Abbey gardens, and of such remarkable size that it almost rivalled the elms and lime trees surrounding it, and when in bloom resembled an enormous garland, stood two young maidens, both of rare beauty, though in totally different styles;—the one being fair-haired and blue-eyed, with a snowy skin tinged with delicate bloom, like that of roses seen through milk, to borrow a simile from old Anacreon; while the other far eclipsed her in the brilliancy of her complexion, the dark splendour of her eyes, and the luxuriance of her jetty tresses, which, unbound and knotted with ribands, flowed down almost to the ground. In age, there was little disparity between them, though perhaps the dark-haired girl might be a year nearer twenty than the other, and somewhat more of seriousness, though not much, sat upon her lovely countenance than on the other's laughing features. Different were they too, in degree, and here social position was infinitely in favour of the fairer girl, but no one would have judged it so if not previously acquainted with their history. Indeed, it was rather the one having least title to be proud (if any one has such title) who now seemed to look up to her companion with mingled admiration and regard; the latter being enthralled at the moment by the rich notes of a thrush poured from a neighbouring lime-tree.

Pleasant was the garden where the two girls stood, shaded by great trees, laid out in exquisite parterres, with knots and figures, quaint flower-beds, shorn trees and hedges, covered alleys and arbours, terraces and mounds, in the taste of the time, and above all an admirably kept bowling-green. It was bounded on the one hand by the ruined chapter-house and vestry of the old monastic structure, and on the other by the stately pile of buildings formerly making part of the Abbot's lodging, in which the long gallery was situated, some of its windows looking upon the bowling-green, and then kept in excellent condition, but now roofless and desolate. Behind them, on the right, half hidden by trees, lay the desecrated and despoiled conventual church. Reared at such cost, and with so much magnificence, by thirteen abbots—the great work having been commenced, as heretofore stated, by Robert de Topcliffe, in 1330, and only completed in all its details by John Paslew; this splendid structure, surpassing, according to Whitaker, "many cathedrals in extent," was now abandoned to the slow ravages of decay. Would it had never encountered worse enemy! But some half century later, the hand of man was called in to accelerate its destruction, and it was then almost entirely rased to the ground. At the period in question, though partially unroofed, and with some of the walls destroyed, it was still beautiful and picturesque—more picturesque, indeed, than in the days of its pride and splendour. The tower with its lofty crocketed spire was still standing, though the latter was cracked and tottering, and the jackdaws roosted within its windows and belfry. Two ranges of broken columns told of the bygone glories of the aisles; and the beautiful side chapels having escaped injury better than other parts of the fabric, remained in tolerable preservation. But the choir and high altar were stripped of all their rich carving and ornaments, and the rain descended through the open rood-loft upon the now grass-grown graves of the abbots in the presbytery. Here and there the ramified mullions still retained their wealth of painted glass, and the grand eastern window shone gorgeously as of yore. All else was neglect and ruin. Briers and turf usurped the place of the marble pavement; many of the pillars were festooned with ivy; and, in some places, the shattered walls were covered with creepers, and trees had taken root in the crevices of the masonry. Beautiful at all times were these magnificent ruins; but never so beautiful as when seen by the witching light of the moon—the hour, according to the best authority, when all ruins should be viewed—when the long lines of broken pillars, the mouldering arches, and the still glowing panes over the altar, had a magical effect.

In front of the maidens stood a square tower, part of the defences of the religious establishment, erected by Abbot Lyndelay, in the reign of Edward III., but disused and decaying. It was sustained by high and richly groined arches, crossing the swift mill-race, and faced the river. A path led through the ruined chapter-house to the spacious cloister quadrangle, once used as a cemetery for the monks, but now converted into a kitchen garden, its broad area being planted out, and fruit-trees trained against the hoary walls. Little of the old refectory was left, except the dilapidated stairs once conducting to the gallery where the brethren were wont to take their meals, but the inner wall still served to enclose the garden on that side. Of the dormitory, formerly constituting the eastern angle of the cloisters, the shell was still left, and it was used partly as a grange, partly as a shed for cattle, the farm-yard and tenements lying on this side.

Thus it will be seen that the garden and grounds, filling up the ruins of Whalley Abbey, offered abundant points of picturesque attraction, all of which—with the exception of the ruined conventual church—had been visited by the two girls. They had tracked the labyrinths of passages, scaled the broken staircases, crept into the roofless and neglected chambers, peered timorously into the black and yawning vaults, and now, having finished their investigations, had paused for awhile, previous to extending their ramble to the church, beneath the wild cherry-tree to listen to the warbling of the birds.

"You should hear the nightingales at Middleton, Alizon," observed Dorothy Assheton, breaking silence; "they sing even more exquisitely than yon thrush. You must come and see me. I should like to show you the old house and gardens, though they are very different from these, and we have no ancient monastic ruins to ornament them. Still, they are very beautiful; and, as I find you are fond of flowers, I will show you some I have reared myself, for I am something of a gardener, Alizon. Promise you will come."

"I wish I dared promise it," replied Alizon.

"And why not, then?" cried Dorothy. "What should prevent you? Do you know, Alizon, what I should like better than all? You are so amiable, and so good, and so—so very pretty; nay, don't blush—there is no one by to hear me—you are so charming altogether, that I should like you to come and live with me. You shall be my handmaiden if you will."

"I should desire nothing better, sweet young lady," replied Alizon; "but—"

"But what?" cried Dorothy. "You have only your own consent to obtain."

"Alas! I have," replied Alizon.

"How can that be!" cried Dorothy, with a disappointed look. "It is not likely your mother will stand in the way of your advancement, and you have not, I suppose, any other tie? Nay, forgive me if I appear too inquisitive. My curiosity only proceeds from the interest I take in you."

"I know it—I feel it, dear, kind young lady," replied Alizon, with the colour again mounting her cheeks. "I have no tie in the world except my family. But I am persuaded my mother will never allow me to quit her, however great the advantage might be to me."

"Well, though sorry, I am scarcely surprised at it," said Dorothy. "She must love you too dearly to part with you."

"I wish I could think so," sighed Alizon. "Proud of me in some sort, though with little reason, she may be, but love me, most assuredly, she does not. Nay more, I am persuaded she would be glad to be freed from my presence, which is an evident restraint and annoyance to her, were it not for some motive stronger than natural affection that binds her to me."

"Now, in good sooth, you amaze me, Alizon!" cried Dorothy. "What possible motive can it be, if not of affection?"

"Of interest, I think," replied Alizon. "I speak to you without reserve, dear young lady, for the sympathy you have shown me deserves and demands confidence on my part, and there are none with whom I can freely converse, so that every emotion has been locked up in my own bosom. My mother fancies I shall one day be of use to her, and therefore keeps me with her. Hints to this effect she has thrown out, when indulging in the uncontrollable fits of passion to which she is liable. And yet I have no just reason to complain; for though she has shown me little maternal tenderness, and repelled all exhibition of affection on my part, she has treated me very differently from her other children, and with much greater consideration. I can make slight boast of education, but the best the village could afford has been given me; and I have derived much religious culture from good Doctor Ormerod. The kind ladies of the vicarage proposed, as you have done, that I should live with them, but my mother forbade it; enjoining me, on the peril of incurring her displeasure, not to leave her, and reminding me of all the benefits I have received from her, and of the necessity of making an adequate return. And, ungrateful indeed I should be, if I did not comply; for, though her manner is harsh and cold to me, she has never ill-used me, as she has done her favourite child, my little sister Jennet, but has always allowed me a separate chamber, where I can retire when I please, to read, or meditate, or pray. For, alas! dear young lady, I dare not pray before my mother. Be not shocked at what I tell you, but I cannot hide it. My poor mother denies herself the consolation of religion—never addresses herself to Heaven in prayer—never opens the book of Life and Truth—never enters church. In her own mistaken way she has brought up poor little Jennet, who has been taught to make a scoff at religious truths and ordinances, and has never been suffered to keep holy the Sabbath-day. Happy and thankful am I, that no such evil lessons have been taught me, but rather, that I have profited by the sad example. In my own secret chamber I have prayed, daily and nightly, for both—prayed that their hearts might be turned. Often have I besought my mother to let me take Jennet to church, but she never would consent. And in that poor misguided child, dear young lady, there is a strange mixture of good and ill. Afflicted with personal deformity, and delicate in health, the mind perhaps sympathising with the body, she is wayward and uncertain in temper, but sensitive and keenly alive to kindness, and with a shrewdness beyond her years. At the risk of offending my mother, for I felt confident I was acting rightly, I have endeavoured to instil religious principles into her heart, and to inspire her with a love of truth. Sometimes she has listened to me; and I have observed strange struggles in her nature, as if the good were obtaining mastery of the evil principle, and I have striven the more to convince her, and win her over, but never with entire success, for my efforts have been overcome by pernicious counsels, and sceptical sneers. Oh, dear young lady, what would I not do to be the instrument of her salvation!"

"You pain me much by this relation, Alizon," said Dorothy Assheton, who had listened with profound attention, "and I now wish more ardently than ever to take you from such a family."

"I cannot leave them, dear young lady," replied Alizon; "for I feel I may be of infinite service—especially to Jennet—by staying with them. Where there is a soul to be saved, especially the soul of one dear as a sister, no sacrifice can be too great to make—no price too heavy to pay. By the blessing of Heaven I hope to save her! And that is the great tie that binds me to a home, only so in name."

"I will not oppose your virtuous intentions, dear Alizon,' replied Dorothy; "but I must now mention a circumstance in connexion with your mother, of which you are perhaps in ignorance, but which it is right you should know, and therefore no false delicacy on my part shall restrain me from mentioning it. Your grandmother, Old Demdike, is in very ill repute in Pendle, and is stigmatised by the common folk, and even by others, as a witch. Your mother, too, shares in the opprobrium attaching to her."

"I dreaded this," replied Alizon, turning deadly pale, and trembling violently, "I feared you had heard the terrible report. But oh, believe it not! My poor mother is erring enough, but she is not so bad as that. Oh, believe it not!"

"I will not believe it," said Dorothy, "since she is blessed with such a daughter as you. But what I fear is that you—you so kind, so good, so beautiful—may come under the same ban."

"I must run this risk also, in the good work I have appointed myself," replied Alizon. If I am ill thought of by men, I shall have the approval of my own conscience to uphold me. Whatever betide, and whatever be said, do not you think ill of me, dear young lady."

"Fear it not," returned Dorothy, earnestly.

While thus conversing, they gradually strayed away from the cherry-tree, and taking a winding path leading in that direction, entered the conventual church, about the middle of the south aisle. After gazing with wonder and delight at the still majestic pillars, that, like ghosts of the departed brethren, seemed to protest against the desolation around them, they took their way along the nave, through broken arches, and over prostrate fragments of stone, to the eastern extremity of the fane, and having admired the light shafts and clerestory windows of the choir, as well as the magnificent painted glass over the altar, they stopped before an arched doorway on the right, with two Gothic niches, in one of which was a small stone statue of Saint Agnes with her lamb, and in the other a similar representation of Saint

Margaret, crowned, and piercing the dragon with a cross. Both were sculptures of much merit, and it was wonderful they had escaped destruction. The door was closed, but it easily opened when tried by Dorothy, and they found themselves in a small but beautiful chapel. What struck them chiefly in it was a magnificent monument of white marble, enriched with numerous small shields, painted and gilt, supporting two recumbent figures, representing Henry de Lacy, one of the founders of the Abbey, and his consort. The knight was cased in plate armour, covered with a surcoat, emblazoned with his arms, and his feet resting upon a hound. This superb monument was wholly uninjured, the painting and gilding being still fresh and bright. Behind it a flag had been removed, discovering a flight of steep stone steps, leading to a vault, or other subterranean chamber.

After looking round this chapel, Dorothy remarked, "There is something else that has just occurred to me. When a child, a strange dark tale was told me, to the effect that the last ill-fated Abbot of Whalley laid his dying curse upon your grandmother, then an infant, predicting that she should be a witch, and the mother of witches."

"I have heard the dread tradition, too," rejoined Alizon; "but I cannot, will not, believe it. An all-benign Power will never sanction such terrible imprecations."

"Far be it from me to affirm the contrary," replied Dorothy; "but it is undoubted that some families have been, and are, under the influence of an inevitable fatality. In one respect, connected also with the same unfortunate prelate, I might instance our own family. Abbot Paslew is said to be unlucky to us even in his grave. If such a curse, as I have described, hangs over the head of your family, all your efforts to remove it will be ineffectual."

"I trust not," said Alizon. "Oh! dear young lady, you have now penetrated the secret of my heart. The mystery of my life is laid open to you. Disguise it as I may, I cannot but believe my mother to be under some baneful influence. Her unholy life, her strange actions, all impress me with the idea. And there is the same tendency in Jennet."

"You have a brother, have you not?" inquired Dorothy.

"I have," returned Alizon, slightly colouring; "but I see little of him, for he lives near my grandmother, in Pendle Forest, and always avoids me in his rare visits here. You will think it strange when I tell you I have never beheld my grandmother Demdike."

"I am glad to hear it," exclaimed Dorothy.

"I have never even been to Pendle," pursued Alizon, "though Jennet and my mother go there frequently. At one time I much wished to see my aged relative, and pressed my mother to take me with her; but she refused, and now I have no desire to go."

"Strange!" exclaimed Dorothy. "Every thing you tell me

strengthens the idea I conceived, the moment I saw you, and which my brother also entertained, that you are not the daughter of Elizabeth Device."

"Did your brother think this?" cried Alizon, eagerly. But she immediately cast down her eyes.

"He did," replied Dorothy, not noticing her confusion. "'It is impossible,' he said, 'that that lovely girl can be sprung from'—but I will not wound you by adding the rest."

"I cannot disown my kindred," said Alizon. "Still, I must confess that some notions of the sort have crossed me, arising, probably, from my mother's extraordinary treatment, and from many other circumstances, which, though trifling in themselves, were not without weight in leading me to the conclusion. Hitherto I have treated it only as a passing fancy, but if you and Master Richard Assheton"—and her voice slightly faltered as she pronounced the name—"think so, it may warrant me in more seriously considering the matter."

"Do consider it most seriously, dear Alizon," cried Dorothy. "I have made up my mind, and Richard has made up his mind, too, that you are not Mother Demdike's grand-daughter, nor Elizabeth Device's daughter, nor Jennet's sister—nor any relation of theirs. We are sure of it, and we will have you of our mind."

The fair and animated speaker could not help noticing the blushes that mantled Alizon's cheeks as she spoke, but she attributed them to other than the true cause. Nor did she mend the matter as she proceeded.

"I am sure you are well born, Alizon," she said, "and so it will be found in the end. And Richard thinks so, too, for he said so to me; and Richard is my oracle, Alizon."

In spite of herself, Alizon's eyes sparkled with pleasure; but she speedily checked the emotion.

"I must not indulge the dream," she said, with a sigh.

"Why not?" cried Dorothy. "I will have strict inquiries made as to your history."

"I cannot consent to it," replied Alizon. "I cannot leave one who, if she be not my parent, has stood to me in that relation. Neither can I have her brought into trouble on my account. What will she think of me, if she learns I have indulged such a notion? She will say, and with truth, that I am the most ungrateful of human beings, as well as the most unnatural of children. No, dear young lady, it must not be. These fancies are brilliant, but fallacious, and, like bubbles, burst as soon as formed."

"I admire your sentiments, though I do not admit the justice of your reasoning," rejoined Dorothy. "It is not on your own account merely, though that is much, that the secret of your birth—if there be one—ought to be cleared up; but, for the sake of those with whom you may be connected. There may be a mother, like mine, weeping for you as lost – a brother, like Richard, mourning you as dead. Think of the sad hearts your restoration will make joyful. As to Elizabeth Device, no consideration should be shown her. If she has stolen you from your parents, as I suspect, she deserves no pity."

"All this is mere surmise, dear young lady," replied Alizon.

At this juncture they were startled, by seeing an old woman come from behind the monument and plant herself before them. Both uttered a cry, and would have fled, but a gesture from the crone detained them. Very old was she, and of strange and sinister aspect, almost blind, bent double, with frosted brows and chin, and shaking with palsy.

"Stay where you are," cried the hag, in an imperious tone. "I want to speak to you. Come nearer to me, my pretty wheans; nearer—nearer."

And as they complied, drawn towards her by an impulse they could not resist, the old woman caught hold of Alizon's arm, and said with a chuckle, "So you are the wench they call Alizon Device, eh!"

"Ay," replied Alizon, trembling like a dove in the talons of a hawk.

"Do you know who I am?" cried the hag, grasping her yet more tightly. "Do you know who I am, I say? If not, I will tell you. I am Mother Chattox of Pendle Forest, the rival of Mother Demdike, and the enemy of all her accursed brood. Now, do you know me, wench? Men call me witch. Whether I am so or not, I have some power, as they and you shall find. Mother Demdike has often defied me—often injured me, but I will have my revenge upon her—ha! ha!"

"Let me go," cried Alizon, greatly terrified.

"I will run and bring assistance," cried Dorothy. And she flew to the door, but it resisted her attempts to open it.

"Come back," screamed the hag. "You strive in vain. The door is fast shut—fast shut. Come back, I say. Who are you?" she added, as the maid drew near, ready to sink with terror. "Your voice is an Assheton's voice. I know you now. You are Dorothy Assheton—whey-skinned, blue-eyed Dorothy. Listen to me, Dorothy. I owe your family a grudge, and, if you provoke me, I will pay it off in part on you. Stir not, as you value your life."

The poor girl did not dare to move, and Alizon remained as if fascinated by the terrible old woman.

"I will tell you what has happened, Dorothy," pursued Mother Chattox. "I came hither to Whalley on business of my own; meddling with no one; harming no one. Tread upon the adder and it will bite; and, when molested, I bite like the adder. Your cousin, Nick Assheton, came in my way, called me 'witch,' and menaced me. I cursed him—ha! ha! And then your brother, Richard—"

MOTHER CHATTOX, ALIZON, AND DOROTHY. P. 136.

"What of him, in Heaven's name?" almost shrieked Alizon.

"How's this?" exclaimed Mother Chattox, placing her hand on the beating heart of the girl.

"What of Richard Assheton?" repeated Alizon.

"You love him, I feel you do, wench," cried the old crone with fierce exultation.

"Release me, wicked woman," cried Alizon.

"Wicked, am I? ha! ha!" rejoined Mother Chattox, chuckling maliciously, "because, forsooth, I read thy heart, and betray its secrets. Wicked, eh! I tell thee wench again, Richard Assheton is lord and master here. Every pulse in thy bosom beats for him—for him alone. But beware of his love. Beware of it, I say. It shall bring thee ruin and despair."

"For pity's sake, release me," implored Alizon.

"Not yet," replied the inexorable old woman, "not yet. My tale is not half told. My curse fell on Richard's head, as it did on Nicholas's. And then the hell-hounds thought to catch me; but they were at fault. I tricked them nicely—ha! ha! However, they took my Nance—my pretty Nance—they seized her, bound her, bore her to the Calder—and there swam her. Curses light on them all!—all!—but chief on him who did it!"

"Who was he?" inquired Alizon, tremblingly.

"Jem Device," replied the old woman—"it was he who bound her—he who plunged her in the river, he who swam her. But I will pinch and plague him for it. I will strew his couch with nettles, and all wholesome food shall be poison to him. His blood shall be as water, and his flesh shrink from his bones. He shall waste away slowly—slowly—slowly—till he drops like a skeleton into the grave ready digged for him. All connected with him shall feel my fury. I would kill thee now, if thou wert aught of his."

"Aught of his! What mean you, old woman?" demanded Alizon.

"Why, this," rejoined Mother Chattox, "and let the knowledge work in thee, to the confusion of Bess Device. Thou art not her daughter."

"It is as I thought," cried Dorothy Assheton, roused by the intelligence from her terror.

"I tell thee not this secret to pleasure thee," continued Mother Chattox, "but to confound Elizabeth Device. I have no other motive. She hath provoked my vengeance, and she shall feel it. Thou art not her child, I say. The secret of thy birth is known to me, but the time is not yet come for its disclosure. It shall out, one day, to the confusion of those who offend me. When thou goest home tell thy reputed mother what I have said, and mark how she takes the information. Ha! who comes here?"

The hag's last exclamation was occasioned by the sudden appearance of Mistress Nutter, who opened the door of the chapel, and, staring in astonishment at the group, came quickly forward.

"What makes you here, Mother Chattox?" she cried.

"I came here to avoid pursuit," replied the old hag, with a cowed manner, and in accents sounding strangely submissive after her late infuriated tone.

"What have you been saying to these girls?" demanded Mistress Nutter, authoritatively.

"Ask them," the hag replied.

"She declares that Alizon is not the daughter of Elizabeth Device," cried Dorothy Assheton.

"Indeed!" exclaimed Mistress Nutter quickly, and as if a spring of extraordinary interest had been suddenly touched. "What reason hast thou for this assertion?"

"No good reason," replied the old woman evasively, yet with evident apprehension of her questioner.

"Good reason or bad, I will have it," cried Mistress Nutter.

"What you, too, take an interest in the wench, like the rest!" returned Mother Chattox. "Is she so very winning?"

"That is no answer to my question," said the lady. "Whose child is she?"

"Ask Bess Device, or Mother Demdike," replied Mother Chattox; "they know more about the matter than me."

"I will have thee speak, and to the purpose," cried the lady, angrily."

"Many an one has lost a child who would gladly have it back again," said the old hag, mysteriously.

"Who has lost one?" asked Mistress Nutter.

"Nay, it passeth me to tell," replied the old woman with affected ignorance. "Question those who stole her. I have set you on the track. If you fail in pursuing it, come to me. You know where to find me."

"You shall not go thus," said Mistress Nutter. "I will have a direct answer now."

And as she spoke she waved her hands twice or thrice over the old woman. In doing this her figure seemed to dilate, and her countenance underwent a marked and fearful change. All her beauty vanished, her eyes blazed, and terror sat on her wrinkled brow. The hag, on the contrary, crouched lower down, and seemed to dwindle less than her ordinary size. Writhing as from heavy blows, and with a mixture of malice and fear in her countenance, she cried, "Were I to speak, you would not thank me. Let me go."

"Answer," vociferated Mistress Nutter, disregarding the caution, and speaking in a sharp piercing voice, strangely contrasting with her ordinary utterance. "Answer, I say, or I will beat thee to the dust."

And she continued her gestures, while the sufferings of the old hag evidently increased, and she crouched nearer and nearer to the ground, moaning out the words, "Do not force me to speak. You will repent it!—you will repent it!"

"Do not torment her thus, madam," cried Alizon, who with Dorothy looked at the strange scene with mingled apprehension and wonderment. Much as I desire to know the secret of my birth, I would not obtain it thus."

As she uttered these words, the old woman contrived to shuffle off, and disappeared behind the tomb.

"Why did you interpose, Alizon," cried Mistress Nutter, somewhat angrily, and dropping her hands. "You broke the power I had over her. I would have compelled her to speak."

"I thank you, gracious lady, for your consideration," replied Alizon, gratefully; "but the sight was too painful."

"What has become of her—where is she gone?" cried Dorothy, peeping behind the tomb. "She has crept into this vault, I suppose."

"Do not trouble yourelf about her more, Dorothy," said Mistress Nutter, resuming her wonted voice and wonted looks. "Let us return to the house. Thus much is ascertained, Alizon, that you are no child of your supposed parent. Wait a little, and the rest shall be found out for you. And, meantime, be assured that I take strong interest in you."

"That we all do," added Dorothy.

"Thank you! thank you!" exclaimed Alizon, almost overpowered.

With this they went forth, and, traversing the shafted aisle, quitted the conventual church, and took their way along the alley leading to the garden.

"Say not a word at present to Elizabeth Device of the information you have obtained, Alizon," observed Mistress Nutter. "I have reasons for this counsel, which I will afterwards explain to you. And do you keep silence on the subject, Dorothy."

"May I not tell Richard?" said the young lady.

"Not Richard—not any one," returned Mistress Nutter, "or you may seriously affect Alizon's prospects."

"You have cautioned me in time," cried Dorothy, "for here comes my brother with our cousin Nicholas."

And as she spoke a turn in the alley showed Richard and Nicholas Assheton advancing towards them.

A strange revolution had been produced in Alizon's feelings by the events of the last half hour. The opinions expressed by Dorothy Assheton, as to her birth, had been singularly confirmed by Mother Chattox; but could reliance be placed on the old woman's assertions? Might they not have been made with mischievous intent? And was it not possible, nay, probable, that, in her place of concealment behind the tomb, the vindictive hag had overheard the previous conversation with Dorothy, and based her own declaration upon it? All these suggestions occurred to Alizon, but the previous idea having once gained admission to her breast, soon established itself firmly there, in spite of doubts and misgivings, and began to mix itself up with new thoughts and wishes, with which other persons were connected; for she could not help fancying she might be well-born, and if so the vast distance heretofore existing between her and Richard Assheton might be greatly diminished, if not altogether removed. So rapid is the progress of thought, that only a few minutes were required for this long train of reflections to pass through her mind, and it was merely put to flight by the approach of the main object of her thoughts.

On joining the party, Richard Assheton saw plainly that something had happened; but as both his sister and Alizon laboured under evident embarrassment, he abstained from making inquiries as to its cause for the present, hoping a better opportunity of doing so would occur, and the conversation was kept up by Nicholas Assheton, who described, in his wonted lively manner, the encounter with Mother Chattox and Nance Redferne, the swimming of the latter, and the trickery and punishment of Potts. During the recital Mistress Nutter often glanced uneasily at the two girls, but neither of them offered any interruption until Nicholas had finished, when Dorothy, taking her brother's hand, said, with a look of affectionate admiration, "You acted like yourself, dear Richard."

Alizon did not venture to give utterance to the same sentiment, but her looks plainly expressed it.

"I only wish you had punished that cruel James Device, as well as saved poor Nance," added Dorothy.

"Hush!" exclaimed Richard, glancing at Alizon.

"You need not be afraid of hurting her feelings," cried the young lady. "She does not mind him now."

"What do you mean, Dorothy?" cried Richard, in surprise.

"Oh, nothing—nothing," she replied, hastily.

"Perhaps you will explain," said Richard to Alizon.

"Indeed I cannot," she answered in confusion.

"You would have laughed to see Potts creep out of the river," said Nicholas, turning to Dorothy; "he looked just like a drowned rat—ha!—ha!"

"You have made a bitter enemy of him, Nicholas," observed Mistress Nutter; "so look well to yourself."

"I heed him not," rejoined the squire; "he knows me now too well to meddle with me again, and I shall take good care how I put myself in his power. One thing I may mention, to show the impotent malice of the knave. Just as he was setting off, he said, 'This is not the only discovery of witchcraft I have made to-day. I have another case nearer home.' What could he mean?"

"I know not," replied Mistress Nutter, a shade of disquietude passing over her countenance. "But he is quite capable of bringing the charge against you or any of us."

"He is so," said Nicholas. "After what has occurred, I wonder whether he will go over to Rough Lee to-morrow?

"Very likely not," replied Mistress Nutter, "and in that case Master Roger Nowell must provide some other person competent to examine the boundary-line of the properties on his behalf."

"Then you are confident of the adjudication being in your favour?" said Nicholas.

"Quite so," replied Mistress Nutter, with a self-satisfied smile.

"The result, I hope, may justify your expectation," said Nicholas; "but it is right to tell you, that Sir Ralph, in consenting to postpone his decision, has only done so out of consideration to you. If the division of the properties be as represented by him, Master Nowell will unquestionably obtain an award in his favour."

"Under such circumstances he may," said Mistress Nutter; "but you will find the contrary turn out to be the fact. I will show you a plan I have had lately prepared, and you can then judge for yourself."

While thus conversing, the party passed through a door in the high stone wall dividing the garden from the court, and proceeded towards the principal entrance of the mansion. Built out of the ruins of the Abbey, which had served as a very convenient quarry for the construction of this edifice, as well as for Portfield, the house was large and irregular, planned chiefly with the view of embodying part of the old abbot's lodging, and consisting of a wide front with two wings, one of which looked into the court, and the other, comprehending the long gallery, into the garden. The old north-east gate of the Abbey, with its lofty archway and embattled walls, served as an entrance to the great court-yard, and at its wicket ordinarily stood Ned Huddlestone, the porter, though he was absent on the present occasion, being occupied with the May-day festivities. Immediately opposite the gateway sprang a flight of stone steps, with a double landing-place and a broad balustrade of the same material, on the lowest pillar of which was placed a large escutcheon sculptured with the arms of the family—argent, a mullet sable—with a rebus on the name—an ash on a tun. The great door to which these steps conducted stood wide open, and before it, on the upper landing-place, were collected Lady Assheton, Mistress Braddyll, Mistress Nicholas Assheton, and some other dames, laughing and conversing together. Some long-eared spaniels, favourites of the lady of the house, were chasing each other up and down the steps, disturbing the slumbers of a couple of fine blood-hounds in the court-yard; or persecuting the proud peafowl that strutted about to display their gorgeous plumage to the spectators.

On seeing the party approach, Lady Assheton came down to meet them.

"You have been long absent," she said to Dorothy; "but I suppose you have been exploring the ruins?"

"Yes, we have not left a hole or corner unvisited," was the reply.

"That is right," said Lady Assheton. "I knew you would make a good guide, Dorothy. Of course you have often seen the old conventual church before, Alizon?"

"I am ashamed to say I have not, your ladyship," she replied.

"Indeed!" exclaimed Lady Assheton; "and yet you have lived all your life in the village?"

"Quite true, your ladyship," answered Alizon; "but these ruins have been prohibited to me."

"Not by us," said Lady Assheton; "they are open to every one."

"I was forbidden to visit them by my mother," said Alizon. And for the first time the word "mother" seemed strange to her.

Lady Assheton looked surprised, but made no remark, and mounting the steps, led the way to a spacious though not very lofty chamber, with huge uncovered rafters, and a floor of polished oak. Over a great fireplace at one side, furnished with immense andirons, hung a noble pair of antlers, and similar trophies of the chase were affixed to other parts of the walls. Here and there were likewise hung rusty skull-caps, breastplates, two-handed and single-handed swords, maces, halberts, and arquebusses, with chain-shirts, buff-jerkins, matchlocks, and other warlike implements, amongst which were several shields painted with the arms of the Asshetons and their alliances. High-backed chairs of gilt leather were ranged against the walls, and ebony cabinets inlaid with ivory were set between them at intervals, supporting rare specimens of glass and earthenware. Opposite the fireplace, stood a large clock, curiously painted and decorated with emblematical devices, with the signs of the zodiac, and provided with movable figures to strike the hours on a bell; while from the centre of the roof hung a great chandelier of stag's horn.

Lady Assheton did not tarry long within the entrance hall, for such it was, but conducted her guests through an arched doorway on the right into the long gallery. One hundred and fifty feet in length, and proportionately wide and lofty, this vast chamber had undergone little change since its original construction by the old owners of the Abbey. Panelled and floored with lustrous oak, and hung in some parts with antique tapestry, representing scriptural subjects, one side was pierced with lofty pointed windows, looking out upon the garden, while the southern extremity boasted a magnificent window, with heavy stone mullions, though of more recent workmanship than the framework, commanding Whalley Nab and the river. The furniture of the apartment was grand but gloomy, and consisted of antique chairs and tables belonging to the Abbey. Some curious ecclesiastical sculptures, wood carvings, and saintly images, were placed at intervals near the walls, and on the upper panels were hung a row of family portraits.

Quitting the rest of the company, and proceeding to the southern window, Dorothy invited Alizon and her brother to place themselves beside her on the cushioned seats of the deep embrasure. Little conversation, however, ensued; Alizon's heart being too full for utterance, and recent occurrences engrossing Dorothy's thoughts, to the exclusion of every thing else. Having made one or two unsuccessful efforts to engage them in talk, Richard likewise lapsed into silence, and gazed out on the lovely scenery before him. The evening has been described as beautiful; and the swift Calder, as it hurried by, was tinged with rays of the declining sun, whilst the woody heights of Whalley Nab were steeped in the same rosy light. But the view failed to interest Richard in his present mood, and after a brief survey, he stole a look at Alizon, and was surprised to find her in tears.

"What saddening thoughts cross you, fair girl?" he inquired, with deep interest.

"I can hardly account for my sudden despondency," she replied; "but I have heard that great happiness is the precursor of dejection, and the saying I suppose must be true, for I have been happier to-day than I ever was before in my life. But the feeling of sadness is now past," she added, smiling.

"I am glad of it," said Richard. "May I not know what has occurred to you?"

"Not at present," interposed Dorothy; "but I am sure you will be pleased when you are made acquainted with the circumstance. I would tell you now if I might."

"May I guess?" said Richard.

"I don't know," rejoined Dorothy, who was dying to tell him "May he?"

"Oh no, no!" cried Alizon.

"You are very perverse," said Richard, with a look of disappointment. "There can be no harm in guessing; and you can please yourself as to giving an answer. I fancy, then, that Alizon has made some discovery."

Dorothy nodded.

"Relative to her parentage?" pursued Richard.

Another nod.

"She has found out she is not Elizabeth Device's daughter?" said Richard.

"Some witch must have told you this," exclaimed Dorothy.

"Have I indeed guessed rightly?" cried Richard, with an eagerness that startled his sister. "Do not keep me in suspense. Speak plainly."

"How am I to answer him, Alizon?" said Dorothy.

"Nay, do not appeal to me, dear young lady," she answered, blushing.

"I have gone too far to retreat," rejoined Dorothy, "and therefore, despite Mistress Nutter's interdiction, the truth shall out.

You have guessed shrewdly, Richard. A discovery *has* been made —a very great discovery. Alizon is not the daughter of Elizabeth Device."

"The intelligence delights me, though it scarcely surprises me," cried Richard, gazing with heartfelt pleasure at the blushing girl; for I was sure of the fact from the first. Nothing so good and charming as Alizon could spring from so foul a source. How and by what means you have derived this information, as well as whose daughter you are, I shall wait patiently to learn. Enough for me you are not the sister of James Device—enough you are not the grandchild of Mother Demdike."

"You know all I know, in knowing thus much," replied Alizon, timidly. "And secrecy has been enjoined by Mistress Nutter, in order that the rest may be found out. But oh! should the hopes I have—perhaps too hastily—indulged, prove fallacious—"

"They cannot be fallacious, Alizon," interrupted Richard, eagerly. "On that score rest easy. Your connexion with that wretched family is for ever broken. But I can see the necessity of caution, and shall observe it. And so Mistress Nutter takes an interest in you?"

"The strongest," replied Dorothy; "but see! she comes this way."

But we must now go back for a short space.

While Mistress Nutter and Nicholas were seated at a table examining a plan of the Rough Lee estates, the latter was greatly astonished to see the door open and give admittance to Master Potts, who he fancied snugly lying between a couple of blankets, at the Dragon. The attorney was clad in a riding-dress, which he had exchanged for his wet habiliments, and was accompanied by Sir Ralph Assheton and Master Roger Nowell. On seeing Nicholas, he instantly stepped up to him.

"Aha! squire," he cried, "you did not expect to see me again so soon, eh! A pottle of hot sack put my blood into circulation, and having, luckily, a change of raiment in my valise, I am all right again. Not so easily got rid of, you see!"

"So it appears," replied Nicholas, laughing.

"We have a trifling account to settle together, sir," said the attorney, putting on a serious look.

"Whenever you please, sir," replied Nicholas, good-humouredly, tapping the hilt of his sword.

"Not in that way," cried Potts, darting quickly back. "I never fight with those weapons—never. Our dispute must be settled in a court of law, sir—in a court of law. You understand, Master Nicholas?"

"There is a shrewd maxim, Master Potts, that he who is his own lawyer has a fool for his client," observed Nicholas, drily. "Would it not be better to stick to the defence of others, rather than practise in your own behalf?"

"You have expressed my opinion, Master Nicholas," observed Roger Nowell; "and I hope Master Potts will not commence any action on his own account till he has finished my business."

"Assuredly not, sir, since you desire it," replied the attorney, obsequiously. "But my motives must not be mistaken. I have a clear case of assault and battery against Master Nicholas Assheton, or I may proceed against him criminally for an attempt on my life."

"Have you given him no provocation, sir?" demanded Sir Ralph, sternly.

"No provocation can justify the treatment I have experienced, Sir Ralph," replied Potts. "However, to show I am a man of peace, and harbour no resentment, however just grounds I may have for such a feeling, I am willing to make up the matter with Master Nicholas, provided—"

"He offers you a handsome consideration, eh?" said the squire.

"Provided he offers me a handsome apology—such as a gentleman may accept," rejoined Potts, consequentially.

"And which he will not refuse, I am sure," said Sir Ralph, glancing at his cousin.

"I should certainly be sorry to have drowned you," said the squire—"very sorry."

"Enough—enough—I am content," cried Potts, holding out his hand, which Nicholas grasped with an energy that brought tears into the little man's eyes.

"I am glad the matter is amicably adjusted," observed Roger Nowell, "for I suspect both parties have been to blame. And I must now request you, Master Potts, to forego your search and inquiries after witches, till such time as you have settled this question of the boundary line for me. One matter at a time, my good sir."

"But, Master Nowell," cried Potts, "my much esteemed and singular good client—"

"I will have no nay," interrupted Nowell, peremptorily.

"Hum!" muttered Potts; "I shall lose the best chance of distinction ever thrown in my way."

"I care not," said Nowell.

"Just as you came up, Master Nowell," observed Nicholas, who was examining a plan of the disputed estates in Pendle Forest, It differs from yours, and, if correct, certainly substantiates Mistress Nutter's claim."

"I have mine with me," replied Nowell, producing a plan, and opening it. "We can compare the two, if you please. The line runs thus:—From the foot of Pendle Hill, beginning with Barley Booth, the boundary is marked by a stone wall, as far as certain fields in the occupation of John Ogden. Is it not so?"

"Is is," replied Nicholas, comparing the statement with the other plan.

"It then runs on in a northerly direction," pursued Nowell, towards Burst Clough, and here the landmarks are certain stones placed in the moor, one hundred yards apart, and giving me twenty acres of this land, and Mistress Nutter ten."

"On the contrary," replied Nicholas. "This plan gives Mistress Nutter twenty acres, and you ten."

"Then the plan is wrong," cried Nowell, sharply.

"It has been carefully prepared," said Mistress Nutter, who had approached the table.

"No matter; it is wrong, I say," cried Nowell, angrily.

"You see where the landmarks are placed, Master Nowell," said Nicholas, pointing to the measurement. "I merely go by them."

"The landmarks are improperly placed in that plan," cried Nowell.

"I will examine them myself to-morrow," said Potts, taking out a large memorandum-book; "there cannot be an error of ten acres—ten perches—or ten feet, possibly, but acres—pshaw!"

"Laugh as you please; but go on," said Mrs. Nutter.

"Well, then," pursued Nicholas, "the line approaches the bank of a rivulet, called Moss Brook—a rare place for woodcocks and snipes that Moss Brook, I may remark—the land on the left consisting of five acres of waste land, marked by a sheepfold, and two posts set up in a line with it, belonging to Mistress Nutter."

"To Mistress Nutter!" exclaimed Nowell, indignantly. "To me, you mean."

"It is here set down to Mistress Nutter," said Nicholas.

"Then it is set down wrongfully," cried Nowell. "That plan is altogether incorrect."

"On which side of the field does the rivulet flow?" inquired Potts.

"On the right," replied Nicholas.

"On the left," cried Nowell.

"There must be some extraordinary mistake," said Potts. "I shall make a note of that, and examine it to-morrow.—N.B. Waste land—sheepfold—rivulet called Moss Brook, flowing on the left."

"On the right," cried Mistress Nutter.

"That remains to be seen," rejoined Potts, "I have made the entry as on the left."

"Go on, Master Nicholas," said Nowell, "I should like to see how many other errors that plan contains."

"Passing the rivulet," pursued the squire, "we come to a footpath leading to the limestone quarry, about which there can be no mistake. Then by Cat Gallows Wood and Swallow Hole; and then by another path to Worston Moor, skirting a hut in the occupation of James Device—ha! ha! Master Jem, are you here? I thought you dwelt with your grandmother at Malkin Tower—excuse me, Master Nowell, but one must relieve the dulness of this plan by an exclamation or so—and here being waste land again, the landmarks are certain stones set at intervals towards Hook Cliff, and giving Mistress Nutter two-thirds of the whole moor, and Master Roger Nowell one-third."

"False again," cried Nowell, furiously. "The two-thirds are mine, the one-third Mistress Nutter's."

"Somebody must be very wrong," cried Nicholas.

"Very wrong indeed," added Potts; "and I suspect that that somebody is—"

"Master Nowell," said Mistress Nutter.

"Mistress Nutter," cried Master Nowell.

"Both are wrong and both right, according to your own showing," said Nicholas, laughing.

"To-morrow will decide the question," said Potts.

"Better wait till then," interposed Sir Ralph. "Take both plans with you, and you will then ascertain which is correct."

"Agreed," cried Nowell. "Here is mine."

"And here is mine," said Mistress Nutter. "I will abide by the investigation."

"And Master Potts and I will verify the statements," said Nicholas.

"We will, sir," replied the attorney, putting his memorandum book in his pocket. "We will."

The plans were then delivered to the custody of Sir Ralph, ho promised to hand them over to Potts and Nicholas on the morrow.

The party then separated; Mistress Nutter shaping her course towards the window where Alizon and the two other young people were seated, while Potts, plucking the squire's sleeve, said, with a very mysterious look, that he desired a word with him in private. Wondering what could be the nature of the communication the attorney desired to make, Nicholas withdrew with him into a corner, and Nowell, who saw them retire, and could not help watching them with some curiosity, remarked that the squire's hilarious countenance fell as he listened to the attorney, while, on the contrary, the features of the latter gleamed with malicious satisfaction.

Meanwhile, Mistress Nutter approached Alizon, and beckoning her towards her, they quitted the room together. As the young girl went forth, she cast a wistful look at Dorothy and her brother.

"You think with me, that that lovely girl is well born?" said Dorothy, as Alizon disappeared.

"It were heresy to doubt it," answered Richard.

"Shall I tell you another secret?" she continued, regarding him fixedly—"if, indeed, it be a secret, for you must be sadly wanting in discernment if you have not found it out ere this. She loves you."

"Dorothy!" exclaimed Richard.

"I am sure of it," she rejoined. "But I would not tell you this, if I were not quite equally sure that you love her in return."

"On my faith, Dorothy, you give yourself credit for wonderful penetration," cried Richard.

"Not a whit more than I am entitled to," she answered. "Nay, it will not do to attempt concealment with me. If I had not been certain of the matter before, your manner now would convince me. I am very glad of it. She will make a charming sister, and I shall be very fond of her."

"How you do run on, madcap!" cried her brother, trying to look displeased, but totally failing in assuming the expression.

"Stranger things have come to pass," said Dorothy; "and one reads in story-books of young nobles marrying village maidens in spite of parental opposition. I dare say you will get nobody's consent to the marriage but mine, Richard."

"I dare say not," he replied, rather blankly.

"That is, if she should not turn out to be somebody's daughter," pursued Dorothy; "somebody, I mean, quite as great as the heir of Middleton, which I make no doubt she will."

"I hope she may," replied Richard.

"Why, you don't mean to say you wouldn't marry her if she didn't!" cried Dorothy. "I'm ashamed of you, Richard."

"It would remove all opposition, at all events," said her brother.

"So it would," said Dorothy; "and now I'll tell you another notion of mine, Richard. Somehow or other, it has come into my head that Alizon is the daughter of—whom do you think?"

"Whom!" he cried.

"Guess," she rejoined.

"I can't," he exclaimed, impatiently.

"Well, then, I'll tell you without more ado," she answered. "Mind, it's only my notion, and I've no precise grounds for it. But, in my opinion, she's the daughter of the lady who has just left the room."

"Of Mistress Nutter!" ejaculated Richard, starting. "What makes you think so?"

"The extraordinary and otherwise unaccountable interest she takes in her," replied Dorothy. "And, if you recollect, Mistress Nutter had an infant daughter who was lost in a strange manner."

"I thought the child died," replied Richard; "but it may be as you say. I hope it is so."

"Time will show," said Dorothy; "but I have made up my mind about the matter."

At this moment Nicholas Assheton came up to them, looking grave and uneasy.

"What has happened?" asked Richard, anxiously.

"I have just received some very unpleasant intelligence," replied Nicholas. "I told you of a menace uttered by that confounded Potts, on quitting me after his ducking. He has now spoken out plainly, and declares he overheard part of a conversation between Mistress Nutter and Elizabeth Device, which took place in the ruins of the convent church this morning, and he is satisfied that—"

"Well!" cried Richard, breathlessly.

"That Mistress Nutter is a witch, and in league with witches," continued Nicholas.

"Ha!" exclaimed Richard, turning deathly pale.

"I suspect the rascal has invented the charge," said Nicholas; "but he is quite unscrupulous enough to make it; and, if made, it will be fatal to our relative's reputation, if not to her life."

"It is false, I am sure of it," cried Richard, torn by conflicting emotions.

"Would I could think so!" cried Dorothy, suddenly recollecting Mistress Nutter's strange demeanour in the little chapel, and the unaccountable influence she seemed to exercise over the old crone. "But something has occurred to-day that leads me to a contrary conviction."

"What is it? Speak!" cried Richard.

"Not now—not now," replied Dorothy.

"Whatever suspicions you may entertain, keep silence, or you will destroy Mistress Nutter," said Nicholas.

"Fear me not," rejoined Dorothy. "Oh, Alizon!" she murmured, "that this unhappy question should arise at such a moment."

"Do you indeed believe the charge, Dorothy?" asked Richard, in a low voice.

"I do," she answered in the same tone. "If Alizon be her daughter, she can never be your wife."

"How?" cried Richard.

"Never—never!" repeated Dorothy, emphatically. "The daughter of a witch, be that witch named Elizabeth Device or Alice Nutter, is no mate for you."

"You prejudge Mistress Nutter, Dorothy," he cried.

"Alas! Richard. I have too good reason for what I say," she answered, sadly.

Richard uttered an exclamation of despair. And on the instant the lively sounds of tabor and pipe, mixed with the jingling of bells, arose from the court-yard, and presently afterwards an attendant entered to announce that the May-day revellers were without, and directions were given by Sir Ralph that they should be shown into the great banqueting-hall below the gallery, which had been prepared for their reception.

CHAPTER VIII.—THE REVELATION.

On quitting the long gallery, Mistress Nutter and Alizon ascended a wide staircase, and, traversing a corridor, came to an antique, tapestried chamber, richly but cumbrously furnished, having a carved oak bedstead with sombre hangings, a few high-backed chairs of the same material, and a massive wardrobe, with shrine-work atop, and two finely sculptured figures, of the size of life, in the habits of Cistertian monks, placed as supporters at either extremity. At one side of the bed the tapestry was drawn aside, showing the entrance to a closet or inner room, and opposite it there was a great yawning fireplace, with a lofty mantelpiece and chimney projecting beyond the walls. The windows were narrow, and darkened by heavy transom bars and small diamond panes while the view without, looking upon Whalley Nab, was obstructed by the contiguity of a tall cypress, whose funereal branches added to the general gloom. The room was one of those formerly allotted to their guests by the hospitable abbots, and had undergone little change since their time, except in regard to furniture; and even that appeared old and faded now. What with the gloomy arras, the shrouded bedstead, and the Gothic wardrobe with its mysterious figures, the chamber had a grim, ghostly air, and so the young girl thought on entering it.

"I have brought you hither, Alizon," said Mistress Nutter, motioning her to a seat, "that we may converse without chance of interruption, for I have much to say. On first seeing you to-day, your appearance, so superior to the rest of the May-day mummers, struck me forcibly, and I resolved to question Elizabeth Device about you. Accordingly I bade her join me in the Abbey gardens. She did so, and had not long left me when I accidentally met you and the others in the Lacy Chapel. When questioned, Elizabeth affected great surprise, and denied positively that there was any foundation for the idea that you were other than her child; but, notwithstanding her asseverations, I could see from her confused manner that there was more in the notion than she chose to admit, and I determined to have recourse to other means of arriving at the truth, little expecting my suspicions would be so soon confirmed by Mother Chattox. To my interrogation of that old woman, you were yourself a party, and I am now rejoiced that you interfered to prevent me from prosecuting my inquiries to the utmost. There was one present from whom the secret of your birth must be strictly kept—at least, for awhile—and my impatience carried me too far."

"I only obeyed a natural impulse, madam," said Alizon; "but I am at a loss to conceive what claim I can possibly have to the consideration you show me."

"Listen to me, and you shall learn," replied Mistress Nutter. "It is a sad tale, and its recital will tear open old wounds, but it must not be withheld on that account. I do not ask you to bury the secrets I am about to impart in the recesses of your bosom. You will do so when you learn them, without my telling you. When little more than your age I was wedded; but not to him I would have chosen if choice had been permitted me. The union I need scarcely say was unhappy—most unhappy—though my discomforts were scrupulously concealed, and I was looked upon as a devoted wife, and my husband as a model of conjugal affection. But this was merely the surface—internally all was strife and misery. Erelong my dislike of my husband increased to absolute hate, while on his part, though he still regarded me with as much passion as heretofore, he became frantically jealous—and above all of Edward Braddyll of Portfield, who, as his bosom friend, and my distant relative, was a frequent visiter at the house. To relate the numerous exhibitions of jealousy that occurred would answer little purpose, and it will be enough to say that not a word or look passed between Edward and myself but was misconstrued. I took care never to be alone with our guest—nor to give any just ground for suspicion—but my caution availed nothing. An easy remedy would have been to forbid Edward the house, but this my husband's pride rejected. He preferred to endure the jealous torment occasioned by the presence of his wife's fancied lover, and inflict needless anguish on her, rather than brook the jeers of a few indifferent acquaintances. The same feeling made him desire to keep up an apparent good understanding with me; and so far I seconded his views, for I shared in his pride, if in nothing else. Our quarrels were all in private, when no eye could see us—no ear listen."

"Yours is a melancholy history, madam," remarked Alizon, in a tone of profound interest.

"You will think so ere I have done," returned the lady, sadly. "The only person in my confidence, and aware of my secret sorrows, was Elizabeth Device, who with her husband, John Device, then lived at Rough Lee. Serving me in the quality of tire-woman and personal attendant, she could not be kept in ignorance of what took place, and the poor soul offered me all the sympathy in her power. Much was it needed, for I had no other sympathy. After awhile, I know not from what cause, unless from some imprudence on the part of Edward Braddyll, who was wild and reckless, my husband conceived worse suspicions than ever of me, and began to treat me with such harshness and cruelty, that, unable longer to endure his violence, I appealed to my father. But he was of a stern and arbitrary nature, and, having forced me into the match, would not listen to my complaints, but bade me submit. 'It was my duty to do so,' he said, and he added some cutting expressions to the effect that I deserved the treatment I experienced, and dismissed me. Driven to desperation, I sought counsel and assistance from one I should most have avoided—from Edward Braddyll—and he proposed flight from my husband's roof—flight with him."

"But you were saved, madam?" cried Alizon, greatly shocked by the narration. "You were saved?"

"Hear me out," rejoined Mistress Nutter. "Outraged as my feelings were, and loathsome as my husband was to me, I spurned the base proposal, and instantly quitted my false friend. Nor would I have seen him more, if permitted; but that secret interview with him was my first and last;—for it had been witnessed by my husband."

"Ha!" exclaimed Alizon.

"Concealed behind the arras, Richard Nutter heard enough to confirm his worst suspicions," pursued the lady; "but he did not hear my justification. He saw Edward Braddyll at my feet—he heard him urge me to fly—but he did not wait to learn if I consented, and, looking upon me as guilty, left his hiding-place to take measures for frustrating the plan, he supposed concerted between us. That night I was made prisoner in my room, and endured treatment the most inhuman. But a proposal was made by my husband, that promised some alleviation of my suffering. Henceforth we were to meet only in public, when a semblance of affection was to be maintained on both sides. This was done, he said, to save my character, and preserve his own name unspotted in the eyes of others, however tarnished it might be in his own. I willingly consented to the arrangement; and thus for a brief space I became tranquil, if not happy. But another and severer trial awaited me."

"Alas, madam!" exclaimed Alizon, sympathisingly.

"My cup of sorrow, I thought, was full," pursued Mistress Nutter; "but the drop was wanting to make it overflow. It came soon enough. Amidst my griefs I expected to be a mother, and with that thought how many fond and cheering anticipations mingled! In my child I hoped to find a balm for my woes: in its smiles and innocent endearments a compensation for the harshness and injustice I had experienced. How little did I foresee that it was to be a new instrument of torture to me; and that I should be cruelly robbed of the only blessing ever vouchsafed me!"

"Did the child die, madam?" asked Alizon.

"You shall hear," replied Mistress Nutter. "A daughter was born to me. I was made happy by its birth. A new existence, bright and unclouded, seemed dawning upon me; but it was like a sunburst on a stormy day. Some two months before this event Elizabeth Device had given birth to a daughter, and she now took my child under her fostering care; for weakness prevented me from affording it the support it is a mother's blessed privilege to bestow. She seemed as fond of it as myself;

and never was babe more calculated to win love than my little Millicent. Oh! how shall I go on? The retrospect I am compelled to take is frightful, but I cannot shun it. The foul and false suspicions entertained by my husband began to settle on the child. He would not believe it to be his own. With violent oaths and threats he first announced his odious suspicions to Elizabeth Device, and she, full of terror, communicated them to me. The tidings filled me with inexpressible alarm; for I knew, if the dread idea had once taken possession of him, it would never be removed, while what he threatened would be executed. I would have fled at once with my poor babe if I had known where to go; but I had no place of shelter. It would be in vain to seek refuge with my father; and I had no other relative or friend whom I could trust. Where then should I fly? At last I bethought me of a retreat, and arranged a plan of escape with Elizabeth Device. Vain were my precautions. On that very night, I was startled from slumber by a sudden cry from the nurse, who was seated by the fire, with the child on her knees. It was long past midnight, and all the household were at rest. Two persons had entered the room. One was my ruthless husband, Richard Nutter; the other was John Device, a powerful ruffianly fellow, who planted himself near the door.

"Marching quickly towards Elizabeth, who had arisen on seeing him, my husband snatched the child from her before I could seize it, and with a violent blow on the chest felled me to the ground, where I lay helpless, speechless. With reeling senses I heard Elizabeth cry out that it was her own child, and call upon her husband to save it. Richard Nutter paused, but re-assured by a laugh of disbelief from his ruffianly follower, he told Elizabeth the pitiful excuse would not avail to save the brat. And then I saw a weapon gleam—there was a feeble piteous cry—a cry that might have moved a demon—but it did not move *him*. With wicked words and blood-imbrued hands he cast the body on the fire. The horrid sight was too much for me, and I became senseless."

"A dreadful tale, indeed, madam!" cried Alizon, frozen with horror,

"The crime was hidden—hidden from the eyes of men, but mark the retribution that followed," said Mistress Nutter; her eyes sparkling with vindictive joy. "Of the two murderers both perished miserably. John Device was drowned in a moss-pool. Richard Nutter's end was terrible, sharpened by the pangs of remorse, and marked by frightful suffering. But another dark event preceded his death, which may have laid a crime the more on his already heavily-burdened soul. Edward Braddyll, the object of his jealousy and hate, suddenly sickened of a malady so strange and fearful, that all who saw him affirmed it the result of witchcraft. None thought of my husband's agency in the dark affair except myself; but knowing he had held many secret conferences about the time with Mother Chattox, I more than suspected him. The sick man died; and from that hour Richard Nutter knew no rest. Ever on horseback, or fiercely carousing, he sought in vain to stifle remorse. Visions scared him by night, and vague fears pursued him by day. He would start at shadows, and talk wildly. To me his whole demeanour was altered; and he strove by every means in his power to win my love. But he could not give me back the treasure he had taken. He could not bring to life my murdered babe. Like his victim, he fell ill on a sudden, and of a strange and terrible sickness. I saw he could not recover, and therefore tended him carefully. He died; and I shed no tear."

"Alas!" exclaimed Alizon, "though guilty, I cannot but compassionate him."

"You are right to do so, Alizon," said Mistress Nutter, rising, while the young girl rose too; "for he was your father."

"My father!" she exclaimed, in amazement. "Then you are my mother?"

"I am—I am," replied Mistress Nutter, straining her to her bosom. "Oh, my child!—my dear child!" she cried. "The voice of nature from the first pleaded eloquently in your behalf, and I should have been deaf to all impulses of affection if I had not listened to the call. I now trace in every feature the lineaments of the babe I thought lost for ever. All is clear to me. The exclamation of Elizabeth Device, which, like my ruthless husband, I looked upon as an artifice to save the infant's life, I now find to be the truth. Her child perished instead of mine. How or why she exchanged the infants on that night remains to be explained, but that she did so is certain; while that she should afterwards conceal the circumstance is easily comprehended, from a natural dread of her own husband as well as of mine. It is possible that from some cause she may still deny the truth, but I can make it her interest to speak plainly. The main difficulty will lie in my public acknowledgment of you. But, at whatever cost, it shall be made."

"Oh! consider it well;" said Alizon, "I will be your daughter in love—in duty—in all but name. But sully not my poor father's honour, which even at the peril of his soul he sought to maintain! How can I be owned as your daughter without involving the discovery of this tragic history?"

"You are right, Alizon," rejoined Mistress Nutter, thoughtfully. "It will bring the dark deed to light. But you shall never return to Elizabeth Device. You shall go with me to Rough Lee, and take up your abode in the house where I was once so wretched—but where I shall now be full of happiness with you. You shall see the dark spots on the hearth, which I took to be your blood."

"If not mine, it was blood spilt by my father," said Alizon with a shudder.

Was it fancy, or did a low groan break upon her ear? It must be imaginary, for Mistress Nutter seemed unconscious of the dismal sound. It was now growing rapidly dark, and the more distant objects in the room were wrapped in obscurity; but Alizon's gaze rested on the two monkish figures supporting the wardrobe.

"Look there, mother," she said to Mistress Nutter.

"Where?" cried the lady, turning round quickly, "Ah! I see. You alarm yourself needlessly, my child. Those are only carved figures of two brethren of the Abbey. They are said, I know not with what truth—to be statues of John Paslew and Borlace Alvetham."

"I thought they stirred," said Alizon.

"It was mere fancy," replied Mistress Nutter. "Calm yourself, sweet child. Let us think of other things—of our newly discovered relationship. Henceforth, to me you are Millicent Nutter; though to others you must still be Alizon Device. My sweet Millicent," she cried, embracing her again and again. "Ah, little—little did I think to see you more!"

Alizon's fears were speedily chased away.

"Forgive me, dear mother," she cried, "if I have failed to express the full delight I experience in my restitution to you. The shock of your sad tale at first deadened my joy, while the suddenness of the information respecting myself so overwhelmed me, that like one chancing upon a hidden treasure, and gazing at it confounded, I was unable to credit my own good fortune. Even now I am quite bewildered; and no wonder, for many thoughts, each of different import, throng upon me. Independently of the pleasure and natural pride I must feel in being acknowledged by you as a daughter, it is a source of the deepest satisfaction to me to know that I am not, in any way, connected with Elizabeth Device—not from her humble station—for poverty weighs little with me in comparison with virtue and goodness—but from her sinfulness. You know the dark offence laid to her charge?"

"I do," replied Mistress Nutter, in a low deep tone, "but I do not believe it."

"Nor I," returned Alizon. "Still, she acts as if she were the wicked thing she is called; avoids all religious offices; shuns all places of worship; and derides the Holy Scriptures. Oh, mother! you will comprehend the frequent conflict of feelings I must have endured. You will understand my horror when I have sometimes thought myself the daughter of a witch."

"Why did you not leave her if you thought so?" said Mistress Nutter, frowning.

"I could not leave her," replied Alizon, "for I then thought her my mother."

Mistress Nutter fell upon her daughter's neck, and wept aloud.

"You have an excellent heart, my child," she said at length, checking her emotion.

"I have nothing to complain of in Elizabeth Device, dear mother," she replied. "What she denied herself, she did not refuse me; and though I have necessarily many and great deficiencies, you will find in me, I trust, no evil principles. And, oh! shall we not strive to rescue that poor benighted creature from the pit? We may yet save her."

"It is too late," replied Mistress Nutter in a sombre tone.

"It cannot be too late," said Alizon, confidently. "She cannot be beyond redemption. But even if she should prove intractable, poor little Jennet may be preserved. She is yet a child, with some good—though, alas! much evil, also—in her nature. Let our united efforts be exerted in this good work, and we must succeed. The weeds extirpated, the flowers will spring up freely, and bloom in beauty."

"I can have nothing to do with her," said Mistress Nutter, in a freezing tone—"nor must you."

"Oh! say not so, mother," cried Alizon. "You rob me of half the happiness I feel in being restored to you. When I was Jennet's sister, I devoted myself to the task of reclaiming her. I hoped to be her guardian angel—to step between her and the assaults of evil—and I cannot, will not, now abandon her. If no longer my sister, she is still dear to me. And recollect that I owe a deep debt of gratitude to her mother—a debt I can never pay."

"How so?" cried Mistress Nutter. "You owe her nothing—but the contrary."

"I owe her a life," said Alizon. "Was not her infant's blood poured out for mine! And shall I not save the child left her, if I can?"

"I shall not oppose your inclinations," replied Mistress Nutter, with reluctant assent; "but Elizabeth, I suspect, will thank you little for your interference.

"Not now, perhaps," returned Alizon; "but a time will come when she will do so."

While this conversation took place, it had been rapidly growing dark, and the gloom at length increased so much, that the speakers could scarcely see each other's faces. The sudden and portentous darkness was accounted for by a vivid flash of lightning, followed by a low growl of thunder rumbling over Whalley Nab. The mother and daughter drew close together, and Mistress Nutter passed her arm round Alizon's neck.

The storm came quickly on, with forked and dangerous lightning, and loud claps of thunder threatening mischief. Presently, all its fury seemed collected over the Abbey. The red flashes hissed, and the peals of thunder rolled overhead. But other terrors were added to Alizon's natural dread of the elemental warfare. Again she fancied the two monkish figures, which had before excited her alarm, moved, and even shook their arms menacingly at her. At first she attributed this wild idea to her overwrought imagination, and strove to convince herself of its fallacy by keeping her eyes steadily fixed upon them. But each succeeding flash only served to confirm her superstitious apprehensions.

Another circumstance contributed to heighten her alarm. Scared most probably by the storm, a large white owl fluttered down the chimney, and after wheeling twice or thrice round the chamber, settled upon the bed, hooting, puffing, ruffling its feathers, and glaring at her with eyes that glowed like fiery coals.

Mistress Nutter seemed little moved by the storm, though she kept a profound silence, but when Alizon gazed in her face, she was frightened by its expression, which reminded her of the terrible aspect she had worn at the interview with Mother Chattox.

All at once Mistress Nutter arose, and, rapid as the lightning playing around her and revealing her movements, made several passes, with extended hands, over her daughter; and on this the latter instantly fell back, as if fainting, though still retaining her consciousness; and, what was stranger still, though her eyes were closed, her power of sight remained.

In this condition she fancied invisible forms were moving about her. Strange sounds seemed to salute her ears, like the gibbering of ghosts, and she thought she felt the flapping of unseen wings around her.

All at once her attention was drawn—she knew not why—towards the closet, and from out it she fancied she saw issue the tall dark figure of a man. She was sure she saw him; for her imagination could not body forth features charged with such a fiendish expression, or eyes of such unearthly lustre. He was clothed in black, but the fashion of his raiments was unlike aught she had ever seen. His stature was gigantic, and a pale phosphoric light enshrouded him. As he advanced, forked lightnings shot into the room, and the thunder split overhead The owl hooted fearfully, quitted its perch, and flew off by the way it had entered the chamber.

The Dark Shape came on. It stood beside Mistress Nutter, and she prostrated herself before it. The gestures of the figure were angry and imperious—those of Mistress Nutter supplicating. Their converse was drowned by the rattling of the storm. At last the figure pointed to Alizon, and the word "midnight" broke in tones louder than the thunder from its lips. All consciousness then forsook her.

How long she continued in this state she knew not, but the touch of a finger applied to her brow seemed to recall her suddenly to animation. She heaved a deep sigh, and looked around. A wondrous change had occurred. The storm had passed off, and the moon was shining brightly over the top of the cypress-tree, flooding the chamber with its gentle radiance, while her mother was bending over her with looks of tenderest affection.

"You are better now, sweet child," said Mistress Nutter. "You were overcome by the storm. It was sudden and terrible."

"Terrible, indeed!" replied Alizon, imperfectly recalling what had passed. "But it was not alone the storm that frightened me. This chamber has been invaded by evil beings. Methought I beheld a dark figure come from out yon closet, and stand before you."

"You have been thrown into a state of stupor by the influence of the electric fluid," replied Mistress Nutter, "and while in that condition visions have passed through your brain. That is all, my child."

"Oh! I hope so," said Alizon.

"Such ecstasies are of frequent occurrence," replied Mistress Nutter. "But, since you are quite recovered, we will descend to Lady Assheton, who may wonder at our absence. You will share this room with me to-night, my child; for, as I have already said, you cannot return to Elizabeth Device. I will make all needful explanations to Lady Assheton, and will see Elizabeth in the morning—perhaps to-night. Reassure yourself, sweet child. There is nothing to fear.

"I trust not, mother," replied Alizon. "But it would ease my mind to look into that closet."

"Do so, then, by all means," replied Mistress Nutter with a forced smile.

Alizon peeped timorously into the little room, which was lighted up by the moon's rays. There was a faded white habit, like the robe of a Cistertian monk, hanging in one corner, and beneath it an old chest. Alizon would fain have opened the chest, but Mistress Nutter called out to her impatiently, "You will discover nothing, I am sure. Come, let us go down-stairs."

And they quitted the room together.

CHAPTER IX.—THE TWO PORTRAITS IN THE BANQUETING-HALL.

THE banqueting-hall lay immediately under the long gallery, corresponding with it in all but height; and though in this respect it fell somewhat short of the magnificent upper room, it was quite lofty enough to admit of a gallery of its own for spectators and minstrels. Great pains had been taken in decorating the hall for the occasion. Between the forest of stags' horns that branched from the gallery rails were hung rich carpets, intermixed with garlands of flowers, and banners painted with the arms of the Assheton family, were suspended from the corners. Over the fireplace, where, despite the advanced season, a pile of turf and wood was burning, were hung two panoplies of arms, and above them, on a bracket, was set a complete suit of mail, once belonging to Richard Assheton, the first possessor of the mansion. On the opposite wall hung two remarkable portraits—the one representing a religious votaress in a loose robe of black, with wide sleeves, holding a rosary and missal in her hand, and having her brow and neck entirely concealed by the wimple, in which her head and shoulders were enveloped. Such of her features as could be seen were of extraordinary loveliness, though of a voluptuous character, the eyes being dark and languishing, and shaded by long lashes, and the lips carnation-hued and full. This was the fair votaress, Isole de Heton, who brought such scandal on the Abbey in the reign of Henry VI. The other portrait was that of an abbot, in the white gown and scapulary of the Cistertian order. The countenance was proud and stern, but tinctured with melancholy. In a small shield at one corner the arms were blazoned—argent, a fess between three mullets, sable, pierced of the field, a crescent for difference—proving it to be the portrait of John Paslew. Both pictures had been found in the abbot's lodgings, when taken possession of by Richard Assheton, but they owed their present position to his descendant, Sir Ralph, who discovering them in an out-of-the-way closet, where they had been cast aside, and struck with their extraordinary merit, hung them up as above stated.

The long oaken table, usually standing in the middle of the hall, had been removed to one side, to allow free scope for dancing and other pastimes, but it was still devoted to hospitable uses, being covered with trenchers and drinking-cups, and spread for a substantial repast. Near it stood two carvers, with aprons round their waists, brandishing long knives, while other yeomen of the kitchen and cellar were at hand to keep the trenchers well supplied, and the cups filled with strong ale, or bragget, as might suit the taste of the guests. Nor were these the only festive preparations. The upper part of the hall was reserved for Sir Ralph's immediate friends, and here, on a slightly raised elevation, stood a cross table, spread for a goodly supper, the snowy napery being ornamented with wreaths and ropes of flowers, and shining with costly vessels. At the lower end of the room, beneath the gallery, which it served to support, was a Gothic screen, embellishing an open armoury, which made a grand display of silver plates and flagons. Through one of the doorways contrived in this screen, the May-day revellers were ushered into the hall by old Adam Whitworth, the white-headed steward.

"I pray you be seated, good masters, and you, too, comely

dames," said Adam, leading them to the table, and assigning each a place with his wand. "Fall to, and spare not, for it is my honoured master's desire you should sup well. You will find that venison pasty worth a trial, and the baked red deer in the centre of the table is a noble dish. The fellow to it was served at Sir Ralph's own table at dinner, and was pronounced excellent. I pray you try it, masters.—Here, Ned Scargill, mind your office, good fellow, and break me that deer. And you, Paul Pimlot, exercise your craft on the venison pasty."

And as trencher after trencher was rapidly filled by the two carvers, who demeaned themselves in their task like men acquainted with the powers of rustic appetite, the old steward addressed himself to the dames.

"What can I do for you, fair mistresses?" he said. "Here be sack possets, junkets and cream, for such as like them—French puffs and Italian puddings, right good, I warrant you, and especially admired by my honourable good lady. Indeed, I am not sure she hath not lent a hand herself in their preparation. Then here be fritters in the court fashion, made with curds of sack posset, eggs and ale, and seasoned with nutmeg and pepper. You will taste them, I am sure, for they are favourites with our sovereign lady, the queen. Here, Gregory, Dickon—bestir yourselves, knaves, and pour forth a cup of sack for each of these dames. As you drink, mistresses, neglect not the health of our honourable good master Sir Ralph, and his lady. It is well—it is well. I will convey to them both your dutiful good wishes. But I must see all your wants supplied. Good Dame Openshaw, you have nought before you. Be prevailed upon to taste these dropt raisins or a fond pudding And you, too, sweet Dame Tetlow. Squire Nicholas gave me special caution to take care of you, but the injunction was unneeded, as I should have done so without it.—Another cup of canary to Dame Tetlow, Gregory. Fill to the brim, knave—to the very brim. To the health of Squire Nicholas," he added in a low tone, as he handed the brimming goblet to the blushing dame; "and be sure and tell him, if he questions you, that I obeyed his behests to the best of my ability. I pray you taste this pippin jelly, dame. It is as red as rubies, but not so red as your lips, or some leach of almonds, which, lily-white though it be, is not to be compared with the teeth that shall touch it."

"Odd's heart! mester steward, yo mun ha' larnt that protty speech fro' th' squoire himself," replied Dame Tetlow, laughing.

"It may be the recollection of something said to me by him, brought to mind by your presence," replied Adam Whitworth, gallantly. "If I can serve you in aught else, sign to me, dame.—Now, knaves, fill the cups—ale or bragget, at your pleasure masters. Drink and stint not, and you will the better please your liberal entertainer and my honoured master."

Thus exhorted, the guests set seriously to work to fulfil the hospitable intentions of the provider of the feast. Cups flowed fast and freely, and erelong little was left of the venison pasty but the outer crust, and nothing more than a few fragments of the baked red deer. The lighter articles then came in for a share of attention, and salmon from the Ribble, jack, trout, and eels from the Hodder and Calder, boiled, broiled, stewed, and pickled, and of delicious flavour, were discussed with infinite relish. Puddings and pastry were left to more delicate stomachs—the solids only being in request with the men. Hitherto, the demolition of the viands had given sufficient employment, but now the edge of appetite beginning to be dulled, tongues were unloosed, and much merriment prevailed. More than eighty in number, the guests were dispersed without any regard to order, and thus the chief actors in the revel were scattered promiscuously about the table, diversifying it with their gay costumes. Robin Hood sat between two pretty female morris-dancers, whose partners had got to the other end of the table; while Ned Huddlestone, the representative of Friar Tuck, was equally fortunate, having a buxom dame on either side of him, towards whom he distributed his favours with singular impartiality. As porter to the Abbey, Ned made himself at home; and, next to Adam Whitworth, was perhaps the most important personage present, continually roaring for ale, and pledging the damsels around him. From the way he went on, it seemed highly probable he would be under the table before supper was over; but Ned Huddlestone, like the burly priest whose gown he wore, had a stout bullet head, proof against all assaults of liquor; and the copious draughts he swallowed, instead of subduing him, only tended to make him more uproarious. Blessed also with lusty lungs, his shouts of laughter made the roof ring again. But if the strong liquor failed to make due impression upon him, the like cannot be said of Jack Roby, who, it will be remembered, took the part of the Fool, and who, having drunk overmuch, mistook the hobby-horse for a real steed, and in an effort to bestride it, fell head-foremost on the floor, and, being found incapable of rising, was carried out to an adjoining room, and laid on a bench. This, however, was the only case of excess; for though the Sherwood foresters emptied their cups often enough to heighten their mirth, none of them seemed the worse for what they drank. Lawrence Blackrod, Mr. Parker's keeper, had fortunately got next to his old flame, Sukey Worseley; while Phil Rawson, the forester, who enacted Will Scarlet, and Nancy Holt, between whom an equally tender feeling subsisted, had likewise got together. A little beyond them sat the gentleman usher and parish clerk, Sampson Harrop, who, piquing himself on his good manners, drank very sparingly, and was content to sup on sweetmeats and a bowl of fleetings, as curds separated from whey are termed in this district. Tom the piper, and his companion the taborer, ate for the next week, but were somewhat more sparing in the matter of drink, their services as minstrels being required later on. Thus the various guests enjoyed themselves according to their bent, and universal hilarity prevailed. It would be strange indeed if it had been otherwise; for what with the good cheer, and the bright eyes around them, the rustics had attained a point of felicity not likely to be surpassed. Of the numerous assemblage more than half were of the fairer sex; and of these the greater portion were young and good-looking, while in the case of the morris-dancers, their natural charms were heightened by their fanciful attire.

Before supper was half over, it became so dark that it was found necessary to illuminate the great lamp suspended from the centre of the roof, while other lights were set on the board, and two flaming torches placed in sockets on either side of the chimney-piece. Scarcely was this accomplished when the storm came on, much to the surprise of the weatherwise, who had not calculated upon such an occurrence, not having seen any indications whatever of it in the heavens. But all were too comfortably sheltered, and too well employed, to pay much attention to what was going on without; and, unless when a flash of lightning more than usually vivid dazzled the gaze, or a peal of thunder more appalling than the rest broke overhead, no alarm was expressed, even by the women. To be sure, a little pretty trepidation was now and then evinced by the younger damsels; but even this was only done with the view of exacting attention on the part of their swains, and never failed in effect. The thunder-storm, therefore, instead of putting a stop to the general enjoyment, only tended to increase it. However the last peal was loud enough to silence the most uproarious. The women turned pale, and the men looked at each other anxiously, listening to hear if any damage had been done. But, as nothing transpired, their spirits revived. A few minutes afterwards word was brought that the Conventual Church had been struck by a thunderbolt, but this was not regarded as a very serious disaster. The bearer of the intelligence was little Jennet, who said she had been caught in the ruins by the storm, and after being dreadfully frightened by the lightning, had seen a bolt strike the steeple, and heard some stones rattle down, after which she ran away. No one thought of inquiring what she had been doing there at the time, but room was made for her at the supper-table next to Sampson Harrop, while the good steward, patting her on the head, filled her a cup of canary with his own hand, and gave her some cates to eat.

"Ey dunna see Alizon" observed the little girl, looking round the table, after she had drunk the wine.

"Your sister is not here, Jennet," replied Adam Whitworth, with a smile. "She is too great a lady for us now. Since she came up with her ladyship from the green she has been treated quite like one of the guests, and has been walking about the garden and ruins all the afternoon with young Mistress Dorothy, who has taken quite a fancy to her. Indeed, for the matter of that, all the ladies seem to have taken a fancy to her, and she is now closeted with Mistress Nutter in her own room."

This was gall and wormwood to Jennet.

"She'll be hard to please when she goes home again, after playing the fine dame here," pursued the steward.

"Then ey hope she'll never come home again," rejoined Jennet, spitefully, "fo' we dunna want fine dames i' our poor cottage."

"For my part I do not wonder Alizon pleases the gentle folks," observed Sampson Harrop, "since such pains have been taken with her manners and education; and I must say she does great credit to her instructor, who, for reasons unnecessary to mention, shall be nameless. I wish I could say the same for you, Jennet; but though you're not deficient in ability, you've no perseverance or pleasure in study."

"Ey knoa os much os ey care to knoa," replied Jennet, "an more than yo con teach me, Mester Harrop. Why is Alizon always to be thrown i' my teeth?"

"Because she's the best model you can have," rejoined Sampson. "Ah! if I'd my own way wi' ye, lass, I'd mend your temper and manners. But you come of an ill stock, ye saucy hussy."

"Ey come fro' th' same stock as Alizon, onny how," said Jennet.

"Unluckily that cannot be denied," replied Sampson; "but you're as different from her as light from darkness."

Jennet eyed him bitterly, and then rose from the table.

"Ey'n go," she said.

"No—no; sit down," interposed the good-natured steward. "The dancing and pastimes will begin presently, and you will see your sister. She will come down with the ladies."

"That's the very reason she wishes to go," said Sampson Harrop. "The spiteful little creature cannot bear to see her sister better treated than herself. Go your ways, then. It is the best thing you can do. Alizon would blush to see you here."

"Then ey'n een stay an vex her," replied Jennet, sharply; "boh ey winna sit near yo onny longer, Mester Sampson Harrop, who ca' yersel gentleman usher, boh who are nah gentleman at aw, nor owt like it, boh merely parish clerk an schoolmester, an a poor schoolmester to boot. Eyn go an sit by Sukey Worseley an Nancy Holt, whom ey see yonder."

"You've found your match, Master Harrop," said the steward, laughing, as the little girl walked away.

"I should account it a disgrace to bandy words with the like of her, Adam," rejoined the clerk, angrily; "but I'm greatly out in my reckoning, if she does not make a second Mother Demdike, and worse could not well befall her."

Jennet's society could have been very well dispensed with by her two friends, but she would not be shaken off. On the contrary, finding herself in the way, she only determined the more pertinaciously to remain, and began to exercise all her powers of teasing, which have been described as considerable, and which on this occasion proved eminently successful. And the worst of it was, there was no crushing the plaguy little insect; any effort made to catch her only resulting in an escape on her part, and a new charge on some undefended quarter, with sharper stinging and more intolerable buzzing than ever.

Out of all patience, Sukey Worseley at length exclaimed, "Ey should loike to see ye swum, crosswise, i' th' Calder, Jennet, as Nance Redferne war this efternoon."

"May be ye would, Sukey," replied the little girl, "boh eym nah so likely to be tried that way as yourself, lass; an if ey war swum ey should sink, while yo, wi' your broad back and shouthers, would be sure to float, an then yo'd be counted a witch."

"Heed her not, Sukey," said Blackrod, unable to resist a laugh, though the poor girl was greatly discomfited by this personal allusion; ye may ha' a broad back o' our own, an the broader the better to my mind, boh mey word on't ye'll never be ta'en fo a witch. Yo're far too comely."

This assurance was a balm to poor Sukey's wounded spirit, and she replied with a well-pleased smile, "Ey hope ey dunna look like one, Lorry."

"Not a bit, lass," said Blackrod, lifting a huge ale-cup to his lips. "Your health, sweetheart."

"What think ye then o' Nance Redferne?" observed Jennet. "Is she neaw comely?—ay, comelier far than fat, fubsy Sukey here—or than Nancy Holt, wi' her yallo hure an frecklet feace—an yet ye ca' her a witch."

"Ey ca' thee one, theaw feaw little whean—an the dowter—an grandowter o' one—an that's more," cried Nancy. "Freckles i' your own feace, ye mismannert minx."

"Ne'er heed her, Nance," said Phil Rawson, putting his arm round the angry damsel's waist, and drawing her gently down. "Every one to his taste, an freckles an yellow hure are so to mine. So dunna fret about it, an spoil your protty lips wi' pouting. Better ha' freckles o' your feace than spots o' your heart, loike that ill-favort little hussy."

"Dunna offend her, Phil," said Nancy Holt, noticing with alarm the malignant look fixed upon her lover by Jennet. "She's dawngerous."

"Firrups tak her!" replied Phil Rawson. "Boh who the dule's that? Ey didna notice him efore, an he's neaw one o' our party."

The latter observation was occasioned by the entrance of a tall personage, in the garb of a Cistertian monk, who issued from one of the doorways in the screen, and glided towards the upper table, attracting general attention and misgiving as he proceeded. His countenance was cadaverous, his lips livid, and his eyes black and deep sunken in their sockets, with a bistre-coloured circle around them. His frame was meagre and bony. What remained of hair on his head was raven black, but either he was bald on the crown, or carried his attention to costume so far as to adopt the priestly tonsure. His forehead was lofty and sallow, and seemed stamped, like his features, with profound gloom. His garments were faded and mouldering, and materially contributed to his ghostly appearance.

"Who is it?" cried Sukey and Nance together.

But no one could answer the question.

"He dusna look loike a bein' o' this warld," observed Blackrod, gaping with alarm, for the stout keeper was easily assailable on the side of superstition; "an there is a mowdy air about him, that gies one the shivers to see. Ey've often heer'd say the Abbey is haanted; an that pale-feaced chap looks like one o' th' owd monks risen fro' his grave to join our revel."

"An see, he looks this way," cried Phil Rawson.

"What flaming een! they mey the very flesh crawl o' one's booans.'

"Is it a ghost, Lorry?" said Sukey, drawing nearer to the stalwart keeper.

"By th' maskins, lass, ey conna tell," replied Blackrod; "boh whotever it be, ey'll protect ye."

"Tak care o' me, Phil," ejaculated Nancy Holt, pressing close to her lover's side.

"Eigh, that I win," rejoined the forester.

"Ey dunna care for ghosts so long as yo are near me, Phil," said Nancy, tenderly.

"Then ey'n never leave ye, Nance," replied Phil.

"Ghost or not," said Jennet, who had been occupied in regarding the new-comer attentively, "ey'n go an speak to it. Ey'm nah afeerd, if yo are."

"Eigh do, Jennet, that's a brave little lass," said Blackrod, glad to be rid of her in any way.

"Stay!" cried Adam Whitworth, coming up at the moment, and overhearing what was said—"you must not go near the gentleman. I will not have him molested, or even spoken with, till Sir Ralph appears."

Meanwhile, the stranger, without returning the glances fixed upon him, or deigning to notice any of the company, pursued his way, and sat down in a chair at the upper table.

But his entrance had been witnessed by others besides the rustic guests and servitors. Nicholas and Richard Assheton chanced to be in the gallery at the time, and, greatly struck by the singularity of his appearance, immediately descended to make inquiries respecting him. As they appeared below, the old steward advanced to meet them.

"Who the devil have you got there, Adam?" asked the squire.

"It passeth me almost to tell you, Master Nicholas," replied the steward; "and, not knowing whether the gentleman be invited or not, I am fain to wait Sir Ralph's pleasure in regard to him."

"Have you no notion who he is?" inquired Richard.

"All I know about him may be soon told, Master Richard," replied Adam. "He is a stranger in these parts, and hath very recently taken up his abode in Wiswall Hall, which has been abandoned of late years, as you know, and suffered to go to decay. Some few months ago an aged couple from Colne, named Hewit, took possession of part of the hall, and were suffered to remain there, though old Katty Hewit, or Mould-heels, as she is familiarly termed by the common folk, is in no very good repute hereabouts, and was driven, it is said from Colne, owing to her practices as a witch. Be that as it may, soon after these Hewits were settled at Wiswall, comes this stranger, and fixes himself in another part of the hall. How he lives no one can tell, but it is said he rambles all night long, like a troubled spirit, about the deserted rooms, attended by Mother Mould-heels; while in the daytime he is never seen."

"Can he be of sound mind?" asked Richard.

"Hardly so, I should think, Master Richard," replied the steward. "As to who he may be there are many opinions; and some aver he is Francis Paslew, grandson of Francis, brother to the abbot, and being a Jesuit priest, for you know the Paslews have all strictly adhered to the old faith—and that is why they have fled the country and abandoned their residence—he is obliged to keep himself concealed."

"If such be the case, he must be crazed indeed to venture here," observed Nicholas; "and yet I am half inclined to credit the report. Look at him, Dick. He is the very image of the old abbot."

"Yon portrait might have been painted for him," said Richard, gazing at the picture on the wall, and from it to the monk as he spoke; "the very same garb, too."

"There is an old monastic robe up-stairs, in the closet adjoining the room occupied by Mistress Nutter," observed the steward, "said to be the garment in which Abbot Paslew suffered death. Some stains are upon it, supposed to be the blood of the wizard Demdike, who perished in an extraordinary manner on the same day."

"I have seen it," cried Nicholas, "and the monk's habit looks precisely like it, and, if my eyes deceive me not, is stained in the same manner."

"I see the spots plainly on the breast," cried Richard. "How can he have procured the robe?"

"Heaven only knows," replied the old steward. "It is a very strange occurrence."

"I will go question him," said Richard.

So saying, he proceeded to the upper table, accompanied by Nicholas. As they drew near, the stranger arose, and fixed a grim look upon Richard, who was a little in advance.

"It is the abbot's ghost!" cried Nicholas, stopping, and detaining his cousin. "You shall not address it."

During the contention that ensued, the monk glided towards a side-door at the upper end of the hall, and passed through it. So general was the consternation, that no one attempted to stay him, nor would any one follow to see whither he went. Released, at length, from the strong grasp of the squire, Richard rushed forth, and not returning, Nicholas, after the lapse of a few minutes, went in search of him, but came back presently, and told the old steward he could neither find him nor the monk.

"Master Richard will be back anon, I dare say, Adam," he remarked; "if not, I will make further search for him; but you had better not mention this mysterious occurrence to Sir Ralph, at all events not until the festivities are over, and the ladies have retired. It might disturb them. I fear the appearance of this monk bodes no good to our family; and what makes it worse is, it is not the first ill omen that has befallen us to-day, Master Richard was unlucky enough to stand on Abbot Paslew's grave!"

"Mercy on us! that was unlucky indeed!" cried Adam, in great trepidation. "Poor dear young gentleman! Bid him take especial care of himself, good Master Nicholas. I noticed just now, that yon fearsome monk regarded him more attentively than you. Bid him be careful, I conjure you, sir. But here comes my honoured master and his guests. Here, Gregory, Dickon, bestir yourselves, knaves; and serve supper at the upper table in a trice."

Any apprehensions Nicholas might entertain for Richard were at this moment relieved, for as Sir Ralph and his guests came in at one door, the young man entered by another. He looked deathly pale. Nicholas put his finger to his lips in token of silence—a gesture which the other signified that he understood.

Sir Ralph and his guests having taken their places at the table, an excellent and plentiful repast was speedily set before them, and if they did not do quite such ample justice to it as the hungry rustics at the lower board had done to the good things provided for them, the cook could not reasonably complain. No allusion whatever being made to the recent strange occurrence, the cheerfulness of the company was uninterrupted; but the noise in the lower part of the hall had in a great measure subsided, partly out of respect to the host, and partly in consequence of the alarm occasioned by the supposed supernatural visitation. Richard continued silent and preoccupied, and neither ate nor drank; but

Nicholas appearing to think his courage would be best sustained by an extra allowance of clary and sack, applied himself frequently to the goblet with that view, and erelong his spirits improved so wonderfully, and his natural boldness was so much increased, that he was ready to confront Abbot Paslew, or any other abbot of them all, wherever they might chance to cross him. In this enterprising frame of mind he drew Richard aside, and questioned him as to what had taken place in his pursuit of the mysterious monk.

"You overtook him, Dick, of course?" he said, "and put it to him roundly why he came hither, where neither ghosts nor Jesuit priests, whichever he may be, are wanted. What answered he, eh? Would I had been there to interrogate him! He should have declared how he became possessed of that old moth-eaten, blood-stained, monkish gown, or I would have unfrocked him, even if he had proved to be a skeleton. But I interrupt you. You have not told me what occurred at the interview?"

"There was no interview," replied Richard, gravely.

"No interview!" echoed Nicholas. "S'blood, man!—but I must be careful, for Doctor Ormerod and Parson Dewhurst are within hearing, and may lecture me on the wantonness and profanity of swearing. By Saint Gregory de Northbury!—no, that's an oath too, and, what is worse, a Popish oath. By—I have several tremendous imprecations at my tongue's end, but they shall not out. It is a sinful propensity, and must be controlled. In a word, then, you let him escape, Dick?"

"If you were so anxious to stay him, I wonder you came not with me," replied Richard; "but you now hold very different language from what you used when I quitted the hall."

"Ah, true—right—Dick," replied Nicholas; "my sentiments have undergone a wonderful change since then. I now regret having stopped you. By my troth! if I meet that confounded monk again, he shall give a good account of himself, I promise him. But what said he to you, Dick? Make an end of your story."

"I have not begun it yet," replied Richard. "But pay attention, and you shall hear what occurred. When I rushed forth, the monk had already gained the entrance-hall. No one was within it at the time, all the serving-men being busied here with the feasting. I summoned him to stay, but he answered not, and, still grimly regarding me, glided towards the outer door, which (I know not by what chance) stood open, and passing through it, closed it upon me. This delayed me a moment; and when I got out, he had already descended the steps, and was moving towards the garden. It was bright moonlight, so I could see him distinctly. And mark this, Nicholas—the two great blood-hounds were running about at large in the court-yard, but they slunk off, as if alarmed at his appearance. The monk had now gained the garden, and was shaping his course swiftly towards the ruined Conventual Church. Determined to overtake him, I quickened my pace; but he gained the old fane before me, and threaded the broken aisles with noiseless celerity. In the choir he paused and confronted me. When within a few yards of him, I paused, arrested by his fixed and terrible gaze. Nicholas, his look froze my blood. I would have spoken, but I could not. My tongue clove to the roof of my mouth for very fear. Before I could shake off this apprehension the figure raised its hand menacingly thrice, and passed into the Lacy Chapel. As soon as he was gone my courage returned, and I followed. The little chapel was brilliantly illuminated by the moon; but it was empty. I could only see the white monument of Sir Henry de Lacy glistening in the pale radiance."

"I must take a cup of wine after this horrific relation," said Nicholas, replenishing his goblet. "It has chilled my blood, as the monk's icy gaze froze yours. Body o' me! but this is strange indeed. Another oath. Lord help me!—I shall never get rid of the infernal—I mean, the evil habit. Will you not pledge me, Dick?"

The young man shook his head.

"You are wrong," pursued Nicholas,—"decidedly wrong. Wine gladdeneth the heart of man, and restoreth courage. A short while ago I was downcast as you, melancholy as an owl, and timorous as a kid, but now I am resolute as an eagle, stout of heart, and cheerful of spirit; and all owing to a cup of wine. Try the remedy, Dick, and get rid of your gloom. You look like a death's-head at a festival. What if you have stumbled on an ill-omened grave! What if you have been banned by a witch! What if you have stood face to face with the devil—or a ghost! Heed them not! Drink, and set care at defiance. And, not to gainsay my own counsel, I shall fill my cup again. For, in good sooth, this is rare clary, Dick; and, talking of wine, you should taste some of the wonderful Rhenish found in the abbot's cellar by our ancestor, Richard Assheton—a century old if it be a day, and yet cordial and corroborative as ever. Those monks were lusty tipplers, Dick. I sometimes wish I had been an abbot myself. I should have made a rare father confessor—especially to a pretty penitent. Here, Gregory, hie thee to the master cellarer, and bid him fill me a goblet of the old Rhenish—the wine from the abbot's cellar. Thou understandest—or, stay, better bring the flask. I have a profound respect for the venerable bottle, and would pay my devoirs to it. Hie away, good fellow!"

"You will drink too much if you go on thus," remarked Richard.

"Not a drop," rejoined Nicholas. "I am blithe as a lark, and would keep so. That is why I drink. But to return to our ghosts. Since this place must be haunted, I would it were visited by spirits of a livelier kind than old Paslew. There is Isole de Heton, for instance. The fair votaress would be the sort of ghost for me. I would not turn my back on her, but face her manfully. Look at her picture, Dick. Was ever countenance sweeter than hers—lips more tempting, or eyes more melting! Is she not adorable? Zounds!" he exclaimed, suddenly pausing, and staring at the portrait—"Would you believe it, Dick? The fair Isole winked at me—I'll swear she did. I mean—I will venture to affirm upon oath, if required, that she winked."

"Pshaw!" exclaimed Richard. "The fumes of the wine have mounted to your brain, and disordered it."

"No such thing," cried Nicholas, regarding the picture as steadily as he could—"she's leering at me now. By the Queen of Paphos! another wink. Nay, if you doubt me, watch her well yourself. A pleasant adventure this—ha!—ha!"

"A truce to this drunken foolery," cried Richard, moving away.

"Drunken! s'death! recall that epithet, Dick," cried Nicholas, angrily. "I am no more drunk than yourself, you dog. I can walk as steadily, and see as plainly, as you; and I will maintain it at the point of the sword, that the eyes of that picture have lovingly regarded me; nay, that they follow me now."

"A common delusion with a portrait," said Richard; they appear to follow *me*."

"But they do not wink at you as they do at me," said Nicholas, "neither do the lips break into smiles, and display the pearly teeth beneath them, as occurs in my case. Grim old abbots frown on you, but fair, though frail, votaresses smile on me. I am the favoured mortal, Dick."

"Were it as you represent, Nicholas," replied Richard, gravely, "I should say, indeed, that some evil principle was at work to lure you through your passions to perdition. But I know they are all fancies engendered by your heated brain, which in your calmer moments you will discard, as I discard them now. If I have any weight with you, I counsel you to drink no more, or you will commit some mad foolery, of which you will be ashamed hereafter. The discreeter course would be to retire altogether; and for this you have ample excuse, as you will have to arise betimes to-morrow, to set out for Pendle Forest with Master Potts."

"Retire!" exclaimed Nicholas, bursting into a loud, contemptuous laugh. "I like thy counsel, lad. Yes, I will retire when I have finished the old monastic Rhenish which Gregory is bringing me. I will retire when I have danced the Morisco with the May Queen—the Cushion Dance with Dame Tetlow—and the Brawl with the lovely Isole de Heton. Another wink, Dick.

By our Lady! she assents to my proposition. When I have done all this, and somewhat more, it will be time to think of retiring. But I have the night before me, Dick—not to be spent in drowsy unconsciousness, as thou recommendest, but in active, pleasurable enjoyment. No man requires less sleep than I do. Ordinarily, I 'retire,' as thou termest it, at ten, and rise with the sun. In summer I am abroad soon after three, and mend that if thou canst, Dick. To-night I shall seek my couch about midnight, and yet I'll warrant me I shall be the first stirring in the Abbey; and, in any case, I shall be in the saddle before thee."

"It may be," replied Richard; "but it was to preserve you from extravagance to-night that I volunteered advice, which, from my knowledge of your character, I might as well have withheld. But let me caution you on another point. Dance with Dame Tetlow, or any other dame you please—dance with the fair Isole de Heton, if you can prevail upon her to descend from her frame and give you her hand; but I object—most decidedly object—to your dancing with Alizon Device."

"Why so?" cried Nicholas; "why should I not dance with whom I please? And what right hast thou to forbid me Alizon? Troth, lad, art thou so ignorant of human nature as not to know that forbidden fruit is the sweetest. It hath ever been so since the fall. I am now only the more bent upon dancing with the prohibited damsel. But I would fain know the principle on which thou erectest thyself into her guardian. Is it because she fainted when thy sword was crossed with that hot-headed fool, Sir Thomas Metcalfe, that thou flatterest thyself she is in love with thee? Be not too sure of it, Dick. Many a timid wench has swooned at the sight of a naked weapon, without being enamoured of the swordsman. The fainting proves nothing. But grant she loves thee—what then? An end must speedily come of it; so better finish at once, before she be entangled in a mesh from which she cannot be extricated without danger. For hark thee, Dick, whatever thou mayst think, I am not so far gone that I know not what I say, neither is my vision so much obscured that I see not some matters plainly enough, and I understand thee and Alizon well, and see through you both. This matter must go no further. It has gone too far already. After to-night you must see her no more. I am serious in this—serious *inter pocula,* if such a thing can be. It is necessary to observe caution, for reasons that will at once occur to thee. Thou canst not wed this girl—then why trifle with her till her heart be broken."

"Broken it shall never be by me!" cried Richard.

"But I tell you it will be broken, if you do not desist at once," rejoined Nicholas. "I was but jesting when I said I would rob you of her in the Morisco, though it would be charity to both, and spare you many a pang hereafter, were I to put my threat into execution. However, I have a soft heart where aught of love is concerned, and, having pointed out the risk you will incur, I shall leave you to follow your own devices. But, for Alizon's sake, stop in time."

"You now speak soberly and sensibly enough, Nicholas," replied Richard, "and I thank you heartily for your counsel; and if I do not follow it by withdrawing at once from a pursuit which may appear to you hopeless, if not dangerous, you will, I hope, give me credit for being actuated by worthy motives. I will at once, and frankly admit, that I love Alizon; and loving her, you may rest assured I would sacrifice my life a thousand times rather than endanger her happiness. But there is a point in her history, with which if you were acquainted, it might alter your view of the case; but this is not the season for its disclosure, neither, I am bound to say, does the circumstance so materially alter the apparent posture of affairs as to remove all difficulty. On the contrary, it leaves an insurmountable obstacle behind it."

"Are you wise, then, in going on?" asked Nicholas.

"I know not," answered Richard, "but I feel as if I were the sport of fate. Uncertain whither to turn for the best, I leave the disposition of my course to chance. But, alas!" he added, sadly, "all seems to point out that this meeting with Alizon will be my last."

"Well, cheer up, lad," said Nicholas. "These afflictions are hard to bear, it is true; but somehow they are got over. Just as if your horse should fling you in the midst of a hedge when you are making a flying leap, you get scratched and bruised, but you scramble out, and in a day or two are on your legs again. Love breaks no bones, that's one comfort. When at your age, I was desperately in love, not with Mistress Nicholas Assheton—Heaven help the fond soul! but with—never mind with whom; but it was not a very prudent match, and so, in my worldly wisdom, I was obliged to cry off. A sad business it was. I thought I should have died of it, and I made quite sure that the devoted girl would die first, in which case we were to occupy the same grave. But I was not driven to such a dire extremity, for before I had kept house a week, Jack Walker, the keeper of Downham, made his appearance in my room, and after telling me of the mischief done by a pair of otters in the Ribble, finding me in a very desponding state, ventured to inquire if I had heard the news. Expecting to hear of the death of the girl, I prepared myself for an outburst of grief, and resolved to give immediate directions for a double funeral, when he informed me—what do you think, Dick?—that she was going to be married to himself. I recovered at once, and immediately went out to hunt the otters, and rare sport we had. But here comes Gregory with the famous old Rhenish. Better take a cup, Dick; this is the best cure for the heartache, and for all other aches and grievances. Ah! glorious stuff—miraculous wine!" he added, smacking his lips with extraordinary satisfaction after a deep draught; "those worthy fathers were excellent judges. I have a great reverence for them. But where can Alizon be all this while? Supper is wellnigh over, and the dancing and pastimes will commence anon, and yet she comes not."

"She is here," cried Richard.

And as he spoke Mistress Nutter and Alizon entered the hall.

Richard endeavoured to read in the young girl's countenance some intimation of what had passed between her and Mistress Nutter, but he only remarked that she was paler than before, and had traces of anxiety about her. Mistress Nutter also looked gloomy and thoughtful, and there was nothing in the manner or deportment of either to lead to the conclusion, that a discovery of relationship between them had taken place. As Alizon moved on, her eyes met those of Richard—but the look was intercepted by Mistress Nutter, who instantly called off her daughter's attention to herself; and, while the young man hesitated to join them, his sister came quickly up to him, and drew him away in another direction. Left to himself, Nicholas tossed off another cup of the miraculous Rhenish, which improved in flavour as he discussed it, and then, placing a chair opposite the portrait of Isole de Heton, filled a bumper, and, uttering the name of the fair votaress, drained it to her. This time he was quite certain he received a significant glance in return, and no one being near to contradict him, he went on indulging the idea of an amorous understanding between himself and the picture, till he had finished the bottle, and obtained as many ogles as he swallowed draughts of wine, upon which he arose and staggered off in search of Dame Tetlow.

Meanwhile, Mistress Nutter having made her excuses to Lady Assheton for not attending the supper, walked down the hall with her daughter, until such time as the dancing and pastimes should commence. As will be readily supposed under the circumstances, this part of the entertainment was distasteful to both of them; but it could not be avoided without entering into explanations, which Mistress Nutter was unwilling to make, and she, therefore, counselled her daughter to act in all respects as if she were still Alizon Device, and in no way connected with her.

"I shall take an early opportunity of announcing my intention to adopt you," she said, "and then you can act differently. Meantime, keep near me as much as you can. Say little to Dorothy or Richard Assheton, and prepare to retire early; for this noisy and riotous assemblage is not much to my taste, and I care not how soon I quit it."

Alizon assented to what was said, and stole a timid glance towards Richard and Dorothy; but the latter, who alone perceived it, instantly averted her head, in such way as to make it evident she wished to shun her regards. Slight as it was, this circumstance occasioned Alizon much pain, for she could not conceive how she had offended her new-made friend, and it was some relief to encounter a party of acquaintances who had risen from the lower table at her approach, though they did not presume to address her while she was with Mistress Nutter, but waited respectfully at a little distance. Alizon, however, flew towards them.

"Ah, Susan!—ah, Nancy!" she cried taking the hand of each—"how glad I am to see you here; and you too, Lawrence Blackrod—and you, Phil Rawson—and you, also, good Master Harrop. How happy you all look!"

"An wi' good reason, sweet Alizon," replied Blackrod. "Boh we began to be afeerd we'd lost ye, an that wad ha' bin a sore mishap—to lose our May Queen—an th' prottiest May Queen os ever dawnced i' this ha', or i' onny other ha' i' Lonkyshiar."

"We ha drunk your health, sweet Alizon," added Phil—"an wishin' ye may be os happy os ye desarve, wi' the mon o' your heart, if onny sich lucky chap there be."

"Thank you—thank you both," replied Alizon, blushing; "and in return I cannot wish you better fortune, Philip, than to be united to the good girl near you, for I know her kindly disposition so well, that I am sure she will make you happy."

"Ey'm satisfied on't myself, replied Rawson; "an ey hope ere long she'll be missus o' a little cot i' Bowland Forest, an that yo'll pay us a visit, Alizon, an see an judge fo' yourself how happy we be. Nance win make a rare forester's wife."

"Not a bit better than my Sukey," cried Lawrence Blackrod. "Ye shanna get th' start o' me, Phil, fo' by th' mess! the very same day os sees yo wedded to Nancy Holt shan find me united to Sukey Worseley. An so Alizon win ha' two cottages i' Bowland Forest to visit i'stead o' one."

"And well pleased I shall be to visit them both," she rejoined, At this moment Mistress Nutter came up.

"My good friends," she said, "as you appear to take so much interest in Alizon, you may be glad to learn that it is my intention to adopt her as a daughter, having no child of my own; and, though her position henceforth will be very different from what it has been, I am sure she will never forget her old friends."

"Never, indeed, never!" cried Alizon, earnestly.

"This is good news, indeed," cried Sampson Harrop, joyfully, while the others joined in his exclamation. "We all rejoice in Alizon's good fortune, and think she richly deserves it. For my own part, I was always sure she would have rare luck, but I did not expect such luck as this."

"What's to become o' me?" cried Jennet, coming from behind a chair, where she had hitherto concealed herself.

"I will always take care of you," replied Alizon, stooping, and kissing her.

"Do not promise more than you may be able to perform, Alizon," observed Mistress Nutter, coldly, and regarding the little girl with a look of disgust; "an ill-favour'd little creature, with the Demdike eyes."

"And as ill-tempered as she is ill-favoured," rejoined Sampson Harrop; "and, though she cannot help being ugly, she might help being malicious."

Jennet gave him a bitter look.

"You do her injustice, Master Harrop," said Alizon. "Poor little Jennet is quick-tempered, but not malevolent."

"Ey con hate weel if ey conna love," replied Jennet, "an con recollect injuries if ey forget kindnesses.—Boh dunna trouble yourself about me, sister. Ey dunna envy ye your luck. Ey dunna want to be adopted by a grand-dame. Ey'm content os ey am. Boh are na ye gettin' on rayther too fast, lass? Mother's consent has to be axed, ey suppose, efore ye leave her."

"There is little fear of her refusal," observed Mistress Nutter.

"Ey dunna knoa that," rejoined Jennet. "If she were to refuse, it wadna surprise me."

"Nothing spiteful she could do would surprise me," remarked Harrop. "But how are you likely to know what your mother will think and do, you forward little hussy?"

"Ey judge fro circumstances," replied the little girl. "Mother has often said she conna weel spare Alizon. An mayhap Mistress Nutter may knoa, that she con be very obstinate when she tays a whim into her head."

"I *do* know it," replied Mistress Nutter; "and, from my experience of her temper in former days, I should be loath to have you near me, who seem to inherit her obstinacy."

"Wi' sich misgivings ey wonder ye wish to tak Alizon, madam," said Jennet; "fo she's os much o' her mother about her os me, onny she dunna choose to show it."

"Peace, thou mischievous urchin," cried Mistress Nutter, losing all patience.

"Shall I take her away?" said Harrop—seizing her hand.

"Ay, do," said Mistress Nutter.

"No, no, let her stay!" cried Alizon, quickly; "I shall be miserable if she goes."

"Oh, ey'm quite ready to go," said Jennet, "fo ey care little fo sich seets os this—boh efore ey leave ey wad fain say a few words to Mester Potts, whom ey see yonder."

"What can you want with him, Jennet," cried Alizon, in surprise.

"Onny to tell him what brother Jem is gone to Pendle fo to-neet," replied the little girl, with a significant and malicious look at Mistress Nutter.

"Ha!" muttered the lady. "There is more malice in this little wasp than I thought. But I must rob it of its sting."

And while thus communing with herself, she fixed a searching look on Jennet, and then raising her hand quickly, waved it in her face.

"Oh!" cried the little girl, falling suddenly backwards.

"What's the matter?" demanded Alizon, flying to her.

"Ey dunna reetly knoa," replied Jennet.

"She's seized with a sudden faintness," said Harrop. "Better she should go home then at once. I'll find somebody to take her."

"Neaw, neaw, ey'n sit down here," said Jennet; "ey shan be better soon."

"Come along, Alizon," said Mistress Nutter, apparently unconcerned at the circumstance.

Having confided the little girl, who was now recovered from the shock, to the care of Nancy Holt, Alizon followed her mother.

At this moment Sir Ralph, who had quitted the supper-table, clapped his hands loudly, thus giving the signal to the minstrels, who, having repaired to the gallery, now struck up a merry tune, and instantly the whole hall was in motion. Snatching up his wand Sampson Harrop hurried after Alizon, beseeching her to return with him, and join a procession about to be formed by the revellers, and of course, as May Queen, and the most important personage in it, she could not refuse. Very short space sufficed the morris-dancers to find their partners; Robin Hood and the foresters got into their places; the hobby-horse curveted and capered; Friar Tuck resumed his drolleries; and even Jack Roby was so far recovered as to be able to get on his legs, though he could not walk very steadily. Marshalled by the gentleman-usher, and headed by Robin Hood and the May Queen, the procession marched round the hall, the minstrels playing merrily the while, and then drew up before the upper table, where a brief oration was pronounced by Sir Ralph. A shout that made the rafters ring again followed the address, after which a couranto was called for by the host, who, taking Mistress Nicholas Assheton by the hand, led her into the body of the hall, whither he was speedily followed by the other guests, who had found partners in like manner.

Before relating how the ball was opened a word must be bestowed upon Mistress Nicholas Assheton, whom I have neglected nearly as much as she was neglected by her unworthy spouse, and I therefore hasten to repair the injustice by declaring that she was a very amiable and very charming woman, and danced delightfully. And recollect, ladies, these were dancing days—I mean days when knowledge of figures as well as skill was required, more than twenty forgotten dances being in vogue, the very names of which may surprise you as I recapitulate them. There was the Passamezzo, a great favourite with Queen Elizabeth, who used to foot it merrily, when, as you are told by Gray—

> "The great Lord-keeper led the brawls,
> And seals and maces danced before him!"

the grave Pavane, likewise a favourite with the Virgin Queen, and which I should like to see supersede the eternal polka at Almack's and elsewhere, and in which—

> "Five was the number of the music's feet
> Which still the dance did with five paces meet;"

the Couranto, with its "current traverses," "sliding passages," and solemn tune, wherein, according to Sir John Davies—

> —"that dancer greatest praise hath won
> Who with best order can all order shun;"

the Lavolta, also delineated by the same knowing hand—

> "Where arm in arm two dancers are entwined,
> And whirl themselves with strict embracements bound,
> And still their feet an anapest do sound."

Is not this very much like a waltz? Yes, ladies, you have been dancing the lavolta of the sixteenth and seventeenth centuries without being aware of it. But there was another waltz still older, called the Sauteuse, which I suspect answered to your favourite polka. Then there were brawls, galliards, paspys, sarabands, country-dances of various figures, cushion dances (another dance I long to see revived), kissing dances, and rounds, any of which are better than the objectionable polka. Thus you will see that there was infinite variety at least at the period under consideration, and that you have rather retrograded than advanced in the saltatory art. But to return to the ball.

Mistress Nicholas Assheton, I have said, excelled in the graceful accomplishment of dancing, and that was probably the reason why she had been selected for the couranto by Sir Ralph, who knew the value of a good partner. By many persons she was accounted the handsomest woman in the room, and in dignity of carriage she was certainly unrivalled. This was precisely what Sir Ralph required, and having executed a few "current traverses and sliding passages" with her, with a gravity and stateliness worthy of Sir Christopher Hatton himself, when graced by the hand of his sovereign mistress, he conducted her, amid the hushed admiration of the beholders, to a seat. Still the dance continued with unabated spirit; all those engaged in it running up and down, or "turning and winding with unlooked-for change." Alizon's hand had been claimed by Richard Assheton, and next to the stately host and his dignified partner, they came in for the largest share of admiration and attention; and if the untutored girl fell short of the accomplished dame in precision and skill, she made up for the want of them in natural grace and freedom of movement, for the display of which the couranto, with its frequent and impromptu changes, afforded ample opportunity. Even Sir Ralph was struck with her extreme gracefulness, and pointed her out to Mistress Nicholas, who, unenvying and amiable, joined heartily in his praises. Overhearing what was said, Mrs. Nutter thought it a fitting opportunity to announce her intention of adopting the young girl; and though Sir Ralph seemed a good deal surprised at the suddenness of the declaration, he raised no objection to the plan; but, on the contrary, applauded it. But another person, by no means disposed to regard it in an equally favourable light, became acquainted with the intelligence at the same time. This was Master Potts, who instantly set his wits at work to discover its import. Ever on the alert, his little eyes, sharp as needles, had detected Jennet amongst the rustic company, and he now made his way towards her, resolved, by dint of cross-questioning and otherwise, to extract all the information he possibly could from her.

The dance over, Richard and his partner wandered towards a more retired part of the hall.

"Why does your sister shun me?" inquired Alizon, with a look of great distress. "What can I have done to offend her? Whenever I regard her she averts her head, and as I approached her just now, she moved away, making it evident she designed to avoid me. If I could think myself in any way different from what I was this morning, when she treated me with such unbounded confidence and kindness, or accuse myself of any offence towards her, even in thought, I could understand it; but as it is, her present coldness appears inexplicable and unreasonable, and gives me great pain. I would not forfeit her regard for worlds, and therefore beseech you to tell me what I have done amiss, that I may endeavour to repair it."

"You have done nothing—nothing whatever, sweet girl," replied Richard. "It is only caprice on Dorothy's part, and except that it distresses you, her conduct, which you justly call 'unreasonable,' does not deserve a moment's serious consideration."

"Oh no! you cannot deceive me thus," cried Alizon. "She is too kind—too well-judging, to be capricious. Something must have occurred to make her change her opinion of me, though what it is I cannot conjecture. I have gained much to-day—more than I had any right to expect; but if I have forfeited the good opinion of your sister, the loss of her friendship will counterbalance all the rest."

"But you have not lost it, Alizon," replied Richard, earnestly. "Dorothy has got some strange notions into her head, which only require to be combated. She does not like Mistress Nutter, and is piqued and displeased by the extraordinary interest which that lady displays towards you. That is all."

"But why should she not like Mistress Nutter?" inquired Alizon.

"Nay, there is no accounting for fancies," returned Richard, with a faint smile. "I do not attempt to defend her, but simply offer the only excuse in my power for her conduct."

"I am concerned to hear it," said Alizon, sadly, "because henceforth I shall be so intimately connected with Mistress Nutter, that this estrangement, which I hoped arose only from some trivial cause, and merely required a little explanation to be set aside, may become widened and lasting. Owing every thing to Mistress Nutter, I must espouse her cause; and if your sister likes her not, she likes me not in consequence, and therefore we must continue divided. But surely her dislike is of very recent date, and cannot have any strong hold upon her; for when she and Mistress Nutter met this morning, a very different feeling seemed to animate her."

"So, indeed, it did," replied Richard, visibly embarrassed and distressed. "And since you have made me acquainted with the new tie and interests you have formed, I can only regret alluding to the circumstance."

"That you may not misunderstand me," said Alizon, "I will explain the extent of my obligations to Mistress Nutter, and then you will perceive how much I am bounden to her. Childless herself, greatly interested in me, and feeling for my unfortunate situation, with infinite goodness of heart she has declared her intention of removing me from all chance of baneful influence, from the family with whom I have been heretofore connected, by adopting me as her daughter."

"I should indeed rejoice at this," said Richard, "were it not that—"

And he stopped, gazing anxiously at her.

"Were not what?" cried Alizon, alarmed by his looks. "What do you mean?"

"Do not press me further," he rejoined; "I cannot answer you. Indeed I have said too much already."

"You have said too much or too little," cried Alizon. "Speak, I implore you. What mean these dark hints which you throw out, and which like shadows elude all attempts to grasp them! Do not keep me in this state of suspense and agitation. Your looks speak more than your words. Oh, give your thoughts utterance!"

"I cannot," replied Richard. "I do not believe what I have heard, and therefore will not repeat it. It would only increase the mischief. But oh! tell me this! Was it, indeed, to remove you from the baneful influence of Elizabeth Device that Mistress Nutter adopted you?"

"Other motives may have swayed her, and I have said they did so," replied Alizon; "but that wish, no doubt, had great weight with her. Nay, notwithstanding her abhorrence of the family, she has kindly consented to use her best endeavours to preserve little Jennet from further ill, as well as to reclaim poor misguided Elizabeth herself."

"Oh! what a weight you have taken from my heart," cried Richard, joyfully. "I will tell Dorothy what you say, and it will at once remove all her doubts and suspicions. She will now be the same to you as ever, and to Mistress Nutter."

"I will not ask you what those doubts and suspicions were,

since you so confidently promise me this, which is all I desire," replied Alizon, smiling; "but any unfavourable opinions entertained of Mistress Nutter are wholly undeserved. Poor lady! she has endured many severe trials and sufferings, and whenever you learn the whole of her history, she will, I am sure, have your sincere sympathy."

"You have certainly produced a complete revolution in my feelings towards her," said Richard, "and I shall not be easy till I have made a like convert of Dorothy."

At this moment a loud clapping of hands was heard, and Nicholas was seen marching towards the centre of the hall, preceded by the minstrels, who had descended for the purpose from the gallery, and bearing in his arms a large red velvet cushion. As soon as the dancers had formed a wide circle round him, a very lively tune called "Joan Sanderson," from which the dance about to be executed sometimes received its name, was struck up, and the squire, after a few preliminary flourishes, set down the cushion, and gave chase to Dame Tetlow, who, threading her way rapidly through the ring, contrived to elude him. This chase, accompanied by music, excited shouts of laughter on all hands, and no one knew which most to admire, the eagerness of the squire, or the dexterity of the lissom dame in avoiding him.

Exhausted at length, and baffled in his quest, Nicholas came to a halt before Tom the Piper, and, taking up the cushion, thus preferred his complaint:—"This dance it can no further go—no further go."

Whereupon the piper chanted in reply,—"I pray you, good sir, why say you so—why say you so?"

Amidst general laughter, the squire tenderly and touchingly responded—"Because Dame Tetlow will not come to—will not come to."

Whereupon Tom the Piper, waxing furious, blew a shrill whistle, accompanied by an encouraging rattle of the tambarine, and enforcing the mandate by two or three energetic stamps on the floor, delivered himself in this fashion:—"She *must* come to, and she SHALL come to. And she must come, whether she will or no."

Upon this two of the prettiest female morris-dancers, taking each a hand of the blushing and overheated Dame Tetlow, for she had found the chase rather warm work, led her forward; while the squire advancing very gallantly placed the cushion upon the ground before her, and as she knelt down upon it, bestowed a smacking kiss upon her lips. This ceremony being performed amidst much tittering and flustering, accompanied by many knowing looks and some expressed wishes among the swains, who hoped that their turn might come next, Dame Tetlow arose, and the squire seizing her hand, they began to whisk round in a sort of jig, singing merrily as they danced—

"Prinkum prankum is a fine dance,
And we shall go dance it once again!
Once again,
And we shall go dance it once again!"

And they made good the words too; for on coming to a stop, Dame Tetlow snatched up the cushion, and ran in search of the squire, who retreating among the surrounding damsels, made sad havoc among them, scarcely leaving a pretty pair of lips unvisited. Oh Nicholas! Nicholas! I am thoroughly ashamed of you, and regret becoming your historian. You get me into an infinitude of scrapes. But there is a rod in pickle for you, sir, which shall be used with good effect presently. Tired of such an unprofitable quest, Dame Tetlow came to a sudden halt, addressed the piper as Nicholas had addressed him, and receiving a like answer, summoned the delinquent to come forward; but as he knelt down on the cushion, instead of receiving the anticipated salute, he got a sound box on the ears, the dame, actuated probably by some feeling of jealousy, taking advantage of the favourable opportunity afforded her of avenging herself. No one could refrain from laughing at this unexpected turn in affairs, and Nicholas, to do him justice, took it in excellent part, and laughed louder than the rest. Springing to his feet, he snatched the kiss denied him by the spirited dame, and led her to obtain some refreshment at the lower table, of which they both stood in need, while the cushion being appropriated by other couples, other boxes on the ear and kisses were interchanged, leading to an infinitude of merriment.

Long before this Master Potts had found his way to Jennet, and as he drew near, affecting to notice her for the first time, he made some remarks upon her not looking very well.

"'Deed, an ey'm nah varry weel," replied the little girl, "boh ey knoa who ey han to thonk fo' my ailment."

"Your sister, most probably," suggested the attorney. "It must be very vexatious to see her so much noticed, and be yourself so much neglected—very vexatious, indeed—I quite feel for you."

"Ey dunna want your feelin'," replied Jennet, nettled by the remark; "boh it wasna my sister os made me ill."

"Who was it then, my little dear," said Potts.

"Dunna 'dear' me," retorted Jennet; "yo're too ceevil by half, os the lamb said to the wolf. Boh sin ye mun knoa, it wur Mistress Nutter."

"Aha! very good—I mean—very bad," cried Potts. "What did Mistress Nutter do to you, my little dear? Don't be afraid of telling me. If I can do any thing for you I shall be very happy. Speak out—and don't be afraid."

"Nay fo' shure, ey'm nah afeerd," returned Jennet. "Boh whot mays ye so inqueesitive? Ye want to get summat out'n me, ey con see that plain enough, an os ye stand there glenting at me wi' your sly little een, ye look loike an owd fox ready to snap up a chicken o' th' furst opportunity."

"Your comparison is not very flattering, Jennet," replied Potts; "but I pass it by for the sake of its cleverness. You are a sharp child, Jennet—a very sharp child. I remarked that from the first moment I saw you. But in regard to Mistress Nutter, she seems a very nice lady—and must be a very kind lady, since she has made up her mind to adopt your sister. Not that I am surprised at her determination, for really Alizon is so superior—so unlike—"

"Me, ye wad say," interrupted Jennet. "Dunna be efeerd to speak out, sir."

"No, no," replied Potts, "on the contrary, there's a very great likeness between you. I saw you were sisters at once. I don't know which is the cleverest or prettiest—but perhaps you are the sharpest. Yes, you are the sharpest, undoubtedly, Jennet. If I wished to adopt any one, which unfortunately I'm not in a condition to do, having only bachelor's chambers in Chancery Lane, it should be you. But I can put you in a way of making your fortune, Jennet, and that's the next best thing to adopting you. Indeed, it's much better in my case."

"May my fortune!" cried the little girl, pricking up her ears, "ey should loike to knoa how ye wad contrive that."

"I'll show you how directly, Jennet," returned Potts. "Pay particular attention to what I say, and think it over carefully, when you are by yourself. You are quite aware that there is a great talk about witches in these parts; and, I may speak it without offence to you, your own family come under the charge. There is your grandmother Demdike, for instance, a notorious witch—your mother, Dame Device, suspected—your brother James suspected."

"Weel, sir," cried Jennet, eyeing him sharply, "what does all this suspicion tend to?"

"You shall hear, my little dear," returned Potts. "It would not surprise me, if every one of your family, including yourself, should be arrested, shut up in Lancaster Castle, and burnt for witches!"

"Alack a day! an this ye ca' makin my fortin," cried Jennet, derisively. "Much obleeged to ye, sir, boh ey'd leefer be without the luck."

"Listen to me," pursued Potts, chuckling, "and I will point out to you a way of escaping the general fate of your family—not merely of escaping it—but of acquiring a large reward. And that is by giving evidence against them—by telling all you know—you understand—eh!"

"Yeigh, ey think ey *do* onderstond," replied Jennet, sullenly. "An so this is your grand scheme, eh, sir?"

"This is my scheme, Jennet," said Potts, "and a notable

scheme it is, my little lass. Think it over. You're an admissible and indeed a desirable witness; for our sagacious sovereign has expressly observed that 'bairns,' (I believe you call children 'bairns' in Lancashire, Jennet; your uncouth dialect very much resembles the Scottish language, in which our learned monarch writes as well as speaks)—'bairns,' says he, 'or wives, or never so defamed persons, may of our law serve for sufficient witnesses and proofs; for who but witches can be proofs, and so witnesses of the doings of witches.'"

"Boh, ey am neaw witch, ey tell ye, mon," cried Jennet, angrily.

"But you're a witch's bairn, my little lassy," replied Potts, "and that's just as bad, and you'll grow up to be a witch in due time—that is, if your career be not cut short. I'm sure you must have witnessed some strange things when you visited your grandmother at Malkin Tower—that, if I mistake not, is the name of her abode?—and a fearful and witch-like name it is;—you must have heard frequent mutterings and curses, spells, charms, and diabolical incantations—beheld strange and monstrous visions—listened to threats uttered against people who have afterwards perished unaccountably."

"Ey've heerd an seen nowt o't sort," replied Jennet; "boh ey' han heerd my mother threaten yo."

"Ah, indeed," cried Potts, forcing a laugh, but looking rather blank afterwards; "and how did she threaten me, Jennet, eh?—But no matter. Let that pass for the moment. As I was saying, you must have seen mysterious proceedings both at Malkin Tower and your own house. A black gentleman with a club foot must visit you occasionally, and your mother must, now and then—say once a week—take a fancy to riding on a broomstick. Are you quite sure you have never ridden on one yourself, Jennet, and got whisked up the chimney without being aware of it? It's the common witch conveyance, and said to be very expeditious and agreeable—but I can't vouch for it myself—ha! ha! Possibly—though you are rather young—but possibly, I say, you may have attended a witch's Sabbath, and seen a huge He-Goat, with four horns on his head, and a large tail, seated in the midst of a large circle of devoted admirers. If you have seen this, and can recollect the names and faces of the assembly, it would be highly important."

"When ey see it, ey shanna forget it," replied Jennet. "Boh ey am nah quite so familiar wi' Owd Scrat os yo seem to suppose."

"Has it ever occurred to you that Alizon might be addicted to these practices?" pursued Potts, "and that she obtained her extraordinary and otherwise unaccountable beauty by some magical process—some charm—some diabolical unguent prepared, as the Lord Keeper of the Privy Seals, the singularly learned

Lord Bacon, declares, from fat of unbaptised babes, compounded with henbane, hemlock, mandrake, moonshade, and other terrible ingredients. She could not be so beautiful without some such aid."

"That shows how little yo knoaw about it," replied Jennet. "Alizon is os good as she's protty, and dunna yo think to wheedle me into sayin' out agen her, fo' yo winna do it. Ey'd dee rayther than harm a hure o' her heaod."

"Very praiseworthy, indeed, my little dear," replied Potts, ironically. "I honour you for your sisterly affection; but, notwithstanding all this, I cannot help thinking she has bewitched Mistress Nutter."

"Licker, Mistress Nutter has bewitched her," replied Jennet.

"Then you think Mistress Nutter is a witch, eh?" cried Potts, eagerly.

"Ey'st neaw tell ye what ey think, mon," rejoined Jennet, doggedly.

"But hear me," cried Potts, "I have my own suspicions, also, nay, more than suspicions."

"If ye're shure, yo dunna want me," said Jennet.

"But I want a witness," pursued Potts, "and if you'll serve as one—"

"Whot'll ye gi' me?" said Jennet.

"Whatever you like," rejoined Potts. "Only name the sum. So you can prove the practice of witchcraft against Mistress Nutter—eh?"

Jennet nodded. "Wad ye loike to knoa why brother Jem is gone to Pendle to-neet?" she said.

"Very much, indeed," replied Potts, drawing still nearer to her. "Very much, indeed."

The little girl was about to speak, but on a sudden a sharp convulsion agitated her frame; her utterance totally failed her; and she fell back in the seat insensible.

Very much startled, Potts flew in search of some restorative, and on doing so, he perceived Mistress Nutter moving away from this part of the hall.

"She has done it," he cried. "A piece of witchcraft before my very eyes. Has she killed the child? No; she breathes, and her pulse beats, though faintly. She is only in a swoon, but a deep and deathlike one. It would be useless to attempt to revive her; she must come to in her own way, or at the pleasure of the wicked woman who has thrown her into this condition. I have now an assured witness in this girl. But I must keep watch upon Mistress Nutter's further movements."

And he walked cautiously after her.

As Richard had anticipated, his explanation was perfectly satisfactory to Dorothy; and the young lady, who had suffered greatly from the restraint she had imposed upon herself, flew to

Alizon, and poured forth excuses, which were as readily accepted as they were freely made. They were instantly as great friends as before, and their brief estrangement only seemed to make them dearer to each other. Dorothy could not forgive herself, and Alizon assured her there was nothing to be forgiven, and so they took hands upon it, and promised to forget all that had passed. Richard stood by, delighted with the change, and wrapped in the contemplation of the object of his love, who, thus engaged, seemed to him more beautiful than he had ever beheld her.

Towards the close of the evening, while all three were still together, Nicholas came up and took Richard aside. The squire looked flushed; and there was an undefined expression of alarm in his countenance.

"What is the matter?" inquired Richard, dreading to hear of some new calamity.

"Have you not noticed it, Dick?" said Nicholas, in a hollow tone. "The portrait is gone."

"What portrait?" exclaimed Richard, forgetting the previous circumstances.

"The portrait of Isole de Heton," returned Nicholas, becoming more sepulchral in his accents as he proceeded; "it has vanished from the wall. See and believe."

"Who has taken it down?" cried Richard, remarking that the picture had certainly disappeared.

"No mortal hand," replied Nicholas. "It has come down of itself. I knew what would happen, Dick. I told you the fair votaress gave me the *clin d'œil*—the wink. You would not believe me then—and now you see your mistake."

"I see nothing but the bare wall," said Richard.

"But you will see something anon, Dick," rejoined Nicholas, with a hollow laugh, and in a dismally deep tone. "You will see Isole herself. I was foolhardy enough to invite her to dance the brawl with me. She smiled her assent, and winked at me thus—very significantly, I protest to you—and she will be as good as her word."

"Absurd!" exclaimed Richard.

"Absurd, sayest thou—thou art an infidel, and believest nothing, Dick," cried Nicholas. "Dost thou not see that the picture is gone? She will be here presently. Ha! the brawl is called for—the very dance I invited her to. She must be in the room now. I will go in search of her. Look out, Dick. Thou wilt behold a sight presently shall make thine hair stand on end."

And he moved away with a rapid but uncertain step.

"The potent wine has confused his brain," said Richard. "I must see that no mischance befalls him."

And, waving his hand to his sister, he followed the squire, who moved on, staring inquisitively into the countenance of every pretty damsel he encountered.

Time had flown fleetly with Dorothy and Alizon, who, occupied with each other, had taken little note of its progress, and were surprised to find how quickly the hours had gone by. Meanwhile several dances had been performed; a Morisco, in which all the May-day revellers took part, with the exception of the queen herself, who, notwithstanding the united entreaties of Robin Hood and her gentleman-usher, could not be prevailed upon to join it: a trenchmore, a sort of long country-dance, extending from top to bottom of the hall, and in which the whole of the rustics stood up: a galliard, confined to the more important guests, and in which both Alizon and Dorothy were included, the former dancing, of course, with Richard, and the latter with one of her cousins, young Joseph Robinson: and a jig, quite promiscuous and unexclusive, and not the less merry on that account. In this way, what with the dances, which were of some duration—the trenchmore alone occupying more than an hour—and the necessary breathing-time between them, it was on the stroke of ten without any body being aware of it. Now this, though a very early hour for a modern party, being about the time when the first guest would arrive, was a very late one even in fashionable assemblages at the period in question, and the guests began to think of retiring, when the brawl, intended to wind up the entertainment, was called. The highest animation still prevailed throughout the company, for the generous host had taken care that the intervals between the dances should be well filled up with refreshments, and large bowls of spiced wines, with burnt oranges and crabs floating in them, were placed on the side-table, and liberally dispensed to all applicants. Thus all seemed destined to be brought to a happy conclusion.

Throughout the evening Alizon had been closely watched by Mistress Nutter, who remarked, with feelings akin to jealousy and distrust, the marked predilection exhibited by her for Richard and Dorothy Assheton, as well as her inattention to her own expressed injunctions in remaining constantly near them. Though secretly displeased by this, she put a calm face upon it, and neither remonstrated by word or look. Thus Alizon, feeling encouraged in the course she had adopted, and prompted by her inclinations, soon forgot the interdiction she had received. Mistress Nutter even went so far in her duplicity as to promise Dorothy, that Alizon should pay her an early visit at Middleton—though inwardly resolving no such visit should ever take place. However, she now received the proposal very graciously, and made Alizon quite happy in acceding to it.

"I would fain have her go back with me to Middleton when I return," said Dorothy, "but I fear you would not like to part with your newly-adopted daughter so soon; neither would it be quite fair to rob you of her. But I shall hold you to your promise of an early visit."

Mistress Nutter replied by a bland smile, and then observed to Alizon that it was time for them to retire, and that she had stayed on her account far later than she intended—a mark of consideration duly appreciated by Alizon. Farewells for the night were then exchanged between the two girls, and Alizon looked round to bid adieu to Richard, but unfortunately, at this very juncture, he was engaged in pursuit of Nicholas. Before quitting the hall she made inquiries after Jennet, and receiving for answer that she was still in the hall, but had fallen asleep in a chair at one corner of the side-table, and could not be wakened, she instantly flew thither and tried to rouse her, but in vain; when Mistress Nutter, coming up the next moment, merely touched her brow, and the little girl opened her eyes and gazed about her with a bewildered look."

"She is unused to these late hours, poor child," said Alizon. "Some one must be found to take her home."

"You need not go far in search of a convoy," said Potts, who had been hovering about, and now stepped up; "I am going to the Dragon myself, and shall be happy to take charge of her."

"You are over-officious, sir," rejoined Mistress Nutter, coldly; "when we need your assistance we will ask it. My own servant, Simon Blackadder, will see her safely home."

And at a sign from her, a tall fellow with a dark, scowling countenance, came from among the other serving-men, and, receiving his instructions from his mistress, seized Jennet's hand, and strode off with her. During all this time, Mistress Nutter kept her eyes steadily fixed on the little girl, who spoke not a word, nor replied even by a gesture to Alizon's affectionate good-night, retaining her dazed look to the moment of quitting the hall.

"I never saw her thus before," said Alizon. "What can be the matter with her?"

"I think I could tell you," rejoined Potts, glancing maliciously and significantly at Mistress Nutter.

The lady darted an ireful and piercing look at him, which seemed to produce much the same consequences as those experienced by Jennet, for his visage instantly elongated, and he sank back in a chair.

"Oh dear!" he cried, putting his hand to his head; "I'm struck all of a heap. I feel a sudden qualm—a giddiness—a sort of don't-know-howishness. Ho, there! some aquavitæ—or imperial water—or cinnamon water—or whatever reviving cordial may be at hand. I feel very ill—very ill, indeed—oh dear!"

While his requirements were attended to, Mistress Nutter moved away with her daughter; but they had not proceeded far when they encountered Richard, who, having fortunately descried them, came up to say good-night.

The brawl, meanwhile, had commenced, and the dancers were whirling round giddily in every direction, somewhat like the couples in a grand polka, danced after a very boisterous, romping, and extravagant fashion.

"Who is Nicholas dancing with?" asked Mistress Nutter suddenly.

"Is he dancing with any one?" rejoined Richard, looking amidst the crowd.

"Do you not see her?" said Mistress Nutter; "a very beautiful woman with flashing eyes: they move so quickly, that I can scarce discern her features; but she is habited like a nun."

"Like a nun!" cried Richard, his blood growing chill in his veins. "'Tis she indeed, then! Where is he?"

"Yonder, yonder, whirling madly round," replied Mistress Nutter.

"I see him now," said Richard, "but he is alone. He has lost his wits to dance in that strange manner by himself. How wild, too, is his gaze!"

"I tell you he is dancing with a very beautiful woman in the habit of a nun," said Mistress Nutter. "Strange I should never have remarked her before. No one in the room is to be compared with her in loveliness—not even Alizon. Her eyes seem to flash fire, and she bounds like the wild roe."

"Does she resemble the portrait of Isole de Heton?" asked Richard, shuddering.

"She does—she does," replied Mistress Nutter. "See! she whirls past us now."

"I can see no one but Nicholas," cried Richard.

"Nor I," added Alizon, who shared in the young man's alarm.

"Are you sure you behold that figure?" said Richard, drawing Mistress Nutter aside, and breathing the words in her ear. "If so, it is a phantom—or he is in the power of the fiend He was rash enough to invite that wicked votaress, Isole de Heton, condemned, it is said, to penal fires for her earthly enormities, to dance with him, and she has come."

"Ha!" exclaimed Mistress Nutter.

"She will whirl him round till he expires," cried Richard; "I must free him at all hazards."

"Stay," said Mistress Nutter; "it is I who have been deceived. Now I look again, I see that Nicholas is alone."

"But the nun's dress—the wondrous beauty—the flashing eyes!" cried Richard. "You described Isole exactly."

"It was mere fancy," said Mistress Nutter. "I had just been looking at her portrait, and it dwelt on my mind, and created the image."

"The portrait is gone," cried Richard, pointing to the empty wall.

Mistress Nutter looked confounded.

And without a word more, she took Alizon, who was full of alarm and astonishment, by the arm, and hurried her out of the hall.

As they disappeared, the young man flew towards Nicholas, whose extraordinary proceedings had excited general amazement. The other dancers had moved out of the way, so that free space was left for his mad gyrations. Greatly scandalised by the exhibition, which he looked upon as the effect of intoxication, Sir Ralph called loudly to him to stop, but he paid no attention to the summons, but whirled on with momently-increasing velocity, oversetting old Adam Whitworth, Gregory, and Dickon, who severally ventured to place themselves in his path, to enforce their master's injunctions, until at last, just as Richard reached him, he uttered a loud cry, and fell to the ground insensible. By Sir Ralph's command he was instantly lifted up and transported to his own chamber.

This unexpected and extraordinary incident put an end to the ball, and the whole of the guests, after taking a respectful and grateful leave of the host, departed—not in "most admired" disorder, but full of wonder. By most persons the squire's "fantastical vagaries," as they were termed, were traced to the vast quantity of wine he had drunk, but a few others shook their heads, and said he was evidently bewitched, and that Mother Chattox and Nance Redferne were at the bottom of it. As to the portrait of Isole de Heton, it was found under the table, and it was said that Nicholas himself had pulled it down; but this he obstinately denied, when afterwards taken to task for his indecorous behaviour; and to his dying day he asserted, and believed, that he had danced the brawl with Isole de Heton. "And never," he would say, "had mortal man such a partner."

From that night the two portraits in the banqueting-hall were regarded with great awe by the inmates of the Abbey.

CHAPTER X.—THE NOCTURNAL MEETING.

On gaining the head of the staircase leading to the corridor, Mistress Nutter, whose movements had hitherto been extremely rapid, paused with her daughter to listen to the sounds arising from below. Suddenly was heard a loud cry, and the music, which had waxed fast and furious in order to keep pace with the frenzied boundings of the squire, ceased at once, showing some interruption had occurred, while from the confused noise that ensued, it was evident the sudden stoppage had been the result of accident. With blanched cheek Alizon listened, scarcely daring to look at her mother, whose expression of countenance, revealed by the lamp she held in her hand, almost frightened her;

and it was a great relief to hear the voices and laughter of the serving-men as they came forth with Nicholas, and bore him towards another part of the mansion; and though much shocked, she was glad when one of them, who appeared to be Nicholas's own servant, assured the others "that it was only a drunken fit, and that the squire would wake up next morning as if nothing had happened."

Apparently satisfied with this explanation, Mistress Nutter moved on; but a new feeling of uneasiness came over Alizon as she followed her down the long dusky corridor, in the direction of the mysterious chamber, where they were to pass the night. The fitful flame of the lamp fell upon many a grim painting depicting the sufferings of the early martyrs; and these ghastly representations did not serve to re-assure her. The grotesque carvings on the panels and ribs of the vaulted roof, likewise impressed her with vague terror, and there was one large piece of sculpture—Saint Theodora subjected to diabolical temptation, as described in the Golden Legend—that absolutely scared her. Their footsteps echoed hollowly overhead, and more than once, deceived by the sound, Alizon turned to see if any one was behind them. At the end of the corridor lay the room once occupied by the superior of the religious establishment, and still known from that circumstance as the "Abbot's Chamber." Connected with this apartment was the beautiful oratory built by Paslew, wherein he had kept his last vigils; and though now no longer applied to purposes of worship, still wearing from the character of its architecture, its sculptured ornaments, and the painted glass in its casements, a dim religious air. The abbot's room was allotted to Dorothy Assheton; and from its sombre magnificence, as well as the ghostly tales connected with it, had impressed her with so much superstitious misgiving, that she besought Alizon to share her couch with her, but the young girl did not dare to assent. Just, however, as Mistress Nutter was about to enter her own room, Dorothy appeared on the corridor, and, calling to Alizon to stay a moment, flew quickly towards her, and renewed the proposition. Alizon looked at her mother, but the latter decidedly, and somewhat sternly, negatived it.

The young girls then said good-night, kissing each other affectionately, after which Alizon entered the room with Mistress Nutter, and the door was closed. Two tapers were burning on the dressing-table, and their light fell upon the carved figures of the wardrobe, which still exercised the same weird influence over her. Mistress Nutter neither seemed disposed to retire to rest immediately, nor willing to talk, but sat down, and was soon lost in thought. After awhile, an impulse of curiosity which she could not resist, prompted Alizon to peep into the closet, and pushing aside the tapestry, partly drawn over the entrance, she held the lamp forward so as to throw its light into the little chamber. A mere glance was all she was allowed, but it sufficed to show her the large oak chest, though the monkish robe lately suspended above it, and which had particularly attracted her attention, was gone. Mistress Nutter had noticed the movement, and instantly and somewhat sharply recalled her.

As Alizon obeyed, a slight tap was heard at the door. The young girl turned pale, for in her present frame of mind any little matter affected her. Nor were her apprehensions materially allayed by the entrance of Dorothy, who, looking white as a sheet said she did not dare to remain in her own room, having been terribly frightened, by seeing a monkish figure in mouldering white garments, exactly resembling one of the carved images on the wardrobe, issue from behind the hangings on the wall, and glide into the oratory, and she entreated Mistress Nutter to let Alizon go back with her. The request was peremptorily refused, and the lady, ridiculing Dorothy for her fears, bade her return; but she still lingered. This relation filled Alizon with inexpressible alarm, for though she did not dare to allude to the disappearance of the monkish gown, she could not help connecting the circumstance with the ghostly figure seen by Dorothy.

Unable otherwise to get rid of the terrified intruder, whose presence was an evident restraint to her, Mistress Nutter, at length, consented to accompany her to her room, and convince her of the folly of her fears, by an examination of the oratory. Alizon went with them, her mother not choosing to leave her behind, and indeed she herself was most anxious to go.

The abbot's chamber was large and gloomy, nearly twice the size of the room occupied by Mistress Nutter, but resembling it in many respects, as well as in the dusky hue of its hangings and furniture, most of which had been undisturbed since the days of Paslew. The very bed, of carved oak, was that in which he had slept, and his arms were still displayed upon it, and on the painted glass of the windows. As Alizon entered she looked round with apprehension, but nothing occurred to justify her uneasiness. Having raised the arras, from behind which Dorothy averred the figure had issued, and discovering nothing but a panel of oak; with a smile of incredulity, Mistress Nutter walked boldly towards the oratory, the two girls, hand in hand, following tremblingly after her; but no fearful object met their view. A dressing-table, with a large mirror upon it, occupied the spot where the altar had formerly stood; but, in spite of this, and of other furniture, the little place of prayer, as has previously been observed, retained much of its original character, and seemed more calculated to inspire sentiments of devotional awe than any other.

After remaining for a short time in the oratory, during which she pointed out the impossibility of any one being concealed there, Mistress Nutter assured Dorothy she might rest quite easy that nothing further would occur to alarm her, and recommending her to lose the sense of her fears as speedily as she could in sleep, took her departure with Alizon.

But the recommendation was of little avail. The poor girl's heart died within her, and all her former terrors returned, and with additional force. Sitting down, she looked fixedly at the hangings till her eyes ached, and then covering her face with her hands, and scarcely daring to breathe, she listened intently for the slightest sound. A rustle would have made her scream—but all was still as death, so profoundly quiet, that the very hush and silence became a new cause of disquietude, and longing for some cheerful sound to break it, she would have spoken aloud but from a fear of hearing her own voice. A book lay before her, and she essayed to read it, but in vain. She was ever glancing fearfully round—ever listening intently. This state could not endure for ever, and feeling a drowsiness steal over her she yielded to it, and at length dropped asleep in her chair. Her dreams, however, were influenced by her mental condition, and slumber was no refuge, as promised by Mistress Nutter, from the hauntings of terror.

At last a jarring sound aroused her, and she found she had been awakened by the clock striking twelve. Her lamp required trimming and burnt dimly, but by its imperfect light she saw the arras move. This could be no fancy, for the next moment the hangings were raised, and a figure looked from behind them; and this time it was not the monk, but a female robed in white. A glimpse of the figure was all Dorothy caught, for it instantly retreated, and the tapestry fell back to its place against the wall.

Scared by this apparition, Dorothy rushed out of the room so hurriedly that she forgot to take her lamp, and made her way, she scarcely knew how, to the adjoining chamber. She did not tap at the door, but trying it, and finding it unfastened, opened it softly, and closed it after her, resolved if the occupants of the room were asleep not to disturb them, but to pass the night in a chair, the presence of some living beings beside her sufficing, in some degree, to dispel her terrors. The room was buried in darkness, the tapers being extinguished.

Advancing on tiptoe she soon discovered a seat, when what was her surprise to find Alizon asleep within it. She was sure it was Alizon—for she had touched her hair and face, and she felt surprised that the contact had not awakened her. Still more surprised did she feel that the young girl had not retired to rest. Again she stepped forward in search of another chair, when a gleam of light suddenly shot from one side of the bed, and the tapestry, masking the entrance to the closet, was slowly drawn aside. From behind it, the next moment, appeared the same female figure, robed in white, that she had previously beheld in the abbot's chamber. The figure held a lamp in one hand, and

ALIZON ALARMED AT THE APPEARANCE OF MRS. NUTTER. P. 192.

a small box in the other, and, to her unspeakable horror, disclosed the livid and contorted countenance of Mistress Nutter.

Dreadful though undefined suspicions crossed her mind, and she feared, if discovered, she should be sacrificed to the fury of this strange and terrible woman. Luckily, where she stood, though Mistress Nutter was revealed to her, she herself was screened from view by the hangings of the bed, and looking around for a hiding-place, she observed that the mysterious wardrobe, close behind her, was open, and without a moment's hesitation, she slipped into the covert and drew the door to, noiselessly. But her curiosity overmastered her fear, and, firmly believing some magical rite was about to be performed, she sought for means of beholding it; nor was she long in discovering a small eyelet-hole in the carving which commanded the room.

Unconscious of any other presence than that of Alizon, whose stupor appeared to occasion her no uneasiness, Mistress Nutter, placed the lamp upon the table, made fast the door, and, muttering some unintelligible words, unlocked the box. It contained two singularly-shaped glass vessels, the one filled with a bright sparkling liquid, and the other with a greenish-coloured unguent. Pouring forth a few drops of the liquid into a glass near her, Mistress Nutter swallowed them, and then taking some of the unguent upon her hands, proceeded to anoint her face and neck with it, exclaiming as she did so, "Emen hetan! Emen hetan!"—words that fixed themselves upon the listener's memory.

Wondering what would follow, Dorothy gazed on, when she suddenly lost sight of Mistress Nutter, and after looking for her as far as her range of vision, limited by the aperture, would extend, she became convinced that she had left the room. All remaining quiet, she ventured, after awhile, to quit her hiding-place, and flying to Alizon, tried to waken her, but in vain. The poor girl retained the same moveless attitude, and appeared plunged in a deathly stupor.

Much frightened, Dorothy resolved to alarm the house, but some fears of Mistress Nutter restrained her, and she crept towards the closet to see whether that dread lady could be there. All was perfectly still; and somewhat emboldened, she returned to the table, where the box, which was left open and its contents unguarded, attracted her attention.

What was the liquid in the phial? What could it do? These were questions she asked herself, and longing to try the effect, she ventured at last to pour forth a few drops and taste it. It was like a potent distillation, and she became instantly sensible of a strange bewildering excitement. Presently her brain reeled, and she laughed wildly. Never before had she felt so light and buoyant, and wings seemed scarcely wanting to enable her to fly. An idea occurred to her. The wondrous liquid might arouse Alizon. The experiment should be tried at once, and, dipping her finger in the phial, she touched the lips of the sleeper, who sighed deeply and opened her eyes. Another drop, and Alizon was on her feet, gazing at her in astonishment, and laughing wildly as herself.

Poor girls! how wild and strange they looked—and how unlike themselves!

"Whither are you going?" cried Alizon.

"To the moon! to the stars!—any where!" rejoined Dorothy, with a laugh of frantic glee.

"I will go with you," cried Alizon, echoing the laugh.

"Here and there!—here and there!" exclaimed Dorothy, taking her hand. "Emen hetan! Emen hetan!"

As the mystic words were uttered they started away. It seemed as if no impediments could stop them; how they crossed the closet, passed through a sliding panel into the abbot's room, entered the oratory, and from it descended, by a secret staircase, to the garden, they knew not—but there they were, gliding swiftly along in the moonlight, like winged spirits. What took them towards the conventual church they could not say. But they were drawn thither, as the ship was irresistibly dragged towards the loadstone rock described in the Eastern legend. Nothing surprised them then, or they might have been struck by the dense vapour, enveloping the monastic ruins, and shrouding them from view; nor was it until they entered the desecrated fabric, that any consciousness of what was passing around returned to them.

Their ears were then assailed by a wild hubbub of discordant sounds, hootings and croakings as of owls and ravens, shrieks and jarring cries as of night-birds, bellowings as of cattle, groans and dismal sounds, mixed with unearthly laughter. Undefined and extraordinary shapes, whether men or women, beings of this world or of another they could not tell, though they judged them the latter, flew past with wild whoops and piercing cries, flapping the air as if with great leathern bat-like wings, or bestriding black, monstrous, misshapen steeds. Fantastical and grotesque were these objects, yet hideous and appalling. Now and then a red and fiery star would whiz crackling through the air, and then exploding break into numerous pale phosphoric lights, that danced awhile overhead, and then flitted away among the ruins. The ground seemed to heave and tremble beneath the footsteps, as if the graves were opening to give forth their dead, while toads and hissing reptiles crept forth.

Appalled, yet partly restored to herself by this confused and horrible din, Alizon stood still and kept fast hold of Dorothy, who, seemingly under a stronger influence than herself, was drawn towards the eastern end of the fane, where a fire appeared to be blazing, a strong ruddy glare being cast upon the broken roof of the choir, and the mouldering arches around it. The noises around them suddenly ceased, and all the uproar seemed concentrated near the spot where the fire was burning. Dorothy besought her friend so earnestly to let her see what was going forward, that Alizon reluctantly and tremblingly assented, and they moved slowly towards the transept, taking care to keep under the shelter of the columns.

On reaching the last pillar, behind which they remained, an extraordinary and fearful spectacle burst upon them. As they had supposed, a large fire was burning in the midst of the choir, the smoke of which, ascending in eddying wreaths, formed a dark canopy overhead, where it was mixed with the steam issuing from a large black bubbling caldron set on the blazing embers. Around the fire were ranged, in a wide circle, an assemblage of men and women, but chiefly the latter, and of these almost all old, hideous, and of malignant aspect, their grim and sinister features looking ghastly in the lurid light. Above them, amid the smoke and steam, wheeled bat and flitter-mouse, horned owl and screech-owl, in mazy circles. The weird assemblage chattered together in some wild jargon, mumbling and muttering spells and incantations, chanting fearfully with hoarse, cracked voices a wild chorus, and anon breaking into a loud and long-continued peal of laughter. Then there was more mumbling, chattering, and singing, and one of the troop producing a wallet, hobbled forward.

She was a fearful old crone; hunchbacked, toothless, blear-eyed, bearded, halt, with huge gouty feet swathed in flannel. As she cast in the ingredients one by one, she chanted thus:—

> "Head of monkey, brain of cat,
> Eye of weasel, tail of rat,
> Juice of mugwort, mastic, myrrh—
> All within the pot I stir."

"Well sung, Mother Mould-heels," cried a little old man, whose doublet and hose were of rusty black, with a short cloak, of the same hue, over his shoulders. "Well sung, Mother Mould-heels," he cried, advancing as the old witch retired, amidst a roar of laughter from the others, and chanting as he filled the caldron:

> "Here is foam from a mad dog's lips,
> Gather'd beneath the moon's eclipse,
> Ashes of a shroud consumed,
> And with deadly vapour fumed.
> These within the mess I cast—
> Stir the caldron—stir it fast!"

A red-haired witch then took his place, singing,

> "Here are snakes from out the river,
> Bones of toad and sea-calf's liver;
> Swine's flesh fatten'd on her brood,
> Wolf's tooth, hare's foot, weasel's blood.
> Skull of ape and fierce baboon,
> And panther spotted like the moon;
> Feathers of the horned owl,
> Daw, pie, and other fatal fowl.
> Fruit from fig-tree never sown.
> Seed from cypress never grown.
> All within the mess I cast,
> Stir the caldron—stir it fast!"

Nance Redferne then advanced, and, taking from her wallet a small clay image, tricked out in attire intended to resemble that of James Device, plunged several pins deeply into its breast, singing as she did so, thus,—

"In his likeness it is moulded,
In his vestments 'tis enfolded.
Ye may know it, as I show it!
In its breast sharp pins I stick,
And I drive them to the quick.
They are in—they are in—
And the wretch's pangs begin.
Now his heart,
Feels the smart;
Through his marrow,
Sharp as arrow,
Torments quiver
He shall shiver,
He shall burn,
He shall toss, and he shall turn.
Unavailingly.
Aches shall rack him,
Cramps attack him;
He shall wail,
Strength shall fail,
Till he die
Miserably!"

As Nance retired, another witch advanced, and sung thus:

"Over mountain, over valley, over woodland, over waste,
On our gallant broomsticks riding we have come with frantic haste,
And the reason of our coming, as ye wot well, is to see
Who this night, as new-made witch, to our ranks shall added be."

A wild burst of laughter followed this address, and another wizard succeeded, chanting thus:

"Beat the water, Demdike's daughter!
Till the tempest gather o'er us;
Till the thunder strike with wonder
And the lightnings flash before us!
Beat the water, Demdike's daughter!
Ruin seize our foes and slaughter!"

As the words were uttered, a woman stepped from out the circle, and throwing back the grey-hooded cloak in which she was enveloped, disclosed the features of Elizabeth Device. Her presence in that fearful assemblage occasioned no surprise to Alizon, though it increased her horror. A pail of water was next set before the witch, and a broom being placed in her hand, she struck the lymph with it, sprinkling it aloft, and uttering this spell:

"Mount, water, to the skies!
Bid the sudden storm arise.
Bid the pitchy clouds advance,
Bid the forked lightnings glance,
Bid the angry thunder growl,
Bid the wild wind fiercely howl!
Bid the tempest come amain,
Thunder, lightning, wind, and rain!"

As she concluded, clouds gathered thickly overhead, obscuring

THE INCANTATION. P. 196.

the stars that had hitherto shone down from the heavens. The wind suddenly arose, but in lieu of dispersing the vapours it seemed only to condense them. A flash of forked lightning cut through the air, and a loud peal of thunder rolled overhead.

Then the whole troop sang together—

"Beat the water, Demdike's daughter!
See the tempests gathers o'er us,
Lightning flashes—thunder crashes,
Wild winds sing in lusty chorus!"

For a brief space the storm raged fearfully, and recalled the terror of that previously witnessed by Alizon, which she now began to think might have originated in a similar manner. The wind raved around the ruined pile, but its breath was not felt within it, and the rain was heard descending in deluging showers without, though no drop came through the open roof. The thunder shook the walls and pillars of the old fabric, and threatened to topple them down from their foundations, but they resisted the shocks. The lightning played around the tall spire springing from this part of the fane, and ran down from its shattered summit to its base, without doing any damage. The red bolts struck the ground innocuously, though they fell at the very feet of the weird assemblage, who laughed wildly at the awful tumult.

Whilst the storm was at its worst, while the lightning was flashing fiercely, and the thunder rattling loudly, Mother Chattox, with a chafing-dish in her hand, advanced towards the fire, and placing the pan upon it, threw certain herbs and roots into it, chanting thus:—

"Here is juice of poppy bruised,
With black hellebore infused;
Here is mandrake's bleeding root,
Mixed with moonshade's deadly fruit;
Viper's bag with venom fill'd,
Taken ere the beast was kill'd;
Adder's skin and raven's feather,
With shell of beetle blent together;
Dragonwort and barbatus,
Hemlock black and poisonous;
Horn of hart, and storax red,
Lapwing's blood, at midnight shed.
In the heated pan they burn,
And to pungent vapours turn.
By this strong suffumigation,
By this potent invocation,
Spirits! I compel you here!
All who list may call appear!"

After a moment's pause, she resumed as follows:—

"White-robed brethren, who of old,
Nightly paced yon cloisters cold,
Sleeping now beneath the mould!
I bid ye rise.

"Abbots! by the weakling fear'd,
By the credulous revered,
Who this mighty fabric rear'd!
I bid ye rise!

"And thou last and guilty one!
By thy lust of power undone,
Whom in death thy fellows shun!
I bid thee come!

"And thou fair one, who disdain'd
To keep the vows thy lips had feign'd;
And thy snowy garments stain'd!
I bid thee come!"

During this invocation, the glee of the assemblage ceased, and they looked around in hushed expectation of the result. Slowly then did a long procession of monkish forms, robed in white, glide along the aisles, and gather round the altar. The brass-covered stones within the presbytery were lifted up, as if they moved on hinges, and from the yawning graves beneath them arose solemn shapes, sixteen in number, each with mitre on head and crosier in hand, which likewise proceeded to the altar. Then a loud cry was heard, and from a side chapel burst the monkish form, in mouldering garments, which Dorothy had seen enter the oratory, and which would have mingled with its brethren at the altar, but they waved it off menacingly. Another piercing shriek followed, and a female shape, habited like a nun, and of surpassing loveliness, issued from the opposite chapel, and hovered near the fire. Content with this proof of her power, Mother Chattox waved her hand, and the long shadowy train glided off as they came. The ghostly abbots returned to their tombs, and the stones closed over them. But the shades of Paslew and Isole de Heton still lingered.

The storm had wellnigh ceased, the thunder rolled hollowly at intervals, and a flash of lightning now and then licked the walls. The weird crew had resumed their rites, when the door of the Lacy chapel flew open, and a tall female figure came forward.

Alizon doubted if she beheld aright. Could that terrific woman in the strangely-fashioned robe of white, girt by a brazen zone graven with mystic characters, with a long glittering blade in her hand, infernal fury in her wildly-rolling orbs, the livid hue of death on her cheeks, and the red brand upon her brow—could that fearful woman, with the black dishevelled tresses floating over her bare shoulders, and whose gestures were so imperious, be Mistress Nutter? Mother no longer, if it indeed were she! How came she there amid that weird assemblage? Why did they so humbly salute her, and fall prostrate before her, kissing the hem of her garment? Why did she stand proudly in the midst of them, and extend her hand, armed with the knife, over them? Was she their sovereign mistress, that they bent so lowly at her coming, and rose so reverentially at her bidding? Was this terrible woman, now seated on a dilapidated tomb, and regarding the dark conclave with the eye of a queen who held their lives in her hands—was she her mother? Oh, no!—no!—it could not be! It must be some fiend that usurped her likeness.

Still, though Alizon thus strove to discredit the evidence of her senses, and to hold all she saw to be delusion, and the work of darkness, she could not entirely convince herself, but imperfectly recalling the fearful vision she had witnessed during her former stupor, began to connect it with the scene now passing before her. The storm had wholly ceased, and the stars again twinkled down through the shattered roof. Deep silence prevailed, broken only by the hissing and bubbling of the caldron.

Alizon's gaze was riveted upon her mother, whose slightest gestures she watched. After numbering the assemblage thrice, Mistress Nutter majestically arose, and motioning Mother Chattox towards her, the old witch tremblingly advanced, and some words passed between them, the import of which did not reach the listener's ear. In conclusion, however, Mistress Nutter exclaimed aloud, in accents of command—"Go, bring it at once, the sacrifice must be made."—And on this, Mother Chattox hobbled off to one of the side chapels.

A mortal terror seized Alizon, and she could scarcely draw breath. Dark tales had been told her that unbaptised infants were sometimes sacrificed by witches, and their flesh boiled and devoured at their impious banquets, and dreading lest some such atrocity was now about to be practised, she mustered all her resolution, determined, at any risk, to interfere, and, if possible, prevent its accomplishment.

In another moment, Mother Chattox returned bearing some living thing, wrapped in a white cloth, which struggled feebly for liberation, apparently confirming Alizon's suspicions, and she was about to rush forward, when Mistress Nutter, snatching the bundle from the old witch, opened, it and disclosed a beautiful bird, with plumage white as driven snow, whose legs were tied together, so that it could not escape. Conjecturing what was to follow, Alizon averted her eyes, and when she looked round again the bird had been slain, while Mother Chattox was in the act of throwing its body into the caldron, muttering a charm as she did so. Mistress Nutter held the ensanguined knife aloft, and casting some ruddy drops upon the glowing embers, pronounced, as they hissed and smoked, the following adjuration:—

"Thy aid I seek, infernal Power!
Be thy word sent to Malkin Tower,
That the beldame old may know
Where I will, thou'dst have her go—
What I will, thou'dst have her do!"

An immediate response was made by an awful voice issuing apparently from the bowels of the earth.

"Thou who seek'st the Demon's aid,
Know'st the price that must be paid."

The queen witch rejoined—

"I do. But grant the aid I crave,
And that thou wishest thou shalt have.
Another worshipper is won,
Thine to be, when all is done."

Again the deep voice spake, with something of mockery in its accents:—

" Enough proud witch, I am content.
To Malkin Tower the word is sent,
Forth to her task the beldame goes,
And where she points the streamlet flows;
Its customary bed forsaking,
Another distant channel making.
Round about like elfets tripping,
Stock and stone, and tree are skipping;
Halting where she plants her staff,
With a wild exulting laugh.
Ho! ho! 'tis a merry sight,
Thou hast given the hag to-night.

Lo! the sheepfold, and the herd,
To another site are stirr'd!
And the rugged limestone quarry,
Where 'twas digg'd may no more tarry;
While the goblin haunted dingle,
With another dell must mingle.
Pendle Moor is in commotion,
Like the billows of the ocean,
When the winds are o'er it ranging,
Heaving, falling, bursting, changing.
Ho! ho! 'tis a merry sight
Thou hast given the hag to-night.

Lo! the moss-pool sudden flies
In another spot to rise;
And the scanty-grown plantation,
Finds another situation,
And a more congenial soil,
Without needing woodman's toil.
Now the warren moves—and see!
How the burrowing rabbits flee,
Hither, thither till they find it,
With another brake behind it.
Ho! ho! 'tis a merry sight
Thou hast given the hag to-night.

Lo! new lines the witch is tracing,
Every well-known mark effacing,
Elsewhere, other bounds erecting,
So the old there's no detecting.
Ho! ho! 'tis a pastime quite,
Thou hast given the hag to-night!

The hind at eve, who wander'd o'er
The dreary waste of Pendle Moor,
Shall wake at dawn, and in surprise,
Doubt the strange sight that meets his eyes.
The pathway leading to his hut
Winds differently,—the gate is shut.
The ruin on the right that stood,
Lies on the left, and nigh the wood;
The paddock fenced with wall of stone,
Well-stock'd with kine, a mile hath flown,
The sheepfold and the herd are gone.
Through channels new the brooklet rushes,
Its ancient course conceal'd by bushes.
Where the hollow was, a mound
Rises from the upheaved ground.
Doubting, shouting with surprise,
How the fool stares, and rubs his eyes!

All's so changed, the simple elf
Fancies he is changed himself!
Ho! ho! 'tis a merry sight
The hag shall have when dawns the light.
But see! she halts and waves her hand.
All is done as thou hast plann'd."

After a moment's pause the voice added,

"I have done as thou hast will'd—
Now be thy path straight fulfill'd."

"It shall be," replied Mistress Nntter, whose features gleamed with fierce exultation. "Bring forth the proselyte!" she shouted.

And at the words, her swarthy serving-man, Blackadder, came forth from the Lacy chapel, leading Jennet by the hand. They were followed by Tib, who, dilated to twice his former size, walked with tail erect, and eyes glowing like carbuncles.

At sight of her daughter a loud cry of rage and astonishment burst from Elizabeth Device, and, rushing forward, she would have seized her, if Tib had not kept her off by a formidable display of teeth and talons. Jennet made no effort to join her mother, but regarded her with a malicious and triumphant grin.

"This is my chilt," screamed Elizabeth. "She canna be baptised without my consent, an ey refuse it. Ey dunna want her to be a witch—at least not yet awhile. What mays yo here, yo little plague?"

"Ey wur brought here, mother," replied Jennet, with affected simplicity.

"Then get whoam at once, and keep there," rejoined Elizabeth, furiously.

"Nay, eyst nah go just yet," replied Jennet. "Ey'd fain be a witch as weel as yo."

"Ho! ho! ho!" laughed the voice from below.

"Nah, nah—ey forbid it," shrieked Elizabeth, "ye shanna be bapteesed. Whoy ha ye brought her here, madam?" she added to Mistress Nutter. "Yo ha' stolen her fro' me. Boh ey protest agen it."

"Your consent is not required," replied Mistress Nutter, waving her off. "Your daughter is anxious to become a witch. That is enough."

"She is not owd enough to act for herself," said Elizabeth.

"Age matters not," replied Mistress Nutter.

"What mun ey do to become a witch?" asked Jennet.

"You must renounce all hopes of heaven," replied Mistress Nutter, "and devote yourself to Satan. You will then be baptised in his name, and become one of his worshippers. You will have power to afflict all persons with bodily ailments—to destroy cattle—blight corn—burn dwellings—and, if you be so minded, kill those you hate, or who molest you. Do you desire to do all this?"

"Eigh, that ey do," replied Jennet. "Ey ha' more pleasure

in evil than in good, an wad rayther see folk weep than laugh; an if cy had the power, ey wad so punish them os jeer at me, that they should rue it to their deein' day."

"All this you shall do, and more," rejoined Mistress Nutter. "You renounce all hopes of salvation, then, and devote yourself, soul and body, to the Powers of Darkness."

Elizabeth, who was still kept at bay by Tib, shaking her arms, and gnashing her teeth, in impotent rage, now groaned aloud; but ere Jennet could answer, a piercing cry was heard, which thrilled through Mistress Nutter's bosom, and Alizon, rushing from her place of concealment, passed through the weird circle, and stood beside the group in the midst of it.

"Forbear, Jennet," she cried; "forbear! Pronounce not those impious words, or you are lost for ever. Come with me, and I will save you."

"Sister Alizon," cried Jennet, staring at her in surprise, "what makes you here?"

"Do not ask—but come," cried Alizon, trying to take her hand.

"Oh! what is this?" cried Mistress Nutter, now partly recovered from the consternation and astonishment into which she had been thrown by Alizon's unexpected appearance. "Why are you here? How have you broken the chains of slumber in which I bound you? Fly—fly—at once, this girl is past your help. You cannot save her. She is already devoted. Fly. I am powerless to protect you here."

"Ho! ho! ho!" laughed the voice.

"Do you not hear that laughter?" cried Mistress Nutter, with a haggard look. "Go!"

"Never, without Jennet," replied Alizon, firmly.

"My child—my child—on my knees I implore you to depart," cried Mistress Nutter, throwing herself before her—"You know not your danger—oh, fly—fly!"

But Alizon continued inflexible.

"Yo are caught i' your own snare, madam," cried Elizabeth Device, with a taunting laugh. "Sin Jennet mun be a witch, Alizon con be bapteesed os weel. Your consent is not required —and age matters not—ha! ha!"

"Curses upon thy malice," cried Mistress Nutter, rising. "What can be done in this extremity?"

"Nothing," replied the voice. "Jennet is mine already. If not brought hither by thee, or by her mother, she would have come of her own accord. I have watched her, and marked her for my own. Besides, she is fated. The curse of Paslew clings to her."

As the words were uttered, the shade of the abbot glided forwards, and, touching the shuddering child upon the brow with its finger, vanished with a lamentable cry.

"Kneel, Jennet," cried Alizon; "kneel, and pray!"

"To me," rejoined the voice; "she can bend to no other power. Alice Nutter, thou hast sought to deceive me, but in vain. I bade thee bring thy daughter here, and in place of her thou offerest me the child of another, who is mine already. I am not to be thus trifled with. Thou knowest my will. Sprinkle water over her head, and devote her to me."

Alizon would fain have thrown herself on her knees, but extremity of horror, or some overmastering influence, held her fast; and she remained with her gaze fixed upon her mother, who seemed torn by conflicting emotions.

"Is there no way to avoid this?" cried Mistress Nutter.

"No way but one," replied the voice. "I have been offered a new devotee, and I claim fulfilment of the promise. Thy daughter or another, it matters not—but not Jennet."

"I embrace the alternative," cried Mistress Nutter.

"It must be done upon the instant," said the voice.

"It shall be," replied Mistress Nutter. And, stretching her arm in the direction of the mansion, she called in a loud imperious voice, "Dorothy Assheton, come hither!"

A minute elapsed, but no one appeared, and, with a look of disappointment, Mistress Nutter repeated the gesture and the words.

Still no one came.

"Baffled!" she exclaimed, "what can it mean?"

"There is a maiden within the south transept, who is not one of my servants," cried the voice. "Call her."

"'Tis she!" cried Mistress Nutter, stretching her arm towards the transept. "This time I am answered," she added, as with a wild laugh Dorothy obeyed the summons.

"I have anointed myself with the unguent, and drank of the potion, ha! ha! ha!" cried Dorothy, with a wild gesture, and wilder laughter.

"Ha! this accounts for her presence here," muttered Mistress Nutter. "But it could not be better. She is in no mood to offer resistance. Dorothy, thou shalt be a witch."

"A witch!" exclaimed the bewildered maiden. "Is Alizon a witch?"

"We are all witches here," replied Mistress Nutter.

Alizon had no power to contradict her.

"A merry company!" exclaimed Dorothy, laughing loudly.

"You will say so anon," replied Mistress Nutter, waving her hand over her, and muttering a spell; "but you see them not in their true forms, Dorothy. Look again—what do you behold now?"

"In place of a troop of old wrinkled crones in wretched habiliments," replied Dorothy, "I behold a band of lovely nymphs in light gauzy attire, wreathed with flowers, and holding myrtle and olive branches in their hands. See they rise, and prepare for the dance. Strains of ravishing music salute the ear. I never heard sounds so sweet and stirring. The round is formed. The dance begins. How gracefully—how lightly they move—ha! ha!"

Alizon could not check her—could not undeceive her—for power of speech as of movement was denied her, but she comprehended the strange delusion under which the poor girl laboured. The figures Dorothy described as young and lovely, were still to her the same loathsome and abhorrent witches; the ravishing music jarred discordantly on her ear, as if produced by a shrill cornemuse; and the lightsome dance was a fantastic round, performed with shouts and laughter by the whole unhallowed crew.

Jennet laughed immoderately, and seemed delighted by the antics of the troop.

"Ey never wished to dance efore," she cried, "boh ey should like to try now."

"Join them, then," said Mistress Nutter.

And to the little girl's infinite delight a place was made for her in the round, and, taking hands with Mother Mould-heels and the red-haired witch, she footed it as merrily as the rest.

"Who is she in the nunlike habit?" inquired Dorothy, pointing to the shade of Isole de Heton, which still hovered near the weird assemblage. "She seems more beautiful than all the others. Will she not dance with me?"

"Heed her not," said Mistress Nutter.

Dorothy, however, would not be gainsaid, but, spite of the caution, beckoned the figure towards her. It came at once, and in another instant its arms were enlaced around her. The same frenzy that had seized Nicholas now took possession of Dorothy, and her dance with Isole might have come to a similar conclusion, if it had not been abruptly checked by Mistress Nutter, who, waving her hand, and pronouncing a spell, the figure instantly quitted Dorothy, and, with a wild shriek, fled.

"How like you these diversions?" said Mistress Nutter to the panting and almost breathless maiden.

"Marvellously," replied Dorothy; "but why have you scared my partner away?"

"Because she would have done you a mischief," rejoined Mistress Nutter. But now let me put a question to you. Are you willing to renounce your baptism, and enter into a covenant with the Prince of Darkness?"

Dorothy did not seem in the least to comprehend what was said to her; but she nevertheless replied, "I am."

"Bring water and salt," said Mistress Nutter to Mother Chattox. "By these drops I baptise you," she added, dipping her fingers in the liquid, and preparing to sprinkle it over the brow of the proselyte.

Then it was that Alizon, by an almost superhuman effort, burst the spell that bound her, and clasped Dorothy in her arms.

"You know not what you do, dear Dorothy," she cried. "I answer for you. You will not yield to the snares and temptations of Satan, however subtly devised. You defy him and all his works. You will make no covenant with him. Though surrounded by his bond-slaves, you fear him not. Is it not so? Speak!"

But Dorothy could only answer with an insane laugh—"I will be a witch."

"It is too late," interposed Mistress Nutter. "You cannot save her. And, remember! she stands in your place. Or you or she must be devoted."

"I will never desert her," cried Alizon, twining her arms round her. "Dorothy—dear Dorothy—address yourself to Heaven."

An angry growl of thunder was heard.

"Beware!" cried Mistress Nutter.

"I am not to be discouraged," rejoined Alizon, firmly. "You cannot gain a victory over a soul in this condition, and I shall effect her deliverance. Heaven will aid us, Dorothy."

A louder roll of thunder was heard, followed by a forked flash of lightning.

"Provoke not the vengeance of the Prince of Darkness," said Mistress Nutter.

"I have no fear," replied Alizon. "Cling to me, Dorothy. No harm shall befall you."

"Be speedy!" cried the voice.

"Let her go," cried Mistress Nutter to Alizon, "or you will rue this disobedience. Why should you interfere with my projects, and bring ruin on yourself! I would save you. What, still obstinate? Nay, then, I will no longer show forbearance. Help me, sisters. Force the new witch from her. But beware how you harm my child."

At these words the troop gathered round the two girls. But Alizon only clasped her hands more tightly round Dorothy; while the latter, on whose brain the maddening potion still worked, laughed frantically at them. It was at this moment that Elizabeth Device, who had conceived a project of revenge, put it into execution. While near Dorothy, she stamped, spat on the ground, and then cast a little mould over her, breathing in her ear, "Thou art bewitched—bewitched by Alizon Device."

Dorothy instantly struggled to free herself from Alizon.

"Oh! do not you strive against me, dear Dorothy," cried Alizon. "Remain with me, or you are lost."

"Hence! off! set me free!" shrieked Dorothy; "you have bewitched me. I heard it this moment."

"Do not believe the false suggestion," cried Alizon.

"It is true," exclaimed all the other witches together. "Alizon has bewitched you, and will kill you. Shake her off—shake her off!"

"Away!" cried Dorothy, mustering all her force. "Away!"

But Alizon was still too strong for her, and, in spite of her efforts at liberation, detained her.

"My patience is wellnigh exhausted," exclaimed the voice.

"Alizon!" cried Mistress Nutter, imploringly.

And again the witches gathered furiously round the two girls.

"Kneel, Dorothy, kneel!" whispered Alizon. And forcing her down, she fell on her knees beside her, exclaiming, with uplifted hands, "Gracious heaven! deliver us."

As the words were uttered, a fearful cry was heard, and the weird troop fled away screaming, like ill-omened birds. The caldron sank into the ground; the dense mist arose like a curtain; and the moon and stars shone brightly down upon the ruined pile.

Alizon prayed long and fervently, with clasped hands and closed eyes, for deliverance from evil. When she looked round again, all was so calm, so beautiful, so holy in its rest, that she could scarcely believe in the recent fearful occurrences. Her hair and garments were damp with the dews of night; and at her feet lay Dorothy, insensible.

She tried to raise her—to revive her, but in vain; when at this moment footsteps were heard approaching, and the next moment Mistress Nutter, accompanied by Adam Whitworth and some other serving-men, entered the choir.

"I see them—they are here!" cried the lady, rushing forward.

"Heaven be praised you have found them, madam!" exclaimed the old steward, coming quickly after her.

"Oh! what an alarm you have given me, Alizon," said Mistress Nutter. "What could induce you to go forth secretly at night in this way with Dorothy! I dreamed you were here, and missing you when I awoke, roused the house and came in search of you. What is the matter with Dorothy? She has been frightened, I suppose. I will give her to breathe at this phial. It will revive her. See, she opens her eyes.

Dorothy looked round wildly for a moment, and then pointing her finger at Alizon, said—

"She has bewitched me."

"Poor thing! she rambles," observed Mistress Nutter to Adam Whitworth, who, with the other serving-men, stared aghast at the accusation; "she has been scared out of her senses by some fearful sight. Let her be conveyed quickly to my chamber, and I will see her cared for."

The orders were obeyed. Dorothy was raised gently by the serving-men, but she still kept pointing to Alizon, and repeatedly exclaimed—

"She has bewitched me!"

The serving-men shook their heads, and looked significantly at each other, while Mistress Nutter lingered to speak to her daughter.

"You look greatly disturbed, Alizon, as if you had been visited by a nightmare in your sleep, and were still under its influence."

Alizon made no reply.

"A few hours' tranquil sleep will restore you," pursued Mistress Nutter, "and you will forget your fears. You must not indulge in these nocturnal rambles again, or they may be attended with dangerous consequences. I may not have a second warning dream. Come to the house."

And, as Alizon followed her along the garden path, she could not help asking herself, though with little hope in the question, if all she had witnessed was indeed nothing more than a troubled dream.

END OF THE FIRST BOOK.

THE LANCASHIRE WITCHES

BOOK THE SECOND.

Pendle Forest.

CHAPTER I.—FLINT.

A LOVELY morning succeeded the strange and terrible night. Brightly shone the sun upon the fair Calder as it winded along the green meads above the bridge, as it rushed rejoicingly over the weir, and pursued its rapid course through the broad plain below the Abbey. A few white vapours hung upon the summit of Whalley Nab, but the warm rays tinging them with gold, and tipping with fire the tree-tops that pierced through them, augured their speedy dispersion. So beautiful, so tranquil, looked the old monastic fane, that none would have deemed its midnight rest had been broken by the impious rites of a foul troop. The choir, where the unearthly scream and the demon laughter had resounded, was now vocal with the melodies of the blackbird, the thrush, and other songsters of the grove. Bells of dew glittered upon the bushes rooted in the walls, and upon the ivy-grown pillars; and gemming the countless spiders' webs stretched from bough to bough, showed they were all unbroken. No traces were visible on the sod where the unhallowed crew had danced their round; nor were any ashes left where the fire had burnt and the caldron had bubbled. The brass-covered tombs of the abbots in the presbytery looked as if a century had passed over them without disturbance; while the graves in the cloister cemetery, obliterated, and only to be detected when a broken coffin or a mouldering bone was turned up by the tiller of the ground, preserved their wonted appearance. The face of nature had received neither impress nor injury from the fantastic freaks and necromantic exhibitions of the witches. Every thing looked as it was left overnight; and the only footprints to be detected were those of the two girls, and of the party who came in quest of them. All else had passed by like a vision or a dream. The rooks cawed loudly in the neighbouring trees, as if discussing the question of breakfast, and the jackdaws wheeled merrily round the tall spire, which sprang from the eastern end of the fane.

Brightly shone the sun upon the noble timber embowering the mansion of the Asshetons; upon the ancient gateway, in the upper chamber of which Ned Huddlestone, the porter, and the burly representative of Friar Tuck, was rubbing his sleepy eyes, preparatory to habiting himself in his ordinary attire; and upon the wide court-yard, across which Nicholas was walking in the direction of the stables. Notwithstanding his excesses overnight, the squire was astir, as he had declared he should be, before day-break; and a plunge into the Calder had cooled his feverish limbs and cured his racking headache, while a draught of ale set his stomach right. Still, in modern parlance, he looked rather "seedy," and his recollection of the events of the previous night was somewhat confused. Aware he had committed many fooleries, he did not desire to investigate matters too closely, and only hoped he should not be reminded of them by Sir Ralph, or worse still, by Parson Dewhurst. As to his poor, dear, uncomplaining wife, he never once troubled his head about her, feeling quite sure she would not upbraid him. On his appearance in the court-yard, the two noble blood-hounds and several lesser dogs came forward to greet him, and, attended by this noisy pack, he marched up to a groom, who was rubbing down his horse at the stable-door.

"Poor Robin," he cried to the steed, who neighed at his approach. "Poor Robin," he said, patting his neck affectionately, "there is not thy match for speed or endurance, for fence or ditch, for beck or stone wall, in the country. Half an hour on thy back will make all right with me; but I would rather take thee to Bowland Forest, and hunt the stag there, than go and perambulate the boundaries of the Rough Lee estates with a rascally attorney. I wonder how the fellow will be mounted."

"If yo be speering about Mester Potts, squoire," observed the groom, "ey con tell ye. He's to ha' little Flint, the Welsh pony."

"Why, zounds, you don't say, Peter!" exclaimed Nicholas, laughing; "he'll never be able to manage him. Flint's the wickedest and most wilful little brute I ever knew. We shall have Master Potts run away with, or thrown into a moss-pit. Better give him something quieter."

"It's Sir Roaph's orders," replied Peter, "an ey darna disobey 'em. Boh Flint's far steadier than when yo seed him last, squoire. Ey dar say he'll carry Mester Potts weel enough, if he dusna mislest him."

"You think nothing of the sort, Peter," said Nicholas. "You expect to see the little gentleman fly over the pony's head, and perhaps break his own at starting. But if Sir Ralph has ordered it, he must abide by the consequences. I sha'n't interfere further. How goes on the young colt you were breaking in? You should take care to show him the saddle in the manger, let him smell it, and jingle the stirrups in his ears, before you put it on his back. Better ground for his first lessons could not be desired than the field below the grange, near the Calder. Sir Ralph was saying yesterday, that the roan mare had pricked her foot. You must wash the sore well with white wine and salt, rub it with the ointment the farriers call ægyptiacum, and then put upon it a hot plaster compounded of flax hards, turpentine, oil and wax, bathing the top of the hoof with bole armeniac and vinegar. This is the best and quickest remedy. And recollect, Peter, that for a new strain, vinegar, bole armeniac, whites of eggs, and bean-flour, make the best salve. How goes on Sir Ralph's black charger, Dragon? A brave horse that, Peter, and the only one in your master's whole stud to compare with my Robin! But Dragon, though of high courage and great swiftness, has not the strength and endurance of Robin—neither can he leap so well. Why, Robin would almost clear the Calder, Peter, and makes nothing of Smithies Brook, near Downham, and you know how wide that stream is. I once tried him at the Ribble, at a narrow point. and if horse could have done it, he would—but it was too much to expect."

"A great deal, ey should say, squoire," replied the groom, opening his eyes to their widest extent. "Whoy, th' Ribble, where yo speak on, mun be twenty yards across, if it be an inch; and no nag os ever wur bred could clear that, onless a witch wur on his back."

"Don't allude to witches, Peter," said Nicholas. "I've had enough of them. But to come back to our steeds. Colour is matter of taste, and a man must please his own eye with bay or grey, chestnut, sorrel, or black; but dun is my fancy. A good horse, Peter, should be clean-limbed, short-jointed, strong-hoofed, out-ribbed, broad-chested, deep-necked, loose-throttled, thin-crested, lean-headed, full-eyed, with wide nostrils. A horse with half these points would not be wrong, and Robin has them all."

"So he has, sure enough, squoire," replied Peter, regarding the animal with an approving eye, as Nicholas enumerated his merits. "Boh, if ey might choose betwixt him an yunk Mester Ruchot Assheton's grey gelding, Merlin, ey knoas which ey'd tak."

"Robin, of course," said Nicholas.

"Nah, squoire, it should be t'other," replied the groom.

"You're no judge of a horse, Peter," rejoined Nicholas, shrugging his shoulders.

"May be not," said the groom, "boh ey'm bound to speak truth. An see! Tum Lomax is bringin' out Merlin. We con put th' two nags soide by soide, if yo choose."

"They shall be put side by side in the field, Peter—that's the way to test their respective merit," returned Nicholas, "and they won't remain long together, I'll warrant you. I offered to make a match for twenty pieces with Master Richard, but he declined the offer. Harkee, Peter, break an egg in Robin's mouth before you put on his bridle. It strengthens the wind, and adds to a horse's power of endurance. You understand?"

"Parfitly, squoire," replied the groom. "By th' mess! that's a secret worth knoain'. Onny more orders?"

"No," replied Nicholas. "We shall set out in an hour—or it may be sooner."

"Aw shan be ready," said Peter. And he added to himself, as Nicholas moved away, "Ey'st tak care Tum Lomax gies an egg to Merlin, an that'll may aw fair, if they chance to try their osses' mettle.

As Nicholas returned to the house, he perceived to his dismay Sir Ralph and Parson Dewhurst standing upon the steps; and convinced, from their grave looks, that they were prepared to lecture him, he endeavoured to nerve himself for the infliction.

"Two to one are awkward odds," said the squire to himself, "especially when they have the 'vantage ground. But I must face them, and make the best fight circumstances will allow. I shall never be able to explain that mad dance with Isole de Heton. No one but Dick will believe me, and the chances are he will not support my story. But I must put on an air of penitence, and sooth to say, in my present state, it is not very difficult to assume."

Thus pondering, with slow step, affectedly humble demeanour, and surprisingly-lengthened visage, he approached the pair who were waiting for him, and regarding him with severe looks.

Thinking it the best plan to open the fire himself, Nicholas saluted them, and said—

"Give you good-day, Sir Ralph, and you too, worthy Master Dewhurst. I scarcely expected to see you so early astir, good sirs; but the morning is too beautiful to allow us to be sluggards. For my own part I have been awake for hours, and have passed the time wholly in self-reproaches for my folly and sinfulness last night, as well as in forming resolutions for self-amendment, and better governance in future."

"I hope you will adhere to those resolutions, then, Nicholas," rejoined Sir Ralph, sternly; "for change of conduct is absolutely necessary, if you would maintain your character as a gentleman. I can make allowance for high animal spirits, and can excuse some licence, though I do not approve of it; but I will not permit decorum to be outraged in my house, and suffer so ill an example to be set to my tenantry."

"Fortunately I was not present at the exhibition," said Dewhurst; but I am told you conducted yourself like one possessed, and committed such freaks as are rarely, if ever, acted by a rational being."

"I can offer no defence, worthy sir, and you my respected relative," returned Nicholas, with a contrite air; "neither can you reprove me more strongly than I deserve, nor than I upbraid myself. I allowed myself to be overcome by wine, and in that condition was undoubtedly guilty of follies I must ever regret."

"Amongst others, I believe you stood upon your head," remarked Dewhurst.

"I am not aware of the circumstance, reverend sir," replied Nicholas, with difficulty repressing a smile; "but as I certainly lost my head, I may have stood upon it unconsciously. But I do recollect enough to make me heartily ashamed of myself, and determine to avoid all such excesses in future."

"In that case, sir," rejoined Dewhurst, "the occurrences of last night, though sufficiently discreditable to you, will not be without profit; for I have observed to my infinite regret, that you are apt to indulge in immoderate potations, and when under their influence to lose due command of yourself, and commit follies which your sober reason must condemn. At such times I scarcely recognise you. You speak with unbecoming levity, and even allow oaths to escape your lips."

"It is too true, reverend sir," said Nicholas; "but, zounds!—a plague upon my tongue—it is an unruly member. Forgive me, good sir, but my brain is a little confused."

"I do not wonder, from the grievous assaults made upon it last night, Nicholas," observed Sir Ralph. "Perhaps you are not aware that your crowning act was whisking wildly round the room by yourself, like a frantic dervish."

"I was dancing with Isole de Heton," said Nicholas.

"With whom?" inquired Dewhurst, in surprise.

"With a wicked votaress, who has been dead nearly a couple of centuries," interposed Sir Ralph; "and who, by her sinful life, merited the punishment she is said to have incurred. This delusion shows how dreadfully intoxicated you were, Nicholas. For the time you had quite lost your reason."

"I am sober enough now, at all events," rejoined Nicholas; "and I am convinced that Isole did dance with me, nor will any arguments reason me out of that belief."

"I am sorry to hear you say so, Nicholas," returned Sir Ralph. "That you were under the impression at the time I can easily understand; but that you should persist in such a senseless and wicked notion is more than I can comprehend."

"I saw her with my own eyes as plainly as I see you, Sir Ralph," replied Nicholas, warmly; "that I declare upon my honour and conscience, and I also felt the pressure of her arms. Whether it may not have been the Fiend in her likeness I will not take upon me to declare—and indeed I have some misgivings on the subject; but that a beautiful creature, exactly resembling the votaress, danced with me, I will ever maintain."

"If so, she was invisible to others, for I beheld her not," said Sir Ralph; "and, though I cannot yield credence to your explanation, yet, granting it to be correct, I do not see how it mends your case."

"On the contrary, it only proves that Master Nicholas yielded to the snares of Satan," said Dewhurst, shaking his head. "I would recommend you long fasting and frequent prayer, my good sir, and I shall prepare a lecture for your special edification, which I will propound to you on your return to Downham, and, if it fails in effect, I will persevere with other godly discourses."

"With your aid, I trust to be set free, reverend sir," returned Nicholas; "but, as I have already passed two or three hours in prayer, I hope they may stand me in lieu of any present fasting, and induce you to omit the article of penance, or postpone it to some future occasion, when I may be better able to perform it; for I am just now particularly hungry, and am always better able to resist temptation with a full stomach than an empty one. As I find it displeasing to Sir Ralph, I will not insist upon my visionary partner in the dance, at least until I am better able to substantiate the fact; and I shall listen to your lectures, worthy sir, with great delight, and, I doubt not, with equal benefit; but in the meantime, as carnal wants must be supplied, and mundane matters attended to, I propose, with our excellent host's permission, that we proceed to breakfast."

Sir Ralph made no answer, but ascended the steps, and was followed by Dewhurst, heaving a deep sigh, and turning up the whites of his eyes, and by Nicholas, who felt his bosom eased of half its load, and secretly congratulated himself upon getting out of the scrape so easily.

In the hall they found Richard Assheton habited in a riding-dress, booted, spurred, and in all respects prepared for the expedition. There were such evident traces of anxiety and suffering about him, that Sir Ralph questioned him as to the cause, and Richard replied that he had passed a most restless night. He did not add, that he had been made acquainted by Adam Whitworth with the midnight visit of the two girls to the conventual church, because he was well aware Sir Ralph would be greatly displeased by the circumstance, and because Mistress Nutter had expressed a wish that it should be kept secret. Sir Ralph, however, saw there was more upon his young relative's mind than he chose to confess, but he did not urge any further admission into his confidence.

Meantime, the party had been increased by the arrival of Master Potts, who was likewise equipped for the ride. The hour was too early, it might be, for him, or he had not rested well like Richard, or had been troubled with bad dreams, but certainly he did not look very well, or in very good-humour. He had slept at the Abbey, having been accommodated with a bed after the sudden seizure which he attributed to the instrumentality of Mistress Nutter. The little attorney bowed obsequiously to Sir Ralph, who returned his salutation very stiffly, nor was he much better received by the rest of the company.

At a sign from Sir Ralph, his guests then knelt down, and a prayer was uttered by the divine—or rather a discourse, for it partook more of the latter character than the former. In the course of it he took occasion to paint in strong colours the terrible consequences of intemperance, and Nicholas was obliged to endure a well-merited lecture of half an hour's duration. But even Parson Dewhurst could not hold out for ever, and, to the relief of all his hearers, he at length brought this discourse to a close.

Breakfast at this period was a much more substantial affair than a modern morning repast, and differed little from dinner or supper, except in respect to quantity. On the present occasion, there were carbonadoes of fish and fowl, a cold chine, a huge pasty, a capon, neat's tongues, sausages, botargos, and other matters as provocative of thirst as sufficing to the appetite. Nicholas set to work bravely. Broiled trout, steaks, and a huge slice of venison pasty, disappeared quickly before him, and he was not quite so sparing of the ale as seemed consistent with his previously-expressed resolutions of temperance. In vain Parson Dewhurst filled a goblet with water, and looked significantly at him. He would not take the hint, and turned a deaf ear to the admonitory cough of Sir Ralph. He had little help from the others, for Richard ate sparingly, and Master Potts made a very poor figure beside him. At length, having cleared his plate, emptied his cup, and wiped his lips, the squire arose, and said he must bid adieu to his wife, and should then be ready to attend them.

While he quitted the hall for this purpose, Mistress Nutter entered it. She looked paler than ever, and her eyes seemed larger, darker, and brighter. Nicholas shuddered slightly as she approached, and even Potts felt a thrill of apprehension pass through his frame. He scarcely, indeed, ventured a look at her, for he dreaded her mysterious power, and feared she could fathom the designs he secretly entertained against her. But she took no notice whatever of him. Acknowledging Sir Ralph's salutation, she motioned Richard to follow her to the further end of the room.

"Your sister is very ill, Richard," she said, as the young man attended her, "feverish, and almost light-headed. Adam Whitworth has told you, I know, that she was imprudent enough, in company with Alizon, to visit the ruins of the conventual church late last night, and she there sustained some fright, which has produced a great shock upon her system. When found, she was fainting, and though I have taken every care of her, she still continues much excited, and rambles strangely. You will be surprised as well as grieved when I tell you, that she charges Alizon with having bewitched her."

"How, madam!" cried Richard. "Alizon bewitch her! It is impossible."

"You are right, Richard," replied Mistress Nutter; "the thing is impossible; but the accusation will find easy credence among the superstitious household here, and may be highly prejudicial, if not fatal to poor Alizon. It is most unlucky she should have gone out in this way, for the circumstance cannot be explained, and in itself serves to throw suspicion upon her."

"I must see Dorothy before I go," said Richard; "perhaps I may be able to soothe her."

"It was for that end I came hither," replied Mistress Nutter; "but I thought it well you should be prepared. Now come with me."

Upon this they left the hall together, and proceeded to the abbot's chamber, where Dorothy was lodged. Richard was greatly shocked at the sight of his sister, so utterly changed was she from the blithe being of yesterday—then so full of health and happiness. Her cheeks burnt with fever, her eyes were unnaturally bright, and her fair hair hung about her face in disorder. She kept fast hold of Alizon, who stood beside her.

"Ah, Richard!" she cried on seeing him, "I am glad you are come. You will persuade this girl to restore me to reason—to free me from the terrors that beset me. She can do so if she will."

"Calm yourself, dear sister," said Richard, gently endeavouring to free Alizon from her grasp.

"No, do not take her from me," said Dorothy, wildly; "I am better when she is near me—much better. My brow does not throb so violently, and my limbs are not twisted so painfully. Do you know what ails me, Richard?"

"You have caught cold from wandering out indiscreetly last night," said Richard.

"I am bewitched!" rejoined Dorothy, in tones that pierced her brother's brain—"bewitched by Alizon Device—by your love—ha! ha! She wishes to kill me, Richard, because she thinks I am in her way. But you will not let her do it."

"You are mistaken, dear Dorothy. She means you no harm," said Richard.

"Heaven knows how much I grieve for her, and how fondly I love her!" exclaimed Alizon, tearfully.

"It is false!" cried Dorothy. "She will tell a different tale when you are gone. She is a witch, and you shall never marry her, Richard—never!—never!"

Mistress Nutter, who stood at a little distance, anxiously observing what was passing, waved her hand several times towards the sufferer, but without effect.

"I have no influence over her," she muttered. "She is really bewitched. I must find other means to quieten her."

Though both greatly distressed, Alizon and Richard redoubled their attentions to the poor sufferer. For a few moments she remained quiet, but with her eyes constantly fixed on Alizon, and then said, quickly and fiercely, "I have been told, if you scratch one who has bewitched you till you draw blood, you will be cured. I will plunge my nails in her flesh."

"I will not oppose you," replied Alizon, gently; "tear my flesh if you will. You should have my life's blood if it would cure you; but if the success of the experiment depends on my having bewitched you, it will assuredly fail."

"This is dreadful," interposed Richard. "Leave her, Alizon, I entreat of you. She will do you an injury."

"I care not," replied the young maid. "I will stay by her till she voluntarily releases me."

The almost tigress fury with which Dorothy had seized upon the unresisting girl here suddenly deserted her, and, sobbing hysterically, she fell upon her neck. Oh, with what delight Alizon pressed her to her bosom!

"Dorothy, dear Dorothy!" she cried.

"Alizon, dear Alizon!" responded Dorothy. "Oh! how could I suspect you of any ill design against me!"

"She is no witch, dear sister, be assured of that!" said Richard.

"Oh, no—no—no! I am quite sure she is not," cried Dorothy, kissing her affectionately.

This change had been wrought by the low-breathed spells of Mistress Nutter.

"The access is over," she mentally ejaculated; "but I must get him away before the fit returns. "You had better go now, Richard," she added aloud, and touching his arm, "I will answer for your sister's restoration. An opiate will produce sleep, and if possible, she shall return to Middleton to-day."

"If I go, Alizon must go with me," said Dorothy.

"Well, well, I will not thwart your desires," rejoined Mistress Nutter. And she made a sign to Richard to depart.

The young man pressed his sister's hand, bade a tender farewell to Alizon, and, infinitely relieved by the improvement which had taken place in the former, and which he firmly believed would speedily lead to her entire restoration, descended to the entrance-hall, where he found Sir Ralph and Parson Dewhurst, who told him that Nicholas and Potts were in the court-yard, and impatient to set out.

Shouts of laughter saluted the ears of the trio as they descended the steps. The cause of the merriment was speedily explained when they looked towards the stables, and beheld Potts struggling for mastery with a stout Welsh pony, who showed every disposition, by plunging, kicking, and rearing, to remove him from his seat, though without success, for the attorney was not quite such a contemptible horseman as might be imagined. A wicked-looking little fellow was Flint, with a rough, rusty-black coat, a thick tail that swept the ground, a mane to match, and an eye of mixed fire and cunning. When brought forth, he had allowed Potts to mount him quietly enough; but no sooner was the attorney comfortably in possession, than he was served with a notice of ejectment. Down went Flint's head and up went his heels; while on the next instant he was rearing aloft, with his fore-feet beating the air, so nearly perpendicular, that the chances seemed in favour of his coming down on his back. Then he whirled suddenly round, shook himself violently, threatened to roll over, and performed antics of the most extraordinary kind, to the dismay of his rider, but to the infinite amusement of the spectators, who were ready to split their sides with laughter —indeed, tears fairly streamed down the squire's cheeks. However, when Sir Ralph appeared, it was thought desirable to put an end to the fun; and Peter, the groom, advanced to seize the restive little animal's bridle, but, eluding the grasp, Flint started off at full gallop, and, accompanied by the two blood-hounds, careered round the court-yard, as if running in a ring. Vainly did poor Potts tug at the bridle. Flint, having the bit firmly between his teeth, defied his utmost efforts. Away he went with the hounds at his heels, as if, said Nicholas, "the devil were behind him." Though annoyed and angry, Sir Ralph could not help laughing at the ridiculous scene, and even a smile crossed Parson Dewhurst's grave countenance as Flint and his rider scampered madly past them. Sir Ralph called to the grooms, and attempts were instantly made to check the furious pony's career; but he baffled them all, swerving suddenly round when an endeavour was made to intercept him, leaping over any trifling obstacle, and occasionally charging any one who stood in his path. What with the grooms running hither and thither, vociferating and swearing, the barking and springing of the hounds, the yelping of lesser dogs, and the screaming of poultry, the whole yard was in a state of uproar and confusion.

"Flint mun be possessed," cried Peter. "Ey never seed him go on i' this way efore. Ey noticed Elizabeth Device near th' stables last neet, an ey shouldna wonder if hoo ha' bewitched him."

"Neaw doubt on't," replied another groom. "Howsomever we mun contrive to ketch him, or Sir Roaph win send us aw abowt our business.

"Ey wish yo'd contrive to do it, then, Tum Lomax," replied Peter, "fo' ey'm fairly blowd. Dang me, if ey ever seed sich hey-go-mad wark i' my born days. What's to be done, squoire?" he added to Nicholas.

"The devil only knows," replied the latter; "but it seems we must wait till the little rascal chooses to stop."

This occurred sooner than was expected. Thinking, possibly, that he had done enough to induce Master Potts to give up all idea of riding him, Flint suddenly slackened his pace, and trotted, as if nothing had happened, to the stable-door; but if he had formed any such notion as the above, he was deceived, for the attorney, who was quite as obstinate and wilful as himself, and who through all his perils had managed to maintain his seat, was resolved not to abandon it, and positively refused to dismount when urged to do so by Nicholas and the grooms.

"He will go quietly enough now, I dare say," observed Potts, "and if not, and you will lend me a hunting-whip, I will undertake to cure him of his tricks."

Flint seemed to understand what was said, for he laid back his ears as if meditating more mischief; but being surrounded by the grooms, he deemed it advisable to postpone the attempt to a more convenient opportunity. In compliance with his request, a heavy hunting-whip was handed to Potts, and, armed with this formidable weapon, the little attorney quite longed for an opportunity of effacing his disgrace. Meanwhile, Sir Ralph had come up and ordered a steady horse out for him; but Master Potts adhered to his resolution, and Flint remaining perfectly quiet, the baronet let him have his own way.

Soon after this, Nicholas and Richard having mounted their steeds, the party set forth. As they were passing through the gateway, which had been thrown wide open by Ned Huddlestone, they were joined by Simon Sparshot, who had been engaged by Potts to attend him on the expedition in his capacity of constable. Simon was mounted on a mule, and brought word that Master Roger Nowell begged they would ride round by Read Hall, where he would be ready to accompany them, as he wished to be present at the perambulation of the boundaries. Assenting to the arrangement, the party set forth in that direction, Richard and Nicholas riding a little in advance of the others.

CHAPTER II.—READ HALL.

THE road taken by the party on quitting Whalley led up the side of a hill, which, broken into picturesque inequalities, and partially clothed with trees, sloped down to the very brink of the Calder. Winding round the broad green plain, heretofore described, with the lovely knoll in the midst of it, and which formed, with the woody hills encircling it, a perfect amphitheatre, the river was ever an object of beauty—sometimes lost beneath overhanging boughs or high banks, anon bursting forth where least expected, now rushing swiftly over its shallow and rocky bed, now subsiding into a smooth full current. The Abbey and the village were screened from view by the lower part of the hill which the horsemen were scaling; but the old bridge and a few cottages at the foot of Whalley Nab, with their thin blue smoke mounting into the pure morning air, gave life and interest to the picture. Hence, from base to summit, Whalley Nab stood revealed, and the verdant lawns opening out amidst the woods feathering its heights, were fully discernible. Placed by Nature as the guardian of this fair valley, the lofty eminence well became the post assigned to it. None of the belt of hills connected with it were so well wooded as their leader, nor so beautiful in form; while some of them were overtopped by the bleak fells of Longridge, rising at a distance behind them.

Nor were those exquisite contrasts wanting, which are only to be seen in full perfection when the day is freshest and the dew is still heavy on the grass. The near side of the hill was plunged in deep shade; thin, gauzy vapour hung on the stream beneath, while on the opposite heights, and where the great boulder stones were visible in the bed of the river, all was sparkling with sunshine. So enchanting was the prospect, that though perfectly familiar with it, the two foremost horsemen drew in the rein to contemplate it. High above them, on a sandbank, through which their giant roots protruded, shot up two tall silver-stemm'd beech-trees, forming with their newly opened foliage a canopy of tenderest green. Further on appeared a grove of oaks scarcely in leaf; and below were several fine sycamores, already green and umbrageous, intermingled with elms, ashes, and horse-chestnuts, and overshadowing brakes, covered with maples, alders, and hazels. The other spaces among the trees were enlivened by patches of yellow flowering and odorous gorse. Mixed with the warblings of innumerable feathered songsters were heard the cheering notes of the cuckoo; and the newly-arrived swallows were seen chasing the flies along the plain, or skimming over the surface of the river. Already had Richard's depression yielded to the exhilarating freshness of the morning, and the same kindly influence produced a more salutary effect on Nicholas than Parson Dewhurst's lecture had been able to accomplish. The worthy squire was a true lover of Nature; admiring her in all her forms, whether arrayed in pomp of wood and verdure, as in the lovely landscape before him, or dreary and desolate, as in the heathy forest wastes they were about to traverse. While breathing the fresh morning air, inhaling the fragrance of the wild-flowers, and listening to the warbling of the birds, he took a well-pleased survey of the scene, commencing with the bridge, passing over Whalley Nab and the mountainous circle conjoined with it, till his gaze settled on Morton Hall, a noble mansion finely situated on a shoulder of the hill beyond him, and commanding the entire valley.

"Were I not owner of Downham," he observed to Richard, "I should wish to be master of Morton." And then, pointing to the green area below, he added, "What a capital spot for a race! There we might try the speed of our nags for the twenty pieces I talked of yesterday; and the judges of the match and those who chose to look on might station themselves on yon knoll, which seems made for the express purpose. Three years ago I remember a fair was held upon that plain, and the foot-races, the wrestling matches, and the various sports and pastimes of the rustics, viewed from the knoll, formed the prettiest sight ever looked upon. But, pleasant as the prospect is, we must not tarry here all day."

Before setting forward, he cast a glance towards Pendle Hill, which formed the most prominent object of view on the left, and lay like a leviathan basking in the sunshine. The vast mass rose up gradually until at its further extremity it attained an altitude of more than 1800 feet above the sea. At the present moment it was without a cloud, and the whole of its broad outline was distinctly visible.

"I love Pendle Hill," cried Nicholas, enthusiastically; "and from whatever side I view it—whether from this place, where I see it from end to end, from its lowest point to its highest; from Padiham, where it frowns upon me; from Clithero, where it smiles; or from Downham, where it rises in full majesty before me—from all points and under all aspects, whether robed in mist or radiant with sunshine, I delight in it. Born beneath its giant shadow, I look upon it with filial regard. Some folks say Pendle Hill wants grandeur and sublimity, but they themselves must be wanting in taste. Its broad, round, smooth mass is better than the roughest, craggiest, shaggiest, most sharply splintered mountain of them all. And then what a view it commands!—Lancaster with its grey old castle on one hand; York with its reverend minster on the other—the Irish Sea and its wild coast—fell, forest, moor, and valley, watered by the Ribble, the Hodder, the Calder, and the Lime—rivers not to be matched for beauty. You recollect the old distich

'Ingleborough, Pendle Hill, and Pennygent,
Are the highest hills between Scotland and Trent.'

This vouches for its height, but there are two other doggerel lines still more to the purpose—

'Pendle Hill, Pennygent, and Ingleborough,
Are three such hills as you'll not find by seeking England thorough.'

With this opinion I quite agree. There is no hill in England like Pendle Hill."

"Every man to his taste, squire," observed Potts; "but to my mind, Pendle Hill has no other recommendation than its size. I think it a great, brown, ugly, lumpy mass, without beauty of form or any striking character. I hate your bleak Lancashire hills, with heathy ranges on the top, fit only for the sustenance of a few poor half-starved sheep; and as to the view from them, it is little else than a continuous range of moors and dwarfed forests. Highgate Hill is quite mountain enough for me, and Hampstead Heath wild enough for any civilised purpose."

"A veritable son of Cockayne!" muttered Nicholas, contemptuously.

Riding on, and entering the grove of oaks, he lost sight of his favourite hill, though glimpses were occasionally caught through the trees of the lovely valley below. Soon afterwards the party turned off on the left, and presently arrived at a gate which admitted them to Read Park. Five minutes' canter over the springy turf then brought them to the house.

The manor of Reved or Read came into the possession of the Nowell family in the time of Edward III., and extended on one side, within a mile of Whalley, from which township it was divided by a deep woody ravine, taking its name from the little village of Sabden, and on the other stretched far into Pendle Forest. The hall was situated on an eminence forming part of the heights of Padiham, and faced a wide valley, watered by the Calder, and consisting chiefly of barren tracts of moor and forest land, bounded by the high hills near Accrington and Rossendale. On the left, some half-dozen miles off, lay Burnley, and the greater part of the land in this direction, being uninclosed and thinly peopled, had a dark dreary look, that served to enhance the green beauty of the well-cultivated district on the right. Behind the mansion, thick woods extended to the very confines of Pendle Forest, of which, indeed, they originally formed part, and here, if the course of the stream, flowing through the gully of Sabden, were followed, every variety of brake, glen, and dingle, might be found. Read Hall was a large and commodious mansion, forming, with a centre and two advancing wings, three sides of a square, between which was a grass-plot ornamented with a dial. The gardens were laid out in the taste of the time, with trim alleys and parterres, terraces and steps, stone statues, and clipped yews.

The house was kept up well and consistently by its owner, who lived like a country gentleman with a good estate, entertained his friends hospitably, but without any parade, and was never needlessly lavish in his expenditure, unless, perhaps, in the instance of the large ostentatious pew erected by him in the parish church of Whalley; and which, considering he had a private chapel at home, and maintained a domestic chaplain to do duty in it, seemed little required, and drew upon him the censure of the neighbouring gossips, who said there was more of pride than religion in his pew. With the chapel at the hall a curious history was afterwards connected. Converted into a dining-room by a descendant of Roger Nowell, the apartment was incautiously occupied by the planner of the alterations before the plaster was thoroughly dried; in consequence of which he caught a severe cold, and died in the desecrated chamber, his fate being looked upon as a judgment.

With many good qualities Roger Nowell was little liked. His

austere and sarcastic manner repelled his equals, and his harshness made him an object of dislike and dread among his inferiors. Besides being the terror of all evil-doers, he was a hard man in his dealings, though he endeavoured to be just, and persuaded himself he was so. A year or two before, having been appointed sheriff of the county, he had discharged the important office with so much zeal and ability, as well as liberality, that he rose considerably in public estimation. It was during this period that Master Potts came under his notice at Lancaster, and the little attorney's shrewdness gained him an excellent client in the owner of Read. Roger Nowell was a widower; but his son, who resided with him, was married, and had a family, so that the hall was fully occupied.

Roger Nowell was turned sixty, but he was still in the full vigour of mind and body, his temperate and active habits keeping him healthy; he was of a spare muscular frame, somewhat bent in the shoulders, and had very sharp features, keen grey eyes, a close mouth, and prominent chin. His hair was white as silver, but his eyebrows were still black and bushy.

Seeing the party approach, the lord of the mansion came forth to meet them, and begged them to dismount for a moment and refresh themselves. Richard excused himself, but Nicholas sprang from his saddle, and Potts, though somewhat more slowly, imitated his example. An open door admitted them to the entrance hall, where a repast was spread, of which the host pressed his guests to partake; but Nicholas declined on the score of having just breakfasted, notwithstanding which he was easily prevailed upon to take a cup of ale. Leaving him to discuss it, Nowell led the attorney to a well-furnished library, where he usually transacted his magisterial business, and held a few minutes' private conference with him, after which they returned to Nicholas, and by this time the magistrate's own horse being brought round, the party mounted once more. The attorney regretted abandoning his seat; for Flint indulged him with another exhibition somewhat similar to the first, though of less duration, for a vigorous application of the hunting-whip brought the wrong-headed little animal to reason.

Elated by the victory he had obtained over Flint, and anticipating a successful issue to the expedition, Master Potts was in excellent spirits, and found a great deal to admire in the domain of his honoured and singular good client. Though not very genuine, his admiration was deservedly bestowed. The portion of the park they were now traversing was extremely diversified and beautiful, with long sweeping lawns studded with fine trees, among which were many ancient thorns, now in full bloom, and richly scenting the gale. Herds of deer were nipping the short grass, browsing the lower spray of the ashes, or couching amid the ferny hollows.

It was now that Nicholas, who had been all along anxious to try the speed of his horse, proposed to Richard a gallop towards a clump of trees about a mile off, and the young man assenting, away they started. Master Potts started too, for Flint did not like to be left behind, but the mettlesome pony was soon distanced. For some time the two horses kept so closely together, that it was difficult to say which would arrive at the goal first; but, by-and-by, Robin got a-head. Though at first indifferent to the issue of the race, the spirit of emulation soon seized upon Richard, and spurring Merlin, the noble animal sprang forward, and was once again by the side of his opponent.

For a quarter of a mile the ground had been tolerably level, and the sod firm; but they now approached a swamp, and, in his eagerness, Nicholas did not take sufficient precaution, and got involved in it before he was aware. Richard was more fortunate, having kept on the right, where the ground was hard. Seeing Nicholas struggling out of the marshy soil, he would have stayed for him; but the latter bade him go on, saying he would soon be up with him, and he made good his words. Shortly after this their course was intercepted by a brook, and both horses having cleared it excellently, they kept well together again for a short time, when they neared a deep dyke which lay between them and the clump of trees. On descrying it, Richard pointed out a course to the left, but Nicholas held on, unheeding the caution. Fully expecting to see him break his neck, for the dyke was of formidable width, Richard watched him with apprehension, but the squire gave him a re-assuring nod, and went on. Neither horse nor man faltered, though failure would have been certain destruction to both. The wide trench now yawned before them—they were upon its edge, and without trusting himself to measure it with his eye, Nicholas clapped spurs into Robin's sides. The brave horse sprang forward and landed him safely on the opposite bank. Hallooing cheerily, as soon as he could check his courser the squire wheeled round, and rode back to look at the dyke he had crossed. Its width was terrific, and fairly astounded him. Robin snorted loudly, as if proud of his achievement, and showed some disposition to return, but the squire was quite content with what he had done. The exploit afterwards became a theme of wonder throughout the country, and the spot was long afterwards pointed out as "Squire Nicholas's Leap;" but there was not another horseman found daring enough to repeat the experiment.

Richard had to make a considerable circuit to join his cousin, and, while he was going round, Nicholas looked out for the others. In the distance, he could see Roger Nowell riding leisurely on, followed by Sparshot and a couple of grooms, who had come with their master from the hall; while midway, to his surprise, he perceived Flint galloping without a rider. A closer examination showed the squire what had happened. Like himself, Master Potts had incautiously approached the swamp, and, getting entangled in it, was thrown, head foremost, into the slough; out of which he was now floundering, covered from head to foot with inky-coloured slime. As soon as they were aware of the accident, the two grooms pushed forward, and one of them galloped after Flint, whom he succeeded at last in catching; while the other, with difficulty preserving his countenance at the woful plight of the attorney, who looked as black as a negro, pointed out a cottage in the hollow which belonged to one of the keepers, and offered to conduct him thither. Potts gladly assented, and soon gained the little tenement, where he was being washed and rubbed down by a couple of stout wenches when the rest of the party came up. It was impossible to help laughing at him, but Potts took the merriment in good part; and, to show he was not disheartened by the misadventure, as soon as circumstances would permit he mounted the unlucky pony, and the cavalcade set forward again.

CHAPTER III.—THE BOGGART'S GLEN.

THE manor of Read, it has been said, was skirted by a deep woody ravine of three or four miles in length, extending from the little village of Sabden, in Pendle Forest, to within a short distance of Whalley; and through this gully flowed a stream which, taking its rise near Barley, at the foot of Pendle Hill, added its waters to those of the Calder at a place called Cock Bridge. In summer, or in dry seasons, this stream proceeded quietly enough, and left the greater part of its stony bed unoccupied; but in winter, or after continuous rains, it assumed all the character of a mountain torrent, and swept every thing before it. A narrow bridle road led through the ravine to Sabden, and along it, after quitting the park, the cavalcade proceeded, headed by Nicholas.

The little river danced merrily past them, singing as it went, the sunshine sparkling on its bright clear waters, and glittering on the pebbles beneath them. Now the stream would chafe and foam against some larger impediment to its course; now it would dash down some rocky height, and form a beautiful cascade; then it would hurry on for some time with little interruption, till stayed by a projecting bank it would form a small deep basin, where, beneath the far-cast shadow of an overhanging oak, or under its huge twisted and denuded roots, the angler might be sure of finding the speckled trout, the dainty greyling, or their mutual enemy, the voracious jack. The ravine was well wooded throughout, and in many parts singularly beautiful, from the disposition of the timber on its banks, as well as from the varied form and charact

POTTS AFTER BEING THROWN FROM HIS HORSE. P. 224

of the trees. Here might be seen an acclivity covered with waving birch, or a top crowned with a mountain ash—there, on a smooth expanse of greensward, stood a range of noble elms, whose mighty arms stretched completely across the ravine. Further on, there were chestnut and walnut trees; willows, with hoary stems and silver leaves, almost encroaching upon the stream; larches upon the heights; and here and there, upon some sandy eminence, a spreading beech-tree. For the most part the bottom of the glen was overgrown with brushwood, and, where its sides were too abrupt to admit the growth of larger trees, they were matted with woodbine and brambles. Out of these would sometimes start a sharp pinnacle, or fantastically-formed crag, adding greatly to the picturesque beauty of the scene. On such points were not unfrequently found perched a hawk, a falcon, or some large bird of prey; for the gully, with its brakes and thickets, was a favourite haunt of the feathered tribe. The hollies, of which there were plenty, with their green prickly leaves and scarlet berries, afforded shelter and support to the blackbird; the thorns were frequented by the thrush; and numberless lesser songsters filled every other tree. In the covert there were pheasants and partridges in abundance, and snipe and wild-fowl resorted to the river in winter. Thither also, at all seasons, repaired the stately heron, to devour the finny race; and thither came, on like errand, the splendidly-plumed kingfisher. The magpie chattered, the jay screamed and flew deeper into the woods as the horsemen approached, and the shy bittern hid herself amid the rushes. Occasionally, too, was heard the deep ominous croaking of a raven.

Hitherto, the glen had been remarkable for its softness and beauty, but it now began to assume a savage and sombre character. The banks drew closer together, and became rugged and precipitous; while the trees met overhead, and, intermingling their branches, formed a canopy impervious to the sun's rays. The stream was likewise contracted in its bed, and its current, which, owing to the gloom, looked black as ink, flowed swiftly on, as if anxious to escape to livelier scenes. A large raven, which had attended the horsemen all the way, now alighted near them, and croaked ominously.

This part of the glen was in very ill repute, and was never traversed, even at noonday, without apprehension. Its wild and savage aspect, its horrent precipices, its shaggy woods, its strangely-shaped rocks and tenebrous depths, where every imperfectly-seen object appeared doubly frightful—all combined to invest it with mystery and terror. No one willingly lingered here, but hurried on, afraid of the sound of his own footsteps. No one dared to gaze at the rocks, lest he should see some hideous hobgoblin peering out of their fissures. No one glanced at the water, for fear some terrible kelpy, with twining snakes for hair and scaly hide, should issue from it and drag him down to devour him with his shark-like teeth. Among the common folk, this part of the ravine was known as "the boggart's glen," and was supposed to be haunted by mischievous beings, who made the unfortunate wanderer their sport.

For the last half-mile the road had been so narrow and intricate in its windings, that the party were obliged to proceed singly; but this did not prevent conversation; and Nicholas, throwing the bridle over Robin's neck, left the surefooted animal to pursue his course unguided, while he himself, leaning back, chatted with Roger Nowell. At the entrance of the gloomy gorge above described, Robin came to a stand, and refusing to move at a jerk from his master, the latter raised himself, and looked forward to see what could be the cause of the stoppage. No impediment was visible, but the animal obstinately refused to go on, though urged both by word and spur. This stoppage necessarily delayed the rest of the cavalcade.

Well aware of the ill reputation of the place, when Simon Sparshot and the grooms found that Robin would not go on, they declared he must see the boggart, and urged the squire to turn back, or some mischief would befall him. But Nicholas, though not without misgivings, did not like to yield thus, especially when urged on by Roger Nowell. Indeed, the party could not get out of the ravine without going back nearly a mile, while Sabden was only half that distance from them. What was to be done? Robin still continued obstinate, and for the first time paid no attention to his master's commands. The poor animal was evidently a prey to violent terror, and snorted and reared, while his limbs were bathed in cold sweat.

Dismounting, and leaving him in charge of Roger Nowell, Nicholas walked on by himself to see if he could discover any cause for the horse's alarm; and he had not advanced far, when his eye rested upon a blasted oak forming a conspicuous object on a crag before him, on a scathed branch of which sat the raven.

Croak! croak! croak!

"Accursed bird, it is thou who hast frightened my horse," cried Nicholas. "Would I had a crossbow or an arquebuss to stop thy croaking."

And as he picked up a stone to cast at the raven, a crashing noise was heard among the bushes high up on the rock, and the next moment a huge fragment dislodged from the cliff rolled down and would have crushed him, if he had not nimbly avoided it.

Croak! croak! croak!

Nicholas almost fancied hoarse laughter was mingled with the cries of the bird.

The raven nodded its head and expanded its wings, and the squire, whose recent experience had prepared him for any wonder, fully expected to hear it speak, but it only croaked loudly and exultingly, or if it laughed, the sound was like the creaking of rusty hinges.

Nicholas did not like it at all, and he resolved to go back; but ere he could do so, he was startled by a buffet on the ear, and turning angrily round to see who had dealt it, he could distinguish no one, but at the same moment received a second buffet on the other ear.

The raven croaked merrily.

"Would I could wring thy neck, accursed bird!" cried the enraged squire.

Scarcely was the vindictive wish uttered than a shower of blows fell upon him, and kicks from unseen feet were applied to his person.

All the while the raven croaked merrily, and flapped his big black wings.

Infuriated by the attack, the squire hit right and left manfully, and dashed out his feet in every direction; but his blows and kicks only met the empty air, while those of his unseen antagonist told upon his own person with increased effect.

The spectacle seemed to afford infinite amusement to the raven. The mischievous bird almost crowed with glee.

There was no standing it any longer. So, amid a perfect hurricane of blows and kicks, and with the infernal voice of the raven ringing in his ears, the squire took to his heels. On reaching his companions he found they had not fared much better than himself. The two grooms were belabouring each other lustily; and Master Potts was exercising his hunting-whip on the broad shoulders of Sparshot, who in return was making him acquainted with the taste of a stout ash-plant. Assailed in the same manner as the squire, and naturally attributing the attack to their nearest neighbours, they waited for no explanation, but fell upon each other. Richard Assheton and Roger Nowell endeavoured to interfere and separate the combatants, and in doing so received some hard knocks for their pains; but all their pacific efforts were fruitless, until the squire appeared, and telling them they were merely the sport of hobgoblins, they desisted, but still the blows fell heavily on them as before, proving the truth of Nicholas's assertion.

Meanwhile the squire had mounted Robin, and, finding the horse no longer exhibit the same reluctance to proceed, he dashed at full speed through the haunted glen; but even above the clatter of hoofs, and the noise of the party galloping after him, he could hear the hoarse exulting croaking of the raven.

As the gully expanded, and the sun once more found its way through the trees, and shone upon the river, Nicholas began to breathe more freely; but it was not until fairly out of the wood that he relaxed his speed. Not caring to enter into any explanation of the occurrence, he rode a little apart to avoid conversation; and as the others, who were still smarting from the blows they had received, were in no very good-humour, a sullen silence prevailed throughout the party, as they mounted the bare hill-side in the direction of the few scattered huts constituting the village of Sabden.

A blight seemed to have fallen upon the place. Roger Nowell, who had visited it a few months ago, could scarcely believe his eyes, so changed was its appearance. His inquiries as to the cause of its altered condition were every where met by the same answer —the poor people were all bewitched. Here a child was ill of a strange sickness, tossed and tumbled in its bed, and contorted its limbs so violently, that its parents could scarcely hold it down. Another family was afflicted in a different manner, two of its number pining away and losing strength daily, as if a prey to some consuming disease. In a third, another child was sick, and vomited pins, nails, and other extraordinary substances. A fourth household was tormented by an imp in the form of a monkey, who came at night and pinched them all black and blue, spilt the milk, broke the dishes and platters, got under the bed, and, raising it to the roof, let it fall with a terrible crash; putting them all in mental terror. In the next cottage there was no end to calamities, though they took a more absurd form. Sometimes the fire would not burn, or when it did it emitted no heat, so that the pot would not boil, nor the meat roast. Then the oatcakes would stick to the bake-stone, and no force could get them away from it till they were burnt and spoiled; the milk turned sour, the cheese became so hard that not even rats' teeth could gnaw it, the stools and settles broke down if sat upon, and the list of petty grievances was completed by a whole side of bacon being devoured in a single night. Roger Nowell and Nicholas listened patiently to a detail of all these grievances, and expressed strong sympathy for the sufferers, promising assistance and redress if possible. All the complainants taxed either Mother Demdike or Mother Chattox with afflicting them, and said they had incurred the anger of the two malevolent old witches by refusing to supply them with poultry, eggs, milk, butter, or other articles, which they had demanded. Master Potts made ample notes of the strange relations, and took down the name of every cottager.

At length, they arrived at the last cottage, and here a man, with a very doleful countenance, besought them to stop and listen to his tale.

"What is the matter, friend?" demanded Roger Nowell, halting with the others. "Are you bewitched, like your neighbours?"

"Troth am ey, your warship," replied the man, "an ey hope yo may be able to deliver me. Yo mun knoa, that somehow ey wor unlucky enough last Yule to offend Mother Chattox, an ever sin then aw's gone wrang wi' me. Th' good-wife con never may butter come without stickin' a redhot poker into t' churn; and last week, when our brindlt sow farrowed, and had fifteen to t' litter, an' fine uns os ever yo seed, seign on um deed. Sad wark! sad wark, mesters. The week efore that t' keaw deed; an th' week efore her th' owd mare, so that aw my stock be gone. Waes me! waes me! Nowt prospers wi' me. My poor dame is besoide hersel, an' th' chilter seems possessed. Ey ha' tried every remedy, boh without success. Ey ha' followed th' owd witch whoam, plucked a hontle o' thatch fro' her roof, sprinklet it wi' sawt an weter, burnt it an' buried th' ess at th' change o' t' moon. No use, mesters. Then again, ey ha' getten a horseshoe, heated it redhot, quenched it i' brine, an' nailed it to t' threshold wi' three nails, heel uppard. No more use nor t'other. Then ey ha' taen sawt weter, and put it in a bottle wi' three rusty nails, needles, and pins, boh ey hanna found that th' witch ha' suffered thereby. An, lastly, ey ha' let myself blood, when the moon wur at full, an in opposition to th' owd hag's planet, an minglin' it wi' sawt, ha' burnt it i' a trivet, in hopes of afflictin' her; boh without avail, fo' ey seed her two days ago, an she flouted me an scoffed at me. What mun ey do, good mesters? What mun ey do?"

"Have you offended any one besides Mother Chattox, my poor fellow?" said Nowell.

"Mother Demdike, may be, your warship," replied the man.

"You suspect Mother Demdike and Mother Chattox of bewitching you," said Potts, taking out his memorandum-book, and making a note in it. "Your name, good fellow?"

"Oamfrey o' Will's o' Ben's o' Tummas' o' Sabden," replied the man.

"Is that all?" asked Potts.

"What more would you have?" said Richard. The description is sufficiently particular."

"Scarcely precise enough," returned Potts. "However, it may do. We will help you in the matter, good Humphrey Etcetera. You shall not be troubled with these pestilent witches much longer. The neighbourhood shall be cleared of them."

"Ey'm reet glad to hear, mester," replied the man.

"You promise much, Master Potts," observed Richard.

"Not a jot more than I am able to perform," replied the attorney.

"That remains to be seen," said Richard. "If these old women are as powerful as represented, they will not be so readily defeated."

"There you are in error, Master Richard," replied Potts. "The devil, whose vassals they are, will deliver them into our hands."

"Granting what you say to be correct, the devil must have little regard for his servants if he abandons them so easily," observed Richard, drily.

"What else can you expect from him?" cried Potts. "It is his custom to ensnare his victims, and then leave them to their fate."

"You are rather describing the course pursued by certain

members of your own profession, Master Potts," said Richard. "The devil behaves with greater fairness to his clients."

"You are not going to defend him, I hope, sir?" said the attorney.

"No; I only desire to give him his due," returned Richard.

"Ha! ha! ha!" laughed Nicholas. "You had better have done, Master Potts; you will never get the better in the argument. But we must be moving, or we shall not get our business done before nightfall. As to you, Numps," he added, to the poor man, "we will not forget you. If any thing can be done for your relief, rely upon it, it shall not be neglected."

"Ay, ay," said Nowell, "the matter shall be looked into—and speedily."

"And the witches brought to justice," said Potts; "comfort yourself with that, good Humphrey Etcetera."

"Ay, comfort yourself with that," observed Nicholas.

Soon after this they entered a wide dreary waste forming the bottom of the valley, lying between the heights of Padiham and Pendle Hill, and while wending their way across it, they heard a shout from the hill-side, and presently afterwards perceived a man, mounted on a powerful black horse, galloping swiftly towards them. The party awaited his approach, and the stranger speedily came up. He was a small man habited in a suit of rusty black, and bore a most extraordinary and marked resemblance to Master Potts. He had the same perky features, the same parchment complexion, the same yellow forehead, as the little attorney. So surprising was the likeness, that Nicholas unconsciously looked round for Potts, and beheld him staring at the new-comer in angry wonder.

CHAPTER IV.—THE REEVE OF THE FOREST.

THE surprise of the party was by no means diminished when the stranger spoke. His voice exactly resembled the sharp cracked tones of the attorney.

"I crave pardon for the freedom I have taken in stopping you, good masters," he said, doffing his cap, and saluting them respectfully; "but, being aware of your errand, I am come to attend you on it."

"And who are you, fellow, who thus volunteer your services?" demanded Roger Nowell, sharply.

"I am one of the reeves of the forest of Blackburnshire, worshipful sir," replied the stranger, "and as such my presence, at the intended perambulation of the boundaries of her property, has been deemed necessary by Mrs. Nutter, as I shall have to make a representation of the matter at the next court of swain-mote."

"Indeed!" exclaimed Nowell, "but how knew you we were coming?"

"Mistress Nutter sent me word last night," replied the reeve, "that Master Nicholas Assheton and certain other gentlemen, would come to Rough Lee for the purpose of ascertaining the marks, meres, and boundaries of her property, early this morning, and desired my attendance on the occasion. Accordingly I stationed myself on yon high ground to look out for you, and have been on the watch for more than an hour."

"Humph!" exclaimed Roger Nowell, "and you live in the forest?"

"I live at Barrowford, worshipful sir," replied the reeve, "but I have only lately come there, having succeeded Maurice Mottisfont, the other reeve, who has been removed by the master forester to Rossendale, where I formerly dwelt."

"That may account for my not having seen you before," rejoined Nowell. "You are well mounted, sirrah. I did not know the master forester allowed his men such horses as the one you ride."

"This horse does not belong to me, sir," replied the reeve; "it has been lent me by Mistress Nutter."

"Aha! I see how it is now," cried Nowell; "you are suborned to give false testimony, knave. I object to his attendance, Master Nicholas."

"Nay, I think you do the man injustice," said the squire. "He speaks frankly and fairly enough, and seems to know his business. The worst that can be said against him is, that he resembles somewhat too closely our little legal friend there. That, however, ought to be no objection to you, Master Nowell, but rather the contrary."

"Well, take the responsibility of the matter upon your own shoulders," said Nowell; "if any ill comes of it I shall blame you."

"Be it so," replied the squire; "my shoulders are broad enough to bear the burthen. You may ride with us, master reeve."

"May I inquire your name, friend?" said Potts, as the stranger fell back to the rear of the party.

"Thomas Potts, at your service, sir," replied the reeve.

"What!—Thomas Potts!" exclaimed the astonished attorney.

"That is my name, sir," replied the reeve, quietly.

"Why, zounds!" exclaimed Nicholas, who overheard the reply, "you do not mean to say your name is Thomas Potts? This is more wonderful still. You must be this gentleman's twin brother."

"The gentleman certainly seems to resemble me very strongly," replied the reeve, apparently surprised in his turn. "Is he of these parts?"

"No, I am not," returned Potts, angrily, "I am from London, where I reside in Chancery-lane, and practise the law, though I likewise attend as clerk of the court at the assizes at Lancaster, where I may possibly, one of these days, have the pleasure of seeing you, my pretended namesake."

"Possibly, sir," said the reeve, with provoking calmness. "I myself am from Chester, and like yourself was brought up to the law, but I abandoned my profession, or rather it abandoned me, for I had few clients; so I took to an honester calling, and became a forester, as you see. My father was a draper in the city I have mentioned, and dwelt in Watergate-street—his name was Peter Potts."

"Peter Potts your father!" exclaimed the attorney, in the last state of astonishment—"Why, he was mine! But I am his only son."

"Up to this moment I conceived myself an only son," said the reeve; "but it seems I was mistaken, since I find I have an elder brother."

"Elder brother!" exclaimed Potts, wrathfully. "You are older than I am by twenty years. But it is all a fabrication. I deny the relationship entirely."

"You cannot make me other than the son of my father," said the reeve, with a smile.

"Well, Master Potts," interposed Nicholas, laughing, "I see no reason why you should be ashamed of your brother. There is a strong family likeness between you. So old Peter Potts, the draper of Chester, was your father, eh? I was not aware of the circumstance before—ha, ha!"

"And, but for this intrusive fellow, you would never have become aware of it," muttered the attorney. "Give ear to me, squire," he said, urging Flint close up to the other's side, and speaking in a low tone, "I do not like the fellow's looks at all."

"I am surprised at that," rejoined the squire, "for he exactly resembles you."

"That is why I do not like him," said Potts; "I believe him to be a wizard."

"You are no wizard to think so," rejoined the squire. And he rode on to join Roger Nowell, who was a little in advance.

"I will try him on the subject of witchcraft," thought Potts. "As you dwell in the forest," he said to the reeve, "you have no doubt seen those two terrible beings, Mothers Demdike and Chattox."

"Frequently," replied the reeve, "but I would rather not talk about them in their own territories. You may judge of their power by the appearance of the village you have just quitted The inhabitants of that unlucky place refused them their customary tributes, and have therefore incurred their resentment. You will meet other instances of the like kind before you have gone far."

"I am glad of it, for I want to collect as many cases as I can of witchcraft," observed Potts.

"They will be of little use to you," observed the reeve.

"How so?" inquired Potts.

"Because if the witches discover what you are about, as they will not fail to do, you will never leave the forest alive," returned the other.

"You think not?" cried Potts.

"I am sure of it," replied the reeve.

"I will not be deterred from the performance of my duty," said Potts. "I defy the devil and all his works."

"You may have reason to repent your temerity," replied the reeve.

And anxious, apparently, to avoid further conversation on the subject, he drew in the rein for a moment, and allowed the attorney to pass on.

Notwithstanding his boasting, Master Potts was not without much secret misgiving; but his constitutional obstinacy made him determine to prosecute his plans at any risk, and he comforted himself by recalling the opinion of his sovereign authority on such matters.

"Let me ponder over the exact words of our British Solomon," he thought. "I have his learned treatise by heart, and it is fortunate my memory serves me so well, for the sagacious prince's dictum will fortify me in my resolution, which has been somewhat shaken by this fellow, whom I believe to be no better than he should be, for all he calls himself my father's son, and hath assumed my likeness, doubtless for some mischievous purpose. 'If the magistrate,' saith the King, 'be slothful towards witches, God is very able to make them instruments to waken and punish his sloth.' No one can accuse me of slothfulness and want of zeal. My best exertions have been used against the accursed creatures. And now for the rest. 'But if, on the contrary, he be diligent in examining and punishing them, God will not permit their master to trouble or hinder so good a work!' Exactly what I have done. I am quite easy now, and shall go on fearlessly as before. I am one of the 'lawful lieutenants' described by the King, and cannot be 'defrauded or deprived' of my office."

As these thoughts passed through the attorney's mind a low derisive laugh sounded in his ears, and, connecting it with the reeve, he looked back and found the object of his suspicions gazing at him, and chuckling maliciously. So fiendishly malignant, indeed, was the gaze fixed upon him, that Potts was glad to turn his head away to avoid it.

"I am confirmed in my suspicions," he thought; "he is evidently a wizard, if he be not—"

Again the mocking laugh sounded in his ears, but he did not venture to look round this time, being fearful of once more encountering the terrible gaze.

Meanwhile the party had traversed the valley, and to avoid a dangerous morass stretching across its lower extremity, and shorten the distance—for the ordinary road would have led them too much to the right—they began to climb one of the ridges of Pendle Hill, which lay between them and the vale they wished to gain. On obtaining the top of this eminence, an extensive view on either side opened upon them. Behind was the sterile valley they had just crossed, its black soil, hoary grass, and heathy wastes, only enlivened at one end by patches of bright sulphur-coloured moss, which masked a treacherous quagmire lurking beneath it. Some of the cottages in Sabden were visible, and, from the sad circumstances connected with them, and which oppressed the thoughts of the beholders, added to the dreary character of the prospect. The day, too, had lost its previous splendour, and there were clouds overhead which cast deep shadows on the ground. But on the crest of Pendle Hill, which rose above them, a sun-burst fell, and attracted attention from its brilliant contrast to the prevailing gloom. Before them lay a deep gully, the sinuosities of which could be traced from the elevated position where they stood, though its termination was hidden by other projecting ridges. Further on, the sides of the mountain were bare and rugged, and covered with shelving stone. Beyond the defile before mentioned, and over the last mountain ridge, lay a wide valley, bounded on the further side by the hills overlooking Colne, and the mountain defile, now laid open to the travellers, exhibiting in the midst of the dark heathy ranges, which were its distinguishing features, some marks of cultivation. In parts it was inclosed and divided into paddocks by stone walls, and here and there a few cottages were collected together, dignified, as in the case of Sabden, by the name of a village. Amongst these were the Hey-houses, an assemblage of small stone tenements, the earliest that arose in the forest; Goldshaw Booth, now a populous place, and even then the largest hamlet in the district; and in the distance Ogden and Barley, the two latter scarcely comprising a dozen habitations, and those little better than huts. In some sheltered nook on the hill-side might be discerned the solitary cottage of a cowherd, and not far from it the certain accompaniment of a sheepfold. Throughout this weird region, thinly peopled it is true, but still of great extent, and apparently abandoned to the powers of darkness, only one edifice could be found where its inhabitants could meet to pray, and this was an ancient chapel at Goldshaw Booth, originally erected in the reign of Henry III, though subsequently in part rebuilt in 1544, and which, with its low grey tower peeping from out the trees, was just discernible. Two halls were in view; one of which, Sabden, was of considerable antiquity, and gave its name to the village; and the other was Hoarstones, a much more recently erected mansion, strikingly situated on an acclivity of Pendle Hill. In general, the upper parts of this mountain monarch of the waste were bare and heathy, while the heights overhanging Ogden and Barley were rocky, shelving, and precipitous; but the lower ridges were well covered with wood, and a thicket, once forming part of the ancieut forest, ran far out into the plain near Goldshaw Booth. Numerous springs burst from the mountain side, and these collecting their forces, formed a considerable stream, which, under the name of Pendle Water, flowed through the valley above described, and, after many picturesque windings, entered the rugged glen in which Rough Lee was situated, and swept past the foot of Mistress Nutter's residence.

Descending the hill, and passing through the thicket, the party came within a short distance of Goldshaw Booth, when they were met by a cowherd, who, with looks of great alarm, told them that John Law, the pedlar, had fallen down in a fit in the clough, and would perish if they did not stay to help him. As the poor man in question was well known both to Nicholas and Roger Nowell, they immediately agreed to go to his assistance, and accompanied the cowherd along a by-road which led through the clough to the village. They had not gone far when they heard loud groans, and presently afterwards found the unfortunate pedlar lying on his back, and writhing in agony. He was a large, powerfully-built man, of middle age, and had been in the full enjoyment of health and vigour, so that his sudden prostration was the more terrible. His face was greatly disfigured, the mouth and neck drawn awry, the left eye pulled down, and the whole power of the same side gone.

"Why, John, this is a bad business," cried Nicholas. "You have had a paralytic stroke, I fear."

"Nah—nah—squoire," replied the sufferer, speaking with difficulty, "it's neaw nat'ral ailment—it's witchcraft."

"Witchcraft!" exclaimed Potts, who had come up, and producing his memorandum book. "Another case. Your name and description, friend?"

"John Law o' Cown, pedlar," replied the man.

"John Law of Colne, I suppose, petty chapman," said Potts, making an entry. "Now, John, my good man, be pleased to tell us by whom you have been bewitched?"

"By Mother Demdike," groaned the man.

"Mother Demdike, ah?" exclaimed Potts, "good! very good. Now, John, as to the cause of your quarrel with the old hag?"

"Ey con scarcely rekillect it, my head be so confused, mester," replied the pedlar.

"Make an effort, John," persisted Potts; "it is most desirable such a dreadful offender should not escape justice."

"Weel, weel, ey'n try an tell it then," replied the pedlar. "Yo mun knoa ey wur crossing the hill fro' Cown to Rough Lee, wi' my pack upon my shouthers, when who should ey meet boh Mother Demdike, an hoo axt me to gi' her some scithers an pins, boh, os ill luck wad ha' it, ey refused. 'Yo had better do it, John,' hoo said, 'or yo'll rue it efore to-morrow neet.' Ey laughed at her, an trudged on, boh when I looked back, an seed her shakin' her skinny hond at me, ey repented and thowt ey would go back, an gi' her the choice o' my wares. Boh my pride wur too strong, an ey walked on to Barley an Ogden, an slept at Bess's o th' Booth, an woke this mornin' stout and strong, fully persuaded th' owd witch's threat would come to nowt. Alack-a-day! ey wur out i' my reckonin', fo' scarcely had ey reached this kloof, o' my way to Sabden, than ey wur seized wi' a sudden shock, os if a thunder-bowt had hit me, an ey lost the use o' my lower limbs, an t' laft soide, an should ha' deed most likely, if it hadna bin fo' Ebil o' Jem's o' Dan's who spied me out, an brought me help."

"Yours is a deplorable case indeed, John," said Richard—"especially if it be the result of witchcraft."

"You do not surely doubt that it is so, Master Richard?" cried Potts.

"I offer no opinion," replied the young man; "but a paralytic stroke would produce the same effect. But, instead of discussing the matter, the best thing we can do will be to transport the poor man to Bess's o' th' Booth, where he can be attended to."

"Tom and I can carry him there, if Abel will take charge of his pack," said one of the grooms.

"That I win," replied the cowherd, unstrapping the box, upon which the sufferer's head rested, and placing it on his own shoulders.

Meanwhile, a gate having been taken from its hinges by Sparshot and the reeve, the poor pedlar, who groaned deeply during the operation, was placed upon it by the men, and borne towards the village, followed by the others, leading their horses.

Great consternation was occasioned in Goldshaw Booth by the entrance of the cavalcade, and still more, when it became known that John Law, the pedlar, who was a favourite with all, had had a frightful seizure. Old and young flocked forth to see him, and the former shook their heads, while the latter were appalled at the hideous sight. Master Potts took care to tell them that the poor fellow was bewitched by Mother Demdike; but the information failed to produce the effect he anticipated, and served rather to repress than heighten their sympathy for the sufferer. The attorney concluded, and justly, that they were afraid of incurring the displeasure of the vindictive old hag by an open expression of interest in his fate. So strongly did this feeling operate, that after bestowing a glance of commiseration at the pedlar, most of them returned, without a word, to their dwellings.

On their way to the little hostel, whither they were conveying the poor pedlar, the party passed the church, and the sexton, who was digging a grave in the yard, came forward to look at them; but on seeing John Law he seemed to understand what had happened, and resumed his employment. A wide-spreading yew-tree grew in this part of the churchyard, and near it stood a small cross rudely carved in granite, marking the spot where, in the reign of Henry VI., Ralph Cliderhow, tenth abbot of Whalley, held a meeting of the tenantry, to check encroachments. Not far from this ancient cross the sexton, a hale old man, with a fresh complexion and silvery hair, was at work, and while the others went on, Master Potts paused to say a word to him.

"You have a funeral here to-day, I suppose, Master Sexton?" he said.

"Yeigh," replied the man, gruffly.

"One of the villagers?" inquired the attorney.

"Neaw; hoo were na o' Goldshey," replied the sexton.

"Where then—who was it?" persevered Potts.

The sexton seemed disinclined to answer; but at length said, "Meary Baldwyn, the miller's dowter o' Rough Lee, os protty a lass os ever yo see, mester. Hoo wur the apple o' her feyther's ee, an he hasna had a dry ee sin hoo deed. Wall-a-dey! we mun aw go, owd an young—owd an young—an protty Meary Baldwyn went young enough. Poor lass! poor lass!" and he brushed the dew from his eyes with his brawny hand.

"Was her death sudden?" asked Potts.

"Neaw, not so sudden, mester," replied the sexton. "Ruchot Baldwyn had fair warnin'. Six months ago Meary wur ta'en ill, an fro' t' furst he knoad how it wad eend."

"How so, friend?" asked Potts, whose curiosity began to be aroused.

"Becose—" replied the sexton, and he stopped suddenly short.

"She was bewitched?" suggested Potts.

The sexton nodded his head, and began to ply his mattock vigorously.

"By Mother Demdike?" inquired Potts, taking out his memorandum book.

The sexton again nodded his head, but spake no word, and, meeting some obstruction in the ground, took up his pick to remove it.

"Another case!" muttered Potts, making an entry. "Mary Baldwyn, daughter of Richard Baldwyn of Rough Lee, aged—How old was she, sexton?"

"Throtteen," replied the man; "boh dunna ax me ony more questions, mester. Th' berrin takes place i' an hour, an ey hanna half digg'd th' grave."

"Your own name, Master Sexton, and I have done?" said Potts.

"Zachariah Worms," answered the man.

"Worms—ha! an excellent name for a sexton," cried Potts. "You provide food for your family, eh, Zachariah?"

"Tut—tut," rejoined the sexton, testily, "go an' moind yer own bus'ness, mon, an' leave me to moind mine."

"Very well, Zachariah," replied Potts. And having obtained all he required, he proceeded to the little hostel, where, finding the rest of the party had dismounted, he consigned Flint to a cowherd, and entered the house.

CHAPTER V.—BESS'S O' TH' BOOTH.

Bess's o' th' Booth—for so the little hostel at Goldshaw was called, after its mistress Bess Whitaker—was far more comfortable and commodious than its unpretending exterior seemed to warrant. Stouter and brighter ale was not to be drunk in Lancashire than Bess brewed; nor was better sherris or clary to be found, go where you would, than in her cellars. The traveller crossing those dreary wastes, and riding from Burnley to Clithero, or from Colne to Whalley, as the case might be, might well halt at Bess's, and be sure of a roast fowl for dinner, with the addition, perhaps, of some trout from Pendle Water, or, if the season permitted, a heath-cock or a pheasant; or, if he tarried there for the night, he was equally sure of a good supper and fair linen. It has already been mentioned, that at this period it was the custom of all classes in the northern counties, men and women, to resort to the alehouses to drink, and the hostel at Goldshaw was the general rendezvous of the neighbourhood. For those who could afford it Bess would brew incomparable sack; but if a guest called for wine, and she liked not his looks, she would flatly tell him her ale was good enough for him, and if it pleased him not he should have nothing. Submission always followed in such cases, for there was no disputing with Bess. Neither would she permit the frequenters of the hostel to sit later than she chose, and would clear the house in a way equally characteristic and effectual. At a certain hour, and that by no means a late one, she would take down a large horsewhip, which hung on a convenient peg in the principal room, and after bluntly ordering her guests to go home, if any resistance were offered, she would lay the whip across their shoulders, and forcibly eject them from the premises; but, as her determined character was well known, this violence was seldom necessary. In strength Bess was a match for any man, and assistance from her cowherds—for she was a farmer as well as hostess—was at hand if required. As will be surmised from the above, Bess was large and masculine-looking, but well-proportioned nevertheless, and possessed a certain coarse kind of beauty, which in earlier years had inflamed Richard Baldwyn, the miller of Rough Lee, who made overtures of marriage to her. These were favourably entertained, but a slight quarrel occurring between them, the lover, in her own phrase, got "his jacket soundly dusted" by her, and declared off, taking to wife a more docile and light-handed maiden. As to Bess, though she had given this unmistakable proof of her ability to manage a husband, she did not receive a second offer, nor, as she had now attained the mature age of forty, did it seem likely she would ever receive one.

Bess's o' th' Booth was an extremely clean and comfortable house. The floor, it is true, was of hard clay, and the windows little more than narrow slits, with heavy stone frames, further darkened by minute diamond panes; but the benches were scrupulously clean, and so was the long oak table in the centre of the principal and only large room in the house. A roundabout fireplace occupied one end of the chamber, sheltered from the draught of the door by a dark oak screen, with a bench on the warm side of it; and here, or in the deep ingle-nooks, on winter nights, the neighbours would sit and chat by the blazing hearth, discussing pots of "nappy ale, good and stale," as the old ballad hath it; and as persons of both sexes came thither, young as well as old, many a match was struck up by Bess's cheery fireside. From the blackened rafters hung a goodly supply of hams, sides of bacon, and dried tongues, with a profusion of oatcakes in a bread-flake; while, in case this store should be exhausted, means of replenishment were at hand in the huge, full-crammed meal-chest standing in one corner. Altogether, there was a look of abundance as well as of comfort about the place.

Great was Bess's consternation when the poor pedlar, who had quitted her house little more than an hour ago, full of health and spirits, was brought back to it in such a deplorable condition; and when she saw him deposited at her door, notwithstanding her masculine character, she had some difficulty in repressing a scream. She did not, however, yield to the weakness, but seeing at once what was best to be done, caused him to be transported by the grooms to the chamber he had occupied over-night, and laid upon the bed. Medical assistance was fortunately at hand; for it chanced that Master Sudall, the chirurgeon of Colne, was in the house at the time, having been brought to Goldshaw by the great sickness that prevailed at Sabden and elsewhere in the neighbourhood. Sudall was immediately in attendance upon the sufferer, and bled him copiously, after which the poor man seemed much easier; and Richard Assheton, taking the chirurgeon aside, asked his opinion of the case, and was told by Sudall that he did not think the pedlar's life in danger, but he doubted whether he would ever recover the use of his limbs.

"You do not attribute the attack to witchcraft, I suppose, Master Sudall?" said Richard.

"I do not like to deliver an opinion, sir," replied the chirurgeon. "It is impossible to decide, when all the appearances are precisely like those of an ordinary attack of paralysis. But a sad case has recently come under my observation, as to which I can have no doubt—I mean as to its being the result of witchcraft—but I will tell you more about it presently, for I must now return to my patient."

It being agreed among the party to rest for an hour at the little hostel, and partake of some refreshment, Nicholas went to look after the horses, while Roger Nowell and Richard remained in the room with the pedlar. Bess Whitaker owned an extensive farm-yard, provided with cow-houses, stables, and a large barn; and it was to the latter place that the two grooms proposed to repair with Sparshot and play a game at loggats on the clay floor. No one knew what had become of the reeve; for, on depositing the poor pedlar at the door of the hostel, he had mounted his horse and ridden away. Having ordered some fried eggs and bacon, Nicholas wended his way to the stable, while Bess, assisted by a stout kitchen wench, busied herself in preparing the eatables, and it was at this juncture that Master Potts entered the house.

Bess eyed him narrowly, and was by no means prepossessed by his looks, while the muddy condition of his habiliments did not tend to exalt him in her opinion.

"Yo mey yersel a' whoam, mon, ey mun say," she observed, as the attorney seated himself on the bench beside her.

"To be sure," rejoined Potts; "where should a man make himself at home, if not at an inn? Those eggs and bacon look very tempting. I'll try some presently; and, as soon as you've done with the frying-pan, I'll have a pottle of sack."

"Neaw, yo winna," replied Bess. "Yo'n get nother eggs nor bacon nor sack here, ey can promise ye. Ele an whoat-kekes mun sarve your turn. Go to t' barn wi' t' other grooms, and play at kittle-pins or nine-holes wi' hin, an ey'n send ye some ele."

"I'm quite comfortable where I am, thank you, hostess," replied Potts, "and have no desire to play at kittle-pins or nine-holes. But what does this bottle contain?"

"Sherris," replied Bess.

"Sherris!" echoed Potts, "and yet you say I can have no sack. Get me some sugar and eggs, and I'll show you how to brew the drink. I was taught the art by my friend, Ben Jonson—rare Ben—ha, ha!"

"Set the bottle down," cried Bess, angrily.

"What do you mean, woman?" said Potts, staring at her in surprise. "I told you to fetch sugar and eggs, and I now repeat the order—sugar, and half-a-dozen eggs at least."

"An ey repeat my order to yo," cried Bess, "to set the bottle down, cr ey'st may ye."

"Make me! ha, ha! I like that," cried Potts. "Let me tell you, woman, I am not accustomed to be ordered in this way. I shall do no such thing. If you will not bring the eggs I shall drink the wine, neat and unsophisticate." And he filled a flagon near him.

"If yo dun, yo shan pay dearly for it," said Bess, putting aside the frying-pan and taking down the horsewhip.

"I daresay I shall," replied Potts merrily; "you hostesses generally do make one pay dearly. Very good sherris this, i' faith!—the true nutty flavour. Now do go and fetch me some eggs, my good woman. You must have plenty, with all the poultry I saw in the farm-yard; and then I'll teach you the whole art and mystery of brewing sack."

"Ey'n teach yo to dispute my orders," cried Bess. And, catching the attorney by the collar, she began to belabour him soundly with the whip.

"Holloa! ho! what's the meaning of this?" cried Potts, struggling to get free. "Assault and battery; ho!"

"Ey'n sawt an batter yo, ay, an baste yo too!" replied Bess, continuing to lay on the whip.

"Why, zounds! this passes a joke," cried the attorney. "How desperately strong she is! I shall be murdered! Help! help! The woman must be a witch."

"A witch! Ey'n teach yo' to ca' me feaw names," cried the enraged hostess, laying on with greater fury.

"Help! help!" roared Potts.

At this moment Nicholas returned from the stables, and, seeing how matters stood, flew to the attorney's assistance.

"Come, come, Bess," he cried, laying hold of her arm, "you've given him enough. What has Master Potts been about? Not insulting you, I hope?"

"Neaw, ey'd tak keare he didna do that, squoire," replied the hostess. "Ey towd him he'd get nowt boh ele here, an' he made free wi't wine bottle, so ey brought down t' whip jist to teach him manners."

"You teach me! you ignorant and insolent hussy," cried Potts, furiously; "do you think I'm to be taught manners by an overgrown Lancashire witch like you? I'll teach you what it is to assault a gentleman. I'll prefer an instant complaint against you to my singular good friend and client, Master Roger, who is in your house, and you'll soon find whom you've got to deal with—"

"Marry—kem—eawt!" exclaimed Bess; "who con it be? Ey took yo fo' one o't grooms, mon."

"Fire and fury!" exclaimed Potts; "this is intolerable. Master Nowell shall let you know who I am, woman."

"Nay, I'll tell you, Bess," interposed Nicholas, laughing. "This little gentleman is a London lawyer, who is going to Rough Lee on business with Master Roger Nowell. Unluckily, he got pitched into a quagmire in Read Park, and that is the reason why his countenance and habiliments have got begrimed."

"Eigh! ey thowt he wur i' a strawnge fettle," replied Bess; "an so he be a lawyer fro' Lunnon, eh? Weel," she added, laughing, and displaying two ranges of very white teeth, "he'll remember Bess Whitaker, t' next time he comes to Pendle Forest."

"And she'll remember me," rejoined Potts.

"Neaw more sawce, mon," cried Bess, "or ey'n raddle thy boans again."

"No you won't, woman," cried Potts, snatching up his horsewhip, which he had dropped in the previous scuffle, and brandishing it fiercely. "I dare you to touch me."

Nicholas was obliged once more to interfere, and as he passed his arms round the hostess's waist, he thought a kiss might tend to bring matters to a peaceable issue, so he took one.

"Ha' done wi' ye, squoire," cried Bess, who, however, did not look very seriously offended by the liberty.

"By my faith, your lips are so sweet that I must have another," cried Nicholas. "I tell you what, Bess, you're the finest woman in Lancashire, and you owe it to the county to get married."

"Whoy so?" said Bess.

"Because it would be a pity to lose the breed," replied Nicholas. "What say you to Master Potts there? Will he suit you?"

"He—pooh! Do you think ey'd put up wi' sich powsement os he! Neaw; when Bess Whitaker, the lonleydey o' Goldshey, weds, it shan be to a mon, and nah to a ninny-hommer."

"Bravely resolved, Bess," cried Nicholas. "You deserve another kiss for your spirit."

"Ha' done, ey say," cried Bess, dealing him a gentle tap that sounded very much like a buffet. "See how yon jobberknow is grinning at ye."

"Jobberknow and ninny-hammer," cried Potts, furiously; "really, woman, I cannot permit such names to be applied to me."

"Os yo please, boh ey'st gi' ye nah better," rejoined the hostess.

"Come, Bess, a truce to this," observed Nicholas; "the eggs and bacon are spoiling, and I'm dying with hunger. There—there," he added, clapping her on the shoulder, "set the dish before us, that's a good soul—a couple of plates, some oatcakes and butter, and we shall do."

And while Bess attended to these requirements, he observed, "This sudden seizure of poor John Law is a bad business."

"'Deed on it is, squoire," replied Bess, "ey wur quite glopp'nt at seet on him. Lorjus o' me! whoy, it's scarcely an hour sin he left here, looking os strong an os 'earty os yersel. Boh it's a kazzardly onsartin loife we lead. Here to-day an gone the morrow, as Parson Houlden says. Wall-a-day!"

"True, true, Bess," replied the squire, and the best plan therefore is, to make the most of the passing moment. So brew us each a lusty pottle of sack, and fry us some more eggs and bacon."

And while the hostess proceeded to prepare the sack, Potts remarked to Nicholas, "I have got another case of witchcraft, squire. Mary Baldwyn, the miller's daughter, of Rough Lee."

"Indeed!" exclaimed Nicholas. "What, is the poor girl bewitched?"

"Bewitched to death—that's all," said Potts.

"Eigh—poor Meary! hoo's to be berried here this mornin," observed Bess, emptying the bottle of sherris into a pot, and placing the latter on the fire.

"And you think she was forespoken?" said Nicholas, addressing her.

"Folk sayn so," replied Bess; "boh I'd leyther howd my tung about it."

"Then I suppose you pay tribute to Mother Chattox, hostess?" cried Potts,—"butter, eggs, and milk from the farm, ale and wine from the cellar, with a flitch of bacon now and then, ey?"

"Nay, by th' maskins! ey gi' her nowt," cried Bess.

"Then you bribe Mother Demdike, and that comes to the same thing," said Potts.

"Weel, yo're neaw so fur fro' t' mark this time," replied Bess, adding eggs, sugar, and spice to the now boiling wine, and stirring up the compound.

"I wonder where your brother, the reeve of the forest, can be, Master Potts!" observed Nicholas. "I did not see either him or his horse at the stables."

"Perhaps the arch impostor has taken himself off altogether," said Potts; "and if so, I shall be sorry, for I have not done with him."

The sack was now set before them, and pronounced excellent, and while they were engaged in discussing it, together with a fresh supply of eggs and bacon, fried by the kitchen wench, Roger Nowell came out of the inner room, accompanied by Richard and the chirurgeon.

"Well, Master Sudall, how goes on your patient?" inquired Nicholas of the latter.

"Much more favourably than I expected, squire," replied the chirurgeon. "He will be better left alone for awhile, and, as I shall not quit the village till evening, I shall be able to look well after him."

"You think the attack occasioned by witchcraft of course, sir?" said Potts.

"The poor fellow affirms it to be so, but I can give no opinion," replied Sudall, evasively.

"You must make up your mind as to the matter, for I think it right to tell you your evidence will be required," said Potts. "Perhaps, you may have seen poor Mary Baldwyn, the miller's daughter of Rough Lee, and can speak more positively as to her case."

"I can, sir," replied the chirurgeon, seating himself beside Potts, while Roger Nowell and Richard placed themselves on the opposite side of the table. "This is the case I referred to a short time ago, when answering your inquiries on the same subject, Master Richard, and a most afflicting one it is. But you shall have the particulars. Six months ago, Mary Baldwyn was as lovely and blooming a lass as could be seen, the joy of her widowed father's heart. A hot-headed, obstinate man is Richard Baldwyn, and he was unwise enough to incur the displeasure of Mother Demdike, by favouring her rival, old Chattox, to whom he gave flour and meal, while he refused the same tribute to the other. The first time Mother Demdike was dismissed without the customary dole, one of his millstones broke, and, instead of taking this as a warning, he became more obstinate. She came a second time, and he sent her away with curses. Then all his flour grew damp and musty, and no one would buy it. Still he remained obstinate, and, when she appeared again, he would have laid hands upon her. But she raised her staff, and the blows fell short. 'I have given thee two warnings, Richard,' she said, 'and thou hast paid no heed to them. Now I will make thee smart, lad, in right earnest. That which thou lovest best thou shalt lose.' Upon this, bethinking him that the dearest thing he had in the world was his daughter Mary, and afraid of harm happening to her, Richard would fain have made up his quarrel with the old witch; but it had now gone too far, and she would not listen to him, but uttering some words, with which the name of the girl was mingled, shook her staff at the house and departed. The next day poor Mary was taken ill, and her father, in despair, applied to old Chattox, who promised him help, and did her best, I make no doubt—for she would have willingly thwarted her rival, and robbed her of her prey; but the latter was too strong for her, and the hapless victim got daily worse and worse. Her blooming cheek grew white and hollow, her dark eyes glistened with unnatural lustre, and she was seen no more on the banks of Pendle water. Before this my aid had been called in by the afflicted father—and I did all I could—but I knew she would die—and I told him so. The information I feared had killed him, for he fell down like a stone—and I repented having spoken. However he recovered, and made a last appeal to Mother Demdike; but the unrelenting hag derided him and cursed him, telling him if he brought her all his mill contained, and added to that all his substance, she would not spare his child. He returned heart-broken, and never quitted the poor girl's bed-side till she breathed her last."

"Poor Ruchot! Robb'd o' his ownly dowter—an neaw woife to cheer him! Ey pity him fro' t' bottom o' my heart," said Bess, whose tears had flowed freely during the narration.

"He is wellnigh crazed with grief," said the chirurgeon. "I hope he will commit no rash act."

Expressions of deep commiseration for the untimely death of the miller's daughter had been uttered by all the party, and they were talking over the strange circumstances attending it, when they were roused by the trampling of horses' feet at the door, and the moment after, a middle-aged man, clad in deep mourning, but put on in a manner that betrayed the disorder of his mind, entered the house. His looks were wild and frenzied, his cheeks haggard, and he rushed into the room so abruptly that he did not at first observe the company assembled.

"Why, Richard Baldwyn, is that you?" cried the chirurgeon.

"What! is this the father?" exclaimed Potts, taking out his memorandum-book; "I must prepare to interrogate him."

"Sit thee down, Ruchot,—sit thee down, mon," said Bess, taking his hand kindly, and leading him to a bench. "Con ey get thee onny thing?"

"Neaw—neaw, Bess," replied the miller; "ey ha lost aw ey vallied i' this warlt, an ey care na how soon ey quit it mysel."

"Neigh, dunna talk on thus, Ruchot," said Bess, in accents of sincere sympathy. "Theaw win live to see happier an brighter days."

"Ey win live to be revenged, Bess," cried the miller, rising suddenly, and stamping his foot on the ground,—"that accursed witch has robbed me o' my 'eart's chief treasure—hoo has crushed a poor innocent os never injured her i' thowt or deed—an has struck the heaviest blow that could be dealt me; but by the heaven above us ey win requite her! A feyther's deep an lasting curse leet on her guilty heoad, an on those of aw her accursed race. Nah rest, neet nor day, win ey know, till ey ha brought em to the stake."

"Right—right—my good friend—an excellent resolution—bring them to the stake!" cried Potts.

But his enthusiasm was suddenly checked by observing the reeve of the forest peeping from behind the wainscot, and earnestly regarding the miller, and he called the attention of the latter to him.

Richard Baldwyn mechanically followed the expressive gestures of the attorney,—but he saw no one, for the reeve had disappeared.

The incident passed unnoticed by the others, who had been too deeply moved by poor Baldwyn's outburst of grief to pay attention to it.

After a little while Bess Whitaker succeeded in prevailing upon the miller to sit down, and when he became more composed he told her that the funeral procession, consisting of some of his neighbours who had undertaken to attend his ill-fated daughter to her last home, was coming from Rough Lee to Goldshaw, but that, unable to bear them company, he had ridden on by himself. It appeared also, from his muttered threats, that he had meditated some wild project of vengeance against Mother Demdike, which he intended to put into execution before the day was over, but Master Potts endeavoured to dissuade him from this course, assuring him that the most certain and efficacious mode of revenge he could adopt would be through the medium of the law, and that he would give him his best advice and assistance in the matter. While they were talking thus, the bell began to toll, and every stroke seemed to vibrate through the heart of the afflicted father, who was at last so overpowered by grief, that the hostess deemed it expedient to lead him into an inner room, where he might indulge his sorrow unobserved.

Without awaiting the issue of this painful scene, Richard, who was much affected by it, went forth, and taking his horse from the stable, with the intention of riding on slowly before the others, led the animal towards the churchyard. When within a short distance of the grey old fabric he paused. The bell continued to toll mournfully, and deepened the melancholy hue of his thoughts. The sad tale he had heard held possession of his mind, and while he pitied poor Mary Baldwyn, he began to entertain apprehensions that Alizon might meet a similar fate. So many strange circumstances had taken place during the morning's ride; he had listened to so many dismal relations, that, coupled with the dark and mysterious events of the previous night, he was quite bewildered, and felt oppressed as if by a hideous nightmare, which it was impossible to shake off. He thought of Mothers Demdike and Chattox. Could these dread beings be permitted to exercise such baneful influence over mankind? With all the apparent proofs of their power he had received, he still strove to doubt, and to persuade himself that the various cases of witchcraft described to him were only held to be such by the timid and the credulous.

Full of these meditations, he tied his horse to a tree and entered the churchyard, and while pursuing a path shaded by a row of young lime-trees leading to the porch, he perceived at a little distance from him, near the cross erected by Abbot Cliderhow, two persons who attracted his attention. One was the sexton, who was now deep in the grave; and the other an old woman, with her back towards him. Neither had remarked his approach, and, influenced by an unaccountable feeling of curiosity, he stood still to watch their proceedings. Presently, the sexton, who was shovelling out the mould, paused in his task; and the old woman, in a hoarse voice, which seemed familiar to the listener, said, "What hast found, Zachariah?"

"That which yo lack, mother," replied the sexton, "a mazzard wi' aw th' teeth in't."

"Pluck out eight, and give them me," replied the hag.

And, as the sexton complied with her injunction, she added, "Now I must have three scalps."

"Here they be, mother," replied Zachariah, uncovering a heap of mould with his spade. "Two brain-pans bleached loike snow, an the third wi' more hewr on it than ey ha' o' my own sconce. Fro' its size an shape ey should tak it to be a female. Ey ha' laid these three skulls aside fo' ye. Whot dun yo mean to do wi' 'em?"

"Question me not, Zachariah," said the hag, sternly; "now give me some pieces of the mouldering coffin, and fill this box with the dust of the corpse it contained."

The sexton complied with her request.

"Now yo ha' getten aw yo seek, mother," he said, "ey wad pray you to tay your departure, fo' the berrin folk win be here presently."

"I'm going," replied the hag, "but first I must have my funeral rites performed—ha! ha! Bury this for me, Zachariah," she said, giving him a small clay figure. "Bury it deep, and as it moulders away, may she it represents pine and wither, till she come to the grave likewise!"

"An whoam doth it represent, mother?" asked the sexton, regarding the image with curiosity. "Ey dunna knoa the feace?"

"How should you know it, fool, since you have never seen her in whose likeness it is made?" replied the hag. "She is connected with the race I hate."

"Wi' the Demdikes?" inquired the sexton.

"Ay," replied the hag, "with the Demdikes. She passes for one of them—but she is not of them. Nevertheless, I hate her as though she were."

"Yo dunna mean Alizon Device?" said the sexton. "Ey ha' heerd say hoo be varry comely an kind-hearted, an ey should be sorry onny harm befell her."

"Mary Baldwyn, who will soon lie there, was quite as comely and kind-hearted as Alizon," cried the hag, "and yet Mother Demdike had no pity on her."

"An that's true," replied the sexton. "Weel, weel; ey'n do your bidding."

"Hold!" exclaimed Richard, stepping forward. "I will not suffer this abomination to be practised."

"Who is it speaks to me?" cried the hag, turning round, and disclosing the hideous countenance of Mother Chattox. "The voice is that of Richard Assheton."

"It is Richard Assheton who speaks," cried the young man, "and I command you to desist from this wickedness. Give me

RICHARD OVERHEARS CHATTOX AND THE SEXTON. P. 247

that clay image," he cried, snatching it from the sexton, and trampling it to dust beneath his feet. "Thus I destroy thy impious handiwork, and defeat thy evil intentions."

"Ah! think'st thou so, lad," rejoined Mother Chattox. "Thou wilt find thyself mistaken. My curse has already alighted upon thee, and it shall work. Thou lov'st Alizon.—I know it. But she shall never be thine. Now, go thy ways."

"I will go," replied Richard—"but you shall come with me, old woman."

"Dare you lay hands on me?" screamed the hag.

"Nay, let her be, mester," interposed the sexton, "yo had better."

"You are as bad as she is," said Richard, "and deserve equal punishment. You escaped yesterday at Whalley, old woman, but you shall not escape me now."

"Be not too sure of that," cried the hag, disabling him for the moment, by a severe blow on the arm from her staff. And shuffling off with an agility which could scarcely have been expected from her, she passed through a gate near her, and disappeared behind a high wall.

Richard would have followed, but he was detained by the sexton, who besought him, as he valued his life, not to interfere, and when at last he broke away from the old man, he could see nothing of her, and only heard the sound of horses' feet in the distance. Either his eyes deceived him, or at a turn in the woody lane skirting the church he descried the reeve of the forest galloping off with the old woman behind him. This lane led towards Rough Lee, and, without a moment's hesitation, Richard flew to the spot where he had left his horse, and, mounting him, rode swiftly along it.

CHAPTER VI.—THE TEMPTATION.

SHORTLY after Richard's departure, a round, rosy-faced personage, whose rusty black cassock, hastily huddled over a dark riding-dress, proclaimed him a churchman, entered the hostel. This was the rector of Goldshaw, Parson Holden, a very worthy little man, though rather, perhaps, too fond of the sports of the field and the bottle. To Roger Nowell and Nicholas Assheton he was of course well known, and was much esteemed by the latter, often riding over to hunt and fish, or carouse, at Downham. Parson Holden had been sent for by Bess to administer spiritual consolation to poor Richard Baldwyn, who she thought stood in need of it, and having respectfully saluted the magistrate, of whom he stood somewhat in awe, and shaken hands cordially with Nicholas, who was delighted to see him, he repaired to the inner room, promising to come back speedily. And he kept his word; for in less than five minutes he reappeared with the satisfactory intelligence that the afflicted miller was considerably calmer, and had listened to his counsels with much edification.

"Take him a glass of aquavitæ, Bess," he said to the hostess. "He is evidently a cup too low, and will be the better for it. Strong water is a specific I always recommend under such circumstances, Master Sudall, and indeed adopt myself, and I am sure you will approve of it.—Harkee, Bess, when you have ministered to poor Baldwyn's wants, I must crave your attention to my own, and beg you to fill me a tankard with your oldest ale, and toast me an oatcake to eat with it.—I must keep up my spirits, worthy sir," he added to Roger Nowell, "for I have a painful duty to perform. I do not know when I have been more shocked than by the death of poor Mary Baldwyn. A fair flower, and early nipped."

"Nipped, indeed, if all we have heard be correct, rejoined Nowell. "The forest is in a sad state, reverend sir. It would seem as if the enemy of mankind, by means of his abominable agents, were permitted to exercise uncontrolled dominion over it. I must needs say, the forlorn condition of the people reflects little credit on those who have them in charge. The powers of darkness could never have prevailed to such an extent if duly resisted."

"I lament to hear you say so, good Master Nowell," replied the rector. "I have done my best, I assure you, to keep my small and widely-scattered flock together, and to save them from the ravening wolves and cunning foxes that infest the country; and if now and then some sheep have gone astray, or a poor lamb, as in the instance of Mary Baldwyn, hath fallen a victim, I am scarcely to blame for the mischance. Rather let me say, sir, that you, as an active and zealous magistrate, should take the matter in hand, and by severe dealing with the offenders, arrest the progress of the evil. No defence, spiritual or otherwise, as yet set up against them, has proved effectual."

"Justly remarked, reverend sir," observed Potts, looking up from the memorandum book in which he was writing, "and I am sure your advice will not be lost upon Master Roger Nowell. As regards the persons who may be afflicted by witchcraft, hath not our sagacious monarch observed, that 'There are three kind of folks who may be tempted or troubled: the wicked for their horrible sins, to punish them in the like measure; the godly that are sleeping in any great sins or infirmities, and weakness in faith, to waken them up the faster by such an uncouth form; and even some of the best, that their patience may be tried before the world as Job's was tried. For why may not God use any kind of extraordinary punishment, when it pleases Him, as well as the ordinary rods of sickness, or other adversities?'"

"Very true, sir," replied Holden. "And we are undergoing this severe trial now Fortunate are they who profit by it!"

"Hear what is said further, sir, by the king," pursued Potts. "'No man,' declares that wise prince, 'ought to presume so far as to promise any impunity to himself.' But further on he gives us courage, for he adds, 'and yet we ought not to be afraid for that, of any thing that the devil and his wicked instruments can do against us, for we daily fight against him in a hundred other ways, and therefore as a valiant captain affrays no more being at the combat, nor stays from his purpose for the rummishing shot of a cannon, nor the small clack of a pistolet; not being certain what may light on him; even so ought we boldly to go forward in fighting against the devil without any greater terror, for these his rarest weapons, than the ordinary, whereof we have daily the proof.'"

"His majesty is quite right," observed Holden, "and I am glad to hear his convincing words so judiciously cited. I myself have no fear of these wicked instruments of Satan."

"In what manner, may I ask, have you proved your courage, sir?" inquired Roger Nowell. "Have you preached against them, and denounced their wickedness, menacing them with the thunders of the Church?"

"I cannot say I have," replied Holden, rather abashed, "but I shall henceforth adopt a very different course.—Ah! here comes the ale!" he added, taking the foaming tankard from Bess; "this is the best cordial wherewith to sustain one's courage in these trying times."

"Some remedy must be found for this intolerable grievance," observed Roger Nowell, after a few moments' reflection. "Till this morning I was not aware of the extent of the evil, but supposed that the two malignant hags, who seem to reign supreme here, confined their operations to blighting corn, maiming cattle, turning milk sour; and even these reports I fancied were greatly exaggerated; but I now find, from what I have seen at Sabden and elsewhere, that they fall very far short of the reality."

"It would be difficult to increase the darkness of the picture," said the chirurgeon; "but what remedy will you apply?"

"The cautery, sir," replied Potts,—"the actual cautery—we will burn out this plague-spot. The two old hags and their noxious brood shall be brought to the stake. That will effect a radical cure."

"It may when it is accomplished, but I fear it will be long ere that happens," replied the chirurgeon, shaking his head doubtfully. "Are you acquainted with Mother Demdike's history, sir?" he added to Potts.

"In part," replied the attorney; "but I shall be glad to hear any thing you may have to bring forward on the subject."

"The peculiarity in her case," observed Sudall, "and the circumstance distinguishing her dark and dread career from that of all other witches is, that it has been shaped out by destiny. When an infant, a malediction was pronounced upon her head by the unfortunate Abbot Paslew. She is also the offspring of a man reputed to have bartered his soul to the Enemy of Mankind, while her mother was a witch. Both parents perished lamentably, about the time of Paslew's execution at Whalley."

"It is a pity their miserable infant did not perish with them," observed Holden. "How much crime and misery would have been spared!"

"It was otherwise ordained," replied Sudall. "Bereft of her parents in this way, the infant was taken charge of and reared by Dame Croft, the miller's wife of Whalley; but even in those early days she exhibited such a malicious and vindictive disposition, and became so unmanageable, that the good dame was glad to get rid of her, and sent her into the forest, where she found a home at Rough Lee, then occupied by Miles Nutter, the grandfather of the late Richard Nutter."

"Aha!" exclaimed Potts, "was Mother Demdike so early connected with that family? I must make a note of that circumstance."

"She remained at Rough Lee for some years," returned Sudall, "and though accounted of an ill disposition, there was nothing to be alleged against her at the time; though afterwards, it was said, that some mishaps that befell the neighbours were owing to her agency, and that she was always attended by a familiar in the form of a rat or a mole. Whether this were so or not, I cannot say; but it is certain that she helped Miles Nutter to get rid of his wife, and procured him a second spouse, in return for which services he bestowed upon her an old ruined tower on his domains."

"You mean Malkin Tower?" said Nicholas.

"Ay, Malkin Tower," replied the chirurgeon. "There is a legend connected with that structure, which I will relate to you anon, if you desire it. But to proceed. Scarcely had Bess Demdike taken up her abode in this lone tower, than it began to be rumoured that she was a witch, and attended sabbaths on the summit of Pendle Hill, and on Rimington Moor. Few would consort with her, and ill-luck invariably attended those with whom she quarrelled. Though of hideous and forbidding aspect, and with one eye lower set than the other, she had subtlety enough to induce a young man named Sothernes to marry her, and two children, a son and a daughter, were the fruit of the union."

"The daughter I have seen at Whalley," observed Potts; "but I have never encountered the son."

"Christopher Demdike still lives, I believe," replied the chirurgeon, "though what has become of him I know not, for he has quitted these parts. He is as ill-reputed as his mother, and has the same strange and fearful look about the eyes."

"I shall recognise him if I see him," observed Potts.

"You are scarcely likely to meet him," returned Sudall, "for, as I have said, he has left the forest. But to return to my story. The marriage state was little suitable to Bess Demdike, and in five years she contrived to free herself from her husband's restraint, and ruled alone in the tower. Her malignant influence now began to be felt throughout the whole district, and by dint of menaces and positive acts of mischief, she extorted all she required. Whosoever refused her requests speedily experienced her resentment. When she was in the fulness of her power, a rival sprang up in the person of Anne Whittle, since known by the name of Chattox, which she obtained in marriage, and this woman disputed Bess Demdike's supremacy. Each strove to injure the adherents of her rival—and terrible was the mischief they wrought. In the end, however, Mother Demdike got the upper hand. Years have flown over the old hag's head, and her guilty career has been hitherto attended with impunity. Plans have been formed to bring her to justice, but they have ever failed. And so in the case of old Chattox. Her career has been as baneful and as successful as that of Mother Demdike."

"But their course is wellnigh run," said Potts, "and the time is come for the extirpation of the old serpents."

"Ah! who is that at the window?" cried Sudall; "but that you are sitting near me, I should declare you were looking in at us."

"It must be Master Potts's brother, the reeve of the forest," observed Nicholas, with a laugh.

"Heed him not," cried the attorney, angrily, "but let us have the promised legend of Malkin Tower."

"Willingly!" replied the chirurgeon. "But before I begin I must recruit myself with a can of ale."

The flagon being set before him, Sudall commenced his story:

The Legend of Malkin Tower.

"On the brow of a high hill forming part of the range of Pendle, and commanding an extensive view over the forest, and the wild and mountainous region around it, stands a stern solitary tower. Old as the Anglo-Saxons, and built as a stronghold by Wulstan, a Northumbrian thane, in the time of Edmund or Edred, it is circular in form and very lofty, and serves as a landmark to the country round. Placed high up in the building the door was formerly reached by a steep flight of stone steps, but these were removed some fifty or sixty years ago by Mother Demdike, and a ladder capable of being raised or let down at pleasure substituted for them, affording the only apparent means of entrance. The tower is otherwise inaccessible, the walls being of immense thickness, with no window lower than five-and-twenty feet from the ground, though it is thought there must be a secret outlet; for the old witch, when she wants to come forth, does not wait for the ladder to be let down. But this may be otherwise explained. Internally there are three floors, the lowest being placed on a level with the door, and this is the apartment chiefly occupied by the hag. In the centre of this room is a trapdoor opening upon a deep vault, which forms the basement story of the structure, and which was once used as a dungeon, but is now tenanted, it is said, by a fiend, who can be summoned by the witch on stamping her foot. Round the room runs a gallery contrived in the thickness of the walls, while the upper chambers are gained by a secret staircase, and closed by movable stones, the machinery of which is only known to the inmate of the tower. All the rooms are lighted by narrow loopholes. Thus you will see that the fortress is still capable of sustaining a siege, and old Demdike has been heard to declare that she would hold it for a month against a hundred men. Hitherto it has proved impregnable.

"On the Norman invasion, Malkin Tower was held by Ughtred, a descendant of Wulstan, who kept possession of Pendle Forest and the hills around it, and successfully resisted the aggressions of the conquerors. His enemies affirmed he was assisted by a demon, whom he had propitiated by some fearful sacrifice made in the tower, and the notion seemed borne out by the success uniformly attending his conflicts. Ughtred's prowess was stained by cruelty and rapine. Merciless in the treatment of his captives, putting them to death by horrible tortures, or immuring them in the dark and noisome dungeon of his tower, he would hold his revels over their heads, and deride their groans. Heaps of treasure, obtained by pillage, were secured by him in the tower. From his frequent acts of treachery, and the many foul murders he perpetrated, Ughtred was styled the 'Scourge of the Normans.' For a long period he enjoyed complete immunity from punishment; but after the siege of York, and the defeat of the insurgents, his destruction was vowed by Ilbert de Lacy, lord of Blackburnshire, and this fierce chieftain set fire to part of the forest in which the Saxon thane and his followers were concealed; drove them to Malkin Tower; took it after an obstinate and prolonged defence, and considerable loss to himself, and put them all to the sword, except the leader, whom he hanged from the top of his own fortress. In the dungeon were found many carcasses, and the greater part of Ughtred's treasure served to enrich the victor.

"Once again, in the reign of Henry VI., Malkin Tower became a robber's stronghold, and gave protection to a freebooter named Blackburn, who, with a band of daring and desperate marauders, took advantage of the troubled state of the country, ravaged it far and wide, and committed unheard of atrocities, even levying contributions upon the Abbeys of Whalley and Salley, and the heads of these religious establishments were glad to make terms with him to save their herds and stores, the rather that all attempts to dislodge him from his mountain fastness, and destroy his band, had failed. Blackburn seemed to enjoy the same kind of protection as Ughtred, and practised the same atrocities, torturing and imprisoning his captives unless they were heavily ransomed. He also led a life of wildest licence, and, when not engaged in some predatory exploit, spent his time in carousing with his followers.

"Upon one occasion it chanced that he made a visit in disguise to Whalley Abbey, and, passing the little hermitage near the church, beheld the votaress who tenanted it. This was Isole de Heton. Ravished by her wondrous beauty, Blackburn soon found an opportunity of making his passion known to her, and his handsome though fierce lineaments pleasing her, he did not long sigh in vain. He frequently visited her in the garb of a Cistertian monk, and, being taken for one of the brethren, his conduct brought great scandal upon the Abbey. The abandoned votaress bore him a daughter, and the infant was conveyed away by the lover, and placed under the care of a peasant's wife, at Barrowford. From that child sprung Bess Blackburn, the mother of old Demdike; so that the witch is a direct descendant of Isole de Heton.

"Notwithstanding all precautions, Isole's dark offence became known, and she would have paid the penalty of it at the stake, if she had not fled. In scaling Whalley Nab, in the woody heights of which she was to remain concealed till her lover could come to her, she fell from a rock, shattering her limbs, and disfiguring her features. Some say she was lamed for life, and became as hideous as she had heretofore been lovely; but this is erroneous, for apprehensive of such a result, attended by the loss of her lover, she invoked the powers of darkness, and proffered her soul in return for five years of unimpaired beauty.

"The compact was made, and when Blackburn came he found her more beautiful than ever. Enraptured, he conveyed her to Malkin Tower, and lived with her there in security, laughing to scorn the menaces of Abbot Eccles, by whom he was excommunicated.

"Time went on, and as Isole's charms underwent no change, her lover's ardour continued unabated. Five years passed in guilty pleasures, and the last day of the allotted term arrived. No change was manifest in Isole's demeanour; neither remorse nor fear were exhibited by her. Never had she appeared more lovely, never in higher or more exuberant spirits. She besought her lover, who was still madly intoxicated by her infernal charms, to give a banquet that night to ten of his trustiest followers. He willingly assented, and bade them to the feast. They ate and drank merrily, and the gayest of the company was the lovely

Isole. Her spirits seemed somewhat too wild even to Blackburn, but he did not check her, though surprised at the excessive liveliness and freedom of her sallies. Her eyes flashed like fire, and there was not a man present but was madly in love with her, and ready to dispute for her smiles with his captain.

"The wine flowed freely, and song and jest went on till midnight. When the hour struck, Isole filled a cup to the brim, and called upon them to pledge her. All arose, and drained their goblets enthusiastically. 'It was a farewell cup,' she said; 'I am going away with one of you.' 'How!' exclaimed Blackburn, in angry surprise. 'Let any one but touch your hand, and I will strike him dead at my feet.' The rest of the company regarded each other with surprise, and it was then discovered that a stranger was amongst them; a tall dark man, whose looks were so terrible and demoniacal that no one dared lay hands upon him. 'I am come,' he said, with fearful significance, to Isole. 'And I am ready,' she answered boldly. 'I will go with you were it to the bottomless pit,' cried Blackburn catching hold of her. 'It is thither I am going,' she answered with a scream of laughter. 'I shall be glad of a companion.'

"When the paroxysm of laughter was over, she fell down on the floor. Her lover would have raised her, when what was his horror to find that he held in his arms an old woman, with frightfully disfigured features, and evidently in the agonies of death. She fixed one look upon him and expired.

"Terrified by the occurrence the guests hurried away, and when they returned next day, they found Blackburn stretched on the floor, and quite dead. They cast his body, together with that of the wretched Isole, into the vault beneath the room where they were lying, and then, taking possession of his treasure, removed to some other retreat.

"Thenceforth, Malkin Tower became haunted. Though wholly deserted, lights were constantly seen shining from it at night, and sounds of wild revelry, succeeded by shrieks and groans, issued from it. The figure of Isole was often seen to come forth, and flit across the wastes in the direction of Whalley Abbey. On stormy nights a huge black cat, with flaming eyes, was frequently descried on the summit of the structure, whence it obtained its name of Grimalkin, or Malkin Tower. The ill-omened pile ultimately came into the possession of the Nutter family, but it was never tenanted, until assigned, as I have already mentioned, to Mother Demdike."

The chirurgeon's marvellous story was listened to with great attention by his auditors. Most of them were familiar with different versions of it; but to Master Potts it was altogether new, and he made rapid notes of it, questioning the narrator as to one or two points which appeared to him to require explanation. Nicholas, as may be supposed, was particularly interested in that part of the legend which referred to Isole de Heton. He now for the first time heard of her unhallowed intercourse with the freebooter Blackburn, of her compact on Whalley Nab with the fiend, of her mysterious connection with Malkin Tower, and of her being the ancestress of Mother Demdike. The consideration of all these points, coupled with a vivid recollection of his own strange adventure with the impious votaress at the Abbey on the previous night, plunged him into a deep train of thought, and he began seriously to consider whether he might not have committed some heinous sin, and, indeed, jeopardised his soul's welfare by dancing with her. "What if I should share the same fate as the robber Blackburn," he ruminated, "and be dragged to perdition by her? It is a very awful reflection. But though my fate might operate as a warning to others, I am by no means anxious to be held up as a moral scarecrow. Rather let me take warning myself, amend my life, abandon intemperance, which leads to all manner of wickedness, and suffer myself no more to be ensnared by the wiles and delusions of the tempter in the form of a fair woman. No—no—I will alter and amend my life."

I regret, however, to say that these praiseworthy resolutions were but transient, and that the squire, quite forgetting that the work of reform, if intended to be really accomplished, ought to commence at once, and by no means be postponed till the morrow, yielded to the seductions of a fresh pottle of sack, which was presented to him at the moment by Bess, and in taking it could not help squeezing the hand of the bouncing hostess, and gazing at her more tenderly than became a married man. Oh! Nicholas—Nicholas—the work of reform, I am afraid, proceeds very slowly and imperfectly with you. Your friend, Parson Dewhurst, would have told you that it is much easier to form good resolutions than to keep them.

Leaving the squire, however, to his cogitations and his sack, the attorney to his memorandum-book, in which he was still engaged in writing, and the others to their talk, we shall proceed to the chamber whither the poor miller had been led by Bess. When visited by the rector, he had been apparently soothed by the worthy man's consolatory advice, but when left alone he speedily relapsed into his former dark and gloomy state of mind. He did not notice Bess, who, according to Holden's directions, placed the aquavitæ bottle before him, but, as long as she stayed, remained with his face buried in his hands. As soon as she was gone he arose, and began to pace the room to and fro. The window was open, and he could hear the funeral bell tolling mournfully at intervals. Each recurrence of the dismal sound added sharpness and intensity to his grief. His sufferings became almost intolerable, and drove him to the very verge of despair and madness. If a weapon had been at hand, he might have seized it, and put a sudden period to his existence. His breast was a chaos of fierce and troubled thoughts, in which one black and terrible idea arose and overpowered all the rest. It was the desire of vengeance, deep and complete, upon her whom he looked upon as the murderess of his child. He cared not how it were accomplished so it were done; but such was the opinion he entertained of the old hag's power, that he doubted his ability to the task. Still, as the bell tolled on, the furies at his heart lashed and goaded him on, and yelled in his ear revenge—revenge! Now, indeed, he was crazed with grief and rage; he tore off handfuls of hair, plunged his nails deeply into his breast, and while committing these and other wild excesses, with frantic imprecations he called down Heaven's judgments on his own head. He was in that lost and helpless state when the enemy of mankind has power over man. Nor was the opportunity neglected; for when the wretched Baldwyn, who, exhausted by the violence of his motions, had leaned for a moment against the wall, he perceived to his surprise that there was a man in the room—a small personage attired in rusty black, whom he thought had been one of the party in the adjoining chamber.

There was an expression of mockery about this person's countenance which did not please the miller, and he asked him, sternly, what he wanted.

"Leave off grinnin, mon," he said, fiercely, "or ey may be tempted to tay yo be t' throttle, an may yo laugh o't wrong side o' your mouth."

"No, no, you will not, Richard Baldwyn, when you know my errand," replied the man. "You are thirsting for vengeance upon Mother Demdike. You shall have it."

"Eigh, eigh, you promised me vengeance efore," cried the miller—"vengeance by the law. Boh ey mun wait lung for it. Ey wad ha' it swift and sure—deep and deadly. Ey wad blast her wi' curses, os hoo blasted my poor Meary. Ey wad strike her deeod at my feet. That's my vengeance, mon."

"You shall have it," replied the other.

"Yo talk differently fro' what yo did just now, mon," said the miller, regarding him narrowly and distrustfully. "An yo look differently too. There's a queer glimmer abowt your een that ey didna notice efore, and that ey mislike."

The man laughed bitterly.

"Leave off grinnin' or begone," cried Baldwyn, furiously. And he raised his hand to strike the man, but he instantly dropped it, appalled by a look which the other threw at him. "Who the dule are yo?"

"The dule must answer you, since you appeal to him," replied the other, with the same mocking smile; "but you are mistaken in supposing that you have spoken to me before. He with whom you conversed in the other room, resembles me in more respects than one, but he does not possess power equal to mine. The law will not aid you against Mother Demdike. She will escape all the snares laid for her. But she will not escape *me*."

"Who are ye?" cried the miller, his hair erecting on his head, and cold damps breaking out upon his brow. "Yo are nah mortal, an nah good, to tawk i' this fashion."

"Heed not who and what I am," replied the other; "I am known here as a reeve of the forest—that is enough. Would you have vengeance on the murtheress of your child?"

"Yeigh," rejoined Baldwyn.

"And you are willing to pay for it at the price of your soul?" demanded the other, advancing towards him.

Baldwyn reeled. He saw at once the fearful peril in which he was placed, and averted his gaze from the scorching glance of the reeve.

At this moment the door was tried without, and the voice of Bess was heard, saying, "Who ha' yo got wi' yo, Ruchot; and whoy ha' yo fastened t' door?"

"Your answer?" demanded the reeve.

"Ey canna gi' it now," replied the miller. "Come in, Bess; come in."

"Ey conna," she replied. "Open t' door, mon."

"Your answer, I say?" said the reeve.

"Gi' me an hour to think on't," said the miller.

"Agreed," replied the other. "I will be with you after the funeral."

And he sprang through the window, and disappeared before Baldwyn could open the door and admit Bess.

CHAPTER VII.—THE PERAMBULATION OF THE BOUNDARIES.

THE lane along which Richard Assheton galloped in pursuit of Mother Chattox, made so many turns, and was, moreover, so completely hemmed in by high banks and hedges, that he could see nothing on either side of him, and very little in advance; but, guided by the clatter of hoofs, he urged Merlin to his utmost speed, fancying he should soon come up with the fugitives. In this, however, he was deceived. The sound that had led him on became fainter and fainter, till at last it died away altogether; and on quitting the lane and gaining the moor, where the view was wholly uninterrupted, no traces either of witch or reeve could be discerned.

With a feeling of angry disappointment, Richard was about to turn back, when a large black greyhound came from out an adjoining clough, and made towards him. The singularity of the circumstance induced him to halt and regard the dog with attention. On nearing him, the animal looked wistfully in his face, and seemed to invite him to follow; and the young man was so struck by the dog's manner, that he complied, and had not gone far when a hare of unusual size and grey with age bounded from beneath a gorse-bush and speeded away, the greyhound starting in pursuit.

Aware of the prevailing notion, that a witch most commonly assumed such a form when desirous of escaping, or performing some act of mischief, such as drying the milk of kine, Richard at once came to the conclusion that the hare could be no other than Mother Chattox; and without pausing to inquire what the hound could be, or why it should appear at such a singular and apparently fortunate juncture, he at once joined the run, and cheered on the dog with whoop and holloa.

Old as it was, apparently, the hare ran with extraordinary swiftness, clearing every stone wall and other impediment in the way, and more than once cunningly doubling upon its pursuers. But every feint and stratagem were defeated by the fleet and sagacious hound, and the hunted animal at length took to the open waste, where the run became so rapid, that Richard had enough to do to keep up with it, though Merlin, almost as furiously excited as his master, strained every sinew to the task.

In this way the chasers and the chased scoured the dark and heathy plain, skirting moss-pool and clearing dyke, till they almost reached the but-end of Pendle Hill, which rose like an impassable barrier before them. Hitherto the chances had seemed in favour of the hare; but they now began to turn, and as it seemed certain she must fall into the hound's jaws, Richard expected every moment to find her resume her natural form. The run having brought him within a quarter of a mile of Barley, the rude hovels composing which little booth were clearly discernible, the young man began to think the hag's dwelling must be among them, and that she was hurrying thither as to a place of refuge. But before this could be accomplished, he hoped to effect her capture, and once more cheered on the hound, and plunged his spurs into Merlin's sides. An obstacle, however, occurred which he had not counted on. Directly in the course taken by the hare lay a deep, disused limestone quarry, completely screened from view by a fringe of brushwood. When within a few yards of this pit, the hound made a dash at the flying hare, but eluding him, the latter sprang forward, and both went over the edge of the quarry together. Richard had well-nigh followed, and in that case would have been inevitably dashed in pieces; but, discovering the danger ere it was too late, by a powerful effort, which threw Merlin upon his haunches, he pulled him back on the very brink of the pit.

The young man shuddered as he gazed into the depths of the quarry, and saw the jagged points and heaps of broken stone that would have received him; but he looked in vain for the old witch, whose mangled body, together with that of the hound, he expected to behold; and he then asked himself whether the chase might not have been a snare set for him by the hag and her familiar, with the intent of luring him to destruction. If so, he had been providentially preserved.

Quitting the pit, his first idea was to proceed to Barley, which was now only a few hundred yards off, to make inquiries respecting Mother Chattox, and ascertain whether she really dwelt there; but, on further consideration, he judged it best to return without further delay to Goldshaw, lest his friends, ignorant as to what had befallen him, might become alarmed on his account; but he resolved, as soon as he had disposed of the business in hand, to prosecute his search after the hag. Riding rapidly, he soon cleared the ground between the quarry and Goldshaw Lane, and was about to enter the latter, when the sound of voices singing a funeral hymn caught his ear, and, pausing to listen to it, he beheld a little procession, the meaning of which he readily comprehended, wending its slow and melancholy way in the same direction as himself. It was headed by four men in deep mourning, bearing upon their shoulders a small coffin, covered with a pall, and having a garland of white flowers in front of it. Behind them followed about a dozen young men and maidens, likewise in mourning, walking two and two, with gait and aspect of unfeigned affliction. Many of the women, though merely rustics, seemed to possess considerable personal attraction; but their features were in a great measure concealed by their large white kerchiefs, disposed in the form of hoods. All carried sprigs of rosemary and bunches of flowers in their hands. Plaintive was the hymn they sang, and their voices, though untaught, were sweet and touching, and went to the heart of the listener.

Much moved, Richard suffered the funeral procession to precede him along the deep and devious lane, and as it winded beneath the hedges, the sight was inexpressibly affecting. Fastening his horse to a tree at the end of the lane, Richard followed on foot. Notice of the approach of the train having been given in the village, all the inhabitants flocked forth to meet it, and there was scarcely a dry eye among them. Arrived within a short distance of the church, the coffin was met by the minister, attended by the clerk, behind whom came Roger Nowell, Nicholas, and the rest of the company from the hostel. With great difficulty poor Baldwyn could be brought to take his place as chief mourner. These arrangements completed, the body of the ill-fated girl was borne into the churchyard, the minister reading the solemn texts appointed for the occasion, and leading the way to the grave, beside which stood the sexton, together with the beadle of Goldshaw and Sparshot. The coffin was then laid on trestles, and amidst profound silence, broken only by the sobs of the mourners, the service was read, and preparations made for lowering the body into the grave.

Then it was that poor Baldwyn, with a wild, heart-piercing cry, flung himself upon the shell containing all that remained of his lost treasure, and could with difficulty be removed from it by Bess and Sudall, both of whom were in attendance. The bunches of flowers and sprigs of rosemary having been laid upon the coffin by the maidens, amidst loud sobbing and audibly expressed lamentations from the bystanders, it was let down into the grave, and earth thrown over it.

Earth to earth; ashes to ashes; dust to dust.

The ceremony was over, the mourners betook themselves to the little hostel, and the spectators slowly dispersed; but the bereaved father still lingered, unable to tear himself away. Leaning for support against the yew-tree, he fiercely bade Bess, who would have led him home with her, begone. The kind-hearted hostess complied in appearance, but remained nigh at hand though concealed from view.

Once more the dark cloud overshadowed the spirit of the wretched man—once more the same infernal desire of vengeance possessed him—once more he subjected himself to temptation. Striding to the foot of the grave he raised his hand, and with terrible imprecations vowed to lay the murtheress of his child as low as she herself was now laid. At that moment he felt an eye like a burning-glass fixed upon him, and, looking up, beheld the reeve of the forest standing on the further side of the grave.

"Kneel down, and swear to be mine, and your wish shall be gratified," said the reeve.

Beside himself with grief and rage, Baldwyn would have complied, but he was arrested by a powerful grasp. Fearing he was about to commit some rash act, Bess rushed forward and caught hold of his doublet.

"Bethink thee whot theaw has just heerd fro' t' minister, Ruchot," she cried in a voice of solemn warning. "'Blessed are the dead that dee i' the Lord, for they rest fro their labours.' An again, 'Suffer us not at our last hour, for onny pains o' death, to fa' fro thee.' Oh Ruchot, dear! fo' the love theaw hadst fo' thy poor chilt, who is now delivert fro' the burthen o' th' flesh, an' dwellin' i' joy an felicity wi' God an his angels, dunna endanger thy precious sowl. Pray that theaw may'st depart hence i' th' Lord, wi' whom are the sowls of the faithful, an Meary's, ey trust, umong the number. Pray that thy eend may be like hers."

"Ey conna pray, Bess," replied the miller, striking his breast. "The Lord has turned his feace fro' me."

"Becose thy heart is hardened, Ruchot," she replied. "Theaw

'rt nourishin' nowt boh black an wicked thowts. Cast em off ye, I adjure thee, an come whoam wi me."

Meanwhile, the reeve had sprung across the grave.

"Thy answer at once," he said, grasping the miller's arm, and breathing the words in his ears. "Vengeance is in thy power. A word, and it is thine."

The miller groaned bitterly. He was sorely tempted.

"What is that mon sayin' to thee, Ruchot?" inquired Bess.

"Dunna ax, boh tak me away," he answered. "Ey am lost else."

"Let him lay a finger on yo if he dare," said Bess, sturdily.

"Leave him alone—yo dunna knoa who he is," whispered the miller.

"Ey con partly guess," she rejoined; "boh ey care nother fo' mon nor dule when ey'm acting reetly. Come along wi' me, Ruchot."

"Fool!" cried the reeve, in the same low tone as before; "you will lose your revenge, but you will not escape me."

And he turned away, while Bess almost carried the trembling and enfeebled miller towards the hostel.

Roger Nowell and his friends had only waited the conclusion of the funeral to set forth, and their horses being in readiness, they mounted them on leaving the churchyard, and rode slowly along the lane leading towards Rough Lee. The melancholy scene they had witnessed, and the afflicting circumstances connected with it, had painfully affected the party, and little conversation occurred until they were overtaken by Parson Holden, who, having been made acquainted with their errand by Nicholas, was desirous of accompanying them. Soon after this, also, the reeve of the forest joined them, and on seeing him, Richard sternly demanded why he had aided Mother Chattox in her flight from the churchyard, and what had become of her.

"You are entirely mistaken, sir," replied the reeve, with affected astonishment. "I have seen nothing whatever of the old hag, and would rather lend a hand to her capture than abet her flight. I hold all witches in abhorrence, and Mother Chattox especially so."

"Your horse looks fresh enough, certainly," said Richard, somewhat shaken in his suspicions. "Where have you been during our stay at Goldshaw? You did not put up at the hostel?"

"I went to Farmer Johnson's," replied the reeve, "and you will find upon inquiry that my horse has not been out of his stables for the last hour. I myself have been loitering about Bess's grange and farmyard, as your grooms will testify, for they have seen me."

"Humph!" exclaimed Richard, "I suppose I must credit assertions made with such confidence, but I could have sworn I saw you ride off with the hag behind you."

"I hope I shall never be caught in such bad company, sir," replied the reeve, with a laugh. "If I ride off with any one, it shall not be with an old witch, depend upon it."

Though by no means satisfied with the explanation, Richard was forced to be content with it; but he thought he would address a few more questions to the reeve.

"Have you any knowledge," he said, "when the boundaries of Pendle Forest were first settled and appointed?"

"The first perambulation was made by Henry de Lacy, about the middle of the twelfth century," replied the reeve. "Pendle Forest, you may be aware, sir, is one of the four divisions of the great forest of Blackburnshire, of which the Lacys were lords, the three other divisions being Accrington, Trawden, and Rossendale, and it comprehends an extent of about twenty-five miles, part of which you have traversed to-day. At a later period, namely in 1311, after the death of another Henry de Lacy, Earl of Lincoln, the last of his line, and one of the bravest of Edward the First's barons, an inquisition was held in the forest, and it was subdivided into eleven vaccaries, one of which is the place to which you are bound, Rough Lee."

"The learned Sir Edward Coke defines a vaccary to signify a dairy," observed Potts.

"Here it means the farm and land as well," replied the reeve; "and the word 'booth,' which is in general use in this district, signifies the mansion erected upon such vaccary: Mistress Nutter's residence, for instance, being nothing more than the booth of Rough Lee: while a 'lawnd,' another local term, is a park inclosed within the forest for the preservation of the deer, and the convenience of the chase, and of such inclosures we have two, namely, the Old and New Lawnd. By a commission in the reign of Henry VII., these vaccaries, originally granted only to tenants at will, were converted into copyholds of inheritance, but—and here is a legal point for your consideration, Master Potts—as it seems very questionable whether titles obtained under letters-patent are secure, not unreasonable fears are entertained by the holders of the lands lest they should be seized, and appropriated by the crown."

"Ah! ah! an excellent idea, Master Reeve," exclaimed Potts, his little eyes twinkling with pleasure. "Our gracious and sagacious monarch would grasp at the suggestion, ay, and grasp at the lands too—ha! ha! Many thanks for the hint, good reeve. I will not fail to profit by it. If their titles are uncertain, the landholders would be glad to compromise the matter with the crown, even to the value of half their estates rather than lose the whole."

"Most assuredly they would," replied the reeve; "and furthermore, they would pay the lawyer well who could manage the matter adroitly for them. This would answer your purpose better than hunting up witches, Master Potts."

"One pursuit does not interfere with the other in the slightest degree, worthy reeve," observed Potts. "I cannot consent to give up my quest of the witches. My honour is concerned in their extermination. But to turn to Pendle Forest—the greater part of it has been disafforested, I presume?"

"It has," replied the other—"and we are now in one of the purlieus."

"Pourallee is the better word, most excellent reeve," said Potts. "I tell you thus much, because you appear to be a man of learning. Manwood, our great authority in such matters, declares a pourallee to be 'a certain territory of ground adjoining unto the forest, mered and bounded with immovable marks, meres, and boundaries, known by matter of record only.' And as it applies to the perambulation we are about to make, I may as well repeat what the same learned writer further saith touching marks, meres, and boundaries, and how they may be known. 'For although,' he saith, 'a forest doth lie open, and not inclosed with hedge, ditch, pale, or stone-wall, which some other inclosures have; yet in the eye and consideration of the law, the same hath as strong an inclosure by those marks, meres, and boundaries, as if there were a brick wall to encircle the same.' Marks, learned reeve, are deemed unremovable—*primo, quia omnes metæ forestæ sunt integræ domino regi*—and those who take them away are punishable for the trespass at the assizes of the forest. *Secundo*, because the marks are things that cannot be stirred, as rivers, highways, hills, and the like. Now, such unremoveable marks, meres, and boundaries we have between the estate of my excellent client, Master Roger Nowell, and that of Mistress Nutter, so that the matter at issue will be easily decided."

A singular smile crossed the reeve's countenance, but he made no observation.

"Unless the lady can turn aside streams, remove hills, and pluck up huge trees, we shall win," pursued Potts, with a chuckle.

Again the reeve smiled, but he forebore to speak.

"You talk of marks, meres, and boundaries, Master Potts," remarked Richard. "Are not the words synonymous?"

"Not precisely so, sir," replied the attorney; "there is a slight difference in their signification, which I will explain to you. The words of the statute are '*metas, meras, et bundas*,'—now *meta*, or mark, is an object rising from the ground, as a church, a wall, or a tree; *mera*, or mere, is the space or interval between the forest and the land adjoining, whereupon the mark may chance to stand; and *bunda* is the boundary, lying on a level with the forest, as a river, a highway, a pool, or a bog."

"I comprehend the distinction," replied Richard. "And now, as we are on this subject," he added to the reeve, "I would gladly know the precise nature of your office?"

"My duty," replied the other, "is to range daily throughout

all the purlieus, or pourallees, as Master Potts more properly terms them, and disafforested lands, and inquire into all trespasses and offences against vert or venison, and present them at the king's next court of attachment or swainmote. It is also my business to drive into the forest such wild beasts as have strayed from it; to attend to the lawing and expeditation of mastiffs; and to raise hue and cry against any malefactors or trespassers within the forest."

"I will give you the exact words of the statute," said Potts—'*Si quis viderit malefactores infra metas forestæ, debet illos capere secundum posse suum, et si non possit, debet levare hutesium et clamorem.*' And the penalty for refusing to follow hue and cry is heavy fine."

"I would that that part of your duty relating to the hock-sinewing, and lawing of mastiffs, could be discontinued," said Richard. "I grieve to see a noble animal so mutilated."

"In Bowland Forest, as you are probably aware, sir," rejoined the reeve, "only the larger mastiffs are lamed, a small stirrup or gauge being kept by the master forester, Squire Robert Parker of Browsholme, and the dog whose foot will pass through it escapes mutilation."

"The practice is a cruel one, and I would it were abolished with some of our other barbarous forest laws," observed Richard.

While this conversation had been going on, the party had proceeded well on their way. For some time the road, which consisted of little more than tracts of wheels along the turf, led along a plain, thrown up into heathy hillocks, and then passing through a thicket, evidently part of the old forest, it brought them to the foot of a hill, which they mounted, and descended into another valley. Here they came upon Pendle Water, and while skirting its banks, could see at a great depth below, the river rushing over its rocky bed like an Alpine torrent. The scenery had now begun to assume a savage and sombre character. The deep rift through which the river ran was evidently the result of some terrible convulsion of the earth, and the rocky strata were strangely and fantastically displayed. On the further side the banks rose up precipitously, consisting for the most part of bare cliffs, though now and then a tree would root itself in some crevice Below this the stream sank over a wide shelf of rock, in a broad full cascade, and boiled and foamed in the stony basin that received it, after which, grown less impetuous, it ran tranquilly on for a couple of hundred yards, and was then artificially restrained by a dam, which, diverting it in part from its course, caused it to turn the wheels of a mill. Here was the abode of the unfortunate Richard Baldwyn, and here had blossomed forth the fair flower so untimely gathered. An air of gloom hung over this once cheerful spot: its very beauty contributing to this saddening effect. The mill-race flowed swiftly and brightly on; but the wheel was stopped, windows and doors were closed, and death kept his grim holiday undisturbed. No one was to be seen about the premises, nor was any sound heard except the bark of the lonely watch-dog. Many a sorrowing glance was cast at this forlorn habitation as the party rode past it, and many a sigh was heaved for the poor girl who had so lately been its pride and ornament; but if any one had noticed the bitter sneer curling the reeve's lip, or caught the malignant fire gleaming in his eye, it would scarcely have been thought that he shared in the general regret.

After the cavalcade had passed the mill, one or two other cottages appeared on the near side of the river, while the opposite banks began to be clothed with timber. The glen became more and more contracted, and a stone bridge crossed the stream, near which, and on the same side of the river as the party, stood a cluster of cottages constituting the little village of Rough Lee.

On reaching the bridge, Mistress Nutter's habitation came in view, and it was pointed out by Nicholas to Potts, who contemplated it with much curiosity. In his eyes it seemed exactly adapted to its owner, and formed to hide dark and guilty deeds. It was a stern, sombre-looking mansion, built of a dark grey stone, with tall square chimneys, and windows with heavy mullions. High stone walls, hoary and moss-grown, ran round the gardens and courts, except on the side of the river, where there was a terrace overlooking the stream, and forming a pleasant summer's walk. At the back of the house were a few ancient oaks and sycamores, and in the gardens were some old clipped yews.

Part of this ancient mansion is still standing, and retains much of its original character, though subdivided and tenanted by several humble families. The garden is cut up into paddocks, and the approach environed by a labyrinth of low stone walls, while miserable sheds and other buildings are appended to it; the terrace is wholly obliterated; and the grange and offices are pulled down, but sufficient is still left of the place to give an idea of its pristine appearance and character. Its situation is striking and peculiar. In front rises a high hill, forming the last link of the chain of Pendle, and looking upon Barrowford and Colne, on the further side of which, and therefore not discernible from the mansion, stood Malkin Tower. At the period in question the lower part of this hill was well wooded, and washed by the Pendle Water, which swept past it through banks picturesque and beautiful, though not so bold and rocky as those in the neighbourhood of the mill. In the rear of the house the ground gradually rose for more than a quarter of a mile, when it obtained a considerable elevation. Following the course of the stream, and looking down the gorge, another hill appeared, so that the house was completely shut in by mountainous acclivities. In winter, when the snow lay on the heights, or when the mists hung upon them for weeks together, or descended in continuous rain, Rough Lee was sufficiently desolate, and seemed cut off from all communication with the outer world; but at the season when the party beheld it, though the approaches were rugged and difficult, and almost inaccessible except to the horseman or pedestrian, bidding defiance to any vehicle except of the strongest construction, still the place was not without a certain charm, mainly, however, derived from its seclusion. The scenery was stern and sombre, the hills were dark and dreary; but the very wildness of the place was attractive, and the old house, with its grey walls, its lofty chimneys, its gardens with their clipped yews, and its rook-haunted trees, harmonised well with all around it.

As the party drew near the house, the gates were thrown open by an old porter with two other servants, who besought them to stay and partake of some refreshment; but Roger Nowell haughtily and peremptorily declined the invitation, and rode on, and the others, though some of them would fain have complied, followed him.

Scarcely were they gone, than James Device, who had been in the garden, issued from the gate and speeded after them.

Passing through a close at the back of the mansion, and tracking a short narrow lane, edged by stone walls, the party, which had received some accessions from the cottages of Rough Lee, as well as from the huts on the hill-side, again approached the river, and proceeded along its banks.

The new-comers, being all of them tenants of Mrs. Nutter, and acting apparently under the directions of James Device, who had now joined the troop, stoutly and loudly maintained that the lady would be found right in the inquiry, with the exception of one old man named Henry Mitton; and he shook his head gravely when appealed to by Jem, and could by no efforts be induced to join him in the clamour.

Notwithstanding this demonstration, Roger Nowell and his legal adviser were both very sanguine as to the result of the survey being in their favour, and Master Potts turned to ascertain from Sparshot that the two plans, which had been rolled up and consigned to his custody, were quite safe.

Meanwhile, the party having followed the course of Pendle Water through the glen for about half a mile, during which they kept close to the brawling current, entered a little thicket, and then striking off on the left, passed over the foot of a hill, and came to the edge of a wide moor, where a halt was called by Nowell.

It being now announced that they were on the confines of the disputed property, preparations were immediately made for the survey; the plans were taken out of a quiver, in which they had been carefully deposited by Sparshot, and handed to Potts, who, giving one to Roger Nowell and the other to Nicholas, and opening his memorandum-book, declared that all was ready, and the two leaders rode slowly forward, while the rest of the troop followed, their curiosity being stimulated to the highest pitch.

Presently Roger Nowell again stopped, and pointed to a woody brake.

"We are now come," he said, "to a wood forming part of my property, and which from an eruption, caused by a spring, that took place in it many years ago, is called Burst Clough."

"Exactly, sir—exactly," cried Potts; "Burst Clough—I have it here—landmarks, five grey stones, lying apart at a distance of one hundred yards or thereabouts, and giving you, sir, twenty acres of moor land. Is it not so, Master Nicholas? The marks are such as I have described, eh?"

"They are, sir," replied the squire; "with this slight difference in the allotment of the land—namely, that Mistress Nutter claims the twenty acres, while she assigns you only ten."

"Ten devils!" cried Roger Nowell, furiously. "Twenty acres are mine, and I will have them."

"To the proof, then," rejoined Nicholas. "The first of the grey stones is here."

"And the second on the left, in that hollow," said Roger Nowell. "Come on, my masters, come on."

"Ay, come on!" cried Nicholas; "this perambulation will be rare sport. Who wins, for a piece of gold, cousin Richard?"

"Nay, I will place no wager on the event," replied the young man.

"Well, as you please," cried the squire; "but I would lay five to one that Mistress Nutter beats the magistrate."

Meanwhile, the whole troop having set forward, they soon arrived at the second stone. Grey and moss-grown, it was deeply imbedded in the soil, and to all appearance had rested undisturbed for many a year.

"You measure from the clough, I presume, sir?" remarked Potts to Nowell.

"To be sure," replied the magistrate; "but how is this?—This stone seems to me much nearer the clough than it used to be."

"Yeigh, so it dun, mester," observed old Mitton.

"It does not appear to have been disturbed, at all events," said Nicholas, dismounting and examining it.

"It would seem not," said Nowell—"and yet it certainly is not in its old place."

"Yo are mistaen, mester," observed Jem Device; "ey knoa th' lond weel, an this stoan has stood where it does fo' t' last twenty year. Ha'n't it, neeburs?"

"Yeigh—yeigh," responded several voices.

"Well, let us go on to the next stone," said Potts, looking rather blank.

Accordingly they went forward, the hinds exchanging significant looks, and Roger Nowell and Nicholas carefully examining their respective maps.

"These landmarks exactly tally with my plan," said the squire, as they arrived at the third stone.

"But not with mine," said Nowell; "this stone ought to be two hundred yards to the right. Some trickery has been practised."

"Impossible!" exclaimed the squire; "these ponderous masses could never have been moved. Besides, there are several persons here who know every inch of the ground, and will give you their unbiassed testimony. What say you, my men? Are these the old boundary stones?"

All answered in the affirmative except old Mitton, who still raised a dissenting voice.

"They be th' owd boundary marks, sure enough," he said; "boh they are neaw i' their owd places."

"It is quite clear that the twenty acres belong to Mistress Nutter," observed Nicholas, "and that you must content yourself with ten, Master Nowell. Make an entry to that effect, Master Potts, unless you will have the ground measured."

"No, it is needless," replied the magistrate, sharply; "let us go on."

During this survey, some of the features of the country appeared changed to the rustics, but how or in what way they could not precisely tell, and they were easily induced by James Device to give their testimony in Mistress Nutter's favour.

A small rivulet was now reached, and another halt being called upon its sedgy banks, the plans were again consulted.

"What have we here, Master Potts—marks or boundaries?" inquired Richard, with a smile.

"Both," replied Potts, angrily. "This rivulet, which I take to be Moss Brook, is a boundary, and that sheepfold and the two posts standing in a line with it are marks. But hold! how is this?" he cried, regarding the plan in dismay; "the five acres of waste land should be on the left of the brook."

"It would doubtless suit Master Nowell better if it were so," said Nicholas; "but as they chance to be on the right, they belong to Mistress Nutter. I merely speak from the plan."

"Your plan is naught, sir," cried Nowell, furiously, "By what foul practice these changes have been wrought I pretend not to say, though I can give a good guess; but the audacious witch who has thus deluded me shall bitterly rue it."

"Hold, hold, Master Nowell!" rejoined Nicholas; "I can make great allowance for your anger, which is natural considering your disappointment, but I will not permit such unwarrantable insinuations to be thrown out against Mistress Nutter. You agreed to abide by Sir Ralph Assheton's award, and you must not complain if it be made against you. Do you imagine that this stream can have changed its course in a single night; or that yon sheepfold has been removed to the further side of it?"

"I do," replied Nowell.

"And so do I," cried Potts; "it has been accomplished by the aid of——"

But feeling himself checked by a glance from the reeve, he stammered out, "of—of Mother Demdike."

"You declared just now that marks, meres, and boundaries, were unremovable, Master Potts," said the reeve, with a sneer; "you have altered your opinion."

The crestfallen attorney was dumb.

"Master Roger Nowell must find some better plea than the imputation of witchcraft to set aside Mistress Nutter's claim," observed Richard.

"Yeigh, that he mun," cried James Device, and the hinds who supported him.

The magistrate bit his lips with vexation.

"There is witchcraft in it, I repeat," he said.

"Yeigh, that there be," responded old Mitton.

But the words were scarcely uttered, when he was felled to the ground by the bludgeon of James Device.

"Ey'd sarve thee i' t' same way, fo' two pins," said Jem, regarding Potts with a savage look.

"No violence, Jem," cried Nicholas, authoritatively—"you do harm to the cause you would serve by your outrageous conduct."

"Beg pardon, squoire," replied Jem, "boh ey winna hear lies towd abowt Mistress Nutter."

"No one shan speak ill on her here," cried the hinds.

"Well, Master Nowell," said Nicholas, "are you willing to concede the matter at once, or will you pursue the investigation further?"

"I will ascertain the extent of the mischief done to me before I stop," rejoined the magistrate, angrily.

"Forward, then," cried Nicholas. "Our course now lies along this footpath, with a croft on the left, and an old barn on the right. Here the plans correspond, I believe, Master Potts?"

The attorney yielded a reluctant assent.

"There is next a small spring and trough on the right, and we then come to a limestone quarry—then by a plantation called Cat Gallows Wood—so named, because some troublesome mouser has been hanged there, I suppose, and next by a deep moss-pit, called Swallow Hole. All right, eh, Master Potts? We shall now enter upon Worston Moor, and come to the hut occupied by Jem Device, who can, it is presumed, speak positively as to its situation."

"Very true," cried Potts, as if struck by an idea. "Let the rascal step forward. I wish to put a few questions to him respecting his tenement. I think I shall catch him now," he added in a low tone to Nowell.

"Here ey be," cried Jem, stepping up with an insolent and defying look. "Whot d'ye want wi' me?"

"First of all I would caution you to speak the truth," commenced Potts, impressively, "as I shall take down your answers in my memorandum book, and they will be produced against you hereafter."

"If he utters a falsehood I will commit him," said Roger Nowell, sharply.

"Speak ceevily, an ey win gi' yo a ceevil answer," rejoined Jem, in a surly tone; "boh ey'm nah to be browbeaten."

"First, then, is your hut in sight?" asked Potts.

"Neaw," replied Jem.

"But you can point out its situation, I suppose?" pursued the attorney.

"Sartinly ey con," replied Jem, without heeding a significant glance cast at him by the reeve. "It stands behind yon kloof, ot soide o' t' moor, wi' a rindle in front."

"Now mind what you say, sirrah," cried Potts. "You are quite sure the hut is behind the clough; and the rindle, which, being interpreted from your base vernacular, I believe means a gutter, in front of it?"

The reeve coughed slightly, but failed to attract Jem's attention, who replied quickly, that he was quite sure of the circumstances.

"Very well," said Potts—"you have all heard the answer. He is quite sure as to what he states. Now, then, I suppose you can tell whether the hut looks to the north or the south; whether the door opens to the moor or to the clough; and whether there is a path leading from it to a spot called Hook Cliff?"

At this moment Jem caught the eye of the reeve, and the look given him by the latter completely puzzled him.

"Ey dunna reetly recollect which way it looks," he answered.

"What! you prevaricating rascal, do you pretend to say that you do not know which way your own dwelling stands," thundered Roger Nowell. "Speak out, sirrah, or Sparshot shall take you into custody at once."

"Ey'm ready, your worship," replied the beadle.

"Weel, then," said Jem, imperfectly comprehending the signs made to him by the reeve, "the hut looks nather to t' south naw to t' north, but to t' west; it feaces t' moor; an there is a path fro' it to Hook Cliff."

As he finished speaking, he saw from the reeve's angry gestures that he had made a mistake, but it was now too late to recall his words. However, he determined to make an effort.

"Now ey bethink me, ey'm naw sure that ey'm reet," he said.

"You must be sure, sirrah," said Roger Nowell, bending his

awful brows upon him. "You cannot be mistaken as to your own dwelling. Take down his description, Master Potts, and proceed with your interrogatories if you have any more to put to him."

"I wish to ask him whether he has been at home to-day," said Potts.

"Answer, fellow," thundered the magistrate.

Before replying, Jem would fain have consulted the reeve, but the latter had turned away in displeasure. Not knowing whether a lie would serve his turn, and fearing he might be contradicted by some of the bystanders, he said he had not been at home for two days, but had returned the night before at a late hour from Whalley, and had slept at Rough Lee.

"Then you cannot tell what changes may have taken place in your dwelling during your absence?" said Potts.

"Of course not," replied Jem, "boh ey dunna see how ony chawnges con ha' happent i' so short a time."

"But I do, if you do not, sirrah," said Potts. "Be pleased to give me your plan, Master Nowell. I have a further question to ask him," he added, after consulting it for a moment.

"Ey win awnser nowt more," replied Jem, gruffly.

"You will answer whatever questions Master Potts may put to you, or you are taken into custody," said the magistrate, sternly.

Jem would have willingly beaten a retreat; but being surrounded by the two grooms and Sparshot, who only waited a sign from Nowell to secure him, or knock him down if he attempted to fly, he gave a surly intimation that he was ready to speak.

"You are aware that a dyke intersects the heath before us, namely, Worston Moor?" said Potts.

Jem nodded his head.

"I must request particular attention to your plan as I proceed, Master Nicholas," pursued the attorney. "I now wish to be informed by you, James Device, whether that dyke cuts through the middle of the moor, or traverses the side; and if so, which side? I desire also to be informed where it commences, and where it ends?"

Jem scratched his head, and reflected a moment.

"The matter does not require consideration, sirrah," cried Nowell. "I must have an instant answer."

"So yo shan," replied Jem; "weel, then, th' dyke begins near a little mound ca'd Turn Heaod, about a hundert yards fro' my dwellin', an runs across th' easterly soide o't moor till it reaches Knowl Bottom."

"You will swear this?" cried Potts, scarcely able to conceal his satisfaction."

"Swere it! eigh," replied Jem.

"Eigh, we'n aw swere it," chorused the hinds.

"I'm delighted to hear it," cried Potts, radiant with delight, "for your description corresponds exactly with Master Nowell's plan, and differs materially from that of Mistress Nutter, as Squire Nicholas Assheton will tell you."

"I cannot deny it," replied Nicholas, in some confusion.

"Ey should ha' said 'westerly' i' stead o' 'yeasterly,'" cried Jem, "boh yo puzzle a mon so wi' your lawyerly questins, that he dusna knoa his reet hond fro' his laft."

"Yeigh, yeigh, we aw meant to say 'yeasterly,'" added the hinds.

"You have sworn the contrary," cried Nowell. "Secure him," he added to the grooms and Sparshot, "and do not let him go till we have completed the survey. We will now see how far the reality corresponds with the description, and what further devilish tricks have been played with the property."

Upon this the troop was again put in motion, James Device walking between the two grooms, with Sparshot behind him.

So wonderfully elated was Master Potts by the successful hit he had just made, and which, in his opinion, quite counterbalanced his previous failure, that he could not help communicating his satisfaction to Flint, and this in such manner, that the fiery little animal, who had been for some time exceedingly tractable and good-natured, took umbrage at it, and threatened to dislodge him if he did not desist from his vagaries—delivering the hint so clearly and unmistakeably that it was not lost upon his rider, who endeavoured to calm him down. In proportion as the attorney's spirits rose, those of James Device and his followers sank, for they felt they were caught in a snare, from which they could not easily escape.

By this time they had reached the borders of Worston Moor, which had been hitherto concealed by a piece of rising ground, covered with gorse and brushwood, and Jem's hut, together with the clough, the rindle, and the dyke, came distinctly into view. The plans were again produced, and, on comparing them, it appeared that the various landmarks were precisely situated as laid down by Mistress Nutter, while their disposition was entirely at variance with James Device's statement.

Master Potts then rose in his stirrups, and calling for silence, addressed the assemblage.

"There stands the hut," he said, "and instead of being behind the clough, it is on one side of it, while the door certainly does *not* face the moor, neither is the rindle in front of the dwelling or near it; while the dyke, which is the main and important boundary line between the properties, runs above two hundred yards further west than formerly. Now, observe the original position of these marks, meres, and boundaries—that is, of this hut, this clough, this rindle, and this dyke—exactly corresponds with the description given of them by the man Device, who dwells in the place, and who is, therefore, a person most likely to be accurately acquainted with the country; and yet, though he has only been absent two days, changes the most surprising have taken place—changes so surprising, indeed, that he scarcely knows the way to his own house, and certainly never could find the path which he has described as leading to Hook Cliff, since it is entirely obliterated. Observe, further, all these extraordinary and incomprehensible changes in the appearance of the country, and in the situation of the marks, meres, and boundaries, are favourable to Mistress Nutter, and give her the advantage she seeks over my honoured and honourable client. They are set down in Mistress Nutter's plan, it is true; but when, let me ask, was that plan prepared? In my opinion it was prepared first, and the changes in the land made after it by diabolical fraud and contrivance. I am sorry to have to declare this to you, Master Nicholas, and to you, Master Richard, but such is my firm conviction."

"And mine, also," added Nowell; "and I here charge Mistress Nutter with sorcery and witchcraft, and on my return I will immediately issue a warrant for her arrest. Sparshot, I command you to attach the person of James Device, for aiding and abetting her in her foul practices."

"I will help you to take charge of him," said the reeve, riding forward.

Probably this was done to give Jem a chance of escape, and if so, it was successful, for as the reeve pushed among his captors, and thrust Sparshot aside, the ruffian broke from them; and running with great swiftness across the moor, plunged into the clough, and disappeared.

Nicholas and Richard instantly gave chase, as did Master Potts, but the fugitive led them over the treacherous bog in such a manner as to baffle all pursuit. A second disaster here overtook the unlucky attorney, and damped him in his hour of triumph. Flint, who had apparently not forgotten or forgiven the joyous kicks he had recently received from the attorney's heels, came to a sudden halt by the side of the quagmire, and, putting down his head, and flinging up his legs, cast him into it. While Potts was scrambling out, the animal galloped off in the direction of the clough, and had just reached it when he was seized upon by James Device, who suddenly started from the covert, and vaulted upon his back.

CHAPTER VIII.—ROUGH LEE.

On returning from their unsuccessful pursuit of James Device, the two Asshetons found Roger Nowell haranguing the hinds, who, on the flight of their leader, would have taken to their heels likewise, if they had not been detained, partly by the energetic efforts of Sparshot and the grooms, and partly by the exhortations and menaces of the magistrate and Holden. As it was, two or three contrived to get away, and fled across the moor, whither the reeve pretended to pursue them; while those left behind were taken sharply to task by Roger Nowell.

"Listen to me," he cried, "and take good heed to what I say, for it concerns you nearly. Strange and dreadful things have come under my observation on my way hither. I have seen a whole village stricken as by a plague—a poor pedlar deprived of the use of his limbs and put in peril of his life—and a young maiden, once the pride and ornament of your own village, snatched from a fond father's care, and borne to an untimely grave. These things I have seen with my own eyes; and I am resolved that the perpetrators of these enormities, Mothers Demdike and Chattox, shall be brought to justice. As to you, the deluded victims of the impious hags, I can easily understand why you shut your eyes to their evil doings. Terrified by their threats you submit to their exactions, and so become their slaves—slaves of the bond-slaves of Satan. What miserable servitude is this! By so doing you not only endanger the welfare of your souls, by leaguing with the enemies of Heaven, and render yourselves unworthy to be classed with a religious and Christian people, but you place your lives in jeopardy by becoming accessories to the crimes of those great offenders, and render yourselves liable to like punishment with them. Seeing, then, the imminency of the peril in which you stand, you will do well to avoid it while there is yet time. Nor is this your only risk. Your servitude to Mistress Nutter is equally perilous. What if she be owner of the land you till, and the flocks you tend! You owe her no fealty. She has forfeited all title to your service—and, so far from aiding her, you ought to regard her as a great criminal, whom you are bound to bring to justice. I have now incontestable proofs of her dealing in the black art, and can show that by witchcraft she has altered the face of this country, with the intent to rob me of my land."

Holden now took up the theme. "The finger of Heaven is pointed against such robbery," he cried. "'Cursed is he,' saith the scripture, 'that removeth his neighbour's landmark.' And again, it is written, 'Cursed is he that smiteth his neighbour secretly.' Both these things hath Mistress Nutter done, and for both shall she incur divine vengeance."

"Neither shall she escape that of man," added Nowell, severely; "for our sovereign lord hath enacted that all persons employing or rewarding any evil spirit, shall be held guilty of felony, and shall suffer death. And death will be her portion, for such demoniacal agency most assuredly hath she employed."

The magistrate here paused for a moment to regard his audience, and reading in their terrified looks that his address had produced the desired impression, he continued with increased severity—

"These wicked women shall trouble the land no longer. They shall be arrested and brought to judgment; and if you do not heartily bestir yourselves in their capture, and undertake to appear in evidence against them, you shall be held and dealt with as accessories in their crimes."

Upon this, the hinds, who were greatly alarmed, declared with one accord their willingness to act as the magistrate should direct.

"You do wisely," cried Potts, who by this time had made his way back to the assemblage, covered from head to foot with ooze, as on his former misadventure. "Mistress Nutter and the two old hags who hold you in thrall would lead you to destruction. For understand it is the firm determination of my respected client, Master Roger Nowell, as well as of myself, not to relax in our exertions till the whole of these pestilent witches who trouble the country be swept away, and to spare none who assist and uphold them."

The hinds stared aghast, for so grim was the appearance of the attorney, that they almost thought Hobthurst, the lubber-fiend, was addressing them.

At this moment old Henry Mitton came up. He had partially recovered from the stunning effects of the blow dealt him by James Device, but his head was cut open, and his white locks were dabbled in blood. Pushing his way through the assemblage, he stood before the magistrate.

"If yo want a witness agen that foul murtheress and witch, Alice Nutter, ca' me, Master Roger Nowell," he said. "Ey con tay my Bible oath that the whole feace o' this keawntry has been chaunged sin yester neet, by her hondywark. Ca' me also to speak to her former life—to her intimacy wi' Mother Demdike an owd Chattox. Ca' me to prove her constant attendance at devils' sabbaths on Pendle Hill, and elsewhere, wi' other black and damning offences—an among 'em the murder, by witchcraft, o' her husband, Ruchot Nutter."

A thrill of horror pervaded the assemblage at this denunciation; and Master Potts, who was being cleansed from his sable stains by one of the grooms, cried out—

"This is the very man for us, my excellent client. Your name and abode, friend?"

"Harry Mitton o' Rough Lee," replied the old man. "Ey ha' dwelt there seventy year an uppards, an ha' known the feyther and granfeyther o' Ruchot Nutter, an also Alice Nutter, when hoo war Alice Assheton. Ca' me, sir, an aw' ye want to knoa ye shan larn."

"We will call you, my good friend," said Potts; "and, if you have sustained any private wrongs from Mistress Nutter, they shall be amply redressed."

"Ey ha' endured much ot her honts," rejoined Mitton; "boh ey dunna speak o' mysel'. It be high time that Owd Scrat should ha' his claws clipt, an honest folk be allowed to live in peace."

"Very true, my worthy friend—very true," assented Potts.

An immediate return to Whalley was now proposed by Nowell; but Master Potts was of opinion that, as they were in the neighbourhood of Malkin Tower, they should proceed thither at once, and effect the arrest of Mother Demdike, after which Mother Chattox could be sought out and secured. The presence of these two witches would be most important, he declared, in the examination of Mistress Nutter. Hue and cry for the fugitive, James Device, ought also to be made throughout the forest."

Confounded by what they heard, Richard and Nicholas had hitherto taken no part in the proceedings, but they now seconded Master Potts's proposition, hoping that the time occupied by the visit to Malkin Tower would prove serviceable to Mistress Nutter; for they did not doubt that intelligence would be conveyed to her by some of her agents, of Nowell's intention to arrest her.

Additional encouragement was given to the plan by the arrival of Richard Baldwyn, who, at this juncture, rode furiously up to the party.

"Weel, han yo settled your business here, Mester Nowell?" he asked, in breathless anxiety.

"We have so far settled it, that we have established proofs of witchcraft against Mistress Nutter," replied Nowell. "Can you speak to her character, Baldwyn?"

"Yeigh, that ey con," rejoined the miller, "an nowt good Ey wish to see aw these mischeevous witches burnt; an that's why ey ha' ridden efter yo, Mester Nowell. Ey want your help os a magistrate agen Mother Demdike. Yo ha a constable wi' ye, and so can arrest her at wonst."

"You have come most opportunely, Baldwyn," observed Potts. "We were just considering whether we should go to Malkin Tower."

"Then decide upon 't," rejoined the miller, "or th' owd hag win escape ye. Tak her unaweares."

"I don't know that we shall take her unawares, Baldwyn," said Potts; "but I am decidedly of opinion that we should go thither without delay. Is Malkin Tower far off?"

"About a mile fro' Rough Lee," replied the miller. "Go back wi' me to t' mill, where yo con refresh yourselves, an ey'n get together some dozen o' my friends, an then we'n aw go up to t' Tower together."

"A very good suggestion," said Potts; "and no doubt Master Nowell will accede to it."

"We have force enough already, it appears to me," observed Nowell.

"I should think so," replied Richard. "Some dozen men, armed, against a poor defenceless old woman, are surely enough."

"Owd, boh neaw defenceless, Mester Ruchot," rejoined Baldwyn. "Yo canna go i' too great force on an expedition like this. Malkin Tower is a varry strong place, os yo'n find."

"Well," said Nowell, "since we are here, I agree with Master Potts, that it would be better to secure these two offenders, and convey them to Whalley, where their examination can be taken at the same time with that of Mistress Nutter. We therefore accept your offer of refreshment, Baldwyn, as some of our party may stand in need of it, and will at once proceed to the mill."

"Well resolved, sir," said Potts.

"We'n tae th' owd witch, dead or alive," cried Baldwyn.

"Alive—we must have her alive, good Baldwyn," said Potts. "You must see her perish at the stake."

"Reet, mon," cried the miller, his eyes blazing with fury; "that's true vengeance. Ey'n ride whoam an get aw ready fo ye. Yo knoa t' road."

So saying, he struck spurs into his horse and galloped off. Scarcely was he gone than the reeve, who had kept out of his sight, came forward.

"Since you have resolved upon going to Malkin Tower," he said to Nowell, "and have a sufficiently numerous party for the purpose, my further attendance can be dispensed with. I will ride in search of James Device."

"Do so," replied the magistrate, "and let hue and cry be made after him."

"It shall be," replied the reeve, "and, if taken, he shall be conveyed to Whalley."

And he made towards the clough, as if with the intention of putting his words into execution.

Word was now given to set forward, and Master Potts having been accommodated with a horse by one of the grooms, who proceeded on foot, the party began to retrace their course to the mill.

They were soon again by the side of Pendle Water, and ere-long reached Rough Lee. As they rode through the close at the back of the mansion, Roger Nowell halted for a moment, and observed with a grim smile to Richard—

"Never more shall Mistress Nutter enter that house. Within a week she shall be lodged in Lancaster Castle, as a felon of the darkest dye, and she shall meet a felon's fate. And not only shall she be sent thither, but all her partners in guilt—Mother Demdike and her accursed brood, the Devices; old Chattox and her grand-daughter, Nance Redferne: not one shall escape."

"You do not include Alizon Device in your list?" cried Richard.

"I include all—I will spare none," rejoined Nowell, sternly.

"Then I will move no further with you," said Richard.

"How!" cried Nowell, "are you an upholder of these witches? Beware what you do, young man. Beware how you take part with them. You will bring suspicion upon yourself, and get entangled in a net from which you will not easily escape."

"I care not what may happen to me," rejoined Richard; "I will never lend myself to gross injustice—such as you are about to practise. Since you announce your intention of including the innocent with the guilty, of exterminating a whole family for the crimes of one or two of its members, I have done. You have made dark accusations against Mistress Nutter, but you have proved nothing. You assert that, by witchcraft, she has changed the features of your land, but in what way can you make good the charge? Old Mitton has, indeed, volunteered himself as a witness against her, and has accused her of most heinous offences; but he has at the same time shown that he is her enemy, and his testimony will be regarded with doubt. I will not believe her guilty on mere suspicion, and I deny that you have aught more to proceed upon."

"I shall not argue the point with you now, sir," replied Nowell, angrily. "Mistress Nutter will be fairly tried, and if I fail in my proofs against her, she will be acquitted. But I have little fear of such a result," he added, with a sinister smile.

"You are confident, sir, because you know there would be every disposition to find her guilty," replied Richard. "She will not be fairly tried. All the prejudices of ignorance and superstition, heightened by the published opinions of the King, will be arrayed against her. Were she as free from crime, or thought of crime, as the new-born babe, once charged with the horrible and inexplicable offence of witchcraft, she would scarce escape. You go determined to destroy her."

"I will not deny it," said Roger Nowell, "and I am satisfied that I shall render good service to society by freeing it from so vile a member. So abhorrent is the crime of witchcraft, that were my own son suspected, I would be the first to deliver him to justice. Like a noxious and poisonous plant, the offence has taken deep root in this country, and is spreading its baneful influence around, so that, if it be not extirpated, it may spring up anew, and cause incalculable mischief. But it shall now be effectually checked. Of the families I have mentioned, not one shall escape; and if Mistress Nutter herself had a daughter, she should be brought to judgment. In such cases, children must suffer for the sins of the parents."

"You have no regard, then, for their innocence?" said Richard, who felt as if a weight of calamity was crushing him down.

"Their innocence must be proved at the proper tribunal," rejoined Nowell. "It is not for me to judge them."

"But you do judge them," cried Richard, sharply. "In making the charge, you know that you pronounce the sentence of condemnation as well. This is why the humane man—why the just man—would hesitate to bring an accusation, even where he suspected guilt—but where suspicion could not possibly attach, he would never suffer himself, however urged on by feelings of animosity, to injure the innocent."

"You ascribe most unworthy motives to me, young sir," rejoined Nowell, sternly. "I am influenced only by a desire to see justice administered, and I shall not swerve from my duty, because my humanity may be called in question by a love-sick boy. I understand why you plead thus warmly for these infamous persons. You are enthralled by the beauty of the young witch, Alizon Device. I noted how you were struck by her yesterday—and I heard what Sir Thomas Metcalfe said on the subject. But take heed what you do. You may jeopardise both soul and body in the indulgence of this fatal passion. Witchcraft is exercised in many ways. Its professors have not only power to maim and to kill, and to do other active mischief, but to ensnare the affections and endanger the souls of their victims, by enticing them to unhallowed love. Alizon Device is comely to view, no doubt, but who shall say whence her beauty is derived? Hell may have arrayed her in its fatal charms. Sin is beautiful, but all-destructive. And the time will come when you may thank me for delivering you from the snares of this seductive siren."

Richard uttered an angry exclamation.

"Not now—I do not expect it—you are too much besotted by her," pursued Nowell; "but I conjure you to cast off this wicked and senseless passion, which, unless checked, will lead you to perdition. You have heard what abominable rites are practised at those unholy meetings called Devil's Sabbaths, and how can you say that some demon may not be your rival in Alizon's love?"

"You pass all licence, sir," cried Richard, infuriated past endurance; "and, if you do not instantly retract the infamous accusation you have made, neither your age nor your office shall protect you."

"I can fortunately protect myself, young man," replied Nowell, coldly; "and if aught were wanting to confirm my suspicions that you were under some evil influence, it would be supplied by your present conduct. You are bewitched by this girl."

"It is false!" cried Richard.

And he raised his hand against the magistrate, when Nicholas quickly interposed.

"Nay, cousin Dick," cried the squire, "this must not be. You must take other means of defending the poor girl, whose innocence I will maintain as stoutly as yourself. But, since Master Roger Nowell is resolved to proceed to extremities, I shall likewise take leave to retire."

"Your pardon, sir," rejoined Nowell; "you will not withdraw till I think fit. Master Richard Assheton, forgetful alike of the respect due to age and constituted authority, has ventured to raise his hand against me, for which, if I chose, I could place him in immediate arrest. But I have no such intention. On the contrary, I am willing to overlook the insult, attributing it to the frenzy by which he is possessed. But both he and you, Master Nicholas, are mistaken if you suppose I will permit you to retire. As a magistrate in the exercise of my office, I call upon you both to aid me in the capture of the two notorious witches, Mothers Demdike and Chattox, and not to desist or depart from me till such capture be effected. You know the penalty of refusal."

"Heavy fine or imprisonment, at the option of the magistrate," remarked Potts.

"My cousin Nicholas will do as he pleases," observed Richard; "but, for my part, I will not stir a step further."

"Nor will I," added Nicholas, "unless I have Master Nowell's solemn pledge that he will take no proceedings against Alizon Device."

"You can give no such assurance, sir," whispered Potts, seeing that the magistrate wavered in his resolution.

"You must go, then," said Nowell, "and take the consequences of your refusal to act with me. Your relationship to Mistress Nutter will not tell in your favour."

"I understand the implied threat," said Nicholas, "and laugh at it. Richard, lad, I am with you. Let him catch the witches himself, if he can. I will not budge an inch further with him."

"Farewell, then, gentlemen," replied Roger Nowell; "I am sorry to part company with you thus, but when next we meet—" and he paused.

"We meet as enemies, I presume" supplied Nicholas.

"We meet no longer as friends," rejoined the magistrate, coldly.

With this he moved forward with the rest of the troop, while the two Asshetons, after a moment's consultation, passed through a gate and made their way to the back of the mansion, where they found one or two men on the look-out, from whom they received intelligence, which induced them immediately to spring from their horses and hurry into the house.

Arrived at the principal entrance of the mansion, which was formed by large gates of open iron-work, admitting a view of the garden and front of the house, Roger Nowell again called a halt, and Master Potts, at his request, addressed the porter and two other serving-men who were standing in the garden, in this fashion—

"Pay attention to what I say to you, my men," he cried in a loud and authoritative voice—"a warrant will this day be issued for the arrest of Alice Nutter of Rough Lee, in whose service you have hitherto dwelt, and who is charged with the dreadful crime of witchcraft, and with invoking, consulting, and covenanting with, entertaining, employing, feeding, and rewarding evil spirits, contrary to the laws of God and man, and in express violation of his Majesty's statute. Now take notice, that if the said Alice Nutter shall at any time hereafter return to this her former abode, or take refuge within it, you are hereby bound to deliver her up forthwith to the nearest constable, to be by him brought before the worshipful Master Roger Nowell of Read, in this county, so that she may be examined by him on these charges. You hear what I have said?"

The men exchanged significant glances, but made no reply.

Potts was about to address them, but to his surprise he saw the central door of the house thrown open, and Mistress Nutter issue from it. She marched slowly and majestically down the broad gravel walk towards the gate. The attorney could scarcely believe his eyes, and he exclaimed to the magistrate with a chuckle—

"Who would have thought of this! We have her safe enough now. Ha! ha!"

But no corresponding smile played upon Nowell's hard lips. His gaze was fixed inquiringly upon the lady.

Another surprise. From the same door issued Alizon Device, escorted by Nicholas and Richard Assheton, who walked on either side of her, and the three followed Mistress Nutter slowly down the broad walk. Such a display seemed to argue no want of confidence. Alizon did not look towards the group outside the gates, but seemed listening eagerly to what Richard was saying to her.

"So, Master Nowell," cried Mistress Nutter, boldly, "since you find yourself defeated in the claims you have made against my property, you are seeking to revenge yourself, I understand, by bringing charges against me as false as they are calumnious. But I defy your malice, and can defend myself against your violence."

"If I could be astonished at any thing in you, madam, I should be at your audacity," rejoined Nowell, "but I am glad that you have presented yourself before me; for it was my fixed intention, on my return to Whalley, to cause your arrest, and your unexpected appearance here enables me to put my design into execution somewhat sooner than I anticipated."

Mistress Nutter laughed scornfully.

"Sparshot," vociferated Nowell, "enter those gates, and arrest the lady in the King's name."

The beadle looked irresolute. He did not like the task.

"The gates are fastened," cried Mistress Nutter.

"Force them open, then," roared Nowell, dismounting and shaking them furiously. "Bring me a heavy stone. By heaven! I will not be baulked of my prey."

"My servants are armed," cried Mistress Nutter, "and the first man who enters shall pay the penalty of his rashness with life. Bring me a petronel, Blackadder."

The order was promptly obeyed by the ill-favoured attendant, who was stationed near the gate.

"I am in earnest, said Mistress Nutter," aiming the petronel, "and seldom miss my mark."

"Give attention to me, my men," cried Roger Nowell. "I charge you in the King's name to throw open the gate."

"And I charge you in mine to keep it fast," rejoined Mistress Nutter. "We shall see who will be obeyed."

One of the grooms now advanced with a large stone taken from an adjoining wall, which he threw with great force against the gates, but though it shook them violently the fastenings continued firm. Blackadder and the two other serving-men, all of whom were armed with halberts, now advanced to the gates, and, thrusting the points of their weapons through the bars, drove back those who were near them.

A short consultation now took place between Nowell and Potts, after which the latter, taking care to keep out of the reach of the halberts, thus delivered himself in a loud voice:—

"Alice Nutter, in order to avoid the serious consequences which might ensue were the necessary measures taken to effect a forcible entrance into your habitation, the worshipful Master Nowell has thought fit to grant you an hour's respite for reflection; at the expiration of which time he trusts that you, seeing the futility of resisting the law, will quietly yield yourself a prisoner. Otherwise, no further leniency will be shown you and those who may uphold you in your contumacy."

Mistress Nutter laughed loudly and contemptuously.

"At the same time," pursued Potts, on a suggestion from the magistrate, "Master Roger Nowell demands that Alizon Device, daughter of Elizabeth Device, whom he beholds in your company, and who is likewise suspected of witchcraft, be likewised delivered up to him."

"Aught more?" inquired Mistress Nutter.

"Only this," replied Potts, in a taunting tone, "the worshipful magistrate would offer a friendly counsel to Master Nicholas Assheton, and Master Richard Assheton, whom, to his infinite surprise, he perceives in a hostile position before him, that they in nowise interfere with his injunctions, but, on the contrary, lend their aid in furtherance of them, otherwise he may be compelled to adopt measures towards them, which must be a source of regret to him. I have furthermore to state, on the part of his worship, that strict watch will be kept at all the approaches of your house, and that no one, on any pretence whatever, during the appointed time of respite, will be suffered to enter it, or depart from it. In an hour his worship will return."

"And in an hour he shall have my answer," replied Mistress Nutter, turning away.

CHAPTER IX.—HOW ROUGH LEE WAS DEFENDED BY NICHOLAS.

WHEN skies are darkest, and storms are gathering thickest overhead, the star of love will oft shine out with greatest brilliancy; and so, while Mistress Nutter was hurling defiance against her foes at the gate, and laughing their menaces to scorn—while those very foes were threatening Alizon's liberty and life—she had become wholly insensible to the peril environing her, and almost unconscious of any other presence save that of Richard, now her avowed lover; for, impelled by the irresistible violence of his feelings, the young man had chosen that moment, apparently so unpropitious, and so fraught with danger and alarm, for the declaration of his passion, and the offer of his life in her service. A few low-murmured words were all Alizon could utter in reply, but they were enough. They told Richard his passion was requited, and his devotion fully appreciated. Sweet were those moments to both—sweet, though sad. Like Alizon, her lover had become insensible to all around him. Engrossed by one thought and one object, he was lost to aught else, and was only at last aroused to what was passing by the squire, who, having good-naturedly removed to a little distance from the pair, now gave utterance to a low whistle, to let them know that Mistress Nutter was coming towards them. The lady, however, did not stop, but motioning them to follow, entered the house.

"You have heard what has passed," she said. "In an hour Master Nowell threatens to return and arrest me and Alizon."

"That shall never be," cried Richard, with a passionate look at the young girl. "We will defend you with our lives."

"Much may be done in an hour," observed Nicholas to Mistress Nutter, "and my advice to you is to use the time allowed you in making good your retreat, so that, when the hawks come back, they may find the doves flown."

"I have no intention of quitting my dovecot," replied Mistress Nutter, with a bitter smile.

"Unless you are forcibly taken from it, I suppose," said the squire; "a contingency not impossible if you await Roger Nowell's return. This time, be assured, he will not go away empty-handed."

"He may not go away at all," rejoined Mistress Nutter, sternly.

"Then you mean to make a determined resistance?" said Nicholas. "Recollect that you are resisting the law. I wish I could induce you to resort to the safer expedient of flight. This affair is already dark and perplexed enough, and does not require further complication. Find any place of concealment, no matter where, till some arrangement can be made with Roger Nowell."

"I should rather urge you to fly, Nicholas," rejoined the lady; "for it is evident you have strong misgivings as to the justice of my cause, and would not willingly compromise yourself. I will not surrender to this magistrate, because, by so doing, my life would assuredly be forfeited, for my innocence could never be established before the iniquitous and bloody tribunal to which I should be brought. Neither, for the same reason, will I surrender Alizon, who, with a refinement of malignity, has been similarly accused. I shall now proceed to make preparations for my defence. Go, if you think fitting—or stay—but if you *do* stay, I shall calculate upon your active services."

"You may," replied the squire. "Whatever I may think, I admire your spirit, and will stand by you. But time is passing, and the foe will return and find us engaged in deliberation when we ought to be prepared. You have a dozen men on the premises on whom you can rely. Half of these must be placed at the back of the house to prevent any entrance from being effected in that quarter. The rest can remain within the entrance hall, and be ready to rush forth when summoned by us; but we will not so summon them unless we are hardly put to it, and their aid is indispensable. All should be well armed, but I trust they will not have to use their weapons. Are you agreed to this, madam?"

"I am," replied Mistress Nutter, "and I will give instant directions that your wishes are complied with. All approaches to the back of the house shall be strictly guarded as you direct, and my trusty man, Blackadder, on whose fidelity and courage I can entirely rely, shall take the command of the party in the hall, and act under your orders. Your prowess will not be unobserved, for Alizon and I shall be in the upper room commanding the garden, whence we can see all that takes place."

A slight smile was exchanged between the lovers; but it was evident, from her anxious looks, that Alizon did not share in Richard's confidence. An opportunity, however, was presently afforded him of again endeavouring to reassure her, for Mistress Nutter went forth to give Blackadder his orders, and Nicholas betook himself to the back of the house to ascertain, from personal inspection, its chance of security.

"You are still uneasy, dear Alizon," said Richard, taking her hand; "but do not be cast down. No harm shall befall you."

"It is not for myself I am apprehensive," she replied, "but for you, who are about to expose yourself to needless risk in this encounter; and, if any thing should happen to you, I shall be for ever wretched. I would far rather you left me to my fate."

"And can you think I would allow you to be borne away a captive to ignominy and certain destruction?" cried Richard. "No, I will shed my heart's best blood before such a calamity shall occur."

"Alas!" said Alizon, "I have no means of requiting your devotion. All I can offer you in return is my love, and that, I fear, will prove fatal to you."

"Oh! do not say so," cried Richard. "Why should this sad presentiment still haunt you? I strove to chase it away just now, and hoped I had succeeded. You are dearer to me than life. Why, therefore, should I not risk it in your defence? And why should your love prove fatal to me?"

"I know not," replied Alizon, in a tone of deepest anguish, "but I feel as if my destiny were evil; and that, against my will, I shall drag those I most love on earth into the same dark gulf with myself. I have the greatest affection for your sister Dorothy, and yet I have been the unconscious instrument of injury to her. And you too, Richard, who are yet dearer to me, are now put in peril on my account. I fear, too, when you know my whole history, you will think of me as a thing of evil, and shun me."

"What mean you, Alizon?" he cried.

"Richard, I can have no secrets from you," she replied; "and though I was forbidden to tell you what I am now about to disclose, I will not withhold it. I was born in this house, and am the daughter of its mistress."

"You tell me only what I guessed, Alizon," rejoined the young man; "but I see nothing in this why I should shun you."

Alizon hid her face for a moment in her hands; and then looking up, said wildly and hurriedly, "Would I had never known the secret of my birth; or, knowing it, had never seen what I beheld last night!"

"What did you behold?" asked Richard, greatly agitated.

"Enough to convince me, that in gaining a mother I was lost myself," replied Alizon; "for oh! how can I survive the shock of telling you I am bound, by ties that can never be dissevered, to one abandoned alike of God and man—who has devoted herself to the Fiend!" Pity me, Richard—pity me, and shun me!"

There was a moment's dreadful pause, which the young man was unable to break.

"Was I not right in saying my love would be fatal to you?" continued Alizon. "Fly from me while you can, Richard. Fly from this house, or you are lost for ever!"

"Never, never! I will not stir without you," cried Richard. "Come with me, and escape all the dangers by which you are menaced, and leave your sinning parent to the doom she so richly merits."

"No, no; sinful though she be, she is still my mother. I cannot leave her," cried Alizon.

"If you stay, I stay, be the consequences what they may," replied the young man; "but you have rendered my arm powerless by what you have told me. How can I defend one whom I know to be guilty?"

"Therefore I urge you to fly," she rejoined.

"I can reconcile myself to it thus," said Richard—"in defending you, whom I know to be innocent, I cannot avoid defending her. The plea is not a good one, but it will suffice to allay my scruples of conscience."

At this moment Mistress Nutter entered the hall, followed by Blackadder and three other men, armed with calivers.

"All is ready, Richard," she said, "and it wants but a few minutes of the appointed time. Perhaps you shrink from the task you have undertaken?" she added, regarding him sharply; "if so, say so at once, and I will adopt my own line of defence."

"Nay, I shall be ready to go forth in a moment," rejoined the young man, glancing at Alizon. "Where is Nicholas?"

"Here," replied the squire, clapping him on the shoulder. "All is secure at the back of the house, and the horses are coming round. We must mount at once."

Richard arose without a word.

"Blackadder will attend to your orders," said Mistress Nutter; "he only waits a sign from you to issue forth with his three companions, or to fire through the windows upon the aggressors, if you see occasion for it."

"I trust it will not come to such a pass," rejoined the squire; "a few blows from these weapons will convince them we are in earnest, and will, I hope, save further trouble."

And as he spoke he took down a couple of stout staves, and gave one of them to Richard.

"Farewell, then, *preux chevaliers*," cried Mistress Nutter, with affected gaiety; "demean yourselves valiantly, and remember that bright eyes will be upon you. Now, Alizon, to our chamber."

Richard did not hazard a look at the young girl as she quitted the hall with her mother, but followed the squire mechanically into the garden, where they found the horses. Scarcely were they mounted than a loud hubbub, arising from the little village, proclaimed that their opponents had arrived, and presently after a large company of horse and foot appeared at the gate.

At sight of the large force brought against them, the countenance of the squire lost its confident and jovial expression. He counted nearly forty men, each of whom was armed in some way or other, and began to fear the affair would terminate awkwardly, and entail unpleasant consequences upon himself and his cousin. He was, therefore, by no means at his ease. As to Richard, he did not dare to ask himself how things would end, neither did he know how to act. His mind was in utter confusion, and his breast oppressed as if by a nightmare. He cast one look towards the upper window, and beheld at it the white face of Mistress Nutter, intently gazing at what was going forward, but Alizon was not to be seen.

Within the last half hour the sky had darkened, and a heavy cloud hung over the house, threatening a storm. Richard hoped it would come on fiercely and fast.

Meanwhile, Roger Nowell had dismounted and advanced to the gate.

"Gentlemen," he cried, addressing the two Asshetons, "I expected to find free access given to me and my followers; but as these gates are still barred against me, I call upon you, as loyal subjects of the King, not to resist or impede the course of law, but to throw them instantly open."

"You must unbar them yourself, Master Nowell," replied Nicholas. "We shall give you no help."

"Nor offer any opposition, I hope, sir?" said the magistrate, sternly.

"You are twenty to one, or thereabout," returned the squire, with a laugh; "we shall stand a poor chance with you."

"But other defensive and offensive preparations have been made, I doubt not," said Nowell; "nay, I descry some armed men through the windows of the hall. Before coming to extremities, I will make a last appeal to you and your kinsman. I have granted Mistress Nutter and the girl with her an hour's delay, in the hope that, seeing the futility of resistance, they would quietly surrender. But I find my clemency thrown away, and undue advantage taken of the time allowed for respite; therefore, I shall show them no further consideration. But to you, my friends, I would offer a last warning. Forget not that you are acting in direct opposition to the law; that we are here armed with full authority and power to carry out our intentions; and that all opposition on your part will be fruitless, and will be visited upon you hereafter with severe pains and penalties. Forget not, also, that your characters will be irrecoverably damaged from your connexion with parties charged with the heinous offence of witchcraft. Meddle not, therefore, in the matter, but go your ways, or, if you would act as best becomes you, aid me in the arrest of the offenders."

"Master Roger Nowell," replied Nicholas, walking his horse slowly towards the gate, "as you have given me a caution, I will give you one in return; and that is, to put a bridle on your tongue when you address gentlemen, or, by my fay, you are likely to get answers little to your taste. You have said that our characters are likely to suffer in this transaction, but, in my humble opinion, they will not suffer so much as your own. The magistrate who uses the arm of the law for purposes of private vengeance, and who brings a false and foul charge against his enemy, knowing that it cannot be repelled, is not entitled to any particular respect or honour. Thus have you acted towards Mistress Nutter. Defeated by her in the boundary question, without leaving its decision to those to whom you had referred it, you instantly accuse her of witchcraft, and seek to destroy her, as well as an innocent and unoffending girl, by whom she is attended. Is such conduct worthy of you, or likely to redound to your credit? I think not. But this is not all. Aided by your crafty and unscrupulous ally, Master Potts, you get together a number of Mistress Nutter's tenants, and, by threats and misrepresentations, induce them to become instruments of your vengeance. But when these misguided men come to know the truth of the case—when they learn that you have no proofs whatever against Mistress Nutter, and that you are influenced solely by animosity to her, they are quite as likely to desert you as to stand by you. At all events, we are determined to resist this unjust arrest, and, at the hazard of our lives, to oppose your entrance into the house."

Nowell and Potts were greatly exasperated by this speech, but they were little prepared for its consequences. Many of those who had been induced to accompany them, as has been shown, wavered in their resolution of acting against Mistress Nutter, but they now began to declare in her favour. In vain Potts repeated all his former arguments. They were no longer of any avail. Of the troop assembled at the gate more than half marched off, and shaped their course towards the rear of the house—with what intention it was easy to surmise—while of those who remained it was very doubtful whether the whole of them would act.

The result of his oration was quite as surprising to Nicholas as to his opponents, and, enchanted by the effect of his eloquence, he could not help glancing up at the window, where he perceived Mistress Nutter, whose smiles showed that she was equally well pleased.

Seeing that, if any further desertions took place, his chances would be at an end, with a menacing gesture at the squire, Roger Nowell ordered the attack to commence immediately.

While some of his men, amongst whom were Baldwyn and old Mitton, battered against the gate with stones, another party, headed by Potts, scaled the walls, which, though of considerable height, presented no very serious obstacles in the way of active assailants. Elevated on the shoulders of Sparshot, Potts was soon on the summit of the wall, and was about to drop into the garden, when he heard a sound that caused him to suspend his intention.

"What are you about to do, cousin Nicholas?" inquired Richard, as the word of assault was given by the magistrate.

"Let loose Mistress Nutter's stag-hounds upon them," replied the squire. "They are kept in leash by a varlet stationed behind yon yew-tree hedge, who only awaits my signal to let them slip; and by my faith it is time he had it."

As he spoke, he applied a dog-whistle to his lips, and, blowing a loud call, it was immediately answered by a savage barking, and alf a dozen hounds, rough-haired, of prodigious size and power, resembling in make, colour, and ferocity, the Irish wolf-hound, bounded towards him.

"Aha!" exclaimed Nicholas, clapping his hands to encourage them: "we could have dispersed the whole rout with these assistants. Hyke, Tristam!—hyke, Hubert! Upon them!—upon them!"

It was the savage barking of the hounds that had caught the ears of the alarmed attorney, and made him desirous to scramble back again. But this was no such easy matter. Sparshot's broad shoulders were wanting to place his feet upon, and while he was bruising his knees against the roughened sides of the wall, in vain attempts to raise himself to the top of it unaided, Hubert's sharp teeth met in the calf of his leg, while those of Tristam were fixed in the skirts of his doublet, and penetrated deeply into the flesh that filled it. A terrific yell proclaimed the attorney's anguish and alarm, and he redoubled his efforts to escape. But, if before it was difficult to get up, the feat was now impossible. All he could do was to cling with desperate tenacity to the coping of the wall, for he made no doubt, if dragged down, he should be torn in pieces. Roaring lustily for help, he besought Nicholas to have compassion upon him; but the squire appeared little moved by his distress, and laughed heartily at his yells and vociferations.

"You will not come again on a like errand, in a hurry, I fancy Master Potts," he said.

"I will not, good Master Nicholas," rejoined Potts; "for pity's sake call off these infernal hounds. They will rend me asunder as they would a fox."

"You were a cunning fox, in good sooth, to come hither," rejoined Nicholas, in a taunting tone; "but will you go hence if I liberate you?"

"I will—indeed I will!" replied Potts.

"And will no more molest Mistress Nutter?" thundered Nicholas.

"Take heed what you promise," roared Nowell from the other side of the wall.

"If you do *not* promise it, the hounds shall pull you down, and make a meal of you!" cried Nicholas.

"I do—I swear—whatever you desire!" cried the terrified attorney.

The hounds were then called off by the squire, and, nerved by fright, Potts sprang upon the wall, and tumbled over it upon the other side, alighting upon the head of his respected and singular good client, whom he brought to the ground.

Meanwhile, all those unlucky persons who had succeeded in scaling the wall were attacked by the hounds, and, unable to stand against them, were chased round the garden, to the infinite amusement of the squire. Frightened to death, and unable otherwise to escape, for the gate allowed them no means of exit, the poor wretches fled towards the terrace overlooking Pendle Water, and, leaping into the stream, gained the opposite bank. There they were safe, for the hounds were not allowed to follow them further. In this way the garden was completely cleared of the enemy, and Nicholas and Richard were left masters of the field.

Leaning out of the window, Mistress Nutter laughingly congratulated them on their success, and, as no further disposition was manifested on the part of Nowell and such of his troop that remained to renew the attack, the contest, for the present at least, was supposed to be at an end.

By this time, also, intimation had been conveyed by the deserters from Nowell's troop, who, it will be remembered, had made their way to the back of the premises, that they were anxious to offer their services to Mistress Nutter; and, as soon as this was told her, she ordered them to be admitted, and descended to give them welcome. Thus things wore a promising aspect for the besieged, while the assailing party were proportionately disheartened.

Long ere this, Baldwyn and old Mitton had desisted from their attempts to break open the gate, and, indeed, rejoiced that such a barrier was interposed between them and the hounds, whose furious onslaughts they witnessed. A bolt was launched against these four-footed guardians of the premises by the bearer of the crossbow, but the man proved but an indifferent marksman, for, instead of hitting the hound, he disabled one of his companions who was battling with him. Finding things in this state, and that neither Nowell nor Potts returned to their charge, while their followers were withdrawn from before the gate, Nicholas thought he might fairly infer that a victory had been obtained. But, like a prudent leader, he did not choose to expose himself till the enemy had absolutely yielded, and he therefore signed to Blackadder and his men to come forth from the hall. The order was obeyed, not only by them, but by the seceders from the hostile troop, and some thirty men issued from the principal door, and, ranging themselves upon the lawn, set up a deafening and triumphant shout, very different from that raised by the same individuals when under the command of Nowell. At the same moment Mistress Nutter and Alizon appeared at the door, and at the sight of them the shouting was renewed.

The unexpected turn in affairs had not been without its effect upon Richard and Alizon, and tended to revive the spirits of both. The immediate danger by which they were threatened had vanished, and time was given for the consideration of new plans. Richard had been firmly resolved to take no further part in the affray than should be required for the protection of Alizon, and, consequently, it was no little satisfaction to him to reflect that the victory had been accomplished without him, and by means which could not afterwards be questioned.

Meanwhile, Mistress Nutter had joined Nicholas, and the gates being unbarred by Blackadder, they passed through them. At a little distance stood Roger Nowell, now altogether abandoned, except by his own immediate followers, with Baldwyn and old Mitton. Poor Potts was lying on the ground, piteously bemoaning the lacerations his skin had undergone.

"Well, you have got the worst of it, Master Nowell," said Nicholas, as he and Mistress Nutter approached the discomfited magistrate, "and must own yourself fairly defeated."

"Defeated as I am, I would rather be in my place than in yours, sir," retorted Nowell, sourly.

"You have had a wholesome lesson read you, Master Nowell," said Mistress Nutter; "but I do not come hither to taunt you. I am quite satisfied with the victory I have obtained, and am anxious to put an end to the misunderstanding between us."

"I have no misunderstanding with you, madam," replied Nowell; "I do not quarrel with persons like you. But be assured, though you may escape now, a day of reckoning will come."

"Your chief cause of grievance against me, I am aware," replied Mistress Nutter, calmly, "is, that I have beaten you in the matter of the land. Now, I have a proposal to make to you respecting it."

"I cannot listen to it," rejoined Nowell, sternly; "I can have no dealings with a witch."

At this moment his cloak was plucked behind by Potts, who looked at him as much as to say, "Do not exasperate her. Hear what she has got to offer."

"I shall be happy to act as mediator between you, if possible," observed Nicholas; "but in that case I must request you, Master Nowell, to abstain from any offensive language."

"What is it you have to propose to me, then, madam?" demanded the magistrate, gruffly.

"Come with me into the house, and you shall hear," replied Mistress Nutter.

Nowell was about to refuse peremptorily, when his cloak was again plucked by Potts, who whispered him to go.

"This is not a snare laid to entrap me, madam?" he said, regarding the lady suspiciously.

"I will answer for her good faith," interposed Nicholas.

Nowell still hesitated, but the counsel of his legal adviser was enforced by a heavy shower of rain, which just then began to descend upon them.

"You can take shelter beneath my roof," said Mistress Nutter "and before the shower is over we can settle the matter."

"And my wounds can be dressed at the same time," said Potts, with a groan, "for they pain me sorely."

"Blackadder has a sovereign balsam, which, with a patch or two of diachylon, will make all right," replied Nicholas, unable to repress a laugh. "Here, lift him up between you," he added to the grooms, "and convey him into the house."

The orders were obeyed, and Mistress Nutter led the way through the now wide-opened gates; her slow and majestic march by no means accelerated by the drenching shower. What Roger Nowell's sensations were at following her in such a way, after his previous threats and boastings, may be easily conceived.

CHAPTER X.—ROGER NOWELL AND HIS DOUBLE.

THE magistrate was ushered by the lady into a small chamber, opening out of the entrance-hall, which, in consequence of having only one small narrow window, with a clipped yew-tree before it, was extremely dark and gloomy. The walls were covered with sombre tapestry, and on entering, Mistress Nutter not only carefully closed the door, but drew the arras before it, so as to prevent the possibility of their conversation being heard outside. These precautions taken, she motioned the magistrate to a chair, and seated herself opposite him.

"We can now deal unreservedly with each other, Master Nowell," she said, fixing her eyes steadily upon him; "and, as our discourse cannot be overheard and repeated, may use perfect freedom of speech."

"I am glad of it," replied Nowell, "because it will save circumlocution, which I dislike; and therefore, before proceeding further, I must tell you, directly and distinctly, that if there be aught of witchcraft in what you are about to propose to me, I will have nought to do with it, and our conference may as well never begin."

"Then you really believe me to be a witch?" said the lady.

"I do," replied Nowell, unflinchingly.

"Since you believe this, you must also believe that I have absolute power over you," rejoined Mistress Nutter, "and might strike you with sickness, cripple you, or kill you if I thought fit."

"I know not that," returned Nowell. "There are limits even to the power of evil beings; and your charms and enchantments, however strong and baneful, may be wholly inoperative against a magistrate in the discharge of his duty. If it were not so, you would scarcely think it worth while to treat with me."

"Humph!" exclaimed the lady. "Now, tell me frankly, what you will do when you depart hence?"

"Ride off with the utmost speed to Whalley," replied Nowell, "and, acquainting Sir Ralph with all that has occurred, claim his assistance; and then, with all the force we can jointly muster, return hither, and finish the work I have left undone."

"You will forego this intention," said Mistress Nutter, with a bitter smile.

The magistrate shook his head.

"I am not easily turned from my purpose," he remarked.

"But you have not yet quitted Rough Lee," said the lady, "and after such an announcement I shall scarce think of parting with you."

"You dare not detain me," replied Nowell. "I have Nicholas Assheton's word for my security, and I know he will not break it. Besides, you will gain nothing by my detention. My absence will soon be discovered, and if living I shall be set free; if dead, avenged."

"That may, or may not be," replied Mistress Nutter; "and in any case I can, if I choose, wreak my vengeance upon you. I am glad to have ascertained your intentions, for I now know how to treat with you. You shall not go hence, except on certain conditions. You have said you will proclaim me a witch, and will come back with sufficient force to accomplish my arrest. Instead of doing this, I advise you to return to Sir Ralph Assheton, and admit to him that you find yourself in error in respect to the boundaries of the land——"

"Never," interrupted Nowell.

"I advise you to do this," pursued the lady, calmly, "and I advise you, also, on quitting this room, to retract all you have uttered to my prejudice, in the presence of Nicholas Assheton and other credible witnesses; in which case I will not only lay aside all feelings of animosity towards you, but will make over to you the whole of the land under dispute, and that without purchase-money on your part.

Roger Nowell was of an avaricious nature, and caught at the bait.

"How, madam!" he cried, "the whole of the land mine without payment?"

"The whole," she replied.

"If she should be arraigned and convicted it will be forfeited to the crown," thought Nowell; "the offer is tempting."

"Your attorney is here, and can prepare the conveyance at once," pursued Mistress Nutter; "a sum can be stated to lend a colour to the proceeding, and I will give you a private memorandum that I will not claim it. All I require is, that you clear me completely from the dark aspersions cast upon my character, and you abandon your projects against my adopted daughter, Alizon, as well as against those two poor old women, Mothers Demdike and Chattox."

"How can I be sure that I shall not be deluded in the matter?" asked Nowell; "the writing may disappear from the parchment you give me, or the parchment itself may turn to ashes. Such things have occurred in transactions with witches. Or it may be that, by consenting to the compact, I may imperil my own soul."

"Tush!" exclaimed Mistress Nutter; "these are idle fears But it is no idle threat on my part, when I tell you you shall not go forth unless you consent."

"You cannot hinder me, woman," cried Nowell, rising.

"You shall see," rejoined the lady, making two or three rapid passes before him, which instantly stiffened his limbs, and deprived him of the power of motion. "Now, stir if you can," she added with a laugh.

Nowell essayed to cry out, but his tongue refused its office. Hearing and sight, however, were left him, and he saw Mistress Nutter take a large volume, bound in black, from the shelf, and open it at a page covered with cabalistic characters, after which she pronounced some words that sounded like an invocation.

As she concluded, the tapestry against the wall was raised, and from behind it appeared a figure in all respects resembling the magistrate: it had the same sharp features, the same keen eyes and bushy eyebrows, the same stoop in the shoulders, the same habiliments. It was, in short, his double.

Mistress Nutter regarded him with a look of triumph.

"Since you refuse, with my injunctions," she said, "your double will prove more tractable. He will go forth and do all I would have you do, while I have but to stamp upon the floor and a dungeon will yawn beneath your feet, where you will lie immured till doomsday. The same fate will attend your crafty associate, Master Potts—so that neither of you will be missed—ha! ha!"

The unfortunate magistrate fully comprehended his danger, but he could now neither offer remonstrance nor entreaty. What was passing in his breast seemed known to Mistress Nutter; for she motioned the double to stay, and, touching the brow of Nowell with the point of her forefinger, instantly restored his power of speech.

"I will give you a last chance," she said. "Will you obey me now?"

"I must, perforce," replied Nowell: "the contest is too unequal."

"You may retire, then," she cried to the double. And stepping backwards, the figure lifted up the tapestry, and disappeared behind it.

"I can breathe, now that infernal being is gone," cried Nowell, sinking into the chair. Oh! madam, you have indeed terrible power."

"You will do well not to brave it again," she rejoined. "Shall I summon Master Potts to prepare the conveyance?"

"Oh! no—no!" cried Nowell. "I do not desire the land. I will not have it. I shall pay too dearly for it. Only let me get out of this horrible place?"

"Not so quickly, sir," rejoined Mistress Nutter. "Before you go hence, I must bind you to the performance of my injunctions. Pronounce these words after me,—'May I become subject to the Fiend if I fail in my promise.'"

"I will never utter them!" cried Nowell, shuddering.

"Then I shall recall your double," said the lady.

"Hold, hold!" exclaimed Nowell. "Let me know what you require of me."

"I require absolute silence on your part, as to all you have seen and heard here, and cessation of hostility towards me and the persons I have already named," replied Mistress Nutter; "and I require a declaration from you, in the presence of the two Asshetons, that you are fully satisfied of the justice of my claims in respect to the land; and that, mortified by your defeat, you have brought a false charge against me, which you now sincerely regret. This I require from you; and you must ratify the promise by the abjuration I have proposed. 'May I become subject to the Fiend if I fail in my promise.'"

The magistrate repeated the words after her. As he finished, mocking laughter, apparently resounding from below, smote his ears.

"Enough!" cried Mistress Nutter, triumphantly; "and now take good heed that you swerve not in the slightest degree from your word, or you are for ever lost."

Again the mocking laughter was heard, and Nowell would have rushed forth, if Mistress Nutter had not withheld him.

"Stay!" she cried, "I have not done with you yet! My witnesses must hear your declaration. Remember!"

And placing her finger upon her lips, in token of silence, she stepped backwards, drew aside the tapestry, and, opening the door, called to the two Asshetons, both of whom instantly came to her, and were not a little surprised to learn that all differences had been adjusted, and that Roger Nowell acknowledged himself entirely in error, retracting all the charges he had brought against her; while, on her part, she was fully satisfied with his explanations and apologies, and promised not to entertain any feelings of resentment towards him.

"You have made up the matter, indeed," cried Nicholas, "and, as Master Roger Nowell is a widower, perhaps a match may come of it. Such an arrangement"——

"This is no occasion for jesting, Nicholas," interrupted the lady, sharply.

"Nay, I but threw out a hint," rejoined the squire. "It would set the question of the land for ever at rest."

"It is set at rest—for ever!" replied the lady, with a side look at the magistrate.

"'May I become subject to the Fiend if I fail in my promise,'" repeated Nowell to himself. "Those words bind me like a chain of iron. I must get out of this accursed house as fast as I can."

As if his thoughts had been divined by Mistress Nutter, she here observed to him, "To make our reconciliation complete, Master Nowell, I must entreat you to pass the day with me. I will give you the best entertainment my house affords—nay, I will take no denial; and you too, Nicholas, and you, Richard, you will stay and keep the worthy magistrate company."

The two Asshetons willingly assented, but Roger Nowell would fain have been excused. A look, however, from his hostess enforced compliance.

"The proposal will be highly agreeable, I am sure, to Master Potts," remarked Nicholas, with a laugh; "for though much better, in consequence of the balsam applied by Blackadder, he is scarcely in condition for the saddle."

"I will warrant him well to-morrow morning," said Mistress Nutter.

"Where is he?" inquired Nowell.

"In the library with Parson Holden," replied Nicholas; "making himself as comfortable as circumstances will permit, with a flask of Rhenish before him."

"I will go to him, then," said Nowell.

"Take care what you say to him," observed Mistress Nutter, in a low tone, and raising her finger to her lips.

Heaving a deep sigh, the magistrate then repaired to the library, a small room panelled with black oak, and furnished with a few cases of ancient tomes. The attorney and the divine were seated at a table, with a big square-built bottle and long-stemmed glasses before them, and Master Potts, with a wry grimace, excused himself from rising on his respected and singular good client's approach.

"Do not disturb yourself," said Nowell, gruffly; "we shall not leave Rough Lee to-day."

"I am glad to hear it," replied Potts, moving the cushions on his chair and eyeing the square-built bottle affectionately.

"Nor to-morrow, it may be—nor the day after—nor at all, possibly," said Nowell.

"Indeed!" exclaimed Potts, starting, and wincing with pain. "What is the meaning of all this, worthy sir?"

"'May I become the subject of the Fiend if I fail in my promise,'" rejoined Nowell, with a groan.

"What promise, worshipful sir?" cried Potts, staring with surprise.

The magistrate got out the words, "My promise to—" and then he stopped suddenly.

"To Mistress Nutter?" suggested Potts.

"Don't ask me," exclaimed Nowell, fiercely. "Don't draw any erroneous conclusions, man. I mean nothing—I say nothing!"

"He is certainly bewitched," observed Parson Holden in an under-tone to the attorney.

"It was by your advice I entered this house," thundered Nowell, "and may all the ill arising from it alight upon your head!"

"My respected client!" implored Potts.

"I am no longer your client!" shrieked the infuriated magistrate. "I dismiss you. I will have nought to do with you more. I wish I had never seen your ugly little face!"

"You were quite right, reverend sir," observed Potts aside to the divine; "he is certainly bewitched, or he never would behave in this way to his best friend. My excellent sir," he added to Nowell, "I beseech you to calm yourself, and listen to me. My motive for wishing you to comply with Mistress Nutter's request was this: We were in a dilemma from which there was no escape, my wounded condition preventing me from flight, and all your followers being dispersed. Knowing your discretion, I apprehended that, finding the tables turned against you, you would not desire to play a losing game, and I therefore counselled apparent submission as the best means of disarming your antagonist. Whatever arrangement you have made with Mistress Nutter is neither morally nor legally binding upon you."

"You think not!" cried Nowell. "'May I become subject to the Fiend if I violate my promise!'"

"What promise have you made, sir?" inquired Potts and Holden together.

"Do not question me," cried Nowell; "it is sufficient that I am tied and bound by it."

The attorney reflected a little, and then observed to Holden, "It is evident some unfair practices have been resorted to with our respected friend, to extort a promise from him which he cannot violate. It is also possible, from what he let fall at first, that an attempt may be made to detain us prisoners within this house, and, for aught I know, Master Nowell may have given his word not to go forth without Mistress Nutter's permission. Under these circumstances, I would beg of you, reverend sir, as an especial favour to us both, to ride over to Whalley, and acquaint Sir Ralph Assheton with our situation."

As this suggestion was made, Nowell's countenance brightened up. The expression was not lost upon the attorney, who perceived he was on the right tack.

"Tell the worthy baronet," continued Potts, "that his old and esteemed friend, Master Roger Nowell, is in great jeopardy—am I not right, sir?"

The magistrate nodded.

"Tell him he is forcibly detained a prisoner, and requires sufficient force to effect his immediate liberation. Tell him, also, that Master Nowell charges Mistress Nutter with robbing him of his land by witchcraft."

"No, no!" interrupted Nowell; "do not tell him that. I no longer charge her with it."

"Then, tell him that I do," cried Potts; "and that Master Nowell has strangely, very strangely, altered his mind."

"'May I become subject to the Fiend if I violate my promise!'" said the magistrate.

"Ay, tell him that," cried the attorney—"tell him the worthy gentleman is constantly repeating that sentence. It will explain all. And now, reverend sir, let me entreat you to set out without delay, or your departure may be prevented."

"I will go at once," said Holden.

As he was about to quit the apartment, Mistress Nutter appeared at the door. Confusion was painted on the countenances of all three.

"Whither go you, sir?" demanded the lady, sharply.

"On a mission which cannot be delayed, madam," replied Holden.

"You annot quit my house at present," she rejoined, peremptorily. "These gentlemen stay to dine with me, and I cannot dispense with your company."

"My duty calls me hence," returned the divine. "With all thanks for your proffered hospitality, I must perforce decline it."

"Not when I command you to stay," she rejoined, raising her hand; "I am absolute mistress here."

"Not over the servants of heaven, madam," replied the divine, taking a Bible from his pocket, and placing it before him. "By this sacred volume I shield myself against your spells, and command you to let me pass."

And as he went forth, Mistress Nutter, unable to oppose him, shrank back.

CHAPTER XI.—MOTHER DEMDIKE.

THE heavy rain, which began to fall as Roger Nowell entered Rough Lee, had now ceased, and the sun shone forth again brilliantly, making the garden look so fresh and beautiful that Richard proposed a stroll within it to Alizon. The young girl seemed doubtful at first whether to comply with the invitation; but she finally assented, and they went forth together alone, for Nicholas, fancying they could dispense with his company, only attended them as far as the door, where he remained looking after them, laughing to himself, and wondering how matters would end. "No good will come of it, I fear," mused the worthy squire, shaking his head, "and I am scarcely doing right in allowing Dick to entangle himself in this fashion. But where is the use of giving advice to a young man who is over head and ears in love? He will never listen to it, and will only resent interference. Dick must take his chance. I have already pointed out the danger to him, and if he chooses to run headlong into the pit, why, I cannot hinder him. After all, I am not much surprised. Alizon's beauty is quite irresistible, and, were all smooth and straightforward in her history, there could be no reason why—pshaw! I am as foolish as the lad himself. Sir Richard Assheton, the proudest man in the shire, would disown his son if he married against his inclinations. No, my pretty youthful pair, since nothing but misery awaits you, I advise you to make the most of your brief season of happiness. I should certainly do so were the case my own."

Meanwhile, the objects of these ruminations had reached the terrace overlooking Pendle Water, and were pacing slowly backwards and forwards along it.

"One might be very happy in this sequestered spot, Alizon," observed Richard. "To some persons it might appear dull, but to me, if blessed with you, it would be little short of Paradise."

"Alas! Richard," she replied, forcing a smile, "why conjure up visions of happiness which never can be realised? But even with you I do not think I could be happy here. There is something about the house which, when I first beheld it, filled me with unaccountable terror. Never since I was a mere infant have I been within it till to-day, and yet it was quite familiar to me—horribly familiar. I knew the hall in which we stood together, with its huge arched fireplace, and the armorial bearings upon it, and could point out the stone on which were carved my father's initials 'R. N.,' with the date '1572.' I knew the tapestry on the walls, and the painted glass in the long range windows. I knew the old oak staircase, and the gallery beyond it, and the room to which my mother led me. I knew the portraits painted on the panels, and at once recognised my father. I knew the great carved oak bedstead in this room, and the high chimney-piece, and the raised hearthstone, and shuddered as I gazed at it. You will ask me how these things could be familiar to me? I will tell you. I had seen them repeatedly in my dreams. They have haunted me for years, but I only to-day knew they had an actual existence, or were in any way connected with my own history. The sight of that house inspired me with a horror I have not been able to overcome; and I have a presentiment that some ill will befall me within it. I would never willingly dwell there.'

"The warning voice within you, which should never be despised, prompts you to quit it," cried Richard; "and I also urge you in like manner."

"In vain," sighed Alizon. "This terrace is beautiful," she added, as they resumed their walk, "and I shall often come hither, if I am permitted. At sunset, this river, and the woody heights above it, must be enchanting; and I do not dislike the savage character of the surrounding scenery. It enhances, by contrast, the beauty of this solitude. I only wish the spot commanded a view of Pendle Hill."

"You are like my cousin Nicholas, who thinks no prospect complete unless that hill forms part of it," said Richard; "but since I find that you will often come hither at sunset, I shall not despair of seeing and conversing with you again, even if I am forbidden the house by Mistress Nutter. That thicket is an excellent hiding-place, and this stream is easily crossed."

"We can have no secret interviews, Richard," replied Alizon; "I shall come hither to think of you, but not to meet you. You must never return to Rough Lee again—that is, not unless some change takes place, which I dare not anticipate—but, hist! I am called. I must go back to the house."

"The voice came from the other side of the river," said Richard—"and, hark! it calls again. Who can it be?"

"It is Jennet," replied Alizon; "I see her now."

And she pointed out the little girl standing beside an alder on the opposite bank.

"Yo didna notice me efore, Alizon," cried Jennet in her sharp tone, and with her customary provoking laugh, "boh ey seed yo plain enuff, an heer'd yo too; and ey heer'd Mester Ruchot say he wad hide i' this thicket, an cross the river to meet ye at sunset. Little pigs, they say, ha' lang ears, an mine werena gi'en me fo' nowt."

"They have somewhat misinformed you in this instance," replied Alizon; "but how, in the name of wonder, did you come here?"

"Varry easily," replied Jennet, "boh ey hanna time to tell ye now. Granny Demdike has sent me hither wi' a message to ye and Mistress Nutter. Boh may be ye winna loike Mester Ruchot to hear what ey ha' getten to tell ye."

"I will leave you," said Richard, about to depart.

"Oh! no, no!" cried Alizon, "she can have nothing to say which you may not hear."

"Shan ey go back to Granny Demdike, an tell her yo're too proud to receive her message?" asked the child.

"On no account," whispered Richard. "Do not let her anger the old hag."

"Speak, Jennet," said Alizon, in a tone of kind persuasion.

"Ey shanna speak onless ye cum ower t' wetur to me," replied the little girl; "an whot ey ha to tell consarns ye mitch."

"I can easily cross," observed Alizon to Richard. "Those stones seem placed on purpose."

Upon this, descending from the terrace to the river's brink, and springing lightly upon the first stone which reared its head above the foaming tide, she bounded to another, and so in an instant was across the stream. Richard saw her ascend the opposite bank, and approach Jennet, who withdrew behind the alder; and then he fancied he perceived an old beldame, partly concealed by the intervening branches of the tree, advance and seize hold of her. Then there was a scream; and the sound had scarcely reached the young man's ears before he was down the bank and across the river, but when he reached the alder, neither Alizon, nor Jennet, nor the old beldame were to be seen.

The terrible conviction that she had been carried off by Mother Demdike then smote him, and though he continued his search for her among the adjoining bushes, it was with fearful misgivings. No answer was returned to his shouts, nor could he discover any trace of the means by which Alizon had been spirited away.

After some time spent in ineffectual search, uncertain what course to pursue, and with a heart full of despair, Richard crossed the river, and proceeded towards the house, in front of which he found Mistress Nutter and Nicholas, both of whom seemed surprised when they perceived he was unaccompanied by Alizon. The lady immediately, and somewhat sharply, questioned him as to what had become of her adopted daughter, and appeared at first to doubt his answer; but at length, unable to question his sincerity, she became violently agitated.

"The poor girl has been conveyed away by Mother Demdike," she cried, "though for what purpose I am at a loss to conceive. The old hag could not cross the running water, and therefore resorted to that stratagem."

"Alizon must not be left in her hands, madam," said Richard.

"She must not," replied the lady. "If Blackadder, whom I have sent after Parson Holden, were here, I would despatch him instantly to Malkin Tower."

"I will go instead," said Richard.

"You had better accept his offer," interposed Nicholas; "he will serve you as well as Blackadder."

"Go I shall, madam," cried Richard; "if not on your account, on my own."

"Come, then, with me," said the lady, entering the house, "and I will furnish you with that which shall be your safeguard in the enterprise."

With this, she proceeded to the closet where her interview with Roger Nowell had been held; and, unlocking an ebony cabinet, took from a drawer within it a small flat piece of gold, graven with mystic characters, and having a slender chain of the same metal attached to it. Throwing the chain over Richard's neck, she said, "Place this talisman, which is of sovereign virtue, near your heart, and no witchcraft shall have power over you. But be careful that you are not by any artifice deprived of it, for the old hag will soon discover that you possess some charm to protect you against her spells. You are impatient to be gone, but I have not yet done," she continued, taking down a small silver bugle from a hook, and giving it him. "On reaching Malkin Tower, wind this horn thrice, and the old witch will appear at the upper window. Demand admittance in my name, and she will not dare to refuse you; or, if she does, tell her you know the secret entrance to her stronghold, and will have recourse to it. And in case this should be needful, I will now disclose it to you, but you must not use it till other means fail. When opposite the door, which you will find is high up in the building, take ten paces to the left, and if you examine the masonry at the foot of the tower, you will perceive one stone somewhat darker than the rest. At the bottom of this stone, and concealed by a patch of heath, you will discover a knob of iron. Touch it, and it will give you an opening to a vaulted chamber, whence you can mount to the upper room. Even then you may experience some difficulty, but with resolution you will surmount all obstacles."

"I have no fear of success, madam," replied Richard, confidently.

And quitting her, he proceeded to the stables, and calling for his horse, vaulted into the saddle, and galloped off towards the bridge.

Fast as Richard rode up the steep hill-side, still faster did the black clouds gather over his head. No natural cause could have produced so instantaneous a change in the aspect of the sky, and the young man viewed it with uneasiness, and wished to get out of the thicket in which he was now involved, before the threatened thunder-storm commenced. But the hill was steep and the road bad, being full of loose stones, and crossed in many places by bare roots of trees. Though ordinarily surefooted, Merlin stumbled frequently, and Richard was obliged to slacken his pace. It grew darker and darker, and the storm seemed ready to burst upon him. The smaller birds ceased singing, and screened themselves under the thickest foliage; the pie chattered incessantly; the jay screamed; the bittern flew past, booming heavily in the air; the raven croaked; the heron arose from the river, and speeded off with his long neck stretched out; and the falcon, who had been hovering over him, sweeped sidelong down and sought shelter beneath an impending rock; the rabbit scudded off to his burrow in the brake; and the hare, erecting himself for a moment, as if to listen to the note of danger, crept timorously off into the long dry grass.

It grew so dark at last that the road was difficult to discern, and the dense rows of trees on either side assumed a fantastic appearance in the deep gloom. Richard was now more than halfway up the hill, and the thicket had become more tangled and intricate, and the road narrower and more rugged. All at once Merlin stopped, quivering in every limb, as if in extremity of error.

Before the rider, and right in his path, glared a pair of red fiery orbs, with something dusky and obscure linked to them; but whether of man or beast he could not distinguish.

Richard called to it. No answer. He struck spurs into the reeking flanks of his horse. The animal refused to stir. Just then there was a moaning sound in the wood, as of some one in pain. He turned in the direction, shouted, but received no answer. When he looked back the red eyes were gone.

Then Merlin moved forward of his own accord, but ere he had gone far, the eyes were visible again, glaring at the rider from the wood. This time they approached, dilating, and increasing in glowing intensity, till they scorched him like burning-glasses. Bethinking him of the talisman, Richard drew it forth. The light was instantly extinguished, and the indistinct figure accompanying it melted into darkness.

Once more Merlin resumed his toilsome way, and Richard was marvelling that the storm so long suspended its fury, when the sky was riven by a sudden blaze, and a crackling bolt shot down and struck the earth at his feet. The affrighted steed reared aloft, and was with difficulty prevented from falling backwards upon his rider. Almost before he could be brought to his feet, an awful peal of thunder burst overhead, and it required Richard's utmost efforts to prevent him from rushing madly down the hill.

The storm had now fairly commenced. Flash followed flash, and peal succeeded peal, without intermission. The rain descended hissing and spouting, and presently ran down the hill in a torrent, adding to the horseman's other difficulties and dangers. To heighten the terror of the scene, strange shapes, revealed by the lightning, were seen flitting among the trees, and strange sounds were heard, though overpowered by the dreadful rolling of the thunder.

But Richard's resolution continued unshaken, and he forced Merlin on. He had not proceeded far, however, when the animal uttered a cry of fright, and began beating the air with his fore hoofs. The lightning enabled Richard to discern the cause of this new distress. Coiled round the poor beast's legs, all whose efforts to disengage himself from the terrible assailant were ineffectual, was a large black snake, seemingly about to plunge its poisonous fangs into the flesh. Again having recourse to the talisman, and bending down, Richard stretched it towards the snake, upon which the reptile instantly darted its arrow-shaped head against him, but instead of wounding him, its forked teeth encountered the piece of gold, and, as if stricken a violent blow, it swiftly untwined itself, and fled, hissing, into the thicket.

Richard was now obliged to dismount and lead his horse. In this way he toiled slowly up the hill. The storm continued with unabated fury: the red lightning played around him, the brattling thunder stunned him, and the pelting rain poured down upon his head. But he was no more molested. Save for the vivid flashes, it had become dark as night, but they served to guide him on his way.

At length he got out of the thicket, and trod upon the turf but it was rendered so slippery by moisture, that he could scarcely keep his feet, while the lightning no longer aided him. Fearing he had taken a wrong course, he stood still, and while debating with himself a blaze of light illumined the wide heath, and showed him the object of his search, Malkin Tower, standing alone, like a beacon, at about a quarter of a mile's distance, on the further side of the hill. Was it disturbed fancy, or did he really behold on the summit of the structure a grisly shape resembling—if it resembled any thing human—a gigantic black cat, with roughened staring skin, and flaming eyeballs?

Nerved by the sight of the tower, Richard was on his steed's back in an instant, and the animal, having in some degree recovered his spirits, galloped off with him, and kept his feet in spite of the slippery state of the road. Erelong, another flash showed the young man that he was drawing rapidly near the tower, and dismounting, he tied Merlin to a tree, and hurried towards the unhallowed pile. When within twenty paces of it, mindful of Mistress Nutter's injunctions, he placed the bugle to his lips, and winded it thrice. The summons, though clear and loud, sounded strangely in the portentous silence.

Scarcely had the last notes died away, when a light shone through the dark red curtains hanging before a casement in the upper part of the tower. The next moment these were drawn aside, and a face appeared, so frightful, so charged with infernal wickedness and malice, that Richard's blood grew chill at the sight. Was it man or woman? The white beard, and the large, broad, masculine character of the countenance, seemed to denote the former, but the garb was that of a female. The face was at once hideous and fantastic—the eyes set across—the mouth awry—the right cheek marked by a mole shining with black hair, and horrible from its contrast to the rest of the visage, and the brow branded as if by a streak of blood. A black thrum cap constituted the old witch's head-gear, and from beneath it her hoary hair escaped in long elf-locks. The lower part of her person was hidden from view, but she appeared to be as broad-shouldered as a man, and her bulky person was wrapped in a tawny-coloured robe. Throwing open the window, she looked forth, and demanded in harsh imperious tones—

"Who dares to summon Mother Demdike?"

"A messenger from Mistress Nutter," replied Richard. "I am come in her name to demand the restitution of Alizon Device, whom thou hast forcibly and wrongfully taken from her."

"Alizon Device is my grand-daughter, and, as such, belongs to me, and not to Mistress Nutter," rejoined Mother Demdike.

"Thou knowest thou speakest false, foul hag!" cried Richard. "Alizon is no blood of thine. Open the door and cast down the ladder, or I will find other means of entrance."

"Try them, then," rejoined Mother Demdike. And she closed the casement sharply, and drew the curtains over it.

After reconnoitring the building for a moment, Richard moved quickly to the left, and counting ten paces, as directed by Mistress Nutter, began to search among the thick grass growing near the base of the tower for the concealed entrance. It was too dark to distinguish any difference in the colour of the masonry, but he was sure he could not be far wrong, and presently his hand came in contact with a knob of iron. He pressed it, but it did not yield to the touch. Again more forcibly, but with like ill success. Could he be mistaken? He tried the next stone, and discovered another knob upon it, but this was as immovable as the first. He went on, and then found that each stone was alike, and that if amongst the number he had chanced upon the one worked by the secret spring, it had refused to act. On examining the structure so far as he was able to do in the gloom, he found he had described the whole circle of the tower, and was about to commence the search anew, when a creaking sound was heard above, and a light streamed suddenly down upon him. The door had been opened by the old witch, and she stood there with a lamp in her hand, its yellow flame illumining her hideous visage, and short, square, powerfully built frame. Her throat was like that of a bull; her hands of extraordinary size; and her arms, which were bare to the shoulder, brawny and muscular.

"What, still outside?" she cried in a jeering tone, and with a wild discordant laugh. "Methought thou affirmedst thou couldst find a way into my dwelling."

"I do not yet despair of finding it," replied Richard.

"Fool!" screamed the hag. "I tell thee it is in vain to attempt it without my consent. With a word, I could make these walls one solid mass, without window or outlet from base to summit. With a word, I could shower stones upon thy head, and crush thee to dust. With a word, I could make the earth swallow thee up. With a word, I could whisk thee hence to the top of Pendle Hill. Ha! ha! Dost fear me now?"

"No," replied Richard, undauntedly. "And the word thou menacest me with shall never be uttered."

"Why not?" asked Mother Demdike, derisively.

"Because thou wouldst not brave the resentment of one whose power is equal to thine own—if not greater," replied the young man.

"Greater it is not—neither equal," rejoined the old hag, haughtily; "but I do not desire a quarrel with Alice Nutter. Only let her not meddle with me."

"Once more, art thou willing to admit me?" demanded Richard.

"Ay, upon one condition," replied Mother Demdike. "Thou shalt learn it anon. Stand aside while I let down the ladder."

Richard obeyed, and a pair of narrow wooden steps dropped to the ground.

"Now mount, if thou hast the courage," cried the hag.

The young man was instantly beside her, but she stood in the doorway, and barred his further progress with her extended staff. Now that he was face to face with her, he wondered at his own temerity. There was nothing human in her countenance, and infernal light gleamed in her strangely-set eyes. Her personal strength, evidently unimpaired by age, or preserved by magical art, seemed equal to her malice; and she appeared as capable of executing any atrocity, as of conceiving it. She saw the effect produced upon him, and chuckled with malicious satisfaction.

"Saw'st thou ever face like mine?" she cried. "No, I wot not. But I would rather inspire aversion and terror than love. Love!—foh! I would rather see men shrink from me, and shudder at my approach, than smile upon me and court me. I would rather freeze the blood in their veins, than set it boiling with passion. Ho! ho!"

"Thou art a fearful being, indeed!" exclaimed Richard, appalled.

"Fearful, am I?" ejaculated the old witch, with renewed laughter. "At last thou own'st it. Why, ay, I *am* fearful. It is my wish to be so. I live to plague mankind—to blight and blast them—to scare them with my looks—to work them mischief. Ho! ho! And now, let us look at thee," she continued, holding the lamp over him. "Why, soh?—a comely youth! And the young maids doat upon thee, I doubt not, and praise thy blooming cheeks, thy bright eyes, thy flowing locks, and thy fine limbs. I hate thy beauty, boy, and would mar it!—would canker thy wholesome flesh, dim thy lustrous eyes, and strike thy vigorous limbs with palsy, till they should shake like mine! I am half-minded to do it," she added, raising her staff, and glaring at him with inconceivable malignity.

"Hold!" exclaimed Richard, taking the talisman from his breast, and displaying it to her. "I am armed against thy malice!"

Mother Demdike's staff fell from her grasp.

"I knew thou wert in some way protected," she cried furiously. "And so it is a piece of gold—with magic characters upon it, eh?" she added, suddenly changing her tone; "Let me look at it."

"Thou seest it plain enough," rejoined Richard. "Now, stand aside and let me pass, for thou perceivest I have power to force an entrance."

"I see it—I see it," replied Mother Demdike, with affected humility. "I see it is in vain to struggle with thee, or rather with the potent lady who sent thee. Tarry where thou art, and I will bring Alizon to thee."

"I almost mistrust thee," said Richard—"but be speedy."

"I will be scarce a moment," said the witch; "but I must warn thee that she is—"

"What—what hast thou done to her, thou wicked hag?" cried Richard, in alarm.

"She is distraught," said Mother Demdike.

"Distraught!" echoed Richard.

"But thou canst easily cure her," said the old hag, significantly.

"Ay, so I can," cried Richard with sudden joy—"the talisman! Bring her to me at once."

Mother Demdike departed, leaving him in a state of indescribable agitation. The walls of the tower were of immense thickness, and the entrance to the chamber towards which the arched doorway led was covered by a curtain of old arras, behind which the hag had disappeared. Scarcely had she entered the room when a scream was heard, and Richard heard his own name pronounced by a voice which, in spite of its agonised tones, he at once recognised. The cries were repeated, and he then heard Mother Demdike call out, "Come hither! come hither!"

Instantly rushing forward and dashing aside the tapestry, he found himself in a mysterious-looking circular chamber, with a massive oak table in the midst of it. There were many strange objects in the room, but he saw only Alizon, who was struggling with the old witch, and clinging desperately to the table. He called to her by name as he advanced, but her bewildered looks proved that she did not know him.

"Alizon—dear Alizon! I am come to free you," he exclaimed.

But in place of answering him she uttered a piercing scream.

"The talisman, the talisman?" cried the hag. "I cannot undo my own work. Place the chain round her neck, and the gold near her heart, that she may experience its full virtue."

Richard unsuspectingly complied with the suggestion of the temptress; but the moment he had parted with the piece of gold the figure of Alizon vanished, the chamber was buried in gloom, and, amidst a hubbub of wild laughter, he was dragged by the powerful arm of the witch through the arched doorway, and flung from it to the ground, the shock of the fall producing immediate insensibility.

CHAPTER XII.—THE MYSTERIES OF MALKIN TOWER.

It was a subterranean chamber; gloomy, and of vast extent, the roof low, and supported by nine ponderous stone columns, to which rings and rusty chains were attached, still retaining the mouldering bones of those they had held captive in life. Amongst others was a gigantic skeleton, quite entire, with an iron girdle round the middle. Fragments of mortality were elsewhere scattered about, showing the numbers who had perished in the place. On either side were cells closed by massive doors, secured by bolts and locks. At one end were three immense coffers made of oak, hooped with iron, and fastened by large padlocks. Near them stood a large armoury, likewise of oak, and sculptured with the ensigns of Whalley Abbey, proving it had once belonged to that establishment. Probably it had been carried off by some robber band. At the opposite end of the vault were two niches, each occupied by a rough-hewn statue—the one representing a warlike figure, with a visage of extraordinary ferocity, and the other an anchoress, in her hood and wimple, with a rosary in her hand. On the ground beneath lay a plain flag, covering the mortal remains of the wicked pair, and proclaiming them to be Isole de Heton and Blackburn, the freebooter. The pillars were ranged in three lines, so as to form, with the arches above them, a series of short passages, in the midst of which stood an altar, and near it a large caldron. In front, elevated on a block of granite, was a marvellous piece of sculpture, wrought in jet, and representing a demon seated on a throne. The visage was human, but the beard that of a goat, while the feet and lower limbs were like those of the same animal. Two curled horns grew behind the ears, and a third, shaped like a conch, sprang from the centre of the forehead, from which burst a blue flame, throwing a ghastly light on the objects surrounding it.

The only discernible approach to the vault was a steep narrow stone staircase, closed at the top by a heavy trapdoor. Other outlet apparently there was none. Some little air was admitted to this foul abode through flues contrived in the walls, the entrances to which were grated, but the light of day never came there. The flame, however, issuing from the brow of the demon image, like the lamps in the sepulchres of the disciples of the Rosy Cross, was ever-burning. Behind the sable statue was a deep well, with water as black as ink, wherein swarmed snakes, and toads, and other noxious reptiles; and as the lurid light fell upon its surface it glittered like a dusky mirror, unless when broken by the horrible things that lurked beneath, or crawled about upon its slimy brim. But snakes and toads were not the only tenants of the vault. At the head of the steps squatted a monstrous and misshapen animal, bearing some resemblance to a cat, but as big as a tiger. Its skin was black and shaggy; its eyes glowed like those of the hyæna; and its cry was like that of the same treacherons beast. Among the gloomy colonnades other swart and bestial shapes could be indistinctly seen moving to and fro.

In this abode of horror were two human beings—one, a young maiden of exquisite beauty; and the other, almost a child, and strangely deformed. The elder, overpowered by terror, was clinging to a pillar for support, while the younger, who might naturally be expected to exhibit the greatest alarm, appeared wholly unconcerned, and derided her companion's fears.

"Oh, Jennet!" exclaimed the elder of the two, "is there no means of escape?"

"None whatever," replied the other. "Yo mun stay here till Granny Demdike cums fo ye."

"Oh! that the earth would open and snatch me from these horrors," cried Alizon. "My reason is forsaking me. Would I could kneel and pray for deliverance! But something prevents me."

"Reet!" replied Jennet. "It's os mitch os yer loife's worth to kneel an pray here, onless yo choose to ge an throw yersel at th' feet o' yon black image."

"Kneel to that idol—never!" exclaimed Alizon. And while striving to call upon heaven for aid, a sharp convulsion seized her, and deprived her of the power of utterance.

"Ey towd yo how it wad be," remarked Jennet, who watched her narrowly. "Yo 're neaw i' a church here, an if yo want to warship, it mun be at yon altar. Dunna yo hear how angry the cats are—how they growl an spit? An see how their een gliss'n! They'll tare yo i' pieces, loike so many tigers, if yo offend em."

"Tell me why I am brought here, Jennet?" inquired Alizon, after a brief pause.

"Granny Demdike will tell yo that," replied the little girl; "boh to my belief," she added, with a mocking laugh, "hoo means to may a witch o' ye, loike aw the rest on us."

"She cannot do that without my consent," cried Alizon, "and I would die a thousand deaths rather than yield it."

"That remains to be seen," replied Jennet, tauntingly. "Yo 're obstinate enuff, nah doubt. Boh Granny Demdike is used to deal wi' sich folk."

"Oh! why was I born?" cried Alizon, bitterly.

"Yo may weel ask that," responded Jennet, with a loud unfeeling laugh; "fo ey see neaw great use yo're on, wi' yer protty feace an bright een, onless it be to may one hate ye."

"Is it possible you can say this to me, Jennet?" cried Alizon. "What have I done to incur your hatred? I have ever loved you, and striven to please and serve you. I have always taken your part against others, even when you were in the wrong. Oh! Jennet, you cannot hate me."

"Boh ey do," replied the little girl, spitefully. "Ey hate yo now warser than onny wan else. Ey hate yo because yo are neaw lunger my sister—becose yo 're a grand ledy's dowter, an a grand ledy yersel. Ey hate yo becose yung Ruchot Assheton loves yo—an becose yo ha better luck i' aw things than ey have, or con expect to have. That's why I hate yo, Alizon. When yo are a witch ey shan love yo, for then we shan be equals once more."

"That will never be, Jennet," said Alizon, sadly, but firmly. "Your grandmother may immure me in this dungeon, and scare away my senses; but she will never rob me of my hopes of salvation."

As the words were uttered, a clang like that produced by a stricken gong shook the vault; the beasts roared fiercely; the black waters of the fountain bubbled up, and were lashed into foam by the angry reptiles; and a larger jet of flame than before burst from the brow of the demon statue.

"Ey ha' warned ye, Alizon," said Jennet, alarmed by these demonstrations; "boh since ye pay no heed to owt ey say, ey'st leave yo to yer fate."

"Oh! stay with me, stay with me, Jennet!" shrieked Alizon. "By our past sisterly affection I implore you to remain! You are some protection to me from these dreadful beings."

"Ey dunna want to protect yo onless yo do os yo're bidd'n," replied Jennet! "Whoy should yo be better than me?"

"Ah! why, indeed?" cried Alizon. "Would I had the power to turn your heart—to open your eyes to evil—to save you, Jennet."

These words were followed by another clang, louder and more brattling than the first. The solid walls of the dungeon were shaken, and the heavy columns rocked; while, to Alizon's affrighted gaze, it seemed as if the sable statue arose upon its ebon throne, and stretched out its arm menacingly towards her. The poor girl was saved from further terror by insensibility.

How long she remained in this condition she could not tell, nor did it appear that any efforts were made to restore her; but when she recovered, she found herself stretched upon a rude pallet within an arched recess, the entrance to which was screened by a piece of tapestry. On lifting it aside she perceived she was no longer in the vault, but in an upper chamber, as she judged, and not incorrectly, of the tower. The room was lofty and circular, and the walls of enormous thickness, as shown by the deep embrasures of the windows; in one of which, the outlet having been built up, the pallet was placed. A massive oak table, two or three chairs of antique shape, and a wooden stool, constituted the furniture of the room. The stool was set near the fireplace, and beside it stood a strangely-fashioned spinning-wheel, which had apparently been recently used; but neither the old hag nor her grand-daughter were visible. Alizon could not tell whether it was night or day; but a lamp was burning upon the table, its feeble light only imperfectly illumining the chamber, and scarcely revealing several strange objects dangling from the huge beams that supported the roof. Faded arras were hung against the walls, representing in one compartment the last banquet of Isole de Heton and her lover, Blackburn; in another, the Saxon

Ughtred hanging from the summit of Malkin Tower; and in a third, the execution of Abbot Paslew. The subjects were as large as life, admirably depicted, and evidently worked at wondrous looms. As they swayed to and fro in the gusts, that found entrance into the chamber through some unprotected loopholes, the figures had a grim and ghostly air.

Weak, trembling, bewildered, Alizon stepped forth, and staggering towards the table sank upon a chair beside it. A fearful storm was raging without—thunder, lightning, deluging rain. Stunned and blinded, she covered her eyes, and remained thus till the fury of the tempest had in some degree abated. She was roused at length by a creaking sound not far from her, and found it proceeded from a trapdoor rising slowly on its hinges.

A thrum cap first appeared above the level of the floor; then a broad, bloated face, the mouth and chin fringed with a white beard like the whiskers of a cat; then a thick, bull throat; then a pair of brawny shoulders; then a square, thick-set frame; and Mother Demdike stood before her. A malignant smile played upon her hideous countenance, and gleamed from her eyes—those eyes so strangely placed by nature, as if to intimate her doom, and that of her fated race, to whom the horrible blemish was transmitted. As the old witch leaped heavily upon the ground, the trapdoor closed behind her.

"Soh, you are better, Alizon, and have quitted your couch, I find," she cried, striking her staff upon the floor. "But you look faint and feeble still. I will give you something to revive you. I have a wondrous cordial in yon closet—a rare restorative—ha! ha! It will make you well the moment it has passed your lips. I will fetch it at once."

"I will have none of it," replied Alizon; "I would rather die."

"Rather die!" echoed Mother Demdike, sarcastically, "because, forsooth, you are crossed in love. But you shall have the man of your heart yet, if you will only follow my counsel, and do as I bid you. Richard Assheton shall be yours, and with your mother's consent, provided—"

"I understand the condition you annex to the promise," interrupted Alizon, "and the terms upon which you would fulfil it: but you seek in vain to tempt me, old woman. I now comprehend why I am brought hither."

"Ay, indeed!" exclaimed the old witch. "And why is it, then, since you are so quick-witted?"

"You desire to make an offering to the evil being you serve," cried Alizon, with sudden energy. "You have entered into some dark compact, which compels you to deliver up a victim in each year to the Fiend, or your own soul becomes forfeit. Thus you have hitherto lengthened out your wretched life, and you hope to extend the term yet further through me. I have heard this tale before, but I would not believe it. Now I do. This is why you have stolen me from my mother—have braved her anger—and brought me to this impious tower."

The old hag laughed hoarsely.

"The tale thou hast heard respecting me is true," she said. "I *have* a compact which requires me to make a proselyte to the power I serve within each year, and if I fail in doing so, I must pay the penalty thou hast mentioned. A like compact exists between Mistress Nutter and the Fiend."

She paused for a moment, to watch the effect of her words on Alizon, and then resumed.

"Thy mother would have sacrificed thee if thou hadst been left with her; but I have carried thee off, because I conceive I am best entitled to thee. Thou wert brought up as my grand-daughter, and therefore I claim thee as my own."

"And you think to deal with me as if I were a puppet in your hands?" cried Alizon.

"Ay, marry, do I," rejoined Mother Demdike, with a scream of laughter "Thou art nothing more than a puppet—a puppet—ho! ho.

"And you deem you can dispose of my soul without my consent?" said Alizon.

"Thy full consent will be obtained," rejoined the old hag.

"Think it not! think it not!" exclaimed Alizon. "Oh! I shall yet be delivered from this infernal bondage."

At this moment the notes of a bugle were heard.

"Saved! saved!" cried the poor girl, starting. "It is Richard come to my rescue!"

"How know'st thou that?" cried Mother Demdike, with a spiteful look.

"By an instinct that never deceives," replied Alizon, as the blast was again heard.

"This must be stopped," said the hag, waving her staff over the maiden, and transfixing her where she sat; after which she took up the lamp, and strode towards the window.

The few words that passed between her and Richard have been already recounted. Having closed the casement and drawn the curtain before it, Mother Demdike traced a circle on the floor, muttered a spell, and then, waving her staff over Alizon, restored her power of speech and motion.

"'Twas he!" exclaimed the young girl, as soon as she could find utterance. "I heard his voice."

"Why, ay, 'twas he, sure enough," rejoined the beldame. "He has come on a fool's errand, but he shall never return from it. Does Mistress Nutter think I will give up my prize the moment I have obtained it, for the mere asking? Does she imagine she can frighten me as she frightens others? Does she know whom she has to deal with? If not, I will tell her. I am the oldest, the boldest, and the strongest of the witches. No mystery of the black art but is known to me. I can do what mischief I will, and my desolating hand has been felt throughout this district. You may trace it like a pestilence. No one has offended me but I have terribly repaid him. I rule over the land like a queen. I exact tributes, and, if they are not rendered, I smite with a sharper edge than the sword. My worship is paid to the Prince of Darkness. This tower is his temple, and yon subterranean chamber the place where the mystical rites, which thou wouldst call impious and damnable, are performed. Countless sabbaths have I attended within it; or upon Rumbles Moor, or on the summit of Pendle Hill, or within the ruins of Whalley Abbey. Many proselytes have I made; many unbaptised babes offered up in sacrifice. I am high-priestess to the Demon, and thy mother would usurp mine office."

"Oh! spare me this horrible recital!" exclaimed Alizon, vainly trying to shut out the hag's piercing voice.

"I will spare thee nothing," pursued Mother Demdike. "Thy mother, I say, would be high-priestess in my stead. There are degrees among witches, as among other sects, and mine is the first. Mistress Nutter would deprive me of mine office; but not till her hair is as white as mine, her knowledge equal to mine, and her hatred of mankind as intense as mine—not till then shall she have it."

"No more of this, in pity!" cried Alizon.

"Often have I aided thy mother in her dark schemes," pursued the implacable hag; "nay, no later than last night I obliterated the old boundaries of her land, and erected new marks to serve her. It was a strong exercise of power; but the command came to me, and I obeyed it. No other witch could have achieved so much, not even the accursed Chattox, and she is next to myself. And how does thy mother purpose to requite me? By thrusting me aside, and stepping into my throne."

"You must be in error," cried Alizon, scarcely knowing what to say.

"My information never fails me," replied the hag, with a disdainful laugh. "Her plans are made known to me as soon as formed. I have those about her who keep strict watch upon her actions, and report them faithfully. I know why she brought thee so suddenly to Rough Lee, though thou know'st it not."

"She brought me there for safety," remarked the young girl, hoping to allay the beldame's fury, "and because she herself desired to know how the survey of the boundaries would end."

"She brought thee there to sacrifice thee to the Fiend!" cried the hag, infernal rage and malice blazing in her eyes. "She failed in propitiating him at the meeting in the ruined church of Whalley last night, when thou thyself wert present, and deliver-

-edst Dorothy Assheton from the snare in which she was taken. And since then all has gone wrong with her. Having demanded from her familiar the cause why all things ran counter, she was told she had failed in the fulfilment of her promise—that a proselyte was required—and that thou alone wouldst be accepted."

"I!" exclaimed Alizon, horror-stricken.

"Ay, thou!" cried the hag. "No choice was allowed her, and the offering must be made to-night. After a long and painful struggle, thy mother consented."

"Oh! no—impossible! you deceive me," cried the wretched girl.

"I tell thee she consented," rejoined Mother Demdike, coldly; "and on this she made instant arrangements to return home, and in spite—as thou know'st—of Sir Ralph and Lady Assheton's efforts to detain her, set forth with thee."

"All this I know," observed Alizon, sadly—"and intelligence of our departure from the Abbey was conveyed to you, I conclude, by Jennet, to whom I bade adieu."

"Thou art right—it was," returned the hag; "but I have yet more to tell thee, for I will lay the secrets of thy mother's dark breast fully before thee. Her time is wellnigh run. Thou wert made the price of its extension. If she fails in offering thee up to-night, and thou art here in my keeping, the Fiend, her master, will abandon her, and she will be delivered up to the justice of man."

Alizon covered her face with horror.

After awhile she looked up, and exclaimed, with unutterable anguish—

"And I cannot help her!"

The unpitying hag laughed derisively.

"She cannot be utterly lost," continued the young girl. "Were I near her, I would show her that heaven is merciful to the greatest sinner who repents; and teach her how to regain the lost path to salvation."

"Peace!" thundered the witch, shaking her huge hand at her, and stamping her heavy foot upon the ground. "Such words must not be uttered here. They are an offence to me. Thy mother has renounced all hopes of heaven. She has been baptised in the baptism of hell, and branded on the brow by the red finger of its ruler, and cannot be wrested from him. It is too late."

"No, no—it never can be too late!" cried Alizon. "It is not even too late for you."

"Thou know'st not what thou talk'st about, foolish wench," rejoined the hag. "Our master would tear us instantly in pieces if but a thought of penitence, as thou callest it, crossed our minds. We are both doomed to an eternity of torture. But thy mother will go first—ay, first. If she had yielded thee up to-night, another term would have been allowed her; but as I hold thee instead, the benefit of the sacrifice will be mine. But, hist! what was that? The youth again! Alice Nutter must have given him some potent counter-charm."

"He comes to deliver me," cried Alizon. "Richard!"

And she arose, and would have flown to the window, but Mother Demdike waved her staff over her, and rooted her to the ground.

"Stay there till I require thee," chuckled the hag, moving, with ponderous footsteps, to the door.

After parleying with Richard, as already related, Mother Demdike suddenly returned to Alizon, and, restoring her to sensibility, placed her hideous face close to her, breathing upon her, and uttering these words, "Be thine eyes blinded and thy brain confused, so that thou mayst not know him when thou seest him, but think him another."

The spell took instant effect. Alizon staggered towards the table, Richard was summoned, and on his appearance the scene took place which has already been detailed, and which ended in his losing the talisman, and being ejected from the tower.

Alizon had been rendered invisible by the old witch, and was afterwards dragged into the arched recess by her, where, snatching the piece of gold from the young girl's neck, she exclaimed triumphantly—

"Now I defy thee, Alice Nutter. Thou canst never recover thy child. The offering shall be made to-night, and another year be added to my long term."

Alizon groaned deeply, but, at a gesture from the hag, she became motionless and speechless.

A dusky indistinctly-seen figure hovered near the entrance of the embrasure. Mother Demdike beckoned it to her.

"Convey this girl to the vault, and watch over her," she said. "I will descend anon."

Upon this the shadowy arms enveloped Alizon, the trapdoor flew open, and the figure disappeared with its inanimate burthen.

CHAPTER XIII.—THE TWO FAMILIARS.

After seeing Richard depart on his perilous mission to Malkin Tower, Mistress Nutter retired to her own chamber, and held long and anxious self-communion. The course of her thoughts may be gathered from the terrible revelations made by Mother Demdike to Alizon. A prey to the most agonising emotions, it may be questioned if she could have endured greater torment if her heart had been consumed by living fire, as in the punishment assigned to the damned in the fabled halls of Eblis. For the first time remorse assailed her, and she felt compunction for the evil she had committed. The whole of her dark career passed in review before her. The long catalogue of her crimes unfolded itself like a scroll of flame, and at its foot were written in blazing characters the awful words, JUDGMENT AND CONDEMNATION! There was no escape—none! Hell, with its unquenchable fires and unimaginable horrors, yawned to receive her; and she felt, with anguish and self-reproach not to be described, how wretched a bargain she had made, and how dearly the brief gratification of her evil passions had been purchased at the cost of an eternity of woe and torture.

This change of feeling had been produced by her newly-awakened affection for her daughter, long supposed dead, and now restored to her, only to be snatched away again in a manner which added to the sharpness of the loss. She saw herself the sport of a juggling fiend, whose aim was to win over her daughter's soul through her instrumentality, and she resolved, if possible, to defeat his purposes. This, she was aware, could only be accomplished by her own destruction, but even this dread alternative she was prepared to embrace. Alizon's sinless nature and devotion to herself had so wrought upon her, that, though she had at first resisted the better impulses kindled within her bosom, in the end they completely overmastered her.

Was it, she asked herself, too late to repent? Was there no way of breaking her compact? She remembered to have read of a young man who had signed away his own soul, being restored to heaven by the intercession of the great reformer of the church, Martin Luther. But, on the other hand, she had heard of many others, who, on the slightest manifestation of penitence, had been rent in pieces by the Fiend. Still the idea recurred to her. Might not her daughter, armed with perfect purity and holiness, with a soul free from stain as an unspotted mirror; might not she, who had avouched herself ready to risk all for her—for she had overheard her declaration to Richard;—might not she be able to work out her salvation? Would confession of her sins and voluntary submission to earthly justice save her? Alas!—no. She was without hope. She had an inexorable master to deal with, who would grant her no grace, except upon conditions she would not assent to.

She would have thrown herself on her knees, but they refused to bend. She would have prayed, but the words turned to blasphemies. She would have wept, but the fountains of tears were dry. The witch could never weep.

Then came despair and frenzy, and, like furies, lashed her with whips of scorpions, goading her with the memory of her abominations and idolatries, and her infinite and varied iniquities. They showed her, as in a swiftly-fleeting vision, all who had suffered wrong by her, or whom her malice had afflicted in body or estate. They mocked her with a glimpse of the paradise she had forfeited. She saw her daughter in a beatified state about to enter its golden portals, and would have clung to her robes in the hope of being carried in with her, but she was driven away by an angel with a flaming sword, who cried out, "Thou hast abjured heaven, and heaven rejects thee. Satan's brand is upon thy brow, and, unless it be effaced, thou canst never enter here. Down to Tophet, thou witch!" Then she implored her daughter to touch her brow with the tip of her finger; and, as the latter was about to comply, a dark demoniacal shape suddenly rose, and, seizing her by the hair, plunged with her down—down—millions of miles—till she beheld a world of fire appear beneath her, consisting of a multitude of volcanoes, roaring and raging like furnaces, boiling over with redhot lava, and casting forth huge burning stones In each of these beds of fire thousands upon thousands of sufferers were writhing, and their groans and lamentations arose in one frightful, incessant wail, too terrible for human hearing.

Over this place of torment the demon held her suspended. She shrieked aloud in her agony, and, shaking off the oppression, rejoiced to find the vision had been caused by her own distempered imagination.

Meanwhile, the storm, which had obstructed Richard as he climbed the hill, had come on, though Mistress Nutter had not noticed it; but now a loud peal of thunder shook the room, and rousing herself she walked to the window. The sight she beheld increased her alarm. Heavy thunder-clouds rested upon the hill-side, and seemed ready to discharge their artillery upon the course which she knew must be taken by the young man.

The chamber in which she stood, it has been said, was large and gloomy, with a wainscoting of dark oak. On one of the panels was painted a picture of herself in her days of youth, innocence, and beauty; and on another, a portrait of her unfortunate husband, who appeared a handsome young man, with a stern countenance, attired in a black velvet doublet and cloak, of the fashion of Elizabeth's day. Between these paintings stood a carved oak bedstead, with a high tester and dark heavy drapery, opposite which was a wide window, occupying almost the whole length of the room, but darkened by thick bars and glass, crowded with armorial bearings, or otherwise deeply dyed. The high mantelpiece and its carvings have been previously described, as well as the bloody hearthstone, where the tragical incident occurred connected with Alizon's early history.

As Mistress Nutter returned to the fireplace, a plaintive cry arose from it, and starting—for the sound revived terrible memories within her breast—she beheld the ineffaceable stains upon the flag traced out by blue phosphoric fire, while above them hovered the shape of a bleeding infant. Horror-stricken, she averted her gaze, but it encountered another object, equally appalling—her husband's portrait; or rather, it would seem, a phantom in its place; for the eyes, lighted up by infernal fire, glared at her from beneath the frowning and contracted brows, while the hand significantly pointed to the hearthstone, on which the sanguinary stains had now formed themselves into the fatal word "VENGEANCE!"

In a few minutes the fiery characters died away, and the portrait resumed its wonted expression; but ere Mistress Nutter had recovered from her terror the back of the fireplace opened, and a tall swarthy man stepped out from it. As he appeared, a flash of lightning illumined the chamber, and revealed his fiendish countenance. On seeing him, the lady immediately regained her courage, and addressed him in a haughty and commanding tone—

"Why this intrusion? I did not summon thee, and do not require thee."

"You are mistaken, madam," he replied; "you had never more occasion for me than at this moment; and, so far from intruding upon you, I have avoided coming near you, even though enjoined to do so by my lord. He is perfectly aware of the change which has just taken place in your opinions, and the anxiety you now feel to break the contract you have entered into with him, and which he has scrupulously fulfilled on his part; but he wishes you distinctly to understand, that he has no intention of abandoning his claims upon you, but will most assuredly enforce them at the proper time. I need not remind you that your term draws to a close, and ere many months must expire; but means of extending it have been offered you, if you choose to avail yourself of them."

"I have no such intention," replied Mistress Nutter, in a decided tone.

"So be it, madam," replied the other; "but you will not preserve your daughter, who is in the hands of a tried and faithful servant of my lord, and what you hesitate to do that servant will perform, and so reap the benefit of the sacrifice."

"Not so," rejoined Mistress Nutter.

"I say yea," retorted the familiar.

"Thou art my slave, I command thee to bring Alizon hither at once."

The familiar shook his head.

"Thou refusest!" cried Mistress Nutter, menacingly.

"Knows't thou not I have the means of chastising thee?"

"You had, madam," replied the other; "but the moment a thought of penitence crossed your breast, the power you were invested with departed. My lord, however, is willing to give you an hour of grace, when, if you voluntarily renew your oaths to him, he will accept them, and place me at your disposal once more; but if you still continue obstinate—"

"He will abandon me," interrupted Mistress Nutter; "I knew

Fool that I was to trust one who, from the beginning, has been a deceiver."

"You have a short memory, and but little gratitude, madam, and seem entirely to forget the important favour conferred upon you last night. At your solicitation, the boundaries of your property were changed, and large slips of land filched from another, to be given to you. But if you fail in your duty, you cannot expect this to continue. The boundary marks will be set up in their old places, and the land restored to its rightful owner."

"I expected as much," observed Mistress Nutter, disdainfully.

"Thus all our pains will be thrown away," pursued the familiar; "and though you may make light of the labour, it is no easy task to change the face of a whole country—to turn streams from their course, move bogs, transplant trees, and shift houses, all of which has been done, and will now have to be undone, because of your inconstancy. I, myself, have been obliged to act as many parts as a poor player to please you, and now you dismiss me at a moment's notice, as if I had played them indifferently, whereas the most fastidious audience would have been ravished with my performance. This morning I was the reeve of the forest, and as such obliged to assume the shape of a rascally attorney. I felt it a degradation, I assure you. Nor was I better pleased when you compelled me to put on the likeness of old Roger Nowell; for, whatever you may think, I am not so entirely destitute of personal vanity as to prefer either of their figures to my own. However, I showed no disinclination to oblige you. You are strangely unreasonable to-day. Is it my lord's fault if your desire of vengeance expires in its fruition—if, when you have accomplished an object, you no longer care for it? You ask for revenge—for power. You have them, and cast them aside like childish baubles!"

"Thy lord is an arch deceiver," rejoined Mistress Nutter; "and cannot perform his promises. They are empty delusions—profitless, unsubstantial as shadows. His power prevails not against any thing holy, as I myself have just now experienced. His money turns to withered leaves; his treasures are dust and ashes. Strong only is he in power of mischief, and even his mischief, like curses, recoils on those who use it. His vengeance is no true vengeance, for it troubles the conscience, and engenders remorse; whereas the servant of heaven heaps coals of fire on the head of his adversary by kindness, and satisfies his own heart."

"You should have thought of all this before you vowed yourself to him," said the familiar; "it is too late to reflect now."

"Perchance not," rejoined Mistress Nutter.

"Beware!" thundered the demon, with a terrible gesture; "any overt act of disobedience, and your limbs shall be scattered over this chamber."

"If I do not dare thee to it, it is not because I fear thee," replied Mistress Nutter, in no way dismayed by the threat. "Thou canst not control my tongue. Thou speakest of the services rendered by thy lord, and I repeat they are like his promises, naught. Show me the witch he has enriched. Of what profit is her worship of the false deity—of what avail the sacrifices she makes at his foul altars? It is ever the same spilling of blood, ever the same working of mischief. The wheels of crime roll on like the car of the Indian idol, crushing all before them. Doth thy master ever help his servants in their need? Doth he not ever abandon them when they are no longer useful, and can win him no more proselytes? Miserable servants—miserable master! Look at the murtherous Demdike and the malignant Chattox, and examine the means whereby they have prolonged their baleful career. Enormities of all kinds committed, and all their families devoted to the Fiend—all wizards or witches! Look at them, I say. What profit to them is their long service? Are they rich? Are they in possession of unfading youth and beauty? Are they splendidly lodged? Have they all they desire? No!—the one dwells in a solitary turret, and the other in a wretched hovel; and both are miserable creatures, living only on the dole wrung by threats from terrified peasants, and capable of no gratification but such as results from practices of malice."

"Is that nothing?" asked the familiar. "To them it is every thing. They care neither for splendid mansions, nor wealth, nor youth, nor beauty. If they did, they could have them all. They care only for the dread and mysterious power they possess, to be able to fascinate with a glance, to transfix by a gesture, to inflict strange ailments by a word, and to kill by a curse. This is the privilege they seek, and this privilege they enjoy."

"And what is the end of it all?" demanded Mistress Nutter, sternly. "Erelong, they will be unable to furnish victims to their insatiate master, who will then abandon them. Their bodies will go to the hangman, and their souls to endless bale!"

The familiar laughed as if a good joke had been repeated to him, and rubbed his hands gleefully.

"Very true," he said; "very true. You have stated the case exactly, madam. Such will certainly be the course of events. But what of that? The old hags will have enjoyed a long term—much longer than might have been anticipated. Mother Demdike, however, as I have intimated, will extend hers, and it is fortunate for her she is enabled to do so, as it would otherwise expire an hour after midnight, and could not be renewed."

"Thou liest!" cried Mistress Nutter—"liest like thy lord, who is the father of lies. My innocent child can never be offered up at his impious shrine. I have no fear for her. Neither he, nor Mother Demdike, nor any of the accursed sisterhood, can harm her. Her goodness will cover her like armour, which no evil can penetrate. Let him wreak his vengeance, if he will, on me. Let him treat me as a slave who has cast off his yoke. Let him abridge the scanty time allotted me, and bear me hence to his burning kingdom; but injure my child, he cannot—shall not!"

"Go to Malkin Tower at midnight, and thou wilt see," replied the familiar, with a mocking laugh.

"I will go there, but it shall be to deliver her," rejoined Mistress Nutter. "And now get thee gone! I need thee no more."

"Be not deceived, proud woman," said the familiar. "Once dismissed, I may not be recalled, while thou wilt be wholly unable to defend thyself against thy enemies."

"I care not," she rejoined; "begone!"

The familiar stepped back, and, stamping upon the hearthstone, it sank like a trapdoor, and he disappeared beneath it, a flash of lightning playing round his dusky figure.

Notwithstanding her vaunted resolution, and the boldness with which she had comported herself before the familiar, Mistress Nutter now completely gave way, and for awhile abandoned herself to despair. Aroused at length by the absolute necessity of action, she again walked to the window and looked forth. The storm still raged furiously without—so furiously, indeed, that it would be madness to brave it, now that she was deprived of her power, and reduced to the ordinary level of humanity. Its very violence, however, assured her it must soon cease, and she would then set out for Malkin Tower. But what chance had she now in a struggle with the old hag, with all the energies of hell at her command?—what hope was there of her being able to effect her daughter's liberation? No matter, however desperate, the attempt should be made. Meanwhile, it would be necessary so see what was going on below ,and ascertain whether Blackadder had returned with Parson Holden. With this view, she descended to the hall, where she found Nicholas Assheton fast asleep in a great arm-chair, and rocked rather than disturbed by the loud concussions of thunder. The squire was, no doubt, overcome by the fatigues of the day, or it might be by the potency of the wine he had swallowed, for an empty flask stood on the table beside him. Mistress Nutter did not awaken him, but proceeded to the chamber where she had left Nowell and Potts prisoners, both of whom rose on her entrance.

"Be seated, gentlemen, I pray you," she said, courteously. "I am come to see if you need any thing; for when this fearful storm abates, I am going forth for a short time."

"Indeed, madam," replied Potts. "For myself I require nothing further; but perhaps another bottle of wine might be agreeable to my honoured and singular good client."

"Speak for yourself, sir," cried Roger Nowell, sharply.

"You shall have it," interposed Mistress Nutter. "I shall be glad of a word with you before I go, Master Nowell. I am sorry this dispute has arisen between us."

"Humph!" exclaimed the magistrate.

"Very sorry," pursued Mistress Nutter; "and I wish to make every reparation in my power."

"Reparation, madam!" cried Nowell. "Give back the land you have stolen from me—restore the boundary lines—sign the deed in Sir Ralph's possession—that is the only reparation you can make."

"I will," replied Mistress Nutter.

"You will!" exclaimed Nowell. "Then the fellow did not deceive us, Master Potts."

"Has any one been with you?" asked the lady, uneasily.

"Ay, the reeve of the forest," replied Nowell. "He told us you would be with us presently, and would make fair offers to us."

"And he told us also *why* you would make them, madam," added Potts, in an insolent and menacing tone; "he told us you would make a merit of doing what you could not help—that your power had gone from you—that your works of darkness would be destroyed—and that, in a word, you were abandoned by the devil, your master."

"He deceived you," replied Mistress Nutter. "I have made you the offer out of pure good-will, and you can reject it or not, as you please. All I stipulate, if you do accept it, is, that you pledge me your word not to bring any charge of witchcraft against me."

"Do not give the pledge," whispered a voice in the ear of the magistrate.

"Did you speak?" he said, turning to Potts.

"No, sir," replied the attorney, in a low tone; "but I thought you cautioned me against—"

"Hush!" interrupted Nowell; "it must be the reeve. We cannot comply with your request, madam," he added, aloud.

"Certainly not," said Potts. We can make no bargain with an avowed witch. We should gain nothing by it; on the contrary, we should be losers, for we have the positive assurance of a gentleman whom we believe to be upon terms of intimacy with a certain black gentleman of your acquaintance, madam, that the latter has given you up entirely, and that law and justice may, therefore, take their course. We protest against our unlawful detention; but we give ourselves small concern about it, as Sir Ralph Assheton, who will be advised of our situation by Parson Holden, will speedily come to our liberation."

"Yes, we are now quite easy on that score, madam," added Nowell; "and to-morrow we shall have the pleasure of escorting you to Lancaster Castle."

"And your trial will come on at the next assizes, about the middle of August," said Potts. "You have only four months to run."

"That is indeed my term," muttered the lady. "I shall not tarry to listen to your taunts," she added, aloud. "You may possibly regret rejecting my proposal."

So saying, she quitted the room.

As she returned to the hall, Nicholas awoke.

"What a devil of a storm!" he exclaimed, stretching himself, and rubbing his eyes. "Zounds! that flash of lightning was enough to blind me, and the thunder wellnigh splits one's ears.

"Yet you have slept through louder peals, Nicholas," said Mistress Nutter, coming up to him. "Richard has not returned from his mission, and I must go myself to Malkin Tower. In my absence, I must entrust you with the defence of my house."

"I am willing to undertake it," replied Nicholas, "provided no witchcraft be used."

"Nay, you need not fear that," said the lady, with a forced smile.

"Well, then, leave it to me," said the squire; "but you will not set out till the storm is over?"

"I must," replied Mistress Nutter; "there seems no likelihood of its cessation, and each moment is fraught with peril to Alizon. If aught happens to me, Nicholas—if I should—whatever mischance may befall me—promise me you will stand by her."

The squire gave the required promise.

"Enough, I hold you to your word," said Mistress Nutter. "Take this parchment. It is a deed of gift, assigning this mansion and all my estates to her. Under certain circumstances you will produce it."

"What circumstances? I am at a loss to understand you, madam," said the squire.

"Do not question me further, but take especial care of the deed, and produce it, as I have said, at the fitting moment. You will know when that arrives. Ha! I am wanted."

The latter exclamation had been occasioned by the appearance of an old woman at the further end of the hall, beckoning to her. On seeing her, Mistress Nutter immediately quitted the squire, and followed her into a small chamber opening from this part of the hall, and into which she retreated.

"What brings you here, Mother Chattox?" exclaimed the lady, closing the door.

"Can you not guess?" replied the hag. "I am come to help you, not for any love I bear you, but to avenge myself on old Demdike. Do not interrupt me. My familiar, Fancy, has told me all. I know how you are circumstanced. I know Alizon is in old Demdike's clutches, and you are unable to extricate her. But I can, and will; because if the hateful old hag fails in offering up her sacrifice before the first hour of day, her term will be out, and I shall be rid of her, and reign in her stead. To-morrow she will be on her way to Lancaster Castle. Ha! ha! The dungeon is prepared for her—the stake driven into the ground—the fagots heaped around it. The torch has only to be lighted. Ho! Ho!"

"Shall we go to Malkin Tower?" asked Mistress Nutter, shuddering.

"No; to the summit of Pendle Hill," rejoined Mother Chattox; "for there the girl will be taken, and there only can we secure her. But first we must proceed to my hut, and make some preparations. I have three scalps and eight teeth, taken from a grave in Goldshaw churchyard this very day. We can make a charm with them.

"You must prepare it alone," said Mistress Nutter; "I can have nought to do with it."

"True—true—I had forgotten," cried the hag, with a chuckling laugh—"you are no longer one of us. Well, then, I will do it alone. But come with me. You will not object to mount upon my broomstick. It is the only safe conveyance in this storm of the devil's raising. Come—away!"

And she threw open the window and sprang forth, followed by Mistress Nutter.

Through the murky air, and borne as if on the wings of the wind, two dark forms are flying swiftly. Over the tops of the tempest-shaken trees they go, and as they gain the skirts of the thicket an oak beneath is shivered by a thunderbolt. They hear the fearful crash, and see the splinters fly far and wide; and the foremost of the two, who, with her skinny arm extended, seems to direct their course, utters a wild scream of laughter, while a raven, speeding on broad black wing before them, croaks hoarsely. Now the torrent rages below, and they see its white waters tumbling over a ledge of rock; now they pass over the brow of a hill; now skim over a dreary waste and dangerous morass. Fearful it is to behold those two flying figures, as the lightning shows them, bestriding their fantastical steed; the one an old hag with hideous lineaments and distorted person, and the other a proud dame, still beautiful, though no longer young, pale as death, and her loose jetty hair streaming like a meteor in the breeze.

The ride is over, and they alight near the door of a solitary hovel. The raven has preceded them, and, perched on the chimney top, flies down it as they enter, and greets them with hoarse croaking. The inside of the hut corresponds with its miserable exterior, consisting only of two rooms, in one of which is a wretched pallet; in the other are a couple of large chests, a crazy table, a bench, a three-legged stool, and a spinning-wheel. A caldron is suspended above a peat fire, smouldering on the hearth. There is only one window, and a thick curtain is drawn across it, to secure the inmate of the hut from prying eyes.

Mother Chattox closes and bars the door, and, motioning Mistress Nutter to seat herself upon the stool, kneels down near

THE RIDE THROUGH THE MURKY AIR.

P. 325.

the hearth, and blows the turf into a flame, the raven helping her, by flapping his big black wings, and uttering a variety of strange sounds, as the sparks fly about. Heaping on more turf, and shifting the caldron, so that it may receive the full influence of the flame, the hag proceeds to one of the chests, and takes out sundry small matters, which she places one by one with great care on the table. The raven has now fixed his great talons on her shoulder, and chuckles and croaks in her ear as she pursues her occupation. Suddenly a piece of bone attracts his attention, and darting out his beak, he seizes it, and hops away.

"Give me that scalp, thou mischievous imp!" cries the hag, "I need it for the charm I am about to prepare. Give it me, I say!"

But the raven still held it fast, and hopped here and there so nimbly that she was unable to catch him. At length, when he had exhausted her patience, he alighted on Mistress Nutter's shoulder, and dropped it into her lap. Engrossed by her own painful thoughts, the lady had paid no attention to what was passing, and she shuddered as she took up the fragment of mortality, and placed it upon the table. A few tufts of hair, the texture of which showed they had belonged to a female, still adhered to the scalp. Mistress Nutter regarded it fixedly, and with an interest for which she could not account.

After sharply chiding the raven, Mother Chattox put forth her hand to grasp the prize she had been robbed of, when Mistress Nutter checked her by observing, "You said you got this scalp from Goldshaw churchyard. Know you ought concerning it?"

"Ay, a good deal," replied the old woman, chuckling. "It comes from a grave near the yew-tree, and not far from Abbot Cliderhow's cross. Old Zachariah Worms, the sexton, digged it up for me. That yellow skull had once a fair face attached to it, and those few dull tufts were once bright flowing tresses. She who owned them died young; but, young as she was, she survived all her beauty. Hollow cheeks and hollow eyes, wasted flesh, and cruel cough, were hers—and she pined and pined away. Folks said she was forespoken, and that I had done it. I, forsooth! She had never done me harm. You know whether I was rightly accused, madam."

"Take it away," cried Mistress Nutter, hurriedly, and as if struggling against some overmastering feeling. "I cannot bear to look at it. I wanted not this horrible reminder of my crimes."

"This was the reason, then, why Ralph stole the scalp from me," muttered the hag, as she threw it, together with some other matters, into the caldron. "He wanted to show you his sagacity. I might have guessed as much."

"I will go into the other room while you make your preparations," said Mistress Nutter, rising; "the sight of them disturbs me. You can summon me when you are ready."

"I will, madam," replied the old hag, "and you must control your impatience, for the spell requires time for its confection."

Mistress Nutter made no reply, but, walking into the inner room, closed the door, and threw herself upon the pallet. Here, despite her anxiety, sleep stole upon her, and though her dreams were troubled, she did not awake till Mother Chattox stood beside her.

"Have I slept long?" she inquired.

"More than three hours," replied the hag.

"Three hours!" exclaimed Mistress Nutter. "Why did you not wake me before? You would have saved me from terrible dreams. We are not too late?"

"No, no," replied Mother Chattox; "there is plenty of time. Come into the other room. All is ready."

As Mistress Nutter followed the old hag into the adjoining room, a strong odour, arising from a chafing-dish, in which herbs, roots, and other ingredients were burning, assailed her, and, versed in all weird ceremonials, she knew that a powerful suffumigation had been made, though with what intent she had yet to learn. The scanty furniture had been cleared away, and a circle was described on the clay floor by skulls and bones, alternated by dried toads, adders, and other reptiles. In the midst of this magical circle, the caldron, which had been brought from the chimney, was placed, and, the lid being removed, a thick vapour arose from it. Mistress Nutter looked around for the raven, but the bird was nowhere to be seen, nor did any other living thing appear to be present beside themselves.

Taking the lady's hand, Mother Chattox drew her into the circle, and began to mutter a spell; after which, still maintaining her hold of her companion, she bade her look into the caldron, and declare what she saw.

"I see nothing," replied the lady, after she had gazed upon the bubbling waters for a few moments. "Ah! yes—I discern certain figures, but they are confused by the steam, and broken by the agitation of the water."

"Caldron—cease boiling! and smoke—disperse!" cried Mother Chattox, stamping her foot. "Now, can you see more plainly?"

"I can," replied Mistress Nutter; "I behold the subterranean chamber beneath Malkin Tower, with its nine ponderous columns, its altar in the midst of them, its demon image, and the well with waters black as Lethe beside it."

"The water within the caldron came from that well," said Mother Chattox, with a chuckling laugh; "my familiar risked his liberty to bring it, but he succeeded. Ha! ha! My precious Fancy, thou art the best of servants, and shalt have my best blood to reward thee to-morrow—thou shalt, my sweetheart, my chuck, my dandyprat. But hie thee back to Malkin Tower, and contrive that this lady may hear, as well as see, all that passes. Away!"

Mistress Nutter concluded that the injunction would be obeyed; but, as the familiar was invisible to her, she could not detect his departure.

"Do you see no one within the dungeon?" inquired Mother Chattox.

"Ah! yes," exclaimed the lady; "I have at last discovered Alizon. She was behind one of the pillars. A little girl is with her. It is Jennet Device, and, from the spiteful looks of the latter, I judge she is mocking her. Oh! what malice lurks in the breast of that hateful child! She is a true descendant of Mother Demdike. But Alizon—sweet, patient Alizon—she seems to bear all her taunts with a meekness and resignation enough to move the hardest heart. I would weep for her if I could. And now Jennet shakes her hand at her, and leaves her. She is alone. What will she do now? Has she no thoughts of escape? Oh, yes! She looks about her distractedly—runs round the vault—tries the door of every cell: they are all bolted and barred—there is no outlet—none!"

"What next?" inquired the hag.

"She shrieks aloud," rejoined Mistress Nutter, "and the cry thrills through every fibre in my frame. She calls upon me for aid—upon me, her mother, and little thinks I hear her, and am unable to help her. Oh! it is horrible. Take me to her, good Chattox—take me to her, I implore you!"

"Impossible!" replied the hag: "you must await the fitting time. If you cannot control yourself, I shall remove the caldron."

"Oh! no, no," cried the distracted lady. "I will be calm. Ah! what is this I see?" she added, belying her former words by sudden vehemence, while rage and astonishment were depicted upon her countenance. "What infernal delusion is practised upon my child! This is monstrous—intolerable. Oh! that I could undeceive her—could warn her of the snare!"

"What is the nature of the delusion?" asked Mother Chattox, with some curiosity. "I am so blind I cannot see the figures on the water."

"It is an evil spirit in my likeness," replied Mistress Nutter.

"In your likeness!" exclaimed the hag. "A cunning device—and worthy of old Demdike—ho! ho!"

"I can scarce bear to look on," cried Mistress Nutter; "but I must, though it tears my heart in pieces to witness such cruelty. The poor girl has rushed to her false parent—has thrown her arms around her, and is weeping on her shoulder. Oh! it is a maddening sight. But it is nothing to what follows. The temptress, with the subtlety of the old serpent, is pouring lies into her ear, telling her they both are captives, and both will perish unless she consents to purchase their deliverance at the price of her soul, and she offers her a bond to sign—such a bond as, alas! thou and I, Chattox, have signed. But Alizon rejects it with horror, and gazes at her false mother as if she suspected the delusion. But the temptress is not to be beaten thus. She renews her entreaties, casts herself on the ground, and clasps my child's knees in humblest supplication. Oh! that Alizon would place her foot upon her neck and crush her. But it is not so the good act. She raises her, and tells her she will willingly die for her; but her soul was given to her by her Creator, and must be returned to him. Oh! that I had thought of this."

"And what answer makes the spirit?" asked the witch.

"It laughs derisively," replied Mistress Nutter; "and proceeds to use all those sophistical arguments, which we have so often heard, to pervert her mind, and overthrow her principles. But Alizon is proof against them all. Religion and virtue support her, and make her more than a match for her opponent. Equally vain are the spirit's attempts to seduce her by the offer of a life of sinful enjoyment. She rejects it with angry scorn. Failing in argument and entreaty, the spirit now endeavours to work upon her fears, and paints, in appalling colours, the tortures she will have to endure, contrasting them with the delight she is voluntarily abandoning, with the lover she might espouse, with the high worldly position she might fill. 'What are worldly joys and honours compared with those of heaven!' exclaims Alizon; 'I would not exchange them.' The spirit then, in a vision, shows her her lover, Richard, and asks her if she can resist his entreaties. The trial is very sore, as she gazes on that beloved form, seeming, by its passionate gestures, to implore her to assent, but she is firm, and the vision disappears. The ordeal is now over. Alizon has triumphed over all their arts. The spirit in my likeness resumes its fiendish shape, and, with a dreadful menace against the poor girl, vanishes from her sight."

"Mother Demdike has not done with her yet," observed Chattox.

"You are right," replied Mistress Nutter. "The old hag descends the staircase leading to the vault, and approaches the miserable captive. With her there are no supplications—no arguments; but commands and terrible threats. She is as unsuccessful as her envoy. Alizon has gained courage and defies her."

"Ha! does she so?" exclaimed Mother Chattox. "I am glad of it."

"The solid floor resounds with the stamping of the enraged witch," pursued Mistress Nutter. "She tells Alizon she will take her to Pendle Hill at midnight, and there offer her up as a sacrifice to the Fiend. My child replies that she trusts for her deliverance to Heaven—that her body may be destroyed—that her soul cannot be harmed. Scarcely are the words uttered than a terrible clangour is heard. The walls of the dungeon seem breaking down, and the ponderous columns reel. The demon statue rises on its throne, and a stream of flame issues from its brow. The doors of the cells burst open, and with the clanking of chains, and other dismal noises, skeleton shapes stalk forth from them, each with a pale blue light above its head. Monstrous beasts, like tiger-cats, with rough black skins and flaming eyes, are moving about, and looking as if they would spring upon the captive. Two gravestones are now pushed aside, and from the cold earth arise the forms of Blackburn, the robber, and his paramour, the dissolute Isole de Heton. She joins the grisly throng now approaching the distracted girl, who falls insensible to the ground."

"Can you see aught more?" asked the hag, as Mistress Nutter still bent eagerly over the caldron.

"No; the whole chamber is buried in darkness," replied the lady; "I can see nothing of my poor child. What will become of her?"

"I will question Fancy," replied the hag, throwing some fresh ingredients into the chafing-dish; and, as the smoke arose, she vociferated, "Come hither, Fancy; I want thee, my fondling, my sweet. Come quickly! ha! thou art here."

The familiar was still invisible to Mistress Nutter, but a slight sound made her aware of his presence.

"And now, my sweet Fancy," pursued the hag, "tell us, if thou canst, what will be done with Alizon, and what course we must pursue to free her from old Demdike?"

"At present she is in a state of insensibility," replied a harsh voice, "and she will be kept in that condition till she is conveyed to the summit of Pendle Hill. I have already told you it is useless to attempt to take her from Malkin Tower. It is too well guarded. Your only chance will be to interrupt the sacrifice."

"But how, my sweet Fancy? how, my little darling?" inquired the hag.

"It is a perplexing question," replied the voice; "for, by showing you how to obtain possession of the girl, I disobey my lord."

"Ay, but you serve me—you please me, my pretty Fancy," cried the hag. "You shall quaff your fill of blood on the morrow, if you do this for me. I want to get rid of my old enemy—to catch her in her own toils—to send her to a dungeon—to burn her—ha! ha! You must help me, my little sweetheart."

"I will do all I can," replied the voice; "but Mother Demdike is cunning and powerful, and high in favour with my lord. You must have mortal aid as well as mine. The officers of justice must be there to seize her at the moment when the victim is snatched from her, or she will baffle all your schemes."

"And how shall we accomplish this?" asked Mother Chattox.

"I will tell you," said Mistress Nutter to the hag. "Let him put on the form of Richard Assheton, and in that guise hasten to Rough Lee, where he will find the young man's cousin, Nicholas, to whom he must make known the dreadful deed about to be enacted on Pendle Hill. Nicholas will at once engage to interrupt it. He can arm himself with the weapons of justice by taking with him Roger Nowell, the magistrate, and his myrmidon, Potts, the attorney, both of whom are detained prisoners in the house by my orders."

"The scheme promises well, and shall be adopted," replied the hag; "but suppose Richard himself should appear first on the scene. Dost know where he is, my sweet Fancy?"

"When I last saw him," replied the voice, "he was lying senseless on the ground, at the foot of Malkin Tower, having been precipitated from the doorway by Mother Demdike. You need apprehend no interference from him."

"It is well," replied Mother Chattox. "Then take his form, my pet, though it is not half as handsome as thy own."

"A black skin and goat-like limbs are to thy taste, I know," replied the familiar, with a laugh.

"Let me look upon him before he goes, that I may be sure the likeness is exact," said Mistress Nutter.

"Thou hearest, Fancy! Become visible to her," cried the hag.

And as she spoke, a figure in all respects resembling Richard stood before them.

"What think you of him? Will he do?" said Mother Chattox.

"Ay," replied the lady; "and now send him off at once. There is no time to lose."

"I shall be there in the twinkling of an eye," said the familiar; "but I own I like not the task."

"There is no help for it, my sweet Fancy," cried the hag. "I cannot forego my triumph over old Demdike. Now, away with thee, and when thou hast executed thy mission, return and tell us how thou hast sped in the matter."

The familiar promised obedience to her commands, and disappeared.

CHAPTER XIV.—HOW ROUGH LEE WAS AGAIN BESIEGED.

Parson Holden, it will be remembered, left Rough Lee, charged by Potts with a message to Sir Ralph Assheton, informing him of his detention and that of Roger Nowell, by Mistress Nutter, and imploring him to come to their assistance without delay. Congratulating himself on his escape, but apprehensive of pursuit, the worthy rector, who, as a keen huntsman, was extremely well mounted, made the best of his way, and had already passed the gloomy gorge through which Pendle Water swept, had climbed the hill beyond it, and was crossing the moor, now alone lying between him and Goldshaw, when he heard a shout behind him, and, turning at the sound, beheld Blackadder and another mounted serving-man issuing from a thicket, and spurring furiously after him. Relying upon the speed of his horse, he disregarded their cries, and accelerated his pace; but, in spite of this, his pursuers gained upon him rapidly.

While debating the question of resistance or surrender, the rector descried Bess Whitaker coming towards him from the opposite direction—a circumstance that greatly rejoiced him; for, aware of her strength and courage, he felt sure he could place as much dependence upon her in this emergency as on any man in the county. Bess was riding a stout, rough-looking nag, apparently well able to sustain her weight, and carried the redoubtable horsewhip with her.

On the other hand, Holden had been recognised by Bess, who came up just as he was overtaken and seized by his assailants, one of whom caught hold of his cassock, and tore it from his back, while the other, seizing hold of his bridle, endeavoured, in spite of his efforts to the contrary, to turn his horse round. Many oaths, threats, and blows were exchanged during the scuffle, which no doubt would have terminated in the rector's defeat, and his compulsory return to Rough Lee, had it not been for the opportune arrival of Bess, who, swearing as lustily as the serving-men, and brandishing the horsewhip, dashed into the scene of action, and, with a few well-applied cuts, liberated the divine. Enraged at her interference, and smarting from the application of the whip, Blackadder drew a petronel from his girdle, and levelled it at her head; but, ere he could discharge it, the weapon was stricken from his grasp, and a second blow on the head from the but-end of the whip felled him from his horse Seeing the fate of his companion, the other serving-man fled, leaving Bess mistress of the field.

The rector thanked her heartily for the service she had rendered him, and complimented her on her prowess.

"Ey'n neaw dun mitch to boast on i' leatherin' them two seawr-feaced rapscallions," said Bess, with becoming modesty "Simon Blackadder an ey ha' had mony a tussle together efore this, fo he's a feaw tempert felly, an canna drink abowt fightin', boh he has awlus found me more nor his match. Boh save us, your reverence, what were the ill-favort gullions ridin' after ye for? Firrups tak 'em! they didna mean to rob ye, surely?"

"Their object was to make me prisoner, and carry me back to Rough Lee, Bess," replied Holden. They wished to prevent my going to Whalley, whither I am bound, to procure help from Sir

Ralph Assheton to liberate Master Roger Nowell and his attorney, who are forcibly detained by Mistress Nutter."

"Yo may spare yer horse an yersel the jorney, then, reverend sir," replied Bess; "for yo'n foind Sir Tummus Metcawfe, wi' some twanty or throtty followers, armed wi' bills, hawberts, petronels, and calivers, at Goldshaw, an they win go wi' ye at wanst, ey'm sartin. Ey heerd sum o' t' chaps say os ow Sir Tummus is goin' to tak' possession o' Mistress Robinson's house, Raydale Ha', i' Wensley Dale, boh nah doubt he'n go furst wi' yer rev'rence, 'specially as he bears Mistress Nutter a grudge."

"At all events, I will ask him," said Holden. "Are he and his followers lodged at your house, Bess?"

"Yeigh," replied the hostess, "some on 'en are i' th' house, some i' th' barn, an some i' th' stables. The place is awtogether owerrun wi' 'em. Ey wur so moydert an wurrotit wi' their ca'in an bawlin fo' ele an drink, that ey swore they shouldna ha' another drawp wi' my consent; an, to be os good os my word, ey clapt key o' t' cellar i' my pocket, an leavin' our Margit to answer 'em, ey set out os yo see, intendin' to go os far as t' mill, an comfort poor deeavely Ruchot Baldwyn in his trouble."

"A most praiseworthy resolution, Bess," said the rector; "but what is to be done with this fellow?" he added, pointing to Blackadder, who, though badly hurt, was trying to creep towards the petronel, which was lying at a little distance from him on the ground.

Perceiving his intention, Bess quickly dismounted, and possessing herself of the weapon, stepped aside, and slipping off one of the bands that confined the hose on her well-shaped leg, grasped the wounded man by the shoulders, and with great expedition tied his hands behind his back. She then lifted him up with as much ease as if he had been an infant, and set him upon his horse, with his face towards the tail. This done, she gave the bridle to the rector, and handing him the petronel at the same time, told him to take care of his prisoner, for she must pursue her journey. And with this, in spite of his renewed entreaties that she would go back with him, she sprang on her horse and rode off.

On arriving at Goldshaw with his prisoner, the rector at once proceeded to the hostel, in front of which he found several of the villagers assembled, attracted by the numerous company within doors, whose shouts and laughter could be heard at a considerable distance. Holden's appearance with Blackadder occasioned considerable surprise, and all eagerly gathered round him to learn what had occurred; but, without satisfying their curiosity, beyond telling them he had been attacked by the prisoner, he left him in their custody, and entered the house, where he found all the benches in the principal room occupied by a crew of half-drunken roysterers, with flagons of ale before them; for, after Bess's departure with the key, they had broken into the cellar, and, broaching a cask, helped themselves to its contents. Various weapons were scattered about the tables or reared against the walls, and the whole scene looked like a carouse by a band of marauders. Little respect was shown the rector, and he was saluted by many a ribald jest as he pushed his way towards the inner room.

Sir Thomas was drinking with a couple of desperadoes, whose long rapiers and tarnished military equipments seemed to announce that they had, at some time or other, belonged to the army, though their ruffianly looks and braggadocio air and discourse, strongly seasoned with oaths and slang, made it evident that they were now little better than Alsatian bullies. They had, in fact, been hired by Sir Thomas for the expedition on which he was bent, as he could find no one in the country upon whom he could so well count as on them. Eyeing the rector fiercely, as he intruded upon their privacy, they glanced at their leader to ask whether they should turn him out; but, receiving no encouragement for such rudeness, they contented themselves with scowling at him from beneath their bent brows, twisting up their shaggy mustaches, and trifling with the hilts of their rapiers. Holden opened his business at once; and as soon as Sir Thomas heard it, he sprang to his feet, and, swearing a great oath, declared he would storm Rough Lee, and burn it to the ground, if Mistress Nutter did not set the two captives free.

"As to the audacious witch herself, I will carry her off, in spite of the devil, her master!" he cried. "How say you, Captain Gauntlet—and you too, Captain Storks, is not this an expedition to your tastes—ha?"

The two worthies appealed to responded joyously, that it was so; and it was then agreed that Blackadder should be brought in and interrogated, as some important information might be obtained from him. Upon this, Captain Gauntlet left the room to fetch him, and presently afterwards returned dragging in the prisoner, who looked dogged and angry, by the shoulders.

"Harkye, fellow," said Sir Thomas, sternly, "if you do not answer the questions I shall put to you, truly and satisfactorily, I will have you taken out into the yard, and shot like a dog. Thus much premised, I shall proceed with my examination. Master Roger Nowell and Master Thomas Potts, you are aware, are unlawfully detained prisoners by Mistress Alice Nutter. Now I have been called upon by the reverend gentleman here to undertake their liberation, but, before doing so, I desire to know from you what defensive and offensive preparations your mistress has made, and whether you judge it likely she will attempt to hold out her house against us?"

"Most assuredly she will," replied Blackadder, "and against twice your force. Rough Lee is as strong as a castle; and as those within it are well-armed, vigilant, and of good courage, there is little fear of its capture. If your worship should propose terms to my mistress for the release of her prisoners, she may possibly assent to them; but if you approach her in hostile fashion, and demand their liberation, I am well assured she will resist you, and well assured, also, she will resist you effectually."

"I shall approach her in no other sort than that of an enemy," rejoined Sir Thomas; "but thou art over confident, knave. Unless thy mistress have a legion of devils at her back, and they hold us in check, we will force a way into her dwelling. Fire and fury! dost presume to laugh at me, fellow? Take him hence, and let him be soundly cudgeled for his insolence, Gauntlet."

"Pardon me, your worship," cried Blackadder, "I only smiled at the strange notions you entertain of my mistress."

"Why, dost mean to deny that she is a witch?" demanded Metcalfe.

"Nay, if your worship will have it so, it is not for me to contradict you," replied Blackadder.

"But I ask thee is she not a servant of Satan?—dost thou not know it?—canst thou not prove it?" cried the knight. "Shall we put him to the torture to make him confess?"

"Ay, tie his thumbs together till the blood burst forth, Sir Thomas," said Gauntlet.

"Or hang him up to yon beam by the heels," suggested Captain Storks.

"On no account," interposed Holden. "I did not bring him hither to be dealt with in this way, and I will not permit it. If torture is to be administered it must be by the hands of justice, into which I require him to be delivered; and then, if he can testify aught against his mistress, he will be made to do it."

"Torture shall never wring a word from me, whether wrongfully or rightfully applied," said Blackadder, doggedly; "though I could tell much if I chose. Now give heed to me, Sir Thomas. You will never take Rough Lee, still less its mistress, without my help."

"What are thy terms, knave?" exclaimed the knight, pondering upon the offer. "And take heed thou triflest not with me, or I will have thee flogged within an inch of thy life, in spite of parson or justice. What are thy terms, I repeat?"

"They are for your worship's ear alone," replied Blackadder.

"Beware what you do, Sir Thomas," interposed Holden. "I hold it my duty to tell you, you are compromising justice in listening to the base proposals of this man, who, while offering to betray his mistress, will assuredly deceive you. You will equally deceive him in feigning to agree to terms which you cannot fulfil."

"Cannot fulfil!" ejaculated the knight, highly offended; "I would have you to know, sir, that Sir Thomas Metcalfe's word is his bond, and that whatsoever he promises he *will* fulfil in spite of the devil! Body o' me! but for the respect I owo your cloth, I would give you a very different answer, reverend sir. But since you have chosen to thrust yourself unasked into the affair, I take leave to say that I *will* hear this knave's proposals, and judge for myself of the expediency of acceding to them. I must pray you, therefore, to withdraw. Nay, if you will not go hence peaceably, you shall perforce. Take him away, gentlemen."

Thus enjoined, the Alsatian captains took each an arm of the rector, and forced him out of the room, leaving Sir Thomas alone with the prisoner. Greatly incensed at the treatment he had experienced, Holden instantly quitted the house, hastened to the rectory, which adjoined the church, and having given some messages to his household, rode off to Whalley, with the intention of acquainting Sir Ralph Assheton with all that had occurred.

Sir Thomas Metcalfe remained closeted with the prisoner for a few minutes, and then coming forth, issued orders that all should get ready to start for Rough Lee without delay; whereupon each man emptied his flagon, pocketed the dice he had been cogging, pushed aside the shuffle-board, left the loggats on the clay floor of the barn, and, grasping his weapon—halbert or caliver, as it might be—prepared to attend his leader. Sir Thomas did not relate, even to the Alsatian captains, what had passed between him and Blackadder; but it did not appear that he placed entire confidence in the latter; for though he caused his hands to be unbound, and allowed him in consideration of his wounded state to ride, he secretly directed Gauntlet and Storks to keep near him, and shoot him through the head if he attempted to escape. Both these personages were provided with horses as well as their leader, but all the rest of the party were on foot. Metcalfe made some inquiries after the rector, but finding he was gone, he did not concern himself further about him. Before starting, the knight, who, with all his recklessness, had a certain sense of honesty, called the girl who had been left in charge of the hostel by Bess, and gave her a sum amply sufficient to cover all the excesses of his men, adding a handsome gratuity to herself.

The first part of the journey was accomplished without mischance, and the party bade fair to arrive at the end of it in safety; but as they entered the gorge, at the extremity of which Rough Lee was situated, a terrific storm burst upon them, compelling them to seek shelter in the mill, from which they were luckily not far distant at the time. The house was completely deserted, but they were well able to shift for themselves, and not over scrupulous in the manner of doing so; and as the remains of the funeral feast were not removed from the table, some of the company sat down to them, while others found their way to the cellar.

The storm was of long continuance, much longer than was agreeable to Sir Thomas, and he paced the room to and fro impatiently, ever and anon walking to the window or door, to see whether it had in any degree abated, and was constantly doomed to disappointment. Instead of diminishing, it increased in violence, and it was now impossible to quit the house with safety. The lightning blazed, the thunder rattled among the overhanging rocks, and the swollen stream of Pendle Water roared at their feet. Blackadder was left under the care of the two Alsatians, but while they had shielded their eyes from the glare of the lightning, he threw open the window, and, springing through it, made good his retreat. In such a storm it was in vain to follow him, even if they had dared to attempt it.

In vain Sir Thomas Metcalfe fumed and fretted—in vain he heaped curses upon the bullies for their negligence—in vain he hurled menaces after the fugitive: the former paid little heed to his imprecations, and the latter was beyond his reach. The notion began to gain ground amongst the rest of the troop that the storm was the work of witchcraft, and occasioned general consternation. Even the knight's anger yielded to superstitious fear, and as a terrific explosion shook the rafters overhead, and threatened to bring them down upon him, he fell on his knees, and essayed, with unaccustomed lips, to murmur a prayer. But he was interrupted; for amid the deep silence succeeding the awful crash, a mocking laugh was heard, and the villainous countenance of Blackadder, rendered doubly hideous by the white lightning, was seen at the casement. The sight restored Sir Thomas at once. Drawing his sword he flew to the window, but before he could reach it Blackadder was gone. The next flash showed what had befallen him. In stepping backwards, he tumbled into the mill-race; and the current, increased in depth and force by the deluging rain, instantly swept him away.

Half an hour after this, the violence of the storm had perceptibly diminished, and Sir Thomas and his companions began to hope that their speedy release was at hand. Latterly the knight had abandoned all idea of attacking Rough Lee, but with the prospect of fair weather his courage returned, and he once more resolved to attempt it. He was moving about among his followers, striving to dispel their fears, and persuade them that the tempest was only the result of natural causes, when the door was suddenly thrown open, giving entrance to Bess Whitaker, who bore the miller in her arms. She stared on seeing the party assembled, and knit her brows, but said nothing till she had deposited Baldwyn in a seat, when she observed to Sir Thomas, that he seemed to have little scruple in taking possession of a house in its owner's absence. The knight excused himself for the intrusion by saying, he had been compelled by the storm to take refuge there with his followers—a plea readily admitted by Baldwyn, who was now able to speak for himself; and the miller next explained that he had been to Rough Lee, and after many perilous adventures, into the particulars of which he did not enter, had been brought away by Bess, who had carried him home. That home he now felt would be a lonely and insecure one unless she would consent to occupy it with him; and Bess, on being thus appealed to, affirmed that the only motive that would induce her to consent to such an arrangement would be her desire to protect him from his mischievous neighbours. While they were thus discoursing, Old Mitton, who it appeared had followed them, arrived wellnigh exhausted, and Baldwyn went in search of some refreshment for him.

By this time the storm had sufficiently cleared off to allow the others to take their departure; and though the miller and Bess would fain have dissuaded the knight from the enterprise, he was not to be turned aside, but, bidding his men attend him, set forth. The rain had ceased, but it was still very dark. Under cover of the gloom, however, they thought they could approach the house unobserved, and obtain an entrance before Mistress Nutter could be aware of their arrival. In this expectation they pursued their way in silence, and soon stood before the gates. These were fastened, but as no one appeared to be on the watch, Sir Thomas, in a low tone, ordered some of his men to scale the walls, with the intention of following himself; but scarcely had a head risen above the level of the brickwork than the flash of an arquebuss was seen, and the man jumped backwards, luckily just in time to avoid the bullet that whistled over him. An alarm was then instantly given, voices were heard in the garden, mingled with the furious barking of hounds. A bell was rung from the upper part of the house, and lights appeared at the windows.

Meanwhile, some of the men, less alarmed than their comrade, contrived to scramble over the wall, and were soon engaged hand to hand with those on the opposite side. But not alone had they to contend with adversaries like themselves. The stag-hounds, which had done so much execution during the first attack upon the house by Roger Nowell, raged amongst them like so many lions, rending their limbs, and seizing their throats. To free themselves from these formidable antagonists was their first business, and by dint of thrust from pike, cut from sword, and ball from caliver, they succeeded in slaughtering two of them, and driving the others, badly wounded, and savagely howling, away. In doing this, however, they themselves had sustained considerable injury. Three of their number were lying on the ground, in no condition, from their broken heads, or shattered limbs, for renewing the combat.

Thus, so far as the siege had gone, success seemed to declare itself rather for the defenders than the assailants, when a new impulse was given to the latter, by the bursting open of the gates, and the sudden influx of Sir Thomas Metcalfe and the rest of his troop. The knight was closely followed by the Alsatian captains, who, with tremendous oaths in their mouths, and slashing blades in their hands, declared they would make minced meat of any one opposing their progress. Sir Thomas was equally truculent in expression and ferocious in tone, and as the whole party laid about them right and left, they speedily routed the defenders of the garden, and drove them towards the house. Flushed by their success, the besiegers shouted loudly, and Sir Thomas roared out, that ere many minutes Nowell and Potts should be set free, and Alice Nutter captured. But before he could reach the main door, Nicholas Assheton, well armed, and attended by some dozen men, presented himself at it. These were instantly joined by the retreating party, and the whole offered a formidable array of opponents, quite sufficient to check the progress of the besiegers. Two or three of the men near Nicholas carried torches, and their light revealed the numbers on both sides.

"What! is it you, Sir Thomas Metcalfe?" cried the squire. "Do you commit such outrages as this—do you break into habitations like a robber, rifle them, and murder their inmates? Explain yourself, sir, or I will treat you as I would a common plunderer; shoot you through the head, or hang you to the first tree if I take you."

"Zounds and fury!" rejoined Metcalfe. "Do you dare to liken me to a common robber and murderer? Take care you do not experience the same fate as that with which you threaten me, with this difference only, that the hangman—the common hangman of Lancaster—shall serve your turn. I am come hither to arrest a notorious witch, and to release two gentlemen who are unlawfully detained prisoners by her; and if you do not instantly deliver her up to me, and produce the two individuals in question, Master Roger Nowell and Master Potts, I will force my way into the house, and all injury done to those who oppose me will rest on your head."

"The two gentlemen you have named are perfectly safe and contented in their quarters," replied Nicholas; "and as to the foul and false aspersions you have thrown out against Mistress Nutter, I cast them back in your teeth. Your purpose in coming hither is to redress some private wrong. How is it you have such a rout with you? How is it I behold two notorious bravos by your side—men who have stood in the pillory, and undergone other ignominious punishment for their offences? You cannot answer, and their oaths and threats go for nothing. I now tell you, Sir Thomas, if you do not instantly withdraw your men, and quit these premises, grievous consequences will ensue to you and them."

"I will hear no more," cried Sir Thomas, infuriated to the last degree. "Follow me into the house, and spare none who oppose you."

"You are not in yet,' cried Nicholas.

And as he spoke a row of pikes bristled around him, holding

the knight at bay, while a hook was fixed in the doublet of each of the Alsatian captains, and they were plucked forward and dragged into the house. This done, Nicholas and his men quickly retreated, and the door was closed and barred upon the enraged and discomfited knight.

CHAPTER XV.—THE PHANTOM MONK.

MANY hours had passed by, and night had come on—a night profoundly dark. Richard was still lying where he had fallen at the foot of Malkin Tower; for though he had regained his sensibility, he was so bruised and shaken as to be wholly unable to move. His limbs, stiffened and powerless, refused their office, and, after each unsuccessful effort, he sank back with a groan.

His sole hope was that Mistress Nutter, alarmed by his prolonged absence, might come to her daughter's assistance, and so discover his forlorn situation; but as time flew by, and nothing occurred, he gave himself up for lost.

On a sudden the gloom was dispersed, and a silvery light shed over the scene. The moon had broken through a rack of clouds, and illumined the tall mysterious tower, and the dreary waste around it. With the light a ghostly figure near him became visible to Richard, which under other circumstances would have excited terror in his breast, but which now only filled him with wonder. It was that of a Cistertian monk; the vestments were old and faded, the visage white and corpse-like. Richard at once recognised the phantom he had seen in the banquet-hall at the Abbey, and had afterwards so rashly followed to the conventual church. It touched him with its icy fingers, and a chillness like death shot through his heart.

"Why dost thou trouble me thus, unhappy spirit?" said the young man. "Leave me, I adjure thee, and let me die in peace!"

"Thou wilt not die yet, Richard Assheton," returned the phantom; "and my intention is not to trouble thee, but to serve thee. Without my aid thou wouldst perish where thou liest, but I will raise thee up, and set thee on thy way."

"Wilt thou help me to liberate Alizon?" demanded Richard.

"Do not concern thyself further about her," replied the phantom; "she must pass through an ordeal with which nothing human may interfere. If she escape it you will meet again. If not, it were better thou shouldst be in thy grave than see her. Take this phial. Drink thou the liquid it contains, and thy strength will return to thee."

"How do I know thou art not sent hither by Mother Demdike

THE PHANTOM MONK. P. 340.

to tempt me?" demanded Richard, doubtfully. "I have already fallen into her snares," he added, with a groan.

"I am Mother Demdike's enemy, and the appointed instrument of her punishment," replied the monk, in a tone that did not admit of question. "Drink, and fear nothing."

Richard obeyed, and the next moment sprang to his feet.

"Thou hast indeed restored me!" he cried. "I would fain reach the secret entrance to the tower."

"Attempt it not, I charge thee!" cried the phantom; "but depart instantly for Pendle Hill."

"Wherefore should I go thither?" demanded Richard.

"Thou wilt learn anon," returned the monk. "I cannot tell thee more now. Dismount at the foot of the hill, and proceed to the beacon. Thou know'st it?"

"I do," replied Richard. "There a fire was lighted which was meant to set all England in a blaze."

"And which led many good men to destruction," said the monk, in a tone of indescribable sadness. "Alas! for him who kindled it. The offence is not yet worked out. But depart without more delay; and look not back."

As Richard hastened towards the spot where he had left Merlin, he fancied he was followed by the phantom; but, obedient to the injunction he received, he did not turn his head. As he mounted the horse, who neighed cheerily as he drew near, he found he was right in supposing the monk to be behind him, for he heard his voice calling out, "Linger not by the way. To the beacon!—to the beacon!"

Thus exhorted, the young man dashed off, and, to his great surprise, found Merlin as fresh as if he had undergone no fatigue during the day. It would almost seem, from his spirit, that he had partaken of the same wondrous elixir which had revived his master. Down the hill he plunged, regardless of the steep descent, and soon entered the thicket where the storm had fallen upon them, and where so many acts of witchcraft were performed. Now, neither accident nor obstacle occurred to check the headlong pace of the animal, though the stones rattled after him as he struck them with his flying hoof. The moonlight quivered on the branches of the trees, and on the tender spray, and all looked as tranquil and beautiful as it had so lately been gloomy and disturbed. The wood was passed, and the last and steepest descent cleared. The little bridge was at hand, and beneath was Pendle Water, rushing over its rocky bed, and glittering like silver in the moon's rays. But here Richard had wellnigh received a check. A party of armed men, it proved, occupied the road leading to Rough Lee, about a bow-shot from the bridge, and as soon as they perceived he was taking the opposite course, with the apparent intention of avoiding them, they shouted to him to stay. This shout made Richard aware of their presence, for he had not before observed them, as they were concealed by the intervention of some small trees; but though surprised at the circumstance, and not without apprehension that they might be there with a hostile design to Mistress Nutter, he did not slacken his pace. A horseman, who appeared to be their leader, rode after him for a short distance, but finding pursuit futile, he desisted, pouring forth a volley of oaths and threats, in a voice that proclaimed him as Sir Thomas Metcalfe. This discovery confirmed Richard in his supposition that mischief was intended Mistress Nutter; but even this conviction, strengthened by his antipathy to Metcalfe, was not sufficiently strong to induce him to stop. Promising himself to return on the morrow, and settle accounts with the insolent knight, he speeded on, and, passing the mill, tracked the rocky gorge above it, and began to mount another hill. Despite the ascent, Merlin never slackened his pace, but, though his master would have restrained him, held on as before. But the brow of the hill attained, Richard compelled him to a brief halt.

By this time the sky was comparatively clear, but small clouds were sailing across the heavens, and at one moment the moon would be obscured by them, and the next, burst forth with sudden effulgence. These alternations produced corresponding effects on the broad, brown, heathy plain extending below, and fantastic shadows were cast upon it, which it needed not Richard's heated imagination to liken to evil beings flying past. The wind, too, lay in the direction of the north end of Pendle Hill, whither Richard was about to shape his course, and the shadows consequently trooped off towards that quarter. The vast mass of Pendle rose in gloomy majesty before him, being thrown into shade, except at its crown, where a flood of radiance rested.

Like an eagle swooping upon his prey, Richard descended into the valley, and like a stag pursued by the huntsman he speeded across it. Neither dyke, morass, nor stone wall checked him, or made him turn aside; and almost as fast as the clouds hurrying above him, and their shadows travelling at his feet, did he reach the base of Pendle Hill.

Making up to a shed, which, though empty, luckily contained a wisp or two of hay, he turned Merlin into it, and commenced the ascent of the hill on foot. After attaining a considerable elevation, he looked down from the giddy heights upon the valley he had just traversed. A few huts, forming the little village of Barley, lay sleeping in the moonlight beneath him, while further off could be just discerned Goldshaw, with its embowered church. A line of thin vapour marked the course of Pendle Water, and thicker mists hovered over the mosses. The shadows were still passing over the plain.

Pressing on, Richard soon came among the rocks protruding from the higher part of the hill, and as the path was here not more than a foot wide, rarely taken except by the sheep and their guartlians, it was necessary to proceed with the utmost caution, as a single false step would have been fatal. After some toil, and not without considerable risk, he reached the summit of the hill.

As he bounded over the springy turf, and inhaled the pure air of that exalted region, his spirits revived, and new elasticity was communicated to his limbs. He shaped his course near the edge of the hill, so that the extensive view it commanded was fully displayed. But his eye rested on the mountainous range on the opposite side of the valley, where Malkin Tower was situated. Even in broad day the accursed structure would have been invisible, as it stood on the further side of the hill, overlooking Barrowford and Colne; but Richard knew its position well, and while his gaze was fixed upon the point, he saw a star shoot down from the heavens and apparently alight near the spot. The circumstance alarmed him, for he could not help thinking it ominous of ill to Alizon.

Nothing, however, followed to increase his misgivings, and erelong he came in sight of the beacon. The ground had been gradually rising, and if he had proceeded a few hundred yards further, a vast panorama would have opened upon him, comprising a large part of Lancashire on the one hand, and on the other an equally extensive portion of Yorkshire. Forest and fell, black moor and bright stream, old castle and stately hall, would have then been laid before him as in a map. But other thoughts engrossed him, and he went straight on. As far as he could discern he was alone on the hill top; and the silence and solitude, coupled with the ill report of the place, which at this hour was said to be often visited by foul hags, for the performance of their unhallowed rites, awakened superstitious fears in his breast.

He was soon by the side of the beacon. The stones were still standing as they had been reared by Paslew, and on looking at them he was astonished to find the hollow within them filled with dry furze, brushwood, and fagots, as if in readiness for another signal. In passing round the circle, his surprise was still further increased by discovering a torch, and not far from it, in one of the interstices of the stones, a dark lantern, in which, on removing the shade, he found a candle burning. It was now clear the beacon was to be kindled that night, though for what end he could not conjecture, and equally clear that he was brought thither to fire it. He put back the lantern into its place, took up the torch, and held himself in readiness.

Half an hour elapsed, and nothing occurred. During this interval it had become dark. A curtain of clouds was drawn over the moon and stars.

Suddenly, a hurtling noise was heard in the air, and it seemed to the watcher as if a troop of witches were alighting at a distance from him.

A loud hubbub of voices ensued—then there was a trampling

of feet, accompanied by discordant strains of music—after which a momentary silence ensued, and a harsh voice asked—

"Why are we brought hither?"

"It is not for a sabbath," shouted another voice, "for there is neither fire nor caldron."

"Mother Demdike would not summon us without good reason," cried a third. "We shall learn presently what we have to do."

"The more mischief the better," rejoined another voice.

"Ay, mischief! mischief! mischief!" echoed the rest of the crew.

"You shall have enough of it to content you," rejoined Mother Demdike. "I have called you hither to be present at a sacrifice."

Hideous screams of laughter followed this announcement, and the voice that had spoken first asked—

"A sacrifice of whom?"

"An unbaptised babe, stolen from its sleeping mother's breast," rejoined another. "Mother Demdike has often played that trick before—ho! ho!"

"Peace!" thundered the hag—"It is no babe I am about to kill, but a full-grown maid—ay, and one of rarest beauty, too. What think ye of Alizon Device?"

"Thy grand-daughter!" cried several voices, in surprise.

"Alice Nutter's daughter—for such she is," rejoined the hag. "I have held her captive in Malkin Tower, and have subjected her to every trial and temptation I could devise, but I have failed in shaking her courage, or in winning her over to our master. All the horrors of the vault have been tried upon her in vain. Even the last terrible ordeal, which no one has hitherto sustained, proved ineffectual. She went through it unmoved."

"Heaven be praised!" murmured Richard.

"It seems I have no power over her soul" pursued the hag; "but I have over her body, and she shall die here, and by my hand. But mind me, not a drop of blood must fall to the ground."

"Have no fear," cried several voices, "we will catch it in our palms and quaff it."

"Hast thou thy knife, Mould-heels?" asked Mother Demdike.

"Ay," replied the other, "it is long and sharp, and will do thy business well. Thy grandson, Jem Device, notched it by killing swine, and my goodman ground it only yesterday. Take it."

"I will plunge it to her heart!" cried Mother Demdike, with an infernal laugh. "And now I will tell you why we have neither fire nor caldron. On questioning the ebon image in the vault as to the place where the sacrifice should be made, I received for answer that it must be here, and in darkness. No human eye but our own must behold it. We are safe on this score, for no one is likely to come hither at this hour. No fire must be kindled, or the sacrifice will result in destruction to us all. Ye have heard, and understand?"

"We do," replied several husky voices.

"And so do I," said Richard, taking hold of the dark lantern.

"And now for the girl," cried Mother Demdike.

CHAPTER XVI.—ONE O'CLOCK!

MISTRESS NUTTER and Mother Chattox were still at the hut, impatiently awaiting the return of Fancy. But nearly an hour elapsed before he appeared.

"What has detained thee so long?" demanded the hag, sharply, as he stood before them.

"You shall hear, mistress," replied Fancy: "I have had a busy time of it, I assure you, and thought I should never accomplish my errand. On arriving at Rough Lee, I found the place invested by Sir Thomas Metcalfe and a host of armed men, who had been sent thither by Parson Holden, for the joint purpose of arresting you, madam," addressing Mistress Nutter, "and liberating Nowell and Potts. The knight was in a great fume; for, in spite of the force brought against it; the house had been stoutly defended by Nicholas Assheton, who had worsted the besieging party, and captured two Alsatian captains, hangers on of Sir Thomas. Appearing in the character of an enemy, I was immediately surrounded by Metcalfe and his men, who swore they would cut my throat unless I undertook to procure the liberation of the two bravos in question, as well as that of Nowell and Potts. I told them I was come for the express purpose of setting free the two last-named gentlemen; but, with respect to the former, I had no instructions, and they must arrange the matter with Master Nicholas himself. Upon this Sir Thomas became exceedingly wroth and insolent, and proceeded to such lengths that I resolved to chastise him, and in so doing performed a feat which will tend greatly to exalt Richard's character for courage and strength."

"Let us hear it, my doughty champion," cried Mother Chattox.

"While Metcalfe was pouring forth his rage, and menacing me with uplifted hand," pursued the familiar, "I seized him by the throat, dragged him from his horse, and in spite of the efforts of his men, whose blows fell upon me thick as hail, and quite as harmlessly, I bore him through the garden to the back of the house, where my shouts soon brought Nicholas and others to my assistance, and after delivering my captive to them, I dismounted. The squire, you will imagine, was astonished to see me, and greatly applauded my prowess. I replied, with the modesty becoming my assumed character, that I had done nothing, and, in reality, the feat was nothing to me; but I told him I had something of the utmost importance to communicate, and which could not be delayed a moment; whereupon he led me to a small room adjoining the hall, while the crestfallen knight was left to vent his rage and mortification on the grooms to whose custody he was committed."

"You acted your part to perfection," said Mistress Nutter.

"Ay, trust my sweet Fancy for that," said the hag—"there is no familiar like him—none whatever."

"Your praises make me blush," rejoined Fancy. "But to proceed. I fulfilled your instructions to the letter, and excited Nicholas's horror and indignation by the tale I told him. I laughed in my sleeve all the while, but I maintained a very different countenance with him. He thought me full of anguish and despair. He questioned me as to my proceedings at Malkin Tower, and I amazed him with the description of a fearful storm I had encountered—of my interview with old Demdike, and her atrocious treatment of Alizon—to all of which he listened with profound interest. Richard himself could not have moved him more—perhaps not so much. As soon as I had finished, he vowed he would rescue Alizon from the murtherous hag, and prevent the latter from committing further mischief; and bidding me come with him, we repaired to the room in which Nowell and Potts were confined. We found them both fast asleep in their chairs; but Nicholas quickly awakened them, and some explanations ensued, which did not at first appear very clear and satisfactory to either magistrate or attorney, but in the end they agreed to accompany us on the expedition, Master Potts declaring it would compensate him for all his mischances if he could arrest Mother Demdike."

"I hope he may have his wish," said Mother Chattox.

"Ay, but he declared that his next step should be to arrest you, mistress," observed Fancy, with a laugh.

"Arrest me!" cried the hag. "Marry, let him touch me, if he dares. My term is not out yet, and, with thee to defend me, my brave Fancy, I have no fear."

"Right!" replied the familiar; "but to go on with my story. Sir Thomas Metcalfe was next brought forward; and after some warm altercation, peace was at length established between him and the squire, and hands were shaken all round. Wine was then called for by Nicholas, who, at the same time, directed that the two Alsatian captains should be brought up from the cellar, where they had been placed for safety. The first part of the order was obeyed, but the second was found impracticable, inasmuch as the two heroes had found their way to the inner cellar, and had emptied so many flasks that they were utterly incapable of moving. While the wine was being discussed, an unexpected arrival took place."

"An arrival!—of whom?" inquired Mistress Nutter, eagerly.

"Sir Ralph Assheton and a large party," replied Fancy. "Parson Holden, it seems, not content with sending Sir Thomas and his rout to the aid of his friends, had proceeded for the same purpose to Whalley, and the result was the appearance of the new party. A brief explanation from Nicholas and myself served to put Sir Ralph in possession of all that had occurred, and he declared his readiness to accompany the expedition to Pendle Hill, and to take all his followers with him. Sir Thomas Metcalfe expressed an equally strong desire to go with him, and of course it was acceded to. I am bound to tell you, madam," added Fancy to Mistress Nutter, "that your conduct is viewed in a most suspicious light by every one of these persons, except Nicholas, who made an effort to defend you."

"I care not what happens to me, if I succeed in rescuing my child," said the lady. "But have they set out on the expedition?"

"By this time, no doubt they have," replied Fancy. "I got off by saying I would ride on to Pendle Hill, and, stationing myself on its summit, give them a signal when they should advance upon their prey. And now, good mistress, I pray you dismiss me. I want to cast off this shape, which I find an incumbrance, and resume my own. I will return when it is time for you to set out."

The hag waved her hand, and the familiar was gone.

Half an hour elapsed, and he returned not. Mistress Nutter became fearfully impatient. Three-quarters, and even the old hag was uneasy. An hour, and he stood before them—dwarfish, fiendish, monstrous.

"It is time," he said, in a harsh voice; but the tones were music in the wretched mother's ears.

"Come, then," she cried, rushing wildly forth.

"Ay, ay, I come," replied the hag, following her. "Not so fast. You cannot go without me."

"Nor either of you without me," added Fancy. "Here, good mistress, is your broomstick."

"Away for Pendle Hill!" screamed the hag.

"Ay, for Pendle Hill!" echoed Fancy.

And there was a whirling of dark figures through the air as before.

Presently they alighted on the summit of Pendle Hill, which seemed to be wrapped in a dense cloud, for Mistress Nutter could scarcely see a yard before her. Fancy's eyes, however, were powerful enough to penetrate the gloom, for stepping back a few yards, he said—

"The expedition is at the foot of the hill, where they have

made a halt. We must wait a few moments, till I can ascertain what they mean to do. Ah! I see. They are dividing into three parties. One detachment, headed by Nicholas Assheton, with whom are Potts and Nowell, is about to make the ascent from the spot where they now stand; another, commanded by Sir Ralph Assheton, is moving towards the but-end of the hill; and the third, headed by Sir Thomas Metcalfe, is proceeding to the right. These are goodly preparations—ha! ha! But, what do I behold? The first detachment have a prisoner with them. It is Jem Device, whom they have captured on the way, I suppose. I can tell from the rascal's looks that he is planning an escape. Patience, madam, I must see how he executes his design. There is no hurry. They are all scrambling up the hill-sides. Some one slips, and rolls down, and bruises himself severely against the loose stones. Ho! ho! it is Master Potts. He is picked up by James Device, who takes him on his shoulders. What means the knave by such attention? We shall see anon. They continue to fight their way upward, and have now reached the narrow path among the rocks. Take heed, or your necks will be broken. Ho! ho! Well done, Jem,—bravo! lad. Thy scheme is out now—ho! ho!"

"What has he done?" asked Mother Chattox.

"Run off with the attorney—with Master Potts," replied Fancy; "disappeared in the gloom, so that it is impossible Nicholas can follow him—ho! ho!"

"But my child!—where is my child?" cried Mistress Nutter, in agitated impatience.

"Come with me, and I will lead you to her," replied Fancy, taking her hand; "and do you keep close to us, mistress," he added to Mother Chattox.

Moving quickly along the heathy plain, they soon reached a small dry hollow, about a hundred paces from the beacon, in the midst of which, as in a grave, was deposited the inanimate form of Alizon. When the spot was indicated to her by Fancy, the miserable mother flew to it, and, with indescribable delight, clasped her child to her breast. But the next moment, a new fear seized her, for the limbs were stiff and cold, and the heart had apparently ceased to beat.

"She is dead!" exclaimed Mistress Nutter, frantically.

"No; she is only in a magical trance," said Fancy; "my mistress can instantly revive her."

"Prithee do so, then, good Chattox," implored the lady.

"Better defer it till we have taken her hence," rejoined the hag.

"Oh! no, now—now! Let me be assured she lives!" cried Mistress Nutter.

Mother Chattox reluctantly assented, and, touching Alizon with her skinny finger, first upon the heart and then upon the brow, the poor girl began to show symptoms of life.

"My child—my child!" cried Mistress Nutter, straining her to her breast; "I am come to save thee!"

"You will scarce succeed, if you tarry here longer," said Fancy. "Away!"

"Ay, come away!" shrieked the hag, seizing Alizon's arm.

"Where are you about to take her?" asked Mistress Nutter.

"To my hut," replied Mother Chattox.

"No, no—she shall not go there," returned the lady.

"And wherefore not?" screamed the hag. "She is mine now, and I say she *shall* go."

"Right, mistress," said Fancy; "and leave the lady here if she objects to accompany her. But be quick."

"You shall not take her from me!" shrieked Mistress Nutter, holding her daughter fast. "I see through your diabolical purpose. You have the same dark design as Mother Demdike, and would sacrifice her; but she shall not go with you, neither will I."

"Tut!" exclaimed the hag, "you have lost your senses on a sudden. I do not want your daughter. But come away, or Mother Demdike will surprise us."

"Do not trifle with her longer," whispered Fancy to the hag; "drag the girl away, or you will lose her. A few moments, and it will be too late."

Mother Chattox made an attempt to obey him, but Mistress Nutter resisted her.

"Curses on her!" she muttered, "she is too strong for me. Do thou help me," she added, appealing to Fancy.

"I cannot," he replied; "I have done all I dare to help you. You must accomplish the rest yourself."

"But, my sweet imp, recollect—"

"I recollect I have a master," interrupted the familiar.

"And a mistress, too," cried the hag; "and she will chastise thee if thou art disobedient. I command thee to carry off this girl."

"I have already told you I dare not, and I now say I will not," replied Fancy.

"Will not!" shrieked the hag. "Thou shalt smart for this. I will bury thee in the heart of this mountain, and make thee labour within it like a gnome. I will set thee to count the sands on the river's bed, and the leaves on the forest trees. Thou shalt know neither rest nor respite."

"Ho! ho! ho!" laughed Fancy, mockingly.

"Dost deride me?" cried the hag. "I will do it, thou saucy jackanapes. For the last time, wilt obey me?"

"No," replied Fancy, "and for this reason—your term is out. It expired at midnight.

"It is false!" shrieked the hag, in accents of mixed terror and rage. "I have months to run, and will renew it."

"Before midnight, you might have done so; but it is now too late—your reign is over," rejoined Fancy. "Farewell, sweet mistress. We shall meet once again, though scarcely under such pleasant circumstances as heretofore."

"It cannot be, my darling Fancy; thou art jesting with me," whimpered the hag; "thou wouldst not delude thy doating mistress thus."

"I have done with thee, foul hag," rejoined the familiar, "and am right glad my service is ended. I could have saved thee, but would not, and delayed my return for that very purpose. Thy soul was forfeited when I came back to thy hut."

"Then curses on thee for thy treachery," cried the hag, "and on thy master, who deceived me in the bond he placed before me."

The familiar laughed hoarsely.

"But what of Mother Demdike?" pursued the hag. "Hast thou no comfort for me? Tell me her hour is likewise come, and I will forgive thee. But do not let her triumph over me."

The familiar made no answer, but, laughing derisively, stamped upon the ground, and it opened to receive him.

"Alizon!" cried Mistress Nutter, who in the mean time had vainly endeavoured to rouse her daughter to full consciousness, "fly with me, my child. The enemy is at hand."

"What enemy?" asked Alizon, faintly. "I have so many, that I know not whom you mean."

"But this is the worst of all—this is Mother Demdike," cried Mistress Nutter. "She would take your life. If we can but conceal ourselves for a short while, we are safe."

"I am too weak to move," said Alizon; "besides, I dare not trust you. I have been deceived already. You may be an evil spirit in the likeness of my mother."

"Oh! no, I am indeed your own—own mother," rejoined Mistress Nutter. "Ask this old woman if it is not so."

"She is a witch herself," replied Alizon. "I will not trust either of you. You are both in league with Mother Demdike."

"We are in league to save thee from her, foolish wench!" cried Mother Chattox, "but thy perverseness will defeat all our schemes."

"Since you will not fly, my child," cried Mistress Nutter, "kneel down, and pray earnestly for deliverance. Pray, while there is yet time."

As she spoke, a growl like thunder was heard in the air, and the earth trembled beneath their feet.

"Nay, now I am sure you are my mother!" cried Alizon, flinging herself into Mistress Nutter's arms; "and I will go with you."

But before they could move, several dusky figures were seen rushing towards them.

"Be on your guard!" cried Mother Chattox; "here comes old Demdike with her troop. I will aid you all I can."

"Down on your knees!" exclaimed Mistress Nutter.

Alizon obeyed, but ere a word could pass her lips, the infuriated hag, attended by her beldame band, stood beside them.

"Ha! who is here?" she cried. "Let me see who dares interrupt my mystic rites."

And raising her hand, the black cloud hanging over the hill was rent asunder, and the moon shone down upon them, revealing the old witch, armed with the sacrificial knife, her limbs shaking with fury, and her eyes flashing with preternatural light. It revealed, also, her weird attendants, as well as the group before her, consisting of the kneeling figure of Alizon, protected by the outstretched arms of her mother, and further defended by Mother Chattox, who planted herself in front of them.

Mother Demdike eyed the group for a moment as if she would annihilate them.

"Out of my way, Chattox!" she vociferated—"out of my way, or I will drive my knife to thy heart." And as her old antagonist maintained her ground, she unhesitatingly advanced upon her, smote her with the weapon, and, as she fell to the ground, stepped over her bleeding body.

"Now what dost thou here, Alice Nutter?" she cried, menacing her with the reeking blade.

"I am come for my child, whom thou hast stolen from me," replied the lady.

"Thou art come to witness her slaughter," replied the witch, fiercely. "Begone, or I will serve thee as I have just served old Chattox."

"I am not sped yet," cried the wounded hag; "I shall live to see thee bound hand and foot by the officers of justice, and, certain thou wilt perish miserably, I shall die content."

"Spit out thy last drops of venom, black viper," rejoined Mother Demdike; "when I have done with the others, I will return and finish thee. Alice Nutter, thou knowest it is vain to struggle with me. Give me up the girl."

"Wilt thou accept my life for hers?" said Mistress Nutter.

"Of what account would thy life be to me?" rejoined Mother Demdike, disdainfully. "If it would profit me to take it, I would do so without thy consent, but I am about to make an oblation to our master, and thou art his already. Snatch her child from her —we waste time," she added, to her attendants.

And immediately the weird crew rushed forward, and in spite of the miserable mother's efforts tore Alizon from her.

"I told you it was in vain to contend with me," said Mother Demdike.

"Oh, that I could call down heaven's vengeance upon thy accursed head!" cried Mistress Nutter; but I am forsaken alike of God and man, and shall die despairing."

"Rave on, thou wilt have ample leisure," replied the hag. "And now bring the girl this way," she added to the beldames; "the sacrifice must be made near the beacon.'

And as Alizon was borne away, Mistress Nutter uttered a cry of anguish.

"Do not stay here," said Mother Chattox, raising herself with difficulty. "Go after her; you may yet save your daughter."

"But how?" cried Mistress Nutter, distractedly. "I have no power now."

As she spoke a dusky form rose up beside her. It was her familiar.

"Will you return to your duty if I help you in this extremity?" he said.

"Ay, do, do!" cried Mother Chattox. "Any thing to avenge yourself upon that murtherous hag."

"Peace!" cried the familiar, spurning her with his cloven foot.

"I do not want vengeance," said Mistress Nutter; "I only want to save my child."

"Then you consent on that condition?" said the familiar.

"No!" replied Mistress Nutter, firmly. "I now perceive I a not utterly lost, since you try to regain me. I have renounce thy master, and will make no new bargain with him. Get henc tempter!"

"Think not to escape us," cried the familiar; "no penitence—no absolution can save thee. Thy name is written on the judgment scroll, and cannot be effaced. I would have aided thee, but, since my offer is rejected, I leave thee."

"You will not let him go!" screamed Mother Chattox. "Oh that the chance were mine!"

"Be silent, or I will beat thy brains out!" said the familiar. "Once more, am I dismissed?"

"Ay, for ever!" replied Mistress Nutter.

And as the familiar disappeared, she flew to the spot where her child had been taken.

About twenty paces from the beacon, a circle had again been formed by the unhallowed crew, in the midst of which stood Mother Demdike, with the gory knife in her hand, muttering spells and incantations, and performing mystical ceremonials.

Every now and then her companions joined in these rites, and chanted a song couched in a wild, unintelligible jargon. Beside the witch knelt Alizon, with her hands tied behind her back, so that she could not raise them in supplication; her hair unbound, and cast loosely over her person, and a thick bandage fastened over her eyes and mouth.

The initiatory ceremonies over, the old hag approached her victim, when Mistress Nutter forced herself through the circle, and cast herself at her feet.

"Spare her!" she cried, clinging to her knees; "it shall be well for thee if thou dost so."

"Again interrupted!" cried the witch, furiously. "This time I will show thee no mercy. Take thy fate, meddlesome woman!"

And she raised the knife, but ere the weapon could descend, it was seized by Mistress Nutter, and wrested from her grasp. In another instant, Alizon's arms were liberated, and the bandage removed from her eyes.

"Now it is my turn to threaten. I have thee in my power, infernal hag!" cried Mistress Nutter, holding the knife to the witch's throat, and clasping her daughter with the other arm. "Wilt let us go?"

"No!" replied Mother Demdike, springing nimbly backwards. "You shall both die. I will soon disarm thee."

And making one or two passes with her hands, Mistress Nutter dropped the weapon, and instantly became fixed and motionless, with her daughter, equally rigid, in her arms. They looked as if suddenly turned to marble.

"Now to complete the ceremonial," cried Mother Demdike, picking up the knife.

And then she began to mutter an impious address preparatory to the sacrifice, when a loud clangour was heard like the stroke of a hammer upon a bell.

"What was that?" exclaimed the witch, in alarm.

"Were there a clock here, I should say it had struck one," replied Mould-heels.

"It must be our master's timepiece," said another witch.

"One o'clock!" exclaimed Mother Demdike, who appeared stupefied with fear, "and the sacrifice not made—then I am lost!"

A derisive laugh reached her ears. It proceeded from Mother Chattox, who had contrived to raise herself to her feet, and, tottering forward, now passed through the appalled circle.

"Ay, thy term is out—thy soul is forfeited like mine—ha! ha!" And she fell to the ground.

"Perhaps it may not be too late," cried Mother Demdike, grasping the knife, and rushing towards Alizon.

But at this moment a bright flame shot up from the beacon.

Astonishment and terror seized the hag, and she uttered a loud cry, which was echoed by the rest of the crew.

The flame mounted higher and higher, and burnt each moment more brightly, illumining the whole summit of the hill. By its light could be seen a band of men, some of whom were on horseback, speeding towards the place of meeting.

Scared by the sight, the witches fled, but were turned by another band advancing from the opposite quarter. They then made towards the spot where their broomsticks were deposited, but ere they could reach it, a third party gained the summit of the hill at this precise point, and immediately started in pursuit of them.

Meanwhile, a young man issuing from behind the beacon, flew

towards Mistress Nutter and her daughter. The moment the flame burst forth, the spell cast over them by Mother Demdike was broken, and motion and speech restored.

"Alizon!" exclaimed the young man, as he came up, "your trials are over. You are safe."

"Oh, Richard!" she replied, falling into his arms, "have we been preserved by you?"

"I am a mere instrument in the hands of Heaven," he replied.

Mother Demdike made no attempt at flight with the rest of the witches, but remained for a few moments absorbed in contemplation of the flaming beacon. Her hand still grasped the murderous weapon she had raised against Alizon, but it had dropped to her side when the fire burst forth. At length she turned fiercely to Richard, and demanded—

"Was it thou who kindled the beacon?"

"It was!" replied the young man.

"And who bade thee do it—who brought thee hither?" pursued the witch.

"An enemy of thine, old woman!" replied Richard. "His vengeance has been slow in coming, but it has arrived at last."

"But who is he? I see him not!" rejoined Mother Demdike.

"You will see him before yon flame expires," said Richard. "I should have come to your assistance sooner, Alizon," he continued, turning to her, "but I was forbidden. And I knew I should best ensure your safety by compliance with the injunctions I had received."

"Some guardian spirit must have interposed to preserve us," replied Alizon; "for such only could have successfully combated with the evil beings from whom we have been delivered."

"Thy spirit is unable to preserve thee now!" cried Mother Demdike, aiming a deadly blow at her with the knife. But, fortunately, the attempt was foreseen by Richard, who caught her arm, and wrested the weapon from her.

"Curses on thee, Richard Assheton!" cried the infuriated hag, —"and on thee too, Alizon Device, I cannot work ye the immediate ill I wish. I cannot make ye loathsome in one another's eyes. I cannot maim your limbs, or blight your beauty. I cannot deliver you over to devilish possession. But I can bequeath you a legacy of hate. What I say will come to pass. Thou, Alizon, wilt never wed Richard Assheton—never! Vainly shall ye struggle with your destiny—vainly indulge hopes of happiness. Misery and despair, and an early grave, are in store for both of you. He shall be to you your worst enemy, and you shall be to him destruction. Think of the witch's prediction and tremble, and may her deadliest curse rest upon your heads."

"Oh, Richard!" exclaimed Alizon, who would have sunk to the ground if he had not sustained her. "Why did you not prevent this terrible malediction?"

"He could not," replied Mother Demdike, with a laugh of exultation; "it shall work, and thy doom shall be accomplished. And now to make an end of old Chattox, and then they may take me where they please."

And she was approaching her old enemy with the intention of putting her threat into execution, when James Device, who appeared to start from the ground, rushed swiftly towards her.

"What art thou doing here, Jem?" cried the hag, regarding him with angry surprise. "Dost thou not see we are surrounded by enemies. I cannot escape them—but thou art young and active. Away with thee!"

"Not without yo, granny," replied Jem. "Ey ha' run os fast os ey could to help yo. Stick fast howld on me," he added, snatching her up in his arms, "an ey'n bring yo clear off yet."

And he set off at a rapid pace with his burthen, Richard being too much occupied with Alizon to oppose him.

CHAPTER XVII.—HOW THE BEACON FIRE WAS EXTINGUISHED.

SOON after this, Nicholas Assheton, attended by two or three men, came up, and asked whither the old witch had flown.

Mistress Nutter pointed out the course taken by the fugitive, who had run towards the northern extremity of the hill, down the sides of which he had already plunged.

"She has been carried off by her grandson, Jem Device," said Mistress Nutter; "be quick, or you will lose her."

"Ay, be quick—be quick!" added Mother Chattox. "Yonder they went, to the back of the beacon."

Casting a look at the wretched speaker, and finding she was too grievously wounded to be able to move, Nicholas bestowed no further thought upon her, but set off with his companions in the direction pointed out. He speedily arrived at the edge of the hill, and, looking down it, sought in vain for any appearance of the fugitives. The sides were here steep and shelving, and some hundred yards lower down were broken into ridges, behind one of which it was possible the old witch and her grandson might be concealed; so, without a moment's hesitation, the squire descended, and began to search about in the hollows, scrambling over the loose stones, or sliding down for some paces with the uncertain boggy soil, when he fancied he heard a plaintive cry. He looked around, but could see no one. The whole side of the mountain was lighted up by the fire from the beacon, which, instead of diminishing, burnt with increased ardour, so that every object was as easily to be discerned as in the day-time; but, notwithstanding this, he could not detect whence the sound proceeded. It was repeated, but more faintly than before, and Nicholas almost persuaded himself it was the voice of Potts calling for help. Motioning to his followers, who were engaged in the search like himself, to keep still, the squire listened intently, and again caught the sound, being this time convinced it arose from the ground. Was it possible the unfortunate attorney had been buried alive? Or had he been thrust into some hole, and a stone placed over it, which he found it impossible to remove? The latter idea seemed the more probable, and Nicholas was guided by a feeble repetition of the noise towards a large fragment of rock, which, on examination, had evidently been rolled from a point immediately over the mouth of a hollow. The squire instantly set himself to work to dislodge the ponderous stone, and, aided by two of his men, who lent their broad shoulders to the task, quickly accomplished his object, disclosing what appeared to be the mouth of a cavernous recess. From out of this, as soon as the stone was removed, popped the head of Master Potts, and Nicholas, bidding him be of good cheer, laid hold of him to draw him forth, as he seemed to have some difficulty in extricating himself, when the attorney cried out—

"Do not pull so hard, squire! That accursed Jem Device has got hold of my legs. Not so hard, sir, I entreat."

"Bid him let go," said Nicholas, unable to refrain from laughing, "or we will unearth him from his badger's hole."

"He pays no heed to what I say to him," cried Potts. "Oh, dear! oh, dear! he is dragging me down again!"

And, as he spoke, the attorney, notwithstanding all Nicholas's efforts to restrain him, was pulled down into the hole. The squire was at a loss what to do, and was considering whether he should resort to the tedious process of digging him out, when a scrambling noise was heard, and the captive's head once more appeared above ground.

"Are you coming out now?" asked Nicholas.

"Alas, no!" replied the attorney, "unless you will make terms with the rascal. He declares he will strangle me, if you do not promise to set him and his grandmother free."

"Is Mother Demdike with him?" asked Nicholas.

"To be sure," replied Potts; "and we are as badly off for room as three foxes in a hole."

"And there is no other outlet said the squire?"

"I conclude not," replied the attorney. "I groped about like a mole when I was first thrust into the cavern by Jem Device, but I could find no means of exit. The entrance was blocked up by the great stone which you had some difficulty in moving, but which Jem could shift at will; for he pushed it aside in a moment, and brought it back to its place, when he returned just now with the old hag; but probably that was effected by witchcraft."

"Most likely," said Nicholas, "But for your being in it, we would stop up this hole, and bury the two wretches alive."

"Get me out first, good Master Nicholas, I implore of you, and then do what you please," cried Potts. "Jem is tugging at my legs as if he would pull them off."

"We will try who is strongest," said Nicholas, again seizing hold of Potts by the shoulders.

"Oh, dear! oh, dear! I can't bear it—let go!" shrieked the attorney. "I shall be stretched to twice my natural length. My joints are starting from their sockets, my legs are coming off—oh! oh!"

"Lend a hand here, one of you," cried Nicholas to the men; "we'll have him out, whatever be the consequence."

"But I won't come!" roared Potts. "You have no right to use me thus. Torture! oh! oh! my loins are ruptured—my back is breaking—I am a dead man.—The hag has got hold of my right leg, while Jem is tugging with all his force at the left."

"Pull away!" cried Nicholas; "he is coming."

"My legs are off," yelled Potts, as he was plucked suddenly forth, with a jerk that threw the squire and his assistants on their backs. "I shall never be able to walk more. No, Heaven be praised!" he added, looking down on his lower limbs, "I have only lost my boots."

"Never mind it, then," cried Nicholas; "but thank your stars you are above ground once more. Hark'ee, Jem!" he continued, shouting down the hole; "If you don't come forth at once, and bring Mother Demdike with you, we'll close up the mouth of this hole in such a way that you sha'n't require another grave. D'ye hear?"

"Yeigh," replied Jem, his voice coming hoarsely and hollowly up like the accents of a ghost. "Am ey to go free if ey comply?"

"Certainly not," replied the squire. "You have a choice between this hole and the hangman's cord at Lancaster, that is all. In either case you will die by suffocation. But be quick—we have wasted time enough already with you."

"Then if that's aw yo'll do fo' me, squire, eyn e'en stay wheere ey am," rejoined Jem.

"Very well," replied Nicholas. "Here, my man, stop up this hole with earth and stones. Master Potts, you will lend a hand to the task."

"Readily, sir," replied the attorney, "though I shall lose the pleasure I had anticipated of seeing that old carrion crow roasted alive."

"Stay a bit, squoire," roared Jem, as preparations were actively made for carrying Nicholas's orders into execution. "Stay a bit, an ey'n cum owt, an bring t' owd woman wi' me."

"I thought you'd change your mind," replied Nicholas,

laughing. "Be upon your guard, he added, in a low tone to the others, "and seize him the moment he appears."

But Jem evidently found it no easy matter to perform his promise, for stifled shrieks and other noises proclaimed that a desperate struggle was going on between him and his grandmother.

"Aha!" exclaimed Nicholas, placing his ear to the hole. "The old hag is unwilling to come forth, and spits and scratches like a cat-a-mountain, while Jem gripes her like a terrier. It is a hard tussle between them, but he is getting the better of it, and is pushing her forth. Now look out."

And as he spoke, Mother Demdike's terrible head protruded from the ground, and, despite of the execrations she poured forth upon her enemies, she was instantly seized by them, drawn out of the cavern, and secured. While the men were thus engaged, and while Nicholas's attention was for an instant diverted, Jem bounded forth as suddenly as a wolf from his lair, and, dashing aside all opposition, plunged down the hill.

"It is useless to pursue him," said Nicholas. "He will not escape. The whole country will be roused by the beacon fire, and hue and cry shall be made after him."

"Right!" exclaimed Potts; "and now let some one creep into that cavern, and bring out my boots, and then I shall be in a better condition to attend you."

The request being complied with, and the attorney being once more equipped for walking, the party climbed the hill-side, and, bringing Mother Demdike with them, shaped their course towards the beacon.

And now to see what had taken place in the interim.

Scarcely had the squire quitted Mistress Nutter than Sir Ralph Assheton rode up to her.

"Why do you loiter here, madam?" he said, in a stern tone, somewhat tempered by sorrow. "I have held back to give you an opportunity of escape. The hill is invested by your enemies. On that side Roger Nowell is advancing, and on this Sir Thomas Metcalfe and his followers. You may possibly effect a retreat in the opposite direction, but not a moment must be lost."

"I will go with you," said Alizon.

"No, no," interposed Richard. "You have not strength for the effort, and will only retard her."

"I thank you for your devotion, my child," said Mistress Nutter, with a look of grateful tenderness; "but it is unneeded. I have no intention of flying. I shall surrender myself into the hands of justice."

"Do not mistake the matter, madam," said Sir Ralph, "and delude yourself with the notion that either your rank or wealth will screen you from punishment. Your guilt is too clearly established to allow you a chance of escape, and, though I myself am acting wrongfully in counselling flight to you, I am led to do so from the friendship once subsisting between us, and the relationship which, unfortunately, I cannot destroy."

"It is you who are mistaken, not I, Sir Ralph," replied Mistress Nutter. "I have no thought of turning aside the sword of justice, but shall court its sharpest edge, hoping by a full avowal of my offences, in some degree to atone for them. My only regret is, that I shall leave my child unprotected, and that my fate will bring dishonour upon her."

"Oh, think not of me, dear mother!" cried Alizon, "but persist unhesitatingly in the course you have laid down. Far rather would I see you act thus—far rather hear the sentiments you have uttered, even though they may be attended by the saddest consequences, than behold you in your former proud position, and impenitent. Think not of me, then. Or, rather, think only how I rejoice that your eyes are at length opened, and that you have cast off the bonds of iniquity. I can now pray for you with the full hope that my intercessions will prevail, and in parting with you in this world shall be sustained by the conviction that we shall meet in eternal happiness hereafter."

Mistress Nutter threw her arms about her daughter's neck, and they mingled their tears together. Sir Ralph Assheton was much moved.

"It is a pity she should fall into their hands," he observed to Richard.

"I know not how to advise," replied the latter, greatly troubled.

"Ah! it is too late," exclaimed the knight; "here come Nowell and Metcalfe. The poor lady's firmness will be severely tested."

The next moment the magistrate and the knight came up, with such of their attendants as were not engaged in pursuing the witches, several of whom had already been captured. On seeing Mistress Nutter, Sir Thomas Metcalfe sprang from his horse, and would have seized her, but Sir Ralph interposed, saying "She has surrendered herself to me. I will be answerable for her safe custody."

"Your pardon, Sir Ralph," observed Nowell; "the arrest must be formally made, and by a constable. Sparshot, execute your warrant."

Upon this, the official, leaping from his horse, displayed his staff and a piece of parchment to Mistress Nutter, telling her she was his prisoner.

The lady bowed her head.

"Shan ey tee her hands, yer warship?" demanded the constable of the magistrate.

"On no account, fellow," interposed Sir Ralph. "I will have no indignity offered her. I have already said I will be responsible for her."

"You will recollect she is arrested for witchcraft, Sir Ralph," observed Nowell

"She shall answer to the charges brought against her. I pledge myself to that," replied Sir Ralph.

"And by a full confession," said Mistress Nutter. "You may pledge yourself to that also, Sir Ralph."

"She avows her guilt," cried Nowell. "I take you all to witness it."

"I shall not forget it," said Sir Thomas Metcalfe.

"Nor I—nor I!" cried Sparshot, and two or three others of the attendants.

"This girl is my prisoner," said Sir Thomas Metcalfe, dismounting, and advancing towards Alizon, "She is a witch, as well as the rest."

"It is false," cried Richard! "and if you attempt to lay hands upon her I will strike you to the earth."

"'Sdeath!" exclaimed Metcalfe, drawing his sword, "I will not let this insolence pass unpunished. I have other affronts to chastise. Stand aside, or I will cut your throat."

"Hold, Sir Thomas," cried Sir Ralph Assheton, authoritatively. "Settle your quarrels hereafter, if you have any to adjust; but I will have no fighting now. Alizon is no witch. You are well aware that she was about to be impiously and cruelly sacrificed by Mother Demdike, and her rescue was the main object of our coming hither."

"Still suspicion attaches to her," said Metcalfe; "whether she be the daughter of Elizabeth Device or Alice Nutter, she comes of a bad stock, and I protest against her being allowed to go free. However, if you are resolved upon it, I have nothing more to say. I shall find other time and place to adjust my differences with Master Richard Assheton."

"When you please, sir," replied the young man, sternly.

"And I will answer for the propriety of the course I have pursued," said Sir Ralph; "but here comes Nicholas with Mother Demdike."

"Demdike taken! I am glad of it," cried Mother Chattox, slightly raising herself as she spoke. "Kill her, or she will 'scape you."

When Nicholas came up with the old hag, both Sir Ralph Assheton and Roger Nowell put several questions to her, but she refused to answer their interrogations; and, horrified by her blasphemies and imprecations, they caused her to be removed to a short distance, while a consultation was held as to the course to be pursued.

"We have made half a dozen of these miscreants prisoners," said Roger Nowell, "and the whole of them had better be taken to Whalley, where they can be safely confined in the old dungeons of the Abbey, and after their examination on the morrow can be removed to Lancaster Castle."

"Be it so," replied Sir Ralph; "but must yon unfortunate

lady," he added, pointing to Mistress Nutter, "be taken with them?"

"Assuredly," replied Nowell. "We can make no distinction among such offenders; or, if there are any degrees in guilt, hers is of the highest class."

"You had better take leave of your daughter," said Sir Ralph to Mistress Nutter.

"I thank you for the hint," replied the lady. "Farewell, dear Alizon," she added, straining her to her bosom. "We must part for some time. Once more before I quit this world, in which I have played so wicked a part, I would fain look upon you—fain bless you, if I have the power—but this must be at the last, when my trials are wellnigh over, and when all is about to close upon me!"

"Oh! must it be thus?" exclaimed Alizon, in a voice half suffocated by emotion.

"It must," replied her mother. "Do not attempt to shake my resolution, my sweet child—do not weep for me. Amidst all the terrors that surround me, I am happier now than I have been for years. I shall strive to work out my redemption by prayers."

"And you will succeed!" cried Alizon.

"Not so!" shrieked Mother Demdike; "the Fiend will have his own. She is bound to him by a compact which nought can annul."

"I should like to see the instrument," said Potts. "I might give a legal opinion upon it. Perhaps it might be avoided; and in any case its production in court would have an admirable effect. I think I see the counsel examining it, and hear the judges calling for it to be placed before them. His infernal Majesty's signature must be a curiosity in its way. Our gracious and sagacious monarch would delight in it."

"Peace!" exclaimed Nicholas; "and take care," he cried, "that no further interruptions are offered by that infernal hag. Have you done, madam?" he added to Mistress Nutter, who still remained with her daughter folded in her arms.

"Not yet," replied the lady. "Oh! what happiness I have thrown away! What anguish—what remorse brought upon myself by the evil life I have led! As I gaze on this fair face, and think it might long, long have brightened my dark and desolate life with its sunshine—as I think upon all this, my fortitude wellnigh deserts me, and I have need of support from on high to carry me through my trial. But I fear it will be denied me. Nicholas Assheton, you have the deed of the gift of Rough Lee in your possession. Henceforth Alizon is mistress of the mansion and domains."

"Provided always they are not forfeited to the crown, which I apprehend will be the case," suggested Potts.

"I will take care she is put in possession of them," said Nicholas.

"As to you, Richard," continued Mistress Nutter, "the time may come when your devotion to my daughter may be rewarded, and I could not bestow a greater boon upon you than by giving you her hand. It may be well I should give my consent now, and, if no other obstacle should arise to the union, may she be yours, and happiness I am sure will attend you!"

Overpowered by conflicting emotions, Alizon hid her face in her mother's bosom, and Richard, who was almost equally overcome, was about to reply, when Mother Demdike broke upon them.

"They will never be united!" she screamed. "Never! I have said it, and my words will come true. Think'st thou a witch like thee can bless an union, Alice Nutter? Thy blessings are curses, thy wishes disappointments and despair. Thriftless love shall be Alizon's, and the grave shall be her bridal bed. The witch's daughter shall share the witch's fate."

These boding words produced a terrible effect upon the hearers.

"Heed her not, my sweet child—she speaks falsely," said Mistress Nutter, endeavouring to re-assure her daughter; but the tone in which the words were uttered showed that she herself was greatly alarmed.

"I have cursed them both, and I will curse them again," yelled Mother Demdike.

"Away with the old screech-owl," cried Nicholas. "Take her to the beacon, and, if she continues troublesome, hurl her into the flame."

And, notwithstanding the hag's struggles and imprecations, she was removed.

"Whatever may betide, Alizon," cried Richard, "my life shall be devoted to you; and, if you should not be mine, I will have no other bride. With your permission, madam," he added, to Mistress Nutter, "I will take your daughter to Middleton, where she will find companionship and solace, I trust, in the attentions of my sister, who has the strongest affection for her."

"I could wish nothing better," replied the lady, "and now to put an end to this harrowing scene. Farewell, my child. Take her, Richard, take her!" she cried, as she disengaged herself from the relaxing embrace of her daughter. "Now, Master Nowell, I am ready."

"It is well, madam," he replied. "You will join the other prisoners, and we will set forth."

But at this juncture a terrific shriek was heard, which drew all eyes towards the beacon.

When Mother Demdike had been removed, in accordance with the squire's directions, her conduct became more violent and outrageous than ever, and those who had charge of her threatened, if she did not desist, to carry out the full instructions they had received, and cast her into the flames. The old hag defied them, and incensed them to such a degree by her violence and blasphemies, that they carried her to the very edge of the fire.

At this moment the figure of a monk, in mouldering white habiliments, came from behind the beacon, and stood beside the old hag. He slowly raised his hood, and disclosed features that looked like those of the dead.

"Thy hour is come, accursed woman!" cried the phantom, in thrilling accents. "Thy term on earth is ended, and thou shalt be delivered to unquenchable fire. The curse of Paslew is fulfilled upon thee, and will be fulfilled upon all thy viperous brood."

"Art thou the abbot's shade?" demanded the hag.

"I am thy implacable enemy," replied the phantom. "Thy judgment and thy punishment are committed to me. To the flames with her!"

Such was the awe inspired by the monk, and such the authority of his tones and gesture, that the command was unhesitatingly obeyed, and the witch was cast, shrieking, into the fire.

She was instantly swallowed up as in a gulf of flame, which raged, and roared, and shot up in a hundred lambent points, as if exulting in its prey.

The wretched creature was seen for a moment to rise up in it in extremity of anguish, with arms extended, and uttering a dreadful yell, but the flames wreathed round her, and she sank for ever.

When those who had assisted at this fearful execution looked around for the mysterious being who had commanded it, they could nowhere behold him.

Then was heard a laugh of gratified hate—such a laugh as only a demon, or one bound to a demon, can utter—and the appalled listeners looked around, and beheld Mother Chattox standing behind them.

"My rival is gone!" cried the hag. "I have seen the last of her. She is burnt—ah! ah!"

Further triumph was not allowed her. With one accord, and as if prompted by an irresistible impulse, the men rushed upon her, seized her, and cast her into the fire.

Her wild laughter was heard for a moment above the roaring of the flames, and then ceased altogether.

Again the flame shot high in air, again roared and raged, again broke into a multitude of lambent points, after which it suddenly expired.

All was darkness on the summit of Pendle Hill.

And in silence and in gloom scarcely more profound than that weighing in every breast, the melancholy troop pursued its way to Whalley.

END OF THE SECOND BOOK.

THE LANCASHIRE WITCHES.

BOOK THE THIRD.

Hoghton Tower.

CHAPTER I.—DOWNHAM MANOR-HOUSE.

On a lovely morning, about the middle of July, in the same year as the events previously narrated, Nicholas Assheton, always astir with the lark, issued from his own dwelling, and sauntered across the smooth lawn in front of it. The green eminence on which he stood was sheltered on the right by a grove of sycamores, forming the boundary of the park, and sloped down into a valley threaded by a small clear stream, whose murmuring, as it danced over its pebbly bed, distinctly reached his ear in the stillness of early day. On the left, partly in the valley, and partly on the side of the acclivity on which the hall was situated, nestled the little village whose inhabitants owned Nicholas as lord; and, to judge from their habitations, they had reason to rejoice in their master; for certainly there was a cheerful air about Downham which the neighbouring hamlets, especially those in Pendle Forest, sadly wanted.

On the left of the mansion, and only separated from it by the garden walls, stood the church, a venerable structure, dating back to a period more remote even than Whalley Abbey. From the churchyard a view, almost similar to that enjoyed by the squire, was obtained, though partially interrupted by the thick rounded foliage of a large tree growing beneath it; and many a traveller who came that way lingered within the hallowed precincts to contemplate the prospect. At the foot of the hill was a small stone bridge crossing the stream.

Across the road, and scarce thirty paces from the church-gate, stood a little alehouse, whose comfortable fireside nook and good liquors were not disdained by the squire. In fact, to his shame be it spoken, he was quite as often to be found there of an evening as at the hall. This had more particularly been the case since the house was tenanted by Richard Baldwyn, who having given up the mill at Rough Lee, and taken to wife Bess Whitaker of Goldshaw Booth, had removed with her to Downham, where he now flourished under the special protection of the squire.

Bess had lost none of her old habits of command, and it must be confessed that poor Richard played a very secondary part in the establishment. Nicholas, as may be supposed, was permitted considerable licence by her, but even he had limits, which she took good care he should not exceed.

The Downham domains were well cultivated; the line of demarcation between them and the heathy wastes adjoining, being clearly traced out, and you had only to follow the course of the brook to see at a glance where the purlieus of the forest ended, and where Nicholas Assheton's property commenced: the one being a dreary moor, with here and there a thicket upon it, but more frequently a dangerous morass, covered with sulphur-coloured moss; and the other consisting of green meadows, bordered in most instances by magnificent timber. The contrast, however, was not without its charm; and while the sterile wastes set off the fair and fertile fields around them, and enhanced their beauty, they offered a wide, uninterrupted expanse, over which the eye could range at will.

On the further side of the valley, and immediately opposite the lawn whereon Nicholas stood, the ground gradually arose, until it reached the foot of Pendle Hill, which here assuming its most majestic aspect, constituted the grand and peculiar feature of the scene. Nowhere could the lordly eminence be seen to the same advantage as from this point, and Nicholas contemplated it with feelings of rapture, which no familiarity could diminish. The sun shone brightly upon its rounded summit, and upon its seamy sides, revealing all its rifts and ridges; adding depth of tint to its dusky soil, laid bare in places by the winter torrents; lending new beauty to its purple heath, and making its grey sod glow as with fire. So exhilarating was the prospect, that Nicholas felt half tempted to cross the valley and scale the hill before breaking his fast; but other feelings checked him, and he turned towards the right. Here, beyond a paddock and some outbuildings, lay the park, small in extent, but beautifully diversified, well stocked with deer, and boasting much noble timber. In the midst was an exquisite knoll, which, besides commanding a fine view of Pendle Hill, Downham, and all the adjacent country, brought within its scope, on the one hand, the ancient castle of Clithero and the heights overlooking Whalley; and, on the other, the lovely and extensive vale through which the Ribble wandered. This, also, was a favourite point of view with the squire, and he had some idea of walking towards it, when he was arrested by a person who came from the house, and who shouted to him, hoarsely but blithely, to stay.

The new-comer was a man of middle age, with a skin almost as tawny as a gipsy's, a hooked nose, black beetling brows, and eyes so strangely set in his head, that they communicated a sinister expression to his countenance. He possessed a burly frame, square, and somewhat heavy, though not so much so as to impede his activity. In deportment and stature, though not in feature, he resembled the squire himself; and the likeness was heightened by his habiliments being part of Nicholas's old wardrobe, the doublet and hose, and even the green hat and boots, being those in which Nicholas made his first appearance in this history. The personage who thus condescended to be fed and clothed at the squire's expense, and who filled a situation something between guest and menial, without receiving the precise attention of the one or the wages of the other, but who made himself so useful to Nicholas that he could not dispense with him—neither, perhaps, would he have been shaken off, even if it had been desired—was named Lawrence Fogg, an entire stranger to the country, whom Nicholas had picked up at Colne, aud whom he had invited to Downham for a few weeks' hunting, and had never been able to get rid of him since.

Lawrence Fogg liked his quarters immensely, and determined to remain in them; and as a means to so desirable an end, he studied all the squire's weak points and peculiarities, and these not being very difficult to be understood, he soon mastered them, and mastered the squire into the bargain, but without allowing his success to become manifest. Nicholas was delighted to find one with tastes so congenial to his own, who was so willing to hunt or fish with him—who could train a hawk as well as Phil Royle, the falconer—diet a fighting-cock as well as Tom Shaw, the cock-master —enter a hound better than Charlie Crouch, the old huntsman—shoot with the long-bow further than any one except himself, and was willing to toss off a pot with him, or sing a merry stave whenever he felt inclined. Such a companion was invaluable, and Nicholas congratulated himself upon the discovery, especially when he found Lawrence Fogg not unwilling to undertake some delicate commissions for him, which he could not well execute himself, and which he was unwilling should reach Mistress Assheton's ears. These were managed with equal adroitness and caution. About the same time, too, Nicholas finding money scarce, and, not liking to borrow it in person, delegated Fogg, and sent him round to his friends to ask for a loan; but, in this instance, the mission was attended with very indifferent success, for not one of them would lend him so small a sum as thirty pounds, all averring they stood in need of it quite as much as himself. Though somewhat inconvenienced by their refusal, Nicholas bore the disappointment with his customary equanimity, and made merry with his friend as if nothing had happened. Fogg showed an equal accommodating spirit in all religious observances, and, though much against his inclination, attended morning discourses and lectures with his patron, and even made an attempt at psalm-singing; but on one occasion, missing the tune and coming in with a bacchanalian chorus, he was severely rebuked by the minister, and enjoined to keep silence in future.

Such was the friendly relation subsisting between the parties when they met together on the lawn on the morning in question.

"Well, Fogg," cried Nicholas, after exchanging salutations with his friend, "what say you to hunting the otter in the Ribble after breakfast? 'Tis a rare day for the sport, and the hounds are in excellent order. There is an old dam and her litter whom we must kill, for she has been playing the very devil with the fish for a space of more than two miles; and if we let her off for another week, we shall have neither salmon, trout, nor umber, as all will have passed down the maws of her voracious brood."

"And that would be a pity, in good sooth, squire," replied Fogg; "for there are no fish like those of the Ribble. Nothing I should prefer to the sport you promise; but I thought you had other business for me to-day? Another attempt to borrow money—eh?"

"Ay, from my cousin, Dick Assheton," rejoined Nicholas; "he will lend me the thirty pounds, I am quite sure. But you had better defer the visit till to-morrow, when his father, Sir Richard, will be at Whalley, and when you can have him to yourself. Dick will not say you nay, depend on't; he is too good a fellow for that. A murrain on those close-fisted curmudgeons, Roger Nowell, Nicholas Townley, and Tom Whitaker. They ought to be delighted to oblige me."

"But they declare they have no money," said Fogg.

"No money!—pshaw!" exclaimed Nicholas; "an idle excuse. They have chests full. Would I had all Roger Nowell's gold, I should not require another supply for years. But, 'sdeath! I will not trouble myself for a paltry thirty pounds."

"If I might venture to suggest, squire, while you are about it, I would ask for a hundred pounds, or even two or three hundred," said Fogg. "Your friends will think all the better of you, and feel more satisfied you intend to repay them."

"Do you think so?" cried Nicholas. "Then, by Plutus, it shall be three hundred pounds—three hundred at interest. Dick will have to borrow the amount to lend it to me; but, no matter, he will easily obtain it. Harkye, Fogg, while you are at Middleton, endeavour to ascertain whether any thing has been arranged about the marriage of a certain young lady to a certain young gentleman. I am curious to know the precise state of affairs in that quarter."

"I will arrive at the truth, if possible, squire," replied Fogg; "but I should scarcely think Sir Richard would assent to his son's union with the daughter of a notorious witch."

"Sir Richard's son is scarcely likely to ask Sir Richard's consent," said Nicholas; "and as to Mistress Nutter, though heavy charges have been brought against her, nothing has been proved, for you know she escaped, or rather was rescued, on her way to Lancaster Castle."

"I am fully aware of it, squire," replied Fogg; "and I more

than suspect a worthy friend of mine had a hand in her deliverance, and could tell where to find her if needful. But that is neither here nor there. The lady is quite innocent, I dare say. Indeed, I am quite sure of it, since you espouse her cause so warmly. But the world is malicious, and strange things are reported of her."

"Heed not the world, Fogg," rejoined Nicholas. "The world speaks well of no man, be his deserts what they may. The world says that I waste my estate in wine, women, and horseflesh—that I spend time in pleasures which might be profitably employed—that I neglect my wife, forget my religious observances, am on horseback when I should be afoot, at the alehouse when I should be at home, at a marriage when I should be at a funeral, shooting when I should be keeping my books—in short, it has not a good word to say for me. And as for thee, Fogg, it says thou art an idle, good-for-nothing fellow; or, if thou art good for aught, it is only for something that leads to evil. It says thou drinkest prodigiously, liest confoundedly, and swearest most profanely; that thou art ever more ready to go to the alehouse than to church, and that none of the girls can 'scape thee. Nay, the slanderers even go so far as to assert thou wouldst not hesitate to say, 'Stand and deliver!' a true man on the highway. That is what the world says of thee. But, hang it! never look chapfallen, man. Let us go to the stables, and then we will in to breakfast; after which we will proceed to the Ribble, and spear the old otter."

A fine old manorial residence was Downham, and beautifully situated, as has been shown, on a woody eminence to the north of Pendle Hill. It was of great antiquity, and first came into the possession of the Assheton family in 1558. Considerable additions had been made to it by its present owner, Nicholas, and the outlay necessarily required, combined with his lavish expenditure, had contributed to embarrass him. The stables were large, and full of horses; the kennels on the same scale, and equally well supplied with hounds, and there was a princely retinue of servants in the yard—grooms, keepers, falconers, huntsmen, and their assistants—to say nothing of their fellows within doors. In short, if it had been your fortune to accompany the squire and his friend round the premises—if you had walked through the stables and counted the horses—if you had viewed the kennels and examined the various hounds—the great Lancashire dogs, tall, shaggy, and heavy, a race now extinct; the Worcestershire hounds, then also in much repute; the greyhounds, the harriers, the beagles, the lurchers, and, lastly, the verminers, or, as we should call them, the terriers,—if you had seen all these, you would not have wondered that money was scarce with him. Still further would your surprise at such a consequence have diminished if you had gone on to the falconry, and seen on the perches the goshawk and her tercel, the sparrowhawk and her musket, under the care of the ostringer; and further on the falcon-gentle, the gerfalcon, the lanner, the merlin, and the hobby, all of which were attended to by the head falconer. It wonld have done you good to hear Nicholas inquiring from his men if they had "set out their birds that morning, and weathered them;" if they had mummy powder in readiness, then esteemed a sovereign remedy; if the lures, hoods, jesses, buets, and all other needful furniture, were in good order; and if the meat were sweet and wholesome. You might next have followed him to the pens where the fighting cocks were kept, and where you would have found another source of expense in the cock-master, Tom Shaw—a knave who not only got high wages from his master, but understood so well the dieting of his birds that he could make them win or lose a battle as he thought proper. Here, again, Nicholas had much to say, and was in raptures with one cock, which he told Fogg he would back to any amount, utterly unconscious of a significant look that passed between his friend and the cock-master.

"Look at him," cried the squire; "how proud and erect he stands! His head is as small as that of a sparrowhawk, his eye large and quick, his body thick, his leg strong in the beam, and his spurs long, rough, and sharp. That is the bird for me. I will take him over to the cockpit at Prescot next week, and match him against any bird Sir John Talbot, or my cousin Braddyll, can bring."

"And yo'n win, squoire," replied the cock-master; "ey ha' been feedin' him these five weeks, so he'll be i' rare condition then, and winna fail yo. Yo may lay what yo loike upon him," he added, with a sly wink at Fogg.

"You may win the thirty pounds you want," observed the latter, in a low tone to the squire.

"Or, mayhap, lose it," replied Nicholas. "I shall not risk so much, unless I get the three hundred from Dick Assheton. I have been unlucky of late. You beat me constantly at tables now, Fogg, and when I first knew you this was not wont to be the case. Nay, never make any excuses, man; you cannot help it. Let us in to breakfast."

With this, he proceeded towards the house, followed by Fogg and a couple of large Lancashire hounds, and, entering at the back of the premises, made his way through the scullery into the kitchen. Here there were plentiful evidences of the hospitality, not to say profusion, reigning throughout the mansion. An open door showed a larder stocked with all kinds of provisions, and before the fire joints of meat and poultry were roasting. Pies were baking in the oven; and over the flames, in the chimney, was suspended a black pot large enough for a witch's caldron. The cook was busied in preparing for the gridiron some freshly-caught trout, intended for the squire's own breakfast; and a kitchen-maid was toasting oatcakes, of which there was a large supply in the bread-flake depending from the ceiling.

Casting a look around, and exchanging a few words with the cook, Nicholas moved on, still followed by Fogg and the hounds, and, tracking a long stone passage, entered the great hall. Here the same disorder and irregularity prevailed as in his own character and conduct. All was litter and confusion. Around the walls were hung breastplates and buff-coats, morions, shields, and two-handed swords; but they were half hidden by fishing-nets, fowling-nets, dogs' collars, saddles and bridles, housings, cross-bows, long-bows, quivers, baldricks, horns, spears, guns, and every other implement then used in the sports of the river or the field. The floor was in an equal state of disorder. The rushes were filled with half-gnawed bones, brought thither by the hounds; and in one corner, on a mat, was a favourite spaniel and her whelps. The squire however was, happily, insensible to the condition of the chamber, and looked around it with an air of satisfaction, as if he thought it the perfection of comfort.

A table was spread for breakfast, near a window looking out upon the lawn, and two covers only were laid, for Mistress Nicholas Assheton did not make her appearance at this early hour. And now was exhibited one of those strange contradictions of which the squire's character was composed. Kneeling down by the side of the table, and without noticing the mocking expression of Fogg's countenance as he followed his example, Nicholas prayed loudly and fervently for upwards of ten minutes, after which he arose and gave a shout which proved that his lungs were unimpaired, and not only roused the whole house, but set all the dogs barking.

Presently a couple of serving-men answered this lusty summons, and the table was covered with good and substantial dishes, which he and his companion attacked with a vigour such as only the most valiant trencherman can display. Already has it been remarked that a breakfast at the period in question resembled a modern dinner; and better proof could not have been afforded of the correctness of the description than the meal under discussion, which comprised fish, flesh, and fowl, boiled, broiled, and roast, together with strong ale and sack. After an hour thus agreeably employed, and while they were still seated, though breakfast had pretty nearly come to an end, a serving-man entered, announcing Master Richard Sherborne of Dunnow. The squire instantly sprang to his feet, and hastened to welcome his brother-in-law.

"Ah! good-day to you, Dick," he cried, shaking him heartily by the hand; "what happy chance brings you here so early? But first sit down and eat—eat, and talk afterwards. Here, Roger, Harry, bring another platter and napkin, and let us have more broiled trout and a cold capon, a pasty, or whatever you can find in the larder. Try some of this gammon meanwhile, Dick. It will help down a can of ale. And now what brings thee hither, lad? Pressing business, no doubt. Thou mayest speak before Fogg. I have no secrets from him. He is my second self."

"I have no secrets to divulge, Nicholas," replied Sherborne, "and I will tell you at once what I am come about. Have you heard that the King is about to visit Hoghton Tower in August?"

"No; this is news to me," replied Nicholas; "does your business relate to his visit?"

"It does," replied Sherborne. "Last night a messenger came to me from Sir Richard Hoghton, entreating me to move you to do him the favour and courtesy to attend him at the King's coming, and wear his livery."

"I wear his livery!" exclaimed Nicholas, indignantly. "'Sdeath! what do you take me for, cousin Dick?"

"For a right good fellow, who I am sure will comply with his friend's request, especially when he finds there is no sort of degradation in it," replied Sherborne. "Why, I shall wear Sir Richard's cloth, and so will several others of our friends. There will be rare doings at Hoghton—masquings, mummings, and all sorts of revels, besides hunting, shooting, racing, wrestling, and the devil knows what. You may feast and carouse to your heart's content. The Dukes of Buckingham and Richmond will be there, and the Earls of Nottingham and Pembroke, and Sir Gilbert Hoghton, the King's great favourite, who married the Duchess of Buckingham's sister. Besides these, you will have all the beauty of Lancashire. I would not miss the sight for thirty pounds."

"Thirty pounds!" echoed Nicholas, as if struck with a sudden thought. "Do you think Sir Thomas Hoghton would lend me that sum if I consent to wear his cloth, and attend him?"

"I have no doubt of it," replied Sherborne; "and if he won't, I will."

"Then I will put my pride in my pocket, and go," said Nicholas. "And now, Dick, dispatch your breakfast as quickly as you can, and then I will take you to the Ribble, and show you some sport with an otter."

Sherborne was not long in concluding his repast, and having received an otter spear from the squire, who had already provided himself and Fogg with like weapons, all three adjourned to the kennels, where they found the old huntsman, Charlie Crouch, awaiting them, attended by four stout varlets, armed with forked staves, meant for the double purpose of beating the river's banks, and striking the poor beast they were about to hunt, and each man having a couple of hounds, well entered for the chase, in leash. Old Crouch was a thin, grey-bearded fellow, but possessed of a tough, muscular frame, which served him quite as well in the long run as the younger, and apparently more vigorous, limbs of his assistants. His cheek was hale, and his eye still bright and quick, and a certain fierceness was imparted to his countenance by a large aquiline nose. He was attired in a greasy leathern jerkin, tight hose of the same material, and had a bugle suspended from his neck, and a sharp hunting-knife thrust into his girdle. In his hand he bore a spear like his master, and was followed by a grey old lurcher, who, though wanting an ear and an eye, and disfigured by sundry scars on throat and back, was hardy, untiring, and sagacious. This ancient dog was called Grip, from his tenacity in holding any thing he set his teeth upon, and he and Crouch were inseparable.

Great was the clamour occasioned by the squire's appearance in the yard. The coupled hounds gave tongue at once, and sang out most melodiously, and all the other dogs within the kennels, or roaming at will about the yard, joined the concert. After much swearing, cracking of whips, and yelping consequent upon the cracking, silence was in some degree restored, and a consultation was then held between Nicholas and Crouch as to where their steps should first be bent. The old huntsman was for drawing the river near a place called Bean Hill Wood, as the trees thereabouts, growing close to the water's edge, it was pretty certain the otter would have her couch amid the roots of some of them. This was objected to by one of the varlets, who declared that the beast lodged in a hollow tree, standing on a bank nearly a mile higher up the stream, and close by the point of junction between Swanside Beck and the Ribble. He was certain of the fact, he avouched, because he had noticed her marks on the moist grass near the tree.

"Hoo goes theere to fish, mon?" cried Crouch, "for it is the natur o' the wary varmint to feed at a distance fro' her lodgin; boh ey'm sure we shan leet on her among the roots o' them big trees o'erhanging th' river near Bean Hill Wood, an if the squire 'll tay my advice, he'n go theere first."

"I put myself entirely under your guidance, Crouch," said Nicholas.

"An yo'n be aw reet, sir," replied the huntsman; "we'n beat the bonks weel, an two o' these chaps shan go up the stream, an two down, one o' one side, and one o' t'other; an i' that manner hoo canna escape us, fo' Grip can swim an dive os weel as onny otter i' aw Englondshiar, an he'n be efter her an her litter the moment they tak to t' wotur. Some folk, os maybe yo ha' seen, squoire, tak howd on a cord by both eends, an droppin it into t' river, draw it slowly along, so that they can tell by th' jerk when th' otter touches it; boh this is an onsartin method, an is nowt like Grip's plan, for wherever yo see him swimmin, t'other beast yo may be sure is nah far ahead."

"A brave dog, but confoundedly ugly!" exclaimed the squire, regarding the old one-eared, one-eyed lurcher with mingled admiration and disgust; "and now, that all is arranged, let us be off."

Accordingly they quitted the court-yard, and, shaping their course in the direction indicated by the huntsman, entered the park, and proceeded along a glade, checkered by the early sunbeams. Here the noise they made in their progress speedily disturbed a herd of deer browsing beneath the trees, and, as the dappled foresters darted off to a thicker covert, great difficulty was experienced by the varlets in restraining the hounds, who struggled eagerly to follow them, and made the welkin resound with their baying.

"Yonder is a tall fellow," cried Nicholas, pointing out a noble buck to Crouch; "I must kill him next week, for I want to send a haunch of venison to Middleton, and another to Whalley Abbey for Sir Ralph."

"Better hunt him, squoire," said Crouch; "he will gi' ye good sport."

Soon after this they attained an eminence, where a charming sweep of country opened upon them, including the finest part of Ribblesdale, with its richly-wooded plains, and the swift and beautiful river from which it derived its name. The view was enchanting, and the squire and his companions paused for a moment to contemplate it, and then, stepping gleefully forward, made their way over the elastic turf towards a small thicket skirting the park. All were in high spirits, for the freshness and beauty of the morning had not been without effect, and the squire's tongue kept pace with his legs as he strode briskly along; but as they entered the thicket in question, and caught sight of the river through the trees, the old huntsman enjoined silence, and he was obliged to put a check upon his loquacity.

When within a bowshot from the water, the party came to a halt, and two of the men were directed by Crouch to cross the stream at different points, and then commence beating the banks, while the other two were ordered to pursue a like course, but to keep on the near side of the river. The hounds were next uncoupled, and the men set off to execute the orders they had received, and soon afterwards the crashing of branches, and the splashing of water, accompanied by the deep baying of the hounds, told they were at work.

Meanwhile, Nicholas and the others had not remained idle. As the varlets struck off in different directions, they went straight on, and forcing their way through the brushwood, came to a high bank overlooking the Ribble, on the top of which grew three or four large trees, whose roots, laid bare on the further side by the swollen currents of winter, formed a convenient resting-place for the fish-loving creature they hoped to surprise. Receiving a hint from Crouch to make for the central tree, Nicholas grasped his spear, and sprang forward; but, quick as he was, he was too late, though he saw enough to convince him that the crafty old huntsman had been correct in his judgment; for a dark, slimy object dropped from out the roots of the tree beneath him, and glided into the water as swiftly and as noiselessly as if its skin had been oiled. A few bubbles rose to the surface of the water, but these were all the indications marking the course of the wondrous diver.

But other eyes, sharper than those of Nicholas, were on the watch, and the old huntsman shouted out, "There heo goes, Grip—efter her, lad, efter her!" The words were scarcely uttered when the dog sprang from the top of the bank and sank under the water. For some seconds no trace could be observed of either animal, and then the shaggy nose of the lurcher was seen nearly fifty yards higher up the river, and after sniffing around for a moment, and fixing his single eye on his master, who was standing on the bank, and encouraging him with his voice and gesture, he dived again.

"Station yourselves on the bank, fifty paces apart," cried Crouch; "run, run, or yo'n be too late, an' strike os quick os leet if yo've a chance. Stay wheere you are, squoire," he added. to Nicholas. "Yo canna be better placed."

All was now animation and excitement. Perceiving from the noise that the otter had been found, the four varlets hastened towards the scene of action, and, by their shouts and the clatter of their staves, contributed greatly to its spirit. Two were on one side of the stream, and two on the other, and up to this moment the hounds were similarly separated; but now most of them had taken to the water, some swimming about, others standing up to the middle in the shallower part of the current, watching with keen gaze for the appearance of their anticipated victim.

Having descended the bank, Nicholas had so placed himself among the huge twisted roots of the tree, that if the otter, alarmed by the presence of so many foes, and unable to escape either up or down the river, should return to her couch, he made certain of striking her. At first there seemed little chance of such an occurrence, for Fogg, who had gone a hundred yards higher up, suddenly dashed into the stream, and, plunging his spear into the mud, cried out that he had hit the beast; but the next moment, when he drew the weapon forth, and exhibited a large rat which he had transfixed, his mistake excited much merriment.

Old Crouch, meantime, did not suffer his attention to be drawn from his dog. Every now and then he saw him come to the surface to breathe, but as he kept within a short distance, though rising at different points, the old huntsman felt certain the otter had not got away, and, having the utmost reliance upon Grip's perseverance and sagacity, he felt confident he would bring the quarry to him if the thing were possible. The varlets kept up an incessant clatter, beating the water with their staves, and casting large stones into it, while the hounds bayed furiously, so that the poor fugitive was turned on whichever side she attempted a retreat.

While this was going on, Nicholas was cautioned by the huntsman to look out, and scarcely had the admonition reached him than the sleek shining body of the otter emerged from the water, and wreathed itself among the roots. The squire instantly dealt a blow which he expected to prove fatal, but his mortification was excessive when he found he had driven the spear-head so deeply into the tree that he could scarcely disengage it, while an almost noiseless plunge told that his prey had escaped. Almost at the same moment that the poor hunted beast had sought its old lodging, the untiring lurcher had appeared at the edge of the bank, and, as the former again went down, he dived likewise.

Secretly laughing at the squire's failure, the old huntsman prepared to take advantage of a similar opportunity if it should present itself, and with this view ensconced himself behind a pollard willow, which stood close beside the stream, and whence he could watch closely all that passed, without being exposed to view. The prudence of the step was soon manifest. After the lapse of a few seconds, during which neither dog nor otter had risen to breathe, a slight, very slight, undulation was perceptible on the surface of the water. Crouch's grasp tightened upon his staff—he waited another moment—then dashed forward, struck down his spear, and raised it aloft, with the poor otter transfixed and writhing upon its point.

Loudly and exultingly did the old man shout at his triumph, and loudly were his vociferations answered by the others. All flew to the spot where he was standing, and the hounds, gathering round him, yelled furiously at the otter, and showed every disposition to tear her in pieces, if they could get at her. Kicking the noisiest and fiercest of them out of the way, Crouch approached the river's brink, and lowered the spear-head till it came within reach of his favourite Grip, who had not yet come out of the water, but stood within his depth, with his one red eye fixed on the enemy he had so hotly pursued, and fully expecting his reward. It now came; his sharp teeth instantly met in the otter's throat, and when Crouch swung them both in the air, he still maintained his hold, showing how well he deserved his name, nor could he be disengaged until long after the sufferings of the tortured animal had ceased.

To say that Nicholas was neither chagrined at his ill success, nor jealous of the old huntsman's superior skill, would be to affirm an untruth; but he put the best face he could upon the matter, and praised Grip very highly, alleging that the whole merit of the hunt rested with him. Old Crouch let him go on, and when he had done, quietly observed that the otter they had destroyed was not the one they came in search of, as they had seen nothing of her litter; and that, most likely, the beast that had done so much mischief had her lodging in the hollow tree near the Swanside Beck, as described by the varlet, and he wished to know whether the squire would like to go and hunt her. Nicholas replied that he was quite willing to do so, and hoped he should have better luck on the second occasion; and with this they set forward again, taking their way along the side of the stream, beating the banks as they went, but without rousing any thing beyond an occasional water-rat, which was killed almost as soon as found by Grip.

Somehow or other, without any one being aware what led to it, the conversation fell upon the two old witches, Mothers Demdike and Chattox, and the strange manner in which their career had terminated on the summit of Pendle Hill—if, indeed, it could be said to have terminated, when their spirits were reported to haunt the spot, and might be seen, it was asserted, at midnight, flitting round the beacon, and shrieking dismally. The restless shades were pursued, it was added, by the figure of a monk in white mouldering robes, supposed to be the ghost of Paslew. It was difficult to understand how these apparitions could be witnessed, since no one, even for a reward, could be prevailed upon to ascend Pendle Hill after nightfall; but the shepherds affirmed they had seen them from below, and that was testimony sufficient to shake the most sceptical. One singular circumstance was mentioned, which must not be passed by without notice; and this was, that when the cinders of the extinct beacon-fire came to be examined, no remains whatever of the two hags could be discovered, though the ashes were carefully sifted, and it was quite certain that the flames had expired long before their bodies could be consumed. The explanation attempted for this marvel was, that Satan had carried them off while yet living, to finish their combustion in a still more fiery region.

Mention of Mother Demdike naturally led to her grandson, Jem Device, who, having escaped in a remarkable manner on the night in question, notwithstanding the hue and cry made after him, had not, as yet, been captured, though he had been occasionally seen at night, and under peculiar circumstances, by various individuals, and amongst others by old Crouch, who, however, declared he had been unable to lay hands upon him.

Allusion was then made to Mistress Nutter, whereupon it was observed that the squire changed the conversation quickly; while sundry sly winks and shrugs were exchanged among the varlets of the kennel, seeming to intimate that they knew more about the matter than they cared to admit. Nothing more, however, was elicited than that the escort conducting her to Lancaster Castle, together with the other witches, after their examination before the magistrates at Whalley, and committal, had been attacked, while it was passing through a woody defile in Bowland Forest, by a party of men in the garb of foresters, and the lady set free

Nor had she been heard of since. What made this rescue the more extraordinary was, that none of the other witches were liberated at the same time, but some of them who seemed disposed to take advantage of the favourable interposition, and endeavoured to get away, were brought back by the foresters to the officers of justice; thus clearly proving that the attempt was solely made on Mistress Nutter's account, and must have been undertaken by her friends. Nothing, it was asserted, could equal the rage and mortification of Roger Nowell and Potts, on learning that their chief prey had thus escaped them; and by their directions, for more than a week, the strictest search was made for the fugitive throughout the neighbourhood, but without effect—no clue could be discovered to her retreat. Suspicion naturally fell upon the two Asshetons, Nicholas and Richard, and Roger Nowell roundly taxed them with contriving and executing the enterprise in person; while Potts told them they were guilty of misprision of felony, and threatened them with imprisonment for life, forfeiture of goods and of rents, for the offence; but as the charge could not be proved against them, notwithstanding all the efforts of the magistrate and attorney, it fell to the ground; and Master Potts, full of chagrin at this unexpected and vexatious termination of the affair, returned to London, and settled himself in his chambers in Chancery Lane. His duties, however, as clerk of the court, would necessarily call him to Lancaster in August, when the assizes commenced, and when he would assist at the trials of such of the witches as were still in durance.

From Mother Demdike it was natural that the conversation should turn to her weird retreat, Malkin Tower; and Richard Sherborne expressed his surprise that the unhallowed structure should be suffered to remain standing after her removal. Nicholas said he was equally anxious with his brother-in-law for its demolition, but it was not so easily to be accomplished as it might appear; for the deserted structure was in such ill repute with the common folk, as well as every one else, that no one dared approach it, even in the daytime. A boggart, it was said, had taken possession of its vaults, and scared away all who ventured near it; sometimes showing himself in one frightful shape, and sometimes in another; now as a monstrous goat, now as an equally monstrous cat, uttering fearful cries, glaring with fiery eyes from out of the windows, or appearing in all his terror on the summit of the tower. Moreover, the haunted structure was frequently lighted up at dead of night, strains of unearthly music were heard resounding from it, and wild figures were seen flitting past the windows, as if engaged in dancing and revelry; so that it appeared that no alteration for the better had taken place there, and that things were still quite as improperly conducted now, as they had been in the time of Mother Demdike, or in those of her predecessors, Isole de Heton and Blackburn, the robber. The common opinion was, that Satan and all his imps had taken up their abode in the tower, and, as they liked their quarters, led a jolly life there, dancing and drinking all night long, it would be useless at present to give them notice to quit, still less to attempt to pull down the house about their ears. Richard Sherborne heard this wondrous relation in silence, but with a look of incredulity; and when it was done he winked slily at his brother-in-law. A strange expression, half comical, half suspicious, might also have been observed on Fogg's countenance; and he narrowly watched the squire as the latter spoke.

"But with the disappearance of the malignant old hags who had so long infested the neighbourhood, had all mischief and calamity ceased, or were people as much afflicted as heretofore? Were there, in short, so many cases of witchcraft, real or supposed?" This was the question next addressed by Sherborne to Nicholas. The squire answered decidedly there were not. Since the burning of the two old beldames, and the imprisonment of the others, the whole district of Pendle had improved. All those who had been smitten with strange illnesses had recovered; and the inhabitants of the little village of Sabden, who had experienced the fullest effects of their malignity, were entirely free from sickness. And not only had they and their families suddenly regained health and strength, but all belonging to them had undergone a similar beneficial change. The kine that had lost their milk now yielded it abundantly; the lame horse halted no longer; the murrain ceased among the sheep; the pigs that had grown lean amidst abundance fattened rapidly; and though the farrows that had perished during the evil ascendency of the witches could not be brought back again, their place promised speedily to be supplied by others. The corn blighted early in the year had sprung forth anew, and the trees nipped in the bud were laden with fruit. In short, all was as fair and as flourishing as it had recently been the reverse. Amongst others, John Law, the pedlar, who had been deprived of the use of his limbs by the damnable arts of Mother Demdike, had marvellously recovered on the very night of her destruction, and was now as strong and as active as ever.

"Such happy results having followed the removal of the witches, it was to be hoped," Sherborne said, "that the riddance would be complete, and that none of the obnoxious brood would be left to inflict future miseries on their fellows. This could not be the case so long as James Device was allowed to go at large; nor while his mother, Elizabeth Device, a notorious witch, was suffered to escape with impunity. There was also Jennet, Elizabeth's daughter, a mischievous and ill-favoured little creature, who inherited all the ill qualities of her parents. These were the spawn of the old snake, and, until they were entirely exterminated, there could be no security against a recurrence of the evil. Again, there was Nance Redferne, old Chattox's grand-daughter, a comely woman enough, but a reputed witch, and an undoubted fabricator of clay images. She was still at liberty, though she ought to be with the rest in the dungeons of Lancaster Castle. It was useless to allege that with the destruction of the old hags all danger had ceased. Common prudence would keep the others quiet now; but the moment the storm passed over, they would resume their atrocious practices, and all would be as bad as ever. No, no! the tree must be utterly uprooted, or it would inevitably burst forth anew."

With these opinions Nicholas generally concurred; but he expressed some sympathy for Nance Redferne, whom he thought far too good-looking to be as wicked and malicious as represented. But however that might be, and however much he might desire to get rid of the family of the Devices, he feared such a step might be attended with danger to Alizon, and that she might in some way or other be implicated with them. This last remark he addressed in an under-tone to his brother-in-law. Sherborne did not at first feel any apprehension on that score, but, on reflection, he admitted that Nicholas was perhaps right; and though Alizon was now the recognised daughter of Mistress Nutter, yet her long and intimate connection with the Device family might operate to her prejudice, while her near relationship to an avowed witch would not tend to remove the unfavourable impression. Sherborne then went on to speak in the most rapturous terms of the beauty and goodness of the young girl who formed the subject of their conversation, and declared he was not in the least surprised that Richard Assheton was so much in love with her. And yet, he added, a most extraordinary change had taken place in her since the dreadful night on Pendle Hill, when her mother's guilt had been proclaimed, and when her arrest had taken place as an offender of the darkest dye. Alizon, he said, had lost none of her beauty, but her light and joyous expression of countenance had been supplanted by a look of profound sadness, which nothing could remove. Gentle and meek in her deportment, she seemed to look upon herself as under a ban, and as if she were unfit to associate with the rest of the world. In vain Richard Assheton and his sister endeavoured to remove this impression by the tenderest assiduities; in vain they sought to induce her to enter into amusements consistent with her years; she declined all society but their own, and passed the greater part of her time in prayer. Sherborne had seen her so engaged, and the expression of her countenance, he declared, was seraphic.

On the extreme verge of a high bank situated at the point of junction between Swanside Beck and the Ribble, stood an old, decayed oak. Little of the once mighty tree beyond the gnarled trunk was left, and this was completely hollow; while there was a great rift near the bottom through which a man might easily creep, and, when once in, stand erect without inconvenience. Beneath the bank the river was deep and still, forming a pool, where the largest and fattest fish were to be met with. In addition to this, the spot was extremely secluded, being rarely visited by the angler on account of the thick copse by which it was surrounded, and which extended along the back, from the point of confluence between the lesser and the larger stream, to Downham mill, nearly half a mile distant.

The sides of the Ribble were here, as elsewhere, beautifully wooded, and as the clear stream winded along through banks of every diversity of shape and character, and covered by forest trees of every description, and of the most luxuriant growth, the effect was enchanting; the more so, that the sun, having now risen high in the heavens, poured down a flood of summer heat and radiance, that rendered these cool shades inexpressibly delightful. Pleasant was it, as the huntsmen leaped from stone to stone, to listen to the sound of the waters rushing past them. Pleasant as they sprang upon some green holm or fairy islet, standing in the midst of the stream, and dividing its lucid waters, to suffer the eye to follow the course of the rapid current, and to see it here sparkling in the bright sunshine, there plunged in shade by the overhanging trees—now fringed with osiers and rushes, now embanked with smoothest sward of emerald green; anon defended by steep rocks, sometimes bold and bare, but more frequently clothed with timber; then sinking down by one of those sudden but exquisite transitions, which nature alone dares display, from this savage and sombre character into the softest and gentlest expression; every where varied, yet every where beautiful.

Through such scenes of silvan loveliness had the huntsmen passed on their way to the hollow oak, and they had ample leisure to enjoy them, because the squire and his brother-in-law being engaged in conversation, as before related, made frequent pauses, and, during these, the others halted likewise; and even the hounds, glad of a respite, stood still, or amused themselves by splashing about amid the shallows without any definite object unless of cooling themselves. Then, as the leaders once more moved forward, arose the cheering shout, the loud deep bay, the clattering of staves, the crashing of branches, and all the other inspiriting noises accompanying the progress of the hunt. But for some minutes these had again ceased, and as Nicholas and Sherborne lingered beneath the shade of a wide-spread beech-tree growing on a sandy hillock near the stream, and seemed deeply interested in their talk—as well they might, for it related to Alizon—the whole troop, including Fogg, held respectfully aloof, and awaited their pleasure to go on.

The signal to move was, at length, given by the squire, who saw they were now not more than a hundred yards from the bank on which stood the hollow tree they were anxious to reach. As the river here made a turn, and swept round the point in question, forming, owing to this detention, the deep pool previously mentioned, the bank almost faced them, and, as nothing intervened, they could almost look into the rift near the base of the tree, forming, they supposed, the entrance to the otter's couch. But, though this was easily distinguished, no traces of the predatory animal could be seen; and though many sharp eyes were fixed upon the spot during the prolonged discourse of the two gentlemen, nothing had occurred to attract their attention, and to prove that the object of their quest was really there.

After some little consultation between the squire and Crouch, it was agreed that the former should alone force his way to the tree, while the others were to station themselves with the hounds at various points of the stream, above and below the bank, so that, if the otter and her litter escaped their first assailant, they should infallibly perish by the hands of some of the others. This being agreed upon, the plan was instantly put into execution—two of the varlets remaining where they were—two going higher up; while Sherborne and Fogg stationed themselves on great stones in the middle of the stream, whence they could command all around them, and Crouch, wading on with Grip, planted himself at the entrance of Swanside Beck into the Ribble.

Meanwhile, the squire having scaled the bank, entered the thick covert encircling it, and, not without some damage to his face and hands from the numerous thorns and brambles growing amongst it, forced his way upwards until he reached the bare space surrounding the hollow tree; and this attained, his first business was to ascertain that all was in readiness below before commencing the attack. A glance showed him on one side old Crouch standing up to his middle in the beck, grasping his long otter spear, and with Grip beating the water in front of him in anxious expectation of employment; and in front Fogg, Sherborne, and two of the varlets, with their hounds so disposed that they could immediately advance upon the otter if it plunged into the river, while its passage up or down would be stopped by their comrades. All this he discerned at a glance; and comprehending from a sign made him by the old huntsman that he should not delay, he advanced towards the tree, and was about to plunge his spear into the hole, hoping to transfix one at least of its occupants, when he was startled by hearing a deep voice apparently issue from the hollows of the timber, bidding him "Beware!"

Nicholas recoiled aghast, for he thought it might be Hobthurst, or the demon of the wood, who thus bespoke him.

"What accursed thing addresses me?" he said, standing on his guard. "What is it? Speak!"

"Get hence, Nicholas Assheton," replied the voice; "an' meddle not wi' them os meddles not wi' thee."

"Aha!" exclaimed the squire, recovering courage, for he thought this did not sound like the language of a demon. "I am known, am I? Why should I go hence, and at whose bidding?"

"Ask neaw questions, mon, boh ge," replied the voice, "or it shan be warse fo' thee. Ey am the boggart o' th' clough, an' if theaw bringst me out, ey'n tear thee i' pieces wi' my claws, an' cast thee into t' Ribble, so that thine own hounts shan eat thee up."

"Ha! say'st thou so, master boggart," cried Nicholas. "For a spirit, thou usest the vernacular of the county fairly enough. But before trying whether thy hide be proof against mortal weapons, I command thee to come forth and declare thyself, that I may judge what manner of thing thou art."

"Thoud'st best lem me be, ey tell thee," replied the boggart, gruffly.

"Ah! methinks I should know those accents," exclaimed the squire; "they marvellously resemble the voice of an offender who has too long evaded justice, and whom I have now fairly entrapped. Jem Device, thou art known, lad, and if thou dost not surrender at discretion, I will strike my spear through this rotten tree, and spit thee as I would the beast I came in quest of."

"An' which yo wad more easily than me," retorted Jem. And suddenly springing from the hole at the foot of the tree, he passed between the squire's legs with great promptitude, and flinging him face foremost upon the ground, crawled to the edge of the bank, and thence dropped into the deep pool below.

The plunge roused all the spectators, who, though they had heard what had passed, and had seen the squire upset in the manner described, had been so much astounded that they could render no assistance; but they now, one and all, bestirred themselves actively to seize the diver when he should rise to the surface. But though every eye was on the look-out, and every arm raised; though the hounds were as eager as their masters, and yelling fiercely, swam round the pool, ready to pounce upon the swimmer as upon a duck, all were disappointed; for, even after a longer interval than their patience could brook, he did not appear.

By this time, Nicholas had regained his legs, and, infuriated by his discomfiture, approached the edge of the bank, and peering down below, hoped to detect the fugitive immediately beneath him, resolved to show him no mercy when he caught him. But he was equally at fault with the others, and after more than five minutes spent in ineffectual search, he ordered Crouch to send Grip into the pool.

The old keeper replied that the dog was not used to this kind of chase, and might not display his usual skill in it; but as the squire would take no nay, he was obliged to consent, and the other hounds were called off lest they should puzzle him. Twice did the shrewd lurcher swim round the pool, sniffing the air, after which he approached the shore, and scented close to the bank;

but still it was evident he could detect nothing, and Nicholas began to despair, when the dog suddenly dived. Expectation was then raised to the utmost, and all were on the watch again, Nicholas leaning over the edge of the bank with his spear in hand, prepared to strike; but the dog was so long in reappearing, that all had given him up for lost, and his master was giving utterance to ejaculations of grief and rage, and vowing vengeance against the warlock, when Grip's grisly head was once more seen above the surface of the water, and this time he had a piece of blue serge in his jaws, proving that he had had hold of the raiments of the fugitive, and that therefore the latter could not be far off, but had most probably got into some hole beneath the bank.

No sooner was this notion suggested than it was acted on by the old huntsman and Fogg, and, wading forward, they pricked the bank with their spears at various points below the level of the water. All at once Fogg fell forward. His spear had entered a hole, and had penetrated so deeply that he had lost his balance. But though soused over head and ears, he had made a successful hit, for the next moment Jem Device appeared above the water, and ere he could dive again his throat was seized by Grip, and while struggling to free himself from the fangs of the tenacious animal, he was laid hold of by Crouch, and the varlets rushing forward to the latter's assistance, the ruffian was captured.

Some difficulty was experienced in rescuing the captive from the jaws of the hounds, who, infuriated by his struggles, and perhaps mistaking him for some strange beast of chase, made their sharp teeth meet in various parts of his person, rending his garments from his limbs, and would no doubt have rent the flesh also, if they had been permitted. At length, after much fighting and struggling, mingled with yells and vociferations, Jem was borne ashore, and flung on the ground, where he presented a wretched spectacle; bleeding, half-drowned, and covered with slime acquired during his occupation of the hole in the bank. But though unable to offer further resistance, his spirit was not quelled, and his eye glared terribly at his captors. Fearing they might have further trouble with him when he recovered from his present exhausted condition, Crouch had his hands bound tightly together with one of the dog leashes, and then would fain have questioned him as to how he managed to breathe in a hole below the level of the water; but Jem refused to satisfy his curiosity, and returned only a sullen rejoinder to any questions addressed to him, until the squire, who had crossed the river at some stepping-stones lower down, came up, and the ruffian then inquired, in a half-menacing tone, what he meant to do with him?

"What do I mean to do with you?" cried Nicholas. "I will tell you, lad. I shall send you at once to Whalley to be examined before the magistrates; and, as the proofs are pretty clear against you, you will be forwarded without any material delay to Lancaster Castle."

"An yo winna rescue me by the way, os yo ha dun a sartin notorious witch an murtheress!" replied Jem, fiercely. "Tak heed whot yo dun, squoire. If ey speak at aw, ey shan speak out, and to some purpose, ey'n warrant ye. If ey ge to Lonkester Castle, ey winna ge alone. Wan o' yer friends shan ge wi' me."

"Cursed villain! I guess thy meaning," replied Nicholas; "but thy vindictive purposes will be frustrated. No credence will be attached to thy false charges; while, as to the lady thou aimest at, she is luckily beyond reach of thy malice."

"Dunna be too sure o' that, squoire," replied Jem. "Ey con put t' officers o' jestis os surely on her track os owd Crouch could set these hounds on an otter. Lay yer account on it, ey winna dee unavenged."

"Heed him not," interposed Sherborne, seeing that the squire was shaken by his threat, and taking him apart; "it will not do to let such a villain escape. He can do you no injury, and as to Mistress Nutter, if you know where she is, it will be easy to give her a hint to get out of the way."

"I don't know that," replied Nicholas, thoughtfully.

"If ey might be so bowd os offer my advice, squoire," said old Crouch, advancing towards his master, "ey'd tee a heavy stoan round the felly's throttle, an chuck him into t' poo', an' he'n tell no teles fo' all his bragging."

"That would silence him effectually, no doubt, Crouch," replied Nicholas, laughing; "but a dog's death is too good for him, and besides I am pretty sure his destiny is not drowning. No, no—at all risks he shall go to Whalley. Harkee, Fogg," he added, beckoning that worthy to him, "I commit the conduct and custody of the prisoner to you. Clap him on a horse, get on another yourself, take these four varlets with you, and deliver him into the hands of Sir Ralph Assheton, who will relieve you of all further trouble and responsibility. But you may add this to the baronet from me," he continued, in an under-tone. "I recommend him to place under immediate arrest Elizabeth Device, the prisoner's mother, and her daughter Jennet. You understand, Fogg—eh?"

"Perfectly," returned the other, with a somewhat singular look; "and your instructions shall be fulfilled to the letter. Have you any thing more to commit to me?"

"Only this," said Nicholas; "you may tell Sir Ralph that I propose to sleep at the Abbey to-night. I shall ride over to Middleton in the course of the day, to confer with Dick Assheton upon what has just occurred, and get the money from him—the three hundred pounds, you understand—and when my errand is done, I will turn bridle towards Whalley. I shall return by

Todmorden, and through the gorge of Cliviger. You may as well tarry for me at the Abbey, for Sir Ralph will be glad of thy company, and we can return together to Downham to-morrow."

As the squire thus spoke, he noticed a singular sparkle in Fogg's ill-set eyes; but he thought nothing of it at the time, though it subsequently occurred to his recollection.

Meanwhile, the prisoner, finding no grace likely to be shown him, shouted out to the squire, that if he were set free, he would make certain important disclosures to him respecting Fogg, who was not what he represented himself; but Nicholas treated the offer with disdain; and the individual mainly interested in the matter, who appeared highly incensed by Jem's malignity, cut a short peg by way of gag, and, thrusting it into the ruffian's mouth, effectually checked any more revelations on his part.

Fogg then ordered the varlets to bring on the prisoner; but as Jem obstinately refused to move, they were under the necessity of taking him on their shoulders, and transporting him in this manner to the stables, where he was placed on a horse, as directed by the squire.

CHAPTER II.—THE PENITENT'S RETREAT.

NICHOLAS and Sherborne returned by a different road from that taken by the others, and loitered so much by the way that they did not arrive at the manor-house until the prisoner and his escort had set out. Probably this was designed, as Nicholas seemed relieved when he learnt they were gone. Having entered the house with his brother-in-law, and conducted him to an apartment opening out of the hall, usually occupied by Mistress Assheton, and where, in fact, they found that amiable lady employed at her embroidery, he left Sherborne with her, and, making some excuse for his own hasty retreat, betook himself to another part of the house.

Mounting the principal staircase, which was of dark oak, with richly-carved railing, he turned into a gallery communicating with the sleeping apartments, and, after proceeding more than half-way down it, halted before a door, which he unlocked, and entered a spacious but evidently disused chamber, hung round with faded tapestry, and containing a large gloomy-looking bedstead. Securing the door carefully after him, Nicholas raised the hangings in one corner of the room, and pressing against a spring, a sliding panel flew open. A screen was placed within, so as to hide from view the inmate of the secret chamber, and Nicholas, having coughed slightly, to announce his presence, received an answer in a low, melancholy female voice, stepped through the aperture, and stood within a small closet.

It was tenanted by a lady, whose features and figure bore the strongest marks of affliction. Her person was so attenuated that she looked little more than a skeleton—her fingers were long and thin—her cheeks hollow and deathly pale—her eyes lustreless and deep sunken in their sockets—and her hair, once jetty as the raven's wing, prematurely blanched. Such was the profound gloom stamped upon her countenance, that it was impossible to look upon her without compassion; while, in spite of her wo-begone looks, there was a noble character about her that elevated the feeling into deep interest, blended with respect. She was kneeling beside a small desk, with an open Bible laid upon it, which she was intently studying when the squire appeared.

"Here is a terrible text for you, Nicholas," she said, regarding him, mournfully. "Listen to it, and judge of its effect on me. Thus it is written in Deuteronomy:—'There shall not be found among you any one that maketh his son or his daughter to pass through the fire, or that useth divination, or an observer of times, or an enchanter, or a witch.' A witch, Nicholas—do you mark the word? And yet more particular is the next verse, wherein it is said;—'Or a charmer, or a consulter with familiar spirits, or a wizard, or a necromancer.' And then cometh the denunciation of divine anger against such offenders in these awful words:—'For all that do these things are an abomination unto the Lord: and because of these abominations, the Lord thy God doth drive them out from before thee.' Again, it is said in Leviticus, that 'the Lord setteth his face against such, to cut them off.' And in Exodus, the law is expressly laid down thus—'THOU SHALT NOT SUFFER A WITCH TO LIVE.' There is no escape for her, you see. By the divine command she must perish, and human justice must carry out the decree. Nicholas, I am one of the offenders thus denounced, thus condemned. I have practised witchcraft, consulted with familiar spirits, and done other abominations in the sight of Heaven; and I ought to pay the full penalty of my offences."

"Do not, I beseech you, madam," replied the squire, "continue to take this view of your case. However you have sinned, you have made amends by the depth and sincerity of your repentance. Your days and nights—for you allow yourself only such rest as nature forces on you, and take even that most unwillingly—are passed in constant prayer. Your abstinence is severer than any anchoress ever practised, for I am sure for the last month you have not taken as much food altogether as I consume in a day; while, not content with this, you perform acts of penance that afflict me beyond measure to think upon, and which I have striven in vain to induce you to forego. There will be no occasion to deliver yourself up to justice, madam; for, if you go on thus, and do not deal with yourself a little more mildly, your accounts with this world will be speedily settled."

"And I should rejoice to think so, Nicholas," replied Mistress Nutter, "if I had any hope in the world to come. But, alas! I have none. I cannot, by any act of penitence and contrition, expiate my offences. My soul is darkened by despair. I know I ought to give myself up—that Heaven and man alike require my life, and I cannot reconcile myself to avoiding my just doom."

"It is the Evil One who puts these thoughts into your head," replied Nicholas, "and who fills your heart with promptings of despair, that he may again obtain the mastery over it. But take a calmer and more consolatory view of your condition. Human justice may require a public sacrifice as an example, but Heaven will be satisfied with contrition in secret."

"I trust so," replied the lady, vainly striving to draw comfort from his words. "Oh, Nicholas! you do not know the temptations I am exposed to in this chamber—the difficulty I experience in keeping my thoughts fixed on one object—the distractions I undergo—the mental obscurations—the faintings of spirit—the bodily prostration—the terrors, the inconceivable terrors, that assail me. Sometimes I wish my spirit would flee away, and be at rest. Rest! there is none for me—none in the grave—none beyond the grave—and therefore I am afraid of death, and still more of the judgment after death! Man might inflict all the tortures he could devise upon this poor frame. I would bear them all with patience, with delight, if I thought they would purchase me immunity hereafter! But with the dread conviction, the almost certainty, that it will be otherwise, I can only look to the final consummation with despair!"

"Again I tell you these suggestions are evil," said Nicholas. "The Son of God, who sacrificed himself for man, and by whose atonement all mankind hope for salvation, has assured us that the greatest sinner who repents shall be forgiven, and, indeed, is more acceptable in the eyes of Heaven than him who has never erred. Far be it from me to attempt to exculpate you in your own eyes, or extenuate your former criminality. You have sinned deeply, so deeply that you may well shrink aghast from the contemplation of your past life—may well recoil in abhorrence from yourself—and may fitly devote yourself to constant prayer and acts of penitence. But having cast off your iniquity, and sincerely repented, I bid you hope—I bid you place a confident reliance in the clemency of an all-merciful power."

"You give me much comfort, Nicholas," said the lady, "and if tears of blood can wash away my sin they shall be shed; but much as you know of my wickedness, even you cannot conceive its extent. In my madness, for it was nothing else, I cast off all hopes of heaven, renounced my Redeemer, was baptised by the demon, and entered into a compact by which—I shudder to speak it—my soul was surrendered to him."

"You placed yourself in fearful jeopardy, no doubt," rejoined Nicholas; "but you have broken the contract in time, and an all-righteous judge will not permit the penalty of the bond to be exacted. Seeing your penitence, Satan has relinquished all claim to your soul."

"I do not think it," replied the lady. "He will contest the point to the last, and it is only at the last that it will be decided."

As she spoke, a sound like mocking laughter reached the ears of Nicholas.

"Did you hear that?" demanded Mistress Nutter, in accents of wildest terror. "He is ever on the watch. I knew it—I knew it."

Clasping her hands together, and fixing her looks on high, she then addressed the most fervent supplications to Heaven for deliverance from evil, and erelong her troubled countenance began to resume its former serenity, proving that the surest balm for a "mind diseased" is prayer. Her example had been followed by Nicholas, who, greatly alarmed, had dropped upon his knees likewise, and now arose with somewhat more composure in his demeanour and aspect.

"I am sorry I do not bring you good news, madam," he said; "but Jem Device has been arrested this morning, and as the fellow is greatly exasperated against me, he threatens to betray your retreat to the officers; and though he is, probably, unacquainted with it notwithstanding his boasting, still he may cause search to be made, and, therefore, I think you had better be removed to some other hiding-place."

"Deliver me up without more ado, I pray you, Nicholas," said the lady.

"You know my resolution on that point, madam," he replied, "and, therefore, it is idle to attempt to shake it. For your daughter's sake, if not for your own, I will save you, in spite of yourself. You would not fix a brand for ever on Alizon's name; you would not destroy her?"

"I would not," replied the wretched lady. "But have you heard from her—have you seen her? Tell me, is she well and happy?"

"She is well, and would be happy, were it not for her anxiety about you," replied Nicholas, evasively. "But for her sake—mine—your own—I must urge you to seek some other place of refuge to night, for if you are discovered here you will bring ruin on us all."

"I will no longer debate the point," replied Mistress Nutter. "Where shall I go?"

"There is one place of absolute security, but I do not like to mention it," replied Nicholas. "Yet still, as it will only be necessary to remain for a day or two, till the search is over, when you can return here, it cannot much matter."

"Where is it?" asked Mistress Nutter.

"Malkin Tower," answered the squire, with some hesitation.

"I will never go to that accursed place," cried the lady. "Send me hence when you will—now, or at midnight—and let me seek shelter on the bleak fells or on the desolate moors, but bid me not go there!"

"And yet it is the best and safest place for you," returned Nicholas, somewhat testily; "and for this reason, that, being reputed to be haunted, no one will venture to molest you. As to Mother Demdike, I suppose you are not afraid of her ghost; and if the evil beings you apprehend were able or inclined to do you mischief, they would not wait till you got there to execute their purpose."

"True," said Mistress Nutter, "I was wrong to hesitate. I will go."

"You will be as safe there as here—ay, and safer," rejoined Nicholas, "or I would not urge the retreat upon you. I am about to ride over to Middleton this morning to see your daughter and Richard Assheton, and shall sleep at Whalley, so that I shall not be able to accompany you to the tower to night; but old Crouch the huntsman shall be in waiting for you, as soon as it grows dusk, in the summer-house, with which, as you know, the secret staircase connected with this room communicates, and he shall have a horse in readiness to take you, together with such matters as you may require, to the place of refuge. Heaven guard you, madam!"

"Amen!" responded the lady.

"And now farewell!" said Nicholas. "I shall hope to see you back again ere many days be gone, when your quietude will not again be disturbed."

So saying, he stepped back, and, passing through the panel, closed it after him.

CHAPTER III.—MIDDLETON HALL.

MIDDLETON HALL, the residence of Sir Richard Assheton, was a large quadrangular structure, built entirely of timber, and painted externally in black and white checker-work, fanciful and varied in design, in the style peculiar to the better class of Tudor houses in South Lancashire and Cheshire. Surrounded by a deep moat, supplied by a neighbouring stream, and crossed by four drawbridges, each faced by a gateway, this vast pile of building was divided into two spacious courts, one of which contained the stables, barns, and offices, while the other was reserved for the family and the guests by whom the hospitable mansion was almost constantly crowded. In the last-mentioned part of the house was a great gallery, with deeply embayed windows filled with painted glass, a floor of polished oak, walls of the same dark lustrous material, hung with portraits of stiff beauties, some in ruff and farthingale, and some in a costume of an earlier period, among whom was Margaret Barton, who brought the manor of Middleton into the family; frowning warriors, beginning with Sir Ralph Assheton, knight-marshal of England in the reign of Edward IV., and surnamed "the black of Assheton-under-line," the founder of the house, and husband of Margaret Barton before mentioned, and ending with Sir Richard Assheton, grandfather of the present owner of the mansion, and one of the heroes of Flodden; grave lawyers, or graver divines—a likeness running through all, and showing they belonged to one line—a huge carved mantelpiece, massive tables of walnut or oak, and black and shining as ebony, set round with high-backed chairs. Here, also, above stairs, there were long corridors looking out through lattices upon the court, and communicating with the almost countless dormitories; while, on the floor beneath, corresponding passages led to all the principal chambers, and terminated in the grand entrance hall, the roof of which being open and intersected by enormous rafters, and crooks of oak, like the ribs of some "tall ammiral," was thought from this circumstance, as well as from its form, to resemble "a ship turned upside down." The lower beams were elaborately carved and ornamented with gilded bosses and sculptured images, sustaining shields emblazoned with the armorial bearings of the Asshetons. As many as three hundred matchlocks, in good and serviceable condition, were ranged round the entrance-hall, besides corselets, Almayne rivets, steel caps, and other accoutrements; this stand of arms having been collected by Sir Richard's predecessor, during the military muster made in the country in 1574, when he had raised and equipped a troop of horse for Queen Elizabeth. Outside the mansion was a garden, charmingly laid out in parterres and walks, and not only carried to the edge of the moat, but continued beyond it till it reached a high knoll crowned with beech-trees. A crest of tall twisted chimneys, a high roof with quaintly carved gables, surmounted by many gilt vanes, may serve to complete the picture of Middleton Hall.

On a lovely summer evening, two young persons of opposite sexes were seated on a bench placed at the foot of one of the largest and most umbrageous of the beech-trees crowning the pleasant eminence before mentioned; and though differing in aspect and character, the one being excessively fair, with tresses as light and fleecy as the clouds above them, and eyes as blue and tender as the skies—and the other distinguished by great manly beauty, though in a totally different style; still there was a sufficiently strong likeness between them, to proclaim them brother and sister. Profound melancholy pervaded the countenance of the young man, whose handsome brow was clouded by care—while the girl, though sad, seemed so only from sympathy.

They were conversing together in deep and earnest tones, showing how greatly they were interested; and, as they proceeded, many an involuntary sigh was heaved by Richard Assheton, while a tear, more than once, dimmed the brightness of his sister's eyes, and her hand sought by its gentle pressure to re-assure him.

They were talking of Alizon, of her peculiar and distressing situation, and of the young man's hopeless love for her. She was the general theme of their discourse, for Richard's sole comfort was in pouring forth his griefs into his sister's willing ear; but new causes of anxiety had been given them by Nicholas, who had arrived that afternoon, bringing intelligence of James Device's capture, and of his threats against Mistress Nutter. The squire had only just departed, having succeeded in the twofold object of his visit—which was, firstly, to borrow three hundred pounds from his cousin—and, secondly, to induce him to attend the meeting at Hoghton Tower. With the first request Richard willingly complied, and he assented, though with some reluctance, to the second, provided nothing of serious moment should occur in the interim. Nicholas tried to rally him on his despondency, endeavouring to convince him all would come right in time, and that his misgivings were causeless; but his arguments were ineffectual, and he was soon compelled to desist. The squire would fain also have seen Alizon, but, understanding she always remained secluded in her chamber till eventide, he did not press the point. Richard urged him to stay over the night, alleging the length of the ride, and the speedy approach of evening, as inducements to him to remain; but on this score the squire was resolute—and having carefully secured the large sum of money he had obtained beneath his doublet, he mounted his favourite steed, Robin, who seemed as fresh as if he had not achieved upwards of thirty miles that morning, and rode off.

Richard watched him cross the drawbridge, and take the road towards Rochdale, and, after exchanging a farewell wave of the hand with him, returned to the hall and sought out his sister.

Dorothy was easily persuaded to take a turn in the garden with her brother, and during their walk he confided to her all he had heard from Nicholas. Her alarm at Jem Device's threat was much greater than his own; and, though she entertained a strong and unconquerable aversion to Mistress Nutter, and could not be brought to believe in the sincerity of her penitence, still, for Alizon's sake, she dreaded lest any harm should befall her, and more particularly desired to avoid the disgrace which would be inflicted by a public execution. Alizon she was sure would not survive such a catastrophe, and therefore, at all risks, it must be averted.

Richard did not share, to the same extent, in her apprehensions, because he had been assured by Nicholas that Mistress Nutter would be removed to a place of perfect security, and because he was disposed, with the squire, to regard the prisoner's threats as mere ravings of impotent malice. Still he could not help feeling great uneasiness. Vague fears, too, beset him, which he found it in vain to shake off, but he did not communicate them to his sister, as he knew the terrifying effect they would have upon her timid nature; and he, therefore, kept the mental anguish he endured to himself, hoping erelong it would diminish in intensity. But in this he was deceived, for, instead of abating, his gloom and depression momently increased.

Almost unconsciously, Richard and his sister had quitted the garden, proceeding with slow and melancholy steps to the beech-crowned knoll. The seat they had chosen was a favourite one with Alizon, and she came thither on most evenings, either accompanied by Dorothy or alone. Here it was that Richard had more than once passionately besought her to become his bride, receiving on both occasions a same meek yet firm refusal. To Dorothy also, who pleaded her brother's cause with all the eloquence and fervour of which she was mistress, Alizon replied that her affections were fixed upon Richard; but that, while her mother lived, and needed her constant prayers, they must not be withheld; and that, looking upon any earthly passion as a criminal interference with this paramount duty, she did not dare to indulge it. Dorothy represented to her that the sacrifice was greater than she was called upon to make, that her health was visibly declining, and that she might fall a victim to her over-zeal; but Alizon was deaf to her remonstrances, as she had been to the entreaties of Richard.

With hearts less burthened, the contemplation of the scene before them could not have failed to give delight to Richard and his sister, and, even amid the adverse circumstances under which it was viewed, its beauty and tranquillity produced a soothing influence.

Evening was gradually stealing on, and all the exquisite tints marking that delightful hour, were spreading over the landscape. The sun was setting gorgeously, and a flood of radiance fell upon the old mansion beneath them, and upon the grey and venerable church, situated on a hill adjoining it. The sounds were all in unison with the hour, and the lowing of cattle, the voices of the husbandmen returning from their work, mingled with the cawing of the rooks newly alighted on the high trees near the church, told them that bird, man, and beast were seeking their home for the night. But though Richard's eye dwelt upon the fair garden beneath him, embracing all its terraces, green slopes, and trim pastures; though it fell upon the moat belting the hall like a glittering zone; though it rested upon the church tower; and, roaming over the park beyond it, finally settled upon the range of hills bounding the horizon, which have not inaptly been termed the English Apennines; though he saw all these things, he thought not of them, neither was he conscious of the sounds that met his ear, and which all spoke of rest from labour, and peace. Darker and deeper grew his melancholy. He began to persuade himself he was not long for this world; and, while gazing upon the beautiful prospect before him, was perhaps looking upon it for the last time.

For some minutes Dorothy watched him anxiously, and at last receiving no answer to her questions, and alarmed by the expression of his countenance, she flung her arms round his neck, and burst into tears. It was now Richard's turn to console her, and he inquired with much anxiety as to the cause of this sudden outburst of grief.

"You yourself are the cause of it, dear Richard," replied Dorothy, regarding him with brimming eyes; "I cannot bear to see you so unhappy. If you suffer this melancholy to grow upon you, it will affect both mind and body. Just now your countenance wore an expression most distressing to look upon. Try to smile, dear Richard, if only to cheer me, or else I shall grow as sad as you. Ah, me! I have known the day, and not long since either, when on a pleasant summer evening like this you would propose a stroll into the park with me; and, when there, would trip along the glades as fleetly as a deer, and defy me to catch you. But you always took care I should, though—ha! ha! Come, there is a little attempt at a smile. That's something. You look more like yourself now. How happy we used to be in those days, to be sure!—and how merry! You would make the courts ring with your blithe laughter, and wellnigh kill me with your jests. If love is to make one mope like an owl, and sigh like the wind through a half-shut casement; if it is to cause one to lose one's rosy complexion and gay spirit, and forget how to dance and sing—take no pleasure in hawking and hunting, or any kind of sport—walk about with eyes fixed upon the ground, muttering, and with disordered attire—if it is to make one silent when one should be talkative, grave when one should be gay, heedless when one should listen—if it is to do all this, defend me from the tender passion! I hope I shall never fall in love."

"I hope you never will, dear Dorothy," replied Richard, pressing her hand affectionately, "if your love is to be attended with such unhappy results as mine. I know not how it is, but I feel unusually despondent this evening, and am haunted by a thousand dismal fancies. But I will do my best to dismiss them, and with your help no doubt I shall succeed."

"There!—there was a smile in earnest!" cried Dorothy,

brightening up. "Oh, Richard! I am quite happy now. And after all I do not see why you should take such a gloomy view of things. I have no doubt there is a great deal, a very great deal, of happiness in store for you and Alizon—I must couple her name with yours, or you will not allow it to be happiness—if you can only be brought to think so. I am quite sure of it; and you shall see how nicely I can make the matter out. As thus. Mistress Nutter is certain to die soon—such a wicked woman cannot live long. Don't be angry with me for calling her wicked, Richard; but you know I never can forget her unhallowed proceedings in the convent church at Whalley, where I was so nearly becoming a witch myself. Well, as I was saying, she cannot live long, and when she goes—and Heaven grant it may be soon!—Alizon, no doubt, will mourn for her though I shall not, and after a decent interval—then, Richard, then she will no longer say you nay, but will make you happy as your wife. Nay, do not look so sad again, dear brother. I thought I should make you quite cheerful by the picture I was drawing."

"It is because I fear it will never be realized that I am sad, Dorothy," replied Richard. "My own anticipations are the opposite of yours, and paint Alizon sinking into an early grave before her mother; while as to myself, if such be the case, I shall not long survive her."

"Nay, now you will make me weep again," cried Dorothy, her tears flowing afresh. "But I will not allow you to indulge such gloomy ideas, Richard. If I seriously thought Mistress Nutter likely to occasion all this fresh mischief, I would cause her to be delivered up to justice, and hanged out of the way. You may look cross at me, but I would. What is an old witch like her, compared with two young handsome persons, dying for love of each other, and yet not able to marry on her account?"

"Dorothy, Dorothy, you must put some restraint on your tongue," said Richard; "you give it sadly too much licence. You forget it is the wish of the unhappy lady you refer to, to expiate her offences at the stake, and that it is only out of consideration to her daughter that she has been induced to remain in concealment. What will be the issue of it all, I dare scarcely conjecture. Wo to her, I fear! Wo to Alizon! Wo to me!"

"Alas! Richard, that you should link yourself to her fate!" exclaimed Dorothy, half mournfully, half reproachfully.

"I cannot help it," he replied. "It is my destiny—a deplorable destiny, if you will—but not to be avoided. That Mistress Nutter will escape the consequences of her crimes, I can scarcely believe. Her penitence is profound and sincere, and that is a great consolation; for I trust she will not perish, body and soul. I should wish her to have some spiritual assistance, but this Nicholas will not for the present permit, alleging that no churchman would consent to screen her from justice when he became aware, as he must by her confession, of the nature and magnitude of her offences. This may be true; but when the wretches who have been leagued with her in iniquity are disposed of, the reason will no longer exist, and I will see that she is cared for. But, apart from her mother, I have another source of anxiety respecting Alizon. It is this: orders have been this day given for the arrest of Elizabeth Device and her daughter, Jennet, and Alizon will be the chief witness against them. This will be a great trouble to her."

"Undoubtedly," rejoined Dorothy, with much concern. "But can it not be avoided?"

"I fear not," said Richard, "and I blamed Nicholas much for his precipitancy in giving the order; but he replied he had been held up latterly as a favourer of witches, and must endeavour to redeem his character by a display of severity. Were it not for Alizon, I should rejoice that the noxious brood should at last be utterly exterminated."

"And so should I, in good sooth," responded Dorothy. "As to Elizabeth Device, she is bad enough for any thing, and capable of almost any mischief: but she is nothing to Jennet, who, I am persuaded, would become a second Mother Demdike if her career were not cut short. You have seen the child, and know what an ill-favoured, deformed little creature she is, with round high shoulders, eyes set strangely in her face, and such a malicious expression—oh! I shudder to think of it."

And she covered her face with her hands, as if to shut out some unpleasant object.

"Poor, predestined child of sin, branded by nature from her birth, and charged with wicked passions, as the snake with venom, I cannot but pity her!" exclaimed Richard. "Compassion is entirely thrown away," he added, with a sudden change of manner, and as if trying to shake off a weakness. "The poisonous fruit must, however, be nipped in the bud. Better she should perish now, even though comparatively guiltless, than hereafter with a soul stained with crime, like her mother."

As he concluded, he put his hand quickly to his side, for a sharp and sudden pang shot through his heart; and so acute was the pain, that, after struggling against it for a moment, he groaned deeply, and would have fallen, if his sister, greatly alarmed, and with difficulty repressing a scream, had not lent him support.

Neither of them were aware of the presence of a little girl, who had approached the place where they were sitting, with footsteps so light that the grass scarcely seemed to bend beneath them, and who, ensconcing herself behind the tree, drank in their discourse with eager ears. She was attended by a large black cat, who, climbing the tree, placed himself on a bough above her.

During the latter part of the conversation, and when it turned upon the arrest of Jennet and her mother, the expression of the child's countenance, malicious enough to begin with, became desperately malignant, and she was only restrained by certain signs from the cat, which appeared to be intelligible to her, from some act of mischief. At last even this failed, and before the animal could descend and check her, she crept round the bole of the tree, so as to bring herself close to Richard, and muttering a spell, made one or two passes behind his back, touched him with the point of her finger, but so lightly that he was unconscious of the pressure, and then hastily retreated with the cat, who glared furiously at her from his flaming orbs.

It was at the moment she touched him that Richard felt as if an arrow were quivering in his heart.

Poor Dorothy's alarm was so great that she could not even scream for assistance, and she feared, if she quitted her brother, he would expire before her return; but the agony, though great, was speedily over, and as the spasm ceased, he looked up, and, with a faint smile, strove to re-assure her.

"Do not be alarmed," he said; "it is nothing—a momentary faintness—that is all."

But the damp upon his brow, and the deathly hue of his cheek, contradicted the assertion, and showed how much he had endured.

"It was more than momentary faintness, dear Richard," replied Dorothy. "It was a frightful seizure—so frightful that I almost feared; but no matter—you know I am easily alarmed. Thank God! here is some colour coming into your cheeks. You are better now, I see. Lean upon me, and let us return to the house."

"I can walk unassisted," said Richard, rising with an effort.

"Do not despise my feeble aid," replied Dorothy, taking his arm under her own. "You will be quite well soon."

"I am quite well now," said Richard, halting after he had advanced a few paces. "The attack is altogether passed. Do you not see Alizon coming towards us? Not a word of this sudden seizure to her. Do you mind, Dorothy?"

Alizon was soon close behind them, and though, in obedience to Richard's injunctions, no allusion was made to his recent illness, she at once perceived he was suffering greatly, and with much solicitude inquired into the cause. Richard avoided giving a direct answer, and, immediately entering upon Nicholas's visit, tried to divert her attention from himself.

So great a change had been wrought in Alizon's appearance and manner during the last few weeks, that she could scarcely be recognised. Still beautiful as ever, her beauty had lost its earthly character, and had become in the highest degree spiritualised and refined. Humility of deportment and resignation of look, blended with an expression of religious fervour, gave her the appearance of one of the early martyrs. Unremitting ardour in the pursuance of her devotional exercises by day, and long vigils at night, had worn down her frame, and robbed it of some of its grace and fulness of outline; but this attenuation had a charm of its own, and gave a touching interest to her figure, which was wanting before. If her cheek was thinner and paler, her eyes looked larger and brighter, and more akin to the stars in splendour; and if she appeared less childlike, less joyous, less free from care, the want of these qualities was more than counterbalanced by increased gentleness, resignation, and serenity.

Deeply interested in all Richard told her of her mother, she was greatly concerned to hear of the intended arrest of Elizabeth and Jennet Device, especially the latter. For this unhappy and misguided child she had once entertained the affection of a sister, and it could not but be a source of grief to her to reflect upon her probable fate.

Little more passed between them, for Richard, feeling his strength again fail him, was anxious to reach the house, and Dorothy was quite unequal to conversation. They parted at the door, and as Alizon, after taking leave of her friends, turned to continue her walk in the garden, Richard staggered into the entrance-hall, and sank upon a chair.

Alizon desired to be alone, for she did not wish to have a witness to the grief that overpowered her, and which, when she had gained a retired part of the garden, where she supposed herself free from all observation, found relief in a flood of tears.

For some minutes she was a prey to violent and irrepressible emotion, and had scarcely regained a show of composure, when she heard herself addressed, as she thought, in the voice of the very child whose unlucky fate she was deploring. Looking round in surprise, and seeing no one, she began to think fancy must have cheated her, when a low malicious laugh, arising from a shrubbery near her, convinced her that Jennet was hidden there. And the next moment the little girl stepped from out the trees.

Alizon's first impulse was to catch the child in her arms, and press her to her bosom; but there was something in Jennet's look that deterred her, and so embarrassed her, that she was unable to bestow upon her the ordinary greeting of affection, or even approach her.

Jennet seemed to enjoy her confusion, and laughed spitefully.

"Yo dunna seem ower glad to see me, sister Alizon," said Jennet, at length.

"*Sister* Alizon!" There was something in the term that now jarred upon the young girl's ears, but she strove to conquer the feeling, as unworthy of her.

"She was once my sister," she thought, "and shall be so still. I will save her, if it be possible. Jennet," she added aloud, "I know not what chance brings you here, and though I may not give you the welcome you expect, I am rejoiced to see you, because I may be the means of serving you. Do not be alarmed at what I am going to tell you. The danger I hope is passed, or at all events may be avoided. Your liberty is threatened, and at the very moment I see you here I was lamenting your supposed condition as a prisoner.

Jennet laughed louder and more spitefully than before, and looked so like a little fury that Alizon's blood ran cold at the sight of it.

"Ey knoa it aw, sister Alizon," she cried, "an that is why ey ha cum'd here. Brother Jem is a pris'ner i' Whalley Abbey. Mother is a pris'ner theere, too. An ey should ha kept em company, if Tib hadna brought me off. Now, listen to me, Alizon, fo' this is my bus'ness wi' yo. Yo mun get mother an Jem out to-neet—eigh, to-neet. Yo con do it, if yo win. An onless yo do—boh ey winna threaten till ey get yer answer."

"How am I to set them free?" asked Alizon, greatly alarmed.

"Yo need only say the word to young Ruchot Assheton, an the job's done," replied Jennet.

"I refuse—positively refuse to do so!" rejoined Alizon, indignantly.

"Varry weel," cried Jennet, with a look of concentrated malice and fury; "then tak the consequences. They win be ta'en to Lonkester Castle, an lose their lives theere. Bo ye shan go, too—ay, an be brunt os a witch—a witch—d'ye mark, wench? eh!"

"I defy your malice!" cried Alizon.

"Defy me!" screamed Jennet. "What, ho! Tib!"

And at the call the huge black cat sprang from out the shrubbery.

"Tear her flesh from her bones!" cried the little girl, pointing to Alizon, and stamping furiously on the ground.

Tib erected his back, and glared like a tiger, but he seemed unwilling or unable to obey the order.

Alizon, who had completely recovered her courage, regarded him fixedly, and apparently without terror.

"Whoy dusna seize her, an tear her i' pieces?" cried the infuriated child.

"He dares not—he has no power over me," said Alizon. "Oh, Jennet! cast him off. Your wicked agent appears to befriend you now, but he will lead you to certain destruction. Come with me, and I will save you."

"Off!" cried Jennet, repelling her with furious gestures. "Off! ey winna ge wi' ye. Ey winna be saved, os yo term it. Ey hate yo more than ever, an wad strike yo dead at my feet, if ey could. Boh as ey conna do it, ey win find some other means o' injurin' ye. Soh look to yersel, proud ledy—look to yersel? Ey ha already smitten you in a place where ye win feel it sore, an ey win repeat the blow. Ey now leave yo, boh we shan meet again. Come along, Tib!"

So saying, she sprang into the shrubbery, followed by the cat, leaving Alizon appalled by her frightful malignity.

ALIZON DEFIES JENNET. P. 398

CHAPTER IV.—THE GORGE OF CLIVIGER.

THE sun had already set as Nicholas Assheton reached Todmorden, then a very small village indeed, and alighting at a little inn near the church, found the ale so good, and so many boon companions assembled to discuss it, that he would fain have tarried with them for an hour or so; but prudence, for once, getting the better of inclination, and suggesting that he had fifteen or sixteen miles still to ride, over a rough and lonely road, part of which lay through the gorge of Cliviger, a long and solitary pass among the English Apennines, and, moreover, had a large sum of money about him, he tore himself away by a great effort.

On quitting the smiling valley of Todmorden, and drawing near the dangerous defile before mentioned, some misgivings crossed him, and he almost reproached himself with foolhardiness in venturing within it at such an hour, and wholly unattended. Several recent cases of robbery, some of them attended by murder, had occurred within the pass; and these now occurred so forcibly to the squire, that he was half inclined to ride back to Todmorden, and engage two or three of the topers he had left at the inn to serve him as an escort as far as Burnley, but he dismissed the idea almost as soon as formed, and, casting one look at the green and woody slopes around him, struck spurs into Robin, and dashed into the gorge.

On the right towered a precipice, on the bare crest of which stood a heap of stones piled like a column—the remains, probably, of a cairn. On this commanding point Nicholas perceived a female figure, dilated to gigantic proportions against the sky, who, as far as he could distinguish, seemed watching him, and making signs to him, apparently to go back; but he paid little regard to them, and soon afterwards lost sight of her.

Precipitous and almost inaccessible rocks, of every variety of form and hue; some springing perpendicularly up like the spire of a church, others running along in broken ridges, or presenting the appearance of high embattled walls; here riven into deep gullies, there opening into wild savage glens, fit spots for robber ambuscade; now presenting a fair smooth surface, now jagged, shattered, shelving, roughened with brushwood; sometimes bleached and hoary, as in the case of the pinnacled crag called the White Kirk; sometimes green with moss or grey with lichen; sometimes, though but rarely, shaded with timber, as in the approach to the cavern named the Earl's Bower; but generally bold and naked, and sombre in tint as the colours employed by the savage Rosa. Such were the distinguishing features of the gorge of Cliviger when Nicholas traversed it. Now the high embankments and mighty arches of a railway fill up its recesses, and span its gullies; the roar of the engine is heard where the cry of the bird of prey alone resounded; and clouds of steam usurp the place of the mist-wreaths on its crags.

Formerly, the high cliffs abounded with hawks; the rocks echoed with their yells and screeches, and the spots adjoining their nests resembled, in the words of the historian of the district, Whitaker, "little charnel-houses for the bones of game." Formerly, also, on some inaccessible point built the rock-eagle, and reared its brood from year to year. The gaunt wolf had once ravaged the glens, and the sly fox and fierce cat-a-mountain still harboured within them. Nor were those the only objects of dread. The superstitious declared the gorge was haunted by a frightful, hirsute demon, yclept Hobthurst.

The general savage character of the ravine was relieved by some spots of exquisite beauty, where the traveller might have lingered with delight, if apprehension of assault from robber, or visit from Hobthurst, had not urged him on. Numberless waterfalls, gushing from fissures in the hills, coursed down their seamy sides, looking like threads of silver as they sprang from point to point. One of the most beautiful of these cascades, issuing from a gully in the rocks near the cavern called the Earl's Bower, fell, in rainy seasons, in one unbroken sheet of a hundred and fifty feet. Through the midst of the gorge ran a swift and brawling stream, known by the appellation of the Calder; but it must not be confounded with the river flowing past Whalley Abbey. The course of this impetuous current was not always restrained within its rocky channel, and when swollen by heavy rains, it would frequently invade the narrow causeway running beside it, and, spreading over the whole width of the gorge, render the road almost impassable.

Through this rocky and sombre defile, and by the side of the brawling Calder, which dashed swiftly past him, Nicholas took his way. The hawks were yelling overhead; the rooks were cawing on the topmost branches of some tall timber, on which they built; a raven was croaking lustily in the wood; and a pair of eagles were soaring in the still glowing sky.

By-and-by, the glen contracted, and a wall of steep rocks on either side hemmed the shuddering traveller in. Instinctively, he struck spurs into his horse, and accelerated his pace.

The narrow glen expands, the precipices fall further back, and the traveller breathes more freely. Still, he does not relax his speed, for his imagination has been at work in the gloom, peopling his path with lurking robbers or grinning boggarts. He begins to fear he shall lose his gold, and execrates his folly for incurring such heedless risk. But it is too late now to turn back.

It grows rapidly dusk, and objects became less and less distinct, assuming fantastical and fearful forms. A blasted tree, clinging to a rock, and thrusting a bare branch across the road, looks to-the squire like a bandit; and a white owl bursting from a bush, scares him as if it had been Hobthurst himself. However, in spite of these and other alarms, for which he is indebted to excited fancy, he hurries on, and is proceeding at a thundering pace, when all at once his horse comes to a stop, arrested by a tall female figure, resembling that seen near the mountain cairn at the entrance of the gorge.

Nicholas's blood ran cold, for though in this case he could not apprehend plunder, he was fearful of personal injury, for he believed the woman to be a witch. Mustering up courage, however, he forced Robin to proceed.

If his progress was meant to be barred, a better spot for the purpose could not have been selected. A narrow road, scarcely two feet in width, ran round the ledge of a tremendous crag, jutting so far into the glen that it almost met the steep barrier of rocks opposite it. Between these precipitous crags dashed the river in a foaming cascade, nearly twelve feet in height, and the steep narrow causeway winding beside it, as above described, was rendered excessively slippery and dangerous from the constant cloud of spray arising from the fall.

At the highest and narrowest point of the ledge, and occupying nearly the whole of its space, with an overhanging rock on one side of her, and a roaring torrent on the other, stood the tall woman, determined apparently, from her attitude and deportment, to oppose the squire's further progress. As Nicholas advanced, he became convinced that it was the same person he had seen near the cairn; but, when her features grew distinguishable, he found to his surprise that it was Nance Redferne.

"Halloa! Nance," he cried. "What are you doing here, lass, eh?"

"Cum to warn ye, squoire," she replied; "yo once did me a sarvice, an ey hanna forgetten it. That's why I watched ye fro' the cairn cliffs, an motioned ye to ge back. Boh ye didna onderstand my signs, or wouldna heed 'em, so ey be cum'd here to stay ye. Yo're i' dawnger, ey tell ye."

"In danger of what, my good woman?" demanded the squire uneasily.

"O' bein' robbed, and plundered o' your gowd," replied Nance; "there are five men waitin' to set upon ye a mile further on, at the Bowder Stoans."

"Indeed!" exclaimed Nicholas; "they will get little for their pains. I have no money about me."

"Dunna think to deceive me, squoire," rejoined Nance; "ey knoa yo ha borrowed three hundert punds i' gowd fro' yung Ruchot Assheton; an os surely os ye ha it aw under your jerkin. so surely win yo lose it, if yo dunna turn back, or ge on without me keepin' ye company."

"I have no objection on earth to your company, Nance, replied the squire; "quite the contrary. But how the devil should these rascals expect me? And, above all, how should they conjecture I should come so well provided? For, sooth to say, such is not ordinarily the case with me."

"Ey knoa it weel, squoire," replied Nance, with a laugh; "boh they ha received sartin information o' your movements."

"There is only one person who could give them such information," cried Nicholas; "but I cannot, will not suspect him."

"If yor're thinkin' o' Lawrence Fogg, yo're na far wide o' th' mark, squoire," replied Nance.

"What! Fogg leagued with robbers—impossible!" exclaimed Nicholas.

"Neaw, it's nah so unpossible os aw that," returned Nance; "yo 'n stare when ey tell yo he has robbed yo mony a time without your being aware on it. Yo were onwise enough to send him round to your friends to borrow money for yo."

"True, so I was. But, luckily, no one would lend me any," said Nicholas.

"There yo're wrong, squoire—fo' unluckily they aw did," replied Nance, with a scarcely-suppressed laugh. "Roger Nowell gied him one hundred; Tummus Whitaker of Holme, another; Ruchot Parker o' Browsholme, another. An more i' th' same way."

"And the rascal pocketed it all, and never brought me back one farthing," cried Nicholas, in a transport of rage. "I'll have him hanged—pshaw! hanging's too good for him. To deceive me, his friend, his benefactor, his patron, in such a manner; to dwell in my house, eat at my table, drink my wine, wear my habiliments, ride my horses, hunt with my hounds! Has the dog no conscience?"

"Varry little, ey'm afear'd," replied Nance.

"And the worst of it is," continued the squire—new lights breaking upon him, "I shall be liable for all the sums he has received. He was my confidential agent, and the lenders will come upon me. It must be six or seven hundred pounds that he has obtained in this nefarious way. Zounds! I shall go mad."

"Yo wur to blame fo' trustin him, squoire," rejoined Nance. "Yo ought to ha' made proper inquiries about him at first, an then yo'd ha' found out what sort o' chap he wur. Boh now ey'n tell ye. Lawrence Fogg is chief o' a band o' robbers, an aw the black an villanous deeds done of late i' this place, ha' been parpetrated by his men. A poor gentleman wur murdert by 'em i' this varry spot th' week efore last, an his body cast into t' river. Fogg, of course, had no hont in the fow deed, boh he would na ha interfered to prevent it if he had bin here, fo' he never scrupled shedding blood. An if he had bin content wi' robbin' yo, squoire, ey wadna ha betrayed him; boh when he proposed to cut your throttle, bekose, os he said, dead men tell neaw teles, ey could howd out nah longer, an resolved to gi' yo warnin."

"What a monstrous and unheard-of villain!" cried the squire. "But is he one of the ambuscade?"

Nance replied in the affirmative.

"Then, by heaven! I will confront him—I will hew him down," pursued Nicholas, griping the hilt of his sword.

"Neaw use, ey tell ye—yo'n be overpowert an kilt," said Nance. "Tak me wi' yo, an ey'n carry yo safely through em aw; boh ge alone, or yo'n ne'er see Downham again. An now it's reet ey should tell ye who Lawrence Fogg really is."

"What new wonder is in store for me?" cried Nicholas. "Who is he?"

"Maybe yo ha heerd tell that Mother Demdike had a son and a dowter," replied Nance; "the dowter bein', of course, Elizabeth Device; and the son, Christopher Demdike, being supposed to be dead. Howsomever, this is not the case, for Lawrence Fogg is he."

"I guessed as much when you began," cried Nicholas. "He has a cursedly bad look about the eyes—a damned Demdike physiognomy. What an infernal villain the fellow must be! without a jot of natural feeling. Why, he has this very day assisted at his nephew's capture, and caused his own sister to be arrested. Oh, I have been properly duped! To lodge a son of that infernal hag in my house—feed him, clothe him, make him my friend—take him, the viper! to my bosom! I have been rightly served. But he shall hang!—he shall hang! That is some consolation, though slight. But how do you know all this, Nance?"

"Dunna ax me," she replied. "Whatever ey ha' been to Christopher Demdike, ey bear him neaw love now; fo', as ey ha towd yo, he is a black-hearted murtherin' villain. Boh lemme get up behind yo, an ey'n bring yo through scatheless. An to-morrow yo may arrest the whole band at Malkin Tower."

"Malkin Tower!" exclaimed the squire, in fresh surprise. "What, have these robbers taken up their quarters there? This accounts for all the strange sights said to have been seen there of late, and which I treated as mere fables. But, ah! a terrible thought crosses me. What have I done? Mistress Nutter will be there to-night. And I have sent her. Death and destruction! she will fall into their hands. I must go there at once. I cannot take any assistance with me. That would betray the poor lady."

"If yo'n trust me, ey'n help yo through the difficulty," replied Nance.

"Get up then quickly, lass, since it must be so," rejoined Nicholas.

With this he moved forward, and giving her his hand, she was instantly seated behind him upon Robin, who seemed no way incommoded by his double burthen, but dashed down the further side of the causeway, in answer to a sharp application of the spur. Passing her arms round the squire's waist, Nance maintained her seat well; and in this way they rattled along, heedless of the increasing difficulties of the road, or the fast-gathering gloom.

The mile was quickly passed, and Nance whispered in the squire's ear that they were approaching the Boulder Stones. Presently they came to a narrow glen, half-filled with huge rocky fragments, detached from the toppling precipices on either side, and forming an admirable place of ambuscade. One rock, larger than the rest, completely commanded the pass, and, as the squire advanced, a thundering voice from it called to him to stay; and the injunction being disregarded, the barrel of a gun was protruded from the bushes covering its brow, and a shot fired at him. Though well aimed, the ball struck the ground beneath his horse's feet, and Nicholas continued his way unmoved, while the faulty marksman jumped down the crag. At the same time four other men started from their places of concealment behind the stones, and, levelling their calivers at the fugitives, fired. The sharp discharges echoed along the gorge, and the shots rattled against the rocks, but none of them took effect, and Nicholas might have gone on without further hindrance; but, despite Nance's remonstrances, who urged him to go on, he pulled up to await the coming of the person who had first challenged him. Scarcely an instant elapsed before he was beside the squire, and presented a petronel at his head. Notwithstanding the gloom, Nicholas recognised him.

"Ah! is it thou, accursed traitor?" cried Nicholas. "I could scarcely believe in thy villainy, but now I am convinced."

"The jade you have got behind you has told you who I am, I see," replied Fogg. "I will settle with her anon. But this will save further explanations with you!"

And he discharged the petronel full at the squire. But the ball rebounded, as if his doublet had been quilted. It was in fact lined with gold. On seeing the squire unhurt, the robber captain uttered an exclamation of rage and astonishment.

"You are mistaken, you see, perfidious villain," cried Nicholas. "You have yet to render an account of all the wrongs you have done me, but meantime you shall not pass unpunished."

And as he spoke, he snatched the petronel from Fogg, and with the but-end dealt him a tremendous blow on the head, felling him to the ground.

By this time the other robbers had descended from the rocks, and, seeing the fall of their leader, rushed forward to avenge him, but Nicholas did not tarry for any further encounter; but, fully satisfied with what he had done, struck spurs into Robin, and galloped off. For a few minutes he could hear the shouts of the men. but they soon afterwards died away.

Little more than half the ravine had been traversed when the rencounter above described took place; but, though the road was still difficult and dangerous, and rendered doubly so by the obscurity, no further hindrance occurred till just as Nicholas was quitting the gloomy intricacies of the gorge, and approaching the more open country beyond it. At this point Robin fell, throwing both him and Nance, and when the animal rose again he was found to be so much injured that it was impossible to mount him. There was no resource but to proceed to Burnley, which was still three or four miles distant, on foot.

In this dilemma, Nance volunteered to provide the squire with another steed, but he resolutely refused the offer.

"No, no—none of your broomsticks for me," he cried; "no devil's horses—I don't know where they may carry me. My own legs must serve me now. I'll just take poor Robin out of the road, and then trudge off for Burnley as fast as I can."

With this, he led the horse to a small green mead skirting the stream, and taking off his saddle and bridle, and depositing them carefully under a tree, he patted the animal on the neck, promising to return for him on the morrow, and then set off at a brisk pace, with Nance walking beside him. They had not gone far, however, when the clattering of hoofs was heard behind them, and it was evident that several horsemen were rapidly approaching. Nance stopped, listened for a moment, and then declaring that it was Demdike and his band in pursuit, seized the squire's arm and drew him out of the road, and under the shelter of some bushes of hazel. The robber captain could only have been stunned, it appeared; and, as soon as he had recovered from the effects of the blow, had mounted his horse, which was concealed, with those of his men, behind the rocks, and started after the fugitives. Such was the construction put upon the matter by Nance, and the event proved it correct. A loud shout from the horsemen, and a sudden halt, proclaimed that poor Robin had been discovered; and this circumstance seemed to give great satisfaction to Demdike, who loudly declared that they were now sure of overtaking the runaways.

"They cannot be far off," he cried; "but they will most likely attempt to hide themselves, so look well about you."

So saying, he rode on, and it was evident from the noise, that the men implicitly obeyed his injunctions. Nothing, however, was found, and ere many minutes Demdike came up, and glancing at the hazels, behind which the fugitives were hidden, he discharged a petronel into the largest tree, but as no movement followed the report, he said—

"I thought I saw something move here, but I suppose I was mistaken. No doubt they have got on further than we expected, or have retired into some of the cloughs, in which case it will be useless to search for them. However, we will make sure of them in this way. Two of you shall form an ambuscade near Holme, and two further on within half a mile of Burnley, and shall remain on the watch till dawn, so that you will be sure to capture them, and when taken, make away with them without hesitation. Unless my skull had been of the strongest, that butcherly squire would have cracked it, so he shall have no grace from me; and as to that treacherous witch, Nance Redferne, she deserves death at our hands, and she shall have her deserts. I have long suspected her, and, indeed, was a fool to trust one of the vile Chattox brood, who are all my natural enemies—but no matter, I shall have my revenge."

The men having promised compliance with their captain's command, he went on—

"As to myself," he said, "I shall go forthwith, and as fast as my horse can carry me, to Malkin Tower, and I will tell you why. It is not that I dislike the game we are upon, but I have better to play just now. Tom Shaw, the cock-master at Downham, who is in my pay, rode over to Whalley this afternoon, to bring me word that a certain lady, who has long been concealed in the Manor-house, will be taken to Malkin Tower to-night. The intelligence is certain, for he had obtained it from Old Crouch, the huntsman, who is to escort her. Thus, Mistress Nutter, for you all know whom I mean, will fall naturally into our hands, and we can wring any sums of money we like out of her; for though she has abandoned her property to her daughter, Alizon, she can no doubt have as much as she wants, and I will take care she asks for plenty, or I will try the effect of some of those instruments of torture which I was lucky enough to find in the dungeons of Malkin Tower, and which were used for a like purpose by my predecessor, Blackburn, the freebooter. Are you content, my lads?"

"Ay, ay, Captain Demdike," they replied.

Upon this the whole party set forward, and were speedily out of hearing. As soon as they thought it prudent to come forth, the squire and Nance emerged from their place of shelter.

"What is to be done?" exclaimed the former, who was almost in a state of distraction. "The villain has announced his intention of going to Malkin Tower, and Mistress Nutter will assuredly fall into his hands. Oh! that I could stop him, or get there before him!"

"Yo shan, if yo like to ride wi' me," said Nance.

"But how—in what way?" asked Nicholas.

"Leave that to me," replied Nance, breaking off a long branch of hazel. "Tak howld o' this," she cried.

The squire obeyed, and was instantly carried off his legs, and whisked through the air at a prodigious rate.

He felt giddy and confused, but did not dare to leave go, lest he should be dashed in pieces, while Nance's wild laughter rang in his ears.

Over the bleached and perpendicular crag—startling the eagle from his eyry—over the yawning gully with the torrent roaring beneath him—over the sharp ridges of the hill—over Townley park—over Burnley steeple—over the wide valley beyond, he went—until at last, bewildered, out of breath, and like one in a dream, he alighted on a brown, bare, heathy expanse, and within a hundred yards of a tall, circular stone structure, which he knew to be Malkin Tower.

CHAPTER V.—THE END OF MALKIN TOWER.

THE shades of night had fallen on Downham manor-house, and with an aching heart, and a strong presentiment of ill, Mistress Nutter prepared to quit the little chamber which had sheltered her for more than two months, and where she would willingly have breathed her latest sigh, if it had been so permitted her. Closing the Bible she had been reading, she placed the sacred volume under her arm, and taking up a small bundle, containing her slender preparations for travel, extinguished the taper, and then descending by a secret staircase, passed through a door, fashioned externally like a cupboard, and entered a summer-house, where she found old Crouch awaiting her.

A few whispered words only passed between her and the huntsman, and informing her that the horses were in waiting at the back of the garden, he took the bundle from her, and would fain have relieved her also of the Bible, but she would not part with it, and pressing it more closely to her bosom, said she was quite ready to attend him.

It was a beautiful, starlight night; the air soft and balmy, and laden with the perfume of the flowers. A nightingale was singing plaintively in an adjoining tree, and presently came a response equally tender from another part of the grove. Mistress Nutter could not choose but listen, and the melody so touched her that she was half suffocated by repressed emotion, for, alas! the relief of tears was denied her.

Motioning her somewhat impatiently to come on, Crouch struck into a sombre alley, edged by clipped yew-trees, and terminating in a plantation, through which a winding path led to the foot of the hill whereon the mansion was situated. By daylight this was a beautiful walk, affording exquisite glimpses through the trees of the surrounding scenery, and commanding a noble view of Pendle Hill, the dominant point in the prospect. But even now to the poor lady, so long immured in her cell-like chamber, and deprived of many of nature's choicest blessings, it appeared delightful. The fresh air, redolent of new-mown hay, fanned her pale cheek and feverish brow, and allayed her agitation and excitement. The perfect stillness, broken only by the lowing of the cattle in the adjoining pastures, by the drowsy hum of the dor-fly, or the rippling of the beck in the valley, further calmed her; and the soothing influence was completed by a contemplation of the serene heavens, wherein were seen the starry host, with the thin bright crescent of the new moon in the midst of them, diffusing a pearly light around her. One blot alone appeared in the otherwise smiling sky, and this was a great, ugly, black cloud, lowering over the summit of Pendle Hill.

Mistress Nutter noticed the portentous cloud, and noticed also its shadow on the hill, which might have been cast by the Fiend himself, so like was it to a demoniacal shape with outstretched wings; but, though shuddering at the idea it suggested, she would not suffer it to obtain possession of her mind, but resolutely fixed her attention on other and more pleasing objects.

By this time they had reached the foot of the hill, and a gate admitted them to a road running by the side of Downham beck. Here they found the horses in charge of a man in the dark red livery of Nicholas Assheton, and who was no other than Tom Shaw, the rascally cock-master. Delivering the bridles to Crouch, the knave hastily strode away, but he lingered at a little distance to see the lady mount; and then leaping the hedge, struck through the plantation towards the hall, chinking the money in his pockets as he went, and thinking how cleverly he had earned it. But he did not go unpunished; for it is a satisfaction to record that, in walking through the woods, he was caught in a gin placed there by Crouch, which held him fast in its iron teeth till morning, when he was discovered by one of the under-keepers while going his rounds, in a deplorable condition, and lamed for life.

Meanwhile, unconscious either of the manner in which she had been betrayed, or of the punishment awaiting her betrayer, Mistress Nutter followed her conductor in silence. For a while the road continued by the side of the brook, and then quitting it, commenced a long and tedious ascent, running between high banks fringed with trees. The overhanging boughs rendered it so dark that Mistress Nutter could scarcely distinguish the old huntsman, though he was not many yards in advance of her, but she heard the tramp of his horse, and that was enough.

All at once, where the boughs were thickest, and the road darkest, she perceived a small fiery object on the bank, and in her alarm called out to the huntsman, who, looking back for a moment, laughed, and told her not to be uneasy, for it was only a glow-worm. Ashamed of her idle fears she rode on, but had not proceeded far, when, looking again at the bank, she saw it studded with the same lights. This time she did not call out or scream, but gazed steadily at the twinkling fires, hoping to get the better of her fears. Her alarm, however, rose to absolute terror, as she beheld the glow-worms—if glow-worms they were—twist together and form themselves into a flaming brand, such as she had seen in her vision, grasped by the angel who had driven her from the gates of Paradise.

Averting her gaze, she would have hastened on, but a hand suddenly laid upon her bridle, held back her horse; and she then perceived a tall dark man, mounted on a sable steed, riding beside her. The supernatural character of the horseman was manifest, inasmuch as no sound was caused by the tread of his steed, nor did he appear to be visible to Crouch when the latter looked back. Mistress Nutter maintained her seat with difficulty. She well knew who was her companion.

"Soh, Alice Nutter," said the horseman at length, in a low deep tone, "you have chosen to shut yourself up in a narrow cell, like a recluse, for more than two months, denying yourself all sort of enjoyment, practising severest abstinence, and passing your whole time in useless prayer—ay, useless, for if you were to pray from now till doomsday—come when it will, a thousand years hence, or to-morrow—it will not save you. When you signed that bond to my master, sentence was recorded against you, and no power can recall it. Why, then, these unavailing lamentations? Why utter prayers which are rejected, and supplications which are scorned? Shake off this weakness, Alice, and be yourself again. Once you had pride enough, and a little of it would now be of service to you. You would then see the folly of this abject conduct—humbling yourself to the dust only to be spurned, and suing for mercy only to be derided. Pray as loud and as long as you will, the ears of Heaven will remain ever deaf to you."

"I hope otherwise," rejoined the lady, meekly.

"Do not deceive yourself," replied the horseman. "The term granted you by your compact will not be abridged, but it is your own fault if it be not extended. Your daughter is destroying herself in the vain hope of saving you. Her prayers are unavailing as your own, and recoil from the Judgment Throne unheard. The youth upon whom her affections are fixed is stricken with a deadly ailment. It is in your power to save them both."

Mistress Nutter groaned deeply.

"It is in your power, I say, to save them," continued the horseman, "by returning to your allegiance to your master. He will forgive your disobedience if you prove yourself zealous in his service; will restore you to your former worldly position; avenge you of your enemies; and accomplish all you may desire with respect to your daughter."

"He cannot do it," replied Mistress Nutter.

"Cannot!" echoed the horseman. "Try him! For many years I have served you as familiar; and you have never set me the task I have failed to execute. I am ready to become your servant again, and to offer you a yet larger range of control. Put no limits to your desires or ambition. If you are tired of this narrow sphere, take a wider. Look abroad. But do not shut yourself up in a narrow cell, and persuade yourself you are accomplishing your ultimate deliverance, when you are only wasting precious time, which might be more advantageously and far more agreeably employed. While laughing at your folly, my master deplores it; and he has, therefore, sent me as to one for whom, notwithstanding all derelictions from duty, he has still a regard, with an offer of full forgiveness, provided you return to him at once, and renew your covenant, proving your sincerity by casting from you the book you hold under your arm."

"Your snares are not laid subtle enough to catch me," replied Mistress Nutter. "I will never part with this holy volume, which is my present safeguard, and on which I build my hopes of salvation—hopes which your very proposals have revived in my breast; for I am well assured your master would not make them if he felt confident of his power over me. No; I defy him and you, and I command you in Heaven's name to get hence, and to tempt me no longer."

As the words were uttered, with a howl of rage and mortification, like the roar of a wild beast, the dark horseman and his steed vanished. Alarmed by the sound, Crouch stopped, and questioned the lady as to its cause; but receiving no satisfactory explanation from her, he bade her ride quickly on, affirming it must be the boggart of the clough.

Soon after this they again came upon Downham beck, and were about to cross it, when their purpose was arrested by a joyous barking, and the next moment Grip came up. The dog, it appeared, had been shut up in the stable, his company not being desired on the expedition; but contriving in some way or other to get out, he had scented his master's course, and in the end overtaken him. Crouch did not know whether to be angry or pleased, and at first gave utterance to an oath, and raised his whip to chastise him, but almost instantly the latter feeling predominated, and he welcomed the faithful animal with a few kind words.

"Ey suppose theaw thowt ey couldna do without thee, Grip," he said, "and mayhap theaw'rt reet."

They are now across the beck, and speeding over the wide brown waste. The huntsman warily shapes his course so as to avoid any limestone-quarries or turf-pits. He points out a jack-o'-lantern dancing merrily on the surface of a dangerous morass, and tells a dismal tale of a traveller lured into it by the delusive light, and swallowed up.

Mistress Nutter pays little heed to him, but ever and anon looks back, as if in dread of some one behind her. But no one is visible, and she only sees the great black cloud still hovering over Pendle Hill.

On—on—they go; their horses' hoofs now splashing through the wet sod, now beating upon the firm but elastic turf. A merry ride it would be if their errand were different, and their hearts free from care. The air is fresh and reviving, and the rapid motion exhilarating. The stars shine out, and the crescent moon is still glittering in the heavens, but the black cloud hangs motionless on Pendle Hill.

Now and then some bird of night flies past them, and they hear the whooping of the owl, and see him skimming like a ghost over the waste. Then more fen fires arise, showing that other treacherous quagmires are at hand; but Crouch skirts them safely. Now the bull-frog croaks in the marsh, and a deep booming tells of a bittern passing by. They see the mighty bird above them, with his wide heavy wings and long neck. Grip howls at him, but is instantly checked by his master, and they gallop on.

They are now by the side of Pendle Water, and within sight of Rough Lee. What tumultuous thoughts agitate the lady's breast! The ground she tramples on was once her own; the woods by the river side were planted by her; the mansion before her once owned her as mistress, and now she dares not approach it. Nor does she desire to do so, for the sight of it brings back terrible recollections, and fills her again with despair.

They are now close upon it, and it appears dark, silent, and deserted. How different from what it was of yore in her husband's days—the husband she had foully slain! Speed on, old huntsman!—lash your panting horse, or the remorseful lady will far outstrip you, for she rides as if the avenging furies were at her heels.

She is rattling over the bridge, and Crouch, toiling after her, and with Grip toiling after him, shouts to her to moderate her pace. She looks back, and beholds the grim old house frowning full upon her, and hurries on. Huntsman and dog are left behind for awhile, but the steep ascent soon compels her to slacken speed, and they come up, Crouch swearing lustily, and Grip, with his tongue out of his mouth, limping as if foot-sore.

The road now leads through a thicket. The horses stumble frequently, for the stones are loose, and the footing consequently uncertain. Crouch has a fall, and ere he can remount the lady is gone. It is useless to hurry after her, and he is proceeding slowly, when Grip, who is a little in advance, growls fiercely, and looks back at his master, as if to intimate that danger is at hand. The huntsman presses on, but he is too late, if, indeed, he could at any time have rendered effectual assistance. A clearing in the thicket shows him the lady dismounted, and surrounded by several wild-looking men armed with calivers. Part of the band bear her shrieking off, and the rest fire at him, but without effect, and then chase him as far as the steepest part of the hill, down which he dashes, followed by Grip. Arrived at the bottom, he pauses to listen if he is pursued, and hearing nothing further to alarm him, debates with himself what is best to be done; and, not liking to alarm the village, for that would be to betray Mistress Nutter, he gets off his horse, ties him to a tree, and with Grip close at his heels, commences the ascent of the hill by a different road from that he had previously taken.

Meanwhile, Mistress Nutter's captors dragged her forcibly towards the tower. Their arms and appearance left her no doubt they were depredators, and she sought to convince them she had neither money nor valuables in her possession. They laughed at her assertions, but made no other reply. Her sole consolation was, that they did not seek to deprive her of her Bible.

On reaching the tower, a signal was given by one of the foremost of the band, and the steps being lowered from the high doorway, she was compelled to ascend them, and being pushed along a short passage, obscured by a piece of thick tapestry, but which was drawn aside as she advanced, she found herself in a circular chamber, in the midst of which was a massive table covered with flasks and drinking-cups, and stained with wine. From the roof, which was crossed by great black beams of oak, was suspended a lamp with three burners, whose light showed that the walls were garnished with petronels, rapiers, poniards, and other murderous weapons; besides these there were hung from pegs long riding-cloaks, sombreros, vizards, and other robber accoutrements, including a variety of disguises, from the clown's frieze jerkin to the gentleman's velvet doublet, ready to be assumed on an emergency. Here and there was an open valise, or a pair of saddle-bags with their contents strewn about the floor, and on a bench were a dice-box and shuffle-board, showing, with the flasks and goblets on the table, how the occupants of the tower passed their time.

A steep ladder-like flight of steps led to the upper chamber, and down these, at the very moment of Mistress Nutter's entrance, descended a stalwart personage, who eyed her fiercely as he leapt upon the floor. There was something in the man's truculent physiognomy, and strange and oblique vision, that reminded her of Mother Demdike.

"Welcome to Malkin Tower, madam," said the robber with a grin, and doffing his cap with affected courtesy. "We have met before, but it is many years ago, and I dare say you have forgotten me. You will guess who I am when I tell you my mother occupied this tower before me."

Finding Mistress Nutter made no remark, he went on.

"I am Christopher Demdike, madam – Captain Demdike, I should say. The brave fellows who have brought you hither are part of my band, and till lately Northumberland and the borders of Scotland used to be our scene of action; but chancing to hear of my worthy old mother's death, I thought we could not do better than take possession of her stronghold, which devolved upon me by right of inheritance. Since our arrival here we have kept ourselves very quiet, and the country folk, taking us for spirits or demons, never approach our hiding-place; while, as all our depredations are confined to distant parts, our retreat has never been suspected."

"This concerns me little," observed Mistress Nutter, coldly.

"Pardon me, madam, it concerns you much, as you will learn anon. But be seated, I pray you," he said, with mock civility. "I am keeping you standing all this while."

But as the lady declined the attention, he went on.

"I was fortunate enough, on first coming back to this part of the country, to pick up an acquaintance with your relative, Nicholas Assheton, who invited me to stay with him at Downham, and was so well pleased with my society that he could not endure to part with me."

"Indeed!" exclaimed Mistress Nutter, "are you the person he called Lawrence Fogg?"

"The same," replied Demdike; "and no doubt you would hear a good report of me, madam. Well, it suited my purpose to stay; for I was very hospitably entertained by the squire, who, except being rather too much addicted to lectures and psalm-singing, is as pleasant a host as one could desire; besides which, he was obliging enough to employ me to borrow money for him, and what I got, I kept, you may be sure."

"I would willingly be spared the details of your knavery," said Mistress Nutter, somewhat impatiently.

"I am coming to an end," rejoined Demdike, "and then, perhaps, you may wish I had prolonged them. All the squire's secrets were committed to me, and I was fully aware of your concealment in the hall, but I could never ascertain precisely where you were lodged. I meant to carry you off, and only awaited the opportunity which has presented itself to-night."

"If you think to obtain money from me, you will find yourself mistaken," said Mistress Nutter. "I have parted with all my possessions."

"But to whom, madam?" cried Demdike, with a sinister smile —"to your daughter. And I am sure she is too gentle, too tender-hearted, to allow you to suffer when she can relieve you. You must get us a good round sum from her, or you will be detained here long. The dungeons are dark and unwholesome, and my band are apt to be harsh in their treatment of captives. They have found in the vaults some instruments of torture belonging to old Blackburn, the freebooter, the efficacy of which in an obstinate case I fear they might be inclined to try. You now begin to see the drift of my discourse, madam, and understand the sort of men you have to deal with—barbarous fellows, madam —inhuman dogs!"

And he laughed coarsely at his own jocularity.

"It may put an end to this discussion," said Mistress Nutter, firmly, "if I declare that no torture shall induce me to make any such demand from my daughter."

"You think, perhaps, I am jesting with you, madam," rejoined Demdike.

"Oh! no, I believe you capable of any atrocity," replied the lady. "You do not, either in feature or deeds, belie your parentage."

"Ah! say you so, madam?" cried Demdike. "You have a sharp tongue, I find. Courtesy is thrown away upon you. What, ho! lads—Kenyon and Lowton, take the lady down to the vaults, and there let her have an hour for solitary reflection. She may change her mind in that time."

"Do not think it," cried Mistress Nutter, resolutely.

"If you continue obstinate, we will find means to move you," rejoined Demdike, in a taunting tone. "But what has she got beneath her arm? Give me the book. What's this?—a Bible! A witch with a Bible! It should be a grimoire. Ha! ha!"

"Give it me back, I implore of you," shrieked the lady "I shall be destroyed, soul and body, if I have it not with me

"What! you are afraid the devil may carry you off without it —ho! ho!" roared Demdike. "Well, that would not suit my purpose at present. Here, take it—and now off with her, lads, without more ado!"

And as he spoke, a trapdoor was opened by one of the robbers, disclosing a flight of steps leading to the subterranean chambers, down which the miserable lady was dragged.

Presently the two men re-appeared with a grim smile on their ruffianly countenances, and, as they closed the trapdoor, one of them observed to the captain that they had chained her to a pillar, by removing the band from the great skeleton, and passing it round her body.

"You have done well, lads," replied Demdike, approvingly; "and now go all of you and scour the hill-top, and return in an hour, and we will decide upon what is to be done with this woman."

The two men then joined the rest of their comrades outside, and the whole troop descended the steps, which were afterwards drawn up by Demdike. This done, the robber captain returned to the circular chamber, and for some time paced to and fro, revolving his dark schemes. He then paused, and placing his ear near the trapdoor, listened, but as no sound reached him, he sat down at the table, and soon grew so much absorbed as to be unconscious that a dark figure was creeping stealthily down the narrow staircase behind him.

"I cannot get rid of Nicholas Assheton," he exclaimed at length. "I somehow fancy we shall meet again; and yet all should be over with him by this time."

"Look round!" thundered a voice behind him. "Nicholas Assheton is not to be got rid of so easily."

At this unexpected summons, Demdike started to his feet, and recoiled aghast, as he saw what he took to be the ghost of the murdered squire standing before him. A second look, however, convinced him that it was no phantom he beheld, but a living man, armed for vengeance, and determined upon it.

"Get a weapon, villain," cried Nicholas, in tones of concentrated fury. "I do not wish to take unfair advantage, even of thee."

Without a word of reply, Demdike snatched a sword from the wall, and the next moment was engaged in deadly strife with the squire. They were well matched, for both were powerful men, both expert in the use of their weapons, and the combat might have been protracted and of doubtful issue but for the irresistible fury of Nicholas, who assaulted his adversary with such vigour and determination that he speedily drove him against the wall, where the latter made an attempt to seize a petronel hanging beside him, but his purpose being divined, he received a thrust through the arm, and, dropping his blade, lay at the squire's mercy.

Nicholas shortened his sword, but forbore to strike. Seizing his enemy by the throat, he hurled him to the ground, and, planting his knee on his chest, called out, "What, ho, Nance!"

"Nance!" exclaimed Demdike,—"then it was that mischievous jade who brought you here."

"Ay," replied the squire, as the young woman came quickly down the steps,—"and I refused her aid in the conflict because I felt certain of mastering thee, and because I would not take odds even against such a treacherous villain as thou art."

"Better dispatch him, squire," said Nance; "he may do yo a mischief yet."

"No—no," replied Nicholas, "he is unworthy of a gentleman's sword. Besides, I have sworn to hang him, and I will keep my word. Go down into the vaults and liberate Mistress Nutter, while I bind him, for we must take him with us. To-morrow, he shall lie in Lancaster Castle with his kinsfolk."

"That remains to be seen," muttered Demdike.

"Be on your guard, squire," cried Nance, as she lifted a small lamp, and raised the trapdoor.

With this caution, she descended to the vaults, while Nicholas looked about for a thong, and perceiving a rope dangling down the wall near him, he seized it, drawing it with some force towards him.

A sudden sound reached his ears—clang! clang! He had rung the alarm-bell violently.

Clang! clang! clang! Would it never stop?

Taking advantage of his surprise and consternation, Demdike got from under him, sprang to his feet, and rushing to the doorway, instantly let fall the steps, roaring out,—

"Treason! to the rescue, my men! to the rescue!"

His cries were immediately answered from without, and it was evident from the tumult that the whole of the band were hurrying to his assistance.

Not a moment was to be lost by the squire. Plunging through the trapdoor, he closed it after him, and bolted it underneath at the very moment the robbers entered the chamber. Demdike's rage at finding him gone was increased, when all the combined efforts of his men failed in forcing open the trapdoor.

"Take hatchets and hew it open!" he cried; "we must have them. I have heard there is a secret outlet below, and though I have never been able to discover it, it may be known to Nance. I will go outside, and watch. If you hear me whistle, come forth instantly."

And, rushing forth, he was making the circuit of the tower, and examining some bushes at its base, when his throat was suddenly seized by a dog, and before he could even utter an exclamation, much less sound his whistle, or use his arms, he was grappled by the old huntsman, and dragged off to a considerable distance, the dog still clinging to his throat.

Meanwhile, Nicholas had hurried down into the vaults, where he found Nance sustaining Mistress Nutter, who was half fainting, and hastily explaining what had occurred, she consigned the lady to him, and then led the way through the central range of pillars, and past the ebon image, until she approached the wall, when, holding up the lamp, she revealed a black marble slab between the statues of Blackburn and Isole. Pressing against it, the slab moved on one side, and disclosed a flight of steps.

"Go up there," cried Nance to the squire, "and when ye get to th' top, yo'n find another stoan, wi' a nob in it. Yo canna miss it. Go on."

"But you!" cried the squire. "Will you not come with us?"

"Ey'n come presently," replied Nance, with a strange smile. "Ey ha summat to do first. That cunning fox Demdike has set a trap fo' himsel an aw his follo vers,—and it's fo' me to ketch 'em. Wait fo' me about a hun lert yorts fro' th' tower. Nab nearer—yo onderstand?"

Nicholas did not very clearly uuderstand, but concluding Nance had some hidden meaning in what she said, he resolved unhesitatingly to obey her. Having got clear of the tower, as directed, with Mistress Nutter, he ran on with her to some distance, when what was his surprise to find Crouch and Grip keeping watch over the prostrate robber chief. A few words from the huntsman sufficed to explain how this had come about, but they were scarcely uttered when Nance rushed up in breathless haste, crying out—"Off! further off! as yo value your lives!"

Seeing from her manner that delay would be dangerous, Nicholas and Crouch laid hold of the prisoner and bore him away between them, while Nance assisted Mistress Nutter along.

They had not gone far when a rumbling sound like that preceding an earthquake was heard.

All looked back towards Malkin Tower. The structure was seen to rock—flames burst from the earth—and with a tremendous explosion heard for miles around, and which shook the ground even where Nicholas and the others stood, the whole of the unhallowed fabric, from base to summit, was blown into the air, some of the stones being projected to an extraordinary distance.

A mine charged with gunpowder, it appeared, had been laid beneath its vaults by Demdike, with a view to its destruction at some future period, and this circumstance being known to Nance, she had fired the train.

Not one of the robbers within the tower escaped. The bodies of all were found next day, crushed, burned, or frightfully mutilated.

CHAPTER VI.—HOGHTON TOWER.

About a month after the occurrence last described, and early on a fine morning in August, Nicholas Assheton and Richard Sherborne rode forth together from the proud town of Preston. Both were gaily attired in doublets and hose of yellow velvet, slashed with white silk, with mantles to match, the latter being somewhat conspicuously embroidered on the shoulder with a wild bull worked in gold, and underneath it the motto, "*Malgré le Tort.*" Followed at a respectful distance by four mounted attendants, the two gentlemen had crossed the bridge over the Ribble, and were wending their way along the banks of a tributary stream, the Darwen, within a short distance of the charming village of Walton-le-Dale, when they perceived a horseman advancing slowly towards them, whom they instantly hailed as Richard Assheton, and pushing forward, were soon beside him. Both were much shocked by the young man's haggard looks, and inquired anxiously as to his health, but Richard bade them, with a melancholy smile, not be uneasy, for all would be well with him erelong.

"All will be over with you, lad, if you don't mind; and that's, perhaps, what you mean," replied Nicholas; "but as soon as the royal festivities at Hoghton are over, I'll set about your cure; and, what's more, I'll accomplish it—for I know where the seat of the disease lies better than Dr. Morphew, your family physician at Middleton. 'Tis near the heart, Dick—near the heart. Ha! I see I have touched you, lad. But, beshrew me, you are very strangely attired—in a suit of sable velvet, with a black Spanish hat and feather, for a festival! You look as if going to a funeral. I am fearful his Majesty may take it amiss. Why not wear the livery of our house?"

"Nay, if it comes to that," rejoined Richard, "why do not you and Sherborne wear it, instead of flaunting like daws in borrowed plumage? I scarce know you in your strange garb, and certainly should not take you for an Assheton, or aught pertaining to our family, from your gaudy colours and the strange badge on your shoulder."

"I don't wonder at it, Dick," said Nicholas; "I scarce know myself; and though the clothes I wear are well made enough, they seem to sit awkwardly on me, and trouble me as much as the shirt of Nessus did Hercules of old. For the nonce I am Sir Richard Hoghton's retainer. I must own I was angry with myself when I saw Sir Ralph Assheton with his long train of gentlemen, all in murrey-coloured cloaks and doublets, at Myerscough Lodge, while I, his cousin, was habited like one of another house. And when I would have excused my apparent defection to Sir Ralph, he answered coldly, 'It was better as it was, for he could scarcely have found room for me among his friends.'"

"Do not fret yourself, Nicholas," rejoined Sherborne; Sir Ralph cannot reasonably take offence at a mere piece of good-nature on your part. But this does not explain why Richard affects a colour so sombre."

"I am the retainer of one whose livery is sombre," replied the young man, with a ghastly smile. "But enough of this," he added, endeavouring to assume a livelier air; "I suppose you are on the way to Hoghton Tower. I thought to reach Preston before you were up, but I might have recollected you are no lag-a-bed, Nicholas, not even after hard drinking overnight, as witness your feats at Whalley. To be frank with you, I feared being led into like excesses, and so preferred passing the night at the quiet little inn at Walton-le-Dale, to coming on to you at the Castle at Preston, which I knew would be full of noisy roysterers."

"Full it was, even to overflowing," replied the squire; "but you should have come, Dick, for, by my troth! we had a right merry night of it. Stephen Hamerton, of Hellyfield Peel, with his wife, and her sister, sweet Mistress Doll Lister, supped with us; and we had music, dancing, and singing, and abundance of good cheer. Nouns! Dick, Doll Lister is a delightful lass, and if you can only get Alizon out of your head, would be just the wife for you. She sings like an angel, has the most captivating sigh-and-die-away manner, and the prettiest rounded figure ever bodice kept in. Were I in your place I should know where to choose. But you will see her at Hoghton to-day, for she is to be at the banquet and masque."

"Your description does not tempt me," said Richard; "I have no taste for sigh-and-die-away damsels. Dorothy Lister, however, is accounted fair enough; but, were she fascinating as Venus herself, in my present mood I should not regard her."

"I' faith, lad, I pity you, if such be the case," shrugging his shoulders, more in contempt than compassion.

"Waste not your sympathy upon me," replied Richard; "but, tell me, how went the show at Preston yesterday?"

"Excellently well, and much to his Majesty's satisfaction," answered the squire. "Proud Preston never was so proud before, and never with such good reason; for if the people be poor, according to the proverb, they take good care to hide their poverty. Bombards were fired from the bridge, and the church bells rang loud enough to crack the steeple, and bring it down about the ears of the deafened lieges. The houses were hung with carpets and arras; the streets strewn ankle deep with sand and sawdust; the cross in the market-place was bedecked with garlands of flowers like a May-pole; and the conduit near it ran wine. At noon there was more firing; and, amidst flourishes of trumpets, rolling of drums, squeaking of fifes, and prodigious shouting, bonnie King Jamie came to the cross, where a speech was made him by Master Breares, the Recorder; after which the corporation presented his Majesty with a huge silver bowl, in token of their love and loyalty. The King seemed highly pleased with the gift, and observed to the Duke of Buckingham, loud enough to be heard by the bystanders, who reported his speech to me, 'God's santie! it's a braw bicker, Steenie, and might serve for a christening-cup, if we had need of siccan a vessel, which, Heaven be praised, we ha'e na!' After this there was a grand banquet in the town-hall; and when the heat of the day was over the King left with his train for Hoghton Tower, visiting the alum mines on the way thither. We are bidden to breakfast by Sir Richard, so we must push on, Dick, for his Majesty is an early riser, like myself. We are to have rare sport to-day. Hunting in the morning, a banquet, and, as I have already intimated, a masque at night, in which Sir George Goring and Sir John Finett will play, and in which I have been solicited to take the drolling part of Jem Tospot—nay, laugh not, Dick, Sherborne says I shall play it to the life—as well as to find some mirthful dame to enact the companion part of Doll Wango. I have spoken with two or three on the subject, and fancy one of them will oblige me. There is another matter on which I am engaged. I am to present a petition to his Majesty from a great number of the lower orders in this county, praying they may be allowed to take their diversions, as of old accustomed, after divine service on Sundays; and, though I am the last man to desire any violation of the Sabbath, being somewhat puritanically inclined, as they now phrase it, yet I cannot think any harm can ensue from lawful recreation and honest exercise. Still, I would any one were chosen to present the petition rather than myself."

"Have no misgivings on the subject," said Richard, "but urge the matter strongly; and if you need support, I will give you all I can, for I feel we are best observing the divine mandate by making the Sabbath a day of rest, and observing it cheerfully. And this, I apprehend, is the substance of your petition?"

"The whole sum and substance," replied Nicholas; "and I have reason to believe his Majesty's wishes are in accordance with it."

"They are known to be so," said Sherborne.

"I am glad to hear it," cried Richard. "God save King James, the friend of the people!"

"Ay, God save King James!" echoed Nicholas; "and if he grant this petition he will prove himself their friend, for he will have all the clergy against him, and will be preached against from half the pulpits in the kingdom."

"Little harm will ensue if it should be so," replied Richard; "for he will be cheered and protected by the prayers of a grateful and happy people."

They then rode on for a few minutes in silence, after which Richard inquired—

"You had brave doings at Myerscough Lodge, I suppose, Nicholas?"

"Ay, marry had we," answered the squire, "and the feasting must have cost Ned Tyldesley a pretty penny. Besides the King and his own particular attendants, there were some dozen noblemen and their followers, including the Duke of Buckingham, who moves about like a king himself, and I know not how many knights and gentlemen. Sherborne and I rode over from Dunnow, and reached the forest immediately after the King had entered it in his coach; so we took a short cut through the woods, and came up just in time to join Sir Richard Hoghton's train as he was riding up to his Majesty. Fancy a wide glade, down which a great gilded coach is slowly moving, drawn by eight horses, and followed by a host of noblemen and gentlemen in splendid apparel, their esquires and pages equally richly arrayed, and equally well mounted; and, after these, numerous falconers, huntsmen, prickers, foresters, and yeomen, with staghounds in leash, and hawk on fist, all ready for the sport. Fancy all this, if you can, Dick, and then conceive what a brave sight it must have been. Well, as I said, we came up in the very nick of time, for presently the royal coach stopped, and Sir Richard Hoghton, calling all his gentlemen around him, and bidding us dismount, and we followed him, and drew up, bareheaded, before the King, while Sir Richard pointed out to his Majesty the boundaries of the royal forest, and told him he would find it as well stocked with deer as any in his kingdom. Before putting an end to the conference, the King complimented the worthy Knight on the gallant appearance of his train, and on learning we were all gentlemen, graciously signified his pleasure that some of us should be presented to him. Amongst others, I was brought forward by Sir Richard, and liking my looks, I suppose, the King was condescending enough to enter into conversation with me; and as his discourse chiefly turned on sporting matters, I was at home with him at once, and he presently grew so familiar with me, that I almost forgot the presence in which I stood. However, his Majesty seemed in no way offended by my freedom, but, on the contrary, clapped me on the shoulder, and said, 'Maister Assheton, for a country gentleman, you're weel-mannered and weel-informed, and I shall be glad to see more of you while I stay in these parts.' After this, the good-natured monarch mounted his horse, and the hunting began, and a famous day's work we made of it, his Majesty killing no fewer than five fine bucks with his own hand."

"You are clearly on the road to preferment, Nicholas," observed Richard, with a smile. "You will outstrip Buckingham himself, if you go on in this way."

"So I tell him," observed Sherborne, laughing; "and, by my faith! young Sir Gilbert Hoghton, who, owing to his connexion by marriage with Buckingham, is a greater man than his father, Sir Richard, looked quite jealous; for the King more than once called out to Nicholas in the chase, and took the wood-knife from him when he broke up the last deer, which is accounted a mark of especial favour."

"Well, gentlemen," said the squire, "I shall not stand in my own light, depend upon it; and, if I should bask in court-sunshine, you shall partake of the rays. If I do become master of the household, in lieu of the Duke of Richmond, or master of the horse and cupbearer to his Majesty, in place of his Grace of Buckingham, I will not forget you."

"We are greatly indebted to you, my Lord Marquess of Downham and Duke of Pendle Hill, that is to be," rejoined Sherborne, taking off his cap with mock reverence; "and perhaps, for the sake of your sweet sister and my spouse, Dorothy, you will make interest to have me appointed gentleman of the bedchamber?"

"Doubt it not—doubt it not," replied Nicholas, in a patronising tone.

"My ambition soars higher than yours, Sherborne," said Richard; "I must be lord-keeper of the privy seal, or nothing."

"Oh! what you will, gentlemen, what you will!" cried Nicholas; "you can ask me nothing I will not grant—always provided I have the means."

A turn in the road now showed them Hoghton Tower, crowning the summit of an isolated and conical hill, about two miles off. Rising proudly in the midst of a fair and fertile plain, watered by the Ribble and the Darwen, the stately edifice seemed to command the whole country. And so King James thought, as, from the window of his chamber, he looked down upon the magnificent prospect around him, comprehending on the one hand the vast forests of Myerscough and Bowland, stretching as far as the fells near Lancaster; and, on the other, an open but still undulating country, beautifully diversified with wood and water, well-peopled and well-cultivated, green with luxuriant pastures, yellow with golden grain, or embowered with orchards, boasting many villages and small towns, as well as two lovely rivers, which, combining their currents at Walton-le-Dale, gradually expanded till they neared the sea, which could be seen gleaming through openings in the distant hills. As the King surveyed this fair scene, and thought how strong was the position of the mansion, situated as it was upon high cliffs springing abruptly from the Darwen, and how favourably circumstanced, with its forests and park, for the enjoyment of the chase, of which he was passionately fond, how capable of defence, and how well adapted for a hunting-seat, he sighed to think it did not belong to the crown. Nor was he wrong in his estimate of its strength, for in after years, during the civil wars, it held out stoutly against the parliamentary forces, and was only reduced at last by treachery, when part of its gate-tower was blown up, destroying an officer and two hundred men, "in that blast most wofully."

Though the hour was so early, the road was already thronged, not only with horsemen and pedestrians of every degree from Preston, but with rude lumbering vehicles from the neighbouring villages of Plessington, Brockholes, and Cuerden, driven by farmers, who, with their buxom dames and cherry-cheeked daughters, decked out in holiday finery, hoped to gain admittance to Hoghton Tower, or, at all events, obtain a peep of the King as he rode out to hunt. Most of these were saluted by Nicholas, who scrupled not to promise them admission to the outer court of the Tower, and even went so far as to offer some of the comelier damsels a presentation to the King. Occasionally, the road was enlivened by strains of music from a band of minstrels, by a song or a chorus from others, or by the gamesome tricks of a party of mummers. At one place, a couple of tumblers and a clown were performing their feats on a cloth stretched on the grass beneath a tree. Here the crowd collected for a few minutes, but presently gave way to loud shouts, attended by the cracking of whips, proceeding from two grooms in the yellow and white livery of Sir Richard Hoghton, who headed some half-dozen carts filled with provisions, carcases of sheep and oxen, turkeys and geese, pullets and capons, fish, bread, and vegetables, all bent for

Hoghton Tower; for though Sir Richard had made vast preparations for his guests, he found his supplies, great as they were, wholly inadequate to their wants. Cracking their whips in answer to the shouts with which they were greeted, the purveyors galloped on, many a hungry wight looking wistfully after them.

Nicholas and his companions were now at the entrance to Hoghton Park, through which the Darwen coursed, after washing the base of the rocky heights on which the mansion was situated. Here four yeomen of the guard, armed with halberts, and an officer, were stationed, and no one was admitted without an order from Sir Richard Hoghton. Possessing a pass, the squire and his companions with their attendants were, of course, allowed to enter; but the throng accompanying them were sent over the bridge, and along a devious road skirting the park, which, though it went more than a mile round, eventually brought them to their destination.

Hoghton Park, though not very extensive, boasted a great deal of magnificent timber, and in some places was so thickly wooded, that, according to Dr. Kuerden, "a man passing through it could scarcely have seen the sun shine at middle of day." Into one of these tenebrous groves the horsemen now plunged, and for some moments were buried in the gloom produced by matted and overhanging boughs. Issuing once more into the warm sunshine, they traversed a long and beautiful silvan glade, skirted by ancient oaks, with mighty arms and gnarled limbs—the patriarchs of the forest. In the open ground on the left were scattered a few ash-trees, and beneath them browsed a herd of fallow deer; while crossing the lower end of the glade was a large herd of red deer, for which the park was famous, the hinds tripping nimbly and timidly away, but the lordly stags, with their branching antlers, standing for a moment at gaze, and disdainfully regarding the intruders on their domain. Little did they think how soon and severely their courage would be tried, or how soon the *mort* would be sounded for their *pryse* by the huntsman. But if, happily for themselves, the poor leathern-coated fools could not foresee their doom, it was not equally hidden from Nicholas, who predicted what would ensue, and pointed out one noble hart which he thought worthy to die by the King's own hand. As if he understood him, the stately beast tossed his antlered head aloft, and plunged into the adjoining thicket; but the squire noted the spot where he had disappeared.

The glade led them into the chase, a glorious hunting-ground of about two miles in circumference, surrounded by an amphitheatre of wood, and studded by noble forest trees. Variety and beauty were lent to it by an occasional knoll crowned with timber, or by numerous ferny dells and dingles. As the horsemen entered upon the chase, they observed at a short distance from them a herd of the beautiful, but fierce wild cattle, originally from Bowland Forest, and still preserved in the park. White and spangled in colour, with short sharp horns, fine eyes, and small shapely limbs, these animals were of untameable fierceness, possessed of great cunning, and ever ready to assault any one who approached them. They would often attack a solitary individual, gore him, and trample him to death. Consequently, they were far more dreaded than the wild-boars, with which, as with every other sort of game, the neighbouring woods were plentifully stocked. Well aware of the danger they ran, the party watched the herd narrowly and distrustfully, and would have galloped on; but this would only have provoked pursuit, and the wild cattle were swifter than any horses. Suddenly, a milk-white bull trotted out from the rest of the herd, bellowing fiercely, lashing his sides with his tail, and lowering his head to the ground, as if meditating an attack. His example was speeedily followed by the others, and the whole herd began to beat the ground and roar loudly. Much alarmed by these hostile manifestations, the party were debating whether to stand the onset, or trust to the fleetness of their steeds for safety; when just as the whole herd, with tails erect and dilated nostrils, were galloping towards them, assistance appeared in the persons of some ten or a dozen mounted prickers, who, armed with long poles pointed with iron, issued with loud shouts from an avenue opening upon the chase. At sight of them, the whole herd wheeled round and fled, but were pursued by the prickers till they were driven into the depths of the furthest thicket. Six of the prickers remained watching over them during the day, in order that the royal hunting-party might not be disturbed, and the woods echoed with the bellowing of the angry brutes.

While this was going forward, the squire and his companions, congratulating themselves on their narrow escape, galloped off, and entered the long avenue of sycamores, from which the prickers had emerged.

At the head of a steep ascent, partly hewn out of the rock, and partly skirted by venerable and majestic trees, forming a continuation of the avenue, rose the embattled gate-tower of the proud edifice they were approaching, and which now held the monarch of the land, and the highest and noblest of his court as guests within its halls. From the top of the central tower of the gateway floated the royal banner, while at the very moment the party reached the foot of the hill, they were saluted by a loud peal of ordnance discharged from the side-towers, proclaiming that the King had arisen; and, as the smoke from the culverins wreathed round the standard, a flourish of trumpets was blown from the walls, and martial music resounded from the court.

Roused by these stirring sounds, Nicholas spurred his horse up the rocky ascent, and followed closely by his companions, who were both nearly as much excited as himself, speedily gained the great gateway—a massive and majestic structure, occupying the centre of the western front of the mansion, and consisting of three towers of great strength and beauty, the mid-tower far overtopping the other two, as in the arms of Old Castile, and sustaining, as was its right, the royal standard. On the platform stood the trumpeters with their silk-fringed clarions, and the iron mouths of the culverins, which had been recently discharged, protruded through the battlements. The arms and motto of the Hoghtons, carved in stone, were placed upon the gateway, with the letters 𝕿. 𝕳., the initials of the founder of the tower. Immediately above the arched entrance was the sculptured figure of a knight slaying a dragon.

In front of the gateway a large crowd of persons were assembled, consisting of the inferior gentry of the neighbourhood, with their wives, daughters, and servants, clergymen, attorneys, chirurgeons, farmers, and tradesmen of all kind from the adjoining towns of Blackburn, Preston, Chorley, Haslingden, Garstang, and even Lancaster. Representatives in some sort or other of almost every town and village in the county might be found amongst the motley assemblage, which, early as it was, numbered several hundreds, many of those from the more distant places having quitted their homes soon after midnight. Admittance was naturally sought by all; but here the same rule was observed as at the park gate, and no one was allowed to enter, even the base court, without authority from the lord of the mansion. The great gates were closed, and two files of halberdiers were drawn up under the deep archway, to keep the passage clear, and quell disturbance in case any should occur; while a gigantic porter, stationed in front of the wicket, rigorously scrutinised the passes. These precautions naturally produced delay; and, though many of the better part of the crowd were entitled to admission, it was not without much pushing and squeezing, and considerable detriment to their gay apparel, that they were enabled to effect their object.

The comfort of those outside the walls had not, however, been altogether neglected by Sir Richard Hoghton, for sheds were reared under the trees, where stout March beer, together with cheese and bread, or oaten cakes and butter, were freely distributed to all applicants; so that, if some were disappointed, few were discontented, especially when told that the gates would be thrown open at noon, when, during the time the King and the nobles feasted in the great banquet-hall, they might partake of a wild bull from the park, slaughtered expressly for the occasion, which was now being roasted whole within the base court. That the latter was no idle promise they had the assurance of thick smoke rising above the walls, laden with the scent of roast meat, and, moreover, they could see through the wicket a great fire blazing and crackling on the green, with a huge carcase on an immense spit before it, and a couple of turn-broaches basting it.

As Nicholas and his companions forced their way through this crowd, which was momently receiving additions as fresh arrivals took place, the squire recognised many old acquaintances, and was nodding familiarly right and left, when he encountered a woman's eye fixed keenly upon him, and to his surprise beheld Nance Redferne. Nance, who had lost none of her good looks, was very gaily attired, with her fine chestnut hair knotted with ribbons, her stomacher similarly adorned, and her red petticoat looped up, so as to display an exceedingly trim ankle and small foot; and, under other circumstances, Nicholas might not have minded staying to chat with her, but just now it was out of the question, and he hastily turned his head another way. As ill luck, however, would have it, a stoppage occurred at the moment, during which Nance forced her way up to him, and, taking hold of his arm, said in a low tone—

"Yo mun tae me in wi' ye, squoire."

"Take you in with me—impossible!" cried Nicholas.

"Nah! it's neaw impossible," rejoined Nance, pertinaciously; "yo con do it, an yo shan. Yo owe me a good turn, and mun repay it now."

"But why the devil do you want to go in?" cried Nicholas, impatiently. "You know the King is the sworn enemy of all witches, and, amongst this concourse, some one is sure to recognise you and betray you. I cannot answer for your safety if I do take you in. In my opinion, you were extremely unwise to venture here at all."

"Ne'er heed my wisdom or my folly, boh do as ey bid yo, or yo'n repent it," said Nance.

"Why, you can get in without my aid," observed the squire, trying to laugh it off. "You can easily fly over the walls."

"Ey ha' left my broomstick a-whoam," replied Nance—"boh no more jesting. Win yo do it?"

"Well, well, I suppose I must," replied Nicholas, "but I wash my hands of the consequences. If ill comes of it, I am not to blame. You must go in as Doll Wango—that is, as a character in the masque to be enacted to-night—d'ye mark?"

Nance signified that she perfectly understood him.

The whole of this hurried discourse, conducted in an undertone, passed unheard and unnoticed by the bystanders. Just then, an opening took place amid the crowd, and the squire pushed through it, hoping to get rid of his companion, but he hoped in vain, for, clinging to his saddle, she went on along with him.

They were soon under the deep groined and ribbed arch of the gate, and Nance would have been here turned back by the foremost halberdier, if Nicholas had not signified somewhat hastily that she belonged to his party. The man smiled, and offered no further opposition; and the gigantic porter next advancing, Nicholas exhibited his pass to him, which appearing sufficiently comprehensive to procure admission for Richard and Sherborne, they instantly availed themselves of the licence, while the squire fumbled in his doublet for a further order for Nance. At last he produced it, and after reading it, the gigantic warder exclaimed, with a smile illumining his broad features—

"Ah! I see;—this is an order from his worship, Sir Richard, to admit a certain woman, who is to enact Doll Wango in the masque. This is she, I suppose?" he added, looking at Nance.

"Ay, ay!" replied the squire.

"A comely wench, by the mass!" exclaimed the porter. "Open the gate."

"No—not yet—not yet, good porter, till my claim be adjusted," cried another woman, pushing forward, quite as young and comely as Nance, and equally gaily dressed. "I am the real Doll Wango, though I be generally known as Dame Tetlow. The squire engaged me to play the part before the King, and now this saucy hussy has taken my place. But I'll have my rights, that I will."

"Odd's heart! two Doll Wangos!" exclaimed the porter, opening his eyes.

"Two!—Nay, beleedy! boh there be three!" exclaimed an immensely tall, stoutly proportioned woman, stepping up, to the increased confusion of the squire, and the infinite merriment of the bystanders, whose laughter had been already excited by the previous part of the scene. "Didna yo tell me at Myerscough to come here, squire, an ey, Bess Baldwyn, should play Doll Wango to your Jem Tospot?"

"Play the devil! for that's what you all seem bent upon doing," exclaimed the squire, impatiently. "Away with you! I can have nothing to say to you!"

"You gave me the same promise at the Castle at Preston last night," said Dame Tetlow.

"I had been drinking, and knew not what I said," rejoined Nicholas, angrily.

"Boh yo promised me a few minutes ago, an yo're sober enough now," cried Nance.

"Ey dunna knoa that," rejoined Dame Baldwyn, looking reproachfully at him. "Boh what ey dun knoa is, that nother o' these squemous queans shan ge in efore me."

And she looked menacingly at them, as if determined to oppose their ingress, much to the alarm of the timorous Dame Tetlow, though Nance returned her angry glances unmoved.

"For Heaven's sake, my good fellow, let them all three in!" said Nicholas, in a low tone to the porter, at the same time slipping a gold piece into his hand, "or there's no saying what may be the consequence, for they're three infernal viragos. I'll take the responsibility of their admittance upon myself with Sir Richard"

"Well, as your worship says, I don't like to see quarrelling amongst women," returned the porter, in a bland tone, "so all three shall go in; and as to who is to play Doll Wango, the master of the ceremonies will settle that, so you need give yourself no more concern about it; but if I were called on to decide," he added, with an amorous leer at Dame Baldwyn, whose proportions so well matched his own, "I know where my choice would light. There, now!" he shouted, "Open wide the gate for Squire Nicholas Assheton of Downham, and the three Doll Wangos."

And, all obstacles being thus removed, Nicholas passed on with the three females amidst the renewed laughter of the bystanders. But he got rid of his plagues as soon as he could; for, dismounting and throwing his bridle to an attendant, he vouchsafed not a word to any of them, but stepped quickly after Richard and Sherborne, who had already reached the great fire with the bull roasting before it.

Appropriated chiefly to stables and other offices, the base court of Hoghton Tower consisted of buildings of various dates, the greater part belonging to Elizabeth's time, though some might be assigned to an earlier period, while many alterations and additions had been recently made, in anticipation of the king's visit. Dating back as far as Henry II., the family had originally fixed their residence at the foot of the hill, on the banks of the Darwen; but in process of time, swayed by prouder notions, they mounted the craggy heights above, and built a tower upon their crest. It is melancholy to think that so glorious a pile, teeming with so many historical recollections, and so magnificently situated, should be abandoned, and suffered to go to decay;—the family having, many years ago, quitted it for Walton Hall, near Walton-le-Dale, and consigned it to the occupation of a few gamekeepers. Bereft of its venerable timber, its courts grass-grown, its fine oak staircase rotting and dilapidated, its domestic chapel neglected, its marble chamber broken and ruinous, its wainscotings and ceilings cracked and mouldering, its paintings mildewed and half effaced, Hoghton Tower presents only the wreck of its former grandeur. Desolate indeed are its halls, and their glory for ever departed! However, this history has to do with it in the season of its greatest splendour; when it glistened with silks and velvets, and resounded with loud laughter and blithe music; when stately nobles and lovely dames were seen in the gallery, and a royal banquet was served in the great hall; when its countless chambers were filled to overflowing, and its passages echoed with hasty feet; when the base court was full of huntsmen and falconers, and enlivened by the neighing of steeds and the baying of hounds; when there was daily hunting in the park, and nightly dancing and diversion in the hall,—it is with

NICHOLAS ASSHETON AND THE THREE DOLL WANGOS. P. 428.

Hoghton Tower at this season that the present tale has to do, and not with it as it is now—silent, solitary, squalid, saddening, but still whispering of the glories of the past, still telling of the kingly pageant that once graced it.

The base court was divided from the court of lodging by the great hall and domestic chapel. A narrow vaulted passage on either side led to the upper quadrangle, the façade of which was magnificent, and far superior in uniformity of design and style to the rest of the structure, the irregularity of which, however, was not unpleasing. The whole frontage of the upper court was richly moulded and filleted, with ranges of mullion and transom windows, capitals, and carved parapets crowned with stone balls. Marble pillars, in the Italian style, had been recently placed near the porch, with two rows of pilasters above them, supporting a heavy marble cornice, on which rested the carved escutcheon of the family. A flight of stone steps led up to the porch, and within was a wide oak staircase, so gentle of ascent that a man on horseback could easily mount it—a feat often practised in later days by one of the descendants of the house. In this part of the mansion all the principal apartments were situated, and here James was lodged. Here also was the green room, so called from its hangings, which he used for private conferences, and which was hung round with portraits of his unfortunate mother, Mary, Queen of Scots; of her implacable enemy, Queen Elizabeth; of his consort, Anne of Bohemia; and of Sir Thomas Hoghton, the founder of the tower. Adjoining it was the Star-Chamber, occupied by the Duke of Buckingham, with its napkin panelling, and ceiling "fretted with golden fires;" and in the same angle were rooms occupied by the Duke of Richmond, the Earls of Pembroke and Nottingham, and Lord Howard of Effingham. Below was the library, whither Doctor Thomas Moreton, Bishop of Chester, and his Majesty's chaplain, with the three puisné judges of the King's Bench, Sir John Doddridge, Sir John Crooke, and Sir Robert Hoghton, all of whom were guests of Sir Richard, resorted; and in the adjoining wing was the great gallery, where the whole of the nobles and courtiers passed such of their time—and that was not much—as was not occupied in feasting or out-of-doors' amusements.

Long corridors ran round the upper stories in this part of the mansion, and communicated with an endless series of rooms, which, numerous as they were, were all occupied, and, accommodation being found impossible for the whole of the guests, many were sent to the new erections in the base court, which had been planned to meet the emergency by the magnificent and provident host. The nobles and gentlemen were, however, far outnumbered by their servants, and the confusion occasioned by the running to and fro of the various grooms of the chambers, was indescribable. Doublets had to be brushed, ruffs plaited, hair curled, beards trimmed, and all with the greatest possible expedition; so that, as soon as day dawned upon Hoghton Tower, there was a prodigious racket from one end of it to the other. Many favoured servants slept in truckle-beds in their masters' rooms; but others, not so fortunate, and unable to find accommodation even in the garrets—for the smallest rooms, and those nearest the roof, were put in requisition—slept upon the benches in the hall, while several sat up all night carousing in the great kitchen, keeping company with the cooks and their assistants, who were busied all the time in preparations for the feasting of the morrow.

Such was the state of things inside Hoghton Tower early on the eventful morning in question, and out of doors, especially in the base court which Nicholas was traversing, the noise, bustle, and confusion were equally great. Wide as was the area, it was filled with various personages, some newly arrived, and seeking information as to their quarters—not very easily obtained, for it seemed every body's business to ask questions, and no one's to answer them—some gathered in groups round the falconers and huntsmen, who had suddenly risen into great importance; others, and these were for the most part smart young pages, in brilliant liveries, chattering, and making love to every pretty damsel they encountered, putting them out of countenance by their licence and strange oaths, and rousing the anger of their parents, and the jealousy of their rustic admirers; others, of a graver sort, with dress of formal cut, and puritanical expression of countenance, shrugging their shoulders, and looking sourly on the whole proceedings—luckily they were in the minority, for the generality of the groups were composed of lively and light-hearted people, bent apparently upon amusement, and tolerably certain of finding it. Through these various groups numerous lackeys were passing swiftly and continuously to and fro, bearing a cap, a mantle, or a sword, and pushing aside all who interfered with their progress, with a "by your leave, my masters—your pardon, fair mistress"—or, "out of my way, knave!" and, as the stables occupied one entire angle of the court, there were grooms without end dressing the horses at the doors, watering them at the troughs, or leading them about amid the admiring or criticising bystanders. The King's horses were, of course, objects of special attraction, and such as could obtain a glimpse of them and of the royal coach thought themselves especially favoured. Besides what was going forward below, the windows looking into the court were all full of curious observers, and much loud conversation took place between those placed at them and their friends underneath. From all this some idea will be formed of the tremendous din that prevailed; but though with much confusion there was no positive disorder, still less brawling, for yeomen of the guard being stationed at various points, perfect order was maintained. Several minstrels, mummers, and merry-makers, in various fantastic habits, swelled the throng, enlivening it with their strains or feats; and amongst other privileged characters admitted was a Tom o' Bedlam, a half-crazed licensed beggar, in a singular and picturesque garb, with a plate of tin engraved with his name attached to his left arm, and a great ox's horn, which he was continually blowing, suspended by a leathern baldric from his neck.

Scarcely had Nicholas joined his companions, than word was given that the king was about to attend morning prayers in the domestic chapel. Upon this, an immediate rush was made in that direction by the crowd; but the greater part were kept back by the guard, who crossed their halberts to prevent their ingress, and a few only were allowed to enter the antechamber leading to the chapel, amongst whom were the squire and his companions.

Here they were detained within it till service was over, and, as prayers were read by the Bishop of Chester, and the whole Court was present, this was a great disappointment to them. At the end of half an hour two very courtly personages came forth, each bearing a white wand, and, announcing that the King was coming forth, the assemblage immediately divided into two lines to allow a passage for the monarch. Nicholas Assheton informed Richard in a whisper that the foremost and stateliest of the two gentlemen was Lord Stanhope of Harrington, the vice-chamberlain, and the other, a handsome young man of slight figure and somewhat libertine expression of countenance, was the renowned Sir John Finett, master of the ceremonies. Notwithstanding his licentiousness, however, which was the vice of the age and the stain of the court, Sir John was a man of wit and address, and perfectly conversant with the duties of his office, of which he has left satisfactory evidence in an amusing tractate, "Finetti Philoxenis."

Some little time elapsed before the King made his appearance, during which the curiosity of such as had not seen him, as was the case with Richard, was greatly excited. The young man wondered whether the pedantic monarch, whose character perplexed the shrewdest, would answer his preconceived notions, and whether it would turn out that his portraits were like him. While these thoughts were passing through his mind, a shuffling noise was heard without, and King James appeared at the doorway. He paused there for a moment to place his plumed and jewelled cap upon his head, and to speak a word with Sir John Finett, and during this Richard had an opportunity of observing him. The portraits *were* like, but the artists had flattered him, though not much. There was great shrewdness of look, but there was also a vacant expression, which seemed to contradict the idea of profound wisdom generally ascribed to him. When in perfect repose, which they were not for more than a minute, the features were thoughtful, benevolent, and pleasing, and Richard began to think him quite handsome, when another change was wrought by some remark of Sir John Finett. As the Master of the Ceremonies told his tale, the King's fine dark eyes blazed with an unpleasant light, and he laughed so loudly and indecorously at the close of the narrative, with his great tongue hanging out of his mouth, and tears running down his cheeks, that the young man was quite sickened. The King's face was thin and long, the cheeks shaven, but the lips clothed with mustaches, and a scanty beard covered his chin. The hair was brushed away from the face, and the cap placed at the back of the head, so as to exhibit a high bald forehead, of which he was prodigiously vain. James was fully equipped for the chase, and wore a green silk doublet, quilted, as all his garments were, so as to be dagger-proof, enormous trunk-hose, likewise thickly stuffed, and buff boots, fitting closely to the leg, and turned slightly over at the knee, with the edges fringed with gold. This was almost the only appearance of finery about the dress, except a row of gold buttons down the jerkin. Attached to his girdle he wore a large pouch, with the mouth drawn together by silken cords, and a small silver bugle was suspended from his neck by a baldric of green silk. Stiffly-starched bands, edged with lace, and slightly turned down on either side of the face, completed his attire. There was nothing majestic, but the very reverse, in the King's deportment, and he seemed only kept upright by the exceeding stiffness of his cumbersome clothes. With the appearance of being corpulent, he was not so in reality, and his weak legs and bent knees were scarcely able to support his frame. He always used a stick, and generally sought the additional aid of a favourite's arm.

In this instance the person selected was Sir Gilbert Hoghton, the eldest son of Sir Richard, and subsequent owner of Hoghton Tower. Indebted for the high court favour he enjoyed partly to his graceful person and accomplishments, and partly to his marriage, having espoused a daughter of Sir John Aston of Cranford, who, as sister of the Duchess of Buckingham, and a descendant of the blood royal of the Stuarts, was a great help to his rapid rise, the handsome young knight was skilled in all manly exercises, and cited as a model of grace in the dance. Constant in attendance upon the court, he frequently took part in the masques performed before it. Like the King, he was fully equipped for hunting; but greater contrast could not have been found than between his tall fine form and the King's ungainly figure. Sir Gilbert had remained behind with the rest of the courtiers in the chapel; but, calling him, James seized his arm, and set forward at his usual shambling pace. As he went on, nodding his head in return to the profound salutations of the assemblage, his eye rolled round them until it alighted on Richard Assheton, and, nudging Sir Gilbert, he asked—

"Wha's that?—a bonnie lad, but waesome pale."

Sir Gilbert, however, was unable to answer the inquiry; but Nicholas, who stood beside the young man, was determined not to lose the opportunity of introducing him, and accordingly moved a step forward, and made a profound obeisance.

"This youth, may it please your Majesty," he said, "is my cousin, Richard Assheton, son and heir of Sir Richard Assheton of Middleton, one of your Majesty's most loyal and devoted servants, and who, I trust, will have the honour of being presented to you in the course of the day."

"We trust so, too, Maister Nicholas Assheton—for that, if we dinna forget, is your ain name," replied James; "and if the sire resembles the son, whilk is not always the case, as our gude freend, Sir Gilbert, is evidence, being as unlike his worthy father as a man weel can be; if, as we say, Sir Richard resembles this callant, he must be a weel-faur'd gentleman. But, God's santie, lad! how cam you in sic sad and sombre abulyiements? Hae ye nae braw claes to put on to grace our coming? Black isna the fashion at our court, as Sir Gilbert will tell ye, and, though a suit o' sables may become you, it's no pleasing in our sight. Let us see you in gayer apparel at dinner."

Richard, who was considerably embarrassed by the royal address, merely bowed, and Nicholas again took upon himself to answer for him.

"Your Majesty will be pleased to pardon him," he said; "but he is unaccustomed to court fashions, having passed all his time in a wild and uncivilized district, where, except on rare and happy occasions like the present, the refined graces of life seldom reach us."

"Weel, we wouldna be hard upon him," said the King, good-naturedly; "and mayhap the family has sustained some recent loss, and he is in mourning."

"I cannot offer that excuse for him, sire," replied Nicholas, who began to flatter himself he was making considerable progress in the monarch's good graces. "It is simply an affair of the heart."

"Puir chiel! we pity him," cried the King. "And sae it is a hopeless suit, young sir?" he added to Richard. "Canna we throw in a good word for ye? Do we ken the lassie, and is she to be here to-day?"

"I am quite at a loss how to answer your Majesty's questions," replied Richard, "and my cousin Nicholas has very unfairly betrayed my secret."

"Hoot, toot! na, lad," exclaimed James; "it wasna he wha betrayed your secret, but our ain discernment that revealed it to us. We kenned your ailment at a glance. Few things are hidden from the King's eye, and we could tell ye mair aboot yoursel', and the lassie you're deeing for, if we cared to speak it; but just now we have other fish to fry, and must awa' and break our fast, of the which, if truth maun be spoken, we stand greatly in need; for creature comforts maun be aye looked to as weel as spiritual wants, though the latter should be ever cared for first, as is our ain rule; and in so doing we offer an example to our subjects, which they will do weel to follow. Later in the day, we will talk further to you on the subject; but, meanwhile, gie us the name of your lassie loo."

"Oh! spare me, your Majesty," cried Richard.

"Her name is Alizon Nutter," interposed Nicholas

"What! a daughter of Alice Nutter of Rough Lee?" exclaimed James.

"The same, sire," replied Nicholas, much surprised at the extent of information manifested by the King.

"Why, saul o' my body! man, she's a witch—a witch! d'ye ken that?" cried the King, with a look of abhorrence; "a mischievous and malignant vermin, with which this pairt of our realm is sair plagued, but which, with God's help, we will thoroughly extirpate. Sae the lass is a daughter of Alice Nutter, ha! That accounts for your grewsome looks, lad. Odd's life! I see it all now. I understand what is the matter with you. Look at him, Sir Gilbert—look at him, I say! Does naething strike you as strange about him?"

"Nothing more than that he is naturally embarrassed by your Majesty's mode of speech," replied the knight.

"You lack the penetration of the King, Sir Gilbert," cried James. "I will tell you what ails him. He is bewitchit—forespoken."

Exclamations were uttered by all the bystanders, and every eye was fixed on Richard, who felt ready to sink to the ground.

"I affirm he is bewitchit," continued the King; "and wha sae likely to do it as the glamouring hizzie that has ensnared him? She has ill bluid in her veins, and can chant deevil's cantrips as weel as the mither, or ony gyre-carline o' them a'."

"You are mistaken, sire," cried Richard, earnestly. "Alizon will be here to-day with my father and sister, and, if you deign to receive her, I am sure you will judge her differently."

"We shall perpend the point of receiving her," replied the King, gravely. "But we are rarely mista'en, young man, and seldom change our opinion except upon gude grounds, and those you arena like to offer us. Belike ye hae been lang ill?"

"Oh! no, your Majesty, I was suddenly seized, about a month ago," replied Richard.

"Suddenly seized—eh!" exclaimed James, winking cunningly at those near him; "and ye swarfit awa' wi' the pain? I guessed it. And whaur was Alizon the while?"

"At that time she was a guest at Middleton," replied Richard; "but it is impossible my illness can in any way be attributed to her. I will answer with my life for her perfect innocence."

"You may have to answer wi' your life for your misplaced faith in her," said the King; "but I tell you naething—naething wicked, at all events—is impossible to witches, and the haill case, even by your own showin', is very suspicious. I have heard somewhat of the story of Alice Nutter, but not the haill truth—but there are folk here wha can enlighten us mair fully. Thus much I do ken—that she is a notorious witch, and a fugitive from justice; though aiblins you, Maister Nicholas Assheton, could give an inkling of her hiding-place if you were so disposed. Nay, never look doited, man," he added, laughing. "I bring nae charges against you. Ye arena on your trial noo. But this is a serious matter, and maun be seriously considered before we dismiss it. You say Alizon will be here to-day. Sae far weel. Canna you contrive to produce the mother, too, Maister Nicholas?"

"Sire!" exclaimed Nicholas.

"Nay, then, we maun gang our ain way to wark," continued James. "We are tauld ye hae a petition to offer us, and our will and pleasure is that you present it afore we go forth to the chase, and after we have partaken of our matutinal refection, whilk we will nae langer delay; for, sooth to say, we are weel nigh famished. Look ye, sirs. Neither of you is to quit Hoghton Tower without our permission had and obtained. We do not place you under arrest, neither do we inhibit you from the chase, or from any other sports; but you are to remain here at our sovereign pleasure. Have we your word that you will not attempt to disobey the injunction?

"You have mine, undoubtedly, sire," replied Richard.

"And mine, too," added Nicholas. "And I hope to justify myself before your Majesty."

"We shall be weel pleased to hear ye do it, man," rejoined the King, laughing, and shuffling on. "But we hae our doubts—we hae our doubts!"

"His Majesty talks of going to breakfast, and says he is famished," observed Nicholas to Sherborne, as the King departed, "but he has completely taken away my appetite."

"No wonder," replied the other.

CHAPTER VII.—THE ROYAL DECLARATION CONCERNING LAWFUL SPORTS ON THE SUNDAY.

NOT many paces after the King marched the Duke of Buckingham, then in the zenith of his power, and in the full perfection of his unequalled beauty, eclipsing all the rest of the nobles in splendour of apparel, as he did in stateliness of deportment. Haughtily returning the salutations made him, which were scarcely less reverential than those addressed to the monarch himself, the prime favourite moved on, all eyes following his majestic figure to the door. Buckingham walked alone, as if he had been a prince of the blood; but after him came a throng of nobles, consisting of the Earl of Pembroke, high chamberlain; the Duke of Richmond, master of the household; the Earl of Nottingham, lord high admiral; Viscount Brackley, Lord Howard of Effingham, Lord Zouche, president of Wales; with the Lords Knollys, Mordaunt, Compton, and Grey of Groby. One or two of the noblemen seemed inclined to question Richard as to what had passed between him and the King; but the young man's reserved and somewhat stern manner deterred them. Next came the three judges, Doddridge, Crooke, and Hoghton, whose countenances wore an enforced gravity; for if any faith could be placed in rubicund cheeks and portly persons, they were not indisposed to self-indulgence and conviviality. After the judges came the Bishop of Chester, the King's chaplain, who had officiated on the present occasion, and who was in his full pontifical robes. He was accompanied by the lord of the mansion, Sir Richard Hoghton, a hale handsome man between fifty and sixty, with silvery hair and beard, a robust but commanding person, a fresh complexion, and features, by no means warranting, from any marked dissimilarity to those of his son, the King's scandalous jest.

A crowd of baronets and knights succeeded, including Sir Arthur Capel, Sir Thomas Brudenell, Sir Edward Montague, Sir Edmund Trafford, sheriff of the county, Sir Edward Mosley, and Sir Ralph Assheton. The latter looked grave and anxious, and, as he passed his relatives, said in a low tone to Richard—

"I am told Alizon is to be here to-day. Is it so?"

"She is," replied the young man; "but why do you ask? Is she in danger? If so, let her be warned against coming."

"On no account," replied Sir Ralph; "that would only increase the suspicion already attaching to her. No; she must face the danger, and I hope will be able to avert it."

"But what *is* the danger?" asked Richard. "In Heaven's name, speak more plainly."

"I cannot do so now," replied Sir Ralph. "We will take counsel together anon. Her enemies are at work; and, if you tarry here a few minutes longer, you will understand whom I mean."

And he passed on.

A large crowd now poured indiscriminately out of the chapel, and amongst it Nicholas perceived many of his friends and neighbours, Mr. Townley of Townley Park, Mr. Parker of Browsholme, Mr. Shuttleworth of Gawthorpe, Sir Thomas Metcalfe, and Roger Nowell. With the latter was Master Potts, and Richard was then at no loss to understand against whom Sir Ralph had warned him. A fierce light blazed in Roger Nowell's keen eyes as he first remarked the two Asshetons, and a smile of gratified vengeance played about his lips; but he quelled the fire in a moment, and, compressing his hard mouth more closely, bowed coldly and ceremoniously to them. Metcalfe did the same. Not so Master Potts. Halting for a moment, he said, with a spiteful look, "Look to yourself, Master Nicholas; and you too, Master Richard. A day of reckoning is coming for both of you."

And with this he sprang nimbly after his client.

"What means the fellow?" cried Nicholas. "But that we are here, as it were, in the precincts of a palace, I would after him and cudgel him soundly for his insolence."

"And wha's that ye'd be after dinging, man?" cried a sharp voice behind him. "No that puir feckless body that has jist skippit aff. If sae, ye'll tak the wrang soo by the lugg, and I counsel you to let him bide, for he's high i' favour wi' the King."

Turning at this address, Nicholas recognised the king's jester, Archie Armstrong, a merry little knave, with light blue eyes, long yellow hair hanging about his ears, and a sandy beard. There was a great deal of mother wit about Archie, and quite as much shrewdness as folly. He wore no distinctive dress as jester—the bauble and coxcomb having been long discontinued—but was simply clad in the royal livery.

"And so Master Potts is in favour with his Majesty, eh, Archie?" asked the squire, hoping to obtain some information from him.

"And sae war you the day efore yesterday, when you hunted at Myerscough," replied the jester.

"But how have I forfeited the King's good opinion?" asked Nicholas. "Come, you are a good fellow, Archie, and will tell me."

"Dinna think to fleech me, man," replied the jester, cunningly. —"I ken what I ken, and that's mair than you'll get frae me wi' a' your speering. The King's secrets are safe wi' Archie—and for a good reason, that he is never tauld them. You're a gude huntsman, and sae is his Majesty; but there's ae kind o' game he likes better than anither, and that's to be found maistly i' these pairts—I mean witches, and sic like fearfu' carlines. We maun hae the country rid o' them, and that's what his Majesty intends, and if you're a wise man you'll lend him a helping hand. But I maun in to disjune."

And with this the jester capered off, leaving Nicholas like one stupefied. He was roused, however, by a smart slap on the shoulder from Sir John Finett.

"What! pondering over the masque, Master Nicholas, or thinking of the petition you have to present to his Majesty?" cried the master of the ceremonies, "Let neither trouble you. The one will be well played, I doubt not, and the other well received, I am sure, for I know the king's sentiments on the subject. But touching the dame, Master Nicholas—have you found one willing and able to take part in the masque?"

"I have found several willing, Sir John," replied Nicholas; "but as to their ability that is another question. However, one of them may do as a make-shift. They are all in the base court, and shall wait on you when you please, and then you can make your election."

"So far well," replied Finett; "it may be that we shall have Ben Jonson here to-day—rare Ben, the prince of poets and masque-writers. Sir Richard Hoghton expects him. Ben is preparing a masque for Christmas, to be called 'The Vision of Delight,' in which his highness the prince is to be a principal actor, and some verses which have been recited to me are amongst the daintiest ever indited by the bard."

"It will be a singular pleasure to me to see him," said Nicholas; "for I hold Ben Jonson in the highest esteem as a poet—ay, above them all, unless it be Will Shakspeare."

"Ay, you do well to except Shakspeare," rejoined Sir John Finett. "Great as Ben Jonson is, and for wit and learning no man surpasses him, he is not to be compared with Shakspeare, who for profound knowledge of nature, and of all the highest qualities of dramatic art, is unapproachable. But ours is a learned court, Master Nicholas, and therefore we have a learned poet; but a right good fellow is Ben Jonson, and a boon companion, though somewhat prone to sarcasm, as you will find if you drink with him. Over his cups he will rail at courts and courtiers in good set terms, I promise you, and I myself have come in for his gibes. However, I love him none the less for his quips, for I know it is his humour to utter them, and so overlook what in another and less deserving person I should assuredly resent. But is not that young man, who is now going forth, your cousin, Richard Assheton? I thought so. The King has had a strange tale whispered in his ear, that the youth has been bewitched by a maiden—Alizon Nutter, I think she is named—of whom he is enamoured. I know not what truth may be in the charge, but the youth himself seems to warrant it, for he looks ghastly ill. A letter was sent to his Majesty at Myerscough, communicating this and certain other particulars with which I am not acquainted; but I know they relate to some professors of the black art in your country, the soil of which seems favourable to the growth of such noxious weeds, and at first he was much disturbed by it, but in the end decided that both parties should be brought hither without being made aware of his design, that he might see and judge for himself in the matter. Accordingly a messenger was sent over to Middleton Hall as from Sir Richard Hoghton, inviting the whole family to the Tower, and giving Sir Richard Assheton to understand it was the King's pleasure he should bring with him a certain young damsel, named Alizon Nutter, of whom mention had been made to him. Sir Richard had no choice but to obey, and promised compliance with his

Majesty's injunctions. An officer, however, was left on the watch, and this very morning reported to his Majesty that young Richard Assheton had already set out with the intention of going to Preston, but had passed the night at Walton-le-Dale, and that Sir Richard, his daughter Dorothy, and Alizon Nutter, would be here before noon."

"His Majesty has laid his plans carefully," replied Nicholas, "and I can easily conjecture from whom he received the information, which is as false as it is malicious. But are you aware, Sir John, upon what evidence the charge is supported—for mere suspicion is not enough?"

"In cases of witchcraft suspicion *is* enough," replied the knight, gravely. "Slender proofs are required. The girl is the daughter of a notorious witch—that is against her. The young man is ailing—that is against her, too. But a witness, I believe. will be produced, though who I cannot say."

"Gracious Heaven! what wickedness there must be in the world when such a charge can be brought against one so good and so unoffending," cried Nicholas. "A maiden more devout than Alizon never existed, nor one holding the crime she is charged with in greater abhorrence. She injure Richard! she would lay down her life for him—and would have been his wife, but for scruples the most delicate and disinterested on her part. But we will establish her innocence before his Majesty, and confound her enemies."

"It is with that hope that I have given you this information sir, of which I am sure you will make no improper use," replied Sir John. "I have heard a similar character to that you have given of Alizon, and am unwilling she should fall a victim to art or malice. Be upon your guard, too, Master Nicholas; for other investigations will take place at the same time, and some matters may come forth in which you are concerned. The King's arms are long, and reach and strike far—and his eyes see clearly when not hoodwinked—or when other people see for him. And now, good sir, you must want breakfast. Here Faryngton," he added to an attendant, "show Master Nicholas Assheton to his lodging in the base court, and attend upon him as if he were your master. I will come for you, sir, when it is time to present the petition to the King."

So saying, he bowed and walked forth, turning into the upper quadrangle, while Nicholas followed Faryngton into the lower court, where he found his friends waiting for him.

Speedily ascertaining where their lodgings were situated, Faryngton led them to a building on the left, almost opposite to the great bonfire, and, ascending a flight of steps, ushered them into a commodious and well-furnished room, looking into the court. This done, he disappeared, but soon afterwards returned with two yeomen of the kitchen, one carrying a tray of provisions upon his head, and the other sustaining a basket of wine under his arm, and a snowy napkin being laid upon the table, trenchers, viands, and flasks were soon arranged in very tempting order—so tempting, indeed, that the squire, notwithstanding his assertion, that his appetite had been taken away, fell to work with his customary vigour, and plied a flask of excellent Bordeaux so incessantly, that another had to be placed before him. Sherborne did equal justice to the good cheer, and Richard not only forced himself to eat, but to the squire's great surprise swallowed more than one deep draught of wine. Having thus administered to the wants of the guests, and seeing his presence was no longer either necessary or desired, Faryngton vanished, first promising to go and see that all was got ready for them in the sleeping apartments. Notwithstanding the man's civility, there was an over-officiousness about him that made Nicholas suspect he was placed over them by Sir John Finett to watch their movements, and he resolved to be upon his guard.

"I am glad to see you drink, lad," he observed to Richard, as soon as they were alone; "a cup of wine will do you good."

"Do you think so?" replied Richard, filling his goblet anew. "I want to get back my spirits and strength—to sustain myself no matter how—to look well—ha! ha! If I can only make this frail machine carry me stoutly through the King's visit, I care not how soon it falls to pieces afterwards."

"I see your motive, Dick," replied Nicholas. "You hope to turn away suspicion from Alizon by this device; but you must not go to excess, or you will defeat your scheme."

"I will do something to convince the King he is mistaken in me—that I am not bewitched," cried Richard, rising and striding across the room. "Bewitched! and by Alizon, too! I could laugh at the charge, but that it is too horrible. Had any other than the King breathed it, I would have slain him."

"His Majesty has been abused by the malice of that knavish attorney, Potts, who has always manifested the greatest hostility towards Alizon," said Nicholas; "but he will not prevail, for she has only to show herself to dispel all prejudice."

"You are right, Nicholas," cried Richard; "and yet the King seems already to have prejudged her, and his obstinacy may lead to her destruction."

"Speak not so loudly, Dick, in Heaven's name!" said the squire, in alarm; "these walls may have ears, and echoes may repeat every word you utter."

"Then let them tell the King that Alizon is innocent," cried Richard, stopping, and replenishing his goblet, "Here's to her health, and confusion to her enemies!"

"I'll drink that toast with pleasure, Dick," replied the squire; "but I must forbid you more wine. You are not used to it, and the fumes will mount to your brain."

"Come and sit down beside us, that we may talk," said Sherborne.

Richard obeyed, and, leaning over the table, asked in a low deep tone, "Where is Mistress Nutter, Nicholas?"

The squire looked towards the door before he answered, and then said—

"I will tell you. After the destruction of Malkin Tower and the band of robbers, she was taken to a solitary hut near Barley Booth, at the foot of Pendle Hill, and the next day was conveyed across Bowland Forest to Poulton in the Fyld, on the borders of Morecambe Bay, with the intention of getting her on board some vessel bound for the Isle of Man. Arrangements were made for this purpose; but when the time came, she refused to go, and was brought secretly back to the hut near Barley, where she has been ever since, though her place of concealment was hidden even from you and her daughter."

"The captain of the robbers, Fogg or Demdike, escaped—did he not?" said Richard.

"Ay, in the confusion occasioned by the blowing up of the Tower he managed to get away," replied Nicholas, "and we were unable to follow him, as our attentions had to be bestowed upon Mistress Nutter. This was the more unlucky, as through his instrumentality Jem and his mother Elizabeth were liberated from the dungeon in which they were placed in Whalley Abbey, prior to their removal to Lancaster Castle, and none of them have been heard of since."

"And I hope will never be heard of again," cried Richard. "But is Mistress Nutter's retreat secure, think you?—May it not be discovered by some of Nowell's emissaries?"

"I trust not," replied Nicholas; "but her voluntary surrender is more to be apprehended, for when I last saw her, on the night before starting for Myerscough, she told me she was determined to give herself up for trial; and her motives could scarce be combated, for she declares that, unless she submits herself to the justice of man, and expiates her offences, she cannot be saved She now seems as resolute in good as she was heretofore resolute in evil."

"If she perishes thus, her self-sacrifice, for thus it becomes, will be Alizon's death-blow," cried Richard.

"So I told her," replied Nicholas—"but she continued inflexible. 'I am born to be the cause of misery to others, and most to those I love most,' she said; 'but I cannot fly from justice. There is no escape for me.'"

"She is right," cried Richard; "there is no escape but the grave, whither we are all three hurrying. A terrible fatality attaches to us."

"Nay, say not so, Dick," rejoined Nicholas; "you are young,

and, though this shock may be severe, yet when it is passed, you will be recompensed, I hope, by many years of happiness."

"I am not to be deceived," said Richard. "Look me in the face, and say honestly if you think me long-lived. You cannot do it. I have been smitten by a mortal illness, and am wasting gradually away. I am dying—I feel it—know it; but though it may abridge my brief term of life, I will purchase present health and spirits at any cost, and save Alizon. Ah!" he exclaimed, putting his hand to his heart, with a fearful expression of anguish.

"What is the matter?" cried the two gentlemen, greatly alarmed, and springing towards him.

But the young man could not reply. Another and another agonising spasm shook his frame, and cold damps broke out upon his pallid brow, showing the intensity of his suffering. Nicholas and Sherborne regarded each other anxiously, as if doubtful how to act.

"Shall I summon assistance?" said the latter in a low tone.

But, softly as the words were uttered, they reached the ears of Richard. Rousing himself by a great effort, he said—

"On no account—the fit is over. I am glad it has seized me now, for I shall not be liable to a recurrence of it throughout the day. Lead me to the window. The air will presently revive me."

His friends complied with the request, and placed him at the open casement.

Great bustle was observable below, and the cause was soon manifest, as the chief huntsman, clad in green, with buff boots drawn high up on the thigh, a horn about his neck, and mounted on a strong black curtal, rode forth from the stables. He was attended by a noble bloodhound, and on gaining the middle of the court, put his bugle to his lips, and blew a loud blithe call that made the walls ring again. The summons was immediately answered by a number of grooms and pages, leading a multitude of richly-caparisoned horses towards the upper end of the court, where a gallant troop of dames, nobles, and gentlemen, all attired for the chase, awaited them; and where, amidst much mirth, and bandying of lively jest and compliment, a general mounting took place, the ladies, of course, being placed first on their steeds. While this was going forward, the hounds were brought from the kennel in couples—relays having been sent down into the park more than an hour before—and the yard resounded with their joyous baying, and the neighing of the impatient steeds. By this time, also, the chief huntsman had collected his forces, consisting of a dozen prickers, six habited like himself in green, and six in russet, and all mounted on stout curtals. Those in green were intended to hunt the hart, and those in russet the wild-boar, the former being provided with hunting-poles, and the latter with spears. Their girdles were well lined with beef and pudding, and each of them, acting upon the advice of worthy Master George Turbervile, had a stone bottle of good wine at the pummel of his saddle. Besides these, there were a whole host of varlets of the chase on foot. The chief falconer, with a long-winged hawk in her hood and jesses upon his wrist, was stationed somewhat near the gateway, and close to him were his attendants, each having on his fist a falcon gentle, a Barbary falcon, a merlin, a goshawk, or a sparrowhawk. Thus all was in readiness, and hound, hawk, and man seemed equally impatient for the sport.

At this juncture, the door was thrown open by Faryngton, who announced Sir John Finett.

"It is time, Master Nicholas Assheton," said the master of the ceremonies.

"I am ready to attend you, Sir John," replied Nicholas, taking a parchment from his doublet, and unfolding it, "the petition is well signed."

"So I see, sir," replied the knight, glancing at it. "Will not your friends come with you?"

"Most assuredly," replied Richard, who had risen on the knight's appearance. And he followed the others down the staircase.

By direction of the master of the ceremonies, nearly a hundred of the more important gentlemen of the county had been got together, and this train was subsequently swelled to thrice the amount, from the accessions it received from persons of inferior rank when its object became known. At the head of this large assemblage Nicholas was now placed, and, accompanied by Sir John Finett, who gave the word to the procession to follow them, he moved slowly up the court. Passing through the brilliant crowd of equestrians, the procession halted at a short distance from the doorway of the great hall, and James, who had been waiting for its approach within, now came forth, amid the cheers and plaudits of the spectators.

Sir John Finett then led Nicholas forward, and the latter, dropping on one knee, said—

"May it please your Majesty, I hold in my hand a petition, signed as, if you will deign to cast your eyes over it, you will perceive, by many hundreds of the lower orders of your loving subjects in this your county of Lancaster, representing that they are debarred from lawful recreations upon Sunday after afternoon service, and upon holidays, and praying that the restrictions imposed in 1579, by the Earls of Derby and Huntingdon, and by William, Bishop of Chester, commissioners to her late Highness, Elizabeth, of glorious memory, your Majesty's predecessor, may be withdrawn."

And with this he placed in the King's hands the petition, which was very graciously received.

"The complaint of our loving subjects in Lancashire shall not pass unnoticed, sir," said James. "Sorry are we to say it, but this county of ours is sair infested wi' folk inclining to Puritanism and Papistry, baith of which sects are adverse to the cause of true religion. Honest mirth is not only tolerable but praiseworthy, and the prohibition of it is likely to breed discontent, and this our enemies ken fu' weel; for when," he continued, loudly and emphatically—"when shall the common people have leave to exercise if not upon Sundays and holidays, seeing they must labour and win their living on all other days?"

"Your Majesty speaks like King Solomon himself," observed Nicholas, amid the loud cheering.

"Our will and pleasure then is," pursued James, "that our good people be not deprived of any lawful recreation that shall not tend to a breach of the laws, or a violation of the Kirk; but that, after the end of divine service, they shall not be disturbed, letted, or discouraged from any lawful recreation—as dancing and sic like, either of men or women, archery, leaping, vaulting, or ony ither harmless recreation; nor frae the having of May-games, Whitsun ales, or morris dancing; nor frae setting up of May-poles, and ither sports, therewith used, provided the same be had in due and convenient time, without impediment or neglect of divine service. And our will further is, that women shall have leave to carry rushes to the church, for the decoring of it, according to auld custom. But we prohibit all unlawful games on Sundays, as bear-baiting and bull-baiting, interludes, and, by the common folk—mark ye that, sir—playing at bowls."*

The royal declaration was received with loud and reiterated cheers, amidst which James mounted his steed, a large black docile-looking charger, and rode out of the court, followed by the whole cavalcade.

Trumpets were sounded from the battlements as he passed through the gateway, and shouting crowds attended him all the way down the hill, until he entered the avenue leading to the park.

At the conclusion of the royal address, the procession headed by Nicholas immediately dispersed, and such as meant to join the chase set off in quest of steeds. Foremost amongst these was the squire himself, and on approaching the stables, he was glad to find Richard and Sherborne already mounted, the former holding his horse by the bridle, so that he had nothing to do but vault upon his back. There was an impatience about Richard, very different from his ordinary manner, that surprised and startled him, and

* This speech is in substance the monarch's actual Declaration concerning Lawful Sports, promulgated in 1618, in a little Tractate, generally known as the "Book of Sports;" by which he would have conferred a great boon on the lower orders, if his kindly purpose had not been misapprehended by some, and ultimately defeated by bigots and fanatics. King James deserves to be remembered with gratitude, if only for this manifestation of sympathy with the enjoyments of the people. He had himself discovered that the restrictions imposed upon them had "set up filthy tipplings and drunkenness, and bred a number of idle and discontented speeches in the alehouses."

the expression of the young man's countenance long afterwards haunted him. The face was deathly pale, except that on either cheek burned a red feverish spot, and the eyes blazed with unnatural light. So much was the squire struck by his cousin's looks, that he would have dissuaded him from going forth; but he saw from his manner that the attempt would fail, while a significant gesture from his brother-in-law told him he was equally uneasy.

Scarcely had the principal nobles passed through the gateway, than, in spite of all efforts to detain him, Richard struck spurs into his horse, and dashed amidst the cavalcade, creating great disorder, and rousing the ire of the Earl of Pembroke, to whom the marshalling of the train was entrusted. But Richard paid little heed to his wrath, and perhaps did not hear the angry expressions addressed to him; for no sooner was he outside the gate, than instead of pursuing the road down which the King was proceeding, and which has been described as hewn out of the rock, he struck into a thicket on the right, and, in defiance of all attempts to stop him, and at the imminent risk of breaking his neck, rode down the precipitous sides of the hill, and reaching the bottom in safety, long before the royal cavalcade had attained the same point, took the direction of the park.

His friends watched him commence this perilous descent in dismay; but, though much alarmed, they were unable to follow him.

"Poor lad! I am fearful he has lost his senses," said Sherborne.

"He is what the King would call 'fey,' and not long for this world," replied Nicholas, shaking his head.

CHAPTER VIII.—HOW KING JAMES HUNTED THE HART AND THE WILD-BOAR IN HOGHTON PARK.

Galloping on fast and furiously, Richard tracked a narrow path of greensward, lying between the tall trees composing the right line of the avenue and the adjoining wood. Within it grew many fine old thorns, diverting him now and then from his course, but he still held on until he came within a short distance of the chase, when his attention was caught by a very singular figure. It was an old man, clad in a robe of coarse brown serge, with a cowl drawn partly over his head, a rope girdle like that used by a cordelier, sandal shoon, and a venerable white beard descending to his waist. The features of the hermit, for such he seemed, were majestic and benevolent. Seated on a bank overgrown with wild thyme, beneath the shade of a broad-armed elm, he appeared so intently engaged in the perusal of a large open volume laid on his knee, that he did not notice Richard's approach. Deeply interested, however, by his appearance, the young man determined to address him, and, reining in his horse, said respectfully, "Save you, father!"

"Pass on, my son," replied the old man, without raising his eyes, "and hinder not my studies."

But Richard would not be thus dismissed.

"Perchance you are not aware, father," he said, "that the King is about to hunt within the park this morning. The royal cavalcade has already left Hoghton Tower, and will be here ere many minutes."

"The king and his retinue will pass along the broad avenue, as you should have done, and not through this retired road," replied the hermit. "They will not disturb me."

"I would fain know the subject of your studies, father?" inquired Richard.

"You are inquisitive, young man," returned the hermit, looking up and fixing a pair of keen grey eyes upon him. But I will satisfy your curiosity, if by so doing I shall rid me of your presence. I am reading the Book of Fate."

Richard uttered an exclamation of astonishment.

"And in it your destiny is written," pursued the old man; "and a sad one it is. Consumed by a strange and incurable disease, which may at any moment prove fatal, you are scarcely likely to survive the next three days, in which case she you love better than existence will perish miserably, being adjudged to have destroyed you by witchcraft."

"It must indeed be the Book of Fate that tells you this," cried Richard, springing from his horse, and approaching close to the old man. "May I cast eyes upon it?"

"No, my son," replied the old man, closing the volume. "You would not comprehend the mystic characters—but no eye, except my own, must look upon them. What is written will be fulfilled. Again, I bid you pass on. I must speedily return to my hermit cell in the forest."

"May I attend you thither, father?" asked Richard.

"To what purpose?" rejoined the old man. "You have not many hours of life. Go, then, and pass them in the fierce excitement of the chase. Pull down the lordly stag—slaughter the savage boar; and, as you see the poor denizens of the forest perish, think that your own end is not far off. Hark! Do you hear that boding cry?"

"It is the croak of a raven newly alighted in the tree above us," replied Richard. "The sagacious bird will ever attend the huntsman in the chase, in the hope of obtaining a morsel when they break up deer."

"Such is the custom of the bird I wot well," said the old man; "but it is not in joyous expectation of the raven's-bone that he croaks now, but because his fell instinct informs him that the living-dead is beneath him."

And, as if in answer to the remark, the raven croaked exultingly; and, rising from the tree, wheeled in a circle above them.

"Is there no way of averting my terrible destiny, father?" cried Richard, despairingly.

"Ay, if you choose to adopt it," replied the old man. "When I said your ailment was incurable, I meant by ordinary remedies, but it will yield to such as I alone can employ. The malignant and fatal influence under which you labour may be removed, and then your instant restoration to health and vigour will follow."

"But how, father—how?" cried Richard, eagerly.

"You have simply to sign your name in this book," rejoined the hermit, "and what you desire shall be done. Here is a pen," he added, taking one from his girdle.

"But the ink?" cried Richard.

"Prick your arm with your dagger, and dip the pen in the blood," replied the old man. "That will suffice."

"And what follows if I sign?" demanded Richard, staring at him.

"Your instant cure. I will give you to drink of a wondrous elixir."

"But to what do I bind myself?" asked Richard.

"To serve me," replied the hermit, smiling; "but it is a light service, and only involves your appearance in this wood once a-year. Are you agreed?"

"I know not," replied the young man distractedly.

"You must make up your mind speedily," said the hermit; "for I hear the approach of the royal cavalcade."

And as he spoke, the mellow notes of a bugle, followed by the baying of hounds, the jingling of bridles, and the trampling of a large troop of horse, were heard at a short distance down the avenue.

"Tell me who you are?" cried Richard.

"I am the hermit of the wood," replied the old man. "Some people call me Hobthurst, and some by other names, but you will have no difficulty in finding me out. Look yonder!" he added, pointing through the trees.

And, glancing in the direction indicated, Richard beheld a small party on horseback advancing across the plain, consisting of his father, his sister, and Alizon, with their attendants.

"'Tis she!—'tis she!" he cried.

"Can you hesitate, when it is to save *her?*" demanded the old man.

"Heaven help me, or I am lost!" fervently ejaculated Richard, gazing on high while making the appeal.

When he looked down again the old man was gone, and he saw only a large black snake gliding off among the bushes.

Muttering a few words of thankfulness for his deliverance, he sprang upon his horse.

"It may be the arch-tempter is right," he cried, "and that but few hours of life remain to me; but if so, they shall be employed in endeavours to vindicate Alizon, and defeat the snares by which she is beset."

With this resolve, he struck spurs into his horse, and set off in the direction of the little troop. Before, however, he could come up to them, their progress was arrested by a pursuivant, who, riding in advance of the royal cavalcade, motioned them to stay till it had passed, and the same person also perceiving Richard's purpose, called to him, authoritatively, to keep back. The young man might have disregarded the injunction, but at the same moment the King himself appeared at the head of the avenue, and remarking Richard, who was not more than fifty yards off on the right, instantly recognised him, and shouted out, "Come hither, young man—come hither!"

Thus, baffled in his design, Richard was forced to comply, and, uncovering his head, rode slowly towards the monarch. As he approached, James fixed on him a glance of sharpest scrutiny.

"Odds life! ye hae been ganging a fine gait, young sir," he cried. "Ye maun be demented to ride down a hill i' that fashion, and as if your craig war of nae account. It's weel ye hae come aff scaithless. Are ye tired o' life—or was it the muckle deil himsel' that drove ye on? Canna ye find an excuse, man? Nay, then, I'll gi'e ye ane. The loadstane will draw nails out of a door, and there be lassies wi' een strang as loadstanes, that drag men to their perdition. Stands the magnet yonder, eh?" he added, glancing towards the little group before them. "Gude faith! the lass maun be a potent witch to exercise sic influence, and we wad fain see the effect she has on you when near. Sir Richard Hoghton," he called out to the knight, who rode a few paces behind him, "we pray you present Sir Richard Assheton and his daughter to us."

Had he dared so to do, Richard would have thrown himself at the King's feet, but all he could venture upon was to say in a low earnest tone, "Do not prejudge Alizon, sire. On my soul she is innocent!"

"The King prejudges nae man," replied James, in a tone of rebuke; "and like the wise prince of Israel, whom it is his wish to resemble, he sees with his ain een, and hears with his ain ears, afore he forms conclusions."

"That is all I can desire, sire," replied Richard. "Far be it from me to doubt your majesty's discrimination or love of justice."

"Ye shall hae proofs of baith, man, afore we hae done," said James. "Ah! here comes our host, an the twa lassies wi' him. She wi' the lintwhite locks is your sister, we guess, and the ither is Alizon—and, by our troth, a weel-faur'd lass. But Satan is aye delusive. We maun resist his snares."

The party now came on, and were formally presented to the monarch by Sir Richard Hoghton. Sir Richard Assheton, a middle-aged gentleman, with handsome features, though somewhat haughty in expression, and stately deportment, was very graciously received, and James thought fit to pay a few compliments to Dorothy, covertly regarding Alizon the while, yet not neglecting Richard, being ready to intercept any signal that should pass between them. None, however, was attempted, for the young man felt he should only alarm and embarrass Alizon by any attempt to caution her, and he therefore endeavoured to assume an unconcerned aspect and demeanour.

"We hae heard the beauty of the Lancashire lassies highly commended," said the King; "but, faith! it passes expectation. Twa lovelier damsels than these we never beheld. Baith are rare specimens o' Nature's handiwark."

"Your Majesty is pleased to be complimentary," rejoined Sir Richard Assheton.

"Na, Sir Richard," returned James. "We arena gien to flichtering, though aften beflummed oursel'. Baith are bonnie lassies, we repeat. An sae this is Alizon Nutter—it wad be Ailsie in our ain Scottish tongue, to which your Lancashire vernacular closely approximates, Sir Richard. Aweel, fair Alizon," he added, eyeing her narrowly, "ye hae lost your mither, we understand?"

The young girl was not discomposed by this question, but answered in a firm, melancholy tone—"Your Majesty, I fear, is too well acquainted with my unfortunate mother's history."

"Aweel, we winna deny having heard somewhat to her disadvantage," replied the King—"but your ain looks gang far to contradict the reports, fair maid."

"Place no faith in them then, sire," replied Alizon, sadly.

"Eh! what!—then you admit your mother's guilt?" cried the King, sharply.

"I neither admit it nor deny it, sire," she replied. "It must be for your Majesty to judge her."

"Weel answered," muttered James,—"but I mustna forget, that the deil himsel' can quote Scripture to serve his purpose. But you hold in abhorrence the crime laid to your mother's charge—eh?" he added aloud.

"In utter abhorrence," replied Alizon.

"Gude—vera gude," rejoined the King. "But, entertaining this feeling, how comes it you screen so heinous an offender frae justice? Nae natural feeling should be allowed to weigh in sic a case."

"Nor should it, sire, with me," replied Alizon—"because I believe my poor mother's eternal welfare would be best consulted if she underwent temporal punishment. Neither is she herself anxious to avoid it."

"Then why does she keep out of the way—why does she not surrender herself?" cried the King.

"Because—" and Alizon stopped.

"Because what?" demanded James.

"Pardon me, sire, I must decline answering further questions on the subject," replied Alizon. "Whatever concerns myself or my mother alone, I will state freely, but I cannot compromise others."

"Aha! then there are others concerned in it?" cried James. "We thought as much. We will interrogate you further hereafter—but a word mair. We trust ye are devout, and constant in your religious exercises, damsel."

"I will answer for that, sire," interposed Sir Richard Assheton. "Alizon's whole time is spent in prayer for her unfortunate mother. If there be a fault it is that she goes too far, and injures her health by her zeal."

"A gude fault that, Sir Richard," observed the King, approvingly.

"It beseems me not to speak of myself, sire," said Alizon, "and I am loth to do so—but I beseech your majesty to believe, that if my life might be offered as an atonement for my mother, I would freely yield it."

"I' gude faith she staggers me in my opinion," muttered James, "and I maun look into the matter mair closely. The lass is far different frae what I imagined her. But the wiles o' Satan arena to be comprehended, and he will put on the semblance of righteousness when seeking to beguile the righteous. Aweel, damsel," he added aloud, "ye speak feelingly and properly, and as a daughter should speak, and we respect your feelings—provided they be sic as ye represent them. And now dispose yourselves for the chase."

"I must pray your Majesty to dismiss me," said Alizon. "It is a sight in which at any time I take small pleasure, and now it is especially distasteful to me. With your permission, I will proceed to Hoghton Tower."

"I also crave your Majesty's leave to go with her," said Dorothy.

"I will attend them," interposed Richard.

"Na, you maun stay wi' us, young sir," cried the King. "Your gude father will gang wi' 'em. Sir John Finett," he added, calling to the master of the ceremonies, and speaking in his ear, "see that they be followed, and that a special watch be kept over Alizon, and also over this youth,—d'ye mark me?—in fact, ower a' the Assheton clan. And now," he cried in a loud voice, "let them blaw the strake."

The chief huntsman having placed the bugle to his lips, and

blown a strike with two winds, a short consultation was held between him and James, who loved to display his knowledge as a woodsman; and while this was going forward, Nicholas and Sherborne having come up, the squire dismounted, and committing Robin to his brother-in-law, approached the monarch.

"If I may be so bold as to put in a word, my liege," he said, "I can show you where a hart of ten is assuredly harboured. I viewed him as I rode through the park this morning, and cannot, therefore, be mistaken. His head is high and well palmed, great beamed and in good proportion, well burred and well pearled. He is stately in height, long, and well fed."

"Did you mark the slot, sir?" inquired James.

"I did, my liege," replied Nicholas. "And a long slot it was; the toes great, with round short joint-bones, large shin-bones, and the dew-claws close together. I will uphold him for a great old hart as ever proffered, and one that shall shew your Majesty rare sport."

"And we'll tak your word for the matter, sir," said James; "for ye're as gude a woodman as any we hae in our dominions. Bring us to him, then."

"Will it please your Majesty to ride towards yon glade?" said Nicholas, "and, before you reach it, the hart shall be roused."

James, assenting to the arrangement, Nicholas sprang upon his steed, and, calling to the chief huntsman, they galloped off together, accompanied by the bloodhound, the royal cavalcade following somewhat more slowly in the same direction. A fair sight it was to see that splendid company careering over the plain, their feathered caps and gay mantles glittering in the sun, which shone brightly upon them. The morning was lovely, giving promise that the day, when further advanced, would be intensely hot, but at present it was fresh and delightful, and the whole company, exhilarated by the exercise, and by animated conversation, were in high spirits; and perhaps amongst the huge party, which numbered nearly three hundred persons, one alone was a prey to despair. But though Richard Assheton suffered thus internally, he bore his anguish with Spartan firmness, resolved, if possible, to let no trace of it be visible in his features or deportment; and he so far succeeded in conquering himself, that the King, who kept a watchful eye upon him, remarked to Sir John Finett as they rode along, that a singular improvement had taken place in the young man's appearance.

"The cavalcade was rapidly approaching the glade at the lower end of the chase, when the lively notes of a horn were heard from the adjoining wood, followed by the deep baying of a bloodhound.

"Aha! they have roused him," cried the King, joyfully placing his own bugle to his lips, and sounding an answer. Upon this the whole company halted in anxious expectation, the hounds baying loudly. The next moment, a noble hart burst from the wood, whence he had been driven by the shouts of Nicholas and the chief huntsman, both of whom appeared immediately afterwards.

"By my faith! a great hart as ever was hunted," exclaimed the King. "There boys, there! to him! to him!"

Dashing after the flying hart, the hounds made the welkin ring with their cries. Many lovely damsels were there, but none thought of the cruelty of the sport—none sympathised with the noble animal they were running to death. The cries of the hounds—now loud and ringing—now deep and doling, accompanied by the whooping of the huntsmen, formed a stirring concert, which found a response in many a gentle bosom. The whole cavalcade was spread widely about, for none were allowed to ride near the King. Over the plain they scoured, fleet as the wind, and the hart seemed making for a fell, forming part of the hill near the mansion. But ere he reached it, the relays stationed within a covert burst forth, and, turning him aside, he once more dashed fleetly across the broad expanse, as if about to return to his old lair. Now he was seen plunging into some bosky dell; and, after being lost to view for a moment, bounding up the opposite bank, and stretching across a tract thickly covered with fern. Here he gained upon the hounds, who were lost in the green wilderness, and their cries were hushed for a brief space—but anon they burst forth anew, and the pack were soon again in full cry, and speeding over the open ground.

At first the cavalcade had kept pretty well together, but on the return the case was very different; and many of the dames, being unable to keep up with the hounds, fell off, and, as a natural consequence, many of the gallants lingered behind, too. Thus only the keenest huntsmen held on. Amongst these, and about fifty yards behind the King, were Richard and Nicholas. The squire was right when he predicted that the hart would show them good sport. Plunging into the wood, the hard-pressed beast knocked up another stag, and took possession of his lair, but was speedily roused again by Nicholas and the chief huntsman. Once more he is crossing the wide plain, with hounds and huntsmen after him—once more he is turned by a new relay; but this time he shapes his course towards the woods skirting the Darwen. It is a piteous sight to see him now; his coat black and glistening with sweat, his mouth embossed with foam, his eyes dull, big tears coursing down his cheeks, and his noble head carried low. His end seems nigh—for the hounds, though weary too, redouble their energies, and the monarch cheers them on. Again the poor beast erects his head—if he can only reach yon coppice he is safe. Despair nerves him, and with gigantic bounds he clears the intervening space, and disappears beneath the branches. Quickly as the hounds come after him, they are at fault.

"He has taken to the soil, sire," cried Nicholas coming up. "To the river—to the river! You may see by the broken branches he has gone this way."

Forcing his way through the wood, James was soon on the banks of the Darwen, which here ran deep and slow. The hart was nowhere to be seen, nor was there any slot on the further side to denote that he had gone forth. It was evident, therefore, that he had swam down the stream. At this moment a shout was heard a hundred yards lower down, proceeding from Nicholas; and, riding in the direction of the sound, the King found the hart at bay on the further side of the stream, and nearly up to his haunches in the water. The King regarded him for a moment anxiously. The poor animal was now in his last extremity, but he seemed determined to sell his life dearly. He stood on a bank projecting into the stream, round which the water flowed deeply, and could not be approached without difficulty and danger. He had already gored several hounds, whose bleeding bodies were swept down the current; and, though the others bayed round him, they did not dare to approach him, and could not get behind him, as a high bank arose in his rear.

"Have I your Majesty's permission to despatch him?" asked Nicholas.

"Ay, marry, if you can, sir," replied James. "But 'ware the tynes!—'ware the tynes!—'If thou be hurt with hart it brings thee to thy bier,' as the auld ballad hath it, and the adage is true, as we oursel's have seen."

Nicholas, however, heeded not the caution, but, drawing his wood-knife, and disencumbering himself of his cloak, he plunged into the stream, and with one or two strokes reached the bank. The hart watched his approach, as if divining his purpose, with a look half menacing, half reproachful, and when he came near, dashed his antlered head at him. Nimbly eluding the blow, which, if it had taken effect, might have proved serious, Nicholas plunged his weapon into the poor brute's throat, who instantly fell with a heavy splash into the water.

"Weel stricken! weel stricken!" shouted James, who had witnessed the performance from the opposite bank. "But how shall we get the carcase here?"

"That is easily done, sire," replied Nicholas. And taking hold of the horns, he guided the body to a low bank, a little below where the King stood.

As soon as it was dragged ashore by the prickers, James put his bugle to his lips and blew a mort. A pryse was thrice sounded by Nicholas, and soon afterwards the whole company came flocking round the spot, whooping the death-note.

Meanwhile, the hounds had gathered round the fallen hart, and were allowed to wreak their fury on him by tearing his throat, happily after sensibility was gone; while Nicholas, again baring his knife, cut off the right fore-foot, and presented it to the King. While this ceremony was performed, the varlets of the kennel having cut down a great heap of green branches, and strewn them on the ground, laid the hart upon them, on his back, and then bore him to an open space in the wood, where he was broken up by the King, who prided himself upon his skill in all matters of woodcraft. While this office was in course of execution a bowl of wine was poured out for the monarch, which he took, adverting, as he did so, to the common superstition, that if a huntsman should break up a deer without drinking, the venison would putrefy. Having drained the cup, he caused it to be filled again, and gave it to Nicholas, saying the liquor was needful to him after the drenching he had undergone. James then proceeded with his task, and just before he completed it, he was reminded, by a loud croak above him, that a raven was at hand, and accordingly taking a piece of gristle from the spoon of the brisket, he cast it on the ground, and the bird immediately pounced down upon it and carried it off in his huge beak.

After a brief interval, the seek was again winded, another hart was roused, and after a short but swift chase, pulled down by the hounds, and dispatched with his own hand by James. Sir Richard Hoghton then besought the King to follow him, and led the way to a verdant hollow surrounded by trees, in which shady and delicious retreat preparations had been made for a slight silvan repast. Upon a mossy bank beneath a tree, a cushion was placed for the King, and before it on the sward was laid a cloth spread with many dainties, including

> "Neats' tongues powder'd well, and jambons of the hog,
> With sausages and savoury knacks to set men's minds agog"—

cold capons, and pigeon pies. Close at hand was a clear cold spring, in which numerous flasks of wine were immersed. A few embers, too, had been lighted, on which carbonadoes of venison were prepared.

No great form or ceremony was observed at the entertainment. Sir John Finett and Sir Thomas Hoghton were in close attendance upon the monarch, and ministered to his wants; but several of the nobles and gentlemen stretched themselves on the sward, and addressed themselves to the viands set before them by the pages. None of the dames dismounted, and few could be prevailed upon to take any refreshment. Besides the flasks of wine, there were two barrels of ale in a small cart, drawn by a mule, both of which were broached. The whole scene was picturesque and pleasing, and well calculated to gratify one so fond of silvan sports as the monarch for whom it was provided.

In the midst of all this tranquillity and enjoyment an incident occurred which interrupted it as completely as if a thunder-storm had suddenly come on. Just when the mirth was at the highest, and when the flowing cup was at many a lip, a tremendous bellowing, followed by the crashing of branches, was heard in the adjoining thicket. All started to their feet at the appalling sound, and the King himself turned pale.

"What in Heaven's name can it be, Sir Richard?" he inquired.

"It must be a drove of wild cattle," replied the baronet, trembling.

"Wild cattle!" ejaculated James, in great alarm; "and sae near us. Zounds! we shall be trampled and gored to death by these bulls of Basan. Sir Richard, ye are a fause traitor thus to endanger the safety o' your sovereign, and ye shall answer for it, if harm comes o' it."

"I am unable to account for it, sire," stammered the frightened baronet. "I gave special directions to the prickers to drive the beasts away."

"Ye shouldna keep sic deevils i' your park, man," cried the monarch. "Eh! what's that?"

Amidst all this consternation and confusion the bellowing was redoubled, and the crashing of branches drew nearer and nearer, and Nicholas Assheton rushed forward with the King's horse, saying, "Mount, sire; mount, and away!"

But James was so much alarmed that his limbs refused to perform their office, and he was unable to put foot in the stirrup. Seeing his condition, Nicholas cried out, "Pardon, my liege; but at a moment of peril like the present, one must not stand on ceremony."

So saying, he took the King round the waist, and placed him on his steed.

At this juncture, a loud cry was heard, and a man in extremity of terror issued from the wood, and dashed towards the hollow. Close on his heels came the drove of wild cattle, and, just as he gained the very verge of the descent, the foremost of the herd overtook him, and lowering his curled head, caught him on the points of his horns, and threw him forwards to such a distance that he alighted with a heavy crash almost at the King's feet. Satisfied, apparently, with their vengeance, or alarmed by the numerous assemblage, the drove instantly turned tail and were pursued into the depths of the forest by the prickers.

Having recovered his composure, James bade some of the attendants raise the poor wretch, who was lying groaning upon the ground, evidently so much injured as to be unable to move without assistance. His garb was that of a forester, and his bulk—for he was stoutly and squarely built—had contributed, no doubt, to the severity of the fall. When he was lifted from the ground, Nicholas instantly recognised in his blackened and distorted features those of Christopher Demdike.

"What?" he exclaimed, rushing towards him. "Is it thou, villain?"

The sufferer only replied by a look of intense malignity.

"Eh! what—d'ye ken wha it is?" demanded James. "By my saul! I fear the puir fellow has maist of his banes broken."

"No great matter if they be," replied Nicholas, "and it may save the application of torture in case your Majesty desires to put any question to him. Chance has most strangely thrown into your hands one of the most heinous offenders in the kingdom, who has long escaped justice, but who will at length meet the punishment of his crimes. The villain is Christopher Demdike, son of the foul hag who perished in the flames on the summit of Pendle Hill, and captain of a band of robbers."

"What! is the knave a warlock and a riever?" demanded James, regarding Demdike with abhorrence, mingled with alarm.

"Both, sire," replied Nicholas, "and an assassin to boot. He is a diabolical villain."

"Let him be taken to Hoghton Tower, and kept in some strong and secure place till we have leisure to examine him," said James,—"and see that he be visited by some skilful chirurgeon, for we wadna hae him dee, and sae rob the woodie."

Demdike, who appeared to be in great agony, now forced himself to speak.

"I can make important disclosures to your Majesty," he said, in hoarse and broken tones, "if you will hear them. I am not the only offender who has escaped from justice," he added, glancing vindictively at Nicholas—"there is another, a notorious witch and murderess, who is still screened from justice. I can reveal her hiding-place."

"Your Majesty will not give heed to such a villain's fabrications?" said Nicholas.

"Are they fabrications, sir?" rejoined James, somewhat sharply. "We maun hear and judge. The snake, though scotched, will still bite, it seems. We hae hangit a Highland cateran without trial afore this, and we may be tempted to tak the law into our ain hands again. Bear the villain hence. See he be disposed of as already directed, and take good care he is strictly guarded. And now gie us a crossbow, Sir Richard Hoghton, and bid the prickers drive the deer afore us, for we wad try our skill as a marksman."

And while Demdike was placed on the litter of green boughs which had recently sustained a nobler burthen in the fallen hart, and in this sort was conveyed to Hoghton Tower, James rode with his retinue towards a long glade, where, receiving a crossbow from the huntsman, he took up a favourable position behind a large oak, and several herds of deer being driven before him, he selected his quarries, and deliberately took aim at them, contriving in the course of an hour to bring down four fat bucks, and to maim as many others, which were pulled down by the hounds. And with this slaughter he was content.

Sir Richard Hoghton then informed his Majesty that a huge boar, which, in sporting phrase, had left the sounder five years, had broken into the park the night before, and had been routing amongst the fern. The age and size of the animal were known by the print of the feet, the toes being round and thick, the edge of the hoof worn and blunt, the heel large, and the guards, or dew-claws, great and open, from all which appearances it was adjudged by the baronet to be "a great old boar, not to be refused."

James at once agreed to hunt him, and the hounds being taken away, six couples of magnificent mastiffs, of the Lancashire breed, were brought forward, and the monarch, under the guidance of Sir Richard Hoghton and the chief huntsman, repaired to an adjoining thicket, in which the boar fed and couched.

On arriving near his den, a boar-spear was given to the King, and the prickers advancing into the wood, presently afterwards reared the enormous brute. Sallying forth, and freaming furiously, he was instantly assailed by the mastiffs; but, notwithstanding the number of his assailants, he made light of them, shaking them from his bristly hide, crushing them beneath his horny feet, thrusting at them with his sharpened tusks, and committing terrible devastation among them.

Repeated charges were made upon the savage animal by James, but it was next to impossible to get a blow at him for some time; and when at length the monarch made the attempt, he struck too low, and hit him on the snout, upon which the infuriated boar, finding himself wounded, sprang towards the horse, and ripped him open with his tusks.

The noble charger instantly rolled over on his side, exposing the royal huntsman to the fury of his merciless assailant, whose tusks must have ploughed his flesh, if at this moment a young man had not ridden forward, and at the greatest personal risk approached the boar, and, striking straight downwards, cleft the heart of the fierce brute with his spear.

Meanwhile, the King, having been disengaged by the prickers from his wounded steed, which was instantly put out of its agony by the sword of the chief huntsman, looked for his deliverer, and, discovering him to be Richard Assheton, was loud in his expressions of gratitude.

"Faith! ye maun claim a boon at our hands," said James. "It maun never be said the King is ungrateful. What can we do for you, lad?"

"For myself nothing, sire," replied Richard.

"But for another meikle—is that what ye wad hae us infer?" cried the King, with a smile. "Aweel, the lassie shall hae strict justice done her; but for your ain sake we maun inquire into the matter. Meantime, wear this," he added, taking a magnificent sapphire ring from his finger, "and, if you should ever need our aid, send it to us as a token."

Richard took the gift, and knelt to kiss the hand so graciously extended to him.

By this time another horse had been provided for the monarch, and the enormous boar, with his feet upwards and tied together, was suspended upon a pole, and borne on the shoulders of four stout varlets as the grand trophy of the chase.

When the royal company issued from the wood a strike of nine was blown by the chief huntsman, and such of the cavalcade as still remained on the field being collected together, the party crossed the chase, and took the direction of Hoghton Tower.

CHAPTER IX.—THE BANQUET.

On the King's return to Hoghton Tower, orders were given by Sir Richard for the immediate service of the banquet; it being the hospitable baronet's desire that festivities should succeed each other so rapidly as to allow of no tedium.

The *coup-d'œil* of the banquet hall on the monarch's entrance was magnificent. Panelled with black lustrous oak, and lighted by mullion windows, filled with stained glass and emblazoned with the armorial bearings of the family, the vast and lofty hall was hung with banners, and decorated with panoplies and trophies of the chase. Three long tables ran down it, each containing a hundred covers. At the lower end were stationed the heralds, the pursuivants, and a band of yeomen of the guard, with the royal badge, a demi-rose crowned, impaled with a demi-thistle, woven in gold on their doublets, and having fringed pole-axes over their shoulders. Behind them was a richly carved oak screen, concealing the passages leading to the buttery and kitchens, in which the clerk of the kitchen, the pantlers, and the yeomen of the cellar and ewery, were hurrying to and fro. Above the screen was a gallery, occupied by the trumpeters and minstrels; and over all was a noble rafter roof. The tables were profusely spread, and glittered with silver dishes of extraordinary size and splendour, as well as with flagons and goblets of the same material, and rare design. The guests, all of whom were assembled, were out-numbered by the prodigious array of serving-men, pages, and yeomen waiters in the yellow and red liveries of the Stuart.

Flourishes of trumpets announced the coming of the monarch, who was preceded by Sir Richard Hoghton, bearing a white wand, and ushered with much ceremony to his place. At the upper end of the hall was a raised floor, and on either side of it an oriel window, glowing with painted glass. On this dais the King's table was placed, underneath a canopy of state, embroidered with the royal arms, and bearing James's kindly motto, "*Beati Pacifici.*" Seats were reserved at it for the Dukes of Buckingham and Richmond, the Earls of Pembroke and Nottingham, the Lords Howard of Effingham and Grey of Groby, Sir Gilbert Hoghton, and the Bishop of Chester. These constituted the favoured guests. Grace having been said by the bishop, the whole company took their seats, and the general stillness hitherto prevailing throughout the vast hall was broken instantaneously by the clatter of trenchers.

A famous feast it was, and worthy of commemoration. Masters Morris and Miller, the two cooks who contrived it, as well as the labourers for the ranges, for the pastries, for the boiled meats, and for the pullets, performed their respective parts to admiration. The result was all that could be desired. The fare was solid and substantial, consisting of dishes which could be cut and come to again. Amongst the roast meats were chines of beef, haunches of venison, gigots of mutton, fatted geese, capons, turkeys, and sucking pigs; amongst the boiled, pullets, lamb, and veal; but baked meats chiefly abounded, and amongst them were to be found red-deer pasty, hare-pie, gammon-of-bacon pie, and baked wild-boar. With the salads, which were nothing more than what would now-a-days be termed "vegetables," were mixed all kinds of soused fish, arranged according to the sewer's directions—"the salads spread about the tables, the fricassees mixed with them, the boiled meats among the fricassees, roast meats amongst the boiled, baked meats amongst the roast, and carbonadoes amongst the baked." This was the first course merely. In the second were all kinds of game and wild-fowl, roast herons three in a dish, bitterns, cranes, bustards, curlews, dotterels, and pewits. Besides these there were lumbar pies, marrow pies, quince pies, artichoke pies, florentines, and innumerable other good things. Some dishes were specially reserved for the King's table, as a baked swan, a roast peacock, and the jowl of a sturgeon soused. These and a piece of roast beef formed the principal dishes.

The attendants at the royal table comprised such gentlemen as wore Sir Richard Hoghton's liveries, and amongst these, of course, were Nicholas Assheton and Sherborne. On seeing the former, the King immediately inquired about his deliverer, and on hearing he was at the lower tables, desired he might be sent for, and, as Richard soon afterwards appeared, having on his return from the chase changed his sombre apparel for gayer attire, James smiled graciously upon him, and more than once, as a mark of especial favour, took the wine-cup from his hands.

The King did ample justice to the good things before him, and especially to the beef, which he found so excellent, that the carver had to help him for the second time. Sir Richard Hoghton ventured to express his gratification that his Majesty found the meat good—"Indeed, it is generally admitted," he said, "that our Lancashire beef is well fed, and well flavoured."

"Weel flavoured!" exclaimed James, as he swallowed the last

juicy morsel; "it is delicious! Finer beef nae man ever put teeth into, an I only wish a' my loving subjects had as gude a dinner as I hae this day eaten. What joint do ye ca' it, Sir Richard?" he asked, with eyes evidently twinkling with a premeditated jest. "This dish," replied the host, somewhat surprised "this, sire, is a loin of beef."

"A loin!" exclaimed James, taking the carving-knife from the sewer, who stood by, "by my faith that is not title honourable enough for joint sae worthy. It wants a dignity, and it shall hae it. Henceforth," he added, touching the meat with the flat of the long blade, as if placing the sword on the back of a knight expectant, "henceforth, it shall be SIR-LOIN, an see ye ca' it sae. Give me a cup of wine, Master Richard Assheton."

All the nobles at the table laughed loudly at the monarch's jest, and as it was soon past down to those at the lower table, the hall resounded with laughter, in which page and attendant of every degree joined, to the great satisfaction of the good-natured originator of the merriment.*

"My dear dad and gossip appears in unwonted good spirits today," observed the Duke of Buckingham.

"An wi' gude reason, Steenie," replied the King, "for we dinna mind when we hae had better sport—always excepting the boar-hunt, when we should hae been rippit up by the cursed creature's tusks but for this braw laddie," he added, pointing to Richard. "Ye maun see what can be done for him, Steenie. We maun hae him at court."

"Your Majesty's wishes have only to be expressed to be fulfilled," replied Buckingham, somewhat drily.

"Were I the lad I wadna place ower meikle dependence on the Duke's promises," remarked Archie Armstrong, in a low tone, to Nicholas.

"Has your Majesty made any further inquiries about the girl suspected of witchcraft?" inquired Buckingham, renewing the conversation.

"Whist, Steenie, whist!" cried James. "Didna ye see her yoursel' this morning?" he added, in a low tone. "Ah! I recollect ye werena at the chase. Aweel, I hae conferred wi' her, an am sair perplexed i' the matter. She is a well-faur'd lassie as ony i' the realm, and answers decorously and doucely. Sooth to say, her looks and manners are mightily in her favour."

"Then you mean to dismiss the matter without further investigation?" observed Buckingham. "I always thought

* "There is a laughable tradition," says Nichols, "still generally current in Lancashire, that our knight-making monarch knighted at the banquet in Hoghton Tower a loin of beef, the part ever since called the sir-loin." And it is added by the same authority, "If the King did not give the sir-loin its name, he might, notwithstanding, have indulged in a pun on the already coined word, the etymology of which was then, as now, as little regarded as the thing signified is well approved."—*Nichols's Progresses of James I.*, vol. iii.

your Majesty delighted to exercise your sagacity in detecting the illusions practised by Satan and his worshippers."

"An sae we do," replied James. "But bend your bonnie head this way till we whisper in your ear. We hae a device for finding it a' out, which canna fail; and when you ken it you will applaud your dear dad's wisdom, and perfit maistery o' the haill science o' kingcraft."

"I would your Majesty would make me acquainted with this notable scheme," replied Buckingham, with ill-concealed contempt. "I might make it more certain of success."

"Na—na—we shanna let the cat out of the bag just yet," returned the King. "We mean it as a surprise to ye a'."

"Then, whatever be the result, it is certain to answer the effect intended," observed the Duke.

"Gae wa'! ye are ever sceptical, Steenie—ever misdoubting your ain dear dad and gossip," rejoined James; "but ye shall find we haena earned the title o' the British Solomon for naething."

Soon after this the King arose, and was ushered to his apartments by Sir Richard Hoghton with the same ceremony as had been observed on his entrance. He was followed by all the nobles; and Nicholas and the others, being released from their duties, repaired to the lower end of the hall to dine. The revel was now sufficiently boisterous; for, as the dames had departed at the same time as the monarch, all restraint was cast aside. The wine-cup flowed freely, and the rafters rang with laughter. Under ordinary circumstances Richard would have shrunk from such a scene; but he had now a part to play, and therefore essayed to laugh at each jest, and to appear as reckless as his neighbours. He was glad, however, when the signal for general dispersion was given; for though Sir Richard Hoghton was unwilling to stint his guests, he was fearful, if they sat too long over their wine, some disturbances might ensue; and indeed, when the revellers came forth and dispersed within the base court, their flushed cheeks, loud voices, and unsteady gait, showed that their potations had already been deep enough.

Meanwhile, quite as much mirth was taking place out of doors as had occurred within the banqueting-hall. As soon as the King sat down to dinner, according to promise the gates were thrown open, and the crowd outside admitted. The huge roast was then taken down, carved, and distributed among them; the only difficulty experienced being in regard to trenchers, and various and extraordinary were the contrivances resorted to to supply the deficiency. This circumstance, however, served to heighten the fun, and, as several casks of stout ale were broached at the same time, universal hilarity prevailed. Still, in the midst of so vast a concourse, many component parts of which had now began to experience the effects of the potent liquor, some little manifestation of disorder might naturally be expected; but all such was speedily quelled by the yeomen of the guard, and other officials appointed for the purpose, and, amidst the uproar and confusion, harmony generally prevailed.

While elbowing his way through the crowd, Nicholas felt his sleeve plucked, and turning, perceived Nance Redferne, who signed him to follow her, and there was something in her manner that left him no alternative but compliance. Nance passed on rapidly, and entered the doorway of a building, where it might be supposed they would be free from interruption.

"What do you want with me, Nance?" asked the squire, somewhat impatiently. "I must beg to observe that I cannot be troubled further on your account, and am greatly afraid aspersions may be thrown on my character, if I am seen talking with you."

"A few words wi' me winna injure your character, squire," rejoined Nance, "an it's on your account an naw on my own that ey ha' brought you here. Ey ha' important information to gie ye. What win yo say when ey tell yo that Jem Device, Elizabeth Device, an' her dowter Jennet are here—aw breedin mischief agen yo, Ruchot Assheton, and Alizon?"

"The devil!" ejaculated Nicholas.

"Eigh, yo'n find it the devil, ey con promise ye, onless their plans be frustrated," said Nance.

"That can be easily done," replied Nicholas. "I'll cause them to be arrested at once."

"Nah, nah—that canna be," rejoined Nance—"Yo mun bide your time."

"What! and allow such miscreants to go at large, and work any malice they please against me and my friends?" replied Nicholas. "Show me where they are, Nance, or I must make you a prisoner."

"Nah! yo winna do that, squire," she replied in a tone of good-humoured defiance. "Ye winna do it for two good reasons: first, becose yo'd be harming a freend who wants to sarve yo, and *win* do so, if yo'n let her; and secondly, becose if yo wur to raise a finger agen me, ey'd deprive yo of speech an motion. When the reet moment comes yo shan strike—boh it's nah come yet. The fruit is nah ripe eneugh to gather. Ey am os anxious os you con be, that the whole o' the Demdike brood should be swept away—an it shan be, if yo'n leave it to me."

"Well, I commit the matter entirely to you," said Nicholas. "Apparently, it cannot be in better hands. But are you aware that Christopher Demdike is a prisoner here in Hoghton Tower? He was taken this morning in the park."

"Ey knoa it," replied Nance; "an ey knoa also why he went there, an it wur my intention to ha' revealed his black design to yo. However, it has bin ordert differently. Boh in respect to t'others, wait till I gie yo the signal. They are disguised; boh even if ye see 'em, an recognise 'em, dunna let it appear till ey gie the word, or yo'n spoil aw."

"Your injunctions shall be obeyed implicitly, Nance," rejoined Nicholas. "I have now perfect reliance upon you. But when shall I see you again?"

"That depends upon circumstances," she replied. "To-neet, may be—may be to-morrow neet. My plans maun be guided by those of others. Boh when next yo see me you win ha' to act."

And, without waiting an answer, she rushed out of the doorway, and, mingling with the crowd, was instantly lost to view; while Nicholas, full of the intelligence he had received, betook himself slowly to his lodgings.

Scarcely were they gone when a door, which had been standing ajar, near them, was opened wide, and disclosed the keen visage of Master Potts.

"Here's a pretty plot hatching—here's a nice discovery I have made!" soliloquised the attorney. "The whole Demdike family, with the exception of the old witch herself, whom I saw burnt on Pendle Hill, are at Hoghton Tower. This shall be made known to the King. I'll have Nicholas Assheton arrested at once, and the woman with him, whom I recognise as Nance Redferne. It will be a wonderful stroke, and will raise me highly in his Majesty's estimation. Yet stay! Will not this interfere with my other plans with Jennet? Let me reflect. I must go cautiously to work. Besides, if I cause Nicholas to be arrested, Nance will escape, and then I shall have no clue to the others. No—no; I must watch Nicholas closely, and take upon myself all the credit of the discovery. Perhaps through Jennet I may be able to detect their disguises. At all events, I will keep a sharp look-out. Affairs are now drawing to a close, and I have only, like a wary and experienced fowler, to lay my nets cleverly to catch the whole covey."

And with these ruminations, he likewise went forth into the base court.

The rest of the day was one round of festivity and enjoyment, in which all classes participated. There were trials of skill and strength, running, wrestling, and cudgeling-matches, with an infinite variety of country games and shows.

Towards five o'clock a rush-cart, decked with flowers and ribbons, and bestridden by men bearing garlands, was drawn up in front of the central building of the tower, in an open window of which sat James—a well-pleased spectator of the different pastimes going forward; and several lively dances were executed by a troop of male and female morris-dancers, accompanied by a tabor and pipe. But though this show was sufficiently attractive, it lacked the spirit of that performed at Whalley; while the character of Maid Marian, which then found so charming a representative in Alizon, was now personated by a man—and if Nicholas Assheton, who was amongst the bystanders, was not deceived, that man was Jem Device. Enraged by this discovery, the squire was about to seize the ruffian; but, calling to mind Nance's counsel, he refrained, and Jem (if it indeed were he) retired with a largess, bestowed by the royal hand as a reward for his uncouth gambols.

The rush-cart and morris-dancers having disappeared, another drollery was exhibited, called the "Fool and his Five Sons," the names of the hopeful offspring of the sapient sire being Pickle Herring, Blue Hose, Pepper Hose, Ginger Hose, and Jack Allspice. The humour of this piece, though not particularly refined, seemed to be appreciated by the audience generally, as well as by the monarch, who laughed heartily at its coarse buffoonery.

Next followed "The Plough and Sword Dance;" the principal actors being a number of grotesque figures armed with swords, some of whom were yoked to a plough, on which sat a piper, playing lustily while dragged along. The plough was guided by a man clothed in a bear-skin, with a fur cap on his head, and a long tail, like that of a lion, dangling behind him. In this hirsute personage, who was intended to represent the wood-demon, Hobthurst, Nicholas again detected Jem Device, and again was strongly tempted to disobey Nance's injunctions, and denounce him—the rather that he recognised in an attendant female, in a fantastic dress, the ruffian's mother, Elizabeth; but he once more desisted.

As soon as the mummers arrived in front of the King, the dance began. With their swords held upright, the party took hands and wheeled rapidly round the plough, keeping time to a merry measure played by the piper, who still maintained his seat. Suddenly the ring was enlarged to double its former size, each man extending his sword to his neighbour, who took hold of the point; after which an hexagonal figure was formed, all the blades being brought together. The swords were then quickly withdrawn, flashing like sunbeams, and a four square figure was presented, the dancers vaulting actively over each other's heads Other variations succeeded, not necessary to be specified—and the sport concluded by a general clashing of swords, intended to represent a melée.

Meanwhile, Nicholas had been joined by Richard Assheton, and the latter was not long in detecting the two Devices through their disguises. On making this discovery he mentioned it to the squire, and was surprised to find him already aware of the circumstance, and not less astonished when he was advised to let them alone; the squire adding he was unable at that time to give his reasons for such counsel, but, being good and conclusive, Richard would be satisfied of their propriety hereafter. The young man, however, thought otherwise, and, notwithstanding his relative's attempts to dissuade him, announced his intention of causing the parties to be arrested at once; and with this design he went in search of an officer of the guard, that the capture might be effected without disturbance. But the throng was so close round the dancers that he could not pierce it, and being compelled to return and take another course, he got nearer to the mazy ring, and was unceremoniously pushed aside by the mummers. At this moment both his arms were forcibly grasped, and a deep voice on the right whispered in his ear—"Meddle not with us, and we will not meddle with you," while similar counsel was given him in other equally menacing tones, though in a different key, on the left. Richard would have shaken off his assailants, and seized them in his turn, but power to do so was wanting to him. For the moment he was deprived of speech and motion; but while thus situated he felt that the sapphire ring given him by the King was snatched from his finger by the first speaker, whom he knew to be Jem Device, while a fearful spell was muttered over him by Elizabeth.

As this occurred at the time when the rattling of the swords engaged the whole attention of the spectators, no one noticed what was going forward except Nicholas, and, before he could get up to the young man, the two miscreants were gone, nor could any one tell what had become of them.

"Have the wretches done you a mischief?" asked the squire, in a low tone, of Richard.

"They have stolen the King's ring, which I meant to use in Alizon's behalf," replied the young man, who by this time had recovered his speech.

"That is unlucky, indeed," said Nicholas. "But we can defeat any ill design they may intend, by acquainting Sir John Finett with the circumstance."

"Let them be," said a voice in his ear. "The time is not yet come."

The squire did not look round, for he well knew that the caution proceeded from Nance Redferne.

And, accordingly, he observed to Richard—"Tarry awhile, and you will be amply avenged."

And with this assurance the young man was fain to be content.

Just then a trumpet was sounded, and a herald stationed on the summit of the broad flight of steps leading to the great hall, proclaimed in a loud voice that a tilting-match was about to take place between Archie Armstrong, jester to his most gracious Majesty, and Davy Droman, who filled the same honourable office to his Grace the Duke of Buckingham, and that a pair of gilt-heel'd chopines would be the reward of the successful combatant. This announcement was received with cheers, and preparations were instantly made for the mock tourney. A large circle being formed by the yeomen of the guard, with an alley leading to it on either side, the two combatants, mounted on gaudy-caparisoned hobby-horses, rode into the ring. Both were armed to the teeth, each having a dish-cover braced around him in lieu of a breastplate, a newly-scoured brass porringer on his head, a large pewter platter instead of a buckler, and a spit with a bung at the point, to prevent mischief, in place of a lance. The Duke's jester was an obese little fellow, and his appearance in this warlike gear was so eminently ridiculous, that it provoked roars of laughter, while Archie was scarcely less ridiculous. After curveting round the arena in imitation of knights of chivalry, and performing "their careers, their prankers, their false trots, their smooth ambles, and Canterbury paces," the two champions took up a position opposite each other, with difficulty, as it seemed, reining in their pawing chargers, and awaiting the signal of attack to be given by Sir John Finett, the judge of the tournament. This was not long delayed, and the "laissez aller" being pronounced, the preux chevaliers started forward with so much fury, and so little discretion, that meeting half-way with a tremendous shock, and butting against each other like two rams, both were thrown violently backwards, exhibiting, amid the shouts of the spectators, their heels, no longer hidden by the trappings of their steeds, kicking in the air. Encumbered as they were, some little time elapsed before they could regain their feet, and their lances having been removed in the mean time, by order of Sir John Finett, as being weapons of too dangerous a description for such truculent combatants, they attacked each other with their broad lathen daggers, dealing sounding blows upon helm, habergeon, and shield, but doing little personal mischief. The strife raged furiously for some time, and, as the champions appeared pretty well matched, it was not easy to say how it would terminate, when chance seemed to decide in favour of Davy Droman; for, in dealing a heavier blow than usual, Archie's dagger snapped in twain, leaving him at the mercy of his opponent. On this the doughty Davy, crowing lustily like chanticleer, called upon him to yield; but Archie was so wroth at his misadventure, that, instead of complying, he sprang forward, and with the hilt of his broken weapon dealt his elated opponent a severe blow on the side of the head, not only knocking off the porringer, but stretching him on the ground beside it. The punishment he had received was enough for poor Davy. He made no attempt to rise, and Archie, crowing in his turn, trampling upon the body of his prostrate foe, and then capering joyously round it, was declared the victor, and received the gilt chopines from the judge, amidst the laughter and acclamations of the beholders.

With this the public sports concluded; and, as evening was drawing on apace, such of the guests as were not invited to pass the night within the Tower, took their departure; while shortly afterwards, supper being served in the banqueting-hall on a scale of profusion and magnificence quite equal to the earlier repast, the King and the whole of his train sat down to it.

CHAPTER X.—EVENING ENTERTAINMENTS.

OTHER amusements were reserved for the evening. While revelry was again held in the great hall; while the tables groaned, for the third time since morning, with good cheer, and the ruby wine, which seemed to gush from inexhaustible fountains, mantled in the silver flagons; while seneschal, sewer, and pantler, with the yeomen of the buttery and kitchen, were again actively engaged in their vocations; while of the three hundred guests more than half, as if insatiate, again vied with each other in prowess with the trencher and the goblet; while in the words of old Taylor, the water poet, but who was no water-drinker—and who thus sang of the hospitality of the men of Manchester, in the early part of the seventeenth century—they had

> "Roast, boil'd, bak'd, too, too much, white, claret, sack.
> Nothing they thought too heavy or too hot,
> Can follow'd can, and pot succeeded pot."

—during this time preparations were making for fresh entertainments out of doors.

The gardens at Hoghton Tower, though necessarily confined in space, owing to their situation on the brow of a hill, were beautifully laid out, and commanded from their balustred terraces magnificent views of the surrounding country. Below them lay the well-wooded park, skirted by the silvery Darwen, with the fair village of Walton-le-Dale immediately beyond it, the proud town of Preston further on, and the single-coned Nese Point rising majestically in the distance. The principal garden constituted a square, and was divided with mathematical precision, according to the formal taste of the time, into smaller squares, with a broad well-kept gravel walk at each angle. These plots were arranged in various figures and devices—such as the cinq-foil, the flower-de-luce, the trefoil, the lozenge, the fret, the diamond, the crossbow, and the oval—all very elaborate and intricate in design. Besides these knots, as they were termed, there were labyrinths, and clipped yew-tree walks, and that indispensable requisite to a garden at the period, a maze. In the centre was a grassy eminence, surmounted by a pavilion, in front of which spread a grass-plot of smoothest turf, ordinarily used as a bowling-green. At the lower end of this a temporary stage was erected, for the masque about to be represented before the King. Torches were kindled, and numerous lamps burned in the branches of the adjoining trees; but they were scarcely needed, for the moon being at the full, the glorious effulgence shed by her upon the scene rendered all other light pale and ineffectual.

After supper, at which the drinking was deeper than at dinner, the whole of the revellers repaired to the garden, full of frolic and merriment, and well-disposed for any diversion in store for them.

The King was conducted to the bowling-green by his host, preceded by a crowd of attendants bearing odoriferous torches; but the royal gait being somewhat unsteady, the aid of Sir Gilbert Hoghton's arm was required to keep the monarch from stumbling. The rest of the bacchanalians followed, and, elated as they were, it will not be wondered that they put very little restraint upon themselves, but shouted, sang, danced, and indulged in all kinds of licence.

Opposite the stage prepared for the masquers a platform had been reared, in front of which was a chair for the King, with seats for the nobles and principal guests behind it. The sides were hung with curtains of crimson velvet fringed with gold; the roof decorated like a canopy; so that it had a very magnificent effect. James lolled back in his chair, and jested loudly and rather indecorously with the various personages as they took their places around him. In less than five minutes the whole of the green was filled with revellers, and great was the pushing and jostling, the laughing and screaming, that ensued among them. Silence was then enjoined by Sir John Finett, who had stationed himself on the steps of the stage, and at this command the assemblage became comparatively quiet, though now and then a half-suppressed titter or a smothered scream would break out. Amid this silence the King's voice could be distinctly heard, and his coarse jests reached the ears of all the astonished audience, provoking many a severe comment from the elders, and much secret laughter from the juniors.

The masque began. Two tutelar deities appeared on the stage. They were followed by a band of foresters clad in Lincoln green, with bows at their backs. The first deity wore a white linen tunic, with flesh-coloured hose and red buskins, and had a purple taffeta mantle over his shoulders. In his hand he held a palm branch, and a garland of the same leaves was woven round his brow. The second household god was a big brawny varlet, wild and shaggy in appearance, being clothed in the skins of beasts, with sandals of untanned cowhide. On his head was a garland of oak leaves; and from his neck hung a horn. He was armed with a hunting-spear and wood-knife, and attended by a large Lancashire mastiff. Advancing to the front of the stage, the foremost personage thus addressed the Monarch—

"This day—great King for government admired!
Which these thy subjects have so much desired—
Shall be kept holy in their heart's best treasure,
And vow'd to James as is this month to Cæsar.
And now the landlord of this ancient Tower,
Thrice fortunate to see this happy hour,
Whose trembling heart thy presence sets on fire,
Unto this house—the heart of all our shire—
Does bid thee cordial welcome, and would speak it
In higher notes, but extreme joy doth break it.
He makes his guests most welcome, in his eyes
Love tears do sit, not he that shouts and cries.

And we the antique guardians of this place,—
I of this house—he of the fruitful chase,—
Since the bold Hoghtons from this hill took name,
Who with the stiff, unbridled Saxons came,
And so have flourish'd in this fairer clime
Successively from that to this our time,
Still offering up to our immortal powers
Sweet incense, wine, and odoriferous flowers;
While sacred Vesta, in her virgin tire,
With vows and wishes tends the hallow'd fire.
Now seeing that thy Majesty is thus
Greater than household deities like us,
We render up to thy more powerful guard,
This Tower. This knight is thine—he is thy ward.
For by thy helping and auspicious hand,
He and his home shall ever, ever stand
And flourish, in despite of envious fate;
And then live, like Augustus, fortunate.
And long, long mayst thou live!—To which both men
And guardian angels cry—"Amen! amen!"

James, who had demeaned himself critically during the delivery of the address, observed at its close to Sir Richard Hoghton, who was standing immediately behind his chair, "We cannot say meikle for the rhymes, which are but indifferently strung together, but the sentiments are leal and gude, and that is a' we care for."

On this the second tutelar divinity advanced, and throwing himself into an attitude, as if bewildered by the august presence in which he stood, exclaimed—

"Thou greatest of mortals!"—

And then stopped, as if utterly confounded.

The King looked at him for a moment, and then roared out—"Weel, gudeman, your commencement is pertinent and true enough; and though we be 'the greatest of mortals,' as ye style us, dinna fash yoursel' about our grandeur, but go on, as if we were nae better nor wiser than your ain simple sel'."

But, instead of encouraging the dumbfounded deity, this speech completely upset him. He hastily retreated; and, in trying to screen himself behind the huntsman, fell back from the stage, and his hound leapt after him. The incident, whether premeditated or not, amused the spectators much more than any speech he could have delivered, and the King joined heartily in the merriment.

Silence being again restored, the first divinity came forward once more, and spoke thus:—

'Dread lord! thy Majesty hath stricken dumb
His weaker god-head; if to himself he come,
Unto thy service straight he will commend
These foresters, and charge them to attend
Thy pleasure in this park, and show such sport
To the chief huntsman and thy princely court,
As the small circle of this round affords,
And be more ready than he was in words." *

* These speeches, given by *Nichols* as derived from the family records of Sir Henry Philip Hoghton, Bart., were actually delivered at a masque represented on occasion of King James's visit to Hoghton Tower

"Weel spoken, and to the purpose, gude fallow," cried James. "And we take this opportunity of assuring our worthy host, in the presence of his other guests, that we have never had better sport in park or forest than we have this day enjoyed—have never eaten better cheer, nor quaffed better wine than at his board—and, altogether, have never been more hospitably welcomed."

Sir Richard was overwhelmed by his Majesty's commendation.

"I have done nothing, my gracious liege," he said, "to merit such acknowledgment on your part, and the delight I experience is only tempered by my utter unworthiness."

"Hoot-toot! man," replied James, jocularly, "ye merit a vast deal mair than we hae said to you. But gude folk dinna always get their deserts. Ye ken that, Sir Richard. And now, hae ye not some ither drolleries in store for us?"

The baronet replied in the affirmative, and soon afterwards the stage was occupied by a new class of performers, and a drollery commenced which kept the audience in one continual roar of laughter so long as it lasted. And yet none of the parts had been studied, the actors entirely trusting to their own powers of comedy to carry it out. The principal character was the Cap Justice, enacted by Sir John Finett, who took occasion in the course of the performance to lampoon and satirise most of the eminent legal characters of the day, mimicking the voices and manner of the three justices—Crooke, Hoghton, and Doddridge—so admirably, that his hearers were wellnigh convulsed; and the three learned gentlemen, who sat near the King, though fully conscious of the ridicule applied to them, were obliged to laugh with the rest. But the unsparing satirist was not content with this, but went on, with most of the other attendants upon the King, and being intimately versed in court scandal, he directed his lash with telling effect. As a contrast to the malicious pleasantry of the Cap Justice, were the gambols and jests of Robin Goodfellow—a merry imp, who, if he led people into mischief, was always ready to get them out of it. Then there was a dance by Bill Huckler, old Crambo, and Tom o' Bedlam, the half-crazed individual already mentioned as being among the crowd in the base court. This was applauded to the echo, and consequently repeated. But the most diverting scene of all was that in which Jem Tospot and the three Doll Wangos appeared. Though given in the broadest vernacular of the county, and scarcely intelligible to the whole of the company, the dialogue of this part of the piece was so lifelike and natural, that every one recognised its truth; while the situations, arranged with the slightest effort, and on the spur of the moment, were extremely ludicrous. The scene was supposed to take place in a small Lancashire alehouse, where a jovial pedlar was carousing, and where, being visited by his three sweethearts—each of whom he privately declared to be the favourite—he had to reconcile their differences, and keep them all in good-humour. Familiar with the character in all its aspects, Nicholas played it to the life; and, to do them justice, Dames Baldwyn, Tetlow, and Nance Redferne, were but little if at all inferior to him. There was a reality in their jealous quarrelling that gave infinite zest to the performance.

"Saul o' my body!" exclaimed James, admiringly, "those are three braw women. Ane of them maun be sax feet if she is an inch, and weel made and weel favourt too. Zounds! Sir Richard, there's nae standing the spells o' your Lancashire Witches. High-born and low-born, they are a' alike. I wad their only witchcraft lay in their een. I should then hae the less fear of 'em. But have you aught mair? for it is growing late, and ye ken we hae something to do in that pavilion."

"Only a merry dance, my liege, in which a man will appear in a dendrological foliage of fronds," replied the baronet.

James laughed at the description, and soon afterwards a party of mummers, male and female, clad in various grotesque garbs, appeared on the stage. In the midst of them was the "dendrological man," enclosed in a framework of green boughs, like that borne by a modern Jack-in-the-green. A ring was formed by the mummers, and the round commenced to lively music.

While the mazy measure was proceeding, Nance Redferne, who had quitted the stage with Nicholas, and now stood close to him among the spectators, said in a low tone, "Look there!"

The squire glanced in the direction indicated, and to his surprise and terror, distinguished, among the crowd at a little distance, the figure of a Cistertian monk.

"He is invisible to every eye except our own," whispered Nance, "and is come to tell me it is time."

"Time for what?" demanded Nicholas.

"Time for you to seize those two accursed Devices, Jem and his mother," replied Nance. "They are both on yon boards. Jem is the man in the tree, and Elizabeth is the owd crone in the red kirtle and high-crowned hat. Yo win knoa her feaw feace when yo pluck off her mask."

"The monk is gone," cried Nicholas; "I have kept my eyes steadily fixed on him, and he has melted into air. What has he to do with the Devices?"

"He is their fate," returned Nance, "an ey ha' acted under his orders. Boh mount, an seize them. Ey win ge wi' ye."

Forcing his way through the crowd, Nicholas ran up the steps, and, followed by Nance, sprang upon the stage. His appearance occasioned considerable surprise; but as he was recognised by the spectators as the jolly Jem Tospot, who had so recently diverted them, and his companion as one of the three Doll Wangos, in anticipation of some more fun they received him with a round of applause. But without stopping to acknowledge it, or being for a moment diverted from his purpose, Nicholas seized the old crone, and, consigning her to Nance, caught hold of the leafy frame in which the man was encased, and pulled him from under it. But he began to think he had unkennelled the wrong fox, for the man, though a tall fellow, bore no resemblance to Jem Device; while, when the crone's mask was plucked off, she was found to be a comely young woman. Meanwhile, all around was in an uproar, and amidst a hurricane of hisses, yells, and other indications of displeasure from the spectators, several of the mummers demanded the meaning of such a strange and unwarrantable proceeding.

"They are a couple of witches," cried Nicholas; "this is Jem Device and his mother Elizabeth."

"My name is nother Jem nor Device," cried the man.

"Nor mine Elizabeth," screamed the woman.

"We know the Devices," cried two or three voices, "and these are none of 'em."

Nicholas was perplexed. The storm increased; threats accompanied the hisses; when luckily he espied a ring on the man's finger. He instantly seized his hand, and held it up to the general gaze.

"A proof!—a proof!" he cried. "This sapphire ring was given by the King to my cousin, Richard Assheton, this morning, and stolen from him by Jem Device."

"Examine their features again" said Nance Redferne, waving her hands over them. "Yo win aw knoa them now."

The woman's face instantly altered. Many years being added to it in a breath. The man changed equally. The utmost astonishment was evinced by all at the transformation, and the bystanders who had spoken before, now cried out loudly—"We know them perfectly now. They are the two Devices."

By this time an officer, attended by a party of halberdiers, had mounted the boards, and the two prisoners were delivered to their custody by Nicholas.

"Howd!" cried the man; "Ey win no longer deny my name. Ey am Jem Device, an this is my mother, Elizabeth. Boh a warse offender than either on us stonds afore yo. This woman is Nance Redferne, grandowter of the owd hag, Mother Chattox. Ey charge her wi' makin' wax images, an' stickin' pins in 'em, wi' intent to kill folk. Hoo wad ha' kilt me mysel', wi' her devilry, if ey hadna bin too strong for her—an' that's why hoo bears me malice, an' has betrayed me to Squoire Nicholas Assheton. Seize her, an' ca' me as a witness agen her."

And as Nance was secured, he laughed malignantly.

"Ey care not," replied Nance. "Ey am now revenged on you both."

While this impromptu performance took place, as much to the surprise of James as of any one else, and while he was desiring Sir Richard Hoghton to ascertain what it all meant—at the very moment that the two Devices and Nance removed from the stage, an usher approached the monarch, and said that Master Potts entreated a moment's audience of his majesty.

"Potts!" exclaimed James, somewhat confused. "Wha is he?—ah, yes! I recollect—a witch-finder. Weel, let him approach."

Accordingly, the next moment the little attorney, whose face was evidently charged with some tremendous intelligence, was ushered into the king's presence.

After a profound reverence, he said, "May it please your Majesty, I have something for your private ear."

"Aweel, then," replied James, "approach us mair closely. What hae ye got to say, sir? Aught mair anent these witches?"

"A great deal, sire," said Potts, in an impressive tone. "Something dreadful has happened—something terrible."

"Eh! what?" exclaimed James, looking alarmed. "What is it, man? Speak!"

"Murder? sire,—murder has been done," said Potts, in low thrilling accents.

"Murder!" exclaimed James, horror-stricken. "Tell us a' about it, and without more ado."

But Potts was still circumspect. With an air of deepest mystery, he approached his head as near as he dared to that of the monarch, and whispered in his ear.

"Can this be true?" cried James. "If sae—it's very shocking—very sad."

"It is too true, as your Majesty will find on investigation," replied Potts. "The little girl I told you of, Jennet Device, saw it done."

"Weel, weel, there is nae accounting for human frailty and wickedness," said James. "Let a' necessary steps be taken at once. We will consider what to do. But—d'ye hear, sir?—dinna let the bairn Jennet go. Haud her fast. D'ye mind that? Now go, and cause the guilty party to be put under arrest."

And on receiving this command Master Potts departed.

Scarcely was he gone than Nicholas Assheton came up to the railing of the platform, and, imploring his Majesty's forgiveness for the disturbance he had occasioned, explained that it had been owing to the seizure of the two Devices, who, for some wicked but unexplained purpose, had contrived to introduce themselves, under various disguises, into the Tower.

"Ye did right to arrest the miscreants, sir," said James. "But hae ye heard what has happened?"

"No, my liege," replied Nicholas, alarmed by the King's manner; "what is it?"

"Come nearer, and ye shall learn," replied James; "for we wadna hae it bruited abroad, though if true, as we canna doubt, it will be known soon enough."

And as the squire bent forward, he imparted some intelligence to him, which instantly changed the expression of the latter to one of mingled horror and rage.

"It is false, sire!" he cried. "I will answer for her innocence with my life. . She could not do it. Your Majesty's patience is abused. It is Jennet who has done it—not she. But I will unravel the terrible mystery. You have the other two wretches prisoners, and can enforce the truth from them."

"We will essay to do so," replied James; "but we have also another prisoner."

"Christopher Demdike?" said Nicholas.

"Ay, Christopher Demdike," rejoined James. "But another besides him—Mistress Nutter. You stare, sir; but it is true. She is in yonder pavilion. We ken fu' weel wha assisted her flight, and wha concealed her. Maister Potts has told us a'. It is weel for you that your puir kinsman, Richard Assheton, did us sic gude service at the boar-hunt to-day. We shall not now be unmindful of it, even though he cannot send us the ring we gave him."

"It is here, sire," replied Nicholas. "It was stolen from him by the villain, Jem Device. The poor youth meant to use it for Alizon. I now deliver it to your Majesty as coming from him in her behalf."

"And we sae receive it," replied the monarch, brushing away the moisture that gathered thickly in his eyes.

At this moment a tall personage, wrapped in a cloak, who appeared to be an officer of the guard, approached the railing.

"I am come to inform your Majesty that Christopher Demdike has just died of his wounds," said this personage.

"And sae he has had a strae death, after a'!" rejoined James. "Weel, we are sorry for it."

"His portion will be eternal bale," observed the officer.

"How know you that, sir?" demanded the King, sharply. "You are not his judge."

"I witnessed his end, sire," replied the officer; "and no man who died as he died can be saved. The Fiend was beside him at the death-throes."

"Save us!" exclaimed James. "Ye dinna say so? God's santie! man, but this is grewsome, and gars the flesh creep on one's banes. Let his foul carcase be taen awa', and hangit on a gibbet on the hill where Malkin Tower aince stood, as a warning to a' sic heinous offenders."

As the King ceased speaking, Master Potts appeared out of breath, and greatly excited.

"She has escaped, sire!" he cried.

"Wha! Jennet!" exclaimed James. "If sae, we will hang you in her stead."

"No, sire—Alizon," replied Potts. "I can nowhere find her; nor—" and he hesitated.

"Weel—weel—it is nae great matter," replied James, as if relieved, and with a glance of satisfaction at Nicholas.

"I know where Alizon is, sire," said the officer.

"Indeed!" exclaimed James. "This fellow is strangely officious," he muttered to himself. "And where may she be, sir?" he added, aloud.

"I will produce her within a quarter of an hour in yonder pavilion," replied the officer, "and all that Master Potts has been unable to find."

"Your Majesty may trust him," observed Nicholas, who had attentively regarded the officer. "Depend upon it he will make good his words."

"You think so?" cried the King. "Then we will put him to the test. You will engage to confront Alizon with her mother?" he added, to the officer.

"I will, sire," replied the other. "But I shall require the assistance of a dozen men."

"Tak twenty, if you will," replied the King,—"I am impatient to see what you can do."

"In a quarter of a minute all shall be ready within the pavilion, sire," replied the officer. "You have seen one masque to-night; —but you shall now behold a different one—the masque of death."

And he disappeared.

Nicholas felt sure he would accomplish his task, for he had recognised in him the Cistertian monk.

"Where is Sir Richard Assheton of Middleton?" inquired the King.

"He left the Tower with his daughter Dorothy, immediately after the banquet," replied Nicholas.

"I am glad of it—right glad," replied the monarch; "the terrible intelligence can be the better broken to them. If it had come upon them suddenly, it might have been fatal—especially to the puir lassie. Let Sir Ralph Assheton of Whalley come to me—and Master Roger Nowell of Read."

"Your Majesty shall be obeyed," replied Sir Richard Hoghton.

The King then gave some instructions respecting the prisoners, and bade Master Potts have Jennet in readiness.

And now to see what terrible thing had happened.

CHAPTER XI.—FATALITY.

ALONG the eastern terrace a youth and maiden were pacing slowly. They had stolen forth unperceived from the revel, and, passing through a door standing invitingly open, had entered the garden. Though overjoyed in each other's presence, the solemn beauty of the night, so powerful in its contrast to the riotous scene they had just quitted, profoundly impressed them. Above, were the deep serene heavens, lighted up by the starry host and their radiant queen—below, the immemorial woods, steeped in silvery mists arising from the stream flowing past them. All nature was hushed in holy rest. In opposition to the flood of soft light emanating from the lovely planet overhead, and which turned all it fell on, whether tree, or tower, or stream, to beauty, was the artificial glare caused by the torches near the pavilion; while the discordant sounds occasioned by the minstrels tuning their instruments, disturbed the repose. As they went on, however, these sounds were lost in the distance, and the glare of the torches was excluded by intervening trees. Then the moon looked down lovingly upon them, and the only music that reached their ears arose from the nightingales. After a pause, they walked on again, hand-in-hand, gazing at each other, at the glorious heavens, and drinking in the thrilling melody of the songsters of the grove.

At the angle of the terrace was a small arbour placed in the midst of a bosquet, and they sat down within it. Then, and not till then, did their thoughts find vent in words. Forgetting the sorrows they had endured, and the perils by which they were environed, they found in their deep mutual love a shield against the sharpest arrows of fate. In low gentle accents they breathed their passion, solemnly plighting their faith before all-seeing Heaven.

Poor souls! they were happy then—intensely happy. Alas! that their happiness should be so short; for those few moments of bliss, stolen from a waste of tears, were all that were allowed them. Inexorable fate still dogged their footsteps.

Amidst the bosquet stood a listener to their converse—a little girl with high shoulders and sharp features, on which diabolical malice was stamped. Two yellow eyes glistened through the leaves beside her, marking the presence of a cat. As the lovers breathed their vows, and indulged in hopes never to be realised, the wicked child grinned, clenched her hands, and, grudging them their short-lived happiness, seemed inclined to interrupt it. Some stronger motive, however, kept her quiet.

What are the pair talking of now?—She hears her own name mentioned by the maiden, who speaks of her with pity, almost with affection—pardons her for the mischief she has done her, and hopes Heaven will pardon her likewise. But she knows not the full extent of the girl's malignity, or even her gentle heart must have been roused to resentment.

The little girl, however, feels no compunction. Infernal malice has taken possession of her heart, and crushed every kindly feeling within it. She hates all those that compassionate her, and returns evil for good.

What are the lovers talking of now? Of their first meeting at Whalley Abbey, when one was May Queen, and by her beauty and simplicity won the other's heart, losing her own at the same time. A bright unclouded career seemed to lie before them then. Wofully had it darkened since. Alas! Alas!

The little girl smiles. She hopes they will go on. She likes to hear them talk thus. Past happiness is ever remembered with a pang by the wretched, and they *were* happy then. Go on—go on!

But they are silent for awhile, for they wish to dwell on that hopeful, that blissful season. And a nightingale, alighting on a bough above them, pours forth its sweet plaint, as if in response to their tender emotions. They praise the bird's song, and it suddenly ceases.

For the little girl, full of malevolence, stretches forth her hand, and it drops to the ground, as if stricken by a dart.

"Is thy heart broken, poor bird?" exclaimed the young man, taking up the hapless songster, yet warm and palpitating. "To die in the midst of thy song—'tis hard."

"Very hard!" replied the maiden, tearfully. "Its fate seems a type of our own."

The little girl laughed, but in a low tone, and to herself.

The pair then grew sad. This slight incident had touched them deeply, and their conversation took a melancholy turn. They spoke of the blights that had nipped their love in the bud—of the canker that had eaten into its heart—of the destiny that so relentlessly pursued them, threatening to separate them for ever.

The little girl laughed merrily.

Then they spoke of the grave—and of hope beyond the grave; and they spoke cheerfully.

The little girl could laugh no longer, for with her all beyond the grave was despair.

After that they spoke of the terrible power that Satan had lately obtained in that unhappy district, of the arts he had employed, and of the votaries he had won. Both prayed fervently that his snares might be circumvented, and his rule destroyed.

During this part of the discourse the cat swelled to the size of a tiger, and his eyes glowed like fiery coals. He made a motion as if he would spring forward, but the voice of prayer arrested him, and he shrank back to his former size.

"Poor Jennet is ensnared by the Fiend," murmured the maiden, "and will perish eternally. Would I could save her!"

"It cannot be," replied the young man. "She is beyond redemption."

The little girl gnashed her teeth with rage.

"But my mother—I do not now despair of her," said Alizon. "She has broken the bondage by which she was enchained, and, if she resists temptation to the last, I am assured will be saved."

"Heaven aid her!" exclaimed Richard.

Scarcely were the words uttered, than the cat disappeared.

"Why, Tib!—where are yo, Tib? Ey want yo!" cried the little girl in a low tone.

But the familiar did not respond to the call.

"Where con he ha' gone?" cried Jennet; "Tib! Tib!"

Still the cat came not.

"Then ey mun do the wark without him," pursued the little girl; "an ey win no longer delay it."

And with this she crept stealthily round the arbour, and, approaching the side where Richard sat, watched an opportunity of touching him unperceived.

As her finger came in contact with his frame, a pang like death shot through his heart, and he fell upon Alizon's shoulder.

"Are you ill?" she exclaimed, gazing at his pallid features, rendered ghastly white by the moonlight.

Richard could make no reply, and Alizon, becoming dreadfully alarmed, was about to fly for assistance, but the young man, by a great effort, detained her.

"Ey mun now run an tell Mester Potts, so that hoo may be found wi' him," muttered Jennet, creeping away.

Just then Richard recovered his speech, but his words were faintly uttered, and with difficulty.

"Alizon," he said, "I will not attempt to disguise my condition from you. I am dying. And my death will be attributed to you—for evil-minded persons have persuaded the King that you have bewitched me, and he will believe the charge now. Oh! if you would ease the pangs of death for me—if you would console my latest moments—leave me, and quit this place, before it be too late."

"Oh! Richard," she cried distractedly, "you ask more than I can perform. If you are indeed in such imminent danger, I will stay with you—will die with you."

"No! live for me—live—save yourself, Alizon," implored the young man. "Your danger is greater than mine. A dreadful death awaits you at the stake! Oh! mercy, mercy, heaven! Spare her—in pity spare her!—Have we not suffered enough? I can no more. Farewell for ever, Alizon—one kiss—the last."

And as their lips met, his strength utterly forsook him, and he fell backwards.

"One grave!" he murmured; "one grave, Alizon!"—And so, without a groan, he expired.

Alizon neither screamed nor swooned, but remained in a state of stupefaction, gazing at the body. As the moon fell upon the placid features, they looked as if locked in slumber.

There he lay—the young, the brave, the beautiful, the loving, the beloved. Fate had triumphed. Death had done his work; but he had only performed half his task.

"One grave—one grave—it was his last wish—it shall be so!" she cried, in frenzied tones. "I shall thus escape my enemies, and avoid the horrible and shameful death to which they would doom me."

And she snatched the dagger from the ill-fated youth's side.

"Now, fate, I defy thee!" she cried, with a fearful laugh.

One last look at that calm beautiful face—one kiss of the cold lips, which can no more return the endearment—and the dagger is pointed at her breast.

But she is withheld by an arm of iron, and the weapon falls from her grasp. She looks up. A tall figure, clothed in the mouldering habiliments of a Cistertian monk, stands beside her. She knows the vestments at once, for she has seen them before, hanging up in the closet adjoining her mother's chamber at Whalley Abbey—and the features of the ghostly monk seem familiar to her.

"Raise not thy hand against thyself," said the phantom, in a tone of awful reproof. "It is the Fiend prompts thee to do it. He would take advantage of thy misery to destroy thee."

"I took thee for the Fiend," replied Alizon, gazing at him with wonder rather than with terror. "Who art thou?"

"The enemy of thy enemies, and therefore thy friend," replied the monk. "I would have saved thy lover if I could, but his destiny was not to be averted. But, rest content, I will avenge him."

"I do not want vengeance—I want to be with him," she replied, frantically embracing the body.

"Thou wilt soon be with him," said the phantom, in tones of deep significance. "Arise, and come with me. Thy mother needs thy assistance."

"My mother!" exclaimed Alizon, clearing the blinding tresses from her brow. "Where is she?"

"Follow me, and I will bring thee to her," said the monk.

"And leave him? I cannot!" cried Alizon, gazing wildly at the body.

"You must. A soul is at stake, and will perish if you come not," said the monk. "He is at rest, and you will speedily rejoin him."

"With that assurance I will go," replied Alizon, with a last look at the object of her love. "One grave—lay us in one grave!"

"It shall be done according to your wish," said the monk.

And he glided on with noiseless footsteps.

Alizon followed him along the terrace.

Presently they came to a dark yew-tree walk, leading to a labyrinth, and tracking it swiftly, as well as the overarched and intricate path to which it conducted, they entered a grotto, whence a flight of steps descended to a subterranean passage, hewn out of the rock. Along this passage, which was of some extent, the monk proceeded, and Alizon followed him.

At last they came to another flight of steps, and here the monk stopped.

"We are now beneath the pavilion, where you will find your

mother," he said. "Mount! the way is clear before you. I have other work to do."

Alizon obeyed; and, as she advanced, was surprised to find the monk gone. He had neither passed her nor ascended the steps, and must, therefore, have sunk into the earth.

CHAPTER XII.—THE LAST HOUR.

WITHIN the pavilion sat Alice Nutter. She was clad in deep mourning, but her dress seemed disordered as if by hasty travel. Her looks were full of anguish and terror; her blanched tresses, once so dark and beautiful, hung dishevelled over her shoulders; and her thin hands were clasped in supplication. Her cheeks were ashy pale, but on her brow was a bright red mark, as if traced by a finger dipped in blood.

A lamp was burning on the table beside her. Near it was a skull, and near this emblem of mortality an hourglass, running fast.

The windows and doors of the building were closed, and it would seem the unhappy lady was a prisoner.

She had been brought there secretly that night, with what intent she knew not; but she felt sure it was with no friendly design towards herself. Early in the day three horsemen had arrived at her retreat in Pendle Forest, and without making any charge against her, or explaining whither they meant to take her, or indeed answering any inquiry, had brought her off with them, and, proceeding across the country, had arrived at a forester's hut on the outskirts of Hoghton Park. Here they tarried till evening, placing her in a room by herself, and keeping strict watch over her; and when the shadows of night fell, they conveyed her through the woods, and by a private entrance to the gardens of the Tower, and with equal secresy to the pavilion, where, setting a lamp before her, they left her to her meditations. All refused to answer her inquiries, but one of them, with a sinister smile, placed the hourglass and skull beside her.

Left alone, the wretched lady vainly sought some solution of the enigma—why she had been brought thither. She could not solve it; but she determined, if her capture had been made by any lawful authorities, to confess her guilt and submit to condign punishment.

Though the windows and doors were closed as before mentioned, sounds from without reached her, and she heard confused and tumultuous noises as if from a large assemblage. For what purpose were they met? Could it be for her execution? No—there were strains of music, and bursts of laughter. And yet she had heard that the burning of a witch was a spectacle in which the populace delighted—that they looked upon it as a show, like any other; and why should they not laugh, and have music at it?

But could she be executed without trial, without judgment? She knew not. All she knew was she was guilty, and deserved to die. But when this idea took possession of her, the laughter sounded in her ears like the yells of demons, and the strains like the fearful harmonies she had heard at weird sabbaths.

All at once she recollected with indescribable terror, that on this very night the compact she had entered into with the Fiend expired. That at midnight, unless by her penitence and prayers she had worked out her salvation, he could claim her. She recollected also, and with increased uneasiness, that the man who had set the hourglass on the table, and who had regarded her with a sinister smile as he did so, had said it was eleven o'clock!

Her last hour then had arrived—nay, was partly spent, and the moments were passing swiftly by.

The agony she endured at this thought was intense. She felt as if reason were forsaking her, and, but for her determined efforts to resist it, such a crisis might have occurred. But she knew that her eternal welfare depended upon the preservation of her mental balance, and she strove to maintain it, and in the end succeeded.

Her gaze was fixed intently on the hourglass. She saw the sand trickling silently but swiftly down, like a current of life-blood, which, when it ceased, life would cease with it. She saw the shining grains above insensibly diminishing in quantity, and, as if she could arrest her destiny by the act, she seized the glass, and would have turned it, but the folly of the proceeding arrested her, and she set it down again.

Then horrible thoughts came upon her, crushing her and overwhelming her, and she felt by anticipation all the torments she would speedily have to endure. Oceans of fire, in which miserable souls were for ever tossing, rolled before her. Yells, such as no human anguish can produce, smote her ears. Monsters of frightful form yawned to devour her. Fiends, armed with terrible implements of torture, such as the wildest imagination cannot paint, menaced her. All hell, and its horrors, was there, its dreadful gulf, its roaring furnaces, its rivers of molten metal, ever burning, yet never consuming its victims. A hot sulphureous atmosphere oppressed her, and a film of blood dimmed her sight.

She endeavoured to pray, but her tongue clove to the roof of her mouth. She looked about for her Bible, but it had been left behind when she was taken from her retreat. She had no safeguard—none.

Still the sand ran on.

New agonies assailed her. Hell was before her again, but in a new form, and with new torments. She closed her eyes. She shut her ears. But she saw it still, and heard its terrific yells.

Again she consults the hourglass. The sand is running on—ever diminishing.

New torments assail her. She thinks of all she loves most on earth—of her daughter! Oh! if Alizon were near her, she might pray for her—might scare away these frightful visions—might save her. She calls to her—but she answers not. No, she is utterly abandoned of God and man, and must perish eternally.

Again she consults the hourglass. One quarter of an hour is all that remains to her. Oh! that she could employ it in prayer! Oh! that she could kneel—or even weep!

A large mirror hangs against the wall, and she is drawn towards it by an irresistible impulse. She sees a figure within it—but she does not know herself. Can that cadaverous object, with the white hair, that seems newly-arisen from the grave, be she? It must be a phantom. No—she touches her cheek, and finds it is real. But, ah! what is this red brand upon her brow? It must be the seal of the demon. She tries to efface it—but it will not come out. On the contrary, it becomes redder and deeper.

Again she consults the glass. The sand is still running on. How many minutes remain to her?

"Ten!" cried a voice, replying to her mental inquiry.—"Ten!"

And, turning, she perceived her familiar standing beside her.

"Thy time is wellnigh out, Alice Nutter," he said. "In ten minutes my lord will claim thee."

"My compact with thy master is broken," she replied, summoning up all her resolution. "I have long ceased to use the power bestowed upon me; but, even if I had wished it, thou hast refused to serve me."

"I have refused to serve you, madam, because you have disobeyed the express injunctions of my master," replied the familiar; "but your apostasy does not free you from bondage. You have merely lost advantages which you might have enjoyed. If you chose to dismiss me I could not help it. Neither I nor my lord have been to blame. We have performed our part of the contract."

"Why am I brought hither?" demanded Mistress Nutter.

"I will tell you," replied the familiar. "You were brought here by order of the King. Your retreat was revealed to him by Master Potts, who learnt it from Jennet Device. The sapient sovereign intended to confront you with your daughter Alizon, who, like yourself, is accused of witchcraft; but he will be disappointed—for when he comes for you, you will be out of his reach—ha! ha!"

And he rubbed his hands at the jest.

"Alizon accused of witchcraft—say'st thou?" cried Mistress Nutter.

"Ay," replied the familiar. "She is suspected of bewitching Richard Assheton, who has been done to death by Jennet Device. For one so young, the little girl has certainly a rare turn for mischief. But no one will know the real author of the crime, and Alizon will suffer for it."

"Heaven will not suffer such iniquity," said the lady.

"As you have nothing to do with heaven, madam, it is needless to refer to it," said the familiar. "But it certainly is rather hard that one so young as Alizon should perish."

"Can you save her?" asked Mistress Nutter.

"Oh! yes, I *could* save her, but she will not let me," replied the familiar, with a grin.

"No—no—it is impossible," cried the wretched woman. "And I cannot help her."

"Perhaps you might," observed the tempter. My master, whom you accuse of harshness, is ever willing to oblige you. You have a few minutes left—do you wish him to aid her? Command me, and I will obey you."

"This is some snare," thought Mistress Nutter; "I will resist it."

"You cannot be worse off than you are," remarked the familiar.

"I know not that," replied the lady. "What would'st thou do?"

"Whatever you command me, madam. I can do nothing of my own accord. Shall I bring your daughter here? Say so, and it shall be done."

"No—thou would'st ensnare me," she replied. "I well know thou hast no power over her. Thou would'st place some phantasm before me. I would see her, but not through thy agency."

"She is here," cried Alizon, opening the door of a closet, and rushing towards her mother, who instantly locked her in her arms.

"Pray for me, my child," cried Mistress Nutter, mastering her emotion, "or I shall be snatched from you for ever. My moments are numbered. Pray—pray!"

Alizon fell on her knees, and prayed fervently.

"You waste your breath," cried the familiar, in a mocking tone. "Never till the brand shall disappear from her brow, and the writing, traced in her blood, shall vanish from this parchment, can she be saved. She is mine."

"Pray, Alizon, pray!" shrieked Mistress Nutter.

"I will tear her in pieces if she does not cease," cried the familiar, assuming a terrible shape, and menacing her with claws like those of a wild beast.

"Pray thou, mother!" cried Alizon.

"I cannot," replied the lady.

"I will kill her if she but makes the attempt," howled the demon.

"But try, mother, try!" cried Alizon.

The poor lady dropped on her knees, and raised her hands in humble supplication—"Heaven forgive me!" she exclaimed.

The demon seized the hourglass.

"The sand is out—her term has expired—she is mine!" he cried.

"Clasp thy arms tightly round me, my child. He cannot take me from thee," shrieked the agonised woman.

"Release her, Alizon, or I will slay thee likewise," roared the demon.

"Never," she replied; "thou canst not overcome me. Ha!" she added joyfully, "the brand has disappeared from her brow."

"And the writing from the parchment," howled the demon; "but I will have her notwithstanding."

And he plunged his claws into Alice Nutter's flesh. But her daughter held her fast.

"Oh! hold me, my child—hold me, or I am lost!" shrieked the lady.

"Be warned, and let her go, or thy life shall pay for her's," cried the demon.

"My life for her's, willingly," replied Alizon.

"Then take thy fate," rejoined the evil spirit.

And placing his hand upon her heart, it instantly ceased to beat.

"Mother, thou art saved—saved!" exclaimed Alizon, throwing out her arms.

And gazing at her for an instant with a seraphic look, she fell backwards, and expired.

"Thou art mine," roared the demon, seizing Mistress Nutter by the hair, and dragging her from her daughter's body, to which she clung desperately.

"Help!—help!" she cried.

"Thou mayst call, but thy cries will be unheeded," rejoined the familiar with mocking laughter.

"Thou liest, false fiend!" said Mistress Nutter. "Heaven will help me now."

And, as she spoke, the Cistertian monk stood before them.

"Hence!" he cried with an imperious gesture to the demon. "She is no longer in thy power. Hence!"

And with a howl of rage and disappointment the familiar vanished.

"Alice Nutter," continued the monk, "thy safety has been purchased at the price of thy daughter's life. But it is of little moment, for she could not live long. Her gentle heart was broken, and, when the demon stopped it for ever, he performed unintentionally a merciful act. She must rest in the same grave with him she loved so well during life. This tell to those who will come to thee anon. Thou art delivered from the yoke of Satan. Full expiation has been made. But earthly justice must be satisfied. Thou must pay the penalty for crimes committed in the flesh, but what thou sufferest here shall avail thee hereafter."

"I am content," she replied.

"Pass the rest of thy life in penitence and prayer," pursued the monk, "and let nothing divert thee from it; for, though free now, thou wilt be subject to evil influence and temptations to the last. Remember this."

"I will—I will," she rejoined.

"And now," he said, "kneel beside thy daughter's body and pray. I will return to thee ere many minutes be passed. One task more, and then my mission is ended."

CHAPTER XIII.—THE MASQUE OF DEATH.

SHORT time as he had to await, James was unable to control his impatience. At last he arose, and, completely sobered by the recent strange events, descended the steps of the platform, and walked on without assistance.

"Let the yeomen of the guard keep back the crowd," he said to an officer, "and let none follow me but Sir Ralph Assheton, Master Nicholas Assheton, and Master Roger Nowell. When I call, let the prisoners be brought forward."

"Your Majesty shall be obeyed," replied the baronet, giving the necessary directions.

James then moved slowly forward in the direction of the pavilion; and, as he went, called Nicholas Assheton to him.

"Wha was that officer?" he asked.

"Your pardon, my liege, but I cannot answer the question," replied Nicholas.

"And why not, sir?" demanded the monarch, sharply.

"For reasons I will hereafter render to your Majesty, and which I am persuaded you will find satisfactory," rejoined the squire.

"Weel, weel, I dare say you are right," said the King. "But do you think he will keep his word?"

"I am sure of it," returned Nicholas.

"The time is come, then!" exclaimed James impatiently, and looking up at the pavilion

"The time is come!" echoed a sepulchral voice.

"Did you speak?" inquired the monarch.

"No, sire," replied Nicholas; "but some one seemed to give you intimation that all is ready. Will it please you to go on?"

"Enter!" cried the voice.

"Wha speaks?" demanded the King. And, as no answer was returned, he continued—"I will not set foot in the structure. It may be a snare of Satan."

At this moment the shutters of the windows flew open, showing that the pavilion was lighted up by many tapers within, while solemn strains of music issued from it.

"Enter!" repeated the voice.

"Have no fear, sire," said Nicholas.

"That canna be the wark o' the deil," cried James. "He does not delight in holy hymns and sweet music."

"That is a solemn dirge for the dead," observed Nicholas, as melodious voices mingled with the music.

"Weel, weel, I will go on at a' hazards," said James.

The doors flew open as the King and his attendants approached, and, as soon as they had passed through them, the valves swung back to their places.

A strange sad spectacle met their gaze. In the midst of the chamber stood a bier, covered with a velvet pall, and on it the bodies of a youth and maiden were deposited. Pale and beautiful were they as sculptured marble, and a smile sat upon their features. Side by side they were lying, with their arms enfolded, as if they had died in each other's embrace. A wreath of yew and cypress was placed above their heads, and flowers were scattered round them.

They were Richard and Alizon.

It was a deeply touching sight, and for some time none spake. The solemn dirge continued, interrupted only by the stifled sobs of the listeners.

"Both gone!" exclaimed Nicholas, in accents broken by emotion; "and so young—so good—so beautiful! Alas! alas!"

"She could not have bewitched him," said the King.

"Alizon was all purity and goodness," cried Nicholas, "and is now numbered with the angels."

"The guilty one is in thy hands, O King!" said the voice. "It is for thee to punish."

"And I will not hold my hand," said James. "The Devices shall assuredly perish. When I go from this chamber, I will have them conveyed under a strong escort to Lancaster Castle. They shall die by the hands of the common executioner."

"My mission, then, is complete," replied the voice. "I can rest in peace."

"Who art thou?" demanded the King.

"One who sinned deeply, but is now pardoned," replied the voice.

The King was for a moment lost in reflection, and then turned to depart. At this moment a kneeling figure, whom no one had hitherto noticed, arose from behind the bier. It was a lady, robed in mourning. So ghastly pale were her features, and so skeleton-like her attenuated frame, that James thought he beheld a spectre, and recoiled in terror. The figure advanced slowly towards him.

"Who, and what art thou, in Heaven's name?" he exclaimed.

"I am Alice Nutter, sire," replied the lady, prostrating herself before him.

"Alice Nutter, the witch!" cried the King. "Why—ay, I recollect thou wert here. I sent for thee, but recent terrible events had put thee clean out of my head. But expect no grace from me, evil woman. I will show thee none."

"I ask none, sire," replied the penitent. "I came to place myself in your hands, that justice may be done upon me."

"Ah!" exclaimed James. "Dost thou, indeed, repent thee of thy iniquities? Dost thou abjure the devil and all his works?"

"I do," replied the lady, fervently. "My compact with the Evil One has been broken by the prayers of my devoted daughter, who sacrificed herself for me, and thereby saved my soul alive. But human justice requires an expiation, and I am anxious to make it."

"Arise, ill-fated woman," said the king, much moved. "You must go to Lancaster, but, in consideration of your penitence, no indignity shall be shown you. You must be strictly guarded, but you shall not be taken with the other prisoners."

"I humbly thank your Majesty," replied the lady. "May I take a last farewell of my child?"

"Do so," replied James.

Alice Nutter then approached the bier, and, after gazing for a moment with deepest fondness upon the features of her daughter, imprinted a kiss upon her marble brow. In doing this her tears fell fast.

"You can weep, I see," observed the King. "You are a witch no longer."

"Ay, Heaven be praised! I can weep," she replied; "and so ease my over-burthened heart. Oh! sire, none but those who have experienced it can tell the agony of being denied this relief of nature. Farewell for ever, my blessed child!" she exclaimed, kissing her brow again; "and you, too, her beloved. Nicholas Assheton—it was her wish to be buried in the same grave with Richard. You will see it done, Nicholas?"

"I will—I will!" replied the squire, in a voice of deepest emotion.

"And I likewise promise it," said Sir Ralph Assheton. "They shall rest together in Whalley churchyard. It is well that Sir Richard and Dorothy are gone," he observed to Nicholas.

"It is indeed," said the squire, "or we should have had another funeral to perform. Pray Heaven it be not so now!"

"Have you any other request to prefer?" demanded the King.

"None whatever, sire," replied the lady, "except that I wish to make full restitution of all the land I have robbed him of, to Master Roger Nowell; and, as some compensation, I would fain add certain lands adjoining, which have been conveyed over to Sir Ralph and Nicholas Assheton, only annexing the condition that a small sum annually be given in dole to the poor of the parish, that I may be remembered in their prayers."

"We will see it done," said Sir Ralph and Nicholas.

"And I will see my part fulfilled," said Nowell. "For any wrong you have done me I now freely and fully forgive you, and may Heaven in its infinite mercy forgive you likewise!"

"Amen!" ejaculated the monarch. And all the others joined in the ejaculation.

The King then moved to the door, which was opened for him by the two Asshetons. At the foot of the steps stood Master Potts, attended by an officer of the guard and a party of halberdiers. In the midst of them, with their hands tied behind their backs, were Jem Device, his mother, Jennet, and poor Nance Redferne. Jem looked dogged and sullen, Elizabeth downcast, but Jennet retained her accustomed malignant expression. Poor Nance was the only one who excited any sympathy. Jennet's malice seemed now directed against Master Potts, whom she charged with having betrayed and deceived her.

"If Tib had na deserted me he should tear thee i' pieces, thou ill-favourt little monster," she cried.

"Monster in your own face, you hideous little wretch," exclaimed the indignant attorney. "If you use such opprobrious epithets I will have you gagged. You will be taken to Lancaster Castle, and hanged."

"Yo are os bad as ey am, and warse," replied Jennet, "and deserve hanging os weel, and the King shan knoa of your tricks," she vociferated, as James appeared at the door of the pavilion. "Yo wished to ensnare Alizon. Yo wished me to kill her. Ey was only your instrument."

"Stop her mouth—gag her!" cried Potts.

"Nah, nah!—they shanna stap my mouth—they shanna gag me," cried Jennet. "Ey win speak out. The King shan hear me. You are as bad os me."

"All malice, your Majesty—all malice," cried the attorney.

"Malice, nae doubt, in great pairt," replied James; "but some truth as weel, I fear, sir. And in any case it will prevent my doing any thing for you."

"There, you have ruined my hopes, you little wretch!" cried Potts, furiously.

"Ey'm reet glad on't," said Jennet. "Yo may tay me to Lonkester Castle, boh yo conna hong me. Ey knoa that fu' weel. Ey shan get out, and then look to yersel, lad; for, os sure os ey'm Mother Demdike's grandowter, ey'n plague the life out o' ye."

"Take the prisoners away, and let them be conveyed under a strict escort to Lancaster Castle," said James.

"And, as the assizes commence next week, quick work will be made with them, your Majesty," observed Potts. "Their guilt can be incontestably proved, so they are sure to be found guilty, sure to be hanged, sire."

As the prisoners were removed, Nance Redferne looked round her, and, catching the eye of Nicholas, made a slight motion with her head, as if bidding him farewell.

The squire returned the mute valediction.

"Poor Nance!" he exclaimed, compassionately, "I sincerely pity her. Would there was any means of saving her!"

"There is none," observed Sir Ralph Assheton. "And you may be thankful you are not brought in as her accomplice."

As Jennet was taken away, she continued to hurl threats and imprecations against Potts.

Another officer of the guard was then summoned, and when he came, James said, "One other prisoner remains within the pavilion. She likewise must be conveyed to Lancaster Castle, but in a litter, and not with the other prisoners."

Attended by Sir Richard Hoghton, the monarch then proceeded to his lodgings in the Tower.

CHAPTER XIV.—"ONE GRAVE."

NOTWITHSTANDING the sad occurrences above detailed, James remained for two more days the guest of Sir Richard Hoghton, enjoying his princely hospitality, hunting in the park, carousing in the great hall, and witnessing all kinds of sports.

Nothing, indeed, was left to remind him of the sad events that had occurred. The prisoners were taken that night to Lancaster Castle, and Master Potts accompanied the escort, to be ready for the assizes. The three judges proceeded thither at the end of the week. The attendance of Roger Nowell, Nicholas, and Sir Ralph Assheton, was also required as witnesses at the trial of the witches.

Sir Richard Assheton and Dorothy had returned, as already stated, to Middleton; and, though the intelligence of the death of Richard and Alizon was communicated to them with infinite caution, the shock to both was very great, especially to Dorothy, who was long—very long—in recovering from it.

Nicholas's vivacity of temperament made him feel the loss of his cousin at first very keenly, but it soon wore off. He vowed amendment and reformation on the model of John Bruen, whose life offered so striking a contrast to his own, that it has very properly been placed in opposition by a reverend moralist; but I regret to say that he did not carry out his praiseworthy intentions. He was apt to make a joke of John Bruen, instead of imitating his example. He professed to devote himself to his excellent wife—but his old habits would break out; and, I am sorry to say, he was often to be found in the alehouse, and was just as fond of horse-racing, cock-fighting, hunting, fishing, and all other sports, as ever. Occasionally he occupied a leisure or a rainy day with a Journal,* parts of which have been preserved; but he set down in it few of the terrible events here related, probably because they were of too painful a nature to be recorded. He died in 1625—at the early age of thirty-five.

But to go back. A few days after the tragical events at Hoghton Tower, the whole village of Whalley was astir. But it

* Published by the Chetham Society, and admirably edited, with notes, exhibiting an extraordinary amount of research and information, by the Rev. F. R. Raines, M.A., F.S.A., of Milnrow Parsonage, near Rochdale.

was no festive occasion—no merry-making—that called forth the inhabitants, for grief sat upon every countenance. The day, too, was gloomy. The feathered summits of Whalley Nab were wreathed in mist, and a fine rain descended in the valley. The Calder looked dull and discoloured as it flowed past the walls of the ancient Abbey. The church bell tolled mournfully, and a large concourse was gathered in the churchyard. Not far from one of the three crosses of Paulinus, which stood nearest the church porch, a grave had been digged, and almost every one looked into it. The grave, it was said, was intended to hold two coffins. Soon after this, a train of mourners issued from the ancient Abbey gateway, and sure enough there were two coffins on the shoulders of the bearers. They were met at the gate by Doctor Ormerod, who was so deeply affected as scarcely to be able to perform the needful offices for the dead. The principal mourners were Sir Richard Assheton of Middleton, Sir Ralph Assheton, and Nicholas. Amid the tears and sobs of all the bystanders, the bodies of Richard and Alizon were committed to the earth—laid together in one grave.

Thus was their latest wish fulfilled. Flowers grew upon the turf that covered them, and there was the earliest primrose seen, and the latest violet. Many a fond youth and trusting maiden have visited their lowly tomb, and many a tear, fresh from the heart, has dropped upon the sod covering the ill-fated lovers.

CHAPTER XV.—LANCASTER CASTLE.

Behold the grim and giant fabric, rebuilt and strengthened by

" Old John of Gaunt, time-honour'd Lancaster ! "

Within one of its turrets called John of Gaunt's Chair, and at eventide, stands a lady under the care of a jailer. It is the last sunset she will ever see—the last time she will look upon the beauties of earth; for she is a prisoner, condemned to die an ignominious and terrible death, and her execution will take place on the morrow. Leaving her alone within the turret, the jailer locks the door and stands outside it. The lady casts a long, lingering look around. All nature seems so beautiful—so attractive. The sunset upon the broad watery sands of Morecambe Bay is exquisite in varied tints. The fells of Furness look black and bold, and the windings of the Lune are clearly traced out. But she casts a wistful glance towards the mountainous ridges of Lancashire, and fancies she can detect amongst the heights the rounded summit of Pendle Hill. Then her gaze settles upon the grey old town beneath her, and, as her glance wanders over it, certain terrible objects arrest it. In the area before the Castle she sees a ring of tall stakes. She knows well their purpose, and counts them. They are thirteen in number. Thirteen wretched beings are to be burned on the morrow. Not far from the stakes are an enormous pile of fagots. All is prepared. Fascinated by the sight, she remains gazing at the place of execution for some time, and when she turns, she beholds a tall dark man standing beside her. At first she thinks it is the jailer, and is about to tell the man she is ready to descend to her cell, when she recognises him, and recoils in terror.

"Thou here—again!" she cried.

"I can save thee from the stake, if thou wilt, Alice Nutter," he said.

"Hence!" she exclaimed. "Thou temptest me in vain. Hence!"

And with a howl of rage the demon disappeared.

Conveyed back to her cell, situated within the dread Dungeon Tower, Alice Nutter passed the whole of that night in prayer. Towards four o'clock, wearied out, she dropped into a slumber; and when the clergyman, from whom she had received spiritual consolation, came to her cell, he found her still sleeping, but with a sweet smile upon her lips—the first he had ever beheld there.

Unwilling to disturb her, he knelt down and prayed by her side. At length the jailer came, and the executioner's aids. The divine then laid his hand upon her shoulder, and she instantly arose.

"I am ready," she said, cheerfully.

"You have had a happy dream, daughter," he observed.

"A blessed dream, reverend sir," she replied. "I thought I saw my children, Richard and Alizon, in a fair garden—oh! how angelic they looked—and they told me I should be with them soon."

"And I doubt not the vision will be realised," replied the clergyman. "Your redemption is fully worked out, and your salvation, I trust, secured. And now you must prepare for your last trial."

"I am fully prepared," she replied: "but will you not go to the others?"

"Alas! my dear daughter," he replied, "they all, excepting Nance Redferne, refuse my services. and will perish in their iniquities."

"Then go to her, sir, I entreat of you," she said; "she may yet be saved. But what of Jennet? Is she, too, to die?"

"No," replied the divine; "being evidence against her relatives, her life is spared."

"Heaven grant she do no more mischief!" exclaimed Alice Nutter.

She then submitted herself to the executioner's assistants, and was led forth. On issuing into the open air a change came over her, and such an exceeding faintness that she had to be supported. She was led towards the stake in this state; but she grew fainter and fainter, and at last fell back in the arms of the men that supported her. Still they carried her on. When the executioner put out his hand to receive her from his aids, she was found to be quite dead. Nevertheless, he tied her to the stake, and her body was consumed. Hundreds of spectators beheld those terrible fires, and exulted in the torments of the miserable sufferers. Their shrieks and blasphemies were terrific, and the place resembled a hell upon earth.

Jennet escaped, to the dismay of Master Potts, who feared she would wreak her threatened vengeance upon him. And, indeed, he did suffer from aches and cramps, which he attributed to her; but which were more reasonably supposed to be owing to rheum caught in the marshes of Pendle Forest. He had, however, the pleasure of assisting at her execution, when some years afterwards retributive justice overtook her.

Jennet was the last of the Lancashire Witches. Ever since then witchcraft has taken a new form with the ladies of the county —though their fascination and spells are as potent as ever. Few can now escape them,—few desire to do so. But to all who are afraid of a bright eye and a blooming cheek, and who desire to adhere to a bachelor's condition—to such I should say, "BEWARE OF THE LANCASHIRE WITCHES!"

THE END.

THE STORIES AND TALES SERIES

Stories and Tales Of Old Merseyside

(Frank Hird, edited Cliff Hayes)

Over 50 stories of Liverpool's characters and incidents PLUS a booklet from 1890 telling of the city's history, well illustrated.

ISBN 1 872226 20 5 £4.95

Stories & Tales Of Old Lancashire

(Frank Hird)

Over 70 fascinating tales told in a wonderful light-hearted fashion. Witches, seiges and superstitions, battles and characters all here.

ISBN 1 872226 21 3 £4.95

Stories and Tales Of Old Manchester

(Frank Hird, edited Cliff Hayes)

A ramble through Manchester's history, many lesser known stories brought to life, informative yet human book. Over 50 stories.

ISBN 1 872226 22 1 £4.95

Stories Of Great Lancastrians

(written Frank Hird)

The lives of 24 great men of the county, told in easy reading style. Complete with sketches and drawings, a good introduction to the famous of Lancashire and Manchester. John Byrom, Arkwright, Tim Bobbins, Duke of Bridgewater.

ISBN 1 872226 23 X £4.95

More Stories Of Old Lancashire

(Frank Hird)

We present another 80 stories in the same easy, readable style, very enjoyable, great. With special section for Preston Guild 1992.

ISBN 1 872226 26 4 £4.95